ISAAC ASIMOV, one of America's great resources, has by now written more than 330 books. No other writer in history has published so much on such a wide variety of subjects, which range from science fiction and murder novels to books on history, the physical sciences, and Shakespeare. Born in the Soviet Union and raised in Brooklyn, he is married and lives in New York City.

MARTIN H. GREENBERG, who has been called "the King of anthologists", now has some 140 to his credit. Greenberg is professor of regional analysis and political science at the University of Wisconsin, Green Bay, USA, where he also teaches a course in the history of science fiction.

CHARLES G. WAUGH is professor of psychology and mass communications at the University of Maine at Augusta, USA. He is a leading authority on science fiction and fantasy and has collaborated on more than 80 anthologies and single-author collections with Isaac Asimov, Martin H. Greenberg, and assorted colleagues.

The Mammoth Book of

# FANTASTIC

## SCIENCE FICTION

**Short Novels of the 1970s**
Edited by Isaac Asimov,
Charles G. Waugh and Martin H. Greenberg

Carroll & Graf Publishers, Inc.
New York

*Carroll & Graf Publishers, Inc.*
*260 Fifth Avenue*
*New York*
*NY 10001*

*First published in Great Britain 1992*

*First Carroll & Graf edition 1992*

*ISBN 0–88184–795–X*

*Printed in Great Britain.*

*10 9 8 7 6 5 4 3 2 1*

# CONTENTS

# ACKNOWLEDGEMENTS

"Born With the Dead" by Robert Silverberg—Copyright (c) 1974 by Agberg, Ltd. Reprinted by permission of the author and Agberg, Ltd.

"The Moon Goddess and the Son" by Donald Kingsbury—Copyright (c) 1979 by Conde Nast Publications, Inc. Reprinted by permission of the author.

"Tin Soldier" by Joan D. Vinge—Copyright (c) 1974 by Joan D. Vinge. Reprinted by permission of the author.

"In the Problem Pit" by Frederik Pohl—Copyright (c) 1973 by Mercury Press, Inc. First appeared in THE MAGAZINE OF FANTASY AND SCIENCE FICTION. Reprinted by permission of the author.

"Riding the Torch" by Norman Spinrad—Copyright (c) 1974 by Norman Spinrad. Reprinted by permission of the author and the Jane Rotrosen Agency.

"Mouthpiece" by Ed Wellen—Copyright (c) 1973 by Mercury Press, Inc.; Copyright (c) 1986 by Edward Wellen. First appeared in THE MAGAZINE OF FANTASY AND SCIENCE FICTION. Reprinted by permission of the author.

"ARM" by Larry Niven—Copyright (c) 1975 by Larry Niven. Reprinted by permission of the author and Spectrum Literary Agency.

"The Persistence of Vision" by John Varley—Copyright (c) 1978 by Mercury Press, Inc. First appeared in THE MAGAZINE OF FANTASY AND SCIENCE FICTION. Reprinted by permission of the Pimlico Agency, Inc.

"The Queen of Air and Darkness" by Poul Anderson—Copyright (c) 1971 by Mercury Press, Inc. Reprinted by permission of the Scott Meredith Literary Agency, Inc., 845 Third Ave., New York, NY 10022.

"The Monster and the Maiden" by Gordon R. Dickson—Copyright (c) 1976 by Random House, Inc. Reprinted by permission of the author.

# BORN WITH THE DEAD

## Robert Silverberg

## 1

And what the dead had no speech for, when living,
They can tell you, being dead: the communication
Of the dead is tongued with fire beyond the language of
   the living.

Eliot: Little Gidding

Supposedly his late wife Sybille was on her way to Zanzibar.
That was what they told him, and he believed it. Jorge Klein
was at that stage in his search when he would believe anything, if
belief would only lead him to Sybille. Anyway, it wasn't so absurd
that she would go to Zanzibar. Sybille had always wanted to go
there. In some unfathomable obsessive way the place had seized
the center of her consciousness long ago. When she was alive it
hadn't been possible for her to go there, but now, loosed from
all bonds, she would be drawn toward Zanzibar like a bird to its
nest, like Ulysses to Ithaca, like a moth to a flame.

The plane, a small Air Zanzibar Havilland FP-803, took off
more than half empty from Dar es Salaam at 0915 on a mild
bright morning, gaily circled above the dense masses of mango
trees, red-flowering flamboyants, and tall coconut palms along the
aquamarine shores of the Indian Ocean, and headed northward on
the short hop across the strait to Zanzibar. This day—Tuesday, the
ninth of March, 1993—would be an unusual one for Zanzibar: five

deads were aboard the plane, the first of their kind ever to visit that fragrant isle. Daud Mahmoud Barwani, the health officer on duty that morning at Zanzibar's Karume Airport, had been warned of this by the emigration officials on the mainland. He had no idea how he was going to handle the situation, and he was apprehensive: these were tense times in Zanzibar. Times are always tense in Zanzibar. Should he refuse them entry? Did deads pose any threat to Zanzibar's ever precarious political stability? What about subtler menaces? Deads might be carriers of dangerous spiritual maladies. Was there anything in the Revised Administrative Code about refusing visas on grounds of suspected contagions of the spirit? Daud Mahmoud Barwani nibbled moodily at his breakfast—a cold chapatti, a mound of cold curried potato—and waited without eagerness for the arrival of the deads.

Almost two and a half years had passed since Jorge Klein had last seen Sybille: the afternoon of Saturday, October 13, 1990, the day of her funeral. That day she lay in her casket as though merely asleep, her beauty altogether unmarred by her final ordeal: pale skin, dark lustrous hair, delicate nostrils, full lips. Iridescent gold and violet fabric enfolded her serene body; a shimmering electrostatic haze, faintly perfumed with a jasmine fragrance, protected her from decay. For five hours she floated on the dais while the rites of parting were read and the condolences were offered—offered almost furtively, as if her death were a thing too monstrous to acknowledge with a show of strong feeling; then, when only a few people remained, the inner core of their circle of friends, Klein kissed her lightly on the lips and surrendered her to the silent dark-clad men whom the Cold Town had sent. She had asked in her will to be rekindled; they took her away in a black van to work their magic on her corpse. The casket, retreating on their broad shoulders, seemed to Klein to be disappearing into a throbbing gray vortex that he was helpless to penetrate. Presumably he would never hear from her again. In those days the deads kept strictly to themselves, sequestered behind the walls of their self-imposed ghettos; it was rare ever to see one outside the Cold Towns, rare even for one of them to make oblique contact with the world of the living.

So a redefinition of their relationship was forced on him. For nine years it had been Jorge and Sybille, Sybille and Jorge, I and thou forming *we*, above all *we*, a transcendental *we*. He had loved her with almost painful intensity. In life they had gone everywhere together, had done everything together, shared research tasks and classroom assignments, thought interchangeable thoughts, expressed tastes that were nearly always identical, so completely had each permeated the other. She was a part of him, he of her, and until the moment of her unexpected death he had assumed it would be like that forever. They were still young, he thirty-eight, she thirty-four, decades to look forward to. Then she was gone. And now they were mere anonymities to one another, she not Sybille but only a dead, he not Jorge but only a warm. She was somewhere on the North American continent, walking about, talking, eating, reading, and yet she was gone, lost to him, and it behooved him to accept that alteration in his life, and outwardly he did accept it, but yet, though he knew he could never again have things as they once had been, he allowed himself the indulgence of a lingering wistful hope of regaining her.

Shortly the plane was in view, dark against the brightness of the sky, a suspended mote, an irritating fleck in Barwani's eye, growing larger, causing him to blink and sneeze. Barwani was not ready for it. When Ameri Kombo, the flight controller in the cubicle next door, phoned him with the routine announcement of the landing, Barwani replied, "Notify the pilot that no one is to debark until I have given clearance. I must consult the regulations. There is possibly a peril to public health." For twenty minutes he let the plane sit, all hatches sealed, on the quiet runway. Wandering goats emerged from the shrubbery and inspected it. Barwani consulted no regulations. He finished his modest meal; then he folded his arms and sought to attain the proper state of tranquillity. These deads, he told himself, could do no harm. They were people like all other people, except that they had undergone extraordinary medical treatment. He must overcome his superstitious fear of them: he was no peasant, no silly clove-picker, nor was Zanzibar an abode of primitives. He would admit them, he would give them their anti-malaria tablets as though they were ordinary tourists, he would send them on their way. Very well. Now he was ready. He phoned Ameri Kombo. "There is no danger," he said. "The passengers may exit."

There were nine altogether, a sparse load. The four warms emerged first, looking somber and a little congealed, like people who had had to travel with a party of uncaged cobras. Barwani knew them all: the German consul's wife, the merchant Chowdhary's son, and two Chinese engineers, all returning from brief holidays in Dar.

He waved them through the gate without formalities. Then came the deads, after an interval of half a minute: probably they had been sitting together at one end of the nearly empty plane and the others had been at the other. There were two women, three men, all of them tall and surprisingly robust-looking. He had expected them to shamble, to shuffle, to limp, to falter, but they moved with aggressive strides, as if they were in better health now than when they had been alive. When they reached the gate, Barwani stepped forward to greet them, saying softly, "Health regulations, come this way, kindly." They were breathing, undoubtedly breathing: he tasted an emanation of liquor from the big red-haired man, a mysterious and pleasant sweet flavor, perhaps anise, from the dark-haired woman. It seemed to Barwani that their skins had an odd waxy texture, an unreal glossiness, but possibly that was his imagination; white skins had always looked artificial to him. The only certain difference he could detect about the deads was in their eyes, a way they had of remaining unnervingly fixed in a single intense gaze for many seconds before shifting. Those were the eyes, Barwini thought, of people who had looked upon the Emptiness without having been swallowed into it. A turbulence of questions erupted within him: What is it like, how do you feel, what do you remember, where did you go? He left them unspoken. Politely he said, "Welcome to the isle of cloves. We ask you to observe that malaria has been wholly eradicated here through extensive precautionary measures, and to prevent recurrence of unwanted disease we require of you that you take these tablets before proceeding further." Tourists often objected to that; these people swallowed their pills without a word of protest. Again Barwani yearned to reach toward them, to achieve some sort of contact that might perhaps help him to transcend the leaden weight of being. But an aura, a shield of strangeness, surrounded these five, and though he was an amiable man who tended to fall into conversations easily with strangers, he passed them on in silence to Mponda the immigration man.

Mponda's high forehead was shiny with sweat, and he chewed at his lower lip; evidently he was as disturbed by the deads as Barwani. He fumbled forms, he stamped a visa in the wrong place, he stammered while telling the deads that he must keep their passports overnight. "I shall post them by messenger to your hotel in the morning," Mponda promised them, and sent the visitors onward to the baggage pickup area with undue haste.

*        *        *

Klein had only one friend with whom he dared talk about it, a colleague of his at UCLA, a sleek supple Parsee sociologist from Bombay named Framji Jijibhoi, who was as deep into the elaborate new subculture of the deads as a warm could get. "How can I accept this?" Klein demanded. "I can't accept it at all. She's out there somewhere, she's alive, she's— "

Jijibhoi cut him off with a quick flick of his fingertips. "No, dear friend," he said sadly, "not alive, not alive at all, merely rekindled. You must learn to grasp the distinction."

Klein could not learn to grasp the distinction. Klein could not learn to grasp anything having to do with Sybille's death. He could not bear to think that she had passed into another existence from which he was totally excluded. To find her, to speak with her, to participate in her experience of death and whatever lay beyond death, became his only purpose. He was inextricably bound to her, as though she were still his wife, as though Jorge-and-Sybille still existed in any way.

He waited for letters from her, but none came. After a few months he began trying to trace her, embarrassed by his own compulsiveness and by his increasingly open breaches of the etiquette of this sort of widowerhood. He traveled from one Cold Town to another—Sacramento, Boise, Ann Arbor, Louisville—but none would admit him, none would even answer his questions. Friends passed on rumors to him, that she was living among the deads of Tucson, of Roanoke, of Rochester, of San Diego, but nothing came of these tales; then Jijibhoi, who had tentacles into the world of the rekindled in many places, and who was aiding Klein in his quest even though he disapproved of its goal, brought him an authoritative-sounding report that she was at Zion Cold Town in southeastern Utah. They turned him away there too, but not entirely cruelly, for he did manage to secure plausible evidence that that was where Sybille really was.

In the summer of '92 Jijibhoi told him that Sybille had emerged from Cold Town seclusion. She had been seen, he said, in Newark, Ohio, touring the municipal golf course at Octagon State Memorial in the company of a swaggering red-haired archaeologist named Kent Zacharias, also a dead, formerly a specialist in the mound-building Hopewellian cultures of the Ohio Valley. "It is a new phase," said Jijibhoi, "not unanticipated. The deads are beginning to abandon their early philosophy of total separatism. We have started to observe them as tourists visiting our world—exploring the life-death interface, as they like to term it. It will be very interesting, dear friend." Klein flew at once to Ohio and without ever actually seeing her, tracked her from Newark to Chillicothe to Marietta, from Marietta into West Virginia, where he lost her trail somewhere between Moundsville and Wheeling. Two months later she was said to be in London, then in Cairo, then Addis Ababa. Early in '93 Klein learned, via the scholarly grapevine—an ex-Californian now at Nyerere University in Arusha—that Sybille was on safari in Tanzania and was planning to go, in a few weeks, across to Zanzibar.

Of course. For ten years she had been working on a doctoral thesis on the establishment of the Arab Sultanate in Zanzibar in the early nineteenth century—studies unavoidably interrupted by other academic chores, by love affairs, by marriage, by financial reverses, by illnesses, death, and other responsibilities—and she had never actually been able to visit the island that was so central to her. Now she was free of all entanglements. Why shouldn't she go to Zanzibar at last? Why not? Of course: she was heading for Zanzibar. And so Klein would go to Zanzibar too, to wait for her.

As the five disappeared into taxis, something occurred to Barwani. He asked Mponda for the passports and scrutinized the names. Such strange ones: Kent Zacharias, Nerita Tracy, Sybille Klein, Anthony Gracchus, Laurence Mortimer. He had never grown accustomed to the names of Europeans. Without the photographs he would be unable to tell which were the women, which the men. Zacharias, Tracy, Klein . . . ah. *Klein.* He checked a memo, two weeks old, tacked to his desk. Klein, yes. Barwani telephoned the Shirazi Hotel—a project that consumed several minutes—and asked to speak with the American who had arrived ten days before, that slender man whose lips had been pressed tight in tension, whose eyes had glittered with fatigue, the one who had asked a little service of Barwani, a special favor, and had dashed him a much-needed hundred shillings as payment in advance. There was a lengthy delay, no doubt while porters searched the hotel, looking in the men's room, the bar, the lounge, the garden, and then the American was on the line. "The person about whom you inquired has just arrived, sir," Barwani told him.

# 2

The dance begins. Worms underneath fingertips, lips beginning to pulse, heartache and throat-catch. All slightly
out of step and out of key, each its own tempo and
rhythm. Slowly, connections. Lip to lip, heart to heart,
finding self in other, dreadfully, tentatively, burning . . .
notes finding themselves in chords, chords in sequence,
cacophony turning to polyphonous contrapuntal chorus, a
diapason of celebration.

                    R. D. Laing: *The Bird of Paradise*

Sybille stands timidly at the edge of the municipal golf course at
Octagon State Memorial in Newark, Ohio, holding her sandals
in her hand and surreptitiously working her toes into the lush,
immaculate carpet of dense, close-cropped lime-green grass. It is
a summer afternoon in 1992, very hot; the air, beautifully translucent, has that timeless midwestern shimmer, and the droplets
of water from the morning sprinkling have not yet burned off the
lawn. Such extraordinary grass! She hadn't often seen grass like
that in California, and certainly not at Zion Cold Town in thirsty
Utah. Kent Zacharias, towering beside her, shakes his head sadly.
"A golf course!" he mutters. "One of the most important prehistoric
sites in North America and they make a golf course out of it! Well,
I suppose it could have been worse. They might have bulldozed
the whole thing and turned it into a municipal parking lot. Look,
there, do you see the earthworks?"

She is trembling. This is her first extended journey outside
the Cold Town, her first venture into the world of the warms
since her rekindling, and she is picking up threatening vibrations
from all the life that burgeons about her. The park is surrounded
by pleasant little houses, well kept. Children on bicycles rocket
through the streets. In front of her, golfers are merrily slamming
away. Little yellow golf carts clamber with lunatic energy over the
rises and dips of the course. There are platoons of tourists who,
like herself and Zacharias, have come to see the Indian mounds.
There are dogs running free. All this seems menacing to her.
Even the vegetation—the thick grass, the manicured shrubs, the
heavy-leafed trees with low-hanging boughs—disturbs her. Nor
is the nearness of Zacharias reassuring, for he too seems inflamed
with undeadlike vitality; his face is florid, his gestures are broad

and overanimated, as he points out the low flat-topped mounds, the grassy bumps and ridges making up the giant joined circle and octagon of the ancient monument. Of course, these mounds are the mainspring of his being, even now, five years post mortem. Ohio is his Zanzibar.

"—once covered four square miles. A grand ceremonial center, the Hopewellian equivalent of Chichén Itzá, of Luxor, of— " He pauses. Awareness of her distress has finally filtered through the intensity of his archaeological zeal. "How are you doing?" he asks gently.

She smiles a brave smile. Moistens her lips. Inclines her head toward the golfers, toward the tourists, toward the row of darling little houses outside the rim of the park. Shudders.

"Too cheery for you, is it?"

"Much," she says.

Cheery. Yes. A cheery little town, a magazine cover town, a chamber-of-commerce town. Newark lies becalmed on the breast of the sea of time: but for the look of the automobiles, this could be 1980 or 1960 or perhaps 1940. Yes. Motherhood, baseball, apple pie, church every Sunday. Yes. Zacharias nods and makes one of the signs of comfort at her. "Come," he whispers. "Let's go toward the heart of the complex. We'll lose the twentieth century along the way."

With brutal imperial strides he plunges into the golf course. Long-legged Sybille must work hard to keep up with him. In a moment they are within the embankment, they have entered the sacred octagon, they have penetrated the vault of the past, and at once Sybille feels they have achieved a successful crossing of the interface between life and death. How still it is here! She senses the powerful presence of the forces of death, and those dark spirits heal her unease. The encroachments of the world of the living on these precincts of the dead become insignificant: the houses outside the park are no longer in view, the golfers are mere foolish incorporeal shadows, the bustling yellow golf carts become beetles, the wandering tourists are invisible.

She is overwhelmed by the size and symmetry of the ancient site. What spirits sleep here? Zacharias conjures them, waving his hands like a magician. She has heard so much from him already about these people these Hopewellians—What did they call themselves? How can we ever know?—who heaped up these ramparts of earth twenty centuries ago. Now he brings them to life for her with gestures and low urgent words. He whispers fiercely:

—Do you see them?

And she does see them. Mists descend. The mounds reawaken; the mound-builders appear. Tall, slender, swarthy, nearly naked, clad in shining copper breastplates, in necklaces of flint disks, in bangles of bone and mica and tortoise shell, in heavy chains of bright lumpy pearls, in rings of stone and terra cotta, in armlets of bears' teeth and panthers' teeth, in spool-shaped metal ear-ornaments, in furry loincloths. Here are priests in intricately woven robes and awesome masks. Here are chieftains with crowns of copper rods, moving in frosty dignity along the long earthen-walled avenue. The eyes of these people glow with energy. What an enormously vital, enormously profligate culture they sustain here! Yet Sybille is not alienated by their throbbing vigor, for it is the vigor of the dead, the vitality of the vanished.

Look, now. Their painted faces, their unblinking gazes. This is a funeral procession. The Indians have come to these intricate geometrical enclosures to perform their acts of worship, and now, solemnly parading along the perimeters of the circle and the octagon, they pass onward, toward the mortuary zone beyond. Zacharias and Sybille are left alone in the middle of the field. He murmurs to her:

—Come. We'll follow them.

He makes it real for her. Through his cunning craft she has access to this community of the dead. How easily she has drifted backward across time! She learns here that she can affix herself to the sealed past at any point; it's only the present, open-ended and unpredictable, that is troublesome. She and Zacharias float through the misty meadow, no sensation of feet touching ground; leaving the octagon, they travel now down a long grassy causeway to the place of the burial mounds, at the edge of a dark forest of wide-crowned oaks. They enter a vast clearing. In the center the ground has been plastered with clay, then covered lightly with sand and fine gravel; on this base the mortuary house, a roofless four-sided structure with walls consisting of rows of wooden palisades, has been erected. Within this is a low clay platform topped by a rectangular tomb of log cribbing, in which two bodies can be seen: a young man, a young woman, side by side, bodies fully extended, beautiful even in death. They wear copper breastplates, copper ear ornaments, copper bracelets, necklaces of gleaming yellowish bears' teeth.

Four priests station themselves at the corners of the mortuary house. Their faces are covered by grotesque wooden masks topped by great antlers, and they carry wands two feet long, effigies of the death-cup mushroom in wood sheathed with copper. One priest commences a harsh, percussive chant. All four lift their wands and abruptly bring them down. It is a signal; the depositing of grave-goods begins. Lines of mourners bowed under heavy sacks approach the mortuary house. They are unweeping, even joyful, faces ecstatic, eyes shining, for these people know what later cultures will forget, that death is no termination but rather a natural continuation of life. Their departed friends are to be envied. They are honored with lavish gifts, so that they may live like royalty in the next world: out of the sacks come nuggets of copper, meteoric iron, and silver, thousands of pearls, shell beads, beads of copper and iron, buttons of wood and stone, heaps of metal ear-spools, chunks and chips of obsidian, animal effigies carved from slate and bone and tortoise shell, ceremonial copper axes and knives, scrolls cut from mica, human jawbones inlaid with turquoise, dark coarse pottery, needles of bone, sheets of woven cloth, coiled serpents fashioned from dark stone, a torrent of offerings, heaped up around and even upon the two bodies.

At length the tomb is choked with gifts. Again there is a signal from the priests. They elevate their wands and the mourners, drawing back to the borders of the clearing, form a circle and begin to sing a somber, throbbing funeral hymn. Zacharias, after a moment, sings with them, wordlessly embellishing the melody with heavy melismas. His voice is a rich *basso cantante*, so unexpectedly beautiful that Sybille is moved almost to confusion by it, and looks at him in awe. Abruptly he breaks off, turns to her, touches her arm, leans down to say:

—You sing too.

Sybille nods hesitantly. She joins the song, falteringly at first, her throat constricted by self-consciousness; then she finds herself becoming part of the rite, somehow, and her tone becomes more confident. Her high clear soprano soars brilliantly above the other voices.

Now another kind of offering is made: boys cover the mortuary house with heaps of kindling—twigs, dead branches, thick boughs, all sorts of combustible debris—until it is quite hidden from sight, and the priests cry a halt. Then, from the forest, comes a woman bearing a blazing firebrand, a girl, actually, entirely naked, her sleek fair-skinned body painted with bizarre horizontal stripes of red and green on breasts and buttocks and thighs, her long glossy black hair flowing like a cape behind her as she runs. Up to the mortuary house she sprints; breathlessly she touches the firebrand to the kindling, here, here, here, performing a wild dance as she goes, and hurls the torch into the center of the pyre. Skyward leap the flames in a ferocious rush. Sybille feels seared by the blast of heat. Swiftly the house and tomb are consumed.

While the embers still glow, the bringing of earth gets under way. Except for the priests, who remain rigid at the cardinal points of the site, and the girl who wielded the torch, who lies like discarded clothing at the edge of the clearing, the whole community takes part. There is an open pit behind a screen of nearby trees; the worshipers, forming lines, go to it and scoop up soil, carrying it to the burned mortuary house in baskets, in buckskin aprons, in big moist clods held in their bare hands. Silently they dump their burdens on the ashes and go back for more.

Sybille glances at Zacharias; he nods; they join the line. She goes down into the pit, gouges a lump of moist black clayey soil from its side, takes it to the growing mound. Back for another, back for another. The mound rises rapidly, two feet above ground level now, three, four, a swelling circular blister, its outlines governed by the unchanging positions of the four priests, its tapering contours formed by the tamping of scores of bare feet. Yes, Sybille thinks, this is a valid way of celebrating death, this is a fitting rite. Sweat runs down her body, her clothes become stained and muddy, and still she runs to the earth-quarry, runs from there to the mound, runs to the quarry, runs to the mound, runs, runs, transfigured, ecstatic.

Then the spell breaks. Something goes wrong, she does not know what, and the mists clear, the sun dazzles her eyes, the priests and the mound-builders and the unfinished mound disappear. She and Zacharias are once again in the octagon, golf carts roaring past them on every side. Three children and their parents stand just a few feet from her, staring, staring, and a boy about ten years old points to Sybille and says in a voice that reverberates through half of Ohio, "Dad, what's wrong with those people? Why do they look so weird?"

Mother gasps and cries, "*Quiet*, Tommy, don't you have any manners?" Dad, looking furious, gives the boy a stinging blow across the face with the tips of his fingers, seizes him by the wrist, tugs him toward the other side of the park, the whole family following in their wake.

Sybille shivers convulsively. She turns away, clasping her hands to her betraying eyes. Zacharias embraces her. "It's all right," he says tenderly. "The boy didn't know any better. It's all right."

"Take me away from here!"

"I want to show you— "

"Some other time. Take me away. To the motel. I don't want to see anything. I don't want anybody to see me."

He takes her to the motel. For an hour she lies face down on the bed, racked by dry sobs. Several times she tells Zacharias she is unready for this tour, she wants to go back to the Cold Town, but he says nothing, simply strokes the tense muscles of her back, and after a while the mood passes. She turns to him and their eyes meet and he touches her and they make love in the fashion of the deads.

# 3

Newness is renewal: *ad hoc enim venit, ut renovemur in illo*; making it new again, as on the first day; *herrlich wie am ersten Tag*. Reformation, or renaissance; rebirth. Life is Phoenix-like, always being born again out of its own death. The true nature of life is resurrection; all life is life after death, a second life, reincarnation. *Totus hic ordo revolubilis testatio est resurrectionis mortuorum*. The universal pattern of recurrence bears witness to the ressurection of the dead.

Norman O. Brown: *Love's Body*

"The rains shall be commencing shortly, gentleman and lady," the taxi driver said, speeding along the narrow highway to Zanzibar Town. He had been chattering steadily, wholly unafraid of his passengers. He must not know what we are, Sybille decided. "Perhaps in a week or two they begin. These shall be the long rains. The short rains come in the last of November and December."

"Yes, I know," Sybille said.

"Ah, you have been to Zanzibar before?"

"In a sense," she replied. In a sense she had been to Zanzibar many times, and how calmly she was taking it, now that the true Zanzibar was beginning to superimpose itself on the template in her mind, on that dream Zanzibar she had carried about so long! She took everything calmly now: nothing excited her, nothing aroused her. In her former life the delay at the airport would have driven her into a fury: a ten-minute flight, and then to be trapped on the runway twice as long! But she had remained tranquil throughout it all, sitting almost immobile, listening vaguely to what Zacharias was saying and occasionally replying as if sending messages from some other planet. And now Zanzibar, so placidly accepted. In the old days she had felt a sort of paradoxical amazement whenever some landmark familiar from childhood geography lessons or the movies or travel posters—the Grand Canyon, the Manhattan skyline, Taos Pueblo—turned out in reality to look exactly as she imagined it would; but now here was Zanzibar, unfolding predictably and unsurprisingly before her, and she observed it with a camera's cool eye, unmoved, unresponsive.

The soft, steamy air was heavy with a burden of perfumes, not only the expected pungent scent of cloves but also creamier fragrances which perhaps were those of hibiscus, frangipani, jacaranda, bougainvillaea, penetrating the cab's open window like probing tendrils. The imminence of the long rains was a tangible pressure, a presence, a heaviness in the atmosphere: at any moment a curtain might be drawn aside and the torrents would start. The highway was lined by two shaggy green walls of palms broken by tin-roofed shacks; behind the palms were mysterious dark groves, dense and alien. Along the edge of the road was the usual tropical array of obstacles: chickens, goats, naked children, old women with shrunken, toothless faces, all wandering around untroubled by the taxi's encroachment on their right-of-way. On through the rolling flatlands the cab sped, out onto the peninsula on which Zanzibar Town sits. The temperature seemed to be rising perceptibly minute by minute; a fist of humid heat was clamping tight over the island. "Here is the waterfront, gentleman and lady," the driver said. His voice was an intrusive hoarse purr, patronizing, disturbing. The sand was glaringly white, the water a dazzling glassy blue; a couple of dhows moved sleepily across the mouth of the harbor, their lateen sails bellying slightly as the gentle sea breeze caught them. "On this side, please— " An enormous white wooden building, four stories high, a wedding cake of long verandahs and cast-iron railings, topped by a vast cupola. Sybille, recognizing it, anticipated the driver's spiel, hearing it like a subliminal pre-echo: "Beit al-Ajaib, the House of Wonders, former government house. Here the Sultan was often make great banquets, here the famous of all Africa came homaging. No longer in use. Next door the old Sultan's Palace, now Palace of People. You wish to go in House of Wonders? Is open: we stop, I take you now."

"Another time," Sybille said faintly. "We'll be here awhile."

"You not here just a day like most?"

"No, a week or more. I've come to study the history of your island. I'll surely visit the Beit al-Ajaib. But not today."

"Not today, no. Very well: you call me, I take you anywhere. I am Ibuni." He gave her a gallant toothy grin over his shoulder and swung the cab inland with a ferocious lurch, into the labyrinth of winding streets and narrow alleys that was Stonetown, the ancient Arab quarter.

All was silent here. The massive white stone buildings presented blank faces to the streets. The windows, mere slits, were shuttered. Most doors—the famous paneled doors of Stonetown, richly carved, studded with brass, cunningly inlaid, each door an ornate Islamic masterpiece—were closed and seemed to be locked. The shops looked shabby, and the small display windows were speckled with dust. Most of the signs were so faded Sybille could barely make them out:

PREMCHAND'S EMPORIUM

MONJI'S CURIOS

ABDULLAH'S BROTHERHOOD STORE

MOTILAL'S BAZAAR

The Arabs were long since gone from Zanzibar. So were most of the Indians, though they were said to be creeping back. Occasionally, as it pursued its intricate course through the maze of Stonetown, the taxi passed elongated black limousines, probably of Russian or Chinese make, chauffeur-driven, occupied by dignified self-contained dark-skinned men in white robes. Legislators, so she supposed them to be, en route to meetings of state. There were no other vehicles in sight, and no pedestrians except for a few women, robed entirely in black hurrying on solitary errands. Stonetown had none of the vitality of the countryside; it was a place of ghosts, she thought, a fitting place for vacationing deads. She glanced at Zacharias, who nodded and smiled, a quick quirky smile that acknowledged her perception and told her that he too had had it. Communication was swift among the deads and the obvious rarely needed voicing.

The route to the hotel seemed extraordinarily involuted, and the driver halted frequently in front of shops, saying hopefully, "You want brass chests, copper pots, silver curios, gold chains from China?" Though Sybille gently declined his suggestions, he continued to point out bazaars and emporiums, offering earnest recommendations of quality and moderate price, and gradually she realized, getting her bearings in the town, that they had passed certain corners more than once. Of course: the driver must be in the pay of shopkeepers who hired him to lure tourists.

"Please take us to our hotel," Sybille said, and when he persisted in his huckstering—"Best ivory here, best lace"—she said it more firmly, but she kept her temper. Jorge would have been pleased by her transformation, she thought; he had all too often been the immediate victim of her fiery impatience. She did not know the specific cause of the change. Some metabolic side-effect of the rekindling process, maybe, or maybe her two years of communion with Guidefather at the Cold Town, or was it, perhaps, nothing more than the new knowledge that all of time was hers, that to let oneself feel hurried now was absurd?

"Your hotel is this," Ibuni said at last.

It was an old Arab mansion—high arches, innumerable balconies, musty air, electric fans turning sluggishly in the dark hallways. Sybille and Zacharias were given a sprawling suite on the third floor, overlooking a courtyard lush with palms, vermilion nandi, kapok trees, poinsettia, and agapanthus. Mortimer, Gracchus, and Nerita had long since arrived in the other cab and were in an identical suite one floor below. "I'll have a bath," Sybille told Zacharias. "Will you be in the bar?"

"Very likely. Or strolling in the garden."

He went out. Sybille quickly shed her travel-sweaty clothes. The bathroom was a Byzantine marvel, elaborate swirls of colored tile, an immense yellow tub standing high on bronze eagle-claw-and-globe legs. Lukewarm water dribbled in slowly when she turned the tap. She smiled at her reflection in the tall oval mirror. There had been a mirror somewhat like it at the rekindling house. On the morning after her awakening, five or six deads had come into her room to celebrate with her her successful transition across the interface, and they had had that big mirror with them; delicately, with great ceremoniousness, they had drawn the coverlet down to show herself to her in it, naked, slender, narrow-waisted, high-breasted, the beauty of her body unchanged, marred neither by dying nor by rekindling, indeed enhanced by it, so that she had become more youthful-looking and even radiant in her passage across that terrible gulf.

—You're a very beautiful woman.

That was Pablo. She would learn his name and all the other names later.

—I feel such a flood of relief. I was afraid I'd wake up and find myself a shriveled ruin.

—That could not have happened, Pablo said.

—And never will happen, said a young woman. Nerita, she was.

—But deads do age, don't they?

—Oh, yes, we age, just as the warms do. But not *just* as.

—More slowly?

—Very much more slowly. And differently. All our biological processes operate more slowly, except the functions of the brain, which tend to be quicker than they were in life.

—Quicker?

—You'll see.

—It all sounds ideal.

—We are extremely fortunate. Life has been kind to us. Our situation is, yes, ideal. We are the new aristocracy.

—The new aristocracy—

Sybille slipped slowly into the tub, leaning back against the cool porcelain, wriggling a little, letting the tepid water slide up as far as her throat. She closed her eyes and drifted peacefully. All of Zanzibar was waiting for her. *Streets I never thought I should visit.* Let Zanzibar wait. Let Zanzibar wait. *Words I never thought to speak. When I left my body on a distant shore.* Time for everything, everything in its due time.

—*You're a very beautiful woman*, Pablo had told her, not meaning to flatter.

Yes. She had wanted to explain to them, that first morning, that she didn't really care all that much about the appearance of her body, that her real priorities lay elsewhere, were "higher," but there hadn't been any need to tell them that. They understood. They understood everything. Besides, she *did* care about her body. Being beautiful was less important to her than it was to those women for whom physical beauty was their only natural advantage, but her appearance mattered to her; her body pleased her and she knew it was pleasing to others, it gave her access to people, it was a means of making connections, and she had always been grateful for that. In her other existence her delight in her body had been flawed by the awareness of the inevitability of its slow steady decay, the certainty of the loss of that accidental power that beauty gave her, but now she had been granted exemption from that: she would change with time but she would not have to feel, as warms must feel, that she was gradually falling apart. Her rekindled body would not betray her by turning ugly. No.

—*We are the new aristocracy*—

After her bath she stood a few minutes by the open window, naked to the humid breeze. Sounds came to her: distant bells, the bright chatter of tropical birds, the voices of children singing in a language she could not identify. Zanzibar! Sultans and spices, Livingstone and Stanley, Tippu Tib the slaver, Sir Richard Burton spending a night in this very hotel room, perhaps. There was a dryness in her throat, a throbbing in her chest: a little excitement coming alive in her after all. She felt anticipation, even eagerness. All Zanzibar lay before her. Very well. Get moving, Sybille, put some clothes on, let's have lunch, a look at the town.

She took a light blouse and shorts from her suitcase. Just then Zacharias returned to the room, and she said, not looking up, "Kent, do you think it's all right for me to wear these shorts here? They're— " A glance at his face and her voice trailed off. "What's wrong?"

"I've just been talking to your husband."

"He's *here*?"

"He came up to me in the lobby. Knew my name. 'You're Zacharias,' he said, with a Bogarty little edge to his voice, like a deceived movie husband confronting the Other Man. 'Where is she? I have to see her.'"

"Oh, no, Kent."

"I asked him what he wanted with you. 'I'm her husband,' he said, and I told him, 'Maybe you were her husband once, but things have changed,' and then— "

"I can't imagine Jorge talking tough. He's such a *gentle* man, Kent! How did he look?"

"Schizoid," Zacharias said. "Glassy eyes, muscles bunching in his jaws, signs of terrific pressure all over him. He knows he's not supposed to do things like this, doesn't he?"

"Jorge knows exactly how he's supposed to behave. Oh, Kent, what a stupid mess! Where is he now?"

"Still downstairs. Nerita and Laurence are talking to him. You don't want to see him, do you?"

"Of course not."

"Write him a note to that effect and I'll take it down to him. Tell him to clear off."

Sybille shook her head. "I don't want to hurt him."

"Hurt him? He's followed you halfway around the world like a lovesick boy, he's tried to violate your privacy, he's disrupted an important trip, he's refused to abide by the conventions that govern the relationships of warms and deads, and you— "

"He loves me, Kent."

"He loved you. All right, I concede that. But the person he loved doesn't exist any more. He has to be made to realize that."

Sybille closed her eyes. "I don't want to hurt him. I don't want you to hurt him either."

"I won't hurt him. Are you going to see him?"

"No," she said. She grunted in annoyance and threw her shorts and blouse into a chair. There was a fierce pounding at her temples, a sensation of being challenged, of being threatened, that she had not felt since that awful day at the Newark mounds. She strode to the window and looked out, half expecting to see Jorge arguing with Nerita and Laurence in the courtyard. But there was no one down there except a houseboy who looked up as if her bare breasts were beacons and gave her a broad dazzling smile. Sybille turned her back to him and said dully, "Go back down. Tell him that it's impossible for me to see him. Use that word. Not that I *won't* see him, not that I *don't want to* see him, not that it isn't *right* for me to see him, just that it's impossible. And then phone the airport. I want to go back to Dar on the evening plane."

"But we've only just arrived!"

"No matter. We'll come back some other time. Jorge is very persistent; he won't accept anything but a brutal rebuff, and I can't do that to him. So we'll leave."

Klein had never seen deads at close range before. Cautiously, uneasily, he stole quick intense looks at Kent Zacharias as they sat side by side on rattan chairs among the potted palms in the lobby of the hotel. Jijibhoi had told him that it hardly showed, that you perceived it more subliminally than by any outward manifestation, and that was true; there was a certain look about the eyes, of course, the famous fixity of the deads, and there was something oddly pallid about Zacharias' skin *beneath* the florid complexion, but if Klein had not known what Zacharias was, he might not have guessed it. He tried to imagine this man, this red-haired red-faced dead archaeologist, this digger of dirt mounds, in bed with Sybille. Doing with her whatever it was that the deads did in their couplings. Even Jijibhoi wasn't sure. Something with hands, with eyes, with whispers and smiles, not at all genital—so Jijibhoi believed. *This is Sybille's lover I'm talking to. This is Sybille's lover.* How strange that it bothered him so. She had had affairs when she was living; so had he; so had everyone; it was the way of life. But he felt threatened, overwhelmed, defeated, by this walking corpse of a lover.

Klein said, "Impossible?"

"That was the word she used."

"Can't I have ten minutes with her?"

"Impossible."

"Would you let me see her for a few moments, at least? I'd just like to find out how she looks."

"Don't you find it humiliating, doing all this scratching around just for a glimpse of her?"

"Yes."

"And you still want it?"

"Yes."

Zacharias sighed. "There's nothing I can do for you. I'm sorry."

"Perhaps Sybille is tired from having done so much traveling. Do you think she might be in a more receptive mood tomorrow?"

"Maybe," Zacharias said. "Why don't you come back then?"

"You've been very kind."

"*De nada.*"

"Can I buy you a drink?"

"Thanks, no," Zacharias said. "I don't indulge any more. Not since— " He smiled.

Klein could smell whiskey on Zacharias' breath. All right, though. All right. He would go away. A driver waiting outside the hotel grounds poked his head out of his cab window and said hopefully, "Tour of the island, gentleman? See the clove plantations, see the athlete stadium?"

"I've seen them already," Klein said. He shrugged. "Take me to the beach."

He spent the afternoon watching turquoise wavelets lapping pink sand. The next morning he returned to Sybille's hotel, but they were gone, all five of them, gone on last night's flight to Dar, said the apologetic desk clerk. Klein asked if he could make a telephone call, and the clerk showed him an ancient instrument in an alcove near the bar. He phone Barwani. "What's going on?" he demanded. "You told me they'd be staying at least a week!"

"Oh, sir, things change," Barwani said softly.

# 4

What portends? What will the future bring? I do not know, I have no presentiment. When a spider hurls itself down from some fixed point, consistently with its nature, it always sees

before it only an empty space wherein it can find no foothold
however much it sprawls. And so it is with me: always before
me an empty space; what drives me forward is a consistency
which lies behind me. This life is topsy-turvy and terrible,
not to be endured.

Søren Kierkegaard: *Either/Or*

Jijibhoi said, "In the entire question of death who is to say what is
right, dear friend? When I was a boy in Bombay it was not unusual
for our Hindu neighbors to practice the rite of suttee, that is, the
burning of the widow on her husband's funeral pyre, and by what
presumption may we call them barbarians? Of course"—his dark
eyes flashed mischievously—"we *did* call them barbarians, though
never when they might hear us. Will you have more curry?"

Klein repressed a sigh. He was getting full, and the curry
was fiery stuff, of an incandescence far beyond his usual level
of tolerance; but Jijibhoi's hospitality, unobtrusively insistent,
had a certain hieratic quality about it that made Klein feel like
a blasphemer whenever he refused anything in his home. He
smiled and nodded, and Jijibhoi, rising, spooned a mound of rice
into Klein's plate, buried it under curried lamb, bedecked it with
chutneys and sambals. Silently, unbidden, Jijibhoi's wife went to
the kitchen and returned with a cold bottle of Heineken. She gave
Klein a shy grin as she set it down before him. They worked well
together, these two Parsees, his hosts.

They were an elegant couple—striking, even. Jijibhoi was a
tall, erect man with a forceful aquiline nose, dark Levantine
skin, jet-black hair, a formidable mustache. His hands and feet
were extraordinarily small; his manner was polite and reserved;
he moved with a quickness of action bordering on nervousness.
Klein guessed that he was in his early forties, though he suspected
his estimate could easily be off by ten years in either direction.
His wife—strangely, Klein had never been told her name—was
younger than her husband, nearly as tall, fair of complexion—a
light-olive tone—and voluptuous of figure. She dressed invariably
in flowing silken saris; Jijibhoi affected western business dress,
suits and ties in style twenty years out of date. Klein had never
seen either of them bareheaded: she wore a kerchief of white linen,
he a brocaded skullcap that might lead people to mistake him for
an Oriental Jew. They were childless and self-sufficient, forming
a closed dyad, a perfect unit, two segments of the same entity,
conjoined and indivisible, as Klein and Sybille once had been.
Their harmonious interplay of thought and gesture made them

a trifle disconcerting, even intimidating, to others. As Klein and Sybille once had been.

Klein said, "Among your people— "

"Oh, very different, very different, quite unique. You know of our funeral custom?"

"Exposure of the dead, isn't it?"

Jijibhoi's wife giggled. "A very ancient recycling scheme!"

"The Towers of Silence," Jijibhoi said. He went to the dining room's vast window and stood with his back to Klein, staring out at the dazzling lights of Los Angeles. The Jijibhois' house, all redwood and glass, perched precariously on stilts near the crest of Benedict Canyon, just below Mulholland: the view took in everything from Hollywood to Santa Monica. "There are five of them in Bombay," said Jijibhoi, "on Malabar Hill, a rocky ridge overlooking the Arabian Sea. They are centuries old, each one circular, several hundred feet in circumference, surrounded by a stone wall twenty or thirty feet high. When a Parsee dies—do you know of this?"

"Not as much as I'd like to know."

"When a Parsee dies, he is carried to the Towers on an iron bier by professional corpse-bearers; the mourners follow in procession, two by two, joined hand to hand by holding a white handkerchief between them. A beautiful scene, dear Jorge. There is a doorway in the stone wall through which the corpse-bearers pass, carrying their burden. No one else may enter the Tower. Within is a circular platform paved with large stone slabs and divided into three rows of shallow, open receptacles. The outer row is used for the bodies of males, the next for those of females, the innermost one for children. The dead one is given a resting-place; vultures rise from the lofty palms in the gardens adjoining the Towers; within an hour or two, only bones remain. Later, the bare, sun-dried skeleton is cast into a pit at the center of the Tower. Rich and poor crumble together there into dust."

"And all Parsees are—ah—buried in this way?"

"Oh, no, no, by no means," Jijibhoi said heartily. "All ancient traditions are in disrepair nowadays, do you not know? Our younger people advocate cremation or even conventional interment. Still, many of us continue to see the beauty of our way."

"—beauty?— "

Jijibhoi's wife said in a quiet voice, "To bury the dead in the ground, in a moist tropical land where diseases are highly contagious, seems not sanitary to us. And to burn a body is to waste its substance. But to give the bodies of the dead to the efficient hungry birds—quickly, cleanly, without fuss—is to us a way of celebrating the economy of nature. To have one's bones mingle in the pit with the bones of the entire community is, to us, the ultimate democracy."

"And the vultures spread no contagions themselves, feeding as they do on the bodies of— "

"Never," said Jijibhoi firmly. "Nor do they contract our ills."

"And I gather that you both intend to have your bodies returned to Bombay when you— " Aghast, Klein paused, shook his head, coughed in embarrassment, forced a weak smile. "You see what this radioactive curry of yours has done to my manners? Forgive me. Here I sit, a guest at your dinner table, quizzing you about your funeral plans!"

Jijibhoi chuckled. "Death is not frightening to us, dear friend. It is—one hardly needs say it, does one?—it is a natural event. For a time we are here, and then we go. When our time ends, yes, she and I will give ourselves to the Towers of Silence."

His wife added sharply, "Better there than the Cold Towns! Much better!"

Klein had never observed such vehemence in her before.

Jijibhoi swung back from the window and glared at her. Klein had never seen that before either. It seemed as if the fragile web of elaborate courtesy that he and these two had been spinning all evening was suddenly unraveling, and that even the bonds between Jijibhoi and his wife were undergoing strain. Agitated now, fluttery, Jijibhoi began to collect the empty dishes, and after a long awkward moment said, "She did not mean to give offense."

"Why should I be offended?"

"A person you love chose to go to the Cold Towns. You might think there was implied criticism of her in my wife's expression of distaste for— "

Klein shrugged. "She's entitled to her feelings about rekindling. I wonder, though— "

He halted, uneasy, fearing to probe too deeply.

"Yes?"

"It was irrelevant."

"Please," Jijibhoi said. "We are old friends."

"I was wondering," said Klein slowly, "if it doesn't make things hard for you, spending all your time among deads, studying them, mastering their ways, devoting your whole career to them, when your wife evidently despises the Cold Towns and everything that goes on in them. If the theme of your work repels her, you must not be able to share it with her."

"Oh," Jijibhoi said, tension visibly going from him, "if it comes to that, I have even less liking for the entire rekindling phenomenon than she."

"You do?" This was a side of Jijibhoi that Klein had never suspected. "It repels you? Then why did you choose to make such an intensive survey of it?"

Jijibhoi looked genuinely amazed. "What? Are you saying one must have personal allegiance to the subject of one's field of scholarship?" He laughed. "You are of Jewish birth, I think, and yet your doctoral thesis was concerned, was it not, with the early phases of the Third Reich?"

Klein winced. "Touché!"

"I find the subculture of the deads irresistible, as a sociologist," Jijibhoi went on. "To have such a radical new aspect of human existence erupt during one's career is an incredible gift. There is no more fertile field for me to investigate. Yet I have no wish, none at all, ever to deliver myself up for rekindling. For me, my wife, it will be the Towers of Silence, the hot sun, the obliging vultures—and finis, the end, no more, terminus."

"I had no idea you felt this way. I suppose if I'd known more about Parsee theology, I might have realized— "

"You misunderstand. Our objections are not theological. It is that we share a wish, an idiosyncratic whim, not to continue beyond the allotted time. But also I have serious reservations about the impact of rekindling on our society. I feel a profound distress at the presence among us of these deads, I feel a purely private fear of these people and the culture they are creating, I feel even an abhorrence for— " Jijibhoi cut himself short. "Your pardon. That was perhaps too strong a word. You see how complex my attitudes are toward this subject, my mixture of fascination and repulsion? I exist in constant tension between those poles. But why do I tell you all this, which if it does not disturb you, must surely bore you? Let us hear about your journey to Zanzibar."

"What can I say? I went, I waited a couple of weeks for her to show up, I wasn't able to get near her at all, and I came home. All the way to Africa and I never even had a glimpse of her."

"What a frustration, dear Jorge!"

"She stayed in her hotel room. They wouldn't let me go upstairs to her."

"They?"

"Her entourage," Klein said. "She was traveling with four other deads, a woman and three men. Sharing her room with the archaeologist, Zacharias. He was the one who shielded her from me, and did it very cleverly, too. He acts as though he owns her. Perhaps he does. What can you tell me, Framji? Do the deads marry? Is Zacharias her new husband?"

"It is very doubtful. The terms 'wife' and 'husband' are not in use among the deads. They form relationships, yes, but pair-bonding seems to be uncommon among them, possibly altogether unknown. Instead they tend to create supportive pseudo-familial groupings of three or four or even more individuals, who— "

"Do you mean that all four of her companions in Zanzibar are her lovers?"?

Jijibhoi gestured eloquently. "Who can say? If you mean in a physical sense, I doubt it, but one can never be sure. Zacharias seems to be her special companion, at any rate. Several of the others may be part of her pseudo-family also, or all, or none. I have reason to think that at certain times every dead may claim a familial relationship to all others of his kind. Who can say? We perceive the doings of these people, as they say, through a glass, darkly."

"I don't see Sybille even that well. I don't even know what she looks like now."

"She has lost none of her beauty."

"So you've told me before. But I want to see her myself. You can't really comprehend, Framji, how much I want to see her. The pain I feel, not able— "

"Would you like to see her right now?"

Klein shook in a convulsion of amazement. "What? What do you mean? Is she— "

"Hiding in the next room? No, no, nothing like that. But I do have a small surprise for you. Come into the library." Smiling expansively, Jijibhoi led the way from the dining room to the small study adjoining it, a room densely packed from floor to ceiling with books in an astonishing range of languages—not merely English, French, and German, but also Sanskrit, Hindi, Gujerati, Farsi, the tongues of Jijibhoi's polyglot upbringing among the tiny Parsee colony of Bombay, a community in which no language once cherished was ever discarded. Pushing aside a stack of dog-eared professional journals, he drew forth a glistening picture-cube, activated its inner light with a touch of his thumb, and handed it to Klein.

The sharp, dazzling holographic image showed three figures in a broad grassy plain that seemed to have no limits and was without trees, boulders, or other visual interruptions, an endlessly unrolling green carpet under a blank death-blue sky. Zacharias stood at the left, his face averted from the camera; he was looking down, tinkering with the action of an enormous rifle. At the far right stood a stocky, powerful-looking dark-haired man whose pale, harsh-featured face seemed all beard and nostrils. Klein recognized him: Anthony Gracchus, one of the deads who had accompanied Sybille to Zanzibar. Sybille stood beside him, clad in khaki slacks and a crisp white blouse. Gracchus' arm was extended; evidently he had just pointed out a target to her, and she was intently aiming a gun nearly as big as Zacharias'.

Klein shifted the cube about, studying her face from various angles, and the sight of her made his fingers grow thick and clumsy, his eyelids to quiver. Jijibhoi had spoken truly: she had lost none of her beauty. Yet she was not at all the Sybille he had known. When he had last seen her, lying in her casket, she had seemed to be a flawless marble image of herself, and she had that same surreal statuary appearance now. Her face was an expressionless mask, calm, remote, aloof; her eyes were glossy mysteries; her lips registered a faint, enigmatic, barely perceptible smile. It frightened him to behold her this way, so alien, so unfamiliar. Perhaps it was the intensity of her concentration that gave her that forbidding marmoreal look, for she seemed to be pouring her entire being into the task of taking aim. By tilting the cube more extremely, Klein was able to see what she was aiming at: a strange awkward bird moving through the grass at the lower left, a bird larger than a turkey, round as a sack, with ash-gray plumage, a whitish breast and tail, yellow-white wings, and short, comical yellow legs. Its head was immense and its black bill ended in a great snubbed hook. The creature seemed solemn, rather dignified, and faintly absurd; it showed no awareness that its doom was upon it. How odd that Sybille should be about to kill it, she who had always detested the taking of life: Sybille the huntress now, Sybille the lunar goddess, Sybille-Diana!

Shaken, Klein looked up at Jijibhoi and said, "Where was this taken? On that safari in Tanzania, I suppose."

"Yes. In February. This man is the guide, the white hunter."

"I saw him in Zanzibar. Gracchus, his name is: He was one of the deads traveling with Sybille."

"He operates a hunting preserve not far from Kilimanjaro,"

Jijibhoi said, "that is set aside exclusively for the use of the deads. One of the more bizarre manifestations of their subculture, actually. They hunt only those animals which— "

Klein said impatiently, "How did you get this picture?"

"It was taken by Nerita Tracy, who is one of your wife's companions."

"I met her in Zanzibar too. But how— "

"A friend of hers is an acquaintance of mine, one of my informants, in fact, a valuable connection in my researches. Some months ago I asked him if he could obtain something like this for me. I did not tell him, of course, that I meant it for you." Jijibhoi looked close. "You seem troubled, dear friend."

Klein nodded. He shut his eyes as though to protect them from the glaring surfaces of Sybille's photograph. Eventually he said in a flat, toneless voice, "I have to get to see her."

"Perhaps it would be better for you if you would abandon— "

"*No.*"

"Is there no way I can convince you that it is dangerous for you to pursue your fantasy of— "

"No," Klein said. "Don't even try. It's necessary for me to reach her. Necessary."

"How will you accomplish this, then?"

Klein said mechanically, "By going to Zion Cold Town."

"You have already done that. They would not admit you."

"This time they will. They don't turn away deads."

The Parsee's eyes widened. "You will surrender your own life? Is this your plan? What are you saying, Jorge?"

Klein, laughing, said, "That isn't what I meant at all."

"I am bewildered."

"I intend to infiltrate. I'll disguise myself as one of them. I'll slip into the Cold Town the way an infidel slips into Mecca." He seized Jijibhoi's wrist. "Can you help me? Coach me in their ways, teach me their jargon?"

"They'll find you out instantly."

"Maybe not. Maybe I'll get to Sybille before they do."

"This is insanity," Jijibhoi said quietly.

"Nevertheless. You have the knowledge. Will you help me?"

Gently Jijibhoi withdrew his arm from Klein's grasp. He crossed the room and busied himself with an untidy bookshelf for some moments, fussily arranging and rearranging. At length he said, "There is little I can do for you myself. My knowledge is broad but not deep, not deep enough. But if you insist on going through with this, Jorge, I can introduce you to someone who may be able to assist you. He is one of my informants, a dead, a man who has rejected the authority of the Guidefathers, a person who is *of* the deads but not *with* them. Possibly he can instruct you in what you would need to know."

"Call him," Klein said.

"I must warn you he is unpredictable, turbulent, perhaps even treacherous. Ordinary human values are without meaning to him in his present state."

"Call him."

"If only I could discourage you from— "

"Call him."

# 5

Quarreling brings trouble. These days lions roar a great deal. Joy follows grief. It is not good to beat children much. You had better go away now and go home. It is impossible to work today. You should go to school every day. It is not advisable to follow this path, there is water in the way. Never mind, I shall be able to pass. We had better go back quickly. These lamps use a lot of oil. There are no mosquitoes in Nairobi. There are no lions here. There are people here, looking for eggs. Is there water in the well? No, there is none. If there are only three people, work will be impossible today.

D.V. Perrott: *Teach Yourself Swahili*

Gracchus signals furiously to the porters and bellows, "*Shika njia hii hii!*" Three turn, two keep trudging along. "*Ninyi nyote!*" he calls. "*Fanga kama hivi!*" He shakes his head, spits, flicks sweat from his forehead. He adds, speaking in a lower voice and in English, taking care that they will not hear him, "Do as I say, you malevolent black bastards, or you'll be deader than I am before sunset!"

Sybille laughs nervously. "Do you always talk to them like that?"

"I try to be easy on them. But what good does it do, what good does any of it do? Come on, let's keep up with them."

It is less than an hour after dawn, but already the sun is very hot, here in the flat dry country between Kilimanjaro and Serengeti. Gracchus is leading the party northward across the high grass, following the spoor of what he thinks is a quagga, but breaking a trail in the high grass is hard work and the porters keep veering away toward a ravine that offers the tempting shade of a thicket of thorn trees, and he constantly has to harass them in order to hold them to the route he wants. Sybille has noticed that Gracchus shouts fiercely to his blacks, as if they were no more than recalcitrant beasts, and speaks of them behind their backs with a rough contempt, but it all seems done for show, all part of his white-hunter role: she has also noticed, at times when she was not supposed to notice, that privately Gracchus is in fact gentle, tender, even loving among the porters, teasing them—she supposes—with affectionate Swahili banter and playful mock-punches. The porters are role-players too: they behave in the traditional manner of their profession, alternately deferential and patronizing to the clients, alternately posing as all-knowing repositories of the lore of the bush and as simple, guileless savages fit only for carrying burdens. But the clients they serve are not quite like the sportsmen of Hemingway's time, since they are deads, and secretly the porters are terrified of the strange beings whom they serve. Sybille has seen them muttering prayers and fondling amulets whenever they accidentally touch one of the deads, and has occasionally detected an unguarded glance conveying unalloyed fear, possibly revulsion. Gracchus is no friend of theirs, however jolly he may get with them: they appear to regard him as some sort of monstrous sorcerer and the clients as fiends made manifest.

Sweating, saying little, the hunters move in single file, first the porters with the guns and supplies, then Gracchus, Zacharias, Sybille, Nerita constantly clicking her camera, and Mortimer. Patches of white cloud drift slowly across the immense arch of the sky. The grass is lush and thick, for the short rains were unusually heavy in December. Small animals scurry through it, visible only in quick flashes, squirrels and jackals and guinea-fowl. Now and then larger creatures can be seen: three haughty ostriches, a pair of snuffling hyenas, a band of Thomson gazelles flowing like a tawny river across the plain. Yesterday Sybille spied two wart hogs, some giraffes, and a serval, an elegant big-eared wildcat that slithered along like a miniature cheetah. None of these beasts may be hunted, but only those special ones that the operators of the preserve have introduced for the special needs of their clients; anything considered native African wildlife, which is to say anything that was living here before the deads leased this tract from the Masai, is protected by government decree. The

Masai themselves are allowed to do some lion-hunting, since this is their reservation, but there are so few Masai left that they can do little harm. Yesterday, after the wart hogs and before the giraffes, Sybille saw her first Masai, five lean, handsome, long-bodied men, naked under skimpy red robes, drifting silently through the bush, pausing frequently to stand thoughtfully on one leg, propped against their spears. At close range they were less handsome—toothless, fly-specked, herniated. They offered to sell their spears and their beaded collars for a few shillings, but the safarigoers had already stocked up on Masai artifacts in Nairobi's curio shops, at astonishingly higher prices.

All through the morning they stalk the quagga, Gracchus pointing out hoofprints here, fresh dung there. It is Zacharias who has asked to shoot a quagga. "How can you tell we're not following a zebra?" he asks peevishly.

Gracchus winks. "Trust me. We'll find zebras up ahead too. But you'll get your quagga. I guarantee it."

Ngiri, the head porter, turns and grins. "*Piga quagga m'uzuri, bwana*," he says to Zacharias, and winks also, and then—Sybille sees it plainly—his jovial confident smile fades as though he has had the courage to sustain it only for an instant, and a veil of dread covers his dark glossy face.

"What did he say?" Zacharias asks.

"That you'll shoot a fine quagga," Gracchus replies.

Quaggas. The last wild one was killed about 1870, leaving only three in the world, all females, in European zoos. The Boers had hunted them to the edge of extinction in order to feed their tender meat to Hottentot slaves and to make from their striped hides sacks for Boer grain, leather *veldschoen* for Boer feet. The quagga of the London zoo died in 1872, that in Berlin in 1875, the Amsterdam quagga in 1883, and none was seen alive again until the artificial revival of the species through breedback selection and genetic manipulation in 1990, when this hunting preserve was opened to a limited and special clientele.

It is nearly noon, now, and not a shot has been fired all morning. The animals have begun heading for cover; they will not emerge until the shadows lengthen. Time to halt, pitch camp, break out the beer and sandwiches, tell tall tales of harrowing adventures with maddened buffaloes and edgy elephants. But not quite yet. The marchers come over a low hill and see, in the long sloping hollow beyond, a flock of ostriches and several hundred grazing zebras. As the humans appear, the ostriches begin slowly and warily to move off, but the zebras, altogether unafraid, continue to graze. Ngiri points and says, "*Piga quagga, bwana.*"

"Just a bunch of zebras," Zacharias says.

Gracchus shakes his head. "No. Listen. You hear the sound?"

At first no one perceives anything unusual. But then, yes, Sybille hears it: a shrill barking neigh, very strange, a sound out of lost time, the cry of some beast she has never known. It is a song of the dead. Nerita hears it too, and Mortimer, and finally Zacharias. Gracchus nods toward the far side of the hollow. There, among the zebras, are half a dozen animals that might almost be zebras, but are not—unfinished zebras, striped only on their heads and foreparts; the rest of their bodies are yellowish brown, their legs are white, their manes are dark-brown with pale stripes. Their coats sparkle like mica in the sunshine. Now and again they lift their heads, emit that weird percussive whistling snort, and bend to the grass again. Quaggas. Strays out of the past relicts, rekindled specters. Gracchus signals and the party fans out along the peak of the hill. Ngiri hands Zacharias his colossal gun. Zacharias kneels, sights.

"No hurry," Gracchus murmurs. "We have all afternoon."

"Do I seem to be hurrying?" Zacharias asks. The zebras now block the little group of quaggas from his view, almost as if by design. He must not shoot a zebra. Of course, or there will be trouble with the rangers Minutes go by. Then the screen of zebras abruptly parts and Zacharias squeezes his trigger. There is a vast explosion; zebras bolt in ten directions, so that the eye is bombarded with dizzying stroboscopic waves of black and white; when the convulsive confusion passes, one of the quaggas is lying on its side, alone in the field, having made the transition across the interface. Sybille regards it calmly. Death once dismayed her, death of any kind, but no longer.

"*Piga m'uzuri!*" the porters cry exultantly.

"*Kufa,*" Gracchus says. "Dead. A neat shot. You have your trophy."

Ngiri is quick with the skinning-knife. That night, camping below Kilimanjaro's broad flank, they dine on roast quagga, deads and porters alike. The meat is juicy, robust, faintly tangy.

Late the following afternoon, as they pass through cooler stream-broken country thick with tall, scrubby gray-green vase-shaped trees, they come upon a monstrosity, a shaggy shambling thing twelve or fifteen feet high, standing upright on ponderous hind legs and balancing itself on an incredibly thick, heavy tail. It leans against a tree, pulling at its top branches with long forelimbs that are tipped with ferocious claws like a row of sickles; it munches voraciously on leaves and twigs. Briefly it notices them, and looks around, studying them with small stupid yellow eyes; then it returns to its meal.

"A rarity," Gracchus says. "I know hunters who have been all over this park without ever running into one. Have you ever seen anything so ugly?"

"What is it?" Sybille asks.

"Megatherium. Giant ground sloth. South American, really, but we weren't fussy about geography when we were stocking this place. We have only four of them, and it costs God knows how many thousands of dollars to shoot one. Nobody's signed up for a ground sloth yet. I doubt anyone will."

Sybille wonders where the beast might be vulnerable to a bullet: surely not in its dim peanut-sized brain. She wonders, too, what sort of sportsman would find pleasure in killing such a thing. For a while they watch as the sluggish monster tears the tree apart. Then they move on.

Gracchus shows them another prodigy at sundown: a pale dome, like some huge melon, nestling in a mound of dense grass beside a stream. "Ostrich egg?" Mortimer guesses.

"Close. Very close. It's a moa egg. World's biggest bird. From New Zealand, extinct since about the eighteenth century."

Nerita crouches and lightly taps the egg. "What an omelet we could make!"

"There's enough there to feed seventy-five of us," Gracchus says. "Two gallons of fluid, easy. But of course we mustn't meddle with it. Natural increase is very important in keeping this park stocked."

"And where's mama moa?" Sybille asks. "Should she have abandoned the egg?"

"Moas aren't very bright," Gracchus answer. "That's one good reason why they became extinct. She must have wandered off to find some dinner. And— "

"Good God," Zacharias blurts.

The moa has returned, emerging suddenly from a thicket. She stands like a feathered mountain above, them, limned by the deep-blue of twilight: an ostrich, more or less, but a magnified ostrich, an ultimate ostrich, a bird a dozen feet high, with a heavy rounded body and a great thick hose of a neck and taloned legs sturdy as saplings. Surely this is Sinbad's rukh, that can fly off with elephants in its grasp! The bird peers at them, sadly contemplating the band of small beings clustered about her egg; she arches her neck as though readying for an attack, and Zacharias reaches for one of the rifles, but Gracchus checks his hand, for the moa is merely rearing back to protest. It utters a deep mournful mooing sound and does not move. "Just back slowly away," Gracchus tells them. "It won't attack. But keep away from the feet; one kick can kill you."

"I was going to apply for a license on a moa," Mortimer says.

"Killing them's a bore," Gracchus tells him. "They just stand there and let you shoot. You're better off with what you signed up for."

What Mortimer has signed up for is an aurochs, the vanished wild ox of the European forests, known to Caesar, known to Pliny, hunted by the hero Siegfried, altogether exterminated by the year 1627. The plains of East Africa are not a comfortable environment for the aurochs and the herd that has been conjured by the genetic necromancers keeps to itself in the wooded highlands, several days' journey from the haunts of quaggas and ground sloths. In this dark grove the hunters come upon troops of chattering baboons and solitary biggeared elephants and, in a place of broken sunlight and shadow, a splendid antelope, a bull bongo with a fine curving pair of horns. Gracchus leads them onward, deeper in. He seems tense: there is peril here. The porters slip through the forest like black wraiths, spreading out in arching crab-claw patterns, communicating with one another and with Gracchus by whistling. Everyone keeps weapons ready in here. Sybille half expects to see leopards draped on overhanging branches, cobras slithering through the undergrowth. But she feels no fear.

They approach a clearing.

"Aurochs," Gracchus says.

A dozen of them are cropping the shrubbery: big short-haired long-horned cattle, muscular and alert. Picking up the scent of the intruders, they lift their heavy heads, sniff, glare. Gracchus and Ngiri confer with eyebrows. Nodding, Gracchus mutters to Mortimer, "Too many of them. Wait for them to thin off." Mortimer smiles. He looks a little nervous. The aurochs has a reputation for attacking without warning. Four, five, six of the beasts slip away, and the others withdraw to the edge of the clearing, as if to plan strategy; but one big bull, sour-eyed and

grim, stands his ground, glowering. Gracchus rolls on the balls
of his feet. His burly body seems, to Sybille, a study in mobility,
in preparedness.

"Now," he says.

In the same moment the bull aurochs charges, moving with
extraordinary swiftness, head lowered, horns extended like spears.
Mortimer fires. The bullet strikes with a loud whonking sound,
crashing into the shoulder of the aurochs, a perfect shot, but the
animal does not fall, and Mortimer shoots again, less gracefully
ripping into the belly, and then Gracchus and Ngiri are firing
also, not at Mortimer's aurochs but over the heads of the others, to
drive them away, and the risky tactic works, for the other animals
go stampeding off into the woods. The one Mortimer has shot
continues toward him, staggering now, losing momentum, and
falls practically at his feet, rolling over, knifing the forest floor
with its hooves.

"*Kufa*," Ngiri says. "*Piga nyati m'uzuri, bwana.*"

Mortimer grins. "*Piga*," he says.

Gracchus salutes him. "More exciting than moa," he says.


"And these are mine," says Nerita three hours later, indicating
a tree at the outer rim of the forest. Several hundred large pigeons
nest in its boughs, so many of them that the tree seems to be
sprouting birds rather than leaves. The females are plain—light-
brown above, gray below—but the males are flamboyant, with
rich, glossy blue plumage on their wings and backs, breasts of
a wine-red chestnut color, iridescent spots of bronze and green
on their necks, and weird, vivid eyes of a bright, fiery orange.
Gracchus says, "Right. You've found your passenger pigeons."

"Where's the thrill in shooting pigeons out of a tree?" Mortimer
asks.

Nerita gives him a withering look. "Where's the thrill in gunning
down a charging bull?" She signals to Ngiri, who fires a shot into
the air. The startled pigeons burst from their perches and fly in
low circles. In the old days, a century and a half ago in the
forests of North America, no one troubled to shoot passenger
pigeons on the wing: the pigeons were food, not sport, and it
was simpler to blast them as they sat, for that way a single hunter
might kill thousands of birds in one day. Thus it took only fifty
years to reduce the passenger pigeon population from uncountable
sky-blackening billions to zero. Nerita is more sporting. This is a
test of her skill, after all. She aims her shotgun, shoots, pumps,

shoots, pumps. Stunned birds drop to the ground. She and her gun are a single entity, sharing one purpose. In moments it is all over. The porters retrieve the fallen birds and snap their necks. Nerita has the dozen pigeons her license allows: a pair to mount, the rest for tonight's dinner. The survivors have returned to their tree and stare placidly, unreproachfully, at the hunters.

"They breed so damned fast," Gracchus mutters. "If we aren't careful, they'll be getting out of the preserve and taking over all of Africa."

Sybille laughs. "Don't worry. We'll cope. We wiped them out once and we can do it again, if we have to."

Sybille's prey is a dodo. In Dar, when they were applying for their licenses, the others mocked her choice: a fat flightless bird, unable to run or fight, so feeble of wit that it fears nothing. She ignored them. She wants a dodo because to her it is the essence of extinction, the prototype of all that is dead and vanished. That there is no sport in shooting foolish dodos means little to Sybille. Hunting itself is meaningless for her.

Through this vast park she wanders as in a dream. She sees ground sloths, great auks, quaggas, moas, heath hens, Javan rhinos, giant armadillos, and many other rarities. The place is an abode of ghosts. The ingenuities of the genetic craftsmen are limitless; someday, perhaps, the preserve will offer trilobites, tyrannosaurs, mastodons, saber-toothed cats, baluchitheria, even—why not?—packs of Australopithecines, tribes of Neanderthals. For the amusement of the deads, whose games tend to be somber. Sybille wonders whether it can really be considered killing, this slaughter of laboratory-spawned novelties. Are these animals real or artificial? Living things, or cleverly animated constructs? Real, she decides. Living. They eat, they metabolize, they reproduce. They must seem real to themselves, and so they are real, realer, maybe, than dead human beings who walk again in their own cast-off bodies.

"Shotgun," Sybille says to the closest porter.

There is the bird, ugly, ridiculous, waddling laboriously through the tall grass. Sybille accepts a weapon and sights along its barrel. "Wait," Nerita says. "I'd like to get a picture of this." She moves slantwise around the group, taking exaggerated care not to frighten the dodo, but the dodo does not seem to be aware of any of them. Like an emissary from the realm of darkness, carrying good news of death to those creatures not yet extinct, it plods diligently across their path. "Fine," Nerita says. "Anthony, point at the dodo, will you, as if you've just noticed it? Kent, I'd like you to look down at your gun, study its bolt or something. Fine. And Sybille, just hold that pose—aiming—yes— "

Nerita takes the picture.

Calmly Sybille pulls the trigger.

"*Kazi imekwisha*," Gracchus says. "The work is finished."

# 6

Although to be driven back upon oneself is an uneasy affair at best, rather like trying to cross a border with borrowed credentials, it seems to be now the one condition necessary to the beginnings of real self-respect. Most of our platitudes notwithstanding, self-deception remains the most difficult deception. The tricks that work on others count for nothing in that very well-lit back alley where one keeps assignations with oneself: no winning smiles will do here, no prettily drawn lists of good intentions.

Joan Didion: On Self-Respect

"You better believe what Jeej is trying to tell you," Dolorosa said. "Ten minutes inside the Cold Town, they'll have your number. Five minutes."

Jijibhoi's man was small, rumpled-looking, forty or fifty years old, with untidy long dark hair and wide-set smoldering eyes. His skin was sallow and his face was gaunt. Such other deads as Klein had seen at close range had about them an air of unearthly serenity, but not this one: Dolorosa was tense, fidgety, a knuckle-cracker, a lip-gnawer. Yet somehow there could be no doubt he was a dead, as much a dead as Zacharias, as Gracchus, as Mortimer.

"They'll have my what?" Klein asked.

"Your number. Your number. They'll know you aren't a dead, because it can't be faked. Jesus, don't you even speak English? Jorge, that's a foreign name. I should have known. Where are you from?"

"Argentina, as a matter of fact, but I was brought to California when I was a small boy. In 1955. Look, if they catch me, they catch me. I just want to get in there and spend half an hour talking with my wife."

"Mister, you don't have any wife any more."

"With Sybille," Klein said, exasperated. "To talk with Sybille, my—my former wife."

"All right. I'll get you inside."

"What will it cost?"

"Never mind that," Dolorosa said. "I owe Jeej here a few favors. More than a few. So I'll get you the drug— "

"Drug?"

"The drug the Treasury agents use when they infiltrate the Cold Towns. It narrows the pupils, contracts the capillaries, gives you that good old zombie look. The agents always get caught and thrown out, and so will you, but at least you'll go in there feeling that you've got a convincing disguise. Little oily capsule, one every morning before breakfast."

Klein looked at Jijibhoi. "Why do Treasury agents infiltrate the Cold Towns?"

"For the same reasons they infiltrate anywhere else," Jijibhoi said. "To spy. They are trying to compile dossiers on the financial dealings of the deads, you see, and until proper life-defining legislation is approved by Congress there is no precise way of compelling a person who is deemed legally dead to divulge— "

Dolorosa said, "Next, the background. I can get you a card of residence from Albany Cold Town in New York. You died last December, okay, and they rekindled you back east because—let's see— "

"I could have been attending the annual meeting of the American Historical Association in New York," Klein suggested. "That's what I do, you understand, professor of contemporary history at UCLA. Because of the Christmas holiday my body couldn't be shipped back to California, no room on any flight, and so they took me to Albany. How does that sound?"

Dolorosa smiled. "You really enjoy making up lies, Professor, don't you? I can dig that quality in you. Okay, Albany Cold Town, and this is your first trip out of there, your drying-off trip—that's what it's called, drying-off—you come out of the Cold Town like a new butterfly just out of its cocoon, all soft and damp, and you're on your own in a strange place. Now, there's a lot of stuff you'll need to know about how to behave, little mannerisms, social graces, that kind of crap, and I'll work on that with you tomorrow and Wednesday and Friday, three sessions; that ought to be enough. Meanwhile let me give you the basics. There are only three things you really have to remember while you're inside:

"(1) Never ask a direct question.

"(2) Never lean on anybody's arm. You know what I mean?

"(3) Keep in mind that to a dead the whole universe is plastic, nothing's real, nothing matters a hell of a lot, it's all only a joke. Only a joke, friend, only a joke."

Early in April he flew to Salt Lake City, rented a car, and drove out past Moab into the high plateau rimmed by red-rock mountains where the deads had built Zion Cold Town. This was Klein's second visit to the necropolis. The other had been in the late summer of '91, a hot, parched season when the sun filled half the sky and even the gnarled junipers looked dazed from thirst; but now it was a frosty afternoon, with faint pale light streaming out of the wintry western hills and occasional gusts of light snow whirling through the iron-blue air. Jijibhoi's route instructions pulsed from the memo screen on his dashboard. Fourteen miles from town, yes, narrow paved lane turns off highway, yes, discreet little sign announcing PRIVATE ROAD, NO ADMITTANCE, yes, a second sign a thousand yards in, ZION COLD TOWN, MEMBERS ONLY, yes, and then just beyond that the barrier of green light across the road, the scanner system, the roadblocks sliding like scythes out of the underground installations, a voice on an invisible loudspeaker saying, "If you have a permit to enter Zion Cold Town, please place it under your left-hand wind-shield wiper."

That other time he had had no permit, and he had gone no farther than this, though at least he had managed a little colloquy with the unseen gatekeeper out of which he had squeezed the information that Sybille was indeed living in that particular Cold Town. This time he affixed Dolorosa's forged card of residence to his windshield, and waited tensely, and in thirty seconds the roadblocks slid from sight. He drove on, along a winding road that followed the natural contours of a dense forest of scrubby conifers, and came at last to a brick wall that curved away into the trees as though it encircled the entire town. Probably it did. Klein had an overpowering sense of the Cold Town as a hermetic city, ponderous and sealed as old Egypt. There was a metal gate in the brick wall; green electronic eyes surveyed him, signaled their approval, and the wall rolled open.

He drove slowly toward the center of town, passing through a zone of what he supposed were utility buildings—storage depots, a power substation, the municipal waterworks, whatever, a bunch of grim windowless one-story cinderblock affairs—and then into the residential district, which was not much lovelier. The streets were laid out on a rectangular grid; the buildings were squat, dreary, impersonal, homogeneous. There was practically no automobile traffic, and in a dozen blocks he saw no more than ten pedestrians, who did not even glance at him. So this was the environment in which the deads chose to spend their second lives. But why such deliberate bleakness? "You will never understand us," Dolorosa had warned. Dolorosa was right. Jijibhoi had told him that Cold Towns were something less than charming, but Klein had not been prepared for this. There was a glacial quality about the place, as though it were wholly entombed in a block of clear ice: silence, sterility, a mortuary calm. Cold Town, yes, aptly named. Architecturally, the town looked like the worst of all possible cheap-and-sleazy tract developments, but the psychic texture it projected was even more depressing, more like that of one of those ghastly retirement communities, one of the innumerable Leisure Worlds or Sun Manors, those childless joyless retreats where colonies of that other kind of living dead collected to await the last trumpet. Klein shivered.

At last, another few minutes deeper into the town a sign of activity, if not exactly of life: a shopping center, flat-topped brown stucco buildings around a U-shaped courtyard, a steady flow of shoppers moving about. All right. His first test was about to commence. He parked his car near the mouth of the U and strolled uneasily inward. He felt as if his forehead were a beacon, flashing glowing betrayals at rhythmic intervals:

FRAUD    INTRUDER    INTERLOPE    SPY

Go ahead, he thought, seize me, seize the impostor, get it over with, throw me out, string me up, crucify me. But no one seemed to pick up the signals. He was altogether ignored. Out of courtesy? Or just contempt? He stole what he hoped were covert glances at the shoppers, half expecting to run across Sybille right away. They all looked like sleepwalkers, moving in glazed silence about their errands. No smiles, no chatter: the icy aloofness of these self-contained people heightened the familiar suburban atmosphere of the shopping center into surrealist intensity, Norman Rockwell with an overlay of Dali or De Chirico. The shopping center looked like all other shopping centers: clothing stores, a bank, a record shop, snack bars, a florist, a TV-stereo outlet, a theater, a five-and-dime. One difference, though, became apparent as Klein wandered from shop to shop: the whole place was automated. There were no clerks anywhere, only the ubiquitous data screens, and no doubt a battery of hidden scanners to discourage shoplifters. (Or did the impulse toward petty theft perish with the body's first death?) The customers selected all the merchandise themselves, checked it out via data screens, touched their thumbs to charge-plates to debit their accounts. Of course. No one was going to waste his precious rekindled existence standing behind a counter to sell tennis shoes or cotton candy. Nor were the dwellers in the Cold Towns likely to dilute their isolation by hiring a labor force of imported warms. Somebody here had to do a little work, obviously—how did the merchandise get into the stores?—but, in general, Klein realized, what could not be done here by machines would not be done at all.

For ten minutes he prowled the center. Just when he was beginning to think he must be entirely invisible to these people, a short, broad-shouldered man, bald but with oddly youthful features, paused in front of him and said, "I am Pablo. I welcome you to Zion Cold Town." This unexpected puncturing of the silence so startled Klein that he had to fight to retain appropriate deadlike imperturbability. Pablo smiled warmly and touched both his hands to Klein's in friendly greeting, but his eyes were frigid, hostile, remote, a terrifying contradiction. "I've been sent to bring you to the lodging-place. Come: your car."

Other than to give directions, Pablo spoke only three times during the five-minute drive. "Here is the rekindling house," he said. A five-story building, as inviting as a hospital, with walls of dark bronze and windows black as onyx. "This is Guidefather's house," Pablo said a moment later. A modest brick building, like a rectory, at the edge of a small park. And, finally: "This is where you will stay. Enjoy your visit." Abruptly he got out of the car and walked rapidly away.

This was the house of strangers, the hotel for visiting deads, a long low cinderblock structure, functional and unglamorous, one of the least seductive buildings in this city of stark disagreeable buildings. However else it might be with the deads, they clearly had no craving for fancy architecture. A voice out of a data screen in the spartan lobby assigned him to a room: a white-walled box, square, high of ceiling. He had his own toilet, his own data screen, a narrow bed, a chest of drawers, a modest closet, a small window that gave him a view of a neighboring building just as drab as this. Nothing had been said about rental; perhaps he was a guest of the city. Nothing had been said about anything. It seemed that he had been accepted. So much for Jijibhoi's gloomy assurance that he would instantly be found out, so much for Dolorosa's insistence that they would have his number in ten minutes or less. He had been in Zion Cold Town for half an hour. Did they have his number?

"Eating isn't important among us," Dolorosa had said.

"But you do eat?"

"Of course we eat. It just isn't *important*."

It was important to Klein, though. Not *haute cuisine*, necessarily, but some sort of food, preferably three times a day. He was getting hungry now. Ring for room service? There were no servants in this city. He turned to the data screen. Dolorosa's first rule: *Never ask a direct question.* Surely that didn't apply to the data screen, only to his fellow deads. He didn't have to observe the niceties of etiquette when talking to a computer. Still, the voice behind the screen might not be that of a computer after all, so he tried to employ the oblique, elliptical conversational style that Dolorosa said the deads favored among themselves:

"Dinner?"

"Commissary."

"Where?"

"Central Four," said the screen.

Central Four? All right. He would find the way. He changed into fresh clothing and went down the long vinyl-floored hallway to the lobby. Night had come; street lamps were glowing; under cloak of darkness the city's ugliness was no longer so obtrusive, and there was even a kind of controlled beauty about the brutal regularity of its streets.

The streets were unmarked, though, and deserted. Klein walked at random for ten minutes, hoping to meet someone heading for the Central Four commissary. But when he did come upon someone, a tall and regal woman well advanced in years, he found himself incapable of approaching her. (*Never ask a direct question. Never lean on anybody's arm.*) He walked alongside her, in silence and at a distance, until she turned suddenly to enter a house. For ten minutes more he wandered alone again. This is ridiculous, he thought: dead or warm, I'm a stranger in town, I should be entitled to a little assistance. Maybe Dolorosa was just trying to complicate things. On the next corner, when Klein caught sight of a man hunched away from the wind, lighting a cigarette, he went boldly over to him. "Excuse me, but— "

The other looked up. "Klein?" he said. "Yes. Of course. Well, so you've made the crossing too!"

He was one of Sybille's Zanzibar companions, Klein realized. The quick-eyed, sharp-edged one—Mortimer. A member of her pseudo-familial grouping, whatever that might be. Klein stared sullenly at him. This had to be the moment when his imposture would be exposed, for only some six weeks had passed since he had argued with Mortimer in the gardens of Sybille's Zanzibar hotel, not nearly enough time for someone to have died and been rekindled and gone through his drying-off. But a moment passed and Mortimer said nothing. At length Klein said, "I just got here. Pablo showed me to the house of strangers and now I'm looking for the commissary."

"Central Four? I'm going there myself. How lucky for you." No sign of suspicion in Mortimer's face. Perhaps an elusive smile revealed his awareness that Klein could not be what he claimed to be. *Keep in mind that to a dead the whole universe is plastic, it's all only a joke.* "I'm waiting for Nerita," Mortimer said. "We can all eat together."

Klein said heavily, "I was rekindled in Albany Cold Town. I've just emerged."

"How nice," Mortimer said.

Nerita Tracy stepped out of a building just beyond the corner—a slim, athletic-looking woman, about forty, with short reddish-brown hair. As she swept toward them, Mortimer said, "Here's Klein, who we met in Zanzibar. Just rekindled, out of Albany."

"Sybille will be amused."

"Is she in town?" Klein blurted.

Mortimer and Nerita exchanged sly glances. Klein felt abashed. *Never ask a direct question.* Damn Dolorosa!

Nerita said, "You'll see her before long. Shall we go to dinner?"

The commissary was less austere than Klein had expected: actually quite an inviting restaurant, elaborately constructed on five or six levels divided by lustrous dark hangings into small, secluded dining areas. It had the warm, rich look of a tropical resort. But the food, which came automat-style out of revolving dispensers, was prefabricated and cheerless—another jarring contradiction. *Only a joke, friend, only a joke.* In any case he was less hungry than he had imagined at the hotel. He sat with Mortimer and Nerita, picking at his meal, while their conversation flowed past him at several times the speed of thought. They spoke in fragments and ellipses, in periphrastics and aposiopeses, in a style abundant in chiasmus, metonymy, meiosis, oxymoron, and zeugma; their dazzling rhetorical techniques left him baffled and uncomfortable, which beyond much doubt was their intention. Now and again they would dart from a thicket of indirection to skewer him with a quick corroborative stab: Isn't that so, they would say, and he would smile and nod, nod and smile, saying, Yes, yes, absolutely. Did they know he was a fake, and were they merely playing with him, or had they, somehow, impossibly, accepted him as one of them? So subtle was their style that he could not tell. A very new member of the society of the rekindled, he told himself, would be nearly as much at sea here as a warm in deadface.

Then Nerita said—no verbal games, this time—"You still miss her terribly, don't you?"

"I do. Some things evidently never perish."

"Everything perishes," Mortimer said. "The dodo, the aurochs, the Holy Roman Empire, the T'ang Dynasty, the walls of Byzantium, the language of Mohenjo-daro."

"But not the Great Pyramid, the Yangtze, the coelacanth, or the skullcap of Pithecanthropus," Klein countered. "Some things persist and endure. And some can be regenerated. Lost languages have been deciphered. I believe the dodo and the aurochs are hunted in a certain African park in this very era."

"Replicas," Mortimer said.

"Convincing replicas. Simulations as good as the original."

"Is that what you want?" Nerita asked.

"I want what's possible to have."

"A convincing replica of lost love?"

"I might be willing to settle for five minutes of conversation with her."

"You'll have it. Not tonight. See? There she is. But don't bother her now." Nerita nodded across the gulf in the center of the restaurant; on the far side, three levels up from where they sat, Sybille and Kent Zacharias had appeared. They stood for a brief while at the edge of their dining alcove, staring blandly and emotionlessly into the restaurant's central well. Klein felt a muscle jerking uncontrollably in his cheek, a damning revelation of undeadlike uncoolness, and pressed his hand over it, so that it twanged and throbbed against his palm. She was like a goddess up there, manifesting herself in her sanctum to her worshipers, a pale shimmering figure, more beautiful even than she had become to him through the anguished enhancements of memory, and it seemed impossible to him that that being had ever been his wife, that he had known her when her eyes were puffy and reddened from a night of study, that he had looked down at her face as they made love and had seen her lips pull back in that spasm of ecstasy that is so close to a grimace of pain, that he had known her crochety and unkind in her illness, short-tempered and impatient in health, a person of flaws and weaknesses, of odors and blemishes, in short a human being, this goddess, this unreal rekindled creature, this object of his quest, this Sybille. Serenely she turned, serenely she vanished into her cloaked alcove. "She knows you're here," Nerita told him. "You'll see her. Perhaps tomorrow." Then Mortimer said something maddeningly oblique, and Nerita replied with the same off-center mystification, and Klein once more was plunged into the river of their easy dancing wordplay, down into it, down and down and down, and as he struggled to keep from drowning, as he fought to comprehend their interchanges, he never once looked toward the place where Sybille sat, not even once, and congratulated himself on having accomplished that much at least in his masquerade.

That night, lying alone in his room at the house of strangers, he wonders what he will say to Sybille when they finally meet, and what she will say to him. Will he dare bluntly to ask her to describe to him the quality of her new existence? That is all that he wants from her, really, that knowledge, that opening of an aperture into her transfigured self; that is as much as he hopes to get from her, knowing as he does that there is scarcely a chance of regaining her, but will he dare to ask, will he dare even that? Of course his asking such things will reveal to her that he is still a warm, too dense and gross of perception to comprehend the life of a dead; but he is certain she will sense that anyway, instantly. What will he say, what will he say? He plays out an imagined script of their conversation in the theater of his mind:

—Tell me what it's like, Sybille, to be the way you are now.
—Like swimming under a sheet of glass.
—I don't follow.
—Everything is quiet where I am, Jorge. There's a peace that passeth all understanding. I used to feel sometimes that I was caught up in a great storm, that I was being buffeted by every breeze, that my life was being consumed by agitations and frenzies, but now, now I'm at the eye of the storm, at the place where everything is always calm. I observe rather than let myself be acted upon.

—But isn't there a loss of feeling that way? Don't you feel that you're wrapped in an insulating layer? Like swimming under glass, you say—that conveys being insulated, being cut off, being almost numb.

—I suppose you might think so. The way it is, is that one no longer is affected by the unnecessary.

—It sounds to me like a limited existence.

—Less limited than the grave, Jorge.

—I never understood why you wanted rekindling. You were such a world-devourer, Sybille, you lived with such intensity, such passion. To settle for the kind of existence you have now, to be only half-alive—

—Don't be a fool, Jorge. To be half-alive is better than to be rotting in the ground. I was so young. There was so much else still to see and do.

—But to see it and do it half-alive?

—Those were your words, not mine. I'm not alive at all. I'm neither less nor more than the person you knew. I'm another kind of being altogether. Neither less nor more, only different.

—Are all your perceptions different?

—Very much so. My perspective is broader. Little things stand revealed as little things.

—Give me an example, Sybille.

—I'd rather not. How could I make anything clear to you? Die and be with us, and you'll understand.

—You know I'm not dead?

—Oh, Jorge, how funny you are!

—How nice that I can still amuse you.

—You look so hurt, so tragic. I could almost feel sorry for you. Come: ask me anything.

—Could you leave your companions and live in the world again?

—I've never considered that.

—Could you?

—I suppose I could. But why should I? This is my world now.

—This ghetto.

—Is that how it seems to you?

—You lock yourselves into a closed society of your peers, a tight subculture. Your own jargon, your own wall of etiquette and idiosyncrasy. Designed, I think, mainly to keep the outsiders off balance, to keep them feeling like outsiders. It's a defensive thing.

The hippies, the blacks, the gays, the deads—same mechanism, same process.

The Jews, too. Don't forget the Jews.

—All right, Sybille, the Jews. With their little tribal jokes, their special holidays, their own mysterious language, yes, a good case in point.

—So I've joined a new tribe. What's wrong with that?

—Did you need to be part of a tribe?

—What did I have before? The tribe of Californians? The tribe of academics?

—The tribe of Jorge and Sybille Klein.

—Too narrow. Anyway, I've been expelled from that tribe. I needed to join another one.

—Expelled?

—By death. After that there's no going back.

—You could go back. Any time.

—Oh, no, no, no, Jorge, I can't, I can't, I'm not Sybille Klein any more, I never will be again. How can I explain it to you? There's no way. Death brings on changes. Die and see, Jorge. Die and see.

Nerita said, "She's waiting for you in the lounge."

It was a big, coldly furnished room at the far end of the other wing of the house of strangers. Sybille stood by a window through which pale, chilly morning light was streaming. Mortimer was with her, and also Kent Zacharias. The two men favored Klein with mysterious oblique smiles—courteous or derisive, he could not tell which. "Do you like our town?" Zacharias asked. "Have you been seeing the sights?" Klein chose not to reply. He acknowledged the question with a faint nod and turned to Sybille. Strangely, he felt altogether calm at this moment of attaining a years-old desire: he felt nothing at all in her presence, no panic, no yearning, no dismay, no nostalgia, nothing, nothing. As though he were truly a dead. He knew it was the tranquility of utter terror.

"We'll leave you two alone," Zacharias said. "You must have so much to tell each other." He went out, with Nerita and Mortimer. Klein's eyes met Sybille's and lingered there. She was looking at him coolly, in a kind of impersonal appraisal. That damnable smile of hers, Klein thought: dying turns them all into Mona Lisas.

She said, "Do you plan to stay here long?"

"Probably not. A few days, maybe a week." He moistened his lips. "How have you been, Sybille? How has it been going?"

"It's all been about as I expected."

*What do you mean by that? Can you give me some details? Are you at all disappointed? Have there been any surprises? What has it been like for you, Sybille? Oh, Jesus—*

*—Never ask a direct question—*

He said, "I wish you had let me visit with you in Zanzibar."

"That wasn't possible. Let's not talk about it now." She dismissed the episode with a casual wave. After a moment she said, "Would you like to hear a fascinating story I've uncovered about the early days of Omani influence in Zanzibar?"

The impersonality of the question startled him. How could she display such absolute lack of curiosity about his presence in Zion Cold Town, his claim to be a dead, his reasons for wanting to see her? How could she plunge so quickly, so coldly, into a discussion of archaic political events in Zanzibar?

"I suppose so," he said weakly.

"It's a sort of Arabian Nights story, really. It's the story of how Ahmad the Sly overthrew Abdullah ibn Muhammad Alawi."

The names were strange to him. He had indeed taken some small part in her historical researches, but it was years since he had worked with her, and everything had drifted about in his mind, leaving a jumbled residue of Ahmads and Hasans and Abdullahs. "I'm sorry," he said. "I don't recall who they were."

Unperturbed, Sybille said, "Certainly you remember that in the eighteenth and early nineteenth centuries the chief power in the Indian Ocean was the Arab state of Oman, ruled from Muscat on the Persian Gulf. Under the Busaidi dynasty, founded in 1744 by Ahmad ibn Said al-Busaidi, the Omani extended their power to East Africa. The logical capital for their African empire was the port of Mombasa, but they were unable to evict a rival dynasty reigning there, so the Busaidi looked toward nearby Zanzibar—a cosmopolitan island of mixed Arab, Indian, and African population. Zanzibar's strategic placement on the coast and its spacious and well-protected harbor made it an ideal base for the East African slave trade that the Busaidi of Oman intended to dominate."

"It comes back to me now, I think."

"Very well. The founder of the Omani Sultanate of Zanzibar was Ahmad ibn Majid the Sly, who came to the throne of Oman in 1811—do you remember?—upon the death of his uncle Abder-Rahman al-Busaidi."

"The names sound familiar," Klein said doubtfully.

"Seven years later," Sybille continued, "seeking to conquer

Zanzibar without the use of force, Ahmad the Sly shaved his beard and mustache and visited the island disguised as a soothsayer, wearing yellow robes and a costly emerald in his turban. At that time most of Zanzibar was governed by a native ruler of mixed Arab and African blood, Abdullah ibn Muhammad Alawi, whose hereditary title was Mwenyi Mkuu. The Mwenyi Mkuu's subjects were mainly Africans, members of a tribe called the Hadimu. Sultan Ahmad, arriving in Zanzibar Town, gave a demonstration of his soothsaying skills on the waterfront and attracted so much attention that he speedily gained an audience at the court of the Mwenyi Mkuu. Ahmad predicted a glowing future for Abdullah, declaring that a powerful prince famed throughout the world would come to Zanzibar, make the Mwenyi Mkuu his high lieutenant, and confirm him and his descendants as lords of Zanzibar forever.

"'How do you know these things?' asked the Mwenyi Mkuu.

"'There is a potion I drink,' Sultan Ahmad replied, 'that enables me to see what is to come. Do you wish to taste of it?'

"'Most surely I do,' Abdullah said, and Ahmad thereupon gave him a drug that sent him into rapturous transports and showed him visions of paradise. Looking down from his place near the footstool of Allah, the Mwenyi Mkuu saw a rich and happy Zanzibar governed by his children's children's children. For hours he wandered in fantasies of almighty power.

"Ahmad then departed, and let his beard and mustache grow again, and returned to Zanzibar ten weeks later in his full regalia as Sultan of Oman, at the head of an imposing and powerful armada. He went at once to the court of the Mwenyi Mkuu and proposed, just as the soothsayer had prophesied, that Oman and Zanzibar enter into a treaty of alliance under which Oman would assume responsibility for much of Zanzibar's external relations—including the slave trade—while guaranteeing the authority of the Mwenyi Mkuu over domestic affairs. In return for his partial abdication of authority, the Mwenyi Mkuu would receive financial compensation from Oman. Remembering the vision the soothsayer had revealed to him, Abdullah at once signed the treaty, thereby legitimizing what was, in effect, the Omani conquest of Zanzibar. A great feast was held to celebrate the treaty, and, as a mark of honor, the Mwenyi Mkuu offered Sultan Ahmad a rare drug used locally, known as borqash, or 'the flower of truth.' Ahmad only pretended to put the pipe to his lips, for he loathed all mind-altering drugs, but Abdullah, as the flower of truth possessed him, looked at Ahmad and recognized the outlines of the soothsayer's face behind the

Sultan's new beard. Realizing that he had been deceived, the Mwenyi Mkuu thrust his dagger, the tip of which was poisoned, deep into the Sultan's side and fled the banquet hall, taking up residence on the neighboring island of Pemba. Ahmad ibn Majid survived, but the poison consumed his vital organs and the remaining ten years of his life were spent in constant agony. As for the Mwenyi Mkuu, the Sultan's men hunted him down and put him to death along with ninety members of his family, and native rule in Zanzibar was therewith extinguished."

Sybille paused. "Is that not a gaudy and wonderful story?" she asked at last.

"Fascinating," Klein said. "Where did you find it?"

"Unpublished memoirs of Claude Richburn of the East India Company. Buried deep in the London archives. Strange that no historian ever came upon it before, isn't it? The standard texts simply say that Ahmad used his navy to bully Abdullah into signing the treaty, and then had the Mwenyi Mkuu assassinated at the first convenient moment."

"Very strange," Klein agreed. But he had not come here to listen to romantic tales of visionary potions and royal treacheries. He groped for some way to bring the conversation to a more personal level. Fragments of his imaginary dialogue with Sybille floated through his mind. *Everything is quiet where I am, Jorge. There's a peace that passeth all understanding. Like swimming under a sheet of glass. The way it is, is that one no longer is affected by the unnecessary. Little things stand revealed as little things. Die and be with us, and you'll understand.* Yes. Chapter Perhaps. But did she really believe any of that? He had put all the words in her mouth; everything he had imagined her to say was his own construct, worthless as a key to the true Sybille. Where would he find the key, though?

She gave him no chance. "I will be going back to Zanzibar soon," she said. "There's much I want to learn about this incident from the people in the back country—old legends about the last days of the Mwenyi Mkuu, perhaps variants on the basic story— "

"May I accompany you?"

"Don't you have your own research to resume, Jorge?" she asked, and did not wait for an answer. She walked briskly toward the door of the lounge and went out, and he was alone.

# 7

I mean what they and their hired psychiatrists call "delu-
sional systems." Needless to say, "delusions" are always
officially defined. We don't have to worry about questions
of real or unreal. They only talk out of expediency. It's
the *system* that matters. How the data arrange themselves
inside it. Some are consistent, others fall apart.
                              Thomas Pynchon: *Gravity's Rainbow*

Once more the deads, this time only three of them, coming over
on the morning flight from Dar. Three was better than five, Daud
Mahmoud Barwani supposed, but three was still more than a
sufficiency. Not that those others, two months back, had caused
any trouble, staying just the one day and flitting off to the mainland
again, but it made him uncomfortable to think of such creatures on
the same small island as himself. With all the world to choose, why
did they keep coming to Zanzibar?

"The plane is here," said the flight controller.

Thirteen passengers. The health officer let the local people
through the gate first—two newspapermen and four legislators
coming back from the Pan-African Conference in Capetown—and
then processed a party of four Japanese tourists, unsmiling owlish
men festooned with cameras. And then the deads: and Barwani
was surprised to discover that they were the same ones as before,
the red-haired man, the brown-haired man without the beard, the
black-haired woman. Did deads have so much money that they
could fly from America to Zanzibar every few months? Barwani
had heard a tale to the effect that each new dead, when he rose from
his coffin, was presented with bars of gold equal to his own weight,
and now he thought he believed it. No good will come of having
such beings loose in the world, he told himself, and certainly none
from letting them into Zanzibar. Yet he had no choice. "Welcome
once again to the isle of cloves," he said unctuously, and smiled
a bureaucratic smile, and wondered, not for the first time, what
would become of Daud Mahmoud Barwani once his days on earth
had reached their end.

"—Ahmad the Sly versus Abdullah Something," Klein said.
"That's all she would talk about. The history of Zanzibar." He
was in Jijibhoi's study. The night was warm and a late-season

rain was falling, blurring the million sparkling lights of the Los
Angeles basin. "It would have been, you know, gauche to ask her
any direct questions. Gauche. I haven't felt so gauche since I was
fourteen. I was helpless among them, a foreigner, a child."

"Do you think they saw through your disguise?" Jijibhoi asked.

"I can't tell. They seemed to be toying with me, to be having
sport with me, but that may just have been their general style with
any newcomer. Nobody challenged me. Nobody hinted I might
be an impostor. Nobody seemed to care very much about me or
what I was doing there or how I had happened to become a dead.
Sybille and I stood face to face, and I wanted to reach out to her,
I wanted her to reach out to me, and there was no contact, none,
none at all, it was as though we had just met at some academic
cocktail party and the only thing on her mind was the new nugget
of obscure history she had just unearthed, and so she told me
all about how Sultan Ahmad outfoxed Abdullah and Abdullah
stabbed the Sultan." Klein caught sight of a set of familiar books
on Jijibhoi's crowded shelves—Oliver and Mathew, *History of East
Africa*, books that had traveled everywhere with Sybille in the years
of their marriage. He pulled forth Volume I, saying, "She claimed
that the standard histories give a sketchy and inaccurate description
of the incident and that she's only now discovered the true story.
For all I know, she was just playing a game with me, telling me
a piece of established history as though it were something nobody
knew till last week. Let me see—Ahmad, Ahmad, Ahmad— "

He examined the index. Five Ahmads were listed, but there
was no entry for a Sultan Ahmad ibn Majid the Sly. Indeed,
an Ahmad ibn Majid was cited, but he was mentioned only in
a footnote and appeared to be an Arab chronicler. Klein found
three Abdullahs, none of them a man of Zanzibar. "Something's
wrong," he murmured.

"It does not matter, dear Jorge," Jijibhoi said mildly.

"It does. Wait a minute." He prowled the listings. Under
*Zanzibar, Rulers*, he found no Ahmads, no Abdullahs; he did
discover a Majid ibn Said, but when he checked the reference
he found that he had reigned somewhere in the second half of the
nineteenth century. Desperately Klein flipped pages, skimming,
turning back, searching. Eventually he looked up and said, "It's
all wrong!"

"The Oxford *History of East Africa?*"

"The details of Sybille's story. Look, she said this Ahmad the
Sly gained the throne of Oman in 1811, and seized Zanzibar seven

years later. But the book says that a certain Seyyid Said al-Busaidi became Sultan of Oman in 1806, and ruled for *fifty years*. He was the one, not this nonexistent Ahmad the Sly, who grabbed Zanzibar, but he did it in 1828, and the ruler he compelled to sign a treaty with him, the Mwenyi Mkuu, was named Hasan ibn Ahmad Alawi, and— " Klein shook his head. "It's an altogether different cast of characters. No stabbings, no assassinations, the dates are entirely different, the whole thing— "

Jijibhoi smiled sadly. "The deads are often mischievous."

"But why would she invent a complete fantasy and palm it off as a sensational new discovery? Sybille was the most scrupulous scholar I ever knew! She would never— "

"That was the Sybille you knew, dear friend. I keep urging you to realize that this is another person, a new person, within her body."

"A person who would lie about history?"

"A person who would tease," Jijibhoi said.

"Yes," Klein muttered. "Who would tease." *Keep in mind that to a dead the whole universe is plastic, nothing's real, nothing matters a hell of a lot.* "Who would tease a stupid, boring, annoyingly persistent ex-husband who has shown up in her Cold Town, wearing a transparent disguise and pretending to be a dead. Who would invent not only an anecdote but even its principals, as a joke, a game, a *jeu d'esprit*. Oh, God. Oh, God, how cruel she is, how foolish I was! It was her way of telling me she knew I was a phony dead. Quid pro quo, fraud for fraud!"

"What will you do?"

"I don't know," Klein said.

What he did, against Jijibhoi's strong advice and his own better judgment, was to get more pills from Dolorosa and return to Zion Cold Town. There would be a fitful joy, like that of probing the socket of a missing tooth, in confronting Sybille with the evidence of her fictional Ahmad, her imaginary Abdullah. Let there be no more games between us, he would say. Tell me what I need to know, Sybille, and then let me go away; but tell me only truth. All the way to Utah he rehearsed his speech, polishing and embellishing. There was no need for it, though, since this time the gate of Zion Cold Town would not open for him. The scanners scanned his forged Albany card and the loudspeaker said, "Your credentials are invalid."

Which could have ended it. He might have returned to Los

Angeles and picked up the pieces of his life. All this semester he had been on sabbatical leave, but the summer term was coming and there was work to do. He did return to Los Angeles, but only long enough to pack a somewhat larger suitcase, find his passport, and drive to the airport. On a sweet May evening a BOAC jet took him over the Pole to London, where, barely pausing for coffee and buns at an airport shop, he boarded another plane that carried him southeast toward Africa. More asleep than awake, he watched the dreamy landmarks drifting past: the Mediterranean, coming and going with surprising rapidity, and the tawny carpet of the Libyan Desert, and the mighty Nile, reduced to a brown thread's thickness when viewed from a height of ten miles. Suddenly Kilimanjaro, mist-wrapped, snow-bound, loomed like a giant double-headed blister to his right, far below, and he thought he could make out to his left the distant glare of the sun on the Indian Ocean. Then the big needle-nosed plane began its abrupt swooping descent, and he found himself, soon after, stepping out into the warm humid air and dazzling sunlight of Dar es Salaam.

Too soon, too soon. He felt unready to go on to Zanzibar. A day or two of rest, perhaps: he picked a Dar hotel at random, the Agip, liking the strange sound of its name, and hired a taxi. The hotel was sleek and clean, a streamlined affair in the glossy 1960's style, much cheaper than the Kilimanjaro, where he had stayed briefly on the other trip, and located in a pleasant leafy quarter of the city, near the ocean. He strolled about for a short while, discovered that he was altogether exhausted, returned to his room for a nap that stretched on for nearly five hours, and awakening groggy, showered and dressed for dinner. The hotel's dining room was full of beefy red-faced fair-haired men, jacketless and wearing open-throated white shirts, all of whom reminded him disturbingly of Kent Zacharias; but these were warms, Britishers from their accents, engineers, he suspected, from their conversation. They were building a damn and a power plant somewhere up the coast, it seemed, or perhaps a power plant without a dam; it was hard to follow what they said. They drank a good deal of gin and spoke in hearty booming shouts. There were also a good many Japanese businessmen, of course, looking trim and restrained in dark-blue suits and narrow ties, and at the table next to Klein's were five tanned curly-haired men talking in rapid Hebrew—Israelis, surely. The only Africans in sight were waiters and bartenders. Klein ordered Mombasa oysters, steak, and a carafe of red wine, and found the food unexpectedly good, but left most of it on his plate. It was late evening in Tanzania, but for him it was ten o'clock in the morning, and his body was confused. He tumbled into bed, meditated vaguely on the probable presence of Sybille just a few air-minutes away in Zanzibar, and dropped into a sound sleep from which he awakened, what seemed like many hours later, to discover that it was still well before dawn.

He dawdled away the morning sightseeing in the old native quarter, hot and dusty, with unpaved streets and rows of tin shacks, and at midday returned to his hotel for a shower and lunch. Much the same national distribution in the restaurant—British, Japanese, Israeli—though the faces seemed different. He was on his second beer when Anthony Gracchus came in. The white hunter, broad-shouldered, pale, densely bearded, clad in khaki shorts, khaki shirt, seemed almost to have stepped out of the picture-cube Jijibhoi had once shown him. Instinctively Klein shrank back, turning toward the window, but too late: Gracchus had seen him. All chatter came to a halt in the restaurant as the dead man strode to Klein's table, pulled out a chair unasked, and seated himself; then, as though a motion-picture projector had been halted and started again, the British engineers resumed their shouting, sounding somewhat strained now. "Small world," Gracchus said. "Crowded one, anyway. On your way to Zanzibar, are you, Klein?"

"In a day or so. Did you know I was here?"

"Of course not." Gracchus' harsh eyes twinkled slyly. "Sheer coincidence is what this is. She's there already."

"She is?"

"She and Zacharias and Mortimer. I hear you wiggled your way into Zion."

"Briefly," Klein said. "I saw Sybille. Briefly."

"Unsatisfactorily. So once again you've followed her here. Give it up, man. Give it up."

"I can't."

"*Can't!*" Gracchus scowled. "A neurotic's word, *can't*. What you mean is *won't*. A mature man can do anything he wants to that isn't a physical impossibility. Forget her. You're only annoying her, this way, interfering with her work, interfering with her— " Gracchus smiled. "With her life. She's been dead almost three years, hasn't she? Forget her. The world's full of other women. You're still young, you have money, you aren't ugly, you have professional standing— "

"Is this what you were sent here to tell me?"

"I wasn't sent here to tell you anything, friend. I'm only trying to save you from yourself. Don't go to Zanzibar. Go home and start your life again."

"When I saw her at Zion," Klein said, "she treated me with contempt. She amused herself at my expense. I want to ask her why she did that."

"Because you're a warm and she's a dead. To her you're a clown. To all of us you're a clown. It's nothing personal, Klein. There's simply a gulf in attitudes, a gulf too wide for you to cross. You went to Zion drugged up like a Treasury man, didn't you? Pale face, bulgy eyes? You didn't fool anyone. You certainly didn't fool *her*. The game she played with you was her way of telling you that. Don't you know that?"

"I know it, yes."

"What more do you want, then? More humiliation?"

Klein shook his head wearily and stared at the tablecloth. After a moment he looked up, and his eyes met those of Gracchus, and he was astounded to realize that he trusted the hunter, that for the first time in his dealings with the deads he felt he was being met with sincerity. He said in a low voice, "We were very close, Sybille and I, and then she died, and now I'm nothing to her. I haven't been able to come to terms with that. I need her, still. I want to share my life with her, even now."

"But you can't."

"I know that. And still I can't help doing what I've been doing."

"There's only one thing you *can* share with her," Gracchus said. "That's your death. She won't descend to your level: you have to climb to hers."

"Don't be asburd."

"Who's absurd, me or you? Listen to me, Klein. I think you're a fool, I think you're a weakling, but I don't dislike you, I don't hold you to blame for your own foolishness. And so I'll help you, if you'll allow me." He reached into his breast pocket and withdrew a tiny metal tube with a safety catch at one end. "Do you know what this is?" Gracchus asked. "It's a self-defense dart, the kind all the women in New York carry. A good many deads carry them, too, because we never know when the reaction will start, when the mobs will turn against us. Only we don't use anesthetic drugs in ours. Listen, we can walk into any tavern in the native quarter and have a decent brawl going in five minutes, and in the confusion I'll put one of these darts into you, and we'll have you in Dar General Hospital fifteen minutes after that, crammed into a deep-freeze unit, and for a few thousand dollars we can ship you unthawed to California, and this time Friday night you'll be undergoing rekindling in, say, San Diego Cold Town. And when you come out of it you and Sybille will be on the same side of the gulf, do you see? If you're destined to get back together with her, ever, that's the only way. That way you have a chance. This way you have none."

"It's unthinkable," Klein said.

"Unacceptable, maybe. But not unthinkable. Nothing's unthinkable once somebody's thought it. You think it some more. Will you promise me that? Think about it before you get aboard that plane for Zanzibar. I'll be staying here tonight and tomorrow, and then I'm going out to Arusha to meet some deads coming in for the hunting, and any time before then I'll do it for you if you say the word. Think about it. Will you think about it? Promise me that you'll think about it."

"I'll think about it," Klein said.

"Good. Good. Thank you. Now let's have lunch and change the subject. Do you like eating here?"

"One thing puzzles me. Why does this place have a clientele that's exclusively non-African? Does it dare to discriminate against blacks in a black republic?"

Gracchus laughed. "It's the blacks who discriminate, friend. This is considered a second-class hotel. All the blacks are at the Kilimanjaro or the Nyerere. Still, it's not such a bad place. I recommend the fish dishes, if you haven't tried them, and there's a decent white wine from Israel that— "

# 8

O Lord, methought what pain it was to drown!
What dreadful noise of water in mine ears!
What sights of ugly death within mine eyes!
Methoughts I saw a thousand fearful wracks;
A thousand men that fishes gnawed upon;
Wedges of gold, great anchors, heaps of pearl,
Inestimable stones, unvalued jewels,
All scatt'red in the bottom of the sea.

Some lay in dead men's skulls, and in the holes
Where eyes did once inhabit there were crept,
As 'twere in scorn of eyes, reflecting gems
That wooed the slimy bottom of the deep
And mocked the dead bones that lay scatt'red by.
                                Shakespeare: *Richard III*

"—Israeli wine," Mick Dongan was saying. "Well, I'll try anything once, especially if there's some neat little irony attached to it. I mean, there we were in Egypt, in *Egypt*, at this fabulous dinner party in the hills at Luxor, and our host is a Saudi prince, no less, in full tribal costume right down to the sunglasses, and when they bring out the roast lamb he grins devilishly and says, 'Of course we could always drink Mouton-Rothschild, but I do happen to have a small stock of select Israeli wines in my cellar, and because I think you are, like myself, a connoisseur of small incongruities, I've asked my steward to open a bottle or two of'—Klein, do you see that girl who just came in?" It is January, 1981, early afternoon, a fine drizzle in the air. Klein is lunching with six colleagues from the history department at the Hanging Gardens atop the Westwood Plaza. The hotel is a huge ziggurat on stilts; the Hanging Gardens is a rooftop restaurant, ninety stories up, in freaky neo-Babylonian décor, all winged bulls and snorting dragons of blue and yellow tile, waiters with long curly beards and scimitars at their hips—gaudy nightclub by dark, campy faculty hangout by day. Klein looks to his left. Yes, a handsome woman, mid-twenties, coolly beautiful, serious-looking, taking a seat by herself, putting a stack of books and cassettes down on the table before her. Klein does not pick up strange girls: a matter of moral policy, and also a matter of innate shyness. Dongan teases him. "Go on over, will you? She's your type, I swear. Her eyes are the right color for you, aren't they?"

Klein has been complaining, lately, that there are too many blue-eyed girls in southern California. Blue eyes are disturbing to him, somehow, even menacing. His own eyes are brown. So are hers: dark, warm, sparkling. He thinks he has seen her occasionally in the library. Perhaps they have even exchanged brief glances. "Go on," Dongan says. "Go *on*, Jorge. Go." Klein glares at him. He will not go. How can he intrude on this woman's privacy? To force himself on her—it would almost be like rape. Dongan smiles complacently; his bland grin is a merciless prod. Klein refuses to be stampeded. But then, as he hesitates, the girl smiles tóo, a quick shy smile, gone so soon he is not altogether sure it happened at all, but he is sure enough, and he finds himself rising, crossing the alabaster floor, hovering awkwardly over her, searching for some inspired words with which to make contact, and no words come, but still they make contact the old-fashioned way, eye to eye, and he is stunned by the intensity of what passes between them in that first implausible moment.

"Are you waiting for someone?" he mutters, shaken.

"No." The smile again, far less tentative. "Would you like to join me?"

She is a graduate student, he discovers quickly. Just got her master's, beginning now on her doctorate—the nineteenth-century East African slave trade, particular emphasis on Zanzibar. "How romantic," he says. "Zanzibar! Have you been there?"

"Never. I hope to go some day. Have you?"

"Not ever. But it always interested me, ever since I was a small boy collecting stamps. It was the last country in my album."

"Not in mine," she says. "Zululand was."

She knows him by name, it turns out. She had even been thinking of enrolling in his course on Nazism and Its Offspring. "Are you South American?" she asks.

"Born there. Raised here. My grandparents escaped to Buenos Aires in '37."

"Why Argentina? I thought that was a hotbed of Nazis."

"Was. Also full of German-speaking refugees, though. All their friends went there. But it was too unstable. My parents got out in '55, just before one of the big revolutions, and came to California. What about you?"

"British family. I was born in Seattle. My father's in the consular service. He— "

A waiter looms. They order sandwiches offhandedly. Lunch seems very unimportant now. The contact still holds. He sees Conrad's *Nostromo* in her stack of books; she is halfway through it, and he has just finished it, and the coincidence amuses them. Conrad is one of her favorites, she says. One of his, too. What about Faulkner? Yes, and Mann, and Virginia Woolf, and they share even a fondness for Hermann Broch, and a dislike for Hesse. How odd. Operas? *Freischütz, Holländer, Fidelio*, yes. "We have very Teutonic tastes," she observes.

"We have very similar tastes," he adds. He finds himself holding her hand.

"Amazingly similar," she says.

Mick Dongan leers at him from the far side of the room; Klein gives him a terrible scowl. Dongan winks. "Let's get out of here," Klein says, just as she starts to say the same thing.

They talk half the night and make love until dawn. "You ought to know," he tells her solemnly over breakfast, "that I decided long ago never to get married and certainly never to have a child."

"So did I," she says. "When I was fifteen."

They were married four months later. Mick Dongan was his best man.

Gracchus said, as they left the restaurant, "You will think things over, won't you?"

"I will," Klein said. "I promised you that."

He went to his room, packed his suitcase, checked out, and took a cab to the airport, arriving in plenty of time for the afternoon flight to Zanzibar. The same melancholy little man was on duty as health officer when he landed, Barwani. "Sir, you have come back," Barwani said. "I thought you might. The other people have been here several days already."

"The other people?"

"When you were here last, sir, you kindly offered me a retainer in order that you might be informed when a certain person reached this island." Barwani's eyes gleamed. "That person, with two of her former companions, is here now."

Klein carefully placed a twenty-shilling note on the health officer's desk.

"At which hotel?"

Barwani's lips quirked. Evidently twenty shillings fell short of expectations. But Klein did not take out another banknote, and after a moment Barwani said, "As before. The Zanzibar House. And you, sir?"

"As before," Klein said. "I'll be staying at the Shirazi."

Sybille was in the garden of the hotel, going over that day's research notes, when the telephone call came from Barwani. "Don't let my papers blow away," she said to Zacharias, and went inside.

When she returned, looking bothered, Zacharias said, "Is there trouble?"

She sighed. "Jorge. He's on his way to his hotel now."

"What a bore," Mortimer murmured. "I thought Gracchus might have brought him to his senses."

"Evidently not," Sybille said. "What are we going to do?"

"What would you like to do?" Zacharias asked.

She shook her head. "We can't allow this to go on, can we?"

The evening air was humid and fragrant. The long rains had come and gone, and the island was in the grip of the new season's lunatic fertility: outside the window of Klein's hotel room some vast twining vine was putting forth monstrous trumpet-shaped yellow flowers, and all about the hotel grounds everything was in blossom, everything was in a frenzy of moist young leaves. Klein's sensibility reverberated to that feeling of universal vigorous thrusting newness; he paced the room, full of energy, trying to devise some feasible stratagem. Go immediately to see Sybille? Force his way in, if necessary, with shouts and alarums, and demand to know why she had told him that fantastic tale of imaginary sultans? No. No. He would do no more confronting, no more lamenting; now that he was here, now that he was close by her, he would seek her out calmly, he would talk quietly, he would invoke memories of their old love, he would speak of Rilke and Woolf and Broch, of afternoons in Puerto Vallarta and nights in Santa Fe, of music heard and caresses shared, he would rekindle not their marriage, for that was impossible, but merely the remembrance of the bond that once had existed, he would win from her some acknowledgment of what had been, and then he would soberly and quietly exorcise that bond, he and she together, they would work to free him by speaking softly of the change that had come over their lives, until, after three hours or four or five, he had brought himself with her help to an acceptance of the unacceptable. That was all. He would demand nothing, he would beg for nothing, except only that she assist him for one evening in ridding his soul of this useless, destructive obsession. Even a dead, even a capricious, wayward, volatile, whimsical, wanton dead, would surely see the desirability of that, and would freely give him her cooperation. Surely. And then home, and then new beginnings, too long postponed.

He made ready to go out.

There was a soft knock at the door. "Sir? Sir? You have visitors downstairs."

"Who?" Klein asked, though he knew the answer.

"A lady and two gentlemen," the bellhop replied. "The taxi has brought them from the Zanzibar House. They wait for you in the bar."

"Tell them I'll be down in a moment."

He went to the iced pitcher on the dresser, drank a glass of cold water mechanically, unthinkingly, poured himself a second, drained that too. This visit was unexpected; and why had she brought her entourage along? He had to struggle to regain that

centeredness, that sense of purpose understood, which he thought
he had attained before the knock. Eventually he left the room.

They were dressed crisply and impeccably this damp night,
Zacharias in a tawny frock coat and pale-green trousers, Mortimer
in a belted white caftan trimmed with intricate brocade, Sybille
in a simple lavender tunic. Their pale faces were unmarred by
perspiration; they seemed perfectly composed, models of poise.
No one sat near them in the bar. As Klein entered, they stood to
greet him, but their smiles appeared sinister, having nothing of
friendliness in them. Klein clung tight to his intended calmness.
He said quietly, "It was kind of you to come. May I buy drinks
for you?"

"We have ours already," Zacharias pointed out. "Let us be your
hosts. What will you have?"

"Pimm's Number Six," Klein said. He tried to match their frosty
smiles. "I admire your tunic, Sybille. You all look so debonair
tonight that I feel shamed."

"You never were famous for your clothes," she said.

Zacharias returned from the counter with Klein's drink. He
took it and toasted them gravely.

After a short while Klein said, "Do you think I could talk
privately with you, Sybille?"

"There's nothing we have to say to one another that can't be
said in front of Kent and Laurence."

"Nevertheless."

"I prefer not to, Jorge."

"As you wish." Klein peered straight into her eyes and saw
nothing there, nothing, and flinched. All that he had meant to
say fled his mind. Only churning fragments danced there: Rilke,
Broch, Puerto Vallarta. He gulped at his drink.

Zacharias said, "We have a problem to discuss, Klein."

"Go on."

"The problem is you. You're causing great distress to Sybille.
This is the second time, now, that you've followed her to Zanzibar,
to the literal end of the earth, Klein, and you've made several
attempts besides to enter a closed sanctuary in Utah under false
pretenses, and this is interfering with Sybille's freedom, Klein,
it's an impossible, intolerable interference."

"The deads are dead," Mortimer said. "We understand the
depths of your feelings for your late wife, but this compulsive
pursuit of her must be brought to an end."

"It will be," Klein said, staring at a point on the stucco wall midway between Zacharias and Sybille. "I want only an hour or two of private conversation with my—with Sybille, and then I promise you that there will be no further— "

"Just as you promised Anthony Gracchus," Mortimer said, "not to go to Zanzibar."

"I wanted— "

"We have our rights," said Zacharias. "We've gone through hell, literally through hell, to get where we are. You've infringed on our right to be left alone. You bother us. You bore us. You annoy us. We hate to be annoyed." He looked toward Sybille. She nodded. Zacharias' hand vanished into the breast pocket of his coat. Mortimer seized Klein's wrist with astonishing suddenness and jerked his arm forward. A minute metal tube glistened in Zacharias' huge fist. Klein had seen such a tube in the hand of Anthony Gracchus only the day before.

"No," Klein gasped. "I don't believe—no!"

Zacharias plunged the cold tip of the tube quickly into Klein's forearm.

"The freezer unit is coming," Mortimer said. "It'll be here in five minutes or less."

"What if it's late?" Sybille asked anxiously. "What if something irreversible happens to his brain before it gets here?"

"He's not even entirely dead yet," Zacharias reminded her. "There's time. There's ample time. I spoke to the doctor myself, a very intelligent Chinese, flawless command of English. He was most sympathetic. They'll have him frozen within a couple minutes of death. We'll book cargo passage aboard the morning plane for Dar. He'll be in the United States within twenty-four hours, I guarantee that. San Diego will be notified. Everything will be all right, Sybille!"

Jorge Klein lay slumped across the table. The bar had emptied the moment he had cried out and lurched forward: the half-dozen customers had fled, not caring to mar their holidays by sharing an evening with the presence of death, and the waiters and bartenders, bigeyed, terrified, lurked in the hallway. A heart attack, Zacharias had announced, some kind of sudden attack, maybe a stroke, where's the telephone? No one had seen the tiny tube do its work.

Sybille trembled. "If anything goes wrong— "

"I hear the sirens now," Zacharias said.

*    *    *

From his desk at the airport Daud Mahmoud Barwani watched the bulky refrigerated coffin being loaded by grunting porters aboard the morning plane for Dar. And then, and then, and then? They would ship the dead man to the far side of the world, to America, and breathe new life into him, and he would go once more among men. Barwani shook his head. These people! The man who was alive is now dead, and these dead ones, who knows what they are? Who knows? Best that the dead remain dead, as was intended in the time of first things. Who could have foreseen a day when the dead returned from the grave? Not I. And who can foresee what we will all become, a hundred years from now? Not I. Not I. A hundred years from now I will sleep, Barwani thought. I will sleep, and it will not matter to me at all what sort of creatures walk the earth.

# 9

We die with the dying:
See, they depart, and we go with them.
We are born with the dead:
See, they return, and bring us with them.
                    T.S. Eliot: *Little Gidding*

On the day of his awakening he saw no one except the attendants at the rekindling house, who bathed him and fed him and helped him to walk slowly around his room. They said nothing to him, nor he to them; words seemed irrelevant. He felt strange in his skin, too snugly contained, as though all his life he had worn ill-fitting clothes and now had for the first time encountered a competent tailor. The images that his eyes brought him were sharp, unnaturally clear, and faintly haloed by prismatic colors, an effect that imperceptibly vanished as the day passed. On the second day he was visited by the San Diego Guidefather, not at all the formidable patriarch he had imagined, but rather a cool, efficient executive, about fifty years old, who greeted him cordially and told him briefly of the disciplines and routines he must master before he could leave the Cold Town. "What month is this?" Klein asked, and Guidefather told him it was June, the seventeenth of June, 1993. He had slept four weeks.

Now it is the morning of the third day after his awakening, and he has guests: Sybille, Nerita, Zacharias, Mortimer, Gracchus.

They file into his room and stand in an arc at the foot of his bed, radiant in the glow of light that pierces the narrow windows. Like demigods, like angels, glittering with a dazzling inward brilliance, and now he is of their company. Formally they embrace him, first Gracchus, then Nerita, then Mortimer. Zacharias advances next to his bedside, Zacharias who sent him into death, and he smiles at Klein and Klein returns the smile, and they embrace. Then it is Sybille's turn: she slips her hand between his, he draws her close, her lips brush his cheek, his touch hers, his arm encircles her shoulders.

"Hello," she whispers.

"Hello," he says.

They ask him how he feels, how quickly his strength is returning, whether he has been out of bed yet, how soon he will commence his drying-off. The style of their conversation is the oblique, elliptical style favored by the deads, but not nearly so clipped and cryptic as the way of speech they normally would use among themselves; they are favoring him, leading him inch by inch into their customs. Within five minutes he thinks he is getting the knack.

He says, using their verbal shorthand, "I must have been a great burden to you."

"You were, you were," Zacharias agrees. "But all that is done with now."

"We forgive you," Mortimer says.

"We welcome you among us," declares Sybille.

They talk about their plans for the months ahead. Sybille is nearly finished with her work on Zanzibar; she will retreat to Zion Cold Town for the summer months to write her thesis. Mortimer and Nerita are off to Mexico to tour the ancient temples and pyramids; Zacharias is going to Ohio, to his beloved mounds. In the autumn they will reassemble at Zion and plan the winter's amusement: a tour of Egypt, perhaps, or Peru, the heights of Machu Picchu. Ruins, archaeological sites, delight them; in the places where death has been busiest, their joy is most intense. They are flushed, excited, verbose—virtually chattering, now. Away we will go, to Zimbabwe, to Palenque, to Angkor, to Knossos, to Uxmal, to Nineveh, to Mohenjo-daro. And as they go on and on, talking with hands and eyes and smiles and even words, even words, torrents of words, they blur and become unreal to him, they are mere dancing puppets jerking about a badly painted stage, they are droning insects, wasps or bees or mosquitoes, with all their talk of travels and festivals, of Boghazköy and Babylon, of Megiddo and Masada, and he ceases to hear them, he tunes them out, he lies there smiling, eyes glazed, mind adrift. It perplexes him that he has so little interest in them. But then he realizes that it is a mark of his liberation. He is freed of old chains now. Will he join their set? Why should he? Perhaps he will travel with them, perhaps not, as the whim takes him. More likely not. Almost certainly not. He does not need their company. He has his own interests. He will follow Sybille about no longer. He does not need, he does not want, he will not seek. Why should he become one of them, rootless, an amoral wanderer, a ghost made flesh? Why should he embrace the values and customs of these people who had given him to death as dispassionately as they might swat an insect, only because he had bored them, because he had annoyed them? He does not hate them for what they did to him, he feels no resentment that he can identify, he merely chooses to detach himself from them. Let them float on from ruin to ruin, let them pursue death from continent to continent; he will go his own way. Now that he has crossed the interface, he finds that Sybille no longer matters to him.

—*Oh, sir, things change*—

"We'll go now," Sybille says softly.

He nods. He makes no other reply.

"We'll see you after your drying-off," Zacharias tells him, and touches him lightly with his knuckles, a farewell gesture used only by the deads.

"See you," Mortimer says.

"See you," says Gracchus.

"Soon," Nerita says.

Never, Klein says, saying it without words, but so they will understand. Never. Never. Never. I will never see any of you. I will never see you, Sybille. The syllables echo through his brain, and the word, *never, never, never,* rolls over him like the breaking surf, cleansing him, purifying him, healing him. He is free. He is alone.

"Goodbye," Sybille calls from the hallway.

"Goodbye," he says.

It was years before he saw her again. But they spent the last days of '99 together, shooting dodos under the shadow of mighty Kilimanjaro.

# THE MOON GODDESS AND THE SON

## Donald Kingsbury

## 1

Diana's ambition to get a job on the moon really started the day she found out that her namesake was the moon goddess. She was six and she crawled out her bedroom window onto the porch roof so she could stare at the full moon in the sky where she belonged. Her father caught her. He was furious because she could have fallen off and hurt herself so he stripped her and tied her to the bed and beat her bleeding with his belt.

The pain blotted out this man, blotted out even the pain itself. She saw a wild boar and she cast an arrow into his heart from her perch safe behind the shield of the moon. But in time the trauma evaporated, leaving only the pain of being touched by a bloodstained bed in Ohio that refused to stop torturing her body with its prodding fingers. When the moon rose so high that her round eyes could no longer see it through the window, she felt abandoned.

On her seventh birthday a high school boy showed her his portable tracking telescope. The cratered mountains of the moon stunned her with their beauty—*her* mountains, *her* craters, *her* plains, *her* rills and streamers. Meticulously she located each of the old Apollo landing sites. In a moment of astral travel she imagined herself in a crater full of trees with lots of nymphs to take care of.

He showed her Jupiter and the Pleiades. Another evening they followed the bright thread of the half-built spaceport as it arrowed through the southern sky in those few minutes before it faded into the Earth's shadow. When it was gone he explained that they could see the spaceport this far north only because it hadn't yet been towed into equatorial orbit.

At eight Diana had a temper tantrum and stoically endured five beatings until her mother papered her wall with a photomontage of the moon's surface. At nine she took up archery in school and worked at it until she became the regional champ for her age. When she was ten she ran away from home to visit a space museum but the police brought her back. After the police were gone her father beat her until even her mother cried. At twelve she ran away from home with her arm in a cast, broken by her father when he found her collection of newspaper stories about families who murdered their children in the night.

She fixed her hair like the March cover girl of *Viva Magazine* and she wore one of her mother's bras stuffed with an extra pair of socks. People gave her rides. She told them she was going to visit her mother in California because her father was out of work.

The best ride she got was from a truck driver whom she targeted at a diesel station in Newton, Iowa, mainly because his rig carried a Washington license plate and she knew vaguely that spaceships were built in Washington. He wasn't supposed to take passengers but she flaunted her spare socks and he broke down and got to liking her over the steak he bought her. She chattered to him about a historical novel called *Diana's Temple*.

An endless ride later, through farmland and broken hills and over decaying interstate highways, they pulled into a rest stop near Elk Mountain to sleep in the cab for the night. Diana tried to seduce her driver because she thought girls were supposed to reward nice men. The cast on her arm got in the way and a sock fell out of her bra.

He laughed, holding her by the chin in a vise grip between thumb and fingers. "Diana was a virgin."

"Yeah, I know." She cringed out of the vise to a position back against the door of the cab.

He didn't want to hurt her feelings. He reached out and pulled her shoulders into his large arm tenderly. "Your virginity is the most valuable thing you have right now. Hang onto it. Grow up a little bit and when you throw it away make sure he's the nicest guy in the world."

"How do you tell the nice guys from the mean ones?"

"Did you ever have any trouble with that?"

"My father always beat me. For *nothing!*"

"Then you know what the bad ones are like."

"What are the good ones like?"

"Me," he laughed.

For a year Diana stayed in a small town near Seattle where they assembled feeder spacecraft for the spaceport as well as cruise missiles for the military. The tiny nine-meter-long automatic lighters rocketed to the spaceport from an equatorial base and flew back on stubby delta wings. Diana was excited at first. She did housework and cared for the children of one of the foremen whose wife was recovering from an auto accident. But this sleepy Earth town was just as far away from the moon as Ohio.

She stole some money and caught a bus for L.A. It was scary panhandling in Hollywood. She got picked up by a pimp she didn't know was a pimp and had to crawl out a window in the middle of the night and sleep under a car like a cat. After three days alone she found a family of runaways and slept on the floor. They were all into stealing and hustling and one of them was into heroin but she found a job as a waitress from which she got fired because she didn't have any papers.

Twilight was panhandling time. Afterwards she took her addict friend to a crowded basement dive so she could have company being depressed. The smoke coiled through the dim light, choking at life. She sat there crazying and suddenly darted toward the ladies' room where she knew they had a little open window where she could breathe for a minute, alone.

A large hand clamped on her shoulder. "You got holes in your head, spending time with that buzzhead? He'll take you for everything you've got."

She whirled on the scruffy young man who had a 1950 hairdo. "What have I got to take? I haven't even got a job."

"Lots of jobs around."

"I don't want to be a whore, smartass."

He smiled sardonically. "A waitress, then?"

"I got fired as a waitress because I don't have any papers."

"How about that!" He shook her hand. "I'm a forger." He escorted her into the ladies' room and, after locking the door, hung his head through the window. "What name you want to be known by?"

"I can change my name?"

"Yeah and you get a birth certificate and a L.A. high school record and a social security number. I figure if we stretched it a bit you could pass for eighteen."

"What do you get out of it?" she asked cynically.

"A girl to ferret around records offices who doesn't arouse suspicion. I need new faces all the time." He laughed. "I'm square. My side lady would kill me if I didn't give every thirteen-year-old an integrity deal."

"Could I get a job on the moon with your papers?"

# 2

Charlie McDougall was an only child with thickly lashed eyes. He first learned to roll his eyes at his parents when he was thirteen—behind their backs. His whole memory of life was of two giants giving him orders that had to be executed on some strict schedule if he didn't want to be driven crazy by shouting directed into his eardrum.

Mama wanted him to become the world's greatest violinist or maybe a dancer who would wow them in Moscow. Papa wanted him to become the greatest space engineer who ever lived, the cutting edge of the Last Hope of Mankind.

During those crucial years when most babies discover the first spark of individuality by playing with the power of the word "no," Charlie had been broken. He learned to obey. He hated the violin and he hated dancing and he hated space but he hated screaming parents even more. Obeying was the only peace he had.

Still, while he became a fine violinist, his strings had a perpetual habit of snapping. He was invariably the best dancer in his class but he was always being thrown out because of his incurable habit of peeking into the girls' dressing room.

For his father he devised even more diabolical tortures. Though he slaved dutifully over his physics and chemistry and math and model building, he refused to read science fiction. On his fifteenth birthday his father tried to seduce him with a luxury hardbound copy of *Dune* with a facsimile Frank Herbert signature.

"You'll love it."

"Hey Papa, that's a great gift. This evening I have some spare time and maybe I'll take a crack at it." When his father went out for a beer, he rolled his eyes.

That evening the old man peeked into his room on tiptoes to

see how the first chapter of *Dune* was going, just as Charlie knew he would. Charlie was engrossed in the eighth chapter of Robert's *Differential Equations* setting up the ninth problem.

"Have you had a chance to look at *Dune*?"

"Tomorrow. I got myself hung up on the breaking mode of long cylinders and I don't want to sleep on it."

The coup had kept Charlie happy for weeks. *Dune* was still on his shelf, unopened.

It was only when he was seventeen that he discovered the perfect shelter from his parents, digital music. Electronic instruments frightened his mother. She had a Ph.D. in musicology from Mills but couldn't tell a fourier compact series from a quartet concert series; a resistor had something to do with the draft, and a chip was what an uncouth person carried on his shoulder. As for Charlie's father, who polished off textbooks like most slow readers polished off light novels, engineered music was in the same category as purple smells or painted cooking.

Waves, repetitions, pulsations, rumblings, the rise of a violin taking off can all be described by a fourier series—an amalgamation of sine and cosine waves of different frequencies and amplitudes. A frequency is a number. An amplitude is a number. Charlie composed by choosing those numbers and deciding when they were to change. His computer executed the commands.

He created his own computer language for simulating instruments. It was a simple matter for him to write a subroutine for oboe or violin or harmonica. He had ten violins on file, four of them matching in sound the finest violins ever crafted, the other six of a haunting timbre that could never come from a material violin, wood lacking the proper resonant qualities. He doodled up new instruments in pensive moments and gave them frivolous names like the pooh and the eeyore and the kanga.

By using his world of numbers as an open sesame to the trance underground, he burrowed assiduously into this dark world his parents couldn't understand. Once when he was twenty and deliriously celebrating the end of his junior year by smashing out in the popular Boston Trance Hall where the show was continuous and the waitresses sported silver pantsuits with cutout buttocks, all seven of his friends became dazzled by the nubility of the singer. She was wearing a golden necklace from which her dress flowed, cupric green, so slashed in a thousand ribbons that one saw both all and none of her body as she sang.

Charlie noted the ordinary voice—slightly brassy with a tendency to slurring—and rashly bet his friends she would date him. Gleefully they put $200 in the pot, impelling him to keep pace by taking her hand as she left the stage.

"You have a zorchy voice—a lot could be done with it."

She smiled coolly and let him hold her fingers just long enough to appear unrude. It gave him time to press his card into that hand, a hand so cold his must have seemed tropical.

## ELECTRONIC MADMAN
## DIGITALIZED MUSIC

Her eyes widened slightly when she read it—DM was a controversial thing on the pop music scene; one loved or hated its sounds and argued endlessly about the awesome scope of its territory. DM projected mystery and resentment. Few musicians could handle its technical demands. But an ambitious woman with an ordinary voice would know what a DM magician could do for her.

She sat down and the cupric cloth rippled, sometimes revealing, sometimes hiding, always teasing. "What do you hear in my voice?"

"You'll have to come to my place and listen. It's beautiful."

"It's not. I don't think my mouth is the right shape."

"But you don't hear what I hear."

"Do you do real time or augmented?"

"Both. I can feed your mike right into the shoebox if that's what you want."

She took his palm and read it silently. Then she looked into his face with the eyes of a judge. "What sign are you?"

"Aquarius."

Her face broke into a smile of relief.

"Fantastic!" And she wouldn't let his hand go. Charlie's friends, conceding, shoved a money-filled envelope into the other hand.

Betty worked with him. He showed her many versions of her voice. He washed her car. He rushed her clothes out for dry cleaning to give her extra sleep. When she had a new gig, he set up for her. He worked late into many nights decoding the structure of her voice until he was able to customize a shoebox that transformed her into a siren at the wave of a mike.

Charlie's new life thrilled him. He spent all his time thinking about seducing Betty. Devious plans grew out of dreams and finally he convinced Betty to let him move into her place in what had once been the maid's room back in the century when Irish labor was plentiful. He promised to cook and do the dishes and not molest her. His theory was that the way to a girl's heart was through her stomach and after a month of being taken care of by a man who loved her, she would melt.

In a mailgram that gave him great pleasure to write he told his father that he was not returning to MIT. Within a week his father arrived in Boston from orbit and charmed Betty off to Mexico City for a vacation. She sent him a card from Xicotencatl wishing he was there. The card was forwarded to New Hampshire where his mother had taken him by the ear, screaming at him all the time, insisting that if he wasn't going to continue his engineering he had to sign up for the Berlin Conservatory. In self-defense he reregistered at MIT, all the while plotting perfect murders.

It took him only two months to utterly crush his mother. He digitalized a secret recording of one of her screaming rages. Slowly he added harmonicas. He mushed the words until their content was lost against a pure emotion. Here he amplified the rage, there he added piteous undertones. Violins played at dramatic moments. Sobbing children filled the silences. He had the tape cut and sold the pressing to a company that pushed it up to thirty-second place on the hit parade.

Charlie figured it would take longer to crush his father. His father was tough. He would have to bide his time and strike at an unexpected moment with overwhelming force.

# 3

It was a nice name. *Diana Grove*. She could go anywhere and do anything with it. Mostly she went to Texas and Arizona because John the Forger's main business was manufacturing new identities for Mexicans. When she became too well known he let her go and she became a waitress.

Rooming with older girls taught Diana how to imitate adult behavior. Her manners became flirtatious. She was a sassy summertime flower to the bees, little caring whether the men she attracted were young or old or handsome or married—but she never dated the same man twice. She had a perfect excuse whenever an admirer wanted a second date.

"But that's the day I'm seeing Larry."

"How about Saturday then?"

"I always go out with George on Saturday."

When too many people wanted her, she changed jobs or room-mates. Eventually she began to move up the coast, carefully picking only the most expensive and popular restaurants. Once in Coos Bay, Oregon, a drunk whacked her around and that so frightened her she flew to San Francisco the very next day.

Not having a job was unimportant. At the airport she bought a paper and answered a classified ad demanding an exceptionally attractive and experienced waitress to work at Namala in the Pacific. Diana was a long-time space buff and knew very well that Namala was one of the equatorial stations that supplied the orbiting spaceport.

The secretary of Ling Enterprises smiled and Diana reciprocated. It helped her nervousness that the secretary was sitting down and she was standing. She could pretend that she was just earning a five-dollar tip.

The speaker beside the video camera spoke in a gentle voice. "Send her in. She's expected."

Diana instantly turned her smile on the camera. It was President Ling speaking. That was very suspicious. Presidents of restaurant chains did *not* interview waitresses. She felt faint and, what was worse, she felt fifteen years old.

When she peered around Mr. Ling's door she found him to be Chinese and ancient. His office was Contemporary American except for the paintings—a battle between Earthmen and beastoid in a jungle under a large red sun, the other a desolate landscape somewhere in the galaxy near a star cluster. The fear went out of her.

"You are another space cookie," she said relieved, all her poise back.

"It's a comfortable disease."

"Do you remember when they landed on the moon?"

He laughed. "I'm so old I remember when they thought landing on the moon was impossible."

"Do you own a restaurant on the moon?"

"No, but when they build one, I'll be running it."

She loved him already. She was his slave. She sat down on the couch and couldn't take her eyes off his face, lined and old and frail and the most fascinating face she'd ever seen.

He moved closer to her, sitting on the desk top. "Are you wondering why a president is interviewing waitresses?"

"Yes," she grinned. "I'm ready to run out the door screaming."

"I have six space-related restaurants and I take a personal interest in them. The frustrated astronaut in me."

"What's Namala like?"

"Hard work for you. Too many men."

"I'm a good girl and surprisingly self-reliant."

"Sometimes you'll need advice. Madam Lilly, who runs my Namala franchise, has large skirts for hiding behind when it is necessary."

"I never need help," said Diana defiantly.

"An unwise consideration."

They talked. He found out all he needed to know and she found out all she needed to know. He offered her the job. She accepted. There was nothing more to say but she didn't want to leave just yet.

He watched her silence as she moved her fingers and played with a ring. "Ah, I've finally caught you when you're not smiling."

"I'm hungry and I want to invite you for lunch," she said with frog's legs in her throat.

He smiled a thousand wrinkles.

"Would your wife mind?" she then asked awkwardly.

"I'm a widower."

"We could to the Calchas. I've worked there. It's beautiful and I miss their food."

She made him talk about himself over too much wine. He was the rebel in his family. His father wanted him to take over the restaurant business and he wanted to be an engineer. He had edited a science fiction fanzine called *Betelgeuse* which went to fourteen issues but when he became engaged to his illustrator who was a Caucasian, his family disowned him. He didn't do well enough in school to get a scholarship and ended up as a city bureaucrat, married, with three lovely mongrel children while he tried to write at night.

Finally his father died and his brothers expanded and took the family fortune into a close brush with disaster and he made a pact with his mother to run the family business. He was good at it. Later he made his breakthrough by discovering how to franchise variety in a world of McDonald's, Johnson's, and Colonel's.

Diana had fun. They ran up quite a bill at Mr. Ling's insistence (he thought he was paying) and she had the best fight of her life taking the bill away from him. To make up for it he bought her beautiful luggage. She sighed and told him she had nothing to put in it, so he bought her clothes. She sighed and told him she had no place to take them because she hadn't rented a hotel room yet, so he gave her the key to his place.

She cooked Mr. Ling a gourmet dinner in his kitchen after

making many phone calls to the office to find out what he liked and when he would be in. They spent the whole meal and three liqueurs discussing the history of Jerusalem. She discovered his wicked sense of humor. He convinced her that there had been a whole order of Chinese Knights who fought in the crusades.

"Don't laugh so hard!" she complained. "You're just lucky I didn't bake a lemon meringue pie for supper or you'd get it right in your kisser!"

Ten o'clock was his bedtime. He excused himself gracefully and escorted her all the way to the guest room where he put an arm around her shoulder and thanked her for a lovely evening before he left her.

Diana peeked. She waited until the light went out under his door and then, dressed only in a candle flame, entered his room. "I've come to kiss you goodnight." It was easy to pretend you were twenty years old when you were nude.

His smile in the candlelight was wistful. "Goddess Diana, I am much too old for such escapades."

"That makes us even. I'm much too young for such escapades." She blew out the candle and slipped under the sheets with him. "Don't die of a heart attack just yet. I want my job on the moon." She snuggled up beside him, deciding that she liked to sleep with men. It was the sleep of innocence.

The next day a great aircraft flew her over the ocean to the equator.

# 4

The rocker-supplied lunar base was an improbable cluster of forms on Mare Imbrium which had lately grown a spiderweb rectenna farm to receive microwaves from a small twenty-five-megawatt solar power station that had been built in low Earth orbit and towed up to the Lagrange 1 position 58,000 km above the moon. Each new addition was part of a single-minded plan. The sole purpose of the base was to build an electromagnetic landing track so that access to the moon might be made cheap. This deep out in space, rockets fueled from Earth were not cheap.

When Byron McDougall took the assignment to construct the initial lunar base he was given one-fourth of the money originally allocated for that task. He was a military man from a military family. He thought like a soldier who could still fight when his supply lines had been cut. McDougall's base had shafts without elevators. He used cast basalt instead of aluminum. Eighty percent of the parts by weight of all imported machines were made of lunar metals and glasses. All food was raised locally. The lunar day was given over to energy intensive tasks such as metals production. The lunar night was given over to effort-intensive tasks such as design work and machining.

From his tiny office Byron called Louise. "Sweetheart, do you have a bottle of champagne tucked away?" He knew she didn't.

"Champagne? You're mad. All I have is a liter of Ralph's turnip rotgut."

"Too bad. How can we celebrate on that? Any last-minute hassles with the SPS?"

"No. We should have power exactly on time."

"Good."

"Your son has been trying to reach you. We'll have the connection set up in fifteen minutes. Do you want to take it there or here?"

"I'm hopping right up to the control room."

Byron switched off, smiling slyly. He took out a half bottle of champagne he had hidden, all he could afford to smuggle in by rocket, but enough to give them a taste of victory. It wasn't really victory: getting the SPS power so they weren't energy starved at night was just another milestone, but one certainly worth celebrating.

Maybe there never would be a final victory. Byron sometimes despaired. Maybe in two years this effort might be a ghost town in spite of all the billions that had been invested in it. Risk funding was so damned erratic. Support waxed and waned in Congress. It had been waning now for years, even though the pay-off was a certainty.

He slipped out of his office, soared up the shaft, caught himself, and made his slow leap into the control room with the bottle high in his hand. "Who's got strong thumbs?"

"How did you get that!" Louise's nature lent itself to exclamations.

"False-bottomed suitcase."

One of the men turned to Byron from the console display with a smile. "The SPS is powered and checking through beautifully. We should get the first beam down soon."

"Is your son as handsome as you?" asked Louise dreamily.

"Why should you care?"

"Braithwaite was telling me he's coming up here to work on the track as soon as he graduates from MIT."

"No, I'm much better looking than my son. You should try older men once in a while."

"Not a chance. You see through all of my tricks. I *might* get away with batting my eyes at your son. He's six years younger than I am."

"Actually you might have a chance. When he gets here I'll set you up. He chases older women—but I've never seen him chase one as bright as you. I once took a girl friend of his off to Mexico City. She was a great lady, but I was bored to death with her chatter."

"Byron! You stole your son's girl friend? How could you be so cruel? And I always thought you were such a *nice* man!"

"I did him a favor. She was using him," he said bitterly.

"He probably needed her!"

That stung Byron's anger. "Like hell he needed her. She didn't have enough sense to send him back to school when he quit to take care of her. For that I could have killed the bitch. I shipped her off to Paris with enough bread to keep her amused."

Louise was grinning. "What was your wife saying about all this?"

"She divorced me."

"Byron!"

He laughed. "Something else to celebrate."

The phone rang. Louise took it and chatted with the operator. "Byron. It's your son."

"Hi, Papa."

"Charlie!"

Two-second pause.

"I'm calling you up to congratulate you. I hear you're not going to need candles at night anymore. Hey, pretty soon you'll have hot running water in the trenches."

"It's pretty good. We'll be powered except for six hours once a month at eclipse."

Two-second pause.

"I just got your comments on my last batch of homework. You're two days faster than my profs. I'm glad I'm getting clever enough with my mistakes so even you can't see them."

"While you're on the line I want you to talk with Braithwaite. You'll be working with him on the lunar track. He's anxious to get you after all he's heard about you."

Byron motioned frantically for Braithwaite to come over while his voice travelled to Earth and his son's came back.

"You still want me to get involved in that thing, eh?"

"You bet. When we get it built this place is going to start to pay for itself. She'll mushroom. We've been tooling up for the track and now that we have the power, we're ready to roll."

The lunar track was an electromagnetic cushion to take fifteen-ton ships in for a horizontal landing at lunar circular velocity. Or shoot them off.

"Say Papa, I'm calling to tell you not to bother to come back to Earth for my graduation."

"But of course I'm coming. I need the vacation."

Two-second pause.

"Yeah, but I just quit school."

"You're at the top of your class!"

Two-second pause.

"I don't want your job. I just want to play around and listen to the birds sing. Why put myself in the position where I need a vacation when I can have one all the time?"

Byron thought frantically. "It's the chance of your lifetime! It will make your career! From this job you can go anywhere!"

Two-second pause. There was no real way to argue over this distance. He had caught a barracuda and the line was too light.

"I never liked engineering. Good luck in your log cabin. I'm hanging up, now."

The line went dead. Byron waited for two seconds, stunned, then he smashed his bottle against the bulkhead wall. Gracefully the champagne foamed as it arced in a slow-motion spatter.

"She's ready," said the operations man, as calmly as if he had witnessed a christening. "There she goes. The grid is powered."

Louise was rushing over to Byron. "It's all right."

Byron was frozen, his hand outstretched where it had grasped sudden defeat from victory. "No," he said in pain.

"Are you going back to Earth to talk to him?"

"No." Byron paused for two thoughtful seconds, his hand slowly sinking. "I had to push him and push him and push him, the little bastard. He did so well, I couldn't resist. If I didn't push him, he didn't move. So I pushed him. God, how I wanted him here under my thumb where I could make a man out of him." He shrugged bitterly. "It's no use. If you have to push a man, he's not going to move anywhere."

"He'll settle out."

"Yeah, he'll settle out. He'll settle out as a third-rate musician."

# 5

Namala was the tropical sea, blue water and a sometimes billowy clouded sky and green islands that, to Diana's airborne eyes, seemed to sleep in the vast moat of the Pacific like a drowsy crocodile. She arrived at sunset while the water was deepening to purple. Never in her life had she been so exhilarated. She was here—part of a base that was shipping goods to the moon to make a home for her that would be there when she found a way to go.

While she waited on the airfield terrace for Madam Lilly, the drowsy crocodile woke. A barrage of delta winged lighters began to lift in roaring flame from the launch area. Then Diana saw to the west the silver thread of the spaceport rising majestically out of the ocean. At first it was only a small thread, a wavering glimmer. On the horizon the spaceport's 150-kilometer length was foreshortened to hardly more than a degree of sky, but, within minutes, as it rose to the thunder of the lighter launches, it grew to stretch its gossamer strand over almost a sixth of the sky—before vanishing into the shadow of the Earth, leaving only stars. She remembered a spider riding a filament of web over the cornfields of Ohio.

Soon another fleet of lighters, electromagnetically ejected from the spaceport as it passed overhead, began a screaming drop out of the blackness, swooping into the floodlamps of the lagoon to be received with the efficiency of a squadron returning to the deck of its aircraft carrier. Some of the lighters were laden with goods manufactured in the factory pods that lined the spaceport's length like factories had once sprung up along a railway spur line. Some of the lighters came down empty.

The ground crews ran a standard maintenance check on each vehicle, inserting a new 500-kilogram payload module, pumping kerosene and oxygen into the tanks, recooling the superconducting coils that would electromagnetically accelerate the lighter once it had been swallowed by the spaceport's electromagnetic interstine on its next spaceward trip. Finally the fresh-readied lighter was rolled to the launch site and pointed at the sky on its own gantry, there to await the return of the spaceport. Every ninety minutes, day and night, this cycle repeated at all of the equatorial stations.

Madam Lilly was standing behind Diana, unwilling to intrude

on the girl's rapture. She turned out to be a hard taskmaster. Her restaurant carried the Ling symbol but like all Ling restaurants it supported its own name, the *Kaleidoscope*, which meant that it was constantly changing its atmosphere. Madam Lilly was a theater person. She could do miracles with a few props and backdrops and screens, but her main focus was on the girls. She costumed them perfectly and taught them gesture and emotion and expression and dialogue.

When Diana arrived they were doing World War II. There was a Rosie the Riveter in slacks and a Sultry Pinup in black negligee. Diana served the veranda in shorts with a tray over her head as a Hep Carhop. Sometimes she chewed gum and she always said "swell" to the customers. The music was "Deep in the heart of Texas . . ." or "Kiss me once . . ."

Namala was a paradise for a girl scared of men. The ratio of single men to women was four to one and she had so many dates that she could easily play one against the other for safety. If that failed, Diana pleaded work. She had to rehearse the movements of a Burmese dancer, or walk like a Persian lady, or catch the subtle way a geisha presented a plate of raw fish. You could find her laughing with her arms around two men, or alone on the beach in the moonlight watching the fireworks supply the spaceport.

The beach could be fun. During the *Kaleidoscope's* twenties' stint Madam Lilly strictly forbade her girls to wear their monokinis and instead had them splashing about in the latest daring flapper bathing suit that exposed the knees. It caused a riot and was very good for business.

Time and the smallness of the Namala community was her enemy. She met a boy named Jack in her martial arts class. He always spoke to her; she consistently ignored him. Their Japanese instructor repeated that the greatest perfection was to defeat an opponent with the minimum of force. Diana was having none of that. She was there to learn how to *demolish* men with the thrust of her heel or the back of her hand. She believed in a safety factor of ten. Break their skulls and then ask questions.

But Jack survived. Smitten, he arranged a surprise birthday party. There were twenty-one candles on the cake even though she was only turning sixteen. She had a fabulous time hugging everyone for their gifts and singing and fooling around. She successfully avoided Jack for three hours, knowing how dangerous a man in love can be.

Her fatal mistake was to need a Kleenex. Jack kept some in his study, which had remained off limits to the party because of the delicate model of the lunar base he kept there. She caught a glimpse of its detail and fell heels over head. Long after the revelry had died she was still in the study, her arms wrapped around Jack, kissing his nose and asking him questions about the lunar electromagnetic landing track.

The affair lasted two weeks, a miracle of involvement for Diana. She went everywhere with him. She haunted the launch site when he was at work. He spent all his money at the *Kaleidoscope*. They went surfing together and kissed at every opportunity. He hinted that he wanted to sleep with her. She hinted that she wanted to wait but to herself decided that he was the nicest guy in the world and she was going to throw her virginity away on him and live happily ever after.

In time they found themselves alone. Unhurriedly, gently he began to undress her. Diana only noticed that he was between her and the door. Since she had been a small girl she had learned to keep herself always between her father and a door. For awhile she tried to suppress her silly need, but the anxiety didn't go away—it became worse. It became imperative. Smiling at her insanity she took Jack in her arms hoping to roll him away from the door, toward the wall, without having to say anything. He chose that moment to be assertive.

Suddenly panicked, Diana threw him off the bed. When he looked up in anger, still commanding the doorway, she was so terrified that she struck him with a reflex karate kick to the head, and ran, not remembering that she ran. The next day he apologized when he found her. She turned away without speaking.

He flew in flowers from the States. He sent her letters. He papered love declarations on the corridor walls of her apartment. He slept on her steps. His intensity frightened her. She stayed awake with images of him murdering her. When he came to the *Kaleidoscope*, the other girls waited on him. Madam Lilly soothed her and told her that it was normal for men to go crazy, that it was nothing to worry about, but Diana worried. Jack persisted. He even sent one of the female mechanics he worked with to talk to her. Diana became so upset that she wrote Mr. Ling a mailgram pleading for a transfer.

The reply bounced back via satellite and was printed up immediately. "Spend a week with me. Ling."

# 6

At the emergency meeting in the main control room of the lunar base Zimmerman told a joke about a congressman that ended with the punch line: "I got no luck at all, nohow. Jist as I was gettin' my ass trained to work without eatin', she has to up and die on me!"

It wasn't a funny joke when you were the ass. They poked at the budget cut and they went over their own expenses from five different angles. No sane way of handling the cut emerged.

During the next shift out on the lunar plain, Byron chewed over his anger in one of the construction trucks along the half-built track. His mind kept wandering off to Earth, that goddess of inconsistency.

One year you had Congress convinced that what you were doing was in the economic self-interest of the United States. You'd ask them if they were *sure* because you wanted them to be *sure* before you went ahead. Yes, they were sure. They backed you to the hilt. They made laws. But the next year they were convinced of something else, riding some new fad.

Back at the base Byron took dinner in his room. He cut off the intercom and tended his climbing vines, still seeking a solution to this latest sudden change in the rules. Adam Smith was wrong; men were not motivated by self-interest—they were too myopic to perceive self-interest farther than an inch away. A man would grab for that cigarette because the pleasure was immediate; the surgeon's knife cutting out his cancerous lung lay an unreal fifteen years in the future.

Byron's eyes blurred and for a moment he beheld a religious vision. A luminous hand was reaching out of the stars and that hand was a mosaic of little men held together by little hands in the pockets of the men above. Each little man was complaining about somebody else's greed. The conquest of space was not, at the moment, a gloriously cooperative venture. It was a war of pickpockets. But war gave him an edge. He smiled. Byron was an old fighter pilot.

His fingers switched off the lights so that he was in total darkness, the bed easy under his body. What did a soldier do when he was cornered? He remembered one of the favorite maxims of his father. "There is no such thing as losing," said that very stern man. It was an absurd maxim, parochially American, but one his father could imbue with a peculiar vitality.

As a ten-year-old Byron had been no fool. "That's what Hitler said at Stalingrad," he argued hotly.

"Ah, but Hitler confused winning with being on the offensive. You and I would have retreated and won."

"We retreated all over the place in Vietnam and lost!"

"Son, recall that you and I were in Germany during that disgraceful affair. Real soldiers aren't so clumsy as to defend something by destroying it."

"What's a real soldier?"

"An ordinary soldier fights well when he is grandly equipped. A *real* soldier can still fight after his supply lines have been cut. A real soldier doesn't even need any help from Congress!"

Once on a 300-kilometer hike with his father he had crumpled, refusing to go farther. The pain was overwhelming.

"A man inured to hell cannot lose."

"He can die," Byron remembered himself whining.

His son-of-a-bitch father had then lifted him up by the hair. "No. You forget. Death comes first. Then hell. Get moving. McDougalls are tough enough to walk out of hell. You're that tough. We make camp in two hours."

Byron walked out of his father's hell into an Air Force recruiting office on his eighteenth birthday. The Air Force groomed him, disciplined him, toughened him, and then sent him to Saudi Arabia to train Bedouins to fly the F-15. It was hell. He found himself drawing upon his father's wisdom and coping with hells because it was all he had. He used that empty time in the desert like a good commander might use a lull in the fighting—to build up his striking power. He sweated out an engineering education by correspondence course.

In those days few Americans cared about space, not even Byron. NASA's program had collapsed to a dismal four-shuttle fleet with no solid funding in sight. Russian space ventures began to show signs of life again and Congress frantically authorized the building of the spaceport, giving Rockwell a contract for 70 modified space shuttles. Byron found himself flying one of them above the Earth, above a vision that shattered his isolation.

He resigned from the Air Force and transferred easily into a spaceport construction crew, engineering with love where no men had built before, 275 kilometers above the silly wars in Africa and Afghanistan and Argentina. That was a boom time. Today it was bust.

*Yes, it is like war*, he thought there in the dark. This was a battle to take the high ground. You won some and you lost some. The battle up the slope always cost more than you wanted to pay. Sometimes the home front got tired of the war. Still you kept on fighting your way higher in the hope that once you reached the peak you could dig in and hold it cheaply.

The first low orbital spaceport had to be built on the money of incredibly expensive orbital rockets, but once in place the 150-kilometer-long, double-barreled spaceport could swallow and electromagnetically accelerate cheap suborbital rocket freighters and spew the unloaded freighters back down again to maintain momentum equilibrium. But that wasn't the end of the battle. That was only a ridge, a defense line, a trench.

The 275 kilometers wasn't high enough. As long as more mass was rising than falling, momentum balancing of the spaceport required a net energy input into the spaceport's mass drivers. That assumed an expensive auxiliary orbiting power plant which tended to limit spaceport capacity. And so the astronautical strategists began to covet the really high ground, the moon. If lunar mass could be delivered to Earth through the spaceport, momentum balancing of the spaceport would cease to depend upon auxiliary power. Capacity would go way up and costs down. If more mass was going down than coming up, the spaceport would generate a net surplus of power. A kilogram of moon delivered to the Earth contains eight times as much energy as a kilogram of the most powerful chemical rocket propellant.

The dust at the bottom of a minor lunar crater holds more energy reserves than in the whole of the Arabian peninsula. The potential energy of the moon is enough to power the wildest space program for millions of years. Damn the cost! Capture the high ground! Economics demanded it!

And so the war went on. Byron McDougall was chief field engineer when the second spaceport was built parallel to the first. It was designed to accelerate vehicles to high orbit beyond the Van Allen belts and to receive the vehicles back from high orbit. He did the job in three years.

By then congressional support was disintegrating. The Russian tortoise had fallen behind again. Wars are not fought on the battlefield alone. They are backed up by a whole support structure. And a loot-hungry populace is impatient with long sieges.

His father had something to say about long wars. "When the enemy's line is solid, endure, survive, and observe. Do not expect a break to appear at an enemy strong point. The breaks appear where *no one* expects trouble. When they appear victory goes to the swiftest. A place which has no strategic importance may achieve importance simply because it is not being defended."

# 7

Every civilization contains eddies of its past, sometimes within walking distance of its major centers. An eddy of the nineteenth century lay tucked away between two mountains of the California Coast Range, below the grasslands where the topography traps enough ocean fog to water a redwood stand. A Chinese family has long owned a log cabin there beside a dammed stream. There is no electricity. The road is dirt. Legend has it that every time a land developer comes this way, the wood nymphs call up a fog from the sea to sift through the redwood forest until it becomes invisible.

When Diana was with her Chinese friend she was all woman. At night she lay cozy with him under heavy blanket, by day she cooked over wood for her sage—flapjacks with sweet fried tomato syrup, and eggs and beans and bacon, even bread from flour and yeast. She kissed him and swam with him behind the dam and massaged him and flattered him.

But when she was by herself she reverted to girl. Deep in the forest she built a shrine out of stone to the goddess of moon and glade so that Diana might properly be worshipped. She tracked animals but they got away. She practiced archery for hours. Once she saw a deer and they both stood frozen, staring at each other in awe in that cathedral of trees.

On their last day she splashed in the cold pool behind the dam and toweled herself sassily in front of her boss because she knew he liked to look at her body even if he couldn't do anything with it. A wondrous evening light sneaked through the redwood needles.

"I have a job for you," he said, lighting the coals for a barbecue.

"You just sit down," she smiled. "I'll take care of everything. What do you want me to cook?"

"I meant a job *opening*. One of my places needs a new girl."

"Are you ever nice to me. Where?"

"You might not want it. It's a costume place. It involves playing up to some crazy men."

"What other kind is there?"

"Put this on," he said, giving her a shining package.

She held it out. "Brass bras!" she hooted. "*Mr. Ling*, I didn't know you ran a skin dive."

"Try it on."

Modestly she held it in front of herself. "I'll show through."

"You'll look beautiful, if slightly kinky."

So she stepped into what there was of it. Her hair spilled out of the helmet, a simple brass band around her forehead that supported oval headpieces which might or might not have been earphones. Her breasts spilled out of their immodest cups and her hips spilled out of their hardly adequate metallic banding. "Where do you get your outrageous ideas?"

He took her by the hand into the cabin and pulled his old copies of *Planet Stories* from a shelf. "Treat them like gold. They are from the forties and early fifties and fragile."

Diana shrieked at the cover of an issue he handed her. "That's me! Brass bras and all! And if that monster goes with the job, I'm quitting yesterday! Where is this restaurant?"

"On the spaceport."

Her heart jumped. "How high is that thing?"

"One hundred sixty-five miles."

"In kilometers! I didn't go to school in the dark ages like you."

"Two hundred seventy-five."

"And how high is the moon?"

"Too high for the restaurant business at the moment. They have to make do with a cafeteria."

"Damn," she said. "Don't forget me when you get your first lunar franchise. I'm going to send you vitamin pills every week. I want to make sure that you'll live that long."

"You haven't said yes to the spaceport yet."

She squeezed his hand. "When have I ever said not to you? I'm so thrilled I'm speechless. What's the name of your restaurant?"

"*Planet Stories*."

# 8

For sixty kilometers the raised track swept across the surface of the Imbrian plain. Since the lunar horizon was only three kilometers away, the track stabbed to the edge of the universe like God's knife separating the light from the darkness.

*If* they were allowed to finish it, within four months graceful ships would be skimming in tangentially at orbital velocity, to be picked up by a travelling platform equipped with superconducting coils, and braked on the maglev track. Right now Byron's staff was installing auxiliary systems, a series of flywheels near the track to soak up the energy of a landing, or feed out energy in the case of a take-off. A fifteen-ton ship moving at 1680 m/sec and decelerating at two Earth gravities generates 500 megawatts of electricity which has to go somewhere.

The flywheels were housed in huts which could be pressurized during construction and maintenance and evacuated during operation. They rotated on magnetic bearings in a vacuum. Their basic frame was built on Earth but the bulk mass for the wheel was made of lunar laminates. It was those laminates that were giving trouble.

Byron was with one of the flywheel crews when he got a call from the main base. "McDougall. Braithwaite here. Louise hasn't been able to find you. She has an urgent call from Earth."

"Goddamn that phone! I've got enough to do seeing if you and Anne are on schedule and under budget, without having to listen to every gripe from Earth."

"Louise said it was a panicky message from Seattle. You're going to be recalled."

"I just got back! Oh for Christ's sake. I suppose they aren't satisfied with the deal I made in Washington. I know damn well it was a stopgap, but it was the best I could do. It has *got* to do for the next four months."

"I think the call was about the crisis," said Braithwaite.

"Which crisis? An old one or a new one?"

"You vac-head. *The revolution.*"

"What revolution?"

"In Saudi Arabia."

"Yeah, yeah, Saudi Arabia is going to revolt when hell freezes over. I know those sand eaters. I know Abdul Zamani, the defense minister. I taught him how to fly the F-15."

"Abdul Zamani is dead. The last I heard the refinery complex at Dhahran was in flames. And God alone knows if the new leaders will continue to sell us oil. We don't yet know which freak Marxist heresy they belong to. Old Poker Face raced in from Camp David and seems to be trying to gather support to send in the marines—but hell, it's already way too late. The Royalists who were yelling for help are already dead."

"You're kidding me?"

"You didn't scan the news this morning? We saw rows of Royal Bodies hanging headless by their feet from the lampposts in Riyadh. The King was murdered three hours ago."

"My God! And you didn't tell me!"

"I automatically assume you know everything."

"I'm coming in. Sweet Jesus!"

Back in the huts of the main base Byron replayed the late news on his console screen. It had been a stunning coup. The battle was over before the Pentagon had even received orders to organize an airlift. And the CIA had heard the news via CBS. Modern Arab coups evidently weren't the clumsy affairs of yesterday.

*Swat, just like that.*

He felt disoriented, remembering the tough men he had trained. Those Saudi fighter pilots had been Royalist to the core. He couldn't imagine a coup succeeding without them and he couldn't imagine them siding with the Palestinians and the Pakistanis and the other immigrants who chafed under Royal rule. But he didn't let his disorientation stop him from sensing that here was an extraordinary battlefield situation to be exploited *immediately*.

Zimmerman came into his office with a worried look. "That's bad news. You heard the news?"

"Yeah. I still don't believe it."

"Look, no American should try already to understand an Arab intrigue."

"You sound upset."

"The House of Saud supported *moderate* terrorists. Me, I'm thinking the new government will maybe support *extreme* terrorists."

"I have a simple philosophy about terrorists—shaved ones and unshaved ones," said Byron. "Give any one of them a buck to do in your blood enemies, and they'll use it to buy a gun to do you in for the *rest* of your money. Bankrolling hatred is a risky line of work."

"You think the terrorists are behind the coup?"

"Zimmerman, I haven't got a clue. Money is power and power is a double-edged sword, that's all I know. There is no denying that the Royalists have been feeding murderers. Maybe that money was used to kill Jews, maybe it turned into graft, maybe it flowed backwards to water the plots in Jidda. Who will ever know? Whatever the basis for the coup, somebody just lost a queen in a big chess game. The USA is up the creek. And we on the moon have been dealt an ace." Byron glanced at his watch. "Hungry?"

"It's cucumber salad today," said Zimmerman disconsolately.

"I'm going to have to crack that whip to get that landing track finished so we can ship in some beef."

"With whose money?"

"You think money will be a problem after today?"

"I see a depression," Zimmerman said gloomily.

Byron was grinning as they drifted off toward the cafeteria. "I see gas rationing in the States, and I'm dying laughing. I'm seeing the pipes bursting in the middle of winter and I'm rolling in the aisles. I'm seeing the Russians trading weapons for Saudi oil and I'm grinning from ear to ear."

"That bad you see it?"

"I used to like Americans," said Byron with amused savagery. "I'm an American. It used to feel great to go to them and say, 'Here's a solution to a problem that hasn't happened yet.' So how do they react? They sniff daisies. Even my son. Zimmerman, if an American jumps out of an airplane, you can't sell him a parachute until *after* he hits the ground. I don't even flap about it anymore. Americans are manic freaks who slack off suicidally between crises and then work their asses to a bone to meet a crisis *after* it has bashed them in the face—all the time bitching bitterly that no one ever told them that the fist was on the way. Well, *I* told them. *I* was on my knees begging them, for Christ's sake. That's the whole story. It's a mania that will kill us all dead one day, and our Constitution besides, that one last crisis too many, but in the meantime it is no use yammering to deaf ears about how to prevent a coming crisis, you just have to be cool and work quietly until you know exactly what to tell them to do *after* the crisis has them screaming in pain—and hope to God they can get their silly asses in gear as fast as they always have before. Don't have the parachutes ready! Know all about splints!"

"Well done!" exclaimed Zimmerman. "I haven't heard you rant that well for three days."

Braithwaite appeared from behind the potted plants and joined them at their table. "Have you phoned Seattle yet?"

"Why should I call Seattle? I know what they are going to say. They're going to send me back to D.C. to try to sell Congress on putting up the risk capital to set up a production line that will crank out one ten-begawatt solar power satellite per month. I'll go; I'll make salvation noises, and our politicians will stand there

with their knees shaking, those Georges who have cut us colonials
down to the bone, and they'll kiss my ass and they'll buy it. Eight
years ago I would have kissed *their* asses."

"You're so happy it depresses me," moped Zimmerman. "The
State Department is having a morbid nightmare, and you're happy."

"Give us a smile, Zim."

"How can I give you a smile? My son is in Israel. I'm worried,"

"Arabs are killing each other and he's worried. Give us a smile.
This is the break we've been praying for. Now the bureaucrats
need us in a bad way."

"You really think D.C. is going to buy anything? With our
luck they'll revoke our return tickets and turn off the air. We'll
starve. Here, maybe have some cucumber salad before it is gone
already."

# 9

The pods were attached all along the sides of the spaceport. Floating
down the central corridor of Pod 43 a customer faced the logo of
*Planet Stories* set into a glass rectangle above liquid crystal credits
for the waitresses such as:

## MOON CRAWLERS
### by Diana Grove

Framed by this layout was the control room of a 1940s class
rocketship battle cruiser. The busy "captain" could be seen in
free fall, perhaps with his hand on the Pressor Beam Rheostat
mixing a whisky sour. Beyond him was a porthole and an awesome
view of the Earth filling half the sky.

Beside the porthole sat a surly Bug Eyed Monster deep in his
cups. He was so lifelike that the unwary frequently approached him
to see if they couldn't detect a defect left by the artist and got the
shock of their lives. The BEM turned with a cat's suppleness, bared
his teeth and snarled at people who came too close. His electronic
innards were, of course, made on the spaceport.

Diana was late for work, the first time in many weeks. It wasn't
her fault. There had been a minor malfunction on the maglev
transport line that carried passengers and freight and empty lighters
along the 150km length of the spaceport. Her apartment, which

she shared with another girl employed in large-scale integrated microelectronics, was 20 km from *Planet Stories*.

She popped through the airlock entrance—a real emergency airlock—whispered hurried words to the "captain" and scooted to the ladies' room where she slipped into her brass scanties and emerged ready to serve. Serving in free fall was freaky but she already knew how to do it with grace.

"Diana!"

She turned. A man with pepper hair and blue eyes was smiling lazily at her. He wore lunar togs. He had a strong aura about him and she thought she saw in his face a gentle fondness for women. That strange heady feeling of love at first sight struck. She let the emotion tingle through her mainly because he was an older man and that made him safe. Three other men hovered with him at a service booth. She glided over, her willingness to serve at a level above and beyond the call of duty.

"What's a Moon Crawler?" he asked.

"How do you know I'm Diana?"

"I've kissed all the other bylines."

"And they rejected your clever pass so you're trying me as a last resort?"

"Byron," said one of the others, "she's armed."

"And beautiful arms they are," said Byron, undiscouraged.

"A Moon Crawler," replied Diana, "is a slimy worm from outer space who telepathically poses as an irresistible woman. All that's left of the man in the morning is his toenails."

"Ouch," said Byron. "Let's hug and make up."

"You wouldn't survive. Now what do you want to order?"

He was amused. "I'm rich and charming and experienced, a classic winner. What did I do to deserve you?"

At the first opportunity Diana asked the "captain" in his Tri-planet Rocketforce uniform, "Who is that distinguished one with those accountant types? He's a regular here, isn't he?"

"McDougall."

"Thanks. That tells me a lot."

"He has a few interesting stories to tell. He's an old fighter pilot. He's an old Rockwell shuttle pilot. He built half of this bird we're flying on. I think he is a close friend of Arnold." Arnold had designed the spaceport. "He's top dog of the moon base construction crew."

"He's really been to the moon?" Her eyes darted to the corner.

"He *commutes* to the moon."

She leaned conspiratorially over the battle cruiser weapons' control array. "Is he married?"

"Divorced."

She shivered at that news. "He likes me, did you notice?"

"Diana sweetheart, listen to me. You have a superlative bod. He's a make-em and leave-em man. He's out of your class."

"What do *you* know about trapping men!" she flared and left with their dinners.

One thing she liked about her job, the girls were supposed to entertain intellectually as well as serve and be sexy. Ling never sent a woman to *Planet Stories* who wasn't a good conversationalist. It was easy to wedge into this group and dominate the chat. She made her points by touching them lightly with excited hands—except McDougall. She let the men fondle her body—except McDougall. But while his companions caressed her brass armor, she flirted with those flecked blue eyes.

Duties called her away, yet she made special trips back to *his* corner. Only as they finished their after-dinner drinks did she tousle Byron's hair and whisper in his ear, "I'm off at 2 A.M. Why don't you pick me up then?" She was trembling with embarrassment.

He smiled. "Too bad I'm not on vacation. This Saudi mess has a stake up all our asses." He scribbled something and handed her a note. "Drop by when you get off. You may have to watch me work."

Diana didn't look at the note until he was gone. It was his Hilton hotel room, the executive suite. She had a flash of anger. *I won't go.* He wanted her to chase him. It was humiliating. *I'll go home and chain myself to the hammock.*

She stared at the wall. On it hung an original *Planet Stories* illustration of the Princess of Io, wearing a World War II hairdo and burlesque costume, racing between the moons of Jupiter on her rocket sled and being pursued. *Some women have all the luck*!.

It was a long ride to the Hilton on the maglev. If you were close to the tubes, you could hear the lighters coming in or being shot out, a kind of humming swoosh that came through your feet, but in the maglev bus, suspended in vacuum, you could hear nothing. She did catch an occasional glimpse of an unloaded lighter, its delta wings retracted, moving along the central transport line in electromagnetic suspension where it was being taken to maintenance or loading or to the ejection breech at the leading edge of the spaceport.

Tremulously, at two-thirty, she was at McDougall's door, knocking. He opened. He seemed confused to see her. Behind him papers were mag-locked to the walls and the combination info-computer console that went with the executive suite was alive with readout.

"Didn't you invite me?" She clutched his note, unsure of herself on his territory.

He shook himself. "I wasn't expecting you."

"I thought you invited me."

He eased her inside. "And I thought you were pulling my leg. You pulled my leg all evening. So I pulled yours. If I'd known you were serious I would have been after you with roses. I hate being stood up."

Slightly mollified she said, "Where would you get roses in space?"

"There are ways, my little Moon Crawler."

She watched the tension lift from his face. A lined face could not hide tension as easily as a young face. *He's happy to have me.* He took her in his arms and held her warmly. She let him. *What am I doing here? He's going to try to lay me. I've got to get out of here.* "Did I interrupt something?"

"You most certainly did."

"I'm sorry. I won't bother you. I'll just watch. I love to watch men work. They're so involved."

"Give me another hour or so. I'm making up a presentation for a congressional committee. Looking at energy alternatives with Saudi oil knocked out."

"I thought we weren't importing as much oil from Saudi Arabia as we used to." *Always get a man to talk about his work.*

"We're not. But try turning off 30 percent of your oil supply when you're all geared up for it. That new crew of camel-smelling sister-beaters are throwing out their American oil men and importing Soviet technicians to put their oil fields back into production. They killed more than 20,000 of their own American-trained men in the battle. And we can't do a damn thing about it."

Her eyes were glowing. "Will they have to build solar power satellites now?"

"There's a good chance."

"They'll just dig more coal," she said disdainfully. "Where I used to live in Ohio, everything was done with coal."

He snorted. "Coal has been having problems for a long time. Do you know how many billions of dollars the government spends on coal-related disabilities every year? I could buy a lunar colony for that budget." He called up a display on the screen. "And look at that. Hydrogen fusion is still 3000 times as expensive as fission. That leaves breeder reactors and solar power satellites. And *we* are clean. It will take a mix of both. It is a pain in the ass figuring out the trade-offs. Time is the factor now. We've got to move *fast* and that changes the trade-offs."

"Is there anything I can do? Sort papers or something?"

"Diana," he said warmly, "you've had a hard day. You've done a whole shift, for God's sake. Get to bed. I'll join you later."

"I'd rather watch." With a cringing fascination she watched the terror that was beginning to rise in her.

"And I'd rather see some rosy cheeks in the morning." He took her behind the room screen and pulled out the bed netting and casually began to undress her.

She froze.

He backed off. "We've made different postulates?"

She was panicky. She didn't know how to explain. "I have to be between you and the door. I'm crazy."

He changed position with her, careful not to touch her, instantly willing to put her at ease. "Is that better?" He was puzzled, and half amused.

She nodded.

"Have you ever made love in space?"

"No."

"You'll enjoy it."

"I'm getting out of here."

"Stay." It was a command. He did not raise his hands.

She stared at those blue eyes which held her, knowing that he would let her go if she had the strength to leave. "I can undress myself." She did so, swiftly, awkwardly, and slipped into the net. "Kiss me goodnight."

Quietly, at six in the morning, he woke her. His body was comfortably warm. That part was like Mr. Ling and she enjoyed it. But Byron's fingers were hungry. That part confused her. She tried to be like the girls in the movies. It didn't work. It was like trying to take control of a runaway horse.

He stopped. "How old did you say you were?"

"Twenty-one."

"You're a virgin."

"Is that bad?"

"Holy Jesus."

"I'm sorry. It's not my fault, I was born that way."

"I'm rattled. You aren't in the space I thought you were in, and I'm astonished that I missed it."

"You don't want me?" She was ready to cry.

He didn't stop making love to her, but he was slower and carefully gentle, less intense, more propitiative, and he took contraceptive precautions because he didn't trust her innocence. The pleasure of it astonished her and she clung to him and wouldn't let go.

"My father used to beat me. I've had a hard time liking men. You're a good lover."

"How would you know? I'm a lousy lover."

"You're so delicious that all that's going to be left of you is toenails."

"Maybe it is just space. The first time you try it on Earth, you'll be shocked—especially if you are stuck with a 200-pound man like me."

"I'm never going back to Earth!"

"I am. In three days."

She began to cry. "Are you going to marry me?"

"Sweet Jesus. I could be your father."

"It doesn't matter. I love you. I remember everything you said. In *Planet Stories* you said you'd never met a woman who could love both you and space. Well, I love you and I love space and I want to settle down on the moon just like you do."

"Wench, we will discuss this later when you are sober."

Diana called up one of the other girls and arranged an exchange of days off. She did her best not to let Byron out of her sight. He didn't seem to mind. She let Byron work. She helped him when she could. But the minute he showed signs of relaxing, she seduced him with every wile she knew. Sex, for two whole days, was her entire universe.

The door slid open. Byron's eyes blazed with blue fire. "Get dressed!" Terrified she slipped into her blouse but his anger couldn't wait and he gathered the collar of the blouse in his fist and shoved her against the wall. "You lied to me!"

She loved him too much to hit him or struggle.

"There is no Diana Grove." He shook her like a dog shakes a rat. "Your name is Osborne and you are sixteen years old. You are jailbait!" He let her go. "Do you realize how much trouble you could get me into?"

"Don't hit me! Don't hit me!" She was cringing.

"You slipped up in some of your stories. I got to thinking. And the company has ways of checking up people. We can't tolerate fools in space. Sixteen. M. God. Sixteen! You should be home with your parents!"

"My father beats me," she said piteously. "That's why I ran away when I was twelve."

Byron remained angry. "Kids always blame their fathers. A favorite sport. Fathers happen to be nice guys. Maybe you just never understood what your father was saying. Maybe you are headstrong and willful and don't see the dangers a father sees. You're young. Fathers know, kid. They *know*."

Her face twisted into agony. "You don't love me anymore."

A single tear rolled out of his eye. "Jesus, what a damn fool I am. Yes, I love you. And I'm responsible for you. I'm leaving tomorrow and you're coming with, me."

Sometimes the sun breaks through the clouds. "You're going to marry me?"

"I'm going to take you home to your family."

The sun can disappear again behind a thundercloud. "I *hate* my father!"   He took Diana in his arms and soothed her. "Can you remember something nice about him?"

"Why should I?"

"For me."

She paused, wanting to please Byron. "He bought me a rug when I wanted one."

"Did you like the rug?"

"Yeah."

"Remember something else nice."

She thought a long time, her eyes staring off in the direction of Arcturus. "He always made lemon and honey for my mother when she was sick."

"See. He's a nice man. It's been a long time. Our minds don't remember some things well because we are committed to proving that our decisions were right. You'll like him. You'll see."

"Mr. Ling will never forgive me," she said petulantly.

"I'm buying your contract."

"You can't make me go!"

"Oh yes I can," he said grimly.

# 10

The snow in Ohio was dirty with coal dust. Coal smells were on the air because the wind blew from that direction. Diana was surprised to see her father smiling, surprised to see him contrite, surprised at the warmth of the welcome he gave to the distinguished Mr. McDougall whose power awed him.

She arrived back in her familiar rat warren of factories and dry cleaning stores and chunky houses on tiny lots with potholes in the streets, a prisoner of the man she loved, determined to be emotionless—instead she cried with her mother. Both her parents lavished her with affection.

It was weird to go back to school with kids who hadn't changed since they were twelve because they hadn't done anything since they were twelve. The boys giggled when they said "books" and the girls were all virgins who thought SPS was a new thing to put in face cream to keep your pores clean.

Diana introverted into thoughts of Byron, suppressing all the evidence that might tell her she had been abandoned. He had hairs on his chest like Samson and she had some of them in an old perfume bottle. He was a hero angel who built stairways to the stars for men who were as yet too savage to understand. His fingers were pleasure, his eyes an ultimate beauty.

In her loneliness she began a letter to him. She wasn't sure she was going to mail it but the poetry of her love ached on her tongue. "Dearest Byron, I had a dream that there was nothing left of you but toenails and woke up in my bed nude (and beautiful as you well know) and imagined sweet touches. . . ." She redrafted the letter again and again, hiding it under the leather blotter on her desk.

One day when she came home from an errand to buy milk, her father chased her up the stairs raging against the depraved McDougall and against his daughter's dirty pornographic mind. He cornered her in her room, crumpling the letter in his fist.

Karate habits told her to take a defensive posture She found herself cringing instead but when his arm lashed out to hit, her reflexes took over. A precisely placed foot smashed into his elbow, breaking it. She never looked back. She grabbed her Diana Grove papers from hiding and leaped through the window onto the porch roof and down onto the ground, rebounding in a run, unprotected against the winter cold.

A man and his wife found her on the highway, half frozen to death, thumbing a ride. They wrapped her in a car blanket and turned up the heat. She told them she was trying to go to her mother in New Hampshire. Only after she said New Hampshire did she remember that Byron's home was there.

The couple were active Christians and though they gave her endless advice about God and finding Jesus they were also practical. They insisted on taking her home, feeding her and finding winter clothes for her from their friends. They insisted on paying her bus fare and when she protested, they merely smiled and told her she could pay them back by helping someone else someday.

On the bus she prepared the scathing lecture with which she intended to axe-murder Byron.

(1) You are a monster!

(2) You seduced me and, not content with just rejecting me, you ruthlessly destroyed the whole wonderful life that I was building up for myself.

(3) And once you smashed my life, you weren't satisfied; you had to deliver me to a sadist for safekeeping, just so you could walk away without any burden.

(4) How am I ever going to get a job like that space port job again?

(5) It's not my fault that I had to pretend to be five years older than I really am. The government is stupid. They won't let me work and they won't take care of me.

*I'll strangle him. He better give me some money. He better give me a job on the moon.*

Halfway to New Hampshire she realized she didn't have a mark on her body and she wouldn't have a story to tell Byron that he would believe. At one of the hourlong rest stops she went out to a brick wall and bashed her head against it until the side of her face was bloody and swollen. When some friendly passengers tried to ask her what had happened she queered them by talking up the joys of head pounding.

Looking like an accident victim and in a state of confusion, she stepped off the bus, penniless, at a roadside terminal in a little New Hampshire town. It was madness to think that Byron would be home. He would be in D.C. or Seattle or anywhere but New Hampshire. She was going to a shuttered home buried in snow. His ex-wife, she knew, was in Florida.

She had a cry in the ladies' room before she went over to the post office and asked about Mr. McDougall. The woman told her

he wasn't home, but that his son was, and a no-good drifter he
had for a son. Diana panhandled a quarter for a phone call and
when she heard the son's voice, hung up without saying a word.
She walked in the snow, ten kilometers, until she reached the
McDougall place.

A dark-haired young man with Byron's blue eyes answered the
door. "You've been walking. Your car is stuck? I have a truck."

"No. I'm your father's mistress."

He tried to say seven things in reply and only a squeak came
out. She walked past him, hugging herself. He rushed after her.
"Hey, you're cold."

"Take me to your radiator."

"You've had an accident."

She touched her face. "The swelling is down. The black eye is
pretty awful, isn't it? My old man beat me up for sleeping with
your old man."

"My father abandoned you?"

"Yeah."

"Didn't he give you a free year in Paris?"

"He gave me a free year in an Ohio coal town."

"You could have asked for more."

"You don't ask for things when you're in love."

"You're too young for him."

"I *don't* think *that* is *any* of your *business*!"

"Are you pregnant?"

"*No*, I'm *not* pregnant," she said through gritted teeth.

"I'll have some hot tea ready in a minute."

She sat down in the kitchen by the radiator and took her boots
off. Her feet were white and numb. "Where is he?"

"I just got a check from Houston, but that was a week ago."

"A lot of good that does me." She started to cry.

"Aw, hey now. It can't be that bad."

"If you come over here with your big blue eyes and try to comfort
me, I'll slug you!"

# 11

Diana sulked in the master bedroom except for meals. Across the
veranda she had a view of snowed-in farmlands, the kind of rolling
landscape rich people purchase when they are bored by the city.
The room had a handcrafted look with walnut trim and carved

walnut doors. It was wholly a woman's room. Perfume bottles were on display, but things like heavy brass hairbrushes were neatly placed in drawers. Two portraits hung over the bed: a woman lit by sun reflected from spring leaves and a man glooming beneath some autumnal overcast in a fighter pilot uniform. The portrait of Mrs. McDougall, Diana hid under the bed. *His* portrait she launched upon the bed, a raft for a lonely girl to cling to in a king-sized ocean of softness.

Sulking made Diana restless. She had never tried it before and didn't like it. After three days she took a couple of hours off to bake a chicken casserole and that was such a relief she began trying on Mrs. McDougall's clothes, modifying the ones she liked on the sewing machine. A timid knock interrupted her concentration sometime during her fourth day of sewing.

"Like to come to the village? I'm going for groceries."

"Thank God! Did Byron finally send you more money?"

"Naw. I did some electrical work at the Hodge farm."

"You worked?" she exclaimed incredulously.

"Yeah, you're eating me out of house and home."

"And here I thought I was starving!"

"So today we'll have steak. I figured that if my father can keep *my* girlfriend in Paris, I can at least buy *his* girlfriend a steak."

In the village she noticed that the highway restaurant needed a waitress and she went in and took the job. It was a drag to live with a wastrel like Charlie who ate macaroni every night, sweet as he was. She was used to money.

Sometimes she hitchhiked home after work. Sometimes Charlie was waiting for her if she paid for the gas. Once he arrived to pick her up and found her being hassled by three toughs who wanted to give her a ride. The leader blew smoke in his face.

"You being bothered by these lung disease cases?" he asked.

"Stay out of this, Charlie. I know karate."

"It's not a job for a lady." He assumed the stance of a battle-tried colonel. "Leave!"

They left.

"How did you do that?" She was amazed.

He laughed. "Ordering men around and saving women and children runs in the family. Old military tradition. I'm considered the sissy of the McDougalls."

Diana decided to become independent of Charlie and bought a fifty-dollar car and pay-by-the-week insurance policy after she had wangled some gas ration tickets. The car got her halfway home.

"Charlie," said a plaintive voice over the phone. "I'm stuck on the Stonefield road at the hairpin. Would it be too much trouble for you to come and get me? Bring a chain."

"A chain?"

"To pull my car."

"Your car!"

"I bought a car."

"How much did you pay?"

She muttered an answer.

"Good God! You can't buy an unrusty hubcap for that!"

"It made noises and quit. Can you fix it?"

He sighed. "Maybe it's the spark plugs. I'll be right down."

The engine had seized. "How much does a new engine cost?" she whined.

"Oh, maybe a thousand dollars."

She cried all the way home. He tried to console her by telling her he could get something for the tires, and maybe sell a few other parts, but she was inconsolable. He began to feel so sorry for her that the next day he towed the car off to a friend's garage and spent all day doing an engine job. That evening he picked her up.

"Where's the truck?"

"I brought the car."

"I didn't know you could fix cars."

"I can't but I used to repair obsolete jet engines at MIT."

"Where did you get the money for parts?"

Charlie grinned like a man who has just won somebody else's gambling money. "My father is a millionaire. I have a kind of credit around here. He grumbles like hell, but he pays the bills."

"I don't understand you. Why do you loaf around when you could get a job as a mechanic?"

"Diana! That's work! I only did it for you."

"You're my nice sweetie pie. How can I sacrifice myself for you?"

"Entertain me in bed."

"I belong to your father!" she said indignantly.

"What kind of garbage is that?" he snarled.

"A girl belongs to the man who took her virginity."

He groaned. "You believe that drivel?"

"I certainly do!"

"You sound like my grandfather."

"Are you in love with me?" she asked warily.

"An inch, going on an inch and a quarter."

As they were thrown around the hairpin turn on Stonefield Road she kissed him. "If I hadn't met your father first, I'd love you an inch and a quarter, too." She kissed him again.

"Watch that stuff. You'll get dirty. I couldn't wash all the grease off."

"I don't care. I want to be nice to you. What was the nicest thing that ever happened to you—besides sex?"

"When Betty let me give her a bath."

Diana screeched. "I'll give you a bath!"

She sudsed him carefully, in no hurry to finish caressing away the black grease. It made her lonely to touch him, and happy at the same time. He tried to convince her to join him in the tub but she refused. When she was toweling him afterwards, he tried to kiss her and she hit him and they had a fight. She ran to the master bedroom and locked the door but hugging Byron's angular portrait proved to be no way to go to sleep. She kept thinking about crazy Charlie.

At four in the morning she wrapped a sheet around her body and shuffled to the kitchen for a glass of milk. She returned by way of Charlie's study, curiosity driving her to rifle through his papers. It was mostly schoolwork—quations, printouts, drawings, projects, experiments.

Charlie appeared at the door in his pajamas. "You're not asleep." He paused. "I'm sorry."

"I'm not mad at you. What are all those things?"

"I used to go to MIT."

"What are you?"

"A lunar engineer. It's not that really; I didn't specialize in lunar construction problems until my last year."

"Is that what these diagrams are?"

"Yeah."

"You never told me."

"It's not important to me."

Like a dash of hot Tabasco the old excitement was in her body as it sauced her blood with adrenaline and a pinch of lust. "Did you flunk?"

"I was the top of my class."

"Why aren't you building houses on the moon? It would be fun."

"Fun? It would be like New Hampshire in January with the air missing. Why take the moon when the worst that can happen to you on Earth is to be staked to an anthill in Nevada."

"But you could go if you wanted?"

"My father would love it. Staking me to an anthill isn't good enough for him."

A small adjustment of her shoulders let one curious nipple peek over the sheet at his blue eyes. "And what's all that electronic junk?"

"My music."

"Is that the weird stuff I hear once in a while?"

"No, the weird stuff is when I'm composing. That's just experiments and subthemes. Sometimes it's a foundation sound on which I'm going to build." Then he added shyly, "I've been composing a piece for you."

"Oh, you *are* in love with me!" she teased. "May I hear it?"

"You sing this wild stuff in the shower. I built it on that. You'll have to forgive me for bugging your shower."

"But I have a slug's voice!"

"Ah, but it's all filtered through my electronic ears and I hear the most beautiful things when I listen to you."

"If you weren't so lazy you could work as a queen's flatterer."

"It's called 'Diana in the Rain.'"

Nothing larval was left in the voice he had transformed with his silken touch. Mostly it wasn't even human. Perhaps a nymph bathing in a mountain waterfall would sing that way. The sound folded and unfolded wings of joy so startling even she failed to recognize herself as the music gripped her with her own emotion. Background instruments fluted in tonal patterns no wooden instrument had ever emitted. Her mind, captured by his net, remembered mythical worlds she had never seen.

He stood breathless, anxious, watching her reaction. Slowly becoming aware of what his metamorphic magic had done to her, she worked out of her percale cocoon with little jerking cries of pleased embarrassment.

"Golly."

He was drugged with happiness, just watching her.

"Don't stare at me like that or I'll turn you into a stag and your own hounds will hunt you down!"

Gently he carried her off to bed but, when responding to his memory of her earlier anger, he withdrew, she would not let him go. What is true one hour is false the next.

"Stay with me and cuddle. As long as I get the door side of the bed. You can make love to me in the morning."

When she woke she found him staring at her with his blue

eyes. She rubbed noses with him. "Hi," he said. "Is it morning yet?"

Their sexing was an awkward disaster. The gravity threw her off and he was a virgin. Alternately they swore at each other and laughed. Finally they decided that at least they knew how to hug.

"It reminds me of a story that my grandfather loves to tell," he sighed. "Once upon a time there was a new recruit for the 43rd Cavalry Regiment and the commanding officer asked him, 'Have you ever ridden before, my boy?' 'No, sir,' said the boy. 'Hmm,' replied the colonel, 'I have just the horse for you; she's never been ridden before, either.'"

"Let's have breakfast and try it again," she said.

For three days Diana ran around in a daze, baking, washing his clothes, laughing at his jokes, buying him presents with her tip money and hugging him every time she met him. The second time she found herself scrubbing the kitchen floor in one week, she frowned. Did sex always make a woman feel this way? Byron had given her goosebumps, too. Were men similarly affected? She peeked out the kitchen window and saw Charlie freezing his fingers off changing a bearing on her right front wheel and that was reassuring.

By Friday she was enough in control of her emotions to begin the Great Plan. (1) Get Charlie a job. (2) Get him to finish school. (3) Get him a job on the moon. (4) Marry him. (5) Have children. She wasn't going to do it by nagging. She hated nagging a man. She'd rather leave a man than nag him. She was going to do it by worshipping him when he moved in the right direction and with patience and humor.

A driver's mother died and he trucked potatoes for three days; Diana let him make love to her for three evenings and three mornings. A neighbor's pipes froze and he joined the plumbing crew; she cooked him a four-course meal. Slyly she began to encourage him to be more ambitious. He took a weekend gig in Concord with his music. But spring came and he was still only doing odd jobs. Happiness gave her patience. They went walking in the woods when the buds sprouted. They splashed nude in the ice-cold brook.

She began to read to him from the papers about the big new push into space. Money was flooding into the effort. Overnight the high frontier had become a business almost half as big as the American cigarette, dope, and cosmetics trade. Charlie was never interested. She hid her hurt.

The Saudi Arabian situation improved. Escaped Royalists had money in America and Europe with which to influence politics at home. Intrigues prospered. Assassinations were frequent. The new leaders found it easier to conquer than to rule, and found some appeasement of the western capitalists necessary. Still the oil situation was grim and as reserves were depleted the United States imposed draconian gasoline rationing. Syntigas plants were pushed to full capacity in spite of a coal strike, suppressed by the Army. But sabotage continued to decimate coal tonnage.

Red tape was cut so that breeder reactors could be put on line in four years but nuisance protests continued to mount. A new tar sands plant was financed for Alberta. Hydrogen fusion power was brought down to $100 per kilowatt hour. A new gas field was discovered at great depth in the Gulf of Mexico. Mainly the economy was gearing up for solar power satellite production.

She read to Charlie the fabulous job offers in the *New York Times*. He wasn't interested. She sulked.

One day like a bolt from Jupiter the father called and Diana listened on the upstairs phone, tears rolling out of her eyes. *There* was a man. He could build. He could fight. His very voice called forth loyalty. He was on the cover of *Time* magazine. He could even be tender to virgins. His kind forged the glory of man. She ached to hold him. Could a woman ever forget her first man?

That noon Diana cooked pies and a mouth-watering lasagna. She made a fresh spring salad of new asparagus tips. She adjusted Charlie's collar. She teased him and in all ways was free and easy with her love. When she went to work she left a note in the truck's windshield wiper. "I have a job on the moon." Which wasn't true. "I'll *always* love you." Which was true for the moment. "Keep in touch."

She stopped at the restaurant only long enough to collect her pay and buy a packet of black-market gas stamps which got her as far as Montana. In Butte she abandoned the car and took a bus to Seattle, curled over two seats with her head pressed against her wadded jacket, dreaming that she was asleep next to Byron's facial stubble.

# 12

For three hours a nervous girl waited in the hotel lobby where that flighty secretary said he was staying. It stunned her when he sailed by, his weathered eyes scanning over her like a reef to be avoided, his wake washing away the hello in her throat. She buttoned the décolleté she had arranged to remind him of her womanhood, and followed him into the waiting elevator, ignoring him while they touched shoulders.

He left the elevator. She followed silently. He stopped and took out his key card. She waited.

"Diana! For the love of God!"

"So you finally noticed," she said petulantly.

"I had you pegged as one of the convention girls," he apologized, somewhat untactfully, switching on the light and walking over to the telephone. "What'll I order for you?"

"Poison darts!"

He spoke into the phone. "A double whisky for room 412. Also an extra glass, a bucket of ice and three bottles of ginger ale." Carefully he cradled the receiver. "So you ran away again?"

"He beat me up the minute you left! I mistook myself for a gong. I escaped by jumping two stories into the snow. A couple of good samaritans found me frozen to death at the end of a trail of blood. I learned about fathers what I already knew."

He was gazing at her with quizzical amusement. "Any scars?"

"No sir!" She snapped her heels. "Regrouped, resupplied, rested, and ready for active duty, you son-of-a-bitch, sir!" A clipped salute finished her report.

"*Now* I remember you," he said amiably. "And how have you been spending your AWOL?"

"Living with your son."

His face crumpled like a piece of paper being prepared for a bureaucrat's wastebasket. "You've seen Charlie?"

"We're lovers."

"Did he send you here for money?"

"Oh Byron! I heard your voice last week on the phone. I became nostalgic. I came here to marry you. We're going to have three children and live on the moon."

"A minute ago you were ready to kill me with poison darts."

"That was a minute ago. I'd be a good wife."

"I'm tempted," he said.

"Yeah?" She unbuttoned her décolleté.

"But my good sense remains. I'll give you a choice. I'll argue with you or I'll send you to an orphan asylum."

"Argue with me."

"You laid Charlie, eh?"

"What's it to you! The last I heard from you, just before you abandoned me to that prick father of mine, you wanted me to live in the coal dust and be virtuous."

Byron was trying to visualize being married to her. "I was thinking that you are young, even for Charlie."

"Yaah! Charlie's young, even for me."

"It wouldn't work between you and me," he said decisively.

"Why not!"

"I'm more than thirty years older than you are. I'm dying. You are beginning to flower."

She undid another button and rummaged around under the bed for his dirty socks which she angrily threw into a plastic bag. "Corpses make good fertilizer for flowers. Your power and my youth; it's a fair exchange. Jesus, Byron," she turned to him with regret, "I swooned when I saw you on *Time*. I was horny for a day."

"You'd tire of an old man."

"But it's men who are fickle. Women aren't like that. They're faithful. When they love a man, they *love* him. I'd be faithful to you. I'd forgive you anything."

He was settling into his decision. "That's what they all say when they are seventeen. When they are twenty-seven it's a different story."

"Already you're complaining about ten glorious years?" she stormed. "I'll bet you think you deserve fifty!"

There was a polite knock on the door.

"Young girls tend to bore experienced men," he reminded her.

She flung open the door and took the double whisky from the bellhop's cart before he had fully entered the room. She set the glass on the dresser, imperiously tipped the man, and poured Byron a ginger ale. "For your liver, old man. So I bore you, do I?"

"You started me thinking about those fifty years."

She half finished the whisky in one slurp.

"Can't I even have a sip of my whisky?" he complained.

"I've decided to blackmail you instead of marry you," she answered calmly.

"Blackmail me!" She had his attention. "We're not even married yet and you're being a bitch. I hope your lawyers are cheaper than my lawyers! You've stolen my whisky. What else do you want?"

"A job on the moon."

His humor left him. "No. That's final. What's your counter-move?"

"You damn fool!" she flared. "Your son is in love with me! He'll follow me to the moon! That's where you want him!"

"And do you love Charlie?"

"No! I can't *stand* drifters. Yes. He's very kind."

Byron gripped her arms in the iron curl of his fingers. "Diana. He *won't* follow you to the moon."

"Yes."

"No. I know my son."

"You've seen him lately with my legs around him?" she lilted sarcastically, not even trying to escape his crushing hold. "I've watched him butter my toast. I've watched him scatter men who were trying to molest me, I've seen his eyes in the morning. You know nothing about your son. You're a dried-up old man, remember, who has forgotten what it's like to be driven by his juices. Charlie would follow me to hell. I planned it that way." She started to cry. "At least he will if we move fast enough before he has time to sober up and get another girl."

"He could follow you and refuse to work."

"Then I'd let him die. No man of mine is a suck." She smiled through her tears. "But for me he'd work. He's a sweet guy, Byron."

He began to march around the room, shaking ice from the ginger ale glass he had exchanged for her arm. "And you think I give a *damn* whether he goes to space? I don't give a *damn* anymore. I used to care. Now I'd be happy if he did anything. *Anything*. Wash cars even. How is his *damned* music going?"

"Like his engineering. He piddles at it."

"Is he healthy?"

"He's fine. I took good care of him. He's probably very unhappy right now."

"Suffering, eh?" Byron was smiling again. "A couple of months in the trenches will do him good. Finish your whisky and let's go. You've earned a dinner in Seattle's only real French restaurant."

At dinner he refused to gossip about his son. He ordered the best meal on the menu, the third most expensive. "It's good to eat like this again. For awhile I didn't even have an expense account."

"I'm on your expense account?"

"You're goddamned right. This year the Saudi Arabian Royal family lucked out and I'm enjoying every minute of their agony. We're tripling the size of the lunar colony. I wouldn't have believed that last year. And you should see the assembly line we're setting up for the solar power satellites; subcontracts all over the nation. It is going to be a boom year for the economy even though oil is short."

Her eyes were grinning. "I heard rumors that next year hydrogen fusion prices will drop to one cent a kilowatt hour."

Byron almost didn't laugh. "How could I let my son marry a girl with such a macabre sense of humor?"

He took her walking along the night beach, barefoot, sometimes on the sand, sometimes over the great driftwood trees, his shoes tied by the shoelaces over his shoulder and hers stuffed in his jacket pockets. The Pacific wind was cold and she sheltered herself behind his body, wondering at his silence that lasted for miles, not daring to invade his thoughts. The waves came and broke and went. Their feet were alternately drowned by foam and then free to make wet tracks in the moonlit sand.

"I'm not sure you'd like it up there. There is no moon in the sky for lovers."

"We can make poems about the Earth."

"You still have your Diana Grove papers?"

"Sure."

"They need to be made more solid. I'll spend some money."

She hugged his arm, thanking him silently, the glory and the triumph rising in her bosom to shout down the Pacific wind.

"I'm shipping out in two weeks. I'll take you with me. Not because of Charlie. Charlie can go to hell. For you. If Charlie follows, well, there'll be a job for him. We're building a second electromagnetic track to separate the take-offs from the landings."

*Blackmail works!* She was amazed. "What will I be doing?"

"Who knows."

"May I stay with you tonight?"

"No!"

"My hotel by the bus station has cockroaches!"

They were halfway back along the beach before he answered. "Zimmerman tells this story about some New York cockroaches that followed him to the moon. He claims to have spaced them and that they didn't die but are running around the crater Aristarchus to this day."

# 13

Rockets were still used to carry passengers and large freight to orbit. The electromagnetic interaction of a vehicle and the spaceport involved momentum transfer and large lighters would have required a more massive spaceport. Since the material of the original spaceport had to be carried to orbit by rocket, cost demanded that, once built, it would be supplied by a swarm of midget freighters which were intrinsically unsuitable for passenger transport.

Diana felt like a veteran. A mere year ago she had first been thrown into space by a rattletrap Rockwell Mark VI transport, a much modified version of the original Rockwell shuttle but still launched essentially by the means pioneered during the 1980s. Today she was aboard a modern impact rocket fresh from the factory at San Diego, its very design younger than her "Grove" identity. Even the upholstery smelled clean.

"How do you like this imp?" asked Byron, cramped beside her, not a patch of their bodies unsupported. Imp was the name by which impact rockets had become known.

"It's super."

"You're not scared?"

"I'm going to heaven!"

"I'm scared to death. I get nervous out of the cockpit."

There were no stewardesses. A robot seat monitored each passenger, checking that regulations were complied with during the countdown. ". . . three . . . two . . . one . . ."

Blastoff crushed them. The imp was, among other things, an oxygen-hydrogen rocket of mass ratio four, carrying enough propellant to reach slightly more than half orbital velocity. The roar cut off. A button tumbled in free fall in front of Diana. Then, as the imp found the apogee of its orbit among the blaze of stars, they met the spaceport, an express to hell passing under them so fast that its linear bulk was already perspective lines piercing infinity at the very moment the four-gravity acceleration hit them.

The imp's magnetically suspended arms had reached down and were receiving oxygen from precision valved nozzles set into a perfectly straight feed pipe laid along the spaceport. The oxygen was hurtling at circular velocity as it entered the imp's ducts. The gas suffered an almost elastic collision against the vehicle, swinging through the ducts, around and out the rear jets with its relative velocity reversed—thus violently thrusting the ship forward without affecting the momentum of the spaceport at all. As the imp began to catch up with the spaceport the impacting oxygen became less and less effective. Then the imp began to inject hydrogen into the reaction chamber, adding fire to the recoil.

Ten percent of the oxygen used by this impact system was already being supplied by the moon. Eventually all of it would be. In the meantime oxygen was imported from the Earth via the hybrid lighters.

"Poor little Byron, you can relax now. We're here."

"Whew! The old shuttle was a piece of cake compared with this sobering ride. I feel like I've just been put up in front of a firing squad and asked to gently kiss a machine gun burst."

"You're such a stick-in-the-mud. You're too old for me."

They ate at the *Planet Stories* with leisurely gusto. Diana got drunk for the first time in her life. She told shaggy-dog stories and, when she had the attention of five booths, tried to dance on the tabletop. If you've ever seen a drunk try to dance on a tabletop in null gravity you may understand the extent to which laughing tears convulsed her audience. When she passed out, Byron towed her back to the Hilton.

The next day they caught a ferry to geosynchronous orbit at the construction site of the first ten-begawatt solar power satellite. For eleven hours the five passengers played poker while the captain distributed sandwiches and made coffee.

There was some more ship maneuvering. When they went into a parking orbit, the captain called Diana into the cockpit. "Take a look." The matchstick framework of the SPS angled away into the star-laden blackness. "It's hard to comprehend how immense it is. Look, see that crane over there? It's a whopping big crane. See the little dot? That's the cabin for two men."

"Wow."

"I'll give you the grand picture. That thing is going to be as big as Manhattan Island. What you see is only five of the eight modules. What's out there would reach from Battery Park to 110th Street at the end of Central Park. The next module, the one that would contain Columbia University off in one corner if it was a piece of New York City, is being assembled in low orbit right now. They bring them up here by pushing hydrogen through porous electrically heated tungsten to get it through the Van Allen belts quickly, and then the rest of the way with ion jets."

McDougall was laughing behind them. "Tell her how to get from the A train to the Seventh Avenue line."

Within the hour they docked with a lunar lander and exchanged lunar oxygen for terran hydrogen. The captain of the lunar lander stuck his head through the hatch, mainly to get a chance to razz McDougall. Byron didn't introduce him to Diana until the visit was over.

"Maltby and I used to fly in Saudi Arabia under the same command. He'll be taking care of you from here in. But don't depend on him. He's a rascal. Take care of yourself. Write Charlie. And don't let them send your bags to Mexico City. Ciao."

Maltby took her back through the tunnel.

"You sit copilot with me."

"Where's your copilot?"

"He's too fat. I left him home. Where would I put you if he was here? This ain't no taxicab. This here boat is a freighter. You want to fly the beast?"

"You're scaring me."

"It seems complicated to you? Shucks, you just say 'giddiap' and the beast goes. She has a brain of her own. She knows where home is. The smell of oats."

"Giddiap," said Diana. Nothing happened.

Maltby did a few quick things with his fingers and the ship swung around. Then he yelled "Giddiap!" with an ear-piercing Texas drawl and the ship roared to life.

This trip, instead of poker, she learned how to play chess. He gave her a two-pawn-and-a-rook handicap and she won one out of five games in the next three days.

The ship faced backwards for the horizontal landing, its rockets firing in tiny vernier adjustments. Lazily the barren moon flowed by, slowly rising to meet them. Only when they were skimming the plain at crater-rim height did their speed become evident. A mile every second. Nearby features ran together in a watercolor blur. Suddenly the track appeared beneath them and she saw, for a split second, the rocket-catching cradle racing up the track toward them. She remembered the spaniel who used to gallop from the neighbor's house to chase her bicycle. The cradle positioned itself underneath them, grabbing with gentle jaws until their ship and the maglev vehicle became one.

Maltby was yelling "Whoa!" at the bloodcurdling top of his Texan voice. Electromagnetic fields cut in to convert fifteen tons of mass flow into an electron flood. Force hit then, two gravities that slowly built to five. The blur beyond the windows resolved into the majesty of the lunar desert, and finally they were moving sedately along a shunt line towards a shed. Maltby was fondly patting the control panel, smiling. "Atta girl."

*I'm here*, she thought and wonder was all within her.

She was assigned to the hydroponic gardens under a scowling beak-nosed boss who went through his chambers constantly tasting tomatoes and carrots and broccoli like a Punch making passes at lady puppets.

"Now that's a strawberry," he cackled. "I have the little buggers fooled that they are living on the slopes of a British Columbian mountain. Taste is everything. To hell with yield. Yield we can leave to the Californians." Slowly his grin grew, showing his upper gums above his jagged teeth.

She decided that her boss was crazy—not that what he *said* was crazy, but he had papered the wall of the small strawberry room with a fantastic view of a British Columbian valley. It didn't take her long to find out that everyone else was crazy, too. In the cafeteria with the construction workers she listened curiously to a conversation beside her. Billy was sick. He'd been anemic for months. His leaves were drying around the edges. *His leaves?*

Byron's friend, Zimmerman, dropped around after work to play scrabble. Diana asked him, "What kind of fruitcake would name a lemon tree Billy?"

Zimmerman nodded. "I hear Billy is pretty sick about it, too. My tree, I named Hershel Ostropolier and he's never been sick a day in his life."

Then there was the tiny cook who had a redwood tree called Paul Bunyan. Weird. But he was into Bonsai so Diana supposed it might be all right. When she bought her own baby orange tree she decided it was *not* going to have a name; however, one evening in a humorous mood when the conversation came around to the Celtic worship of trees, she toasted her tree with a local version of Irish Mist. "To my true Irish friend!" Henceforth her orange tree was invariably referred to as "the Irishman."

It wasn't easy living on the moon. The corridors were cramped. The rooms were small. There was no place to go. She missed Charlie and hiking through the New Hampshire woods.

Worse, an enormous sense of loss began to plague her. She had no direction, no purpose to her life, which had always known a fierce purpose. It was awful. It was like being a compass that had smashed its way through to the north magnetic pole and was now spinning, aimless. One night she dreamed about the truck driver who had taken her to Washington when she was twelve. In the dream he said with an ironic smile, "Better be careful what you want, kid—you may get it!"

Somehow the most important thing in her life became the study of plants. She was going to become a genius and bring life to the moon. She borrowed botany books and began to memorize all the names. She began to read biology books and agricultural texts and every hydroponic book in the library of her boss. Studying became an urgent compulsion. There wasn't even time to socialize, and finally no time to sleep.

One afternoon, looking for a scrabble game, Zimmerman found her wandering around the landing track control room trying to explain a theory of hers that no one could understand.

# 14

Every time she woke up and tried to get out of bed so she could go back to work, they held her down and shot her full of drugs again. Once she escaped and turned up for work in her pajamas. They brought her back and put her to sleep. This time she was going to be more cunning. She'd pretend to be asleep until the drugs were all worn off and *then* she'd get up and go to work.

She peeked.

"Ah, you're awake," said Charlie.

She opened her eyes in wide disbelief. "Charlie! What are you doing here?"

"The old man called me up. He told me to get off my ass and take care of you. It was like listening to a wire brush cleaning out the hole between my ears."

"Are you on *their* side?"

"I don't know from nothing. I got here an hour ago. Tomorrow I'm out working on the new track. The old man got me a job as a laborer, the rat."

"Get me out of here, Charlie. I have to go back to work."

"You're on a paid vacation and you're complaining?"

"They'll fire me." She was terrified.

"Nobody is going to fire you with my old man backing you."

"What happened to me? They won't tell me."

"You were wandering around passionately trying to convince

people that milkweed was going to save the moon. The flowers are edible or something."

"I wasn't! I don't believe you!" She hid under her covers in shame.

"Yeah, you were really around the bend."

"I don't understand," she said through the covers.

"Neither does the doctor. But I do. You ought to see the loonies wandering around MIT during final exam time."

"You'll take care of me?"

"Do you think I'll let you out of my sight again? You gave me the shock of my life. For a week I thought I was strong enough to dismiss you. Then a funny thing began to happen. The sweet flowered fields of New Hampshire dissolved away into the flowered fields of hell. And the moon up there in the sky began to take on a heavenly beauty."

"Can I go back to work? I could finish the afternoon shift if I started now."

"Maybe tomorrow. We have to settle things between us. Like who is this Irishman you're living with?"

"That's not my Irishman! That's my orange tree!"

"I'm competing with an orange tree? Do you think I have a chance?"

She laughed as Charlie tried to walk her home. He needed low-gravity locomotion lessons. Once he collided with one of the awkwardly placed potted trees. "Charlie! Excuse yourself to Jezebel." He looked at her askance as she patted the pear tree. "There, there, Jezebel. Everything is going to be all right." Then she burst into tears.

Select friends gave Diana a homecoming party. Her boss arrived with a bowl of strawberries so delicious they needed neither sugar nor cream. Zimmerman leaned against the wall stealing more than his share. Louise was there and Maltby brought his guitar and his regular copilot. The Irishman moved into one corner to make room for them all.

Later Charlie explained to her the profounder truths of the universe as he saw them. "Some unsolved problem starts to push you. A couple of weeks without sleep and the borderline between the real world and imagination begins to fuzz. You fall asleep on your feet. You begin to treat real people as if they were the ghosts of your dreams and that's when the guys in the white coats come after you. Happens all the time at MIT in May. So if you get eight hours of sleep, I'll let you go to work. Otherwise, no."

"Make love to me. That'll put me to sleep."

"Thanks."

"Is that what happened to you at MIT?"

"Naw. I was pushing to get my father's ass. Sweet revenge. Haven't you ever wanted to strangle your father?"

"Oh yes!" she said brightly.

"I was going to get 100 percent in every course my last year just to rub that martinet's nose in the robot he'd made out of me. But no matter how much I strove I just couldn't make it as a robot. I couldn't get past 98 percent. It drove me crazy. It was like continually jumping in front of my father's Buick to prove to him what a bad driver he was and always coming out between the wheels without a scratch."

"You're crazier than I am!"

"I owe it all to my father." He was smiling.

"I like Byron!"

"That's because you're a girl." He sighed. "Maybe one of these days I'll make my peace with the old prick."

"You could have finished school. It was in your own best interest."

He shrugged. "I wasn't doing it for me."

"Why didn't you do more with your music?"

"My music was something they *didn't* want, so it was a reaction, too, I guess."

"What *do* you want then?"

"You."

"Oh Charlie! That's not enough and you know it!"

"Maybe it is. Men are more romantic than women. Women only pretend to be romantic because they know men like it."

"Are you calling me a fake?" she bridled.

"No. You made it very clear that what you wanted to do was sit on a peak 380,000 kilometers high and look down on the rest of us."

"Screw you!" She strode to the furthest corner of the room, which wasn't very far away, and sat with her arms crossed, confronting him belligerently.

"Don't you think it's romantic that I climbed a peak that high just to ask you to marry me?"

She smiled mischievously, still with her arms crossed. "You haven't passed the other tests yet. You have to learn how to work first. Then *maybe* I'll marry you."

Within two years Charlie worked his way to assistant chief

construction engineer. He was known with awe as the 100 percent man; the man who got the job perfect the first time. He lived with Diana and refused to take an SPS construction job because it would take him away from her.

Diana began to write papers on taste in high yield crops. For a lark she sent some tomatoes to a California fair and won first prize. She had seven projects going at once. Some people suspected that she never slept. Then, when necessity moved the command center out of the original Spartan diggings into much larger quarters, Diana made some frantic calls to Byron before someone else could find a use for the space. Charlie did the conversion design work. Zimmerman did the politicking. Ling, her old friend Ling, put up the money.

The place is called *Diana's Grove*. There are trees everywhere, not big trees, but what they lack in size they make up for in lushness. Some of them bear fruit—lemons and oranges and figs. There are vines and bamboo stands, even a brook that flows in too dreamlike a manner to gurgle. The benches are real wood. The food is the best in the solar system—just don't ask for beef. Nymphs with names like Callisto serve the tables wearing Roman hairdos and wispy gowns.

Diana, when she comes, makes her appearance in a white tunic with a quiver over her shoulder. She knows everyone. Often she has a dinner party in one of the alcoves and brings people together who should be together, sometimes for major or minor politicking, sometimes because she delights in the clash of disparate views, sometimes because she is a secret matchmaker, sometimes for trivial reasons—an old professor of Charlie's needs company or one of her friends needs to discuss curtains. She is fiercely protective of the girls who work for her.

If you've ever heard the music at *Diana's Grove* you know that Charlie has risen into the league of the greatest. He claims it is just a hobby. The compositions can be as simple as birds chattering in the morning from somewhere beyond the leaves—a heron's cry, a sightseeing flock southbound, a lone warbler—or it can be a conversation stopping argument between the gods.

Infrequently Charlie still proposes to Diana. She smiles her teasing smile, even though they already have one child, and writes him out a new contract in a flourishing script that promises she will be faithful to him for at least the next fortnight. He grumbles that living with her is like being an untenured professor.

The solar power satellites are winking on all around the equator, half of their mass coming from the moon now. All of the oxygen used by the space fleet is manufactured on the moon. America is prosperous, doing what it has always done best, selling high technology to the rest of the world. Her economy has achieved power independence and resource independence. The investment is considerable but it is, as yet, not well defended. Both McDougalls belong to an unofficial defense ministry which considers problems that Pentagon thinking is too archaic to handle. Serious decisions have to be made to secure the high ground in the face of a Russian resurgence into space. Such duties take Charlie back to the homeworld once a year.

Diana never goes with him. She is a minor Earth deity who worked hard for her promotion to moon goddess and she is well content with her position.

# TIN SOLDIER

## Joan D. Vinge

The ship drifted down the ragged light-robe of the Pleiades, dropped like a perfect pearl into the midnight water of the bay. And reemerged, to bob gently in a chain of gleaming pearls stretched across the harbor toward the port. The port's unsleeping Eye blinked once, the ship replied. New Piraeus, pooled among the hills, sent tributaries of light streaming down to the bay to welcome all comers, full of sound and brilliance and rash promise. The crew grinned, expectant, faces peering through the transparent hull; someone giggled nervously.

The sign at the heavy door flashed a red one-legged toy; TIN SOLDIER flashed blue below it. EAT. DRINK. COME BACK AGAIN. In green. And they always did, because they knew they could.

"Soldier, another round, please!" came over canned music.

The owner of the Tin Soldier, also known as Tin Soldier, glanced up from his polishing to nod and smile, reached down to set bottles out on the bar. He mixed the drinks himself. His face was ordinary, with eyes that were dark and patient, and his hair was coppery barbed wire bound with a knotted cloth. Under the curling copper, under the skin, the back of his skull was a plastic plate. The quick fingers of the hand on the goose-necked bottle were plastic, the smooth arm was prosthetic. Sometimes he imagined he heard clicking as it moved. More than half his body was artificial. He looked to be about twenty-five; he had looked the same fifty years ago.

He set the glasses on the tray and pushed, watching as it drifted across the room, and returned to his polishing. The agate surface of the bar showed cloudy permutations of color, grain-streak and whorl and chalcedony depths of mist. He had discovered it in the desert to the east—a shattered imitation tree, like a fellow traveler trapped in stasis through time. They shared the joke with the ??? clientele.

"—come see our living legend!"

He looked up, saw her coming in with the crew of the *Who Got Her—709*, realized he didn't know her. She hung back as they crowded around, her short ashen hair like beaten metal in the blue-glass lantern light. *New*, he thought. Maybe eighteen, with eyes of quicksilver very wide open. He smiled at her as he welcomed them, and the other women pulled her up to the agate bar. "Come on, little sister," he heard Harkané say, "you're one of us too." She smiled back at him.

"I don't know you . . . but your name should be Diana, like the silver Lady of the Moon." His voice caught him by surprise.

Quicksilver shifted. "It's not."

*Very new.* And realizing what he'd almost done again, suddenly wanted it more than anything. Filled with bitter joy he said. "What is your name?"

Her face flickered, but then she met his eyes and said, smiling. "My name is Brandy."

"Brandy . . ."

A knowing voice said, "Send us the usual, Soldier. Later, yes—?"

He nodded vaguely, groping for bottles under the counter ledge. Wood screeked over stone as she pulled a stool near and slipped onto it, watching him pour. "You're very neat." She picked nuts from a bowl.

"*Long* practice."

She smiled, missing the joke.

He said. "Brandy's a nice name. And I think somewhere I've heard it— "

"The whole thing is Branduin. My mother said it was very old."

He was staring at her. He wondered if she could see one side of his face blushing. "What will you drink?"

"Oh . . . do you have any—brandy? It's a wine, I think; nobody's ever had any. But because it's my name, I always ask."

He frowned. "I don't . . . hell, I do! Stay there."

He returned with the impossible bottle, carefully wiped away its gray coat of years and laid it gleaming on the bar. Glintings of maroon speared their eyes. "All these years, it must have been waiting. That's where I heard it . . . genuine vintage brandy, from Home."

"From Terra—really? Oh, thank you!" She touched the bottle, touched his hand. "I'm going to be lucky."

Curving glasses blossomed with wine; he placed one in her palm. "*Ad astra.*" She lifted the glass.

"*Ad astra*; to the stars." He raised his own, adding silently, *Tonight* . . .

They were alone. Her breath came hard as they climbed up the newly cobbled streets to his home, up from the lower city where the fluorescent lamps were snuffing out one by one.

He stopped against a low stone wall. "Do you want to catch your breath?" Behind him in the empty lot a weedy garden patch wavered with the popping street lamp.

"Thank you." She leaned downhill against him, against the wall. "I got lazy on my training rides. There's not much to do on a ship; you're supposed to exercise, but . . ." Her shoulder twitched under the quilted bluesilver. He absorbed her warmth.

Her hand pressed his lightly on the wall. "What's your name? You haven't told me, you know."

"Everyone calls me Soldier."

"But that's not your name." Her eyes searched his own, smiling.

He ducked his head, his hand caught and tightened around hers. "Oh . . . no, it's not. It's Maris." He looked up. That's an old name, too. It *means* "soldier, consecrated to the god of war. I never liked it much."

"From 'Mars'? Sol's fourth plane, the god of war." She bent back her head and peered up into the darkness. Fog hid the stars.

"Yes."

"Were you a soldier?"

"Yes. Everyone was a soldier—every man—where I came from. War was a way of life."

"An attempt to reconcile the blow to the masculine ego?"

He looked at her.

She frowned in concentration. "After it was determined that men were physically unsuited to spacing, and women came to a new position of dominance as they monopolized this critical area, the Terran culture foundation underwent severe strain. As a result, many new and not always satisfactory cultural systems are evolving in the galaxy . . . One of these is what might be termed a backlash of exaggerated *machismo*— "

"'—and the rebirth of the warrior/chattel tradition.'"

"You've read that book too." She looked crestfallen.

"I read a lot. *New Ways for Old*, by Ebert Ntaka?"

"Sorry . . . I guess I got carried away. But, I just read it— "

"No." He grinned. "And I agree with old Ntaka, too. Glatte— what a sour name—was an unhealthy planet. But that's why I'm here, not there."

"Ow—!" She jerked loose from his hand. "Ohh, oh . . . God, you're strong!" She put her fingers in her mouth.

He fell over apologies; but she shook her head, and shook her hand. "No, it's all right . . . really, it just surprised me. Bad memories?"

He nodded, mouth tight.

She touched his shoulder, raised her fingers to his lips. "Kiss it, and make it well?" Gently he caught her hand, kissed it; she pressed against him. "It's very late. We should finish climbing the hill . . .?"

"No." Hating himself, he set her back against the wall.

"No? But I thought— "

"I know you did. Your first space, I asked your name; you wanted me to; tradition says you lay the guy. But I'm a cyborg, Brandy. . . . It's always good for a laugh on the poor greenie, they've pulled it a hundred times."

"A cyborg?" The flickering gray eyes raked his body.

"It doesn't show with my clothes on."

"Oh . . ." Pale lashes were beating very hard across the eyes now. She took a breath, held it. "Do—you always let it get this far? I mean— "

"No. Hell, I don't know why I . . . I owe you another apology. Usually I never ask the name. If I slip, I tell them right away; nobody's ever held to it. I don't count." He smiled weakly.

"Well. Why? You mean you can't— "

"I'm not all plastic." He frowned, numb fingers rapping stone. "God. I'm not. Sometimes I wish I was, but I'm not."

"No one? They never want to?"

"Branduin"—he faced the questioning eyes—"you'd better go back down. Get some sleep. Tomorrow laugh it off, and pick up some flashy Tail in the bar and have a good time. Come see me again in twenty-five years, when you're back from space, and tell me what you saw." Hesitating, he brushed her cheek with his true hand; instinctively she bent her head to the caress. "Goodbye." He started up the hill.

"Maris— "

He stopped, trembling.

"Thank you for the brandy. . . ." She came up beside him and caught his belt. "You'll probably have to tow me up the hill."

He pulled her to him and began to kiss her, hands touching her body incredulously.

"It's getting—very, very late. Let's hurry."

Maris woke, confused, to the sound of banging shutters. Raising his head, he was struck by the colors of dawn, and the shadow of Brandy standing bright-edged at the window. He left the rumpled bed and crossed cold tiles to join her. "What are you doing?" He yawned.

"I wanted to watch the sun rise, I haven't seen anything but night for months. Look, the fog's lifting already: the sun burns it up, it's on fire, over the mountains— "

He smoothed her hair, pale gold under a corona of light. "And embers in the canyon."

She looked down, across ends of gray mist slowly reddening, and back. "Good morning." She began to laugh. "I'm glad you don't have any neighbors down there!" They were both naked.

He grinned. "That's what I like about the place." He put his arms around her. She moved close in the circle of coolness and warmth.

They watched the sunrise from the bed.

In the evening she came into the bar with the crew of the *Kiss and Tell—736*. They waved to him, nodded to her and drifted into blue shadows; she perched smiling before him. It struck him suddenly that nine hours was a long time.

"That's the crew of my training ship. They want some white wine, please, any kind, in a bottle."

He reached under the bar. "And one brandy, on the house?" He sent the tray off.

"Hi, Maris . . ."

"Hi, Brandy."

"To misty mornings." They drank together.

"By the way"—she glanced at him slyly—"I passed it around that people have been missing something. You."

"Thank you," meaning it. "But I doubt if it'll change any minds."

"Why not?"

"You read Ntaka—xenophobia; to most people in most cultures cyborgs are unnatural, the next thing up from a corpse. You'd have to be a necrophile— "

She frowned.

"—or extraordinary. You're the first extraordinary person I've met in a hundred years."

The smile formed, faded. "Maris—you're not exactly twenty-five, are you? How old are you?"

"More like a hundred and fifteen." He waited for the reaction.

She stared. "But, you look like twenty-five! You're real—don't you age?"

"I age. About five years for every hundred." He shrugged. "The prosthetics slow the body's aging. Perhaps it's because only half my body needs constant regeneration; or it may be an effect of the anti-rejection treatment. Nobody really understands it. It just happens sometimes."

"Oh." She looked embarrassed. "That's what you meant by 'come back and see me' . . . and they meant—Will you really live a thousand years?"

"Probably not. Something vital will break down in another three or four centuries, I guess. Even plastic doesn't last forever."

"Oh . . ."

"Live longer and enjoy it less. Except for today. What did you do today? Get any sleep?"

"No— " She shook away disconcertion. "A bunch of us went out and gorged. We stay on wake-ups when we're in port, so we don't miss a minute; you don't need to sleep. Really they're for emergencies, but everybody does it."

Quick laughter almost escaped him; he hoped she'd missed it. Serious, he said, "You want to be careful with those things. They can get to you."

"Oh, they're all right." She twiddled her glass, annoyed and suddenly awkward again, confronted by the Old Man.

*Hell, it can't matter.* . . . He glanced toward the door.

"Brandy! There you are." And the crew came in. "Soldier, you must come sit with us later; but right now we're going to steal Brandy away from you."

He looked up with Brandy to the brown face, brown eyes, and salt-white hair of Harkané, Best Friend of the Mactav on the *Who*

*Got Her—709.* Time had woven deep nets of understanding around her eyes; she was one of his oldest customers. Even the shape of her words sounded strange to him now: "Ah, Soldier, you make me feel young, always. . . . Come, little sister, and join your family; share her, Soldier."

Brandy gulped brandy; her boots clattered as she dropped off the stool. "Thank you for the drink," and for half a second the smile was real. "Guess I'll be seeing you—Soldier." And she was leaving, ungracefully, gratefully.

Soldier polished the agate bar, ignoring the disappointed face it showed him. And later watched her leave, with a smug, black-eyed Tail in velvet knee pants.

Beyond the doorway yellow-green twilight seeped into the bay, the early crowds began to come together with the night. "H'lo, Maris . . .?" Silver dulled to lead met him in a face gone hollow; thin hands trembled, clenched, trembled in the air.

"Brandy— "

"What've you got for an upset stomach?" She was expecting laughter.

"Got the shakes, huh?" He didn't laugh.

She nodded. "You were right about the pills, Maris. They make me sick. I got tired, I kept taking them. . . ." Her hands rattled on the counter.

"And that was pretty dumb, wasn't it?" He poured her a glass of water, watched her trying to drink, pushed a button under the counter. "Listen, I just called you a ride—when it comes, I want you to go to my place and go to bed."

"But— "

"I won't be home for hours. Catch some sleep and then you'll be all right, right? This is my door lock." He printed large numbers on a napkin. "Don't lose this."

She nodded, drank, stuffed the napkin up her sleeve. Drank some more, spilling it. "My mouth is numb." An abrupt chirp of laughter escaped; she put up a shaky hand. "I—won't lose it."

Deep gold leaped beyond the doorway, sunlight on metal. "Your ride's here."

"Thank you, Maris." The smile was crooked but very fond. She tacked toward the doorway.

She was still there when he came home, snoring gently in the bedroom in a knot of unmade blankets. He went silently out of the room, afraid to touch her, and sank into a leather-slung chair. Filled with rare and uneasy peace, he dozed, while the starlit mist of the Pleiades' nebulosity passed across the darkened sky toward morning.

"Maris, why didn't you wake me up? You didn't have to sleep in a *chair* all night." Brandy stood before him wrestling with a towel, eyes puffy with sleep and hair flopping in sodden plumb-bobs from the shower. Her feet made small puddles on the braided rug.

"I didn't mind. I don't need much sleep."

"That's what I told *you*."

"But I meant it. I never sleep more than three hours. You needed the rest, anyway."

"I know . . . damn— " She gave up and wrapped the towel around her head. "You're a fine guy, Maris."

"You're not so bad yourself."

She blushed. "Glad you approve. Ugh, your rug—I got it all wet," She disappeared into the bedroom.

Maris stretched unwillingly, stared up into ceiling beams bronzed with early sunlight. He sighed faintly. "You want some breakfast?"

"Sure, I'm starving! Oh, wait— " A wet head reappeared. "Let me make you breakfast? Wait for me."

He sat watching as the apparition in silver-blue flightsuit ransacked his cupboards. "You're kind of low on raw materials."

"I know." He brushed crumbs off the table. "I eat instant breakfasts and frozen dinners; I hate to cook."

She made a face.

"Yeah, it gets pretty old after half a century . . . they've only had them on Oro for half a century. They don't get any better, either."

She stuck something into the oven. "I'm sorry I was so stupid about it."

"About what?"

"About . . . a hundred years. I guess it scared me. I acted like a bitch."

"No, you didn't."

"Yes, I did! I know I did." She frowned.

"Okay, you did. . . . I forgive you. When do we eat?"

They ate, sitting side by side.

"Cooking seems like an odd spacer's hobby." Maris scraped his plate appreciatively. "When can you cook on a ship?"

"Never. It's all prepared and processed. So we can't overeat.

That's why we love to eat and drink when we're in port. But I can't cook now either—no place. So it's not really a hobby, I guess, any more. I learned how from my father—he loved to cook. . . ." She inhaled, eyes closed.

"Is your mother dead?"

"No— " She looked startled. "She just doesn't like to cook."

"She wouldn't have liked Glatte, either." He scratched his crooked nose.

"Calicho—that's my home, it's seven light years up the cube from this corner of the Quadrangle. It's . . . a pretty nice place. I guess Niaka would call it 'healthy,' even . . . there's lots of room, like space: that helps. Cold and not very rich, but they get along. My mother and father always shared their work . . . they have a farm." She broke off more bread.

"What did they think about you becoming a spacer?"

"They never tried to stop me, but I don't think they wanted me to. I guess when you're so tied to the land it's hard to imagine wanting to be so free. . . . It made them sad to lose me—it made me sad to lose them; but, I had to go. . . ."

Her mouth began to quiver suddenly. "You know, I'll never get to see them again, I'll never have time, our trips take so long, they'll grow old and die. . . ." Tears dripped onto her plate. "And I miss my h-home— " Words dissolved into sobs she clung to him in terror.

He rubbed her back helplessly, wordlessly, left unequipped to deal with loneliness by a hundred years alone.

"M-Maris, can I come and see you always, will you always, always be here when I need you, and be my friend?"

"Always." He rocked her gently. "Come when you want, stay as long as you want, cook dinner if you want, I'll always be here. . . ."

. . . Until the night, twenty-five years later, when they were suddenly clustered around him at the bar, hugging, badgering, laughing, the crew of the *Who Got Her—709*.

"Hi, Soldier!"

"Soldier, have we— "

"Look at this, Soldier— "

"What happened to— "

"Brandy?" he said stupidly. "Where's Brandy?"

"Honestly, Soldier, you really never *do* forget a face, do you?"

"Ah-ha, I bet it's not her *face* he remembered!"

"She was right with us." Harkané peered easily over the heads around her. "Maybe she stopped off somewhere."

"Maybe she's caught a Tail *already?*" Nilgiri was impressed.

"She could if anybody could, the little rascal." Wynmet rolled her eyes.

"Oh, just send us the usual, Soldier. She'll be along eventually. Come sit with us when she does." Harkané waved a rainbow-tipped hand. "Come, sisters, gossip is not tasteful before we've had a drink."

"That little rascal."

Soldier began to pour drinks with single-minded precision, until he noticed that he had the wrong bottle. Cursing, he drank them himself, one by one.

"Hi, Maris."

He pushed the tray away.

"*Hi*, Maris." Fingers appeared in front of his face; he started. "Hey."

"Brandy!"

Patrons along the bar turned to stare, turned away again.

"Brandy— "

"Well sure; weren't you expecting me? Everybody else is already here."

"I know. I thought—I mean, they said . . . maybe you were out with somebody already," trying to keep it light, "and— "

"Well, really, Maris, what do you take me for?" She was insulted. "I just wanted to wait till everybody else got settled, so I could have you to myself. Did you think I'd forget you? Unkind." She hefted a bright mottled sack onto the bar. "Look, I brought you a present!" Pulling it open, she dumped heaping confusion onto the counter. "Books, tapes, buttons, all kinds of things to look at. You said you'd read out the library five times; so I collected everywhere, some of them should be new. . . . Don't you like them?"

"I . . ." He coughed. "I'm crazy about them! I'm—over-whelmed. Nobody ever brought me anything before. Thank you. Thanks very much. And welcome back to New Piraeus!"

"Glad to be back!" She stretched across the bar, hugged him, kissed his nose. She wore a new belt of metal inlaid with stones. "You're just like I remembered."

"You're more beautiful."

"Flatterer." She beamed. Ashen hair fell to her breasts; angles had deepened on her face. The quicksilver eyes took all things in now without amazement. "I'm twenty-one today, you know."

"No kidding? That calls for a celebration. Will you have brandy?"

"Do you still have some?" The eyes widened slightly. "Oh, yes! We should make it a tradition, as long as it lasts."

He smiled contentedly. They drank to birthdays, and to stars.

"Not very crowded tonight, is it?" Brandy glanced into the room, tying small knots in her hair. "Not like last time."

"It comes and it goes. I've always got some fisherfolk, they're heavy on tradition. . . . I gave up keeping track of ship schedules."

"We don't even believe our own; they never quite fit. We're a month late here."

"I know—happened to notice it. . . ." He closed a bent cover, laid the book flat. "So anyway, how did you like your first Quadrangle?"

"Beautiful—oh, Maris, if I start I'll never finish, the City in the Clouds on Paris, the Freeport on Sanalareta . . . and the Pleiades . . . and the depths of night, ice and fire." Her eyes burned through him toward infinity. "You can't imagine— "

"So they tell me."

She searched his face for bitterness, found none. He shook his head. "I'm a man and a cyborg; that's two League rules against me that I can't change—so why resent it? I enjoy the stories." His mouth twitched up.

"Do you like poetry?"

"Sometimes."

"Then—may I show you mine? I'm writing a cycle of poems about space; maybe someday I'll have a book. I haven't shown them to anybody else, but if you'd like— "

"I'd like it."

"I'll find them, then. Guess I should be joining the party, really, they'll think I'm antisocial"—she winced—"and they'll talk about me! It's like a small town, we're as bad as lubbers."

He laughed. "Don't—you'll disillusion me. See you later. Uh . . . listen, do you want arrangements like before? For sleeping."

"Use your place? Could I? I don't want to put you out."

"Hell, no. You're welcome to it."

"I'll cook for you— "

"I bought some eggs."

"It's a deal! Enjoy your books." She wove a path between the tables, nodded to sailor and spacer; he watched her laughing face merge and blur, caught occasional flashes of silver. Stuffing books into the sack, he set it against his shin behind the bar. And some time later, watched her go out with a Tail.

The morning of the thirteenth day he woke to find Brandy sleeping soundly in the pile of hairy cushions by the door. Curious, he glanced out into a water-gray field of fog. It was the first time she had come home before dawn. *Home*? Carefully he lifted her from the pillows; she sighed, arms found him, in her sleep she began to kiss his neck. He carried her to the bed and put her down softly, bent to . . . *No*. He turned away, left the room. He had slept with her only once. Twenty-five or three years ago, without words, she had told him they would not be lovers again. She kept the customs; a spacer never had the same man more than once.

In the kitchen he heated a frozen dinner, and ate alone.

"What's that?" Brandy appeared beside him, mummified in a blanket. She dropped down on the cushions where he sat barefoot, drinking wine and ignoring the TD.

"Three-dimensional propaganda: the Oro Morning Mine Report. You're up pretty early—it's hardly noon."

"I'm not sleepy." She took a sip of his wine.

"Got in pretty early, too. Anything wrong?"

"No . . . just—nothing happening, you know. Ran out of parties, everybody's pooped but me." She cocked her head. "What is this, anyway . . . an inquisition? 'Home awfully *early*, aren't you—?'" She glared at him and burst into laughter.

"You're crazy." He grinned.

"Whatever happened to your couch?" She prodded cushions.

"It fell apart. It's been twenty-five years, you know."

"Oh. That's too bad. . . . Maris, may I read you my poems?" Suddenly serious, she produced a small, battered notebook from the folds of her blanket.

"Sure." He leaned back, watching subtle transformations occur in her face. And felt them begin to occur in himself, growing pride and a tender possessiveness.

> . . . Until, lost in darkness, we
> dance the silken star-song.

It was the final poem. "That's 'Genesis.' It's about the beginning of a flight . . . and a life." Her eyes found the world again, found dark eyes quietly regarding her.

"'Attired with stars we shall forever sit, triumphing over Death, and Chance, and thee, O Time.'" He glanced away, pulling the tassel of a cushion. "No . . . Milton, not Maris—I could never do that."

He looked back, in wonder. "They're beautiful, you are beautiful. Make a book. Gifts are meant for giving, and you are gifted."

Pleasure glowed in her cheeks. "You really think someone would want to read them?"

"Yes." He nodded, searching for the words to tell her. "Nobody's ever made me—see that way . . . as though I . . . go with you. Others would go, if they could. Home to the sky."

She turned with him to the window; they were silent. After a time she moved closer, smiling. "Do you know what I'd like to do?"

"What?" He let out a long breath.

"See your home." She set her notebook aside. "Let's go for a walk in New Piraeus. I've never really seen it by day—the real part of it. I want to see its beauty up close, before it's all gone. Can we go?"

He hesitated. "You sure you want to—?"

"Sure. Come on, lazy." She gestured him up.

And he wondered again why she had come home early.

So on the last afternoon he took her out through the stone-paved winding streets, where small whitewashed houses pressed for footholds. They climbed narrow steps, panting, tasted the sea wind, bought fruit from a leathery smiling woman with a basket.

"Mmm— " Brandy licked juice from the crimson pith. "Who was that woman? She called you 'Sojer,' but I couldn't understand the rest . . . I couldn't even understand you! Is the dialect that slurred?"

He wiped his chin. "It's getting worse all the time, with all the newcomers. But you get used to everything in the lower city. . . . An old acquaintance, I met her during the epidemic, she was sick."

"Epidemic? What epidemic?"

"Oro Mines was importing workers—they started before your last visit, because of the bigger raw-material demands. One of the new workers had some disease we didn't; it killed about a third of New Piraeus."

"Oh, my God— "

"That was about fifteen years ago. . . . Oro's labs synthesized a vaccine, eventually, and they repopulated the city. But they still don't know what the disease was."

"It's like a trap, to live on a single world."

"Most of us have to. . . . It has its compensations."

She finished her fruit, and changed the subject. "You helped take care of them, during the epidemic?"

He nodded. "I seemed to be immune, so— "

She patted his arm. "You are very good."

He laughed; glanced away. "Very plastic would be more like it."

"Don't you ever get sick?"

"Almost never. I can't even get very drunk. Someday I'll probably wake up entirely plastic."

"You'd still be very good." They began to walk again. "What did she say?"

"She said, 'Ah, Soldier, you've got a lady friend.' She seemed pleased."

"What did you say?"

"I said, 'That's right.'" Smiling, he didn't put his arm around her; his fingers kneaded emptiness.

"Well, I'm glad she was pleased. . . . I don't think most people have been."

"Don't look at them. Look out there." He showed her the sea, muted greens and blues below the ivory jumble of the flat-roofed town. To the north and south mountains like rumpled cloth reached down to the shore—

"Oh, the sea—I've always loved the sea; at home we were surrounded by it, on an island. Space is like the sea, boundless, constant, constantly changing . . ."

"—spacer!" Two giggling girls made a wide circle past them in the street, dark skirts brushing their calves.

Brandy blushed, frowned, sought the sea again. "I—think I'm getting tired. I guess I've seen enough."

"Not much on up there but the new, anyway." He took her hand and they started back down. "It's just that we're a rarity up this far." A heavy man in a heavy caftan pushed past them; in his cold eyes Maris saw an alien wanton and her overaged Tail.

"They either leer, or they censure." He felt her nails mark his flesh. "What's their problem?"

"Jealousy . . . mortality. You threaten them, you spacers. Don't you ever think about it? Free and beautiful immortals— "

"They know we aren't immortal; we hardly live longer than anybody else."

"They also know you come here from a voyage of twenty-five years looking hardly older than when you left. Maybe they don't recognize you, but they *know*. And they're twenty-five years older. . . . Why do you think they go around in sacks?"

"To look ugly. They must be dreadfully repressed." She tossed her head sullenly.

"They are; but that's not why. It's because they want to hide the changes. And in their way to mimic you, who always look the same. They've done it since I can remember; you're all they have to envy."

She sighed: "I've heard on Elder they paint patterns on their skin, to hide the change. Ntaka called them 'youth-fixing,' didn't he?" Anger faded, her eyes grew cool like the sea, gray-green. "Yes, I think about it . . . especially when we're laughing at the lubbers, and their narrow lives. And all the poor panting awestruck Tails, sometimes they think they're using us, but we're always using them. . . . Sometimes I think we're very cruel."

"Very like a god—Silver Lady of the Moon."

"You haven't called me that since—that night . . . all night." Her hand tightened painfully: he said nothing. "I guess they envy a cyborg for the same things. . . ."

"At least it's easier to rationalize—and harder to imitate." He shrugged. "We leave each other alone, for the most part."

"And so we must wait for each other, we immortals. It's still a beautiful town; I don't care what they think."

He sat, fingers catching in the twisted metal of his thick bracelet, listening to her voice weave patterns through the hiss of running water. Washing away the dirty looks. . . . Absently he reread the third paragraph on the page for the eighth time; and the singing stopped.

"Maris, do you have any— "

He looked up at her thin, shining body, naked in the doorway. "Brandy, goddamn it! You're not between planets—you want to show it all to the whole damn street?"

"But I always— " Made awkward by sudden awareness, she fled.

He sat and stared at the sun-hazed windows, entirely aware that there was no one to see in. Slowly the fire died, his breathing eased.

She returned shyly, closing herself into quilted blue-silver, and sank onto the edge of a chair. "I just never think about it." Her voice was very small.

"It's all right." Ashamed, he looked past her. "Sorry I yelled at you. . . . What did you want to ask me?"

"It doesn't matter." She pulled violently at her snarled hair.

"Ow! Dammit!" Feeling him look at her. She forced a smile. "Uh, you know, I'm glad we picked up Mirna on Treone; I'm not the little sister anymore. I was really getting pretty tired of being the greenie for so long. She's— "

"Brandy— "

"Hm?"

"Why don't they allow cyborgs on crews?"

Surprise caught her. "It's a regulation."

He shook his head. "Don't tell me 'It's a regulation,' tell me why."

"Well . . ." She smoothed wet hair-strands with her fingers. "They tried it, and it didn't work out. Like with men—they couldn't endure space, they broke down, their hormonal balance was wrong. With cyborgs, stresses between the real and the artificial in the body were too severe, they broke down too. . . . At the beginning they tried cyborganics, as a way to let men keep space, like they tried altering the hormone balance. Neither worked. Physically or psychologically, there was too much strain. So finally they just made it a regulation, no men on space crews."

"But that was over a thousand years ago—cyborganics has improved. I'm healthier and live longer than any normal person. And stronger." He leaned forward, tight with agitation.

"And slower. We don't need strength, we have artificial means. And anyway, a man would still have to face more stress, it would be dangerous."

"Are there any female cyborgs on crews?"

"No."

"Have they ever even tried it again?"

"No— "

"You see? The League has a lock on space, they keep it with archaic laws. They don't want anyone else out there!" Sudden resentment shook his voice.

"Maybe . . . we don't." Her fingers closed, opened, closed over the soft heavy arms of the chair; her eyes were the color of twisting smoke. "Do you really blame us? Spacing is our life, it's our strength. We have to close the others out, everything changes and changes around us, there's no continuity—we only have each other. That's why we have our regulations, that's why we dress alike, look alike, act alike; there's nothing else we *can* do, and stay sane. We have to live apart, always." She pulled her hair forward, tying nervous knots. "And—that's why we never take the same lover twice, too. We have needs we have to satisfy; but we can't afford to . . . form relationships, get involved, tied. It's a danger, it's an instability. . . . You do understand that, don't you, Maris; that it's why I don't— " She broke off, eyes burning him with sorrow and, below it, fear.

He managed a smile. "Have you heard me complain?"

"Weren't you just . . .?" She lifted her head.

Slowly he nodded, felt pain start. "I suppose I was." *But I don't change.* He shut his eyes suddenly, before she read them. *But that's not the point, is it?*

"Maris, do you want me to stop staying here?"

"No—No . . . I understand, it's all right. I like the company." He stretched, shook his head. "Only, wear a towel, all right? I'm only human."

"I promise . . . that I will keep my eyes open, in the future."

He considered the future that would begin with dawn when her ship went up, and said nothing.


He stumbled cursing from the bedroom to the door, to find her waiting there, radiant and wholly unexpected. "Surprise!" She laughed and hugged him, dislodging his half-tied robe.

"My God—hey!" He dragged her inside and slammed the door. "You want to get me arrested for indecent exposure?" He turned his back, making adjustments, while she stood and giggled behind him.

He faced her again, fogged with sleep, struggling to believe. "You're early—almost two weeks?"

"I know. I couldn't wait till tonight to surprise you. And I did, didn't I?" She rolled her eyes. "I heard you coming to the door!"

She sat curled on his aging striped couch, squinting out the window as he fastened his sandals. "You used to have so much room. Houses haven't filled up your canyon, have they?" Her voice grew wistful.

"Not yet. If they ever do, I won't stay to see it. . . . How was your trip this time?"

"Beautiful, again . . . I can't imagine it ever being anything else. You could see it all a hundred times over, and never see it all—

> Through your crystal eye,
> Mactav, I watch the midnight's
> star turn inside out . . .

Oh, guess what! My poems—I finished the cycle during the voyage . . . and it's going to be published, on Treone. They said very nice things about it."

He nodded smugly. "They have good taste. They must have changed, too."

"'A renaissance in progress'—meaning they've put on some *ver*-ry artsy airs, last decade; their Tails are really something else. . . ." Remembering, she shook her head. "It was one of them that told me about the publisher."

"You showed him your poems?" Trying not to—

"Good grief, no; he was telling me about *his*. So I thought. What have I got to lose?"

"When do I get a copy?"

"I don't know." Disappointment pulled at her mouth. "Maybe I'll never even get one; after twenty-five years they'll be out of print. 'Art is long, and Time is fleeting' . . . Longfellow had it backward. But I made you some copies of the poems. And brought you some more books, too. There's one you should read; it replaced Ntaka years ago on the Inside. I thought it was inferior, but who are we . . . What are you laughing about?"

"What happened to that freckle-faced kid in pigtails?"

"*What?*" Her nose wrinkled.

"How old are you now?"

"Twenty-four. Oh— " She looked pleased.

"Madame Poet, do you want to go to dinner with me?"

"Oh, *food*, oh yes!" She bounced, caught him grinning, froze. "I would love to. Can we go to Good Eats?"

"It closed right after you left."

"Oh . . . the music was wild. Well, how about that seafood place, with the fish name—?"

He shook his head. "The owner died. It's been twenty-five years."

"Damn, we can never keep anything." She sighed. "Why don't I just make us a dinner—*I'm* still here. And I'd like that."

That night, and every other night, he stood at the bar and watched her go out, with a Tail or a laughing knot of partiers. Once she waved to him; the stem of a shatterproof glass snapped in his hand; he kicked it under the counter, confused and angry.

But three nights in the two weeks she came home early. This time, pointedly, he asked her no questions. Gratefully, she told him no lies, sleeping on his couch and sharing the afternoon. . . .

\*　　\*　　\*

They returned to the flyer, moving in step along the cool jade sand of the beach. Maris looked toward the sea's edge, where frothy fingers reached, withdrew, and reached again. "You leave tomorrow, huh?"

Brandy nodded. "Uh-huh."

He sighed.

"Maris, if— "

"What?"

"Oh—nothing." She brushed sand from her boot.

He watched the sea reach, and withdraw, and reach—

"Have you ever wanted to see a ship? Inside, I mean." She pulled open the flyer door, her body strangely intent.

He followed her. "Yes."

"Would you like to see mine—the *Who Got Her*?"

"I thought that was illegal?"

"'No waking man shall set foot on a ship of the spaceways.' It is a League regulation . . . but it's based on a superstition that's at least a thousand years old—'Men on ships is bad luck.' Which is silly here. Your presence on board in port isn't going to bring us disaster."

He looked incredulous.

"I'd like you to see our life, Maris, as I see yours. There's nothing wrong with that. And besides"—she shrugged—"no one will know; because nobody's there right now."

He faced a wicked grin, and did his best to match it. "I will if you will."

They got in; the flyer drifted silently from the cove. New Piraeus rose to meet them from beyond the ridge; the late sun struck gold from hidden windows.

"I wish it wouldn't change—oh . . . there's another new one. It's a skyscraper!"

He glanced across the bay. "Just finished; maybe New Piraeus is growing up—thanks to Oro Mines. It hardly changed over a century; after all those years, it's a little scary."

"Even after three . . . or twenty-five?" She pointed. "Right down there, Maris—there's our airlock."

The flyer settled on the water below the looming semi-transparent hull of the *WGH—709*.

Maris gazed up and back. "It's a lot bigger than I ever realized."

"It masses twenty thousand tons, empty." Brandy caught hold of the hanging ladder. "I guess we'll have to go up this . . . okay?" She looked over at him.

"Sure. Slow, maybe, but sure."

They slipped in through the lock, moved soft-footed down hallways past dim cavernous storerooms.

"Is the whole ship transparent?" He touched a wall, plastic met plastic. "How do you get any privacy?"

"Why are you whispering?"

"I'm no—*I'm not*. Why are you?"

"*Shhh!* Because it's so *quiet*." She stopped, pride beginning to show on her face. "The whole ship can be almost transparent, like now; but usually it's not. All the walls and the hull are polarized; you can opaque them. These are just holds, anyway, they're most of the ship. The passenger stasis cubicles are up there. Here's the lift. We'll go up to the control room."

"Brandy!" A girl in red with a clipboard turned on them outraged, as they stepped from the lift. "Brandy, what the hell do you mean by—Oh. Is that you, Soldier? God, I thought she'd brought a man on board."

Maris flinched. "Hi, Nilgiri."

Brandy was very pale beside him. "We just came out to—uh, look in on Mactav, she's been kind of moody lately, you know. I thought we could read to her. . . . What are *you* doing here?" And a whispered, "Bitch."

"Just that—checking up on Mactav. Harkané sent me out." Nilgiri glanced at the panels behind her, back at Maris, suddenly awkward. "Uh—look, since I'm already here don't worry about it, okay? I'll go down and play some music for her. Why don't you—uh, show Soldier around the ship, or something. . . ." Her round face was reddening like an apple. "Bye?" She slipped past them and into the lift, and disappeared.

"*Damn*, sometimes she's such an ass."

"She didn't mean it."

"Oh, I should have— "

"—done just what you did; she *was* sorry. And at least we're not trespassing."

"God, Maris, how do you stand it? They must do it to you all the time. Don't you resent it?"

"Hell, yes, I resent it. Who wouldn't? I just got tired of, getting mad. . . . And besides"—he glanced at the closed doors—"besides, nobody needs a mean bartender. Come on, show me around the ship."

Her knotted fingers uncurled, took his hand. "This way, please; straight ahead of you is our control room." She pulled him forward beneath the daybright dome. He saw a handprinted sign above the central panel, NO-MAN'S LAND. "From here we program our computer; this area here is for the AAFAL drive, first devised by Ursula, an early spacer who— "

"What's awful about it?"

"What?"

"Every spacer I know calls the ship's drive 'awful.'"

"Oh—Not 'awful,' AAFAL: Almost As Fast As Light. Which it is. That's what we call it; there's a technical name too."

"Um." He looked vaguely disappointed. "Guess I'm used to— " He made it into curiosity again, as he watched her smiling with delight. "I—suppose it's different from antigravity?" Seventy years before she was born, he had taught himself the principles of starship technology.

"Very." She giggled suddenly. "The 'awfuls' and the 'aghs.' *hmm* . . . We do use an AG unit to leave and enter solar systems; it operates like the ones in flyers, it throws us away from the planet, and finally the entire system, until we reach AAFAL ignition speeds. With the AG you can only get fractions of the speed of light, but it's enough to concentrate interstellar gases and dust. Our force nets feed them through the drive unit, where they're converted to energy, which increases our speed, which makes the unit more efficient . . . until we're moving almost as fast as light.

"We use the AG to protect us from acceleration forces, and after deceleration to guide us into port. The start and finish can take up most of our trip times; the farther out in space you are, the less AG feedback you get from the system's mass, and the less your velocity changes. It's a beautiful time, though—you can see the AG forces through the polarized hill, wrapping you in shifting rainbow. . . .

"And you are isolated"—she leaned against a silent panel and punched buttons; the room began to grow dark—"in absolute night . . . and stars." And stars appeared, in the darkness of a planetarium show; fire-gnats lighting her face and shoulders and his own. "How do you like our stars?"

"Are we in here?"

Four streaks of blue joined lights in the air. "Here . . . in space by this corner of the Quadrangle. This is our navigation chart for the Quadrangle run; see the bowed leg and brightness, that's the Pleiades. Patris . . . Sanalareta . . . Treone . . . back to Oro. The other lines zigzag too, but it doesn't show. Now come with me. . . . With a flare of energy, we open our AAFAL nets in space— "

He followed her voice into the night, where flickering tracery seined motes of interstellar gas, and impossible nothingness burned with infinite energy, potential transformed and transforming. With the wisdom of a thousand years a ship of the League fell through limitless seas, navigating the shifting currents of the void, beating into the sterile winds of space. Stars glittered like snow on the curving hull, spitting icy dangers of light that moved imperceptibly into spectral blues before him, reddened as he looked behind: imperceptibly time expanded, velocity increased and with it power. He saw the haze of silver on his right rise into their path, a wall of liquid shadow . . . the Pleiades, an endless bank of burning fog kindled from within by shrouded islands of fire. Tendrils of shimmering mists curved outward across hundreds of billions of kilometers, the nets found bountiful harvest, drew close hurled the ship into the edge of cloud.

Nebulosity wrapped him in clinging haloes of colored light ringed him in brilliance, as the nets fell inward toward the ship, burgeoning with energy, shielding its fragile nucleas from the soundless fury of its passage. Acceleration increased by hundredfolds, around him the Doppler shifts deepened toward cerulean and crimson; slowly the clinging brightness wove into parabolas of shining smoke, whipping past until the entire flaming mass of cloud and stars seemed to sweep ahead, shriveling toward blue-whiteness, trailing embers.

And suddenly the ship burst once more into a void, a universe warped into a rubber bowl of brilliance stretching past him, drawing away and away before him toward a gleaming point of darkness. The shrunken nets seined near-vacuum and were filled; their speed approached $0.999c$ . . . held constant, as the conversion of matter of energy ceased within the ship . . . and in time, with a flicker of silver force, began once more to fall away. Slowly time unbowed, the universe cast off its alienness. One star grew steadily before them: the sun of Patris.

A sun rose in ruddy splendor above the City in the Clouds on Patris, nine months and seven light-years from Oro. . . . And again, Patris fell away; and the brash gleaming Freeport of Sanalareta; they crept toward Treone through gasless waste, groping for current and mote across the barren ship-wakes of half a millennium. . . . And again—

Maris found himself among fire-gnat stars, on a ship in the bay of New Piraeus. And realized she had stopped speaking. His hand rubbed the copper snarl of his hair, his eyes bright as a child's. "You didn't tell me you were a witch in your spare time."

He heard her smile, "Thank you. Mactav makes the real magic, though; her special effects are fantastic. She can show you the whole inhabited section of the galaxy, with all the trade polyhedra, like a dew-flecked cobweb hanging in the air." Daylight returned to the panel. "Mactav—that's her bank, there—handles most of the navigation, life support, all that, too. Sometimes it seems like we're almost along for the ride! But of course we're along for Mactav."

"Who or what is Mactav?" Maris peered into a darkened screen, saw something amber glimmer in its depths, drew back.

"You've never met her, neither have we—but you were staring her right in the eye." Brandy stood beside him. "She must be listening to Giri down below. . . . Okay, okay!—a Mactavia unit is the brain, the nervous system of a ship, she monitors its vital signs, calculates, adjusts. We only have to ask—sometimes we don't even have to do that. The memory is a real spacer woman's, fed into the circuits . . . someone who died irrevocably, or had reached retirement, but wanted to stay on. A human system is wiser, more versatile—and lots cheaper—than anything all-machine that's ever been done."

"Then your Mactav is a kind of cyborg."

She smiled. "Well, I guess so; in a way— "

"But the Spacing League's regulations still won't allow cyborgs in crews."

She looked annoyed.

He shrugged. "Sorry. Dumb thing to say. . . . What's that red down there?"

"Oh, that's our 'stomach': the AAFAL unit, where"—she grinned 3—"we digest stardust into energy. It's the only thing that's never transparent; the red is the shield."

"How does it work?"

"I don't really know. I can make it go, but I don't understand why—I'm only a five-and-a-half technician now. If I was a six I could tell you." She glanced at him sidelong. "Aha! I finally impressed you!"

He laughed. "Not so dumb as you look." He had qualified as a six half a century before, out of boredom.

"You'd better be kidding!"

"I am." He followed her back across the palely opalescing floor, looking down, and down. "Like walking on water . . . why transparent?"

She smiled through him at the sky. "Because it's so beautiful outside."

They dropped down through floors, to come out in a new hall. Music came faintly to him.

"This is where my cabin— "

Abruptly the music became an impossible agony of sound torn with screaming.

"God!" And Brandy was gone from beside him, down the hallway and through a flickering wall.

He found her inside the door, rigid with awe. Across the room the wall vomited blinding waves of color, above a screeching growth of crystal organ pipes. Nilgiri crouched on the floor, hands pressed against her stomach, shrieking hysterically. "Stop it, Mactav! Stop it! Stop it! Stop it!"

He touched Brandy's shoulder; she looked up and caught his arm; together they pulled Nilgiri, wailing, back from bedlam to the door.

"Nilgiri! Nilgiri, what happened!" Brandy screamed against her ear.

"Mactav, Mactav!"

"*Why*?"

"She put a . . . charge through it, she's crazy-mad . . . sh-she thinks . . . Oh, *stop* it, Mactav!" Nilgiri clung, sobbing.

Maris started into the room, hands over his ears. "How do you turn it off?"

"Maris, wait!"

"*How*, Brandy?"

"It's electrified, don't touch it!"

"*How*?"

"On the left, on the left, three switches—Maris, *don't*—Stop it, Mactav, stop— "

He heard her screaming as he lowered his left hand, hesitated, battered with glaring sound; sparks crackled as he flicked switches on the organ panel, once, twice, again.

"—it-it-it-it!" Her voice echoed through silent halls. Nilgiri slid down the doorjamb and sat sobbing on the floor.

"Maris, are you all right?"

He heard her dimly through cotton. Dazed with relief, he backed away from the gleaming console, nodding, and started across the room.

"*Man*," the soft hollow voice echoed echoed echoed. "What are you doing in here?"

"Mactav?" Brandy was gazing uneasily to his left.

He turned; across the room was another artificial eye, burning amber.

"Branduin, you brought him onto the ship; how could you do this thing? It is forbidden!"

"Oh, God." Nilgiri began to wail again in horror. Brandy knelt and caught Nilgiri's blistered hands; he saw anger hardened over her face. "Mactav, how could you!"

"Brandy." He shook his head; took a breath, frightened. "Mactav—I'm not a man. You're mistaken."

"Maris, no . . ."

He frowned. "I'm one hundred and forty-one years old . . . half my body is synthetic. I'm hardly human, any more than you are. Scan and see." He held up his hands.

"The part of you that matters is still a man."

A smile caught at his mouth. "Thanks."

"Men are evil, men destroyed . . ."

"Her, Maris," Brandy whispered. "They destroyed her."

The smile wavered. "Something more we have in common." His false arm pressed his side.

The golden eye regarded him. "Cyborg."

He sighed, went to the door. Brandy stood to meet him. Nilgiri huddled silently at her feet, staring up.

"Nilgiri." The voice was full of pain; they looked back. "How can I forgive myself for what I've done? I will never, never do such a thing again . . . never. Please, go to the infirmary; let me help you."

Slowly, with Brandy's help, Nilgiri got to her feet. "All right. It's all right, Mactav. I'll go on down now."

"Girl, do you want us—?"

Nilgiri shook her head, hands curled in front of her. "No, Brandy, it's okay. She's all right now. Me too—I think." Her smile quivered. "Ouch . . ." She started down the corridor toward the lift.

"Branduin, Maris, I apologize also to you. I'm—not usually like this, you know. . . ." Amber faded from her eye.

"Is she gone?"

Brandy nodded.

"That's the first bigoted computer I ever met."

And she remembered. "Your *hand*?"

Smiling, he held it out to her. "No harm; see? It's a nonconductor."

She shivered. Hands cradled the hand that ached to feel. "Mactav really isn't like that, you know. But something's been wrong lately, she gets into moods; we'll have to have her looked at when we get to Sanalareta."

"Isn't it dangerous?"

"I don't think so—not really. It's just that she has special problems; she's in there because she didn't have any choice, a strife-based culture killed her ship. She was very young, but that was all that was left of her."

"A high technology." A grimace; memory moved in his eyes.

"They were terribly apologetic, they did their best."

"What happened to them?"

"We cut contact—that's regulation number one. We have to protect ourselves."

He nodded, looking away. "Will they ever go back?"

"I don't know. Maybe, someday." She leaned against the doorway. "But that's why Mactav hates men; men, and war—and combined with the old taboo . . . I guess her memory suppressors weren't enough."

Nilgiri reappeared beside them. "All better." Her hands were bright pink. "Ready for anything!"

"How's Mactav acting?"

"Super-solicitous. She's still pretty upset about it, I guess."

Light flickered at the curving junctures of the walls, ceiling, floor. Maris glanced up. "Hell, it's getting dark outside. I expect I'd better be leaving; nearly time to open up. One last night on the town?" Nilgiri grinned and nodded; he saw Brandy hesitate.

"Maybe I'd better stay with Mactav tonight, if she's still upset. She's got to be ready to go up tomorrow." Almost-guilt firmed resolution on her face.

"Well . . . I could stay, if you think . . ." Nilgiri looked unhappy.

"No. It's my fault she's like this; I'll do it. Besides, I've been out having a fantastic day, I'd be too tired to do it right tonight. You go on in. Thank you, Maris! I wish it wasn't over so soon." She turned back to him, beginning to put her hair into braids; quicksilver shone.

"The pleasure was all mine." The tight sense of loss dissolved in warmth. "I can't remember a better one either . . . or more exciting. . . ." He grimaced.

She smiled and took his hands; Nilgiri glanced back and forth between them. "I'll see you to the lock."

Nilgiri climbed down through the glow to the waiting flyer. Maris braced back from the top rung to watch Brandy's face, bearing a strange expression, look down through whipping strands of loose hair. "Goodbye, Maris."

"Goodbye, Brandy."

"It was a short two weeks, you know?"

"I know."

"I like New Piraeus better than anywhere; I don't know why."

"I hope it won't be too different when you get back."

"Me too. . . . See you in three years?"

"Twenty-five."

"Oh, yeah. Time passes so quickly when you're having fun— " Almost true, almost not. A smile flowered.

"Write while you're away. Poems, that is." He began to climb down, slowly.

"I will. . . . Hey, my stuff is at— "

"I'll send it back with Nilgiri." He settled behind the controls; the flyer grew bright and began to rise. He waved; so did Nilgiri. He watched her wave back, watched her in his mirror until she became the vast and gleaming pearl that was the *Who Got Her—709*. And felt the gap that widened between their lives, more than distance, more than time.


"Well, now that you've seen it, what do you think?"

Late afternoon, first day, fourth visit, seventy-fifth year . . . mentally he tallied. Brandy stood looking into the kitchen. "It's—different."

"I know. It's still too new; I miss the old wood beams. They were rotting, but I miss them. Sometimes I wake up in the morning and don't know where I am. But I was losing my canyon."

She looked back at him, surprising him with her misery. "Oh . . . At least they won't reach you for a long time, out here."

"We can't walk home any more, though."

"No." She turned away again. "All—all your furniture is built in?"

"*Um.* It's supposed to last as long as the house."

"What if you get tired of it?"

He laughed. "As long as it holds me up, I don't care what it looks like. One thing I like, though." He pressed a plate on the wall, looking up. "The roof is polarized. Like your ship. At night you can watch the stars."

"Oh!" She looked up and back, he watched her mind pierce the high cloud-fog, pierce the day, to find stars. "How wonderful! I've never seen it anywhere else."

It had been his idea, thinking of her. He smiled.

"They must really be growing out here, to be doing things like this now." She tried the cushions of a molded chair. "Hmm . . ."

"They're up to two and a half already, they actually do a few things besides mining now. The Inside is catching up, if they can bring us this without a loss. I may even live to see the day when we'll be importing raw materials, instead of filling everyone else's mined-out guts. If there's anything left of Oro by then. . . ."

"Would you stay to see that?"

"I don't know." He looked at her. "It depends. Anyway, tell me about this trip." He stretched out on the chain-hung wall seat. "You know everything that's new with me already: one house." And waited for far glory to rise up in her eyes.

They flickered down, stayed the color of fog. "Well—some good news, and some bad news, I guess."

"Like how?" Feeling suddenly cold.

"Good news"—her smile warmed him—"I'll be staying nearly a month this time. We'll have more time to—do things, if you want to."

"How did you manage that?" He sat up.

"That's more good news. I have a chance to crew on a different ship, to get out of the Quadrangle and see things I've only dreamed of, new worlds— "

"And the bad news is how long you'll be gone."

"Yes."

"How many years?"

"It's an extended voyage, following up trade contacts; if we're lucky, we might be back in the stellar neighborhood in thirty-five years . . . thirty-five years tau—more than two hundred, here. If we're not so lucky, maybe we won't be back this way at all."

"I see." He stared unblinking at the floor, hands knotted between his knees. "It's—an incredible opportunity, all right . . . especially for your poetry. I envy you. But I'll miss you."

"I know." He saw her teeth catch her lip. "But we can spend time together, we'll have a lot of time before I go. And—well, I've brought you something, to remember me." She crossed the room to him.

It was a star, suspended burning coldly in scrolled silver by an artist who knew fire. Inside she showed him her face, laughing, full of joy.

"I found it on Treone . . . they really are in renaissance. And I liked that holo, I thought you might— "

Leaning across silver he found the silver of her hair, kissed her once on the mouth, felt her quiver as he pulled away. He lifted the woven chain, fixed it at his throat. I have something for you, too."

He got up, returned with a slim book the color of red wine, put it in her hands.

"My poems!"

He nodded, his fingers feeling the star at his throat. "I managed to get hold of two copies—it wasn't easy. Because they're too well known now; the spacers carry them, they show them but they won't give them up. You must be known on more worlds than you could ever see."

"Oh, I hadn't even heard. . . ." She laughed suddenly. "My fame preceded me. But next trip— " She looked away. "No. I won't be going that way anymore."

"But you'll be seeing new things, to make into new poems." He stood, trying to loosen the tightness in his voice.

"Yes . . . Oh, yes, I know. . . ."

"A month is a long time."

A sudden sputter of noise made them look up. Fat dapples of rain were beginning to slide, smearing dust over the flat roof.

"Rain! not fog; the season's started." They stood and watched the sky fade overhead, darken, crack and shudder with electric light. The rain fell harder, the ceiling rippled and blurred; he led her to the window. Out across the smooth folded land a liquid curtain billowed, slaking the dust-dry throat of the canyons, renewing the earth and the spicy tight-leaf scrub. "I always wonder if it's ever going to happen. It always does." He looked at her, expecting quicksilver, and found slow tears. She wept silently, watching the rain.

For the next two weeks they shared the rain, and the chill bright air that followed. In the evenings she went out, while he stood behind the bar, because it was the last time she would have leave with the crew of the *Who Got Her*. But every morning he found her sleeping, and every afternoon she spent with him. Together they traced the serpentine alleyways of the shabby, metamorphosing lower city or roamed the docks with the windburned, fisherfolk. He took her to meet Makerrah, whom he had seen as a boy mending nets by hand, as a fishnet-clad Tail courting spacers at the Tin Soldier, as a sailor and fisherman, for almost forty years.

Makerrah, now growing heavy and slow as his wood-pulled boat, showed it with pride to the sailor from the sky; they discussed nets, eating fish.

"This world is getting old. . . ." Brandy had come with him to the bar as the evening started.

Maris smiled. "But the night is young." And felt pleasure stir with envy.

"True, true . . ." Pale hair cascaded as her head bobbed. "But, you know, when . . . if I was gone another twenty-five years, I probably wouldn't recognize this *street*. The Tin Soldier really is the only thing that doesn't change." She sat at the agate counter, face propped in her hands, musing.

He stirred drinks. "It's good to have something constant in your life."

"I know. We appreciate that too, more than anybody." She glanced away into the dark-raftered room. "They really always do come back here first, and spend more time in here . . . and knowing that they *can* means so much, that you'll be here, young and real and remembering them. A sudden hunger blurred her sight.

"It goes both ways." He looked up.

"I know that, too. . . . You know, I always meant to ask: why did you call it the 'Tin Soldier'? I mean, I think I see . . . but why 'tin'?"

"Sort of a private joke, I guess. It was in a book of folk tales I read, *Andersen's Fairy Tales*"—he looked embarrassed—"I'd *read* everything else. It was a story about a toy shop, about a tin soldier with one leg, who was left on the shelf for years. . . . He fell in love with a toy ballerina who only loved dancing, never him. In the end, she fell into the fire, and he went after her—she burned to dust, heartless; he melted into a heart-shaped lump. . . ." He laughed carefully, seeing her face. "A footnote said sometimes the story had a happy ending; I like to believe that."

She nodded, hopeful. "Me too. . . . Where did your stone bar come from? It's beautiful; like the edge of the Pleiades, depths of mist."

"Why all the questions?"

"I'm appreciating. I've loved it all for years, and never said anything. Sometimes you love things without knowing it, you take them for granted. It's wrong to let that happen . . . so I wanted you to know." She smoothed the polished stone with her hand.

He joined her tracing opalescences. "It's petrified wood—some kind of plant life that was preserved in stone, minerals replaced its structure. I found it in the desert."

"Desert?"

"East of the mountains. I found a whole canyon full of them. It's an incredible place, the desert."

"I've never seen one. Only heard about them, barren and deadly; it frightened me."

"While you cross the most terrible desert of them all?—between the stars."

"But it's not barren."

"Neither is this one. It's winter here now. I can take you to see the trees, if you'd like it." He grinned. "If you dare."

Her eyebrows rose. "I dare! We could go tomorrow, I'll make us a lunch."

"We'd have to leave early, though. If you were wanting to do the town again tonight . . ."

"Oh, that's all right; I'll take a pill."

"Hey— "

She winced. "Oh, well . . . I found a kind I could take. I used them all the time at the other ports, like the rest."

"Then why— "

"Because I liked staying with you. I deceived you, now you know, true confession. Are you mad?"

His face filled with astonished pleasure. "Hardly . . . I have to admit, I used to wonder what— "

"*Sol*-dier!" He looked away, someone gestured at him across the room. "More wine, please!" He raised a hand.

"Brandy, come on, there's a party— "

She waved. "Tomorrow morning, early?" Her eyes kept his face.

"Uh-huh. See you— "

"—later." She slipped down and was gone.

The flyer rose silently, pointing into the early sun. Brandy sat beside him, squinting down and back through the glare as New Piraeus grew narrow beside the glass-green bay. "Look, how it falls behind the hills, until all you can see are the land and the sea, and no sign of change. It's like that when the ship goes up, but it happens so fast you don't have time to savor it." She turned back to him, bright-eyed. "We go from world to world but we never see them; we're always looking up. It's good to look down, today."

They drifted higher, rising with the climbing hills, until the rumpled olive-red suede of the seacoast grew jagged, blotched green-black and gray and blinding white.

"Is that really snow?" She pulled at his arm, pointing.

He nodded. "We manage a little."

"I've only seen snow once since I left Calicho, once it was winter on Treone. We wrapped up in furs and capes even though we didn't have to, and threw snowballs with the Tails. . . . But it was cold most of the year on our island, on Calicho—we were pretty far north, we grew special kinds of crops . . . and us kids had hairy hornbeats to plod around on. . . ." Lost in memories, she rested against his shoulder; while he tried to remember a freehold on Glatte, and snowy walls became jumbled whiteness climbing a hill by the sea.

They had crossed the divide; the protruding batholith of the peaks degenerated into parched, crumbling slopes of gigantic rubble. Ahead of them the scarred yellow desolation stretched away like an infinite canvas, into mauve haze. "How far does it go?"

"It goes on forever. . . . Maybe not this desert, but this merges into others that merge into others—the whole planet is a desert, hot or cold. It's been desiccating for eons; the sun's been rising off the main sequence. The sea by New Piraeus is the only large body of free water left now, and that's dropped half an inch since I've been here. The coast is the only habitable area, and there aren't many towns there even now."

"Then Oro will never be able to change too much."

"Only enough to hurt. See the dust? Open-pit mining, for seventy kilometers north. And that's a little one."

He took them south, sliding over the eroded face of the land to twist through canyons of folded stone, sediments contorted by the palsied hands of tectonic force; or flashing across pitted flatlands lipping on pocket seas of ridged and shadowed blow-sand.

They settled at last under a steep outcurving wall of frescoed rock layered in red and green. The wide, rough bed of the sandy wash was pale in the chill glare of noon, scrunching underfoot as they began to walk. Pulling on his leather jacket, Maris showed her the kaleidoscope of ages left tumbled in stones over the hills they climbed, shouting against the lusty wind of the ridges. She cupped them in marveling hands, hair streaming like silken banners past her face; obligingly he put her chosen few into his pockets. "Aren't you cold?" He caught her hand.

"No, my suit takes care of me. How did you ever learn to know all these, Maris?"

Shaking his head, he began to lead her back down. "There's more here than I'll ever know. I just got a mining tape on geology at the library. But it made it mean more to come out here . . . where you can see eons of the planet laid open, one cycle settling on another. To know the time it took, the life history of an entire world: it helps my perspective, it makes me feel—young."

"We think we know worlds, but we don't, we only see people: change and pettiness. We forget the greater constancy, tied to the universe. It would humble our perspective, too . . ." Pebbles boiled and clattered; her hand held his strongly as his foot slipped. He looked back, chagrined, and she laughed. "You don't really have to lead me here, Maris. I was a mountain goat on Calicho, and I haven't forgotten it all."

Indignant, he dropped her hand. "You lead."

Still laughing, she led him to the bottom of the hill.

And he took her to see the trees. Working their way over rocks up the windless branch wash, they rounded a bend and found them, tumbled in static glory. He heard her indrawn breath. "Oh, Maris— " Radiant with color and light she walked among them, while he wondered again at the passionless artistry of the earth. Amethyst and agate, crystal and mimicked wood-grain, hexagonal trunks split open to bare subtleties of mergence and secret nebulosities. She knelt among the broken bits of limb, choosing colors to hold up to the sun.

He sat on a trunk, picking agate pebbles. "They're sort of special friends of mine; we go down in time together, in strangely familiar bodies . . ." He studied them with fond pride. "But they go with more grace."

She put her colored chunks on the ground. "No . . . I don't think so. They had no choice."

He looked down, tossing pebbles.

"Let's have our picnic here."

They cleared a space and spread a blanket, and picnicked with the trees. The sun warmed them in the windless hollow, and he made a pillow of his jacket; satiated, they lay back head by head, watching the cloudness green-blue sky.

"You pack a good lunch."

"Thank you. It was the least I could do"—her hand brushed his arm; quietly his fingers tightened on themselves—"to share your secrets; to learn that the desert isn't barren, that it's immense, timeless, full of—mysteries. But no life?"

"No—not anymore. There's no water, nothing can live. The

only things left are in or by the sea, or they're things we've brought. Across our own lifeless desert-sea."

"'Though inland far we be, our souls have sight of that immortal sea which brought us hither.'" Her hand stretched above him, to catch the sky.

"Wordsworth. That's the only thing by him I ever liked much."

They lay together in the warm silence. A piece of agate came loose, dropped to the ground with a clink; they started.

"Maris— "

"*Hmm?*"

"Do you realize we've known each other for three-quarters of a century?"

"Yes . . ."

"I've almost caught up with you, I think. I'm twenty-seven. Soon I'm going to start passing you. But at least—now you'll never have to see it show." Her fingers touched the rusty curls of his hair.

"It would never show. You couldn't help but be beautiful."

"Maris . . . sweet Maris."

He felt her hand clench in the soft wave of his shirt, move in caresses down his body. Angrily he pulled away, sat up, half his face flushed. "Damn—!"

Stricken, she caught at his sleeve. "No, no— " Her eyes found his face, gray filled with grief. "No . . . Maris . . . I—want you." She unsealed her suit, drew blue-silver from her shoulders, knelt before him. "I want you."

Her hair fell to her waist, the color of warm honey. She reached out and lifted his hand with tenderness; slowly he leaned forward, to bare her breasts and her beating heart, felt the softness set fire to his nerves. Pulling her close, he found her lips, kissed them long and longingly; held her against his own heart beating, lost in her silken hair. "Oh, God, Brandy . . ."

"I love you, Maris . . . I think I've always loved you." She clung to him, cold and shivering in the sunlit air. "And it's wrong to leave you and never let you know."

And he realized that fear made her tremble, fear bound to her love in ways he could not fully understand. Blind to the future, he drew her down beside him and stopped her trembling with his joy.

In the evening she sat across from him at the bar, blue-haloed with light, sipping brandy. Their faces were bright with wine and melancholy bliss.

"I finally got some more brandy, Brandy . . . a couple of years ago. So we wouldn't run out. If we don't get to it, you can take it with you." He set the dusty red-splintered bottle carefully on the bar.

"You could save it, in case I do come back, as old as your grandmaw, and in need of some warmth . . ." Slowly she rotated her glass, watching red leap up the sides. "Do you suppose by then my poems will have reached Home? And maybe somewhere. Inside, Ntaka will be reading *me*."

"The Outside will be the Inside by then . . . Besides, Ntaka's probably already dead. Been dead for years."

"Oh. I guess." She pouted, her eyes growing dim and moist. "Damn, I wish . . . I wish."

"Branduin, you haven't joined us yet tonight. It is our last together." Harkané appeared beside her, lean dark face smiling in a cloud-mass of blued white hair. She sat down with her drink.

"I'll come soon." Clouded eyes glanced up, away.

"Ah, the sadness of parting keeps you apart? I know." Harkané nodded. "We've been together so long; it's hard, to lose another family." She regarded Maris. "And a good bartender must share everyone's sorrows, yes, Soldier—? But bury his own. Oh—they would like some more drinks— "

Sensing dismissal, he moved aside: with long-practiced skill he became blind and deaf, pouring wine.

"Brandy, you are so unhappy—don't you want to go on this other voyage?"

"Yes, I do—But . . ."

"But you don't. It is always so when there is choice. Sometimes we make the right choice, and though we're afraid we go on with it anyway. And sometimes we make the wrong choice, and go on with it anyway because we're afraid not to. Have you changed your mind?"

"But I can't change— "

"Why not? We will leave them a message. They will go on and pick up their second compatible."

"Is it really that easy?"

"No . . . not quite. But we can do it, if you want to stay."

Silence stretched; Maris sent a tray away, began to wipe glasses, fumbled.

"But I *should*."

"Brandy. If you go only out of obligation, I will tell you something. I want to retire. I was going to resign this trip, at Sanalareta;

but if I do that, Maclav will need a new Best Friend. She's getting old and cantankerous, just like me; these past few years her behavior has begun to show the strain she is under. She must have someone who can feel her needs. I was going to ask you, I think you understand her best; but I thought you wanted this other thing more. If not, I ask you now to become the new Best Friend of the *Who Got Her*."

"But Harkané, you're not old— "

"I am eighty-six. I'm too old for the sporting life anymore; I will become a Mactav; I've been lucky, I have an opportunity."

"Then . . . yes—I do want to stay! I accept the position."

In spite of himself Maris looked up, saw her face shining with joy and release. "Brandy—?"

"Maris, I'm not going!"

"I know!" He laughed, joined them.

"Soldier." He looked up, dark met dark, Harkané's eyes that saw more than surfaces. "This will be the last time that I see you; I am retiring, you know. You have been very good to me all these years, helping me be young; you are very kind to us all. . . . Now, to say goodbye, I do something in return." She took his hand, placed it firmly over Brandy's, shining with rings on the counter. "I give her back to you. Brandy—join us soon, we'll celebrate." She rose mildly and moved away to the crowded room.

Their hands twisted, clasped tight on the counter.

Brandy closed her eyes. "God, I'm so glad!"

"So am I."

"Only the poems . . ."

"Remember once you told me, 'you can see it all a hundred times, and never see it all'?"

A quicksilver smile. "And it's true. . . . Oh, Maris, now this is my last night! And I have to spend it with them, to celebrate."

"I know. There's—no way I can have you forever, I suppose. But it's all right." He grinned. "Everything's all right. What's twenty-five years, compared to two hundred?"

"It'll seem like three."

"It'll seem like twenty-five. But I can stand it. . . ."


He stood it, for twenty-four more years, looking up from the bar with sudden eagerness every time new voices and the sound of laughter spilled into the dim blue room.

"Soldier! Soldier, you're still— "

"We missed you like— "

"—two whole weeks of— "

"—want to buy a whole *sack* of my own— "

The crew of the *DOM—428* pressed around him, their fingers proving he was real; their lips brushed a cheek that couldn't feel and one that could, long loose hair rippling over the agate bar. He hugged four at a time. "Aralea! Vlasa! Elsah, what the hell have you done to your hair now—and Ling-shan! My God, you're pretty, like always. Cathe— " The memory bank never forgot a shining fresh-scrubbed face, even after thirty-seven years. Their eyes were very bright as he welcomed them, and their hands left loving prints along the agate bar.

"—still have your stone bar; I'm so glad, don't ever sell it— "

"And what's new with you?" Elsah gasped, and ecstatic laughter burst over him.

He shook his head, hands up, laughing too. "—go prematurely *deaf*? First round on the house; only one at a time, huh?"

Elsah brushed strands of green-tinged waist-length hair back from her very green eyes. "Sorry, Soldier. We've just said it *all* to each other, over and over. And gee, we haven't seen you for four years!" Her belt tossed blue-green sparks against her green quilted flight-suit.

"Four years? Seems more like thirty-seven." And they laughed again, appreciating, because it was true. "Welcome back to the Tin Soldier. What's your pleasure?"

"Why you of course, me darlin'," said black-haired Brigit, and she winked.

His smile barely caught on a sharp edge; he winked back. "Just the drinks are on the house, lass." The smile widened and came unstuck.

More giggles.

"Ach, a pity!" Brigit pouted. She wore a filigree necklace, like the galaxy strung over her dark-suited breast. "Well, then, I guess a little olive beer, for old time's sake."

"Make it two."

"Anybody want a pitcher?"

"Sure, why not?"

"Come sit with us in a while, Soldier. Have we got things to tell you!"

He jammed the clumsy pitcher under the spigot and pulled down as they drifted away, watching the amber splatter up its frosty sides.

"Alta, hi! Good timing! How are things on the *Extra Sexy Old—115?*"

"Oh, good enough; how's Chrysalis—has it changed much?"

The froth spilled out over his hand; he let the lever jerk up, licked his fingers and wiped them on his apron.

"It's gone wild this time, you should see what they're wearing for clothes. My God, you would not believe— "

He hoisted the slimy pitcher onto the bar and set octagonal mugs on a tray.

"Aralea, did you hear what happened to the— "

He lifted the pitcher again, up to the tray's edge.

"—*Who Got her—709?*"

The pitcher teetered.

"Their Mactav had a nervous breakdown on landing at Sanalareta. Branduin died, the poet, the one who wrote— "

Splinters and froth exploded on the agate bar and slobbered over the edge, *tinkle, crash.*

Stunned blank faces turned to see Soldier, hands moving ineffectually in a puddle of red-flecked foam. He began to brush it off onto the floor, looking like a stricken adolescent. "Sorry . . . sorry about that."

"Ach, Soldier, you really blew it!"

"Got a mop? Here, we'll help you clean it up . . . hey, you're bleeding—?" Brigit and Ling-shan were piling chunks of pitcher onto the bar.

Soldier shook his head, fumbling a towel around the one wrist that bled. "No . . . no, thanks, leave it, huh? I'll get you another pitcher . . . it doesn't matter. Go on!" They looked at him. "I'll send you a pitcher; thanks." He smiled.

They left, the smile stopped. *Fill the pitcher.* He filled a pitcher, his hand smarting. *Clean up, damn it.* He cleaned up, wiping off disaster while the floor absorbed and fangs of glass disappeared under the bar. As the agate bartop dried he saw the white-edged shatter flower, tendrils of hairline crack shooting out a handbreadth on every side. He began to track them with a rigid finger, counting softly. . . . *She loved me, she loved me not, she loved me—*

"Two cepheids and a wine, Soldier!"

"Soldier, come hear what we saw on Chrysalis if you're through!"

He nodded and poured, blinking hard. *Goddamn sweet-smoke in here . . . goddamn everything!* Elsah was going out the door with a boy in tight green pants and a starmap-tattooed body. He stared them into fluorescent blur. And remembered Brandy going out the door too many times. . . .

"Hey, *Sol*-dier, what are you doing?"

He blinked himself back.

"Come sit with us?"

He crossed the room to the nearest bulky table and the remaining crew of the *Dirty Old Man—428*.

"How's your hand?" Vlasa soothed it with a dark, ringed finger.

"It only hurts when I laugh."

"*You* really are screwed up!" Ling-shan's smile wrinkled. "Oh, Soldier, why look so glum?"

"I chipped my bar."

"Ohhh . . . nothing but bad news tonight. Make him laugh, somebody, we can't go on like this!"

"Tell him the joke you heard on Chrysalis— "

"—from the boy with a cat's-eye in his navel? Oh. Well, it seems there was . . ."

His fingers moved reluctantly up the laces of his patchwork shirt and began to untangle the thumb-sized star trapped near his throat. He set it free; his hand tightened across the stubby spines, feeling only dull pressure. Pain registered from somewhere else.

"—'Oh, they fired the pickle slicer too!'"

He looked up into laughter.

"It's a tech-one joke, Soldier," Ling-Shan said helpfully.

"Oh . . . I see." He laughed, blindly.

"Soldier, we took pictures of our black hole!" Vlasa pulled at his arm. "From a respectable distance, but it was bizarre— "

"Holograms— " somebody interrupted.

"And you should see the effects!" Brigit said. "When you look into them you feel like your eyes are being— "

"Soldier, another round, please?"

"Excuse me." He pushed back his chair. "Later?" Thinking, *God won't this night ever end?*


His hand closed the lock on the pitted tavern door at last; his woven sandal skidded as he stepped into the street. Two slim figures, one all in sea-blue, passed him and red hair flamed; he recognized Marena, intent and content arm in arm with a gaudy, laughing Tail. Their hands were in each other's back pockets. They were going uphill; he turned down, treading carefully on the time- and fog-slicked cobbles. He limped slightly. Moist wraiths of

sea fog twined the curving streets, turning the street lights into dark
angels under fluorescing haloes. Bright droplets formed in his hair
as he walked. His footsteps scratched to dim echoes; the laughter
faded, leaving him alone with memory.

The presence of dawn took him by surprise, as a hand brushed
his shoulder.

"Sojer, 'tis you?"

Soldier looked up fiercely into a gray-bristled face.

"Y'all right? What'ree doin' down here at dawn, lad?"

He recognized old Makerrah the fisherman, finally. Lately it
amused the old man to call him "lad."

"Nothin' . . . nothin'." He pulled away from the brine-warped
rail. The sun was rising beyond the mountains, the edge of fog
caught the colors of fire and was burned away. It would be a hot
day. "G'bye, ol' man." He began to walk.

"Y'sure y're all right?"

Alone again he sat with one foot hanging, feeling the suck and
swell of water far below the pier. *All right . . .?* When had he ever
been all right? And tried to remember into the time before he had
known her, and could find no answer.

There had never been an answer for him on his own world, on
Glatte; never even a place for him. Glatte, with a four-point-five
technology, and a neo-feudal society, where the competition for
that technology was a cultural rationale for war. All his life he
had seen his people butchered and butchering, blindly, trapped by
senseless superstition. And hated it, but could not escape the bitter
ties that led him to his destruction. Fragments of that former life
were all that remained now, after two centuries, still clinging to the
fact of his alienness. He remembered the taste of fresh-fallen snow
. . . remembered the taste of blood. And the memory filled him
of how it felt to be nineteen, and hating war, and blown to pieces
. . . to find yourself suddenly half-prosthetic, with the pieces that
were gone still hurting in your mind; and your stepfather's voice,
with something that was not pride, saying you were finally a real
man. . . . Soldier held his breath unaware. His name was Maris,
consecrated to war; and when at last he understood why, he left
Glatte forever.

He paid all he had to the notorious spacer women; was carried
in stasis between the stars, like so much baggage. He wakened
to Oro, tech one-point-five, no wars and almost no people. And
found out that now to the rest of humanity he was no longer

quite human. But he had stayed on Oro for ninety-six years, aging only five, alone. Ninety-six years; a jumble of whiteness climbing a hill, constant New Piraeus; a jumble of faces in dim blue lantern light, patterning a new life. A pattern endlessly repeated, his smile welcoming, welcoming with the patience of the damned, all the old/new faces that needed him but never wanted him, while he wanted and needed them all. And then she had come to Oro, and after ninety-six years the pattern was broken. Damned Tin Soldier fell in love, after too many years of knowing better, with a ballerina who danced between the stars.

He pressed his face abruptly against the rail, pain flickered. *God, still real*; *thought it all turned to plastic, damn, damn. . . .* And shut out three times twenty-five more years of pattern, of everyone else's nights and cold, solitary mornings trying to find her face. Ninety-one hundred days to carry the ache of returned life, until she would come again, and—

"See? That's our ship. The third one in line."

Soldier listened, unwillingly. A spacer in lavender stood with her Tail where the dock angled to the right, pointing out across the bay.

"Can't we go see it?" Blue glass glittered in mesh across the boy's back as he draped himself over the rail.

"Certainly not. Men aren't allowed on ships; it's against regulations. And anyway—I'd rather stay here." She drew him into the corner; amethyst and opal wrapped her neck in light. They began to kiss, hands wandering.

Soldier got up slowly and left them, still entwined, to privacy. The sun was climbing toward noon; above him as he walked, the skyline of New Piraeus wavered in the hazed and heated air. His eyes moved up and back toward the forty-story skeleton of the Universal Bank under construction, dropped to the warehouses, the docks, his atrophying ancient lower city. Insistent through the cry of sea birds he could hear the hungry whining of heavy machinery, the belly of a changing world. *And still I triumph over Death, and Chance, and thee, O Time—*

"But I can't stand it." His hands tightened on wood. "I stood it for ninety-six years; on the shelf." Dolefully the sea birds mocked him, creaking in the gray-green twilight, *now, now*—Wind probed the openings of his shirt like the cold fingers of sorrow. *Was dead, for ninety-six years before she came.*

For hours along the rail he had watched the ships in the bay;

while he watched, a new ship had come slipping down, like the sun's tear. Now they grew bright as the day ended, setting a bracelet on the black water. Stiffness made him lurch as he turned away, to artificial stars clustered on the wall of night.

Choking on the past, he climbed the worn streets, where the old patterns of a new night reached him only vaguely, and his eyes found nothing that he remembered anymore. Until he reached the time-eaten door, the thick, peeling mud-brick wall beneath the neon sign. His hand fondled the slippery lock, as it had for two hundred years. TIN SOLDIER . . . loved a ballerina. His hand slammed against the lock. *No—this bar is closed tonight.*

The door slid open at his touch; Soldier entered his quiet house. And stopped, hearing the hollow mutter of the empty night, and found himself alone for the rest of his life.

He moved through the rooms by starlight, touching nothing, until he came to the bedroom door. Opened it, the cold latch burning his hand. And saw her there, lying asleep under the silver robe of the Pleiades. Slowly he closed the door, waited, opened it once more and filled the room with light.

She sat up, blinking, a fist against her eyes and hair falling ash-golden to her waist. She wore a long soft dress of muted flowers, blue and green and earth tones. "Maris? I didn't hear you, I guess I went to sleep."

He crossed the room, fell onto the bed beside her, caressing her, covering her face with kisses. "They said you were dead . . . all day I thought— "

"I am." Her voice was dull, her eyes dark-ringed with fatigue.

"No."

"I am. To them I am. I'm not a spacer anymore; space is closed to me forever. That's what it means to be 'dead'. To lose your life. . . . Mactav—went crazy. I never thought we'd even get to port. I was hurt badly, in the accident." Fingers twined loops in her hair, pulled—

"But you're all right."

She shook her head. "No." She held out her hand, upturned; he took it, curled its fingers into his own, flesh over flesh, warm and supple. "It's plastic, Maris."

He turned the hand over, stroked it, folded the long limber fingers. "It can't be— "

"It's numb. I barely feel you at all. They tell me I may live for hundreds of years." Her hand tightened into a fist. "And I *am* a whole woman, but they forbid me to go into space again! I can't be crew, I can't be a Mactav, I can only be baggage. And—I can't even say it's unfair. . . ." Hot tears burned her face. "I didn't know what to do, I didn't know—if I should come. If you'd want a . . . ballerina who'd been in fire."

"You even wondered?" He held her close again, rested her head on his shoulder, to hide his own face grown wet.

A noise of pain twisted in her throat, her arms tightened. "Oh, Maris. Help me . . . please, help me, help me. . . ."

He rocked her silently, gently, until her sobbing eased, as he had rocked a homesick teenager a hundred years before.

"How will I live . . . on one world for centuries, always remembering. How do you bear it?"

"By learning what really matters. . . . Worlds are not so small. We'll go to other worlds if you want—we could see Home. You'd be surprised how much credit you build up over two hundred years." He kissed her swollen eyes, her reddened cheeks, her lips. "And maybe in time the rules will change."

She shook her head, bruised with loss. "Oh, my Maris, my wise love—love me, tie me to the earth."

He took her prosthetic hand, kissed the soft palm and fingers. *And make it well* . . . And knowing that it would never be easy, reached to dim the lights.

# IN THE PROBLEM PIT

## Frederik Pohl

### David

Before I left the apartment to meet my draft call I had packed up the last of Lara. She had left herself all over our home: perfumes, books, eye shadow, Tampax, ivory animals she had forgotten to take and letters from him that she had probably meant for me to read. I didn't read them. I packed up the whole schmear and sent it off to her in Djakarta, with longing and hatred.

Since I was traveling at government expense, I took the hyperjet and then a STOL to the nearest city and a cab from there. I paid for the whole thing with travel vouchers, even the cab, which enormously annoyed the driver; I didn't tip him. He bounced off down the road muttering in Spanish, racing his motor and double-clutching on the switchbacks, and there I was in front of the pit facility, and I didn't want to go on in. I wasn't ready to talk to anybody about any problems, especially mine.

There was an explosion of horns and gunned motors from down the road. Somebody else was arriving, and the drivers were fighting about which of them would pull over to let the other pass. I made up my mind to slope off. So I looked for a cubbyhole to hide my pack and sleeping bag in and found it behind a rock, and I left the stuff there and was gone before the next cab arrived. I didn't know where I was going, exactly. I just wanted to walk up the trails around the mountains in the warm afternoon rain.

It was late afternoon, which meant it was, I calculated, oh,

something like six in the morning in Djakarta. I could visualize
Lara sound asleep in the heat, sprawled with the covers kicked
off, making that little ladylike whistle that served her in place of
a snore. (I could not visualize the other half of the bed.)

I was hurting. Lara and I had been married for six years, counting
two separations. And the way trouble always does, it had screwed
up my work. I'd had this commission from the library in St. Paul,
a big, complicated piece for over the front foyer. Well, it hadn't
gone well, being more Brancusi and interior-decorator art than me,
but still it had been a lot of work and just about finished. And
then when I had it in the vacuum chamber and was floating the
aluminum plating onto it, I'd let the pressure go up, and air got
in, and of course the whole thing burned.

So partly I was thinking about whether Lara would come back
and partly whether there was any chance I could do a whole new
sculpture and plate it and deliver it before the library purchasing
commission got around to canceling my contract, and partly I
wasn't thinking at all, just huffing and puffing up those trails
in the muggy mist. I could see morning glories growing. I picked
up a couple and put them in my pocket. The long muscles in my
thighs were beginning to burn, and I was fighting my breathing.
So I slowed down, spending my concentration on pacing my steps
and my breathing so that I could keep my head away from where
the real pain was. And then I found myself almost tripping over a
rusted bent old sign that said *Pericoloso* in one language and *Danger*
in another.

The sign spoke truth.

In front of me was a cliff and a catwalk stretching out over what
looked like a quarter of a mile of space.

I had blundered on to the old telescope. I could see the bowl way
down below, all grown over with bushes and trees. And hanging in
the air in front of me, suspended from three cables, was a thing like a
rusty trolley car, with spikes sticking out of the lower part of it.

No one was around; I guess they don't use the telescope any
more. I couldn't go any farther unless I wanted to go out on the
catwalk, which I didn't, and so I sat down and breathed hard. As
I began to get caught up on my oxygen debt, I began to think
again; and since I didn't want to do that, I pulled the crushed
morning glories out of my pocket and chewed on a few seeds.

Well, I had forgotten where I was. In Minneapolis you grow
them in a window box. You have to pound them and crush
them and soak them and squeeze them, hundreds of seeds at a

time, before you get anything. But these had grown in a tropical climate.

I wasn't stoned or tripping, really. But I was—oh, I guess the word is "anesthetized." Nothing hurt any more. It wasn't just an absence of hurting, it was a positive *not* hurting, like when you've broken a tooth and you've finally got to the dentist's office and he's squirted in the novocaine and you can feel that not-hurting spread like a golden glow across your jaw, blotting up the ache as it goes.

I don't know how long I sat there, but by the time I remembered I was supposed to report in at the pit the shadows were getting long.

So I missed dinner, I missed signing in properly, I got there just in time for the VISTA guard to snap at me, "Why the hell can't you be on time, Charlie?" and I was the last one down the elevators and into the pit. Everybody else was gathered there already in a big room that looked like it had been chopped out of rock, which I guess it had, with foam cushions scattered around the floor and, I guess, 12 or 14 people scattered around on the cushions, all with their bodies pointed toward an old lady in black slacks and a black turtleneck, but their faces pointed toward me.

I flung down my sleeping bag and sat on it and said, "Sorry."

She said, rather nicely, "Actually, we were just beginning."

And everybody looked at me begrudgingly, as though they had no choice but to wait while I blew my nose or built myself a nest out of straws or whatever I was going to do to delay them all still further, but I just sat there, trying not to look stoned, and after a while she began to talk.

## Tina's Talk

Hello. My name is Tina Wattridge, and I'm one of your resource people.

I'm not the leader of this group. There isn't any leader. If the group ever decides it has to have a leader, well, it can pick one. Or if you want to be a leader, you can pick yourself. See if anybody follows. But I'm not it, I'm only here to be available for answering questions or giving information.

First, I will tell you what you already know. The reason you are all here is to solve problems.

(She paused for a moment, scratching her nose and smiling, and then went on.)

Thank you. A lot of groups start complaining and making jokes right there, and you didn't. That's nice, because I didn't organize this group, and although I must say I think the groups work out well, it isn't my fault that you're here. And I appreciate your not blaming it on me.

Still, you are here, and we are expected to state some problems and solve them, and we will stay right here until we do that, or enough of it so that whoever's watching us is satisfied enough to let us go. That might be a couple of weeks. I had a group once that got out in 72 hours, but don't expect that. Anyway, you won't know how long it is. The reason we are in these caves is to minimize contact with the external world, including all sorts of times cues. And if any of you have managed to smuggle watches past the VISTA people, please give them to me now. They're not allowed here.

I saw some of you look interested when I talked about who is watching us, and so I ought to say right now I don't know how they watch or when, and I don't care. They do watch. But they don't interfere. The first word we will get fròm them is when the VISTA duty people unlock the elevator and come down and tell us we can go home.

Food. You can eat whenever you want to, on demand. If you want to establish meal hours, any group of you can do so. If you want to eat singly, whenever you want to, fine. Either way you simply sign in in the dining room—"sign in" means you type your names on the monitor; they'll know who you are; just the last name will do—and order what you want to eat. Your choices are four: "Breakfast," "snack," "light meal" and "full meal." It doesn't matter what order you eat them in or when you want them. When you put in your order, they make them and put them in the dumbwaiter. Dirty dishes go back in the dumbwaiter except for the disposable ones, which go in the trash chute. You can ask for certain special dishes—the way you want your eggs, for instance—but in general you take what they give you. It's all explained on the menu.

Sleep. You sleep when you want to, where you want to. In these three rooms—this one, the problem pit and the eating room, as well as the pool and showers—the lights are permanently on. In the two small rooms out past the bathrooms and laundry the lights can be controlled, and whoever is in the room can turn them on or off any way you like. If you can't agree, you'll just have to work it out.

(She could see them building walls between themselves and her, and quickly she tried to reduce them.)

Listen, it's not as bad as it sounds. I always hate this part because it sounds like I'm giving you orders, but I'm not; those are just the ground rules and they bind me too. And, honestly, you won't all hate it, or not all of it. I've done this 15 times now, and I look forward to coming back!

All right, let's see. Showers, toilets and all are over there. Washer-dryers are next to them. I assume you all did what you were told and brought wash-and-wear clothes, as well as sleeping bags and so on; if you didn't, you'll have to figure out what to do about it yourselves. When you want to wash your clothes, put your stuff in one of the net bags and put it in the machine. If there's something already in the machine, just take it out and leave it on the table. The owner will pick it up when he wants it, no doubt. You can do three or four people's wash in a single cycle without any trouble. They're big machines. And there's plenty of water—you people who come from the Southwest and the Plains States don't have to worry. Incidentally, the sequenced water-supply system that you use there to conserve potable water was figured out right in this cave. The research and development people had to work it over hard, to get the fluidic controls responsive enough, but the basic idea came from here; so, you see, there's a point to all this.

(She lit a cigarette and looked cheerfully around at the group, pleased that they were not resisting, less pleased that they were passive. She was a tall and elderly red-headed woman, who usually managed to look cheerful without smiling.)

That brings me to computation facilities, for those of you who want to work on something that needs mathematical analysis or data access. I will do a certain amount of keyboarding for you, and I'll be there to help—that's basically my job, I guess. There are two terminals in the pit room. They are on-line, real-time, shared-time programs, and those of you who are familiar with ALGOL, COBOL, and so on can use them direct. If you can't write a program in computer language, you can either bring it to me—up to a point—or you can just type out what you want in clear. First, you type the words HELP ME; then you say what you want; then you type THAT'S ALL. The message will be relayed to a programmer, and he will help you if I can't, or if you don't want me to. You can blind-type your queries if you don't want me looking over your shoulder. And sign your last name to everything. And, as always, if more of you want to use the terminals than we have terminals, you'll have to work it out among you. I don't care how.

Incidentally, the problem pit is there because some groups like to sit face to face in formal surroundings. Sometimes it helps. Use it or not, as you like. You can solve problems anywhere in these chambers. Or outside, if you want to go outside. You can't leave through the elevator, of course, because that's locked now. Where you can go is into the rest of the cave system. But if you do that, it's entirely your own responsibility. These caves run for at least 80 miles and maybe more, right down under the sea. We're at least ten miles by the shortest route from the public ones where the tourists come. I doubt you could find your way there. They aren't lighted, and you can very easily get lost. And there are no, repeat no, communications facilities or food available there. Three people have got lost and died in the past year, although most people do manage to find their way back—or are found. But don't count on being found. No one will even start looking for you until we're all released, and then it can take a long time.

My personal advice—no, I'm sorry. I was going to say that my personal advice is to stay here with the rest of us, but it is, as I say, your decision to make, and if you want to go out you'll find two doors that are unlocked.

Now, there are two other resource people here. The rest of you are either draftees or volunteers. You all know which you are, and for any purposes I can think of it doesn't matter.

I'll introduce the two other pros. Jerry Fein is a doctor. Stand up, will you, Jerry? If any of you get into anything you can't handle, he'll help if he can.

And Marge Klapper over there is a physiotherapist. She's here to help, not to order you around, but—advice and personal opinion again, not a rule—I think you'll benefit from letting her help you. The rest of you can introduce yourselves when we get into our first session. Right now I'll turn you over to—what? Oh, thanks, Marge. Sorry.

The pool. It's available for any of you, any time, as many of you as want to use it. It's kept at 78 degrees, which is two degrees warmer than air temperature. It's a good place to have fun and get the knots out, but, again, you can use it for any purpose you like. Some groups have had active, formal problem-solving sessions in it, and that's all right too.

Now I think that's it, so I'll turn you over to Marge.

## Marge Interacting

Marge Klapper was 24 years old, pretty, married but separated, slightly pregnant but not by her husband, and a veteran of eight problem-group marathons.

She would have challenged every part of the description of her, except the first and the last, on the grounds that each item defined her in terms of her relationship to men. She did not even like to be called "pretty." She wasn't in any doubt that she was sexually attractive, of course. She simply didn't accept the presumption that it was only her physical appearance that made her so. The men she found sexually attractive came in all shapes and sizes, one because he was so butchy, one because of his sense of humor, one because he wrote poems that turned into bars of music at the end. She didn't much like being called a physiotherapist, either; it was her job classification, true, but she was going for her master's in Gestalt psychology and was of half a mind to become an M.D. Or else to have the baby that was just beginning to grow inside her; she had not yet reached a decision about that.

"Let's get the blood flowing," she said to all of them, standing up and throwing off her shorty terry-cloth robe. Under it she wore a swimsuit with a narrow bikini bottom and a halter top. She would have preferred to be nude, but her breasts were too full for unsupported calisthenics. She thought the way they flopped around was unaesthetic, and at times it could be actively painful. Also, some of the group were likely to be shy about nudity, she knew from experience. She liked to let them come to it at their own pace.

Getting them moving was the hard part. She had got to the pit early and chatted with some of them ahead of time, learning some of the names, picking out the ones who would work right away, identifying the difficult ones. One of the difficult ones was the little dark Italian man who was "in construction," he had said, whatever that meant; she had sat down next to him on purpose, and now she pulled him up next to her and said:

"All right. Let's start nice and slow and get some of the fug out of our heads. This is easy: we'll just reach."

She lifted her arms over her head, up on tiptoe, fingers upstretched. "High as you can go," she said. "Look up. Let's close our eyes and feel for the roof."

But what Marge was feeling for was the tension and needs of the group. She could almost taste, almost smell, their feelings. What Ben Ittri, next to her, was feeling was embarrassment and fear. The shaggy man who had come in late: a sort of numb pain, so much pain that it had drowned out his receptors. The fat girl, Dolores: anger. Marge could identify with that anger; it was man-directed anger.

She put the group through some simple bending energetics, or at least did with those who would cooperate. She had already taken a census of her mind. Not counting the three professionals, there were five in the group who were really with the kinetics. She supposed they were the volunteers, and probably they had had experience of previous sessions. The other eight, the ones she assumed were draftees, were a spectrum of all the colors of disengagement. The fat girl simply did not seem physically able to stand on tiptoes, though her anger carried her through most of the bending and turning; it was like a sack of cement bending, Marge thought, but she could sense the bones moving under the fat. The bent old black man who sat obstinately on the floor, regarding the creases on his trousers, was a different kind of problem; Marge had not been able to see how to deal with him.

She began moving around the room, calling out instructions. "Now bend sidewise from the waist. You can do it with your hands up like this, or you might be more comfortable with your hands on your hips. But see how far you can go. Left. Right. Left— "

They were actually responding rather well, considering. She stopped in front of a slight black youth in a one-piece Che Guevara overall. "It's fun if we do it together," she said, reaching out for his hands. He flinched away, then apologetically allowed her to take his hands and bend with him. "It's like a dance," she said, smiling, but feeling the tension in his arms and upper torso as he allowed himself unwillingly to turn with her. Marge was not used to that sort of response from males, except from homosexuals, or occasionally the very old ones who had been brought up under the Protestant ethic. He didn't seem to be either of those. "You know my name," she said softly. "It's Marge."

"Rufous," he said, looking away from her. He was acutely uncomfortable; reluctantly she let him go and moved on. She felt an old annoyance that these sessions would not allow her to probe really deeply into the hangups she uncovered, but of course that was not their basic purpose; she could only do that if the people themselves elected to work on that problem.

The other black man, the one who was so obdurately sitting on the floor, had not moved; Marge confronted him and said, "Will you get up and do something with me?"

For a moment she thought he was going to refuse. But then, with dignity, he stood up, took her hands and bent with her, bending left, bending right. He was as light as a leaf but strong, wire rather than straw. "Thank you," she said, and dropped his hands, pleased. "Now," she said to the group, "we're going to be together for quite a while, so let's get to know each other, please. Let's make a circle and put our arms around each other. Right up close! Close as you can get! All of us. Please?"

It was working out nicely, and Marge was very satisfied. Even the old black man was now in the circle, his arms looped around the shoulders of the fat girl on one side and a middle-aged man who looked like an Irish tenor on the other. The group was so responsive, at least compared to most groups in the first hour of their existence as groups, that for a moment Marge considered going right into the pool, or nonverbal communication—but no, she thought, that's imposing my will on them; I won't push it.

"All right, that's wonderful," she said. "Thank you all."

Tina said, "From here on, it's all up to you. All of you. There's tea and coffee and munch over there if anyone wants anything. Marge, thank you; that was fun."

"Anytime," called Marge, stretching her legs against the wall. "I mean that. If any of you ever want to work out with me, just say. Or if you see me doing anything and want to join in, please do."

"Now," said Tina, "if anybody wants to start introducing himself or talking about a problem, I, for one, would like to listen."

## Introductions

The hardest thing to learn to do was wait.

Tina Wattridge worked at doing it. She pushed a throw pillow over to the floor next to the corner of a couch and sat on it, cross-legged, her back against the couch. Tina's opinion of Marge Klapper was colored by the fact that she had a granddaughter only seven or eight years younger than Marge, which, Tina was aware, led her to think of the therapist as immature; nevertheless, there was something in the notion that the state of the body controlled the state of the mind, and Tina let her consciousness seep into her toes, the tendons on the soles of her feet, her ankles, her knees, all the way up her body, feeling what they felt and letting them relax. It was good in itself, and it kept her from saying anything. If she waited long enough, someone would speak . . .

"Well, does anybody mind if I go first?"

Tina recognized the voice, was surprised and looked up. It was Jerry Fein. It was not against the rules for one of the pros to start, because there were no rules, exactly. But it was unusual. Tina looked at him doubtfully. She had never worked with him before. He was the plumpish kind of young man who looks older than he is; he looked about forty, and for some reason Tina was aware that she didn't like him.

"The thing is," said Dr. Fein, haunching himself backward on the floor so that he could see everyone in the group at once, "I do have a problem. It's a two-part problem. The first part isn't really a problem, except in personal terms, for me. I got a dose from a dear friend two months ago." He shrugged comically. "Like shoemaker's children that never have shoes, you know? I think we doctors get the idea somewhere in med school that when we get into practice we'll be exempt from diseases, they're only things that happen to patients. Well, anyway, it turned out to be syphilis, and so I had to get the shots and all. It's not too bad a thing, you know, but it isn't a lot of fun because there are these resistant strains of spirochetes around, and I had one of the toughest of them, Mary Bet 13 it's called—so it didn't clear up overnight. But it is cleared up," he added reassuringly. "I mention this in case any of you should be worrying. I mean about maybe using the same drinking glass or something.

"But the part of the problem I want to throw in front of you is, why should anybody get syphilis in the first place? I mean, if there are any diseases in the world we could wipe out in thirty days from a standing start, syphilis and gonorrhea are the ones. But we don't. And I've been thinking about it. The trouble is people won't report themselves. They won't report their contacts even more positively. And they never, *never* think of getting an examination until they're already pretty sure they've got a dose. So if any of you can help me with this public health problem that's on my mind, I'd like to hear."

It was like talking into a tape recorder in an empty room; the group soaked up the words, but nothing changed in their faces or attitudes. Tina closed her eyes, half hoping that someone would respond to the doctor, half that someone else would say something. But the silence grew. After a moment the doctor got up and poured himself a cup of coffee, and when he sat down again his face was as blank as the others.

The man next to Tina stirred and looked around. He was young and extremely good-looking, with the fair hair and sharp-featured face of a Higher Youth. His name was Stanwyck. Tina had negative feelings toward him, too, for some reason she could not identify; one of the things she didn't like about Jerry Fein was his sloppiness—he was wearing two shirts, one over the other, like a Sicilian peasant. One of the things she didn't like about Stanwyck was his excessive neatness; like the old black man, Bob Sanger, he was wearing a pressed business suit.

But Stanwyck didn't speak.

The fat girl got up, fixed herself a cup of tea with sugar and milk, took a handful of raisins out of a bowl and went back to her place on the floor.

"I think I might as well talk," said somebody at last. (Tina exhaled, which made her realize she had been holding her breath.)

It was the elderly black man, Sanger. He was sitting, hugging his knees to himself, and he stayed that way all the time he was talking. He did not look up but addressed his words to his knees, but his voice was controlled and carrying. "I am a volunteer for this group," he said, "and I think you should know that I asked to join because I am desperate. I am seventy-one years old. For more than forty years I have been the owner and manager of a dental-supply manufacturing company, Sanger Hygiene Products, of Fresno, California. I do not have any response to make to what was said by the gentleman before me, nor am I very sympathetic to him. I am satisfied that God's Word is clear on the wages of sin. Those who transgress against His commandments must expect the consequences, and I have no desire to make their foulness less painful for them. But mine is, in a sense, also a public health problem; so perhaps it is not inappropriate for me to propose it to you now."

"Name?" Tina murmured.

He did not look up at her, but he said, "Yes, Mrs. Wattridge, of course. My name is Bob Sanger. My problem is that halidated sugar and tooth-bud transplants have effectively depleted the market for my products. As you all may be aware, there simply is not a great demand for dental therapy any more. What work is done is preventive and does not require the bridges and caps and plates we make in any great volume. So we are in difficulties such that, at the present projection, my company will have crossed the illiquidity level in at most twelve months, more likely as little as four; and my problem is to avoid bankruptcy."

He rubbed his nose reflectively against one knife-creased knee and added, "More than three hundred people will be out of work if I close the plant. If you would not care to help me for my sake, perhaps you will for theirs."

"Oh, Bob, cut the crap," cried the fat girl, getting up for more raisins. "You don't have to blackmail us!"

He did not look at her or respond in any way. She stood by the coffee table with a handful of raisins for a moment, looking around, and then grinned and said:

"You know, I have the feeling I just volunteered to go next."

She waited for someone to contradict her, or even to agree with her. No one did, but after a moment she went on. "Well why not? My name is Dolores Belli. That's bell-*eye*, not bell-*ee*. I've already heard all the jokes and they're not too funny; I know I'm fat, so what else is new? I'm not sensitive about it," she explained. "But I *am* kind of tired of the subject. Okay. Now about problems. I'll help any way I can, and I do want to think about what both of you have said, Jerry and Bob. Nothing occurs to me right now, but I'll see if I can make something occur, and then I'll be back. I don't have any particular problem of my own to offer, I'm afraid. In fact, I wouldn't be here if I hadn't been drafted. Or truthfully," she said, smiling, "I do have a problem. I missed dinner. I'd like to see what the food is like here. Is that all right?"

When no one volunteered an answer, she said sharply, "Tina? Is it all right?"

"It's up to you, Dolores," said Tina gently.

"Sure it is. Well, let's get our feet wet. Anybody want to join me?"

A couple of the others got up, and then a third, all looking somewhat belligerent about it. They paused at the door, and one of them, a man with long hair and a Zapata mustache, said, "I'll be back, but I really am starving. My name is David Jaretski. I do have a problem on my mind. It's personal. I don't seem to be able to keep my marriage together, although maybe that's because I don't seem to be able to keep my life together. I'll talk about it later." He thought of adding something else but decided against it; he was still feeling a little stoned and not yet ready either to hear someone else's troubles or trust the group with his own.

The man next to him was good-looking in the solid, self-assured way of a middle-aged Irish tenor. He said, in a comfortable, carrying voice, "I'm Bill Murtagh. I ran for Congress last year and got my tail whipped, and I guess that's what I'll be hoping to talk to you folks about later on."

He did not seem disposed to add to that, and so the other woman who had stood up spoke. Her blond schoolgirl hair did not match the coffee-and-cream color of her skin or the splayed shape of her nose, but she was strikingly attractive in a short jacket and flared pants. "My name's Barbara Devereux," she said. "I'm a draftee. I haven't figured out a problem yet." She started to leave with the others, then turned back. "I don't like this whole deal much," she said thoughtfully. "I'm not sure I'm coming back. I might prefer going into the caves."

## The Cast of Characters

In Terre Haute, Indiana, at the Headquarters of SAD, the Social Affairs Department, in the building called the Heptagon, Group 95–114 had been put together with the usual care. The total number was 16, of whom three were professional resource people, five were volunteers and the remainder selectees. Nine were male, seven female. The youngest had just turned 18; the oldest 71. Their homes were in eight of the 54 states; and they represented a permissible balance of religions, national origins, educational backgrounds and declared political affiliations.

These were the people who made up the 114th group of the year:

BELLI, Dolores. 19. White female, unmarried. Volunteer (who regretted it and pretended she had been drafted; the only one who knew this was untrue was Tina Wattridge, but actually none of the others really cared). As a small child her father had called her Dolly-Belly because she was so cutely plump. She wanted very much to be loved. The men who appealed to her were all-American jocks, and none of them had ever shown the slightest interest in her.

DEL LA GARZA, Caspar. 51. White male. Widower, no surviving children. Draftee. In Harlingen, Texas, where he had lived most of his life, he was assistant manager of an A&P supermarket, a volunteer fireman and a member of the Methodist Church. He had few close friends, but everyone liked him.

DEVEREUX, Barbara. 31. Black female, unmarried. Draftee. Although she had been trained as an architect and had for a time been employed as a fashion artist, she was currently working for a life insurance agent in Elgin, Illinois, processing premiums. With any luck she would have had seven years of marriage and at least one child by now, but the man she loved had been killed serving with the National Guard during the pollution riots of the '80s.

FEIN, Gerald, M.D. 38. White male. Professional resource person, now in his third problem marathon. Jerry Fein was either separated or partially married, depending on how you looked at it; he and his wife had opted for an open marriage, but for more than a year they had not actually lived in the same house. Still, they had never discussed any formal change in the relationship. His wife, Aline, was also a doctor—they had met in medical school—and he often spoke complimentarily of her success, which was much more rapid and impressive than his own.

GALIFINIAKIS, Rose. 44. White female, married, no children. She had been into the Christ Reborn movement in her twenties, New Maoism in her thirties and excursions into commune living, Scientology and transcendental meditation since then, through all of which she had maintained a decorous home and conventional social life for her husband, who was an accountant in the income tax department of the state of New Mexico. She had volunteered for the problem marathon in the hope that it would be something productive and exciting to do.

ITTRI, Benjamin. 32. White male. Draftee. Ittri was a carpenter, but so was Jesus of Nazareth. He thought about that a lot on the job.

JARETSKI, David. 33. White male, listed as married but de facto wifeless, since Lara had run off with a man who traveled in information for the government. Draftee. David was a sculptor, computer programmer and former acid head.

JEFFERSON, Rufous, III. 18. Black male, unmarried. Draftee. Rufous was studying for the priesthood in the Catholic Church in an old-rite seminary which retained the vows of celibacy and poverty and conducted its masses in Latin.

KLAPPER, Marjorie, B.A., Mem. Am. Guild Ther. 24. White female, separated. Professional resource person. Five weeks earlier, sailing after dark with a man she did not know well but really liked, Marge Klapper had decided not to bother with anything and see if she happened to get pregnant. She had, and was now faced with the problem of deciding what to do about it, including what to say to her husband, who thought they had agreed to avoid any relationship with anybody, including each other, until they worked things out.

LIM, Felice. 30. White female, married, one child. Technically a draftee, but she had waived exemption (on grounds of dependent child at home—her husband had vacation time coming and had offered to take care of the baby). Felice Lim had quite a nice natural soprano voice and had wanted to be an opera singer, but either she had a bad voice teacher or the voice simply would not develop. It was sweet and true, but she could not fill a hall, and so she got married.

MENCHEK, Philip. 48. White male, married, no children. Draftee. Menchek was an associate professor of English Literature in a girl's college in South Carolina and rather liked the idea of the problem marathon. If he hadn't been drafted, he might have volunteered, but this way there was less chance of a disagreement with his wife.

MURTAGH, William. 45. White male, married (third time), five children (aggregate of all marriages). Volunteer. Murtagh, when a young college dropout who called himself Wee Willie Wu, had been a section leader in the Marin County Cultural Revolution. It was the best time of his life. His original True Maoists had occupied a nine-bedroom mansion on the top of a mountain in Belvedere, overlooking the Bay, with a private swimming pool they used for struggling with political opponents and a squash court for mass meetings. But they were only able to stay on Golden Gate Avenue for a month. Then they were defeated and disbanded as counterrevolutionaries by the successful East Is Red Cooperative Mao Philosophical Commune, who had helicopters and armored cars. Expelled and homeless, Murtagh had dropped out of the revolutionary movement and back into school, got his degree at San Jose State and became an attorney.

SANGER, Robert, B.Sc., M.A. 71. Black male. Wife deceased, one child (male, also deceased), two grandchildren. Volunteer. Bob Sanger's father, a successful orthodontic dentist in Parsippany, New Jersey, celebrated his son's birth, which happened to occur on the day Calvin Coolidge was elected to his own full term as President, by buying a bottle of bootleg champagne. It was a cold day for November, and Dr. Sanger slipped on the ice. He dropped the bottle. It shattered. A week later the family learned that everyone drinking champagne out of that batch had gone blind, since it had been cooked up out of wood alcohol, ethylene glycol, Seven-Up and grape squeezings. They nicknamed the baby "Lucky Bob". to celebrate. Lucky Bob was, in fact, lucky. He got his master's degree just when the civil rights boom in opportunities for black executives was at its peak. He had accumulated seed capital just when President Nixon's Black Capitalism program was spewing out huge hunks of investment cash. He was used to being lucky, and the death of his industry, coming at the end of his own long life, threw him more than it might have otherwise.

STANWYCK, Devon. 26. White male, unmarried. Volunteer. Stanwyck was the third generation to manage the family real estate agency, a member of three country clubs and a leading social figure in Bucks County, Pennsylvania. When he met Ben Ittri, he said, "I didn't know carpenters would be at this marathon." His grandfather had brought his father up convinced that he could never do anything well enough to earn the old man's respect; and the father, skills sharpened by thirty years of pain, did the same to his son.

TEITLEBAUM, Khanya. 32. White female, divorced, no children. Draftee. Khanya Teitlebaum was a loving big Male-mute of a woman, six feet four inches tall and stronger than any man she had ever known. She was an assistant personnel manager for a General Motors auto-assembly plant in an industrial park near Baton Rouge, Louisiana, where she kept putting cards through the sorter, looking for a man who was six feet or more and unmarried.

WATTRIDGE, Albertina. 62. White female, married, one child, one grandchild. Professional resource person. A curious thing about Tina, who had achieved a career of more than thirty years as a group therapist and psychiatric counselor for undergraduates at several universities before joining the SAD problem-marathon staff, was that she had been 28 years old and married for almost four before she realized that every human being had a navel. Somehow, the subject had never come up in conversation, and she had always been shy of physical exposure. At first she had thought her belly button a unique and personal physical disfigurement. After marriage she had regarded it as a wondrous and fearful coincidence that her husband bore the same blemish. It was not until her daughter was born that she discovered what it was for.

## David Again

It was weird never knowing what time it was. It didn't take long to lose all connection with night and day; I think it happened almost when I got off the elevator. Although that may have been because of the morning glory seeds.

It was sort of like a six-day bash, you know, between exams and when you get your grades, when no one bothers to go to classes but no one can afford to leave for home yet. I would be in the pool with the girls, maybe. We'd get out, and get something to eat, and talk for a while, and then Barbie would yawn, and look at the bare place on her wrist the way she did, and say, "Well, how about if we get a little sleep?" So we'd go into one of the sleeping rooms and straighten out our bags and get in. And just about then somebody else would sit up and stretch and yawn, and poke the person next to him. And they'd get up. And a couple of others would get up. And pretty soon you'd smell bacon and eggs coming down the dumbwaiter, and then they'd all be jumping and turning with Marge Klapper just as you were dropping off.

Barbie and Dolly-Belly and I stayed tight with each other for a long time. We hadn't picked each other out, it just happened that way. I felt very self-conscious that first night in the common room, still flying a little and expecting everybody could see what I was doing. It wasn't that they were so sexually alluring to me. There were other women in the group who, actually, were more my type, a girl from New Mexico who had that long-haired, folk-singer look, a lot like Lara. Even Tina. I couldn't figure her age very well. She might easily have been fifty or more. But she had a gorgeous teenage kind of figure and marvelous skin. But I wasn't motivated to go after them, and they didn't show any special interest in me.

Barbie was really very good-looking, but I'd never made it with a black girl. Some kind of leftover race prejudice, which may come from being born in Minnesota among all those fair-haired WASPs, I suppose. Whatever it was, I didn't think of her that way right at first, and then after that there were the three of us together almost every minute. We kept our sleeping bags in the same corner, but we each stayed in our own.

And Dolly-Belly herself could have been quite pretty, in a way, if all that fat didn't turn you off. She easily weighed two hundred pounds. There was a funny thing about that. I had inside my head an unpleasant feeling about both fat women and black women, that they would smell different in a repulsive way. Well, it wasn't true. We could smell each other very well almost all the time, not only because our sleeping bags were so close together but holding each other, or doing non-verbal things, or just sitting back to back, me in the middle and one of the girls propped on each side of me, in group, and all I ever smelled from either of them was Tigress from Barbie and Aphrodisia from Dolly-Belly. And yet in my head I still had that feeling.

There was no time, and there was no place outside the group. Just the sixteen of us experiencing each other and ourselves. Every once in a while somebody would say something about the outside world. Willie Murtagh would wonder out loud what the Rams had done. Or Dev Stanwyck would come by with Tina and say, "What do you think about building underground condominium homes in abandoned strip mines, and then covering them over with landscaping?" We didn't see television; we didn't know if it was raining or hot or the world had come to an end. We hadn't heard if the manned Grand Tour fly-by had anything to say about the rings of Saturn, which it was about due to be approaching, or whether Donnie Osmond had announced his candidacy for the presidency. We, or at least the three of us, were living in and with each other, and about anything else we just didn't want to know.

Fortunately for the group, most of the others were more responsible than we were. Tina and Dev would almost always be in the problem pit, hashing over everybody's problems all the time. So would Bob Sanger, sitting by himself in one of the top rows, silent unless somebody spoke to him directly, or to his problem, or rarely when he had a constructive and well-thought-out comment to offer. So would Jerry Fein and that big hairy bird, Khanya. Almost everybody would be working hard a lot of the time, except for Willie Murtagh, who did God knows what by himself but was almost never in sight after the three of us decided we didn't like him much, that first night, and the young black kid, Rufous, who spent a lot of his time in what looked like meditation but I later found out was prayer. And the three of us.

I don't mean we copped out entirely. Sometimes we would look in on them. Almost any hour there would be four or five of them in the big pit, with the chairs arranged in concentric circles facing in so that no matter where you sat you were practically looking right in the face of everyone else. We even took part. Now and then we did. Sometimes we'd even offer problems. Barbie got the idea of making them up, like, "I'm worried," she said once, "that the Moon will fall on us. Could we build some kind of a big net and hang it between mountains, like?" That didn't go over a bit. Then Dolly tried a sort of complicated joke about how the CIA should react if Amazonia intervened in the Ecuadorian elections, with the USIS parachuting disc jockeys into the Brazilian bulge to drive them crazy with concentrated-rock music. I didn't like that a bit; the USIS part made me think of

Lara's boy friend, which made me remember to hurt. I didn't want to hurt.

I guess that's why we all three of us stayed with made-up problems, and other people's problems: because we didn't want to hurt. But I didn't think of that at the time.

"Of course," Dolly-Belly said one time, when she and I were rocking Barbie in the pool, "we're not going to get out of here until Joe Good up there in the Heptagon marks our papers and says we pass."

I concentrated on sliding Barbie headward, slowing her down, sliding her back. The long blond hair streamed out behind her when she was going one way, wrapped itself around her face when she was going the other. She looked beautiful in the soft pool light, although it was clear, if it had needed to be clear, that she was a natural blond. "So?" I said.

Barbie caught the change in rhythm or something, opened her eyes, lifted one ear out of the water to hear what we were saying.

"So what's the smart thing for us to do, my David? Get down to work and get out faster? Or go on the way we're going?"

Barbie wriggled off our hands and stood up. "Why are we worrying? They'll let the whole group go at the same time anyway," she said.

Dolly-Belly said sadly, "You know, I think that's what's worrying me. I kind of like it here. Hey! Now you two swing me!"

## Preliminary Reports

The one part of the job that Tina didn't like was filing interim reports with the control monitors up at the old radio-telescope computation center. It seemed to her sneaky. The whole thing about the group was that it built up trust within itself, and the trust made it possible for the people to speak without penalty. And every time Tina found the computer terminals unoccupied and dashed in to file a report she was violating that trust.

However, rules were rules. Still dripping from the pool, where nearly all the group were passing each other hand to hand down a chain, she sat before the console, pulled the hood over her fingers, set the machine for blind-typing and began to type. Nothing appeared on the paper before her, but the impulses went out to the above-ground monitors. Of course, with no one else nearby that much secrecy was not really essential, but Tina had trained herself to be a methodical person. She checked her watch, pinned inside her bra—another deceit—and logged in:

Day 4, hour 0352. WATTRIDGE reporting. INTERACTION good, CONSENSUALITY satisfactory. No incapacitating illnesses or defections.

Seven individuals have stated problem areas of general interest, as follows:

DE LA GARZA. Early detection of home fires. Based on experience as a volunteer fireman (eight years), he believes damage could be reduced "anyway half" if the average time of reporting could be made ten minutes earlier. GROUP proposed training in fire detection and diagnosis for householders.

(That had been only a few hours before, when most of the group were lying around after a session with Marge's energetics. The little man had really come to life then. "See, most people, they think a fire is what happens to somebody else; so when they smell smoke, or the lights go out because wires have melted and a fuse blows, or whatever, they spend 20 minutes looking for cigarettes burning in the ashtrays, or putting new fuses in. And then half the time they run down to the kitchen and get a pan of water and try to put it out themselves. So by the time we get there it's got a good start, and there's three, four thousand dollars just in water damage getting it out, even if we can save the house.")

FEIN. National or world campaign to wipe out VD. States that failure to report disease and contacts is only barrier to complete control of syphilis and gonorrhea. GROUP proposal for free examinations every month, medallion in the form of bracelet or necklace charm to be issued to all persons disease-free or accepting treatment.

(That one had started as a joke. That big girl, Khanya, said, "What you really need is a sort of kosher stamp that everybody has to wear." And then the group had got interested, and the idea of issuing medallions had come out of it.)

LIM. Part-time professional assistance for amateur theater and music groups. States that there are many talented musicians who cannot compete for major engagements but would be useful as backup for school, community or other music productions. Could be financed by government salaries repaid from share of admissions.

MURTAGH. Failure of electorate to respond to real issues in voting. Statement of problem as yet unclear; no GROUP proposals have emerged.

SANGER. Loss of market for dental supplies. GROUP currently considering solutions.

STANWYCK. Better utilization of prime real estate by combining function. GROUP has proposed siting new homes underground, and/or building development home with flat joined roofs with landscaping on top. Interaction continuing.

(Tina wanted to go on with Dev Stanwyck's problem, because she was becoming aware that she cared a great deal about solving problems for him, but her discipline was too good to let her impose her personal feelings in the report. And anyway, Tina did not believe that the problem Dev stated was anywhere near the real problems he felt.)

TEITLEBAUM. Stated problem as unsatisfactory existing solitaire games. (Note: There is a personality problem here presumably due to unsatisfactory relationships with other sex). GROUP proposed telephone links to computer chess-checker, or card-playing programs, perhaps to be furnished as a commercial service of phone company.

PERSONALITY PROBLEMS exhibited by nine group members, mostly marital, career or parental conflicts. Some resolution apparent.

TRANSMISSION ENDS.

No one had disturbed Tina, and she pushed the hood away from the keyboard and clicked off the machine without rising. She sat there for a moment, staring at the wall. The group was making real progress in solving problems, but it seemed to her strange that it also appeared to have generated one in herself. All therapists had blind spots about their own behaviour. But even a blind person could see that Tina Wattridge was working herself in pretty deep with a boy not much too old to be her grandchild, Devon Stanwyck.

## *David Cathecting the Leader*

One time when we were just getting ready to go to sleep, we went into the room we liked—not that there was much difference between them, but this one they had left the walls pretty natural, and there were nice, transparent, waterfally rock formations that looked good with the lights low—and Tina and Dev Stanwyck were sitting by themselves in a corner. It seemed as though Dev was crying. We didn't pay much attention, because a lot of people cried, now and then, and after a while they went out without saying anything, and we got to sleep. And then, later on, Barbie and I were eating some of the frozen steaks and sort of kidding Dolly-Belly about her fruit and salads, and we heard a noise in the shower, and I went in, and there were Tina and Dev again. Only this time it looked as though Tina was crying. When I came back I told the girls about it. It struck me as odd; Tina letting Devon cry was one thing, Devon holding Tina while she was crying was another.

"I think they're in love," said Dolly-Belly.

"She's twice as old as he is," I said.

"More than that, for God's sake. She's pushing sixty."

"And what has that got to do with it, you two Nosy Parkers? How does it hurt you?"

"Peace, Barbie," I said. "I only think it's trouble. You'd have to be blind not to see she's working herself in pretty deep."

"You've got something against being in love?" Barbie demanded, her brown eyes looking very black.

I got up and threw the rest of my "light meal, steak" away. I wasn't hungry any more. I said, "I just don't want them to get hurt."

After a while Dolly said, "David. Why do you assume being in love is the same as being hurt?"

"Oh, cut it out, Dolly-Belly! She's too old for him, that's all."

Barbie said, "Who wants to go in the pool?"

We had just come out of the pool.

Dolly said, "David, dear. What kind of a person was your wife?"

I sat down and said, "Has one of you got a cigarette?" Barbie did, and gave it to me. "Well," I said, "she looked kind of like Felice. A little younger. Blue eyes. We were married six years, and then she just didn't want to live with me any more."

I wasn't really listening to what I was saying, I was listening to myself, inside. Trying to diagnose what I was feeling. But I was having trouble. See, for a couple of weeks I'd always known what I felt about Lara, because I hurt. It was almost like an ache, as though somebody were squeezing me around the chest. It was a kind of wriggly feeling in my testicles, as though they were gathering themselves up out of harm's way, getting ready for a fight. It was as if I was five years old and somebody had stolen my tricycle. All of those things. And the thing was that I could feel them all, every one, but I suddenly realized I hadn't *been* feeling them. I had forgotten to hurt at all, a lot of the time.

I had not expected that would happen.

Along about that time, I do not know if there was a casual relationship, I became aware of the fact that I was feeling pretty chipper pretty much of the time, and I began to like it. Only sometimes when I was trying to get to sleep, or when I happened to think about going back to Minnesota and remembered there was nobody there to go back to, I hurt. But I could handle it because I knew it would go away again. The cure for Lara was Barbie and Dolly-Belly, even though I had not even kissed either of them, except in a friendly good-night way.

Time wore on, we could only tell how much by guessing from things like the fact that we all ran out of cigarettes. Dolly's were the last to go. She shared with us, and then she complained that Barbie was smoking them twice as fast as she was, and I was hitting them harder than that; she'd smoke two or three cigarettes, and I'd have finished the pack. It was our mixed-up time sense, maybe? Then Rufous came and shared a meal with us once and heard us talking about it, and later he took me aside and offered to trade me a carton for a couple of bananas. I grabbed the offer, ordered bananas, picked them off the dumbwaiter, handed them to Rufous, took the cigarettes and was smoking one before it occurred to me that he could have ordered bananas for himself if he'd wanted them. Barbie said he knew that, he just wanted to give me something, but he didn't want me to feel obligated.

We were all running out of everything we'd brought in with us. There wasn't any dope. Dolly-Belly had brought in some grass, and I guess some of the others had too, but it was gone. Dolly smoked hers up all by herself the first night, or anyway the first time between when we decided we were sleepy and when we got to sleep finally, before we were really close enough to share.

We were all running out, except Willie the Weeper. He had

cigarettes. I saw them. But he didn't smoke them. He also had a pocket flask that he kept nipping out of. And he kept ordering fruit off the dumbwaiter, which surprised me when I thought about it because I didn't see him eating any. "He's making cave drippings somewhere," Dolly told me.

"What's cave drippings?"

"It's like when you make homemade wine. Only you drink it as soon as it ferments. Any kind of fruit will do, they say."

"How do you know so much about it if you've never been here before?"

"Oh, screw you, David, are you calling me a liar?"

"No. Honestly not, Dolly-Belly. Get back to cave drippings."

"Well. It's kind of the stuff you made when you're in the Peace Corps in the jungle and you've run out of beer and hash. I bet you a thousand dollars Willie's got some stewing away somewhere. Only I don't smell it." And she splashed out of the pool and went sniffing around the connecting caves, still bare. There was a lot of Dolly-Belly to be bare, and quite a few of the people didn't care much for group nudity even then. But she didn't care.

Out of all the people in our group, 16 of us altogether, Willie was about the only one I didn't really care for. I mean, I didn't like him. He was one of those guys my father used to bring home for dinner when I was little. So very tolerant of kids, so very sure we'd change. So very different in what they did from the face they showed the world. Willie was always bragging about his revolutionary youth and his commitment to Goodness and Truth, one of those fake nine-percenters that, if you could see his income tax form, wasn't pledging a penny behind what he had to give. Even when he came in with us that first night and as much as asked us for help, you couldn't believe him. He wasn't asking what he did wrong, he was asking why the voters in his district were such perverse fools that they voted for his opponent.

Some of the others were strange, in their ways. But we got along. Little Rufous stayed to himself, praying mostly. That big broad Khanya would drive you crazy with how she had poltergeists in her house if you'd let her. Dev Stanwyck was a grade-A snob, but he was tight with Tina most of the time, and he couldn't have been all lousy, because she was all right. I guess the hardest to get along with was the old black millionaire, or ex-millionaire, or maybe-about-to-be-ex-millionaire, Bob Sanger. He didn't seem to like any part of us or the marathon. But he was always polite, and I never saw anybody ask him for anything that he didn't try to give. And so everybody tried to help him.

## Some Solutions for Sanger

After several days, only Tina knew exactly how many, the group found itself united in a desire to deal with the problems of Bob Sanger, and so a marathon brainstorming took place in the problem pit. Every chair was occupied at one time or another. Some 61 proposals were written down by Rose Galifiniakis, who appointed herself recorder because she had a pencil.

The principal solutions proposed were the following:

1. Reconvert to the manufacture of medical and surgical equipment, specifically noble-metal joints for prostheses, spare parts for cyborgs, surgical instruments "of very high quality" and "self-warming jiggers that they stick in you when you have your Papp test, that are always so goddamn cold you scream and jump right out of the stirrups."

2. Take all the money out of the company treasury and spend it on advertising to get kids crazy about cotton candy.

3. Hire a promoter and start a national fad for the hobby of collecting false teeth, bridges, etc., "which you can then sell by mail and save all the dealers' commissions."

4. Reconvert to making microminiaturized parts for guided missiles "in case somebody invents a penetration device to get through everybody's antimissile screens."

5. Hire a lobbyist and get the government to stockpile dental supplies in case there is another Cultural Revolution with riots and consequently lots of broken teeth.

6. Start a saturation advertising campaign pitched to the sado-maso trade about "getting sexual jollies out of home dentistry."

7. Start a fashion for wearing different-colored teeth to match dresses for formal wear. "You could make caps, sort of, out of that plastic kind of stuff you used to make the pink parts of sets of false choppers out of."

8. Move the factory to the Greater Los Angeles area in order to qualify for government loans, subsidies, and tax exemptions under the Aid to Impoverished Areas bill.

9. Get into veterinarian dentistry, particularly for free clinics for the millions of cats roaming the streets of depopulated cities "that some old lady might leave you a million dollars to take care of."

10. Revive the code duello, with fistfights instead of swords.

There were 51 others that were unanimously adjudged too dumb to be worth even writing down, and Rose obediently crossed them out. Bob Sanger did not say that. He listened patiently and aloofly to all of them, even the most stupid of them. The only effect he showed as the marathon wore on was that he went on looking thinner and blacker and smaller all the time.

Of the ten which survived the initial rounds, Numbers 2, 3, 6, 7, and 10 were ruled out for lack of time to develop their impact. Bob thanked the group for them, but pointed out that advertising campaigns took time, maybe years, and he had only weeks. "Especially when they involve basic changes in folkways," agreed Willie Murtagh. "Anyway, seriously. Those are pretty crazy to begin with. You need something real and tangible and immediate, like the idea I threw into the hopper about the Aid to Impoverished Areas funding."

"I do appreciate your helpfulness," said Bob. "It is a matter of capital and, again, time. I have not the funds to relocate the entire plant."

"Surely a government loan— "

"Oh, drop it, Willie," said Marge Klapper. "Time, remember? How fast are you going to get SAD to move? No, Bob, I understand what you're saying. What about the idea of the cats? I was in Newark once and there were like thousands of them."

"I regret to inform you that many of my competitors have anticipated you in this, at least insofar as the emphasis of veterinary dentistry in concerned," said Bob politely. "As to the notion of getting some wealthy person to establish a foundation, I know of no such person. Also the matter of stockpiling supplies has been anticipated. It is this that has kept us going since '92."

Rufous Jefferson looked up from his worry beads long enough to say, "I don't like that idea of making missiles, Mr. Sanger."

"It wouldn't work," said Willie the Weeper positively. "I know. You couldn't switch over *and* get the government back in the missile business in time anyway."

"Besides," said Dolly-Belly, "everybody's got plenty of missiles put away already. No, forget it, fellows, we've bombed out except for one thing. It's your only chance, Bob. You've got to go for that surgical stuff. *And* that self-warming jigger. You don't know, Bob, you're not a woman, but I swear to God every time I go to my gynaecologist I leap right up the wall when he touches me with that thing. Brrr!"

"Dumb," said Tina affectionately. "Dolores, dear, I bet you go to a man gynaecologist."

"Well, sure," said Dolly defensively. "It's kind of a sex thing with me, I don't like to have women messing me around there."

"All right, but if you went to a woman doctor she'd know what it feels like. How could a man know? *He never* gets that kind of an examination."

Bob Sanger uncrossed his legs and recrossed them the other way. "Excuse me," he said with a certain amount of pain in his voice. "I am afraid I'm not quite following what you are saying."

Tina said with tact, "It's for vaginal examination, Bob. In order to make a proper examination they use a dilator, which is kept sterile, of course, so it has to be metal. And it's cold. *My* doctor keeps the sterile dilators in a little jar next to an electric light so they're warm . . . but she's a woman. She knows what it feels like. Long ago, when I was pregnant, I went to a male obstetrician, and it's just like they say, Bob. You jump. You really do. A self-warming dilator would make a million dollars."

Sanger averted his eyes. His face seemed darker than usual; perhaps he was blushing. "It is an interesting idea," he said, and then added reluctantly, "but I'm afraid there are some difficulties. I can't quite see a place for it in our product line. Self-warming, you say? That would make them quite expensive, and perhaps hard to sterilize, as well. Let me think. I can envision perhaps marketing some sort of little cup containing a sterile solution maintained at body temperature by a thermostat. But would doctors buy it? Assuming we were able to persuade them of the importance of it—and I accept your word, ladies," he added hastily. "Even so. Why wouldn't a doctor just keep them by an electric light, as Tina's does?"

"Come on, Bob. Don't you have a research department?" Willie demanded.

"I do, yes. What I don't have is time. Still it could have been a useful addition to our line, under other circumstances, I am sure," Bob said politely, once again addressing the crease in his trousers.

Then nobody said anything for a while until Tina took a deep breath, let go of Dev Stanwyck's hand and stood up. "Sorry, Bob," she said gently. "We'll try more later. Now how about the pool?"

And the group dispersed, some yelling and stripping off their clothes, and slapping and laughing as they headed for the pool chamber, one or two to eat, Bob Sanger remaining behind, tossing a dumbbell from hand to hand and looking angrily at his kneecap, left alone.

## David Cathecting the Group

They keep the pool at blood temperature, just like one of Tina's thingamabobs. As, in spite of everything, the walls stay cold—I suppose because of the cold miles and miles of rock behind them—it stays all steamy and dewy in there. And the walls are unfinished, pretty much the way God left them when he poked the caves out of the Puerto Rican rock. Some places they look like dirty green mud, like the bottom of a creek. Some places they look like diamonds. There is one place that is like a frozen waterfall, and one like icicles melting off the roof; and when they built the pool and lighted it, they put colored lights behind the rocks in some places, and you can switch them to go on and off at random. We liked that a lot. We went racing in, and Dolly-Belly pushed me in right on top of Barbie and went to turn on the lights, and then she came leaping like a landslide into the pool almost on top of both of us. Half the water in the pool came surging out, it looked like. But it all drains right back and gets churned around some way to kill the bugs and fungi, and so we jumped and splashed most of it out again and yelled and dived and then settled down to just holding each other, half drowsing, until the pool got too crowded and we felt ourselves being pushed into a corner and decided to get out.

We put some clothes on and sort of stood in the corridor, between the pool and the showers, trying to make up our minds what to do.

"Want to get some sleep?" Barbie asked, but not very urgently. Neither of us said yes.

"How about eating something?" I offered.

Dolly-Belly said politely, "No thanks. I'm not hungry now." I found one of Rufous the Third's cigarettes and we passed it around, trying to keep it dry although the girls' hair kept dripping on it, and then we noticed that we were in front of the door that opens into the empty caves. And we realized we had all been looking at it, and then at each other, and then at the door again.

So Dolly tried the knob, and it turned. I pushed on the door, and it opened. And Barbie stepped through, and we followed.

It closed behind us.

We were alone in the solid dark and cold of the caves. A little line of light ran around three sides of the door we had just come through; and if we listened closely, we could hear, very faintly, an occasional word or sound from the people behind it. That was all. Outside of that, nothing.

Barbie took one of my hands. I reached out and took Dolly's with the other.

We stood silently for a moment, waiting to see if our eyes would become dark-adapted, but it was no use. The darkness was too complete. Dolly-Belly was twisting around at the end of our extended arms' length, and after a moment she said, "I can feel along a wall here. There's a kind of a rope. Watch where you step."

Someone had put duckboards down sometime. Although we couldn't see a thing, we could feel what we were doing. I had socks on; the girls were barefoot. Since I had one hand in the hand of each of them, I couldn't guide myself by the rope or the wall, as Barbie and Dolly could, but we went very slowly.

We had done a sensitivity thing a while earlier, two sleeps and about 11 meals earlier, I think, blindfolding each of us in turn and letting ourselves be led around to smell and hear and feel things. It was like that. In the same way, none of us wanted to talk. We were extending our other senses, listening, and feeling, and smelling.

Then Dolly-Belly stopped and said, "End of the rope." She disengaged her fingers and bent down. Barbie came up beside me, and I slipped my hand free of hers and around her waist.

Dolly said, "I think there are some steps going down. Be careful, hear? It's scary."

I let go of Barbie, passed myself in front of Dolly, felt with my toes, knelt down and explored with my fingertips. It was queasy, all right. I felt as though I were falling over forward, not being able to see where I might be falling. There were wooden steps there, all right. But how far down they went and what was at the end of them and how long they had been rotting away there and what shape they were in, I could not tell.

So we juggled ourselves around cautiously and sat on the top step, which was just wide enough for the three of us, even Dolly-Belly. We listened to the silence and looked at the emptiness, until Barbie said suddenly:

"I hear something."

And Dolly said, "I smell something. What do you hear?"

"What do you smell?"

"Sort of like vinegar."

"What I hear is sort of like somebody breathing."

And a light flared up at us from the bottom of the stairs, blinding us by its abruptness although it was only a tiny light, and the voice of Willie the Weeper said, "Great balls o' fahr, effen 'tain't the Revenooers come to bust up mah li'l ol' still!"

I flung my head away from the light and yelled, "Willie, for Christ's sake! What are you doing here?"

"Dumb question, my David," said Barbie beside me. "Don't you remember about cave drippings? Willie's got himself a supply of home brew out here."

"Right," said Willie benevolently. "Thought I recognized your voice, my two-toned sepia queen. Say, how are your roots doing?"

Barbie didn't say a word, and neither did any of the rest of us. After a moment Willie may have felt a little ashamed of himself, because he flicked off his light. "I've only got the one battery," he explained apologetically from the darkness. "Oh, wait a minute. Take a look." And he turned on the little penlight again, shined it at arm's length on himself, and then against the wall, where he had four fruit bowls covered by dinner plates and a bunch of paper cups. "I thought you might like to see my little popskull plant," he said pridefully, turning the light off again. "Care for a shot?"

"Why not?" said Barbie, and we all three eased ourselves down to the lower steps and accepted a paper cup of the stuff, sharing it among us.

"Straining it was the hard part," said Willie. "You may notice a certain indefinable piquancy to the bouquet. I had to use my underwear."

Barbie, just swallowing, coughed and giggled. "Not bad, Willie. Here, try it, David. It's a little bit like Dutch gin."

To me it tasted like the liquid that accumulates in the bottom of the vegetable bins in a refrigerator, and I said so.

"Right, that's what I mean. My compliments to the vintner, Willie. Do you come here a lot?"

"No. Oh, well, maybe, I guess so. I don't like being hassled around in there." I couldn't see his face in the darkness, but I could imagine it: angry and defensive. So, to make it worse, I said,

"I thought you volunteered for this."

"Hell! I didn't know it would be like this."

"What did you think it would be like, Willie?" Barbie asked. But her voice wasn't mocking.

He said, with pauses, "I suppose, in a way . . . I suppose I thought it would be kind of like the revolution. I don't suppose you remember. You're probably too young, and anyway it was mostly on the West Coast. But we were all together then, you know . . . I mean, even the ones we were fighting and struggling were part of it. Chaos, chaos, and out of it came some good things. We struggled with the chief of police of San Francisco in the middle of Market Street, and afterwards he was all bruised and bleeding, but he thanked me."

We didn't say anything. He was right, we were too young to have been involved except watching it on TV, where it didn't seemed like another entertainment.

"And then," said Willie, "nothing ever went right." And he didn't say anything more for a long time, until Dolly-Belly said:

"Can I have another shot of drippings?"

And then we just sat for a while, thinking about Willie, and finally not thinking about anything much. I didn't feel blind any more, even with the light off. Just that bit from Willie's flash had given me some sense of domain. I could remember the glimpse I had got: the flat, unreflective black wall off to my right, just past Dolly-Belly, the wooden steps down (there had been nine of them), the duckboards along the rough shelf above us, the faint occasional drip of water from the bumps in the cave roof over us, the emptiness off to the left past where the light from Willie's penlamp did any good, Willie's booze factory down below. With a girl on either side of me I didn't even feel cold, except for my feet, and after a while Willie put his hand on one of them. It felt warm and I liked it, but I heard myself saying, "You've got the wrong foot, Willie. Barbie's on my left, Dolly's on my right."

After a moment he said, "I knew it was yours. I'm already holding one of Dolly's." But he took it away.

Barbie said thoughtfully, "If you'd been a voter in your district, Willie, who would you have voted for?"

"Do you think I haven't asked myself that?" he demanded. "You're right. I would have voted for Tom Gdansk."

Dolly said, "It's time for a refill, Willie friend." And we all churned around getting our paper cups topped off and readjusting ourselves and when Willie prudently turned the penlight off again, we were all sitting together against the wall, touching and drinking, and talking. Willie was doing most of the talking. I didn't say much. I wasn't holding back; it was just that I had had the perception that it was more important for Willie to talk than for me to respond. I let the talk wash over me. Time slowed and shuddered to a stop.

It came to me that we four were sitting there because it was meant from the beginning of time that we should be sitting there, and that sitting there was the thing and the only thing that we were ordained to do. My spattered statue for the library? It didn't matter. It was in a different part of reality. Not the part we four were in just then. Willie's worries about being not-loved? It mattered that he was telling us about it (he was back to his third birthday, when his older brother's whooping cough had canceled Willie's party), but it didn't matter that it had happened. Dolly's fatness? *N'importe.* Barbie's fitful soft weeping, over she never said what? *De nada.* Lara leaving me for the USIS goon? *Machts nicht* . . . well, no. That did amount to something real and external. I could feel it working inside me.

But I was not prepared to let it interfere with the groupness of our group, which was a real and immanent thing in itself. After a while, Dolly began to hum to herself. She had a bad, reedy voice, but she wasn't pushing it, and it fitted in nicely behind Willie's talking and Barbie's weeping. We eased each other, all four of us. It must have been in some part Willie's terrible foul brew, but it could not have been all that; it was weak stuff and tasted so awful you could drink it only one round at a time. It was, in some ways, the finest time of my life.

"Time," I said wonderingly. "And time, and time, and all of the kinds of time." I don't suppose it meant anything, but it seemed to at that—yes. At that time. And for a time we talked timelessly about time, which, in my perception, had the quality of a mobile or a medallion or a coffee-table book, in that it was something one discussed for its pleasant virtues but not something that constrained one.

Except that there too there was some sort of inner activity, like stomach rumblings, going on all the time.

While we were there, what was happening in those external worlds we had left? In the world in the caves behind us? Had the group been judged and passed and discharged while we were gone? If it had, how would we ever know?

But Barbie said (and I had not known I had asked her, or spoken out loud) that that was unlikely because, as far as she could see, our group had done damn-all about solving any problems, especially its own, and if we were to be excused only after performance, we had all the performance yet to perform. Everybody knew the numbers.

Most groups got out in some three weeks. But what was three weeks? Twenty-one sleeps? But we slept when we chose, and no two of us had exactly the same number. Sixty-three meals? Dolly had stopped eating almost entirely. How could you tell? Only by the solutions of problems, maybe. If you knew what standards were applied, and who the judges were. But I could see little of that happening, like Barbie, like all of us, I was still trapped in my own internal problems that, even there, came funneling in by some undetectable pipeline from that larger external world beyond the caves. And I had solved no part of them. Lara was still gone and would still be gone. Whatever time it was in Djakarta, she was there. Whatever was appropriate to that time, she was doing, with her USIS man and not with me, for I was not any part of her life and never would be again. She probably never thought of me, even. Or if she did, only with anger. "I feel bad about the anger," I said out loud, only then realizing I had been talking out loud for some time, "because I earned it richly and truly. I own it and acknowledge it as mine."

"So do you want to do anything about it?" asked somebody, Dolly I think, or maybe Willie.

I considered that for a timeless stretch. "Only to tell her about it," I said finally, "to tell her what's true, that I earned it."

"Do you want her back?" asked Willie. (Or Barbie.)

I considered that for a long time. I don't know whether I ever answered the question, or what I said. But I began to see what the answer was, at least. Really I didn't want her back. Not exactly. At least, I didn't want the familiar obligatory one-to-oneness with Lara, the getting up with Lara in the morning, the making the coffee for Lara, the sharing the toast with Lara, the following Lara to the bus twenty minutes after, the calling Lara at her office from my office, wondering who Lara was seeing for lunch, being home before Lara and waiting for Lara to come in, sharing a strained dinner with Lara, watching TV with Lara, fighting with Lara, swallowing resentments against Lara; I didn't even want going to bed with Lara or those few moments, so brief and in recollection so illusory, when Lara and I were peacefully at one or pleasuring each other with some discovery or joy. Drowsily I began to feel that I wanted nothing from Lara except the privilege of letting go of her without anger or pain; letting go of all pain, maybe, so that I did not have to have it eating at me.

But how much of this I said, or heard, I do not know, I only remember bits and tableaux. I remember Willie the Weeper actually weeping, softly and easingly like Barbie. I remember that there was a point when there was no more of the cave drippings left except some little bit that had just begun to work. I remember kissing Dolly, who was crying in quite a different and more painful way, and then I only remember waking up.

At first I was not sure where I was. For a moment I thought we had all got ourselves dead drunk and wandering, and perhaps had gone out into the cave and got ourselves lost in some deadly, foolish way. It scared me. How could we ever get back?

But it wasn't that way, as I perceived as soon as I saw that we were huddled in a corner of one of the sleeping rooms. I was not alone in my sleeping bag; Barbie was there with me, her arms around me and her face beautiful and slack. There was a weight across our feet which I thought was Dolly.

But it wasn't. It was Willie Murtagh, wrapped in his own bag, stretched flat and snoring, and Dolly was not anywhere around.

## Aspects of External Reality

*Geology*. About a hundred million years before the birth of Christ, during the period called the Upper Cretaceous when the Gulf of Mexico swelled to drown huge parts of the Southern United States, a series of volcanic eruptions racked the sea that would become the Caribbean. The chains of islands called the Greater and Lesser Antilles were born.

As the molten rock boiled forth and the pressure dropped, great bubbles of trapped gas evolved, some bursting free into the air, others remaining imprisoned as the cooling and hardening of the lava raced against the steady upward crawl of the gas. In time the rock cooled and became agelessly hard. The rains drenched it, the seas tore at it, the winds scoured it, and all of them brought donations: waveborne insects, small animals floating on bits of vegetation or sturdily swimming, air-borne dust, bird-borne seeds. After a time the islands became densely overgrown with reeds and grasses, orchids and morning-glories, bamboo, palm, cedar, ebony, calabash, whitewood; it was a place of karst topography, so wrinkled and seamed that it was like a continent's worth of landscaping crammed into a single island, and overgrown everywhere.

Under the rock the bubbles remained; and as the peaks weathered, some of the bubbles thinned and balded at the top, opened, and collapsed, leaving great, round, open valleys like craters. When astronomers wanted to build the biggest damned radio telescope the world had ever seen, they found one of these opened-out bubbles. They trimmed it and smoothed it and drained it and inlaid it with wire mesh to become the thousand-foot dish of the Arecibo Observatory. Countless other bubbles remained. Those that had been farther under the surface remained under the surface and were hidden until animals found them, then natives, then pirates, then geologists and spelunkers, who explored them and declared them to be perhaps the biggest chain of connected caverns ever found in the earth. Tourists gaped. Geologists plumbed. Astronomers peered, in their leisure hours. And then, when all radio telescopy was driven to the far side of the Moon by a thousand too many radio-dispatched taxicabs and a million too many radar ovens, the observatory no longer served a function and was abandoned.

But the caves remained.

*Physical Description.* After examining nearly all of the Puerto Rican cave system, a group of four linked caverns was selected and suitably modified. By blasting and hammering they were shaped and squared. Concrete flowed into the lower parts of the flooring to make them level. Wiring reached out to the generators of the old observatory, and then there were lighting, power, and communications facilities. In a separate cavern near the surface, almost burst through to the air, rack upon rack of salt crystals were stored; in the endless Puerto Rican sun the salt accepted heat, and when warmth was needed below, air was pumped through the salt. Decorators furnished and painted the chambers. Plumbers and masons installed fixtures and the pool. Water? There was endless water from the inexhaustible natural springs in the mountains. Drainage? The underground rivers that flowed off to the sea carried everything away. (When the astronomers came to build their telescope, they found that the valley had become a stagnant lake; its natural drain, through underground channels to the sea, had become blocked. Divers opened it, and the water swept sweetly away.) Two short elevator shafts, one for use and one for backup, completed the construction program. The result was an isolation pit exempt from the diurnal swing and the seasonal shift, without time or external stimuli, without distraction.

*Support facilities.* Maintenance, care and supervision of the problem pits is provided by a detachment of 50 VISTA volunteers, working out their substitute for military service. They tended the pumps, kept the machinery in repair, and did the housekeeping for the inmates. Their duties were quite light. The climate was humid but pleasant, especially in the northern hemisphere's winter months. Except for the long jackknifing drive to the city of Arecibo on the coast, for beer and company, the VISTA detachment was well pleased to be where they were. The principal everyday task was cooking, and that was no problem; it was all TV dinners, basically, prefabricated and prefrozen. All the duty chefs had to do was take the orders, pull them out of the freezers, pop them in the microwave ovens, and put them on the dumbwaiter. Plus, of course, something like scrambling eggs and buttering toast from time to time. There were seldom problems of any importance. The attempt of the United Brotherhood of Government Employees, in 1993, to organize the paramilitary services was the most traumatic event in the detachment's history. There had been a strike. Twenty-two persons, comprising the ongoing group of problem personnel, were temporarily marooned in the caves. For 18 days they were without food, light or communications, except for a few dumbwaiter loads of field rations smuggled down by one of the strikers. The inconvenience was considerable, but there were no deaths.

*Monitoring and evaluation.* Technical supervision is carried on by administratively separate personnel. There are two main areas of technical project control.

The first, employing sophisticated equipment originally designed for observatory use but substantially modified, is based near the old thousand-foot dish in the former administration and technical headquarters. Full information retrieval and communications capabilities exist, with on-line microwave links to the Heptagon, in Terre Haute, Indiana, via synchronous satellite. This is the top headquarters and decision-making station, and the work there is carried on by an autonomous division of SAD with full independent departmental status. The personnel of both technical supervision installations are interchangeable, and generally rotate duty from Indiana to Puerto Rico, six months or a year at a time.

The personnel of the technical project control centers are primarily professionals, including graduate students in social sciences and a large number of career civil service scientists in many disciplines. While stationed in Puerto Rico, most of these live along the coast with their families and commute to the observatory center by car or short-line STOL flight. They do not ordinarily associate with the VISTA crews, and only exceptionally have any firsthand contact with the members of the problem-solving groups, even the professional resource people included. This was not the original policy. At first the professionals actually participating in the groups were drawn by rota from the administrative personnel. It was found that the group identity was weakened by identification with the outside world, and so after the third year of operation the group-active personnel were kept separate, both administratively and physically. When off duty the group-active professionals are encouraged to return to their own homes and engage in activities unrelated to the work of the problem pits. The problem pits were originally sponsored by a consortium consisting of the Rand Corporation, the Hudson Institute, Cornell University, the New York Academy of Sciences, and the Puerto Rican Chamber of Commerce, under a matched-funds grant shared by SAD and the Rockefeller Foundation. In 1994 it was decided that they could and should be self-financing, and so a semipublic stock corporation similar to COMSAT and the fusion-power corporations was set up. All royalties and licensing fees are paid to the corporation, which by law distributes 35 percent of income as dividends to its stockholders, 11 percent to the State of Puerto Rico, and 4 percent to the federal government, reinvesting the balance in research-and-development exploitation.

*Results to date*. The present practice of consensual labor arbitration, the so-called "Nine Percent" income tax act, eight commercially developed board games, some 125 therapeutic personality measures, 51 distinct educational programs (including the technique of teaching elementary schoolchildren foreign languages through folksinging), and more than 1,800 other useful discoveries or systems have come directly from the problem-solving sessions in the Arecibo caves and elsewhere and from research along lines suggested by these sessions.

Here are two examples:

*The Nine Percent Law*. After the California riots, priority was assigned to social studies concerning "involvement," as the phrase of the day put it. Students, hereditarily unemployed aerospace workers, old people, and other disadvantaged groups who had united and overthrown civil government along most of the Pacific Coast for more than 18 months, were found to be suffering from the condition called *anomie*, characterized by a feeling that they were not related to the persons or institutions in their environment and had no means of control or participation in the events of the day. In a series of problem-pit sessions the plan was proposed which ultimately was adopted as the Kennedy-Moody Act of 1993, sometimes called "The Nine Percent Law." Under this act taxpayers are permitted to direct a proportion of their income tax to a specific function of government, e.g., national defense, subsidization of scientific research, education, highways, etc. A premium of 1 percent of the total tax payable is charged for each 10 percent which is allocated in this way, up to a limit of 9 percent of the base tax (which means allocating 90 percent of the tax payable). The consequences of this law are well known, particularly as to the essential disbanding of the DoD.

*The militia draft.* After the 1991 suspension of Selective Service had caused severe economic dislocation because of the lack of employment for youths not serving under the draft, a problem-pit session proposed resuming the draft and using up to 60 percent of draftees, on a volunteer basis, as adjuncts to local police forces all over the nation. It had been observed that law enforcement typically attracted rigid and often punitive psychological types, with consequent damage to the police-civilian relations, particularly with minority groups. The original proposal was that all police forces cease recruiting and that all vacancies be filled with national militia draftees. However, the increasing professionalization of police work made that impractical, and the present system of assigning militia in equal numbers to every police force was adopted. The success of the program may be judged from the number of other nations which have since come to imitate it.

In recent years some procedural changes have been made, notably in giving preference to nongoal-oriented problem-solving sessions, in which all participants are urged to generate problems as well as solutions. A complex scoring system, conducted in Terre Haute, gives credits for elapsed time, for definition of problems, for intensity of application and for (estimated) value of proposals made. As the group activity inevitably impinges on personality problems, a separate score is given to useful or beneficial personality changes which occur among the participants. When the score reaches a given numerical value (the exact value of which has never been made public), the group is discharged and a new one convened.

The procedures used in the problem pits are formative, eclectic and heuristic. Among the standard procedures are sensitivity training, encounter, brainstorming, and head-cloning. More elaborate forms of problem-solving and decision-making, such as Delphi, relevance-tree construction, and the calculus of statement, have been used experimentally from time to time. At present they are not considered to be of great value in the basic pit sessions, although each of them retains a place in the later R&D work carried on by professional teams, either in Terre Haute or, through subcontracting, in many research institutions around the country.

*Selection procedures.* Any citizen is eligible to volunteer and, upon passing a simple series of physical and psychological tests designed to determine fitness for the isolation experience, may be called as openings occur. Nearly all volunteers are accepted and actually participate in a pit session within 10 months to one year after application, although in periods when the number of volunteers is high, some proportion are used in sessions in other places than Arecibo, under slightly different ground rules.

In order to maintain a suitable ethnic, professional, religious, sexual, and personality mix, and as part of a randomizing procedure, about one half of all participants are selectees. These are chosen through Selective Service channels in the first instance, comprising all citizens who have not otherwise discharged their military obligation. Of course, the number thus provided is far in excess of need, and so a secondary lottery is then held. Those persons thus chosen are given the battery of tests required of volunteers, and those who pass remain subject to call for the remainder of their lives. As a matter of policy, many of the youngest age groups are given automatic deferments for a period of years, to provide a proper age mix for each working group.

*Summary and future plans.* The problem-pit sessions have proven so productive that there have been many attempts to expand them to larger formats, e.g., the so-called "Universal Town Meeting." These have achieved considerable success in special areas, but at the cost of limiting spontaneity and interpersonal interaction. Some studies have criticized the therapeutic aspects of pit sessions as distractive and irrelevant to their central purpose. Yet experimental sessions conducted on a purely problem-solving basis have been uniformly less productive, perhaps due to the emergence of a professionalist elite group who dominate such sessions; as their expertise is acquired through professional exposure over a period of time, their contributions are often too conventional and thus limited. The fresh, if uninformed, thoughts of nonexperts give the pit sessions their special qualities of innovation and daring. Most observers feel that the interpersonal quality of the sessions cannot be achieved on a mass scale except with the comcomitant danger of violence, personal danger and property destruction, as in the California Cultural Revolution. However, studies are still being pursued with the end in view of enlarging the scope and effectiveness of the sessions.

In conclusion, we can only agree with the oft-quoted extemporaneous rhyme offered by Sen. Moody at the ceremonies attendant on the tenth anniversary of the establishment of the problem pits:

> The pits are quirky,
> Perfection they're not.
> The best you can say's
> They're the best we've got.

## The Statement of Tina's Problem

In Tina Wattridge's head lived a dozen people, all of whom were her and all of whom fought like tigers for sole ownership. Pit Leader Tina moved among the group, offering encouragement here, advice there, bringing one person to interact with another. Mother Tina remembered, after a third of a century, the costive agony of childbirth and the inexpressible love that drowned her when they first laid her daughter in her arms. Tina the Spy eavesdropped and snooped, and furtively slipped into the communications room to type out her reports on group progress. Homemaker Tina loathed the cockroach yellow paint on the walls of the main social room and composed unsent demands to the control authorities for new mats for the pool chamber, where the dank and the hard use had eaten them into disgraceful tatters. And all the Tinas were Tina Wattridge, and when they battled among themselves for her, she felt fragmented and paralyzed. When she felt worst was when one of the long-silent Tina's came arrogantly to the fore and drove her in a direction she had long forgotten. It was happening now. She knew what a spectacle she must seem to everyone present, most of all to the other parts of herself, but she could not help herself; she was in love; could not possibly be in love; was.

And while she was numb to everything but the external love and the interior pain of reproach, her group was exploding in a dozen directions. She couldn't cope; somehow she did cope, moment by moment, but always at the cost of feeling that there she had spent the last erg of energy, the last moiety of will and had nothing left—until another demand came. And they came every minute, it seemed. Bob Sanger shouting and trembling, demanding that the group be terminated and he be let to get back to his collapsing business. David Jaretski and Barbara Devereux screaming that their friend Dolores had blundered off into the caves to die. Marge Klapper (who should have known better!) whispering that she wanted to get out now, right now, to have the other man's baby pumped out of her so she could go back to the man she was married to. And back and forth to the teletypes, sneaking in reports; and worrying about every person there; and most of the time, all of the time, with her mind full of Dev Stanwyck and their utterly preposterous, utterly overpowering love.

She could not sleep. She would lie down exhausted, more often than not with Dev beside her, and sometimes there would be sex, fast and total, and sometimes there would be his passionate attempt to explain and justify all of his life. Sometimes nothing but exhaustion alone; she would feel herself falling away into sleep and hear Dev's breathing deepen beside her. And then some voice from the other room, or some memory, or some discomfort from the fold of the sleeping bag would come. Not much. Enough. Enough to pull her back from sleep, fighting angrily against it, and in a minute she would be wide awake with her mind furiously circling into a kind of panic.

Then she would get up, trying not to disturb Dev, trying to avoid the rest of the group, and head for the only place in the caves where she could have privacy, the toilets. And with the door locked, in the end stall, she would reach behind the flush tank and slide one piece of molding over another and take out the rough copies of her reports, trying to force her mind back onto her job.

Day 1, hour 2300. WATTRIDGE reporting. FEIN introduced VD epidemiology problem; no group uptake. SANGER states problem of approaching bankruptcy in dental findings industry; n.g.u. JEFFERSON made no overt statement but indicates sexual inadequacy problem. JARETSKI marital situation; wife has left him. ITTRI despondent career status; attributes lack of education. MURTAGH states criticism of Congressional election procedure; n.g.u. GROUP interaction in weak normal range.

They had all been strangers then. Dev Stanwyck's name did not even appear in that first report!

Day 4, hour 2220. WATTRIDGE reporting. KLAPPER and BELLI hostility; fought with bats without resolution. GROUP effective in bioenergetics and immersion therapy. Some preliminary diagnoses:

DEVEREUX passive-aggressive, deep frustration feelings. BELLI compulsive and anal-retentive. STANWYCK latent homosexual father-dominated. (Note: I have personal feelings toward STANWYCK. I think of him as a son.)

She flipped hastily through the pages of the notebook, trying to ignore the fact that somebody was silently moving around outside the toilet door, apparently listening. Then she found the page she was looking for:

Day 13, hour 2330. WATTRIDGE reporting. Clique formation: BELLI-DEVEREUX-JARETSKI: semisexual triad, some boding to rest of group. STANWYCK-ITTRI, bivalent pairing, sociopersonal conflict vs. joint hostility to rest of group, little interaction. FEIN-KLAPPER-SANGER, weak professional communality of interest in medical areas; unstable bond, with individual links to other group members. No overt sexual interaction observed. Problem-solving: SANGER received full group brainstorm but did not consider any proposal satisfactory; forwarded for analysis. FEIN received approximately 30 minutes intensive discussion, no formal proposals but interaction taking place. ITTRI: Has become able to perceive own failure to make use of adult-education and other resources, accepts suggestions for courses and new career orientation. (Note: BELLI noticed in the pool that I was wearing my watch. I tried to persuade her that it was only an ornament and did not keep time. However, she told some of the others. STANWYCK in particular has been observing me closely, making these transmissions difficult even with blind-typing.)

And there it was, an absolute fraud! It hadn't happened that way at all. It had been Dev Stanwyck who had noticed it first, Dolly Belli only a day later; and Tina remembered cringingly with what anger and passion she had blown up at Dolly's half-joking question. It had stopped the questioning, all right; Dolly climbed out of the pool without another word, and her friends followed her. What else had it stopped: How close had Dolly been to opening up to the group at large?

And where had the anger come from? It was only when Tina had realized that the anger was all out of proportion to the stimulus that she had plumbed in her mind for another source and found it transferred from her own feelings about Dev Stanwyck.

Slowly she turned to a blank page and began her latest report:

*     *     *

Day 17, hour 2300. WATTRIDGE reporting. BELLI still missing. Tensions peaking. GROUP interaction maintaining plateau in high normal range. Sexual pairing marked: JARETSKI-DEVEREUX, KLAPPER-FEIN (temporary and apparently discontinued), ITTRI-TEITLEBAUM. Also WATTRIDGE-STANWYCK. (Note: I find this professionally disconcerting and am attempting to disengage. I am too old for him!)

She put down the pencil and wrinkled her eyes; repentance oft I swore, yes, but was I sober when I swore? How could she disengage herself from someone a third her age who found that she turned him on? And how could she not?

The breathing outside stopped for a moment, and then Dev's voice said, "Tina, is that you in there?"

She could not answer; some maiden shyness kept her from speaking while sitting on a toilet, or else she simply did not know what to say to Dev.

"I think you better come out," he went on. "Something's happening."

## Hassling Willie

In the main social room Marge Klapper was facing Willie Murtagh across a mat. Both were tense and angry, which troubled Marge more than Willie because she did not like to be professionally inept. The one-night stand with Jerry Fein had left her upset, especially as Jerry didn't want to let it stay a one-night stand; she was angry; she wanted to get out to get rid of her souvenir of one other one-night stand; she wanted to go back to her husband and find out if the marriage could be made to work; and, most difficult of all, she wanted to do all those things while retaining her self-image as a competent professional intact. So she reached out for Willie:

"Do you want to fight?"

He stood angrily mute and shook his head.

She dropped the soft, inflated plastic bats and put a professional smile on her face. "Shall we push? Would you like to go in the pool?"

"No." He wasn't helping at all. He was uptight and souring the whole group with his tensions and giving her nothing to work on—nothing, she realized, except that intensity with which he was looking at her, as though hoping the next word out of her mouth would be what he wanted. So she tried again. She stepped up on the edge of the mat and said sweetly to Willie, "Would you like to try something with me? Let's jump."

Willie said, "Oh, Christ."

"Go on," Jerry Fein put in helpfully. "Shake the tensions out."

"Stay out of this, Jerry!" Marge snapped. And then forced herself to relax. "Like this, Willie," she said, jumping, coming down, jumping again. "Try it."

He glowered, looked around the room and gave a half-hearted hop.

"Great!" cried Marge. "Higher!"

He shrugged and jumped a mighty leap, twice as high as hers. Then another. "Beautiful, Willie," said Marge breathlessly. "Keep it up!" It was like an invisible seesaw, first Marge in the air, then Willie, Marge again; he began to move his feet like a Russian dancer, coming down with one knee half bent, then the other, turning his body from side to side. "Make a noise, Willie!" Marge yelled triumphantly, and demonstrated: "Yow! Whee! Hoooo!"

The whole group was joining in—anyway, that part of it that was in the room, all yelling with Willie. Marge felt triumphant and fulfilled; and then Tina had to come in and spoil it all.

"Sorry, Marge," she called from the doorway. "Listen, everybody. Does anybody know where Barbie and David are?"

"In the pool?" somebody guessed helpfully.

"No. I looked everywhere."

Marge panted angrily, "Tina, do you have to take attendance right now?"

"I'm sorry, Marge. But I'm afraid they've gone into the caves after Dolly. Is anyone else missing?"

The group looked around at itself. "Rufous!" cried Jerry Fein. "Where's he?"

Dev Stanwyck, as always tagging along after Tina, said in his superior way, "We've already checked the sleeping rooms. Rufous is there. Anybody else?"

No answer for a moment, and then three or four people at once: "Bob Sanger!"

Tina looked around, then nodded grimly. "Thanks." And she disappeared, Stanwyck hurrying after.

Nevertheless, the interruption had wrecked Marge's mood. And hadn't done any good for Willie, either; he was collapsed on the floor, staring into space.

"Well," said Marge heartily, "want to get back to it, Willie?"

He looked up and said, "I know where they are. It's kind of my fault." He straightened up and said, "Hell, it's *exactly* my fault. I was trying to get with that colored girl, and I said something I shouldn't have. Dolly took it the wrong way and split for the caves, and I—well, I told David it was his fault, so he went after her. I didn't actually think he'd take Barbie with him."

"Or Sanger," said someone.

"I don't know anything about Sanger. But I know where they are. They're wandering."

Tina said from the entrance, "No, not in the caves, they aren't." All at once she looked every year of her age. "They're outside," she said. "I just heard from the VISTA crew; they identified four persons leaving the caves about a quarter of a mile from here, one alone, then three more about an hour ago."

"At least they're outside," said Willie thankfully.

"Oh, yes," said Tina, "they're outside. In the dark. Wandering around. Did you look at the terrain when you came in, Willie?" She absentmindedly pressed her hands against her face. It smeared her make-up, but she was no longer aware she had it on. "One other thing," she said. "You can all go home now. The word just came down over the teletype; our group is discharged with thanks and, how did they say it?—oh, yes. 'Tell them it was a good job well done,'" she said.

## Running Home

I didn't really believe Willie even when it was clearly to his advantage to tell the truth, but it was the way he said: follow the piece of string he had laid out, exploring the caves to keep from exploring his own head, and you came to a rock slope, very steep but with places where somebody had once cut handholds into it, and at the end of the handholds you found yourself out in the fresh air. When we got out we were all beat. Bob Sanger was the worst off of us, which was easy to figure when you considered he was a pretty old guy who hadn't done anything athletic for about as long as Barbie and I had been alive. But he was right with us. "I'll leave you now," he said. "I do appreciate your help."

"Cut it out, Bob," wheezed Barbie. "Where do you think you're going?"

It had turned out to be night, and a very dark night with a

feeble tepid rain coming down, too—perhaps they had no other kinds around there. I couldn't see his face, but I could imagine his expression, very remote and contented with whatever interior decisions he had reached. "I'll make my own way, thank you," he said politely. "It is only a matter of finding a road, and then following it downhill, I imagine."

"Then what?" I demanded. "We're AWOL, you know."

"That's why I have attorneys, Mr. Jaretski," he said cheerfully.

"Sitting on the bottom of the hill waiting for you?"

"Of course not. Really, you should not worry about me. I took the precaution of retaining my money belt when we checked our valuables. U.S. currency will get me to Ponce, and from there there are plenty of flights to the mainland. I'll be in California in no more than eight or nine hours, I should think."

"Listen, Bob!" I exploded—but stopped; Barbie squeezed my shoulder.

"Bob," she said, in a tone quite different from mine, "it isn't just that we're worried about you. We're worried about Dolly. Please help us find her."

Silence. I wished I could have seen his face. Then he said, "Please believe me, I am not ungrateful. But consider these facts. First, as I explained to all of you when we started this affair, it is of considerable importance to me to keep my company solvent. I believe that I have reasoned out a way to do so, and *I have no spare time.* I have no idea how much time we've wasted, and it may already be too late. Second, this is a big island. It is quite hopeless to search it for one girl with a long start, with no lights and no idea of where she has gone. I would help you if I could. I can't."

I said, trying to crawl down from my anger, "We don't have any other way to do it, Bob. I think I know where she is; anyway, that's where I want to look. But three of us can look fifty percent better than two."

"Call the VISTA crew," he said.

"I don't know where they are."

"Anyway, you're assuming she may be in some kind of danger. She is quite capable of taking care of herself."

"Capable, yes. Motivated, no. She's jealous and angry, Bob. Barbie and I were shacked up and it— " I hesitated; I didn't know exactly how to say it. "It spoiled things for her," I said. "I think she might do something crazy."

Sanger spluttered, "Your f-fornications are your own business, Mr. Jaretski! I must go. I— "

He hesitated and became, for him, confidential. "I believe that the discussion of my problem has in fact borne fruit. The, ah, gynaecological instruments are an area in which I had little knowledge."

"You've invented a warmer for the thingy?" Barbie asked, interestedly.

"For the speculum, yes. A warmer, no. It isn't necessary. Metal conducts heat so rapidly that if it isn't warm it feels cold. Plastic such as our K-14A is as strong as metal, as poreless and thus readily sterilized as metal and has a very low thermal conductivity. I think—well. The remainder of what I think is properly my own business, Miss Devereux, and I want to get back to my own business to implement it before it is too late."

"Jesus, Bob," I said, really angry, "don't you feel anything at all? You got something good out of the group. Don't you want to help?"

I could hear him walking away. "Not in the least," he said.

"Won't you at least come over to the radio mirror with us to look? There's a road there . . ."

But he didn't even answer.

And we had wasted enough time, more than enough time. I took Barbie's hand, and we started off to where the faint sky glow suggested there were buildings. There was nothing much else in these hills; it had to be either the administration buildings around the radio dish or the cave entrance, and either way I could find my way from there. Of course, Dolly might not have gone to the dish. But where else would she go? Down the hill to civilization, maybe, but in that case she would be all right. But if she had gone to the dish, if she had been listening when I told her about the slippery catwalk and the five-hundred-foot drop—no, there was not much more time to waste.

There was no road near the outcropping with the crevice through which we had come. People had been there before. There was a sort of bruised part of the undergrowth that might have been a kind of path. It didn't help much. We bulldozed our way through the brush, with wet branches slapping at us and wet vines and bushes wrapping themselves around our legs; a little of that was plenty, on the up-and-down hillsides, but after half an hour or so we did hit a road. Something like a road, anyway; two parallel ruts that presumably were used from time to time, because the vegetation

had not quite obliterated it. It circled a hill, and from the far side
of it I could see not one but two glowing spots in the cloud. The
nearer and brighter one looked like the entrance to the pit. Ergo,
the other was where we wanted to go.

I think it took us a couple of hours to get there, and we didn't
have the breath for much talking. We were lower down than I had
been before. The suspended thing that looked like an old trolley
car slung from wires was now higher up than we were; the rain
had stopped, and the clouds were beginning to lighten with dawn
coming. I stopped, gasping, and Barbie leaned against me, and
the two of us stared around the great round bowl.

"I don't see her," Barbie said.

I didn't see her either. That was not all bad. The good part
was that I didn't see her body spread out over the rusting wire
mesh at the bottom of the bowl. "Maybe she didn't come here
after all," I said.

"Where else would she go?"

"She could have got lost." Or she could have blundered down
the mountains looking for a road. Or she could have found another
cliff to jump off.

But I didn't think so, and then Barbie said, very softly, "Oh,
look up there, my David. What's that that's moving?"

I looked. It was still gray and I could not be sure; but, yes,
there was something moving.

It was actually in the big metal instrument cage, whatever it
was.

I said, "I don't know, Barb. Let's go find out."

It was easy to say that, hard to do; the catwalk started out from
the side of a hill but unfortunately not the hill we were on; we had
to skirt one and circle around another before we reached the end
of the catwalk. That was twenty minutes or so, I guess; and by
then the day was brighter. And that was not all good. The bad
part was that I could see the catwalk very clearly. It had not been
used much for, I would guess, ten or fifteen years. Maybe more.
It had a plank floor with spaces between the planks and spaces
where planks seemed to have rotted out and fallen off. It had a
wire-net side-barrier: rusty. The cables themselves, the overhead
ones from which it was slung and the smaller ones that bound it
to them, looked sturdy enough, but what good would that do us
if the boards split under us and we fell through?

There were, however, only two alternatives, and neither of them
was any good. The tangible alternative was a sort of bucket car that

rose from the administration buildings to the machine cage, but to get to that meant going halfway around the bowl, and who could know if it would be working? The intangible alternative was to turn away. So in effect we had no alternatives, and I took Barbie's hand and led her out onto the catwalk. By the time we were ten yards along it, we became aware of wind (we had not felt it before) and the rain (which slammed into us from the side). And we became aware that the whole suspended walk was swaying, and making creaking, testy, failing sounds as it swayed. We walked as lightly as we could . . .

I was almost surprised when we discovered that we were at the machine cage. Down between our feet was a whole lot of emptiness, with the wire mesh and the greenery poking through at the end. Over us was the machinery. And I didn't know what to do next.

Barbie did; she called, "Dolly, dear, are you up there?"

There was no answer.

I tried: "Dolly, please come down! We want you."

No answer, except what might have been the wind blowing, and might have been a sob.

Barbie looked at me. "Do you want to go up and look around?"

I shook my head. There was a metal ladder, but it went into a hatch and the hatch was shut. I really didn't like the idea of climbing those few extra feet, but most of all I didn't like the idea of driving Dolly farther and farther away, until I drove her maybe out of some window. I yelled, "Dolly, we didn't come all this way just to say good-bye. We want you with us, Dolly!" I hadn't asked Barbie if that was true; it didn't matter.

Silence that prolonged itself, and then there was a grating sound and the hatch opened. Dolly peered down at us, looking cross but otherwise not unusual. "Crap," she said. "Okay, you've soothed your consciences. Now go back to bed."

Barbie, holding on to the ladder—the whole structure was vibrating now—looked up at her and said, "Dolly, are you mad because David and I went to bed?"

With dignity Dolly said, "I have nothing to be angry about. Not to mention I'm used to it."

"Because it wasn't that big a deal, Dolly," Barbie went on. "It just happened that way. It could have been you and David, and I wouldn't have been mad."

"You're not me," said Dolly, and added, very carefully and precisely, "you're not a girl that's always been fifty pounds too fat, that everybody laughs at, that buys the kind of clothes you wear all the time and tries them on in front of a mirror, and then throws them out and cries herself to sleep."

She stopped there. Neither Barbie nor I said anything for a moment. Then I started, "Dolly dear— " But Barbie put her hand on my shoulder and stopped me.

She gathered her thoughts and then said, "Dolly, that's right, I'm not you. I'm me, but maybe you don't know what it's like to be me, either. Would you like me to tell you who I am? I'm a girl who really looked forward to this group, which took all the guts I had, because it meant letting myself hope for something, and then ran out of courage and never asked anybody for the help I wanted. I'm a black girl, Dolly, and that may not seem like much of a bad thing to you, but I happen to be a black girl who's going to die of it. Or to put it another way, Dolly dear, you're a girl who can make plans for Christmas, and I'm a girl who won't be here then."

You hear words like that, and for a minute you don't know what it is you've heard. I stood there, one hand holding on to the ladder, looking at Barbie with the expression of polite interest you give someone who is telling you a complicated story of which you have not yet seen the point. I couldn't make that expression go off my face. I couldn't find the right expression to replace it with.

Dolly said, "What the hell are you talking about?" And her voice was suddenly shrill.

"What I say," said Barbie. "It's what they call sickle-cell anemia. You white folks don't get it much, but us black folks, we get it. You know. All God's chillun got hemoglobin, but where your hemoglobin has something they call glutamic acid, my hemoglobin has something they call valine. Sounds like nothing much? Yeah, Dolly, but we die of it. Used to be we died before we grew up, most of the time, but they do things better now. I'm thirty-one, and they say I've got, oh, easily another five or six months."

Dolly's face pulled back out of the hatch, and her voice, muffled, yelled, "Wait a minute," and Dolly's legs and bottom appeared as she lowered herself down the ladder. When she got there, all she said was Barbie's name, and put her arms around both of us.

I don't know how long we stayed like that, but it was a long time. And might have been longer if we hadn't heard voices and looked up and saw people coming toward us along the catwalk. A hell of a lot of people, a dozen or so, and we looked again, and it was Bob Sanger leading all the rest.

"Why, son of a bitch," said Barbie in deep surprise. "You

know what he did? He went and got the group to see if we needed help."

And Dolly said, "And you know what? We do. We all do." And then she said, "Dear Barbie. We could all be dead before Christmas. If David will have us, let's stick together a while. I mean—a while. As long as we want to." And before Barbie could say anything, she went on. "You know, I volunteered for this group. I didn't exactly ever say what I wanted, but I can tell you two. I guess I could tell all of them, and maybe I will." She took a deep breath. "What I wanted," she said, "was to find out how to be loved."

And I said, "You are."

## The Wrap-Up

*Tina Wattridge Final Report.* Attached are the analysis sheets, work-ups, recommendations, and SR-4 situation cards.

There is one omission. I left out Jerry Fein's solution to his own problem. If you refer to D6H2140, you will find the problem stated (epidemiological control measures for VD). He ultimately provided his own solution, quote his words from my notes: "Suppose we make a monthly check for VD for the whole population. Everybody who shows up and is clear on the tests gets a little button to wear, like in the shape of a heart, with a date. You know, like the inspection sticker in a car. It could be like a charm bracelet for girls, maybe love beads for men. And if you don't pass the test that month, or start treatment if you fail, you don't get to wear the emblem." The reason I did not forward it was not that I thought it a bad idea; actually, I thought it kind of cute, and with the proper promotion it might work. What I did think, in fact what I was sure of, was that it was a setup. Jerry planted the problem and had the solution in his head when he came in, I guess to get brownie points. Maybe he wants my job. Maybe he just wanted to end the session sooner. Anyway he was playing games, and the reason I'm passing it on now is that I've come to the conclusion that I don't really care if he was playing games. It's still not a bad idea and is forwarded for R&D consideration.

One final personal note: Dev Stanwyck kissed me sweetly and weepily good-bye and took off for Louisiana with the Teitlebaum girl. I hated it, but there it is, and anyway—Well, I don't mind his being young enough to be my youngest son, but I was beginning to kind of mind being his mother. When I was a little girl, I saw an old

George Arliss movie on TV; he played an Indian rajah who had tried
to abduct an English girl for his harem, and after his plot was foiled,
at the end of the picture, he said something that I identify with right
now. He looked into the camera and lit a cigarette and said, "Ah,
well. She would have been a damn nuisance anyhow."

All in all, it was a good group. I'm taking two weeks accumulated
leave effective tomorrow. Then I'll be ready for the next one.

# RIDING THE TORCH

## Norman Spinrad

## 1

Flashing rainbows from his skintight mirror suit, flourishing a swirl of black cape, Jofe D'mahl burst through the shimmer screen that formed the shipside wall of his grand salon to the opening bars of Beethoven's *Fifth Symphony*. The shimmer rippled through the spectrum as his flesh passed through it, visually announcing his presence with quicksilver strobes of dopplering light. Heads turned, bodies froze, and the party stopped for a good long beat as he greeted his guests with an ironic half-bow. The party resumed its rhythm as he walked across the misty floor toward a floating tray of flashers. He had made his entrance.

D'mahl selected a purple sphere, popped the flasher into his mouth, and bit through an exquisite brittle sponginess into an overwhelming surge of velvet, a gustatory orgasm. A first collection by one Lina Wolder, Jiz had said, and as usual she had picked a winner. He tapped the name into his memory banks, keying it to the sensorium track of the last ten seconds, and filed it in his current party listing. Yes indeed, a rising star to remember.

Tapping the floater to follow him, he strode through the knee-high multicolored fog, nodding, turning, bestowing glances of his deep green eyes, savoring the ambience he had brought into being.

D'mahl had wheedled Hiro Korakin himself into designing the grand salon as his interpretation of D'mahl's own personality.

Korakin had hung an immense semicircular slab of simmed emerald out from the hull of the ship itself and had blistered this huge balcony in transparent plex, giving D'mahl's guests a breathtaking and uncompromising view of humanity's universe. As *Excelsior* was near the center of the Trek, the great concourse of ships tiaraed the salon's horizon line, a triumphant jeweled city of coruscating light. Ten kilometers bow-ward, the hydrogen interface was an auroral skin stretched across the unseemly nakedness of interstellar space.

But to look over the edge of the balcony, down the sleek and brilliantly lit precipice of *Excelsior's* cylindrical hull, was to be confronted by a vista that sucked slobbering at the soul: the bottomless interstellar abyss, an infinite black pit in which the myriad stars were but iridescent motes of unimportant dust, a nothingness that went on forever in space and time. At some indefinable point down there in the blackness, the invisible output of *Excelsior's* torch merged with those of two thousand and thirty-nine other ships to form an ethereal comet's tail of all-but-invisible purplish fire that dwindled off into a frail thread which seemed to go on forever down into the abyss: the wake of the Trek, reeling backward in space and time for hundreds of light-years and nearly ten centuries, a visible track that the eye might seemingly follow backward through the ages to the lost garden, Earth.

Jofe D'mahl knew full well that many of his guests found this prime reality visualization of their basic existential position unsettling, frightening, perhaps even in bad taste. But that was *their* problem; D'mahl himself found the view bracing, which, of course, justifiably elevated his own already high opinion of himself. Korakin wasn't considered the best psychetect on the Trek for nothing.

But D'mahl himself had decorated the salon, with the inevitable assistance of Jiz Rumoku. On the translucent emerald floor he had planted a tinkling forest of ruby, sapphire, diamond, and amethyst trees—cunningly detailed sims of the ancient life-forms that waved flashing crystal leaves with every subtle current of air. He had topped off the effect with the scented fog that picked up blue, red, and lavender tints from the internally incandescent trees, and customarily kept the gravity at .8 g to sync with the faerie mood. To soften the crystal edges, Jiz had gotten him a collection of forty fuzzballs: downy globs in subdued green, brown, mustard, and gray that floated about randomly at floor level until someone sat in them. If Korakin had captured D'mahl's clear-eyed core, Jofe had expressed the neobaroque style of his recent sensos, and to D'mahl, the combined work of art sang of the paradox that was the Trek. To his guests, it sang of the paradox that was Jofe D'mahl. Egowise, D'mahl himself did not deign to make this distinction.

The guest list was also a work of art in D'mahl's neobaroque style: a constellation of people designed to rub purringly here, jangle like broken glass there, generate cross-fertilization someplace else, keep the old karmic kettle boiling. Jans Ryn was displaying herself as usual to a mixed bag that included *Excelsior's* chief torchtender, two dirtdiggers from *Kantuck*, and Tanya Daivis, the velvet asp. A heated discussion between Dalta Reed and Trombleau, the astrophysicist from *Glade*, was drawing another conspicuous crowd. Less conspicuous guests were floating about doing less conspicuous things. The party needed a catalyst to really start torching up lights.

And at 24.00 that catalyst would zap itself right into their sweet little taps—the premiere tapping of Jofe D'mahl's new senso, *Wandering Dutchmen*. D'mahl had carved something prime out of the void, and he knew it.

"—by backbreeding beyond the point of original radiation, and then up the line to the elm— "

"—like a thousand suns, as they said at Alamagordo, Jans, and it's only a bulkhead and a fluxfield away— "

"—how Promethean you must feel— "

"Jof, this nova claims he's isolated a spectral pattern synced to organic life," Dalta called out, momentarily drawing D'mahl into her orbit.

"In a starscan tape?" D'mahl asked dubiously.

"In theory," Trombleau admitted.

"Where've I heard that one before?" D'mahl said, popping another of the Wolder flashers. It wriggled through his teeth, then exploded in a burst of bittersweet that almost immediately faded into a lingering smoky aftertaste. Not bad, D'mahl thought, dancing away from Trombleau's open mouth before he could get sucked into the argument.

D'mahl flitted through the mists, goosed Arni Simkov, slapped Darius Warner on the behind, came upon a group of guests surrounding John Benina, who had viewpointed the Dutchman. They were trying to pump him about the senso, but John knew that if he blatted before the premiere, his chances of working with Jofe D'mahl again were exactly zip.

"Come on, Jofe, tell us something about *Wandering Dutchmen*," begged a woman wearing a cloud of bright-yellow mist. D'mahl couldn't remember her with his flesh, but didn't bother tapping for it. Instead, he bit into a cubical flasher that atomized at the touch of his teeth, whiting out every synapse in his mouth for a mad micropulse. Feh.

"Two hints," D'mahl said. "John Benina played one of the two major viewpoints, and it's a mythmash."

A great collective groan went up, under cover of which D'mahl ricocheted away in the direction of Jiz Rumoku, who was standing in a green mist with someone he couldn't make out.

Jiz Rumoku was the only person privileged to bring her own guests to D'mahl's parties, and just about the only person not involved in the production who had any idea of what *Wandering Dutchmen* was about. If Jofe D'mahl could be said to have a souler (a dubious assumption), she was it.

She was dressed, as usual, in tomorrow's latest fashion: a pants suit of iridescent, rigid-seeming green-and-purple material, a mosaic of planar geometric forms that approximated the curves of her body like a medieval suit of armor. But the facets of her suit articulated subtly with her tiniest motion—a fantastic insectile effect set off by a tall plumelike crest into which her long black hair had been static-molded.

But D'mahl's attention was drawn to her companion, for he was obviously a voidsucker. He wore nothing but blue briefs and thin brown slippers; there was not a speck of hair on his body, and his bald head was tinted silver. But persona aside, his eyes alone would have instantly marked him: windows of blue plex into an infinite universe of utter blackness confined by some topological legerdemain inside his gleaming skull.

D'mahl tapped the voidsucker's visual image to the banks. "I.D.," he subvoced. The name "Haris Bandoora" appeared in his mind. "Data brief," D'mahl subvoced.

"Haris Bandoora, fifty standard years, currently commanding Scoutship Bela-37, returned to Trek 4.987 last Tuesday. Report unavailable at this real-time."

Jiz had certainly come up with something tasty this time, a voidsucker so fresh from the great zilch that the Council of Pilots hadn't yet released his report.

"Welcome back to civilization, such as it is, Commander Bandoora," D'mahl said.

Bandoora turned the vacuum of his eyes on D'mahl. "Such as it is," he said, in a cold clear voice that seemed to sum up, judge, and dismiss all of human history in four dead syllables.

D'mahl looked away from those black pits, looked into Jiz's almond eyes, and they cross-tapped each other's sensoriums for a moment in private greeting. Jofe saw his own mirrored body, felt the warmth it evoked in her. He kissed his lips with Jiz's, tasting the electric smokiness of the flashers he had eaten. As their lips parted, they broke their taps simultaneously.

"What's in that report of yours that the Pilots haven't released to the banks yet, Bandoora?" D'mahl asked conversationally. (How else could you make small talk with a voidsucker?)

Bandoora's thin lips parted in what might have been a smile, or just as easily a grimace of pain. D'mahl sensed that the man's emotional parameters were truly alien to his experience, prime or simmed. He had never paid attention to the voidsuckers before, and he wondered why. There was one beyond senso to be made on the subject!

"They've found a planet," Jiz said. "There's going to be a blanket bulletin at 23.80."

"Drool," D'mahl said, nuancing the word with most of the feelings that this flash stirred up. The voidsuckers were always reporting back with some hot new solar system, turning the Trek for a few months while they high-geed for a telltale peek, then turning the Trek again for the next Ultima Thule just as the flash hit that the last one was the usual slokyard of rock and puke-gas. The voidsuckers had been leading the Trek in a zigzag stagger through space from one vain hope to another for the better part of a millennium; the latest zig was therefore hardly a cosmic flash in Jofe D'mahl's estimation. But it *would* be a three-month wonder at least, and tapping out a blanket bulletin just before the premiere was a prime piece of upstaging, a real boot in the ego. Drool.

"The probabilities look good on this one," Bandoora said.

"They always do, don't they?" D'mahl said snidely. "And it always turns out the same. If there's a rock in the habitable zone, it's got gravity that'd pull your head off, or the atmosphere is a tasty mixture of hydrogen cyanide and fluorine. Bandoora, don't you ever get the feeling that some nonexistent cosmic personage is trying to tell you something you don't want to hear?"

Bandoora's inner expression seemed to crinkle behind his impassive flesh. A tic made his lower lip tremble. What did I do *this* time? D'mahl wondered. These voidsuckers must be far beyond along some pretty strange vectors.

Jiz forced a laugh. "The torch Jof is riding is all ego," she said. "He's just singed because the bulletin is going to bleed some H from his premiere. Isn't that right, Jof, you egomonster, you?"

"Don't knock ego," D'mahl said. "It's all that stands between us and the lamer universe we have the bad taste to be stuck in. Since my opinion of myself is the only thing I know of higher in the karmic pecking order than my own magnificent being, my ego is the only thing I've found worth worshiping. Know what that makes me?"

"Insufferable?" Jiz suggested.

"A human being," D'mahl said. "I'm stuck with it, so I might as well enjoy it."

"A bulletin from the Council of Pilots." The words intruded themselves into D'mahl's mind with a reasonable degree of gentleness, an improvement over the days when the Pilots had felt they had the right to snap you into full sensory fugue on the spot whenever the spirit moved them. "Ten . . . nine . . . eight . . . seven . . ." D'mahl pulled over a green fuzzball and anchored the floating cloud of particles by planting his posterior in it. Jiz and Bandoora sat down flanking him. "Six . . . five . . . four . . ."

Whichever guests were standing found themselves seats; there was no telling how long one of these bulletins would last. The Pilots have a grossly exaggerated sense of their own importance, D'mahl thought. And what does that make them?

". . . three . . . two . . . one . . ."

Human beings.

D'mahl sat on a bench at the focus of a small amphitheater. Tiered around him were two thousand and forty people wearing the archaic blue military tunics, dating back to the time when Ship's Pilot was a paramilitary rank rather than an elective office. D'mahl found the uniformity of dress stultifying and the overhead holo of the day sky of an Earthlike planet banal and oppressive, but then he found most Pilots, with their naïve notion of the Trek's existential position, somewhat simpleminded and more than a little pathetic.

Ryan Nakamura, a white-haired man who had been Chairman of the Council of Pilots longer than anyone cared to remember, walked slowly toward him, clapped him on the shoulder with both hands, and sat down beside him. Nakamura smelled of some noxious perfume designed to sim wisdom-odors of moldy parchment and decayed sweetness. As an artist, D'mahl found the effect competent if painfully obvious; as a citizen, he found it patronizing and offensive.

Nakamura leaned toward him, and as he did, the amphitheater vanished and they sat cozily alone on an abstract surface entirely surrounded by a firmament of tightly packed stars.

"Jofe, Scoutship Bela-37 has returned to the Trek and reported that a solar system containing a potentially habitable planet is located within a light-year and a half of our present position," Nakamura said solemnly.

D'mahl wanted to yawn in the old bore's face, but of course the viewpoint player hunched him intently toward Nakamura instead as the Chairman blatted on. "The Council has voted 1,839 to 201 to alter the vector of the Trek toward this system, designated 997-Beta, pending the report of the telltale."

D'mahl sat midway up in the amphitheater as Nakamura continued formally from a podium on the floor below. "It is our earnest hope that our long trek is at last nearing its successful completion, that in our own lifetimes men will once more stand on the verdant hills of a living planet, with a sky overhead and the smells of living things in our nostrils. We conclude this bulletin with brief excerpts from the report of Haris Bandoora, commander of Bela-37."

Behind the podium, Nakamura faded into Haris Bandoora. "Bela-37 was following a course thirty degrees from the forward vector of the Trek," Bandoora said tonelessly. "Torching at point nine . . ."

D'mahl stood on the bridge of Bela-37—a small round chamber rimmed with impressive-looking gadgetry, domed in somewhat bluish plex to compensate for the doppler shift, but otherwise visually open to the terrifying glory of the deep void. However, one of the four voidsuckers on the bridge was a woman who easily upstaged the stellar spectacle as far as D'mahl was concerned. She wore briefs and slippers and was totally bald, like the others, and her skull was tinted silver, but her preternaturally conical breasts and shining, tightly muscled flesh made what ordinarily would have been an ugly effect into an abstract paradigm of feminine beauty. Whether the warmth he felt was his alone, or his reaction plus that of the viewpoint player, apparently Bandoora himself, was entirely beside the point.

"Ready to scan and record system 997-Beta," the stunning creature said. D'mahl walked closer to her wanting to dive into those bottomless voidsucker eyes. Instead, he found his lips saying, with Bandoora's voice: "Display it, Sidi."

Sidi did something to the control panel before her (how archaic!) and the holo of a yellow star about the diameter of a human head appeared in the geometric center of the bridge. D'mahl exchanged tense glances with his crew, somatically felt his expectation rise.

"The planets . . ." he said.

Five small round particles appeared, rotating in compressed time around the yellow sun.

"The habitable zone . . ."

A transparent green torus appeared around the holo of 997-Beta. The second planet lay within its boundaries.

There was an audible intake of breath, and D'mahl felt his own body tremble. "The second planet," Bandoora's voice ordered. "At max."

The holo of the star vanished, replaced by a pale fuzzy holo of the second planet, about four times its diameter. The planet seemed to be mottled with areas of brown, green, blue, yellow, and purple, but the holo was washed out and wavered as if seen through miles of heat-haze.

A neuter voice recited instrument readings. "Estimated gravity 1.2 gs plus or minus ten percent . . . estimated mean temperature thirty-three degrees centigrade plus or minus six degrees . . . estimated atmospheric composition: helium, nitrogen, oxygen as major constituents . . . percentages indeterminate from present data . . . traces of carbon dioxide, argon, ammonia, water vapor . . . estimated ratio of liquid area to solid surface 60–40 . . . composition of oceans indeterminate from present data. . . ."

D'mahl felt the tension in his body release itself through his vocal cords in a wordless shout that merged with the whoops of his companions. He heard his lips say, with Bandoora's voice: "That's the best prospect any scoutship's turned up within my lifetime."

D'mahl was seated in the amphitheater as Bandoora addressed the Council. "A probe was immediately dispatched to 997-Beta-II. Bela-37 will leave within twenty days to monitor the probe data wavefront. We estimate that we will be able to bring back conclusive data within half a standard year."

D'mahl was an abstract viewpoint in black space. A huge hazy holo of 997-Beta-II hovered before him like a ghostly forbidden fruit as the words in his mind announced: "This concludes the bulletin from the Council of Pilots."

Everyone in Jofe D'mahl's grand salon immediately began babbling, gesticulating, milling about excitedly. Head after head turned in the direction of D'mahl, Jiz, and Bandoora. D'mahl felt a slow burn rising, knowing to whom the fascinated glances were directed.

"Well, what do you think of *that*, Jof!" Jiz said, with a sly knife edge in her voice.

"Not badly done," D'mahl said coolly. "Hardly art, but effective propaganda, I must admit."

Once again, Bandoora seemed strangely stricken, as if D'mahl's words had probed some inner wound.

"The planet, Jof, the *planet*!"

Fighting to control a building wave of anger, D'mahl managed an arch smile. "I was paying more attention to Sidi," he said. "Voidsuckers come up with planets that look that good from a distance much more often than you see bodies that look that good that close."

"You think the future of the human race is a rather humorous subject," Bandoora said loudly, betraying annoyance for the first time.

D'mahl tapped the time at 23.981. His guests were all blatting about the prospects of at last finding a viable mudball, and *Wandering Dutchmen* was about to begin! Leaping to his feet, he shouted: "Bandoora, you've been out in the big zilch too long!" The sheer volume of his voice focused the attention of every guest on his person. "If *I* were confined in a scoutship with Sidi, I'd have something better than slok planets on my mind!"

"You're a degenerate and an egomaniac, D'mahl!" Bandoora blatted piously, drawing the laughter D'mahl had hoped for.

"Guilty on both counts," D'mahl said. "Sure I'm an egomaniac—like everyone else, I'm the only god there is. Of course I'm a degenerate, and so is everyone else—soft protoplasmic machines that begin to degenerate from day one!"

All at once D'mahl had penetrated the serious mood that the bulletin had imposed on his party, and by donning it and taking it one step beyond, had recaptured the core. "We're stuck where we are and with what we are. We're Flying Dutchmen on an endless sea of space, we're Wandering Jews remembering what we killed for all eternity— "

A great groan went up, undertoned with laughter at the crude bridge to the impending premiere, overtoned with sullenness at the reminder of just who and what they were. D'mahl had blown it—or at least failed to entirely recover—and he knew it, and the knowledge was a red nova inside his skull. At this moment of foul karma, 24.000 passed into realtime, and on tap frequency E-6—

You are standing at the base of a gentle verdant hill on whose tree-dotted summit a man in a loincloth is being nailed to a cross. Each time the mallet descends, you feel piercing pains in your wrists. You stand in an alleyway in ancient Jerusalem holding a jug of water to your breast as Jesus is dragged to his doom, and you feel his terrible hopeless thirst parching your throat. You are back at Calvary listening to the beat of the mallet, feeling the lightnings of pain in your wrists, the taste of burning sands in your mouth.

You are on the quarterdeck of an ancient wooden sailing ship tasting the salt wind of an ocean storm. The sky roils and howls under an evil green moon. Your crew scurries about the deck and rigging, shouting and moaning in thin spectral voices, creatures of tattered rags and ghostly transparent flesh. Foam flies into your face, and you wipe it off with the back of your hand, seeing through your own flesh as it passes before your eyes. You feel laughter at the back of your throat, and it bubbles out of you—too loud, too hearty, a maniac's howl. You raise your foglike fist and brandish it at the heavens. Lightning bolts crackle. You shake your fist harder and inhale the storm wind like the breath of a lover.

You look up the slope of Calvary as the final stroke of the mallet is driven home and you feel the wooden handle and the iron spike in your own hands. The cross is erected, and it is you who hang from it, and the sky is dissolved in a deafening blast of light brighter than a thousand suns. And you are trudging on an endless plain of blowing gray ash under a sky the color of rusting steel. The jagged ruins of broken buildings protrude from the swirling dust, and the world is full of maimed and skeletal people marching from horizon to horizon without hope. But your body has the plodding leaden strength of a thing that knows it cannot die. Pain in your wrists, and ashes in your mouth. The people around you begin to rot on their feet, to melt like Dali watches, and then only you remain, custodian of a planetary corpse. A ghostly sailing ship approaches you, luffing and pitching on the storm-whipped ash.

The quarterdeck pitches under your feet and skies howl. Then the storm clouds around the moon melt away to reveal a cool utter blackness punctuated by myriad hard points of light, and the quarterdeck becomes a steel bulkhead under your feet and you are standing in an observation bubble of a primitive first generation torchship. Around your starry horizon are dozens of other converted asteroid freighters, little more than fusion torchtubes with makeshift domes, blisters, and toroid decks cobbled to their surfaces—the distant solar ancestors of the Trek.

You turn to see an ancient horror standing beside you: an old, old man, his face scarred by radiation, his soul scarred by bottomless guilt, and his black eyes burning coldly with eternal ice.

You are standing in an observation bubble of a first-generation torchship. Below, the Earth is a brownish, singed, cancerous ball still stewing in the radiation of the Slow Motion War. Somewhere a bell is tolling, and you can feel the tug of the bellrope in your hands. Turning, you see a lean, sinister man with a face all flat planes and eyes like blue coals. His face fades into fog for a moment, and only those mad eyes remain solid and real.

"Hello, Dutchman," you say.

"Hello, Refugee."

"I'm usually called Wanderer."

"That's no longer much of a distinction," the Dutchman says. "All men are wanderers now."

"We're all refugees too. We've killed the living world that gave us birth. Even you and I may never live to see another." The bite of the nails into your wrists, the weight of the mallet in your hand. Thirst, and the tolling of a far-off bell.

You are the Dutchman, looking out into the universal night; a generation to the nearest star, a century to the nearest hope of a living world, forever to the other side. Thunder rolls inside your head and lightnings flash behind your eyes. "We've got these decks under our feet, the interstellar wind to ride, and fusion torches to ride it with," you say. "Don't whine to me, I've never had more." You laugh a wild maniac howl. "And I've got plenty of company, now."

You are the Wanderer, looking down at the slain Earth, listening to the bell toll, feeling the dead weight of the mallet in your hand. "So do I, Dutchman, so do I."

The globe of the Earth transforms itself into another world: a brown-and-purple planetary continent marbled with veins and lakes of watery blue. Clad in a heavy spacesuit, you are standing on the surface of the planet: naked rock on the shore of a clear blue lake, under a violet sky laced with thin gray clouds like jet contrails. A dozen other suited men are fanned out across the plain of fractured rock, like ants crawling on a bone pile.

"Dead," you say. "A corpse-world."

Maniac laughter beside you. "Don't be morbid, Wanderer. Nothing is dead that was never alive."

You kneel on a patch of furrowed soil cupping a wilted pine seedling in your hands. The sky above you is steel plating studded with overhead floodlights, and the massive cylindrical body of the torchtube skewers the watertank universe of this dirtdigger deck. The whole layout is primitive, strictly first-generation Trek. Beside you, a young girl in green dirtdigger shorts and shirt is sitting disconsolately on the synthetic loam, staring at the curved outer bulkhead of the farm deck.

"I'm going to live and die without ever seeing a sky or walking in a forest," she says. "What am I doing here? What's all this for?"

"You're keeping the embers of Earth alive," you say in your ancient's voice. "You're preserving the last surviving forms of organic life. Some day your children or your children's children will plant these seeds in the living soil of a new Earth."

"Do you really believe that?" she says earnestly, turning her youthful strength on you like a sun. "That we'll find a living planet some day?"

"You must believe. If you stop believing, you'll be with us here in this hell of our own creation. We Earthborn were life's destroyers. Our children must be life's preservers."

She looks at you with the Wanderer's cold eternal eyes, and her face withers to a parchment of ancient despair. "For the sake of our bloodstained souls?" she says, then becomes a young girl once more.

"For the sake of your own, girl, for the sake of your own."

You float weightless inside the huddled circle of the Trek. The circular formation of ships is a lagoon of light in an endless sea of black nothingness. Bow-ward of the Trek, the interstellar abyss is hidden behind a curtain of gauzy brilliance: the hydrogen interface, where the combined scoopfields of the Trek's fusion torches form a permanent shock wave against the attenuated interstellar atmosphere. Although the Trek's ships have already been modified and aligned to form the hydrogen interface, the ships are still the same converted asteroid freighters that left Sol; this is no later than Trek Year 150.

But inside the circle of ships, the future is being launched. The *Flying Dutchman*, the first torchship to be built entirely on the Trek out of matter winnowed and transmuted from the interstellar medium, floats in the space before you, surrounded by a gnat swarm of intership shuttles and men and women in voidsuits. A clean, smooth cylinder ringed with windowed decks, it seems out of place among the messy jury-rigging of the first-generation torchships, an intrusion from the future.

Then an all-but-invisible purple flame issues from the *Dutchman's* torchtube and the first Trekborn ship is drawing its breath of life.

Another new torchship appears beside the *Flying Dutchman*, and another and another and another, until the new Trekborn ships outnumber the converted asteroid freighters and the hydrogen interface has more than doubled in diameter. Now the area inside the Trek is a vast concourse of torchships, shuttles, suited people, and the dancing lights of civilized life.

You are standing on a bulkhead catwalk overlooking the floor of a dirtdigger deck: a sparse forest of small pines and oaks, patches of green grass, a few rows of flowers. Above is a holo of a blue Earth sky with fleecy white clouds. Dirtdiggers in their traditional green move about solemnly, tending the fragile life-forms, measuring their growth. Your nostrils are filled with the incense odor of holiness.

And you sit at a round simmed marble table on a balcony café halfway up the outer bulkhead of an amusement deck sipping a glass of simmed burgundy. A circle of shops and restaurants rings the floor below, connected by radial paths to an inner ring of shops around the central torchtube shaft. Each resulting wedge of floor is a different bright color, each is given over to a different amusement: a swimming pool, a bandstand, a zero-g dance-plate, carnival rides, a shimmer maze. Noise rises. Music plays.

Across from you sits the Wanderer, wearing dirtdigger green and an expression of bitter contempt. "Look at them," he says. "We're about to approach another planet, and they don't even know where they are."

"And where is that, Refugee?"

"Who should know better than you, Dutchman?" he says. And the people below turn transparent, and the bulkheads disappear, and you are watching zombies dancing on a platform floating in the interstellar abyss. Nothing else lives, nothing else moves, in all that endless immensity.

Manic laughter tickles your throat.

A planet appears as a pinpoint, then a green-and-brown mottled sphere with fleecy white clouds, and then you are standing on its surface among a party of suited men trudging heavily back to their shuttleship. Hard brown rock veined with greenish mineral streakings under a blue-black sky dotted with pastel-green clouds. You are back on your balcony watching specters dance in the endless galactic night.

"Great admiral, what shall you say when hope is gone?" the Wanderer says.

And you are down among the specters, grown ten feet tall, a giant shaking your fist against the blackness, at the dead planet, howling your defiance against the everlasting night. "Sail on! Sail on! Sail on and on!"

"No more ships! No more ships! Soil or death!" You are marching at the head of a small army of men and women in dirtdigger green as it bursts into the amusement deck from the deck below, bearing crosses wrapped with simmed grape leaves. Each chanted shout sends nails through your wrists.

And you are leading your carnival of ghosts on a mad dance through a dirtdigger deck, carelessly trampling on the fragile life-forms, strewing gold and silver confetti, flashers, handfuls of jewels—the bounty of the fusion torch's passage through the interstellar plankton.

You are in a droptube falling through the decks of a ship. Amusement decks, residential decks, manufacturing decks, sifting decks—all but the control and torchtender decks—have been rudely covered over with synthetic loam and turned into makeshift dirtdigger decks. The growth is sparse, the air has a chemical foulness, metal surfaces are beginning to corrode, and the green-clad people have the hunched shoulders and sunken eyes of the unwholesomely obsessed. The vine-covered cross is everywhere.

You are rising through a lift-tube on another ship. Here the machinery is in good repair, the air is clean, the bulkheads shiny, and the decks of the ship glory in light and sound and surfaces of simmed ruby, emerald, sapphire, and diamond. The people are birds-of-paradise in mirror suits, simmed velvets and silks in luxurious shades and patterns, feathers and leathers, gold, silver, and brass. But they seem to be moving to an unnatural rhythm, dancing a mad jig to a phantom fiddler, and their flesh is as transparent as unpolarized plex.

You are floating in space in the center of the Trek; behind you, the Trekborn ships are a half-circle diadem of jeweled brilliance. In front of you floats the Wanderer, and behind him the old converted asteroid freighters, tacky and decayed, pale greenery showing behind every blister and viewport.

"Your gardens are dying, Wanderer."

"Yours never had life, Dutchman," he says, and you can see stars and void through your glassy flesh, through the ghost-ships behind you.

Two silvery headbands appear in the space between you in a fanfare of music and a golden halo of light. Large, crude, designed for temporary external wear, they are the first full sensory transceivers, ancestors of the surgically implanted tap. They glow and pulse like live things, like the gift of the nonexistent gods.

You pick one of the headbands, laugh, place it on the Wanderer's head. "With this ring, I thee wed."

Unblinkingly, he places the other band on yours. "Bear my crown of thorns," he says.

You stand on the bridge of a torchship, the spectral Dutchman at your side. Beyond the plex, the stars are a million live jewels, a glory mirrored in the lights of the Trek.

You kneel among tiny pine trees in a dirtdigger deck beside the Wanderer, and they become a redwood forest towering into the blue skies of lost Earth, and you can feel the pain of the nails in your ghostly wrists, hearing the tolling of a far-off bell, feel the body's sadness, smell the incense of irredeemable loss.

You rise through a lift-tube, the Dutchman's hand in yours, and you hear the hum of energy as you pass through deck after jeweled and gleaming deck, hear the sounds of human laughter and joy, see crystal trees sprouting and rising from the metal deckplates. The flesh of the spectral people solidifies and the Dutchman's hand becomes pink and solid. When you look at his face, your own Wanderer's eyes look back, pain muted by a wild joy.

You float in the center of the Trek with the Wanderer as the ships around you rearrange themselves in an intricate ballet: Trekborn and converted asteroid freighters in hundreds of magical *pas de deux*, reintegrating the Trek.

You are droptubing down through the decks of a dirtdigger ship, watching green uniforms transform themselves into the bird-of-paradise plumage of the Trekborn ships, watching the corrosion disappear from the metal, watching crystal gazebos, shimmer mazes, and bubbling brooks appear, as shrines to sadness become gardens of joy.

And you are sitting across a round simmed marble table from the Dutchman on a balcony café halfway up the bulkhead of an amusement deck. The central torchtube shaft is overgrown with ivy. The pool, bandstand, shimmer mazes, dance-plates, and carnival rides are laid out in a meadow of green grass shaded by pines and oaks. The bulkheads and upper decking dissolve, and this garden square stands revealed as a tiny circle of life lost in the immensity of the eternal void.

"We're Wanderers in the midnight of the soul," the Dutchman says. "Perhaps we're guardians of the only living things that ever were."

"Flying Dutchmen on an endless sea, perhaps the only gods there be."

And you are a detached viewpoint watching this circle of life drift away into the immensity of space, watching the Trek dwindle away until it is nothing more than one more abstract pinpoint of light against the galactic darkness. Words of pale fire appear across the endless starfield:

# WANDERING DUTCHMEN
## by Jofe D'mahl

There was an unmistakable note of politeness in the clicking of tongues in Jofe D'mahl's grand salon. The applause went on for an appropriate interval (*just appropriate*), and then the guests were up and talking, a brightly colored flock of birds flitting and jabbering about the jeweled forest.

". . . you could see that it had well-defined continents, and the green areas *must* be vegetation . . ."

". . . oxygen, sure, but can we breathe all that helium?"

Standing between Jiz Rumoku and Bandoora, Jofe D'mahl found himself in the infuriating position of being a vacuum beside the focus of attention. Eyes constantly glanced in their direction for a glimpse of Bandoora, but no gaze dared linger long, for at the side of the voidsucker, D'mahl was sizzling toward nova, his eyes putting out enough hard radiation to melt plex.

But Bandoora himself was looking straight at him, and D'mahl sensed some unguessable focus of alien warmth pulsing up at him from the depths of those unfathomable eyes. "I'm sorry the Pilots' bulletin ruined your premiere," he said.

"*Really?*" D'mahl snarled. "What makes you think your precious blatt has so much importance?" he continued loudly. There was no reason for the guests not to stare now; D'mahl was shouting for it. "You dreeks expect us to slaver like Pavlov's dogs every time you turn up some reeking mudball that looks habitable until you get close enough to get a good whiff of the dead stink of poison gas and naked rock. Your blatt will be a six-month nova, Bandoora. Art is forever."

"Forever may be a longer time than you realize, D'mahl,"

Bandoora said calmly. "Other than that, I agree with you entirely. I found *Wandering Dutchmen* quite moving." Were those actually *tears* forming in his eyes? "Perhaps more moving than even you can imagine."

Silence reigned now as the attention of the guests became totally focused on this small psychodrama. Some of the bolder ones began to inch closer. D'mahl found that he could not make out Bandoora's vector; in this little ego contest, there seemed to be no common set of rules.

"I'd like to atone for interfering with the premiere of a great work of art," Bandoora said. "I'll give you a chance to make the greatest senso of your career, D'mahl." There was a thin smile on his lips, but his eyes were so earnest as to appear almost comical.

"What makes you think *you* can teach *me* anything about sensos?" D'mahl said. "Next thing, you'll be asking me for a lesson in voidsucking." A titter of laughter danced around the salon.

"Perhaps I've already gotten it, D'mahl," Bandoora said. He turned, began walking through the colored mists and crystal trees toward the transparent plex that blistered the great balcony, focusing his eyes on D'mahl through the crowd, back over his shoulder. "I don't know anything about sensos, but I can show you a reality that will make anything you've experienced pale into nothingness. Capture it on tape if you dare." A massed intake of breath.

"*If I dare!*" D'mahl shouted, exploding into nova. "Who do you think you're scaring with your cheap theatrics, Bandoora? I'm Jofe D'mahl, I'm the greatest artist of my time, I'm riding the torch of my own ego, and I know it. *If I dare*! What do you think any of us have to do *but* dare, you poor dreek? Didn't you understand *anything* of what you just experienced?"

Bandoora reached the plex blister, turned, stood outlined against the starry darkness, the blaze of the concourse of ships. His eyes seemed to draw a baleful energy from the blackness. "No theatrics, D'mahl," Bandoora said. "No computer taps, no sensos, no illusions. None of the things all you people live by. *Reality*, D'mahl, the real thing. Out there. The naked void."

He half turned, stretched out his right arm as if to embrace the darkness. "Come with us on Bela-37, D'mahl," he said. "Out there in your naked mind where nothing exists but you and the everlasting void. *Wandering Dutchmen* speaks well of such things—for a senso by a man who was simming it. What might you do with your own sensorium tape of the void itself—if you dared record it through your own living flesh? Do you dare, D'mahl, do you dare face the truth of it with your naked soul?"

"Jof— "

D'mahl brushed Jiz aside. "*Simming it!*" he bellowed in red rage. "Do I dare!" The reality of the grand salon, even the ego challenge hurled at him before his guests, burned away in the white-hot fire of the deeper challenge, the gauntlet Bandoora had flung at the feet of his soul. *I can face this thing, can you? Can you truly carve living art out of the dead void, not metaphorically, but out of the nothingness itself, in the flesh, in realtime? Or are you simming it? Are you a fraud?*

"I told you, Bandoora," he said, hissing through his rage, "I've got nothing to do *but* dare."

The guests oohed, Jiz shook her head, Bandoora nodded and smiled. Jofe D'mahl felt waves of change ripple through his grand salon, through himself, but their nature and vector eluded the grasp of his mind.

# 2

As he flitted from *Excelsior* to *Brigadoon* across a crowded sector of the central Trek, it seemed to Jofe D'mahl that the bubble of excitement in which he had been moving since the premiere party had more tangibility than the transparent shimmer screen of his void-bubble. The shimmer was visible only as the interface between the hard vacuum of space and the sphere of air it contained, but the enhancement of his persona was visible on the face of every person he saw. He was being tapped so frequently by people he had never met in senso or flesh that he had finally had to do something 180 degrees from his normal vector: tap a screening program into his banks that rejected calls from all people not on a manageable approved list. He was definitely the Trek's current nova.

Even here, among the bubbled throngs flitting from ship to ship or just space-jaunting, D'mahl felt as if he were outshining the brilliance of the concourse of torchships, even the hydrogen interface itself, as most of the people whose trajectories came within visible range of his own saluted him with nods of their heads or subtle sidelong glances.

It almost made up for the fact that it wasn't *Wandering Dutchmen* that had triggered his nova but his public decision to dare six standard months with the voidsuckers—away from the Trek, out of tap contact with the banks, alone in his mind and body like a primitive pre-tap man. Waller Nan Pei had achieved the same effect by announcing his public suicide a month in advance, but blew out his torch forever by failing to go through with it. D'mahl knew there could be no backing out now.

He flitted past *Paradisio*, accepted the salutations of the passengers on a passing shuttle, rounded *Ginza*, throttled back his g-polarizer, and landed lightly on his toes on *Brigadoon*'s main entrance stage. He walked quickly across the ruby ledge, passed through the shimmer, collapsed his bubble, and took the nearest droptube for Jiz Rumoku's gallery on twelvedeck, wondering what the place would look like this time.

Thanks to Jiz's aura, *Brigadoon* was the chameleonship of the Trek; whole decks were completely done over about as often as the average Trekker redid his private quarters. Fashions and flashes tended to spread from *Brigadoon* to the rest of the Trek much as they spread from Jiz's gallery to the decks of her ship. Recently, a motion to change the ship's name to *Quicksilver* had come within fifty votes of passage.

Dropping through the decks, D'mahl saw more changes than he could identify without tapping for the previous layouts, and he had been on *Brigadoon* about a standard month ago. Threedeck had been living quarters tiered around a formalized rock garden; now it was a lagoon with floating houseboats. Sixdeck had been a sim of the ancient Tivoli; now the amusements were arranged on multileveled g-plates over a huge slow-motion whirlpool of syrupy rainbow-colored liquid. Ninedeck had been a ziggurat-maze of living quarters festooned with ivy; now it was a miniature desert of static-molded gold and silver dust-dunes, latticed into a faerie filigree of cavelike apartments. Fluidity seemed to be the theme of the month.

Twelvedeck was now a confection of multicolored energy. The walls of the shops and restaurants were tinted shimmer screens in scores of subtle hues, and the central plaza around the torchtube shaft was an ever-changing meadow of slowly moving miniature fuzzballs in blue, green, purple, yellow, and magenta. The torchtube itself was a cylindrical mirror, and most of the people were wearing tinted mirror suits, fogrobes, or lightcloaks. It was like being inside a rainbow, and D'mahl felt out of sync in his comparatively severe blue pants, bare chest, and cloth-of-gold cloak.

Jiz Rumoku's gallery was behind a sapphire-blue waterfall that cascaded from halfway up the curved bulkhead to a pool of mist spilling out across the floor of the deck. D'mahl stepped through it, half expecting to be soaked. Mercifully, the waterfall proved to be a holo, but with Jiz, you never knew.

"You who are about to die salute us," Jiz said. She was lying in a blushing-pink fuzzball, naked except for blinding auroras of broad-spectrum light coyly hiding her breasts and loins. The pink fuzzball floated in a lazy ellipse near the center of the gallery, which was now a circular area contained by a shimmer screen around its circumference that rippled endless spectral changes. The ceiling was a holo of roiling orange fire, the floor a mirror of some soft substance.

"Better in fire than in ice," D'mahl said. "My motto." They cross-tapped, and D'mahl lay in the fuzzball feeling an electric glow as his body walked across the gallery and kissed Jiz's lips.

"Voidsucking isn't exactly my idea of fire, Jof," Jiz said as they simultaneously broke their taps.

"This is?" D'mahl said, sweeping his arm in an arc. Dozens of floaters in sizes ranging from a few square centimeters to a good three meters square drifted in seemingly random trajectories around the gallery, displaying objects and energy-effects ranging from tiny pieces of static-molded gemdust jewelry to boxes of flashers, fogrobes, clingers, holopanes that were mostly abstract, and several large and very striking fire-sculptures. The floaters themselves were all transparent plex, and very few of the "objects" on them were pure matter.

"I cog that people are going to be bored with matter for a while," Jiz said, rising from the fuzzball. "After all, it's nothing but frozen energy. Flux is the coming nova, energy-matter interface stuff. It expresses the spirit of the torch, don't you think? Energy, protons, electrons, neutrons, and heavy element dust from the interstellar medium transmuted into whatever 'we please. This current collection expresses the transmutational state itself."

"I like to have a few things with hard surfaces around," D'mahl said somewhat dubiously.

"You'll see, even your place will be primarily interface for the next standard month or so. You'll put it in sync."

"No I won't, Oh creator of tomorrow's flash," D'mahl said, kissing her teasingly on the lips. "While everyone else is going transmutational, I'll be out there in the cold hard void, where energy and matter know their places and stick to them."

Jiz frowned, touched his cheek. "You're really going through with it, aren't you?" she said. "Months of being cooped up in some awful scoutship, sans tap, sans lovers, sans change. . . ."

"Perhaps at least not sans lovers," D'mahl said lightly, thinking of Sidi. But Jiz, he saw, was seriously worried. "What's the matter, Jiz?"

"What do you actually know about the voidsuckers?"

"What's to know? They man the scoutships. They look for habitable planets. They live the simplest lives imaginable."

"Have you tapped anything on them?"

"No. I'm taking a senso recorder along, of course, and I'll have to use myself as major viewpoint, so I don't want any sensory preconceptions."

"I've tapped the basic sensohistory of the voidsuckers Jof. There's nothing else in the banks. Doesn't that bother you?"

"Should it?"

"Tap it, Jof."

"I told you— "

"I know, no sensory preconceptions. But I'm asking you to tap it anyway. I have, and I think you should." Her eyes were hard and unblinking, and her mouth was hardened into an ideogram of resolve. When Jiz got that look, D'mahl usually found it advisable to follow her vector, for the sake of parsimony, if nothing else.

"All right," he said. "For you, I'll sully my pristine consciousness with sordid facts. Voidsuckers, basic history," he subvoced.

He stood in an observation blister watching a scoutship head for the hydrogen interface. The scout was basically a torchship-size fusion tube with a single small toroid deck amidship and a bridge bubble up near the intake. "Trek Year 301," a neuter voice said. "The first scoutship is launched by the Trek's. Crewed by five volunteers, it is powered by a full-size fusion torch though its mass is only one-tenth that of a conventional torchship. Combined with its utilization of the Trek's momentum, this enables it rapidly to reach a terminal velocity approaching .87 lights."

D'mahl was a detached observer far out in space watching the scoutship torch ahead of the Trek. Another scoutship, then another, and another, and finally others too numerous to count easily, torched through the hydrogen interface and ahead of the Trek, veering off at angles ranging from ten to thirty degrees, forming a conical formation. The area of space enclosed by the cone turned bright green as the voice said: "By 402, the scoutships numbered forty-seven, and the still-current search pattern had been regularized. Ranging up to a full light-year from the Trek and remote-surveying solar systems from this expanded cone of vision, the scoutship system maximized the number of potential habitable planets surveyed in a given unit of time."

Now D'mahl sat on the bridge of a scoutship looking out the plex at space. Around him, two men and a woman in blue voidsucker shorts were puttering about with instrument consoles. "In 508, a new innovation was introduced." A small drone missile shot slightly ahead of the scoutship, which then began to veer off. "Scoutships now dispatched telltale probes to potentially habitable planets, returning at once to the Trek."

D'mahl was a viewpoint in space watching a stylized diorama of the Trek, a scoutship, a telltale, and a solar system. The scout was torching back to the Trek while the telltale orbited a planet, broadcasting a red wavefront of information Trekward. The scout reached the Trek, which altered its vector toward the telltale's solar system. The scout then left the Trek to monitor the oncoming telltale wavefront. "By turning the Trek toward a prospective system, then returning to monitor the telltale wavefront by scoutship, our fully evolved planetary reconnaissance system now maximizes the number of solar systems investigated in a given time period and also minimizes the reporting time for each high-probability solar system investigated."

D'mahl was aboard a scoutship, playing null-g tennis with an attractive female voidsucker. He was in a simple commissary punching out a meal. He was lying on a grav-plate set at about .25 g in small private sleeping quarters. He was a female voidsucker making love to a tall powerful man in null-g. "The scout's quarters, though comfortable and adequate to maintain physical and mental health, impose some hardship on the crew owing to space limitations," the neuter voice said. "Tap banks are very limited and access to the central Trek banks impossible. Scout crews must content themselves with simple in-flesh amusements. All Trekkers owe these selfless volunteers a debt of gratitude."

Jofe D'mahl looked into Jiz Rumoku's eyes. He shrugged. "So?" he said. "What does that tell me that I didn't already know?"

"Nothing, Jof, not one damned thing! The voidsuckers have been out there in the flesh for over half a millennium, spending most of their lives with no tap connection to the Trek, to everything that makes the only human civilization there is what it is. What's their karmic vector? What's inside their skulls? Why are they called voidsuckers, anyway? Why isn't there anything in the banks except that basic history tape?"

"Obviously because no one's gone out there with them to make a real senso," D'mahl said. "They're certainly not the types to produce one themselves. That's why I'm going, Jiz. I think Bandoora was right—there's a beyond senso to be made on the voidsuckers, and it may be the only virgin subject matter left."

A little of the intensity went out of Jiz's expression. "Ego, of course, has nothing to do with it," she said.

"Ego, of course, has everything to do with it," D'mahl replied.

She touched a hand to his cheek. "Be careful, Jof," she said quite softly.

Moved, D'mahl put his hand over hers, kissed her lightly on the lips, feeling, somehow, like an Earthbound primitive. "What's there to be afraid of?" he said with equal tenderness.

"I don't know, Jof, and I don't know how to find out. That's what scares me."

Jofe D'mahl felt a rising sense of vectorless anticipation as the shuttle bore him bow-ward toward Bela-37, a silvery cylinder glinting against the auroral background of the hydrogen interface as it hung like a Damoclean sword above him. Below, the ships of the Trek were receding, becoming first a horizon-filling landscape of light and flash, then a disk of human warmth sharply outlined against the cold black night. It occurred to him that Trekkers seldom ventured up here where the scoutships parked, close by the interface separating the Trek from the true void. It was not hard to see why.

"Long way up, isn't it?" he muttered.

The shuttle pilot nodded. "Not many people come up here," he said. "Voidsuckers and maintenance crews mostly. I come up here by myself sometimes to feel the pressure of the void behind the interface and look down on it all like a god on Olympus." He laughed dryly. "Maybe I've ferried one voidsucker too many."

Something made D'mahl shudder, then yearn for the communion of the tap—the overwhelmingly rich intermeshing of time, space, bodies, and realities from which he was about to isolate himself for the first time in his life. The tap is what we live by, he thought, and who so more than I?

"Jiz Rumoku," he subvoced, and he was in her body, standing beside a fire-sculpture in her gallery with a chunky black man in a severe green velvet suit. "Hello, Jiz," he said with her vocal cords. "Hello and good-bye."

He withdrew his tap from her body, and she followed into his, high above the Trek. "Hello, Jof. It's sure a long way up." She kissed his hand with his lips. "Take care," his voice said. Then she broke the tap, and D'mahl was alone in his flesh as the shuttle decelerated, easing up alongside Bela-37's toroid main deck.

"This is it," the shuttle pilot said. "You board through the main shimmer." D'mahl gave the pilot an ironic salute, erected his voidbubble, grabbed his kit and senso recorder, and flitted across a few meters of space to Bela-37's main entrance stage.

Stepping through the shimmer, he was surprised to find himself in a small closetlike room with no drop-tube shaft in evidence. A round door in the far bulkhead opened and a tall, pale voidsucker stepped inside. "I'm Ban Nyborg, D'mahl," he said. He laughed rather humorlessly. "This is an airlock," he said. "Safety feature."

Automatically, D'mahl tapped for a definition of the new word: *double-doored chamber designed to facilitate ship entry and exit, obsoleted by the shimmer screen.* "How quaint," he said, following Nyborg through the open door.

"Lose power, lose your shimmer, this way you keep your air," Nyborg said, leading D'mahl down a dismal blue pastel corridor. "Radial passageway," Nyborg said. "Leads to circular corridor around the torchtube. Five other radials, tubes to the bridge and back, that's the ship." They reached the circumtorchtube corridor, done in washed-out blue and yellow, walked sixty degrees around it past some instrument consoles and an orange radial corridor, then another sixty degrees and halfway up a green radial to a plain matter door.

Nyborg opened the door and D'mahl stepped into a grim little room. There was a g-plate, a blue pneumatic chair, a tall simmed walnut chest, a shaggy red rug, and, beyond an open door, toilet facilities. The ceiling was deep gray, and three of the walls were grayish tan. The fourth was a holo of the interstellar abyss itself—pinpoint stars and yawning blackness—and it faced the g-plate.

"Bandoora's quarters," Nyborg said. "He's doubling with Sidi."

"Charming," D'mahl grunted. "I'm touched."

"Ship's got three tap frequencies: library, communications, external visual. Bridge is off limits now. You can tap our departure on external." Nyborg turned, walked unceremoniously out of the little cell, and closed the door behind him.

D'mahl shuddered. The walls and ceiling seemed to be closing in on him as if to squeeze him into the reality of the holo. He found himself staring into the starfield, leaning toward it as if it were pulling him down into it.

He blinked, feeling the strangeness of the sensation, which drew his attention away from the holo and to his senso recorder. Ought to get all this down. He turned the recorder on, dropped in a hundred-hour pod of microtape, keyed it to his own sensorium. But the initial moment of vertigo had passed; now he was just in an excruciatingly dull little room with a big starfield holo on one wall.

D'mahl set the g-plate for .1 g, just enough to hold him in place, and lay down on the padding. He found himself staring into the starfield holo again from this position. Did Bandoora actually like being sucked at by that thing?

Bandoora tapped him, audio only: "Welcome to Bela-37, D'mahl. We're about to torch through the interface. Perhaps you'd care to tap it."

"Thanks," D'mahl tapped back through the scout's com frequency, "but I'd rather record it in the flesh from the bridge."

"Sorry, but the bridge is off limits to you now," Bandoora said, and broke the tap.

"Drool!" D'mahl snarled to no one, and irritably tapped the scout's external visual frequency.

He was a disembodied viewpoint moving through the silent frictionless darkness of space. It was like being in a voidbubble and yet not like being in a void-bubble, for here he was disconnected from all internal and external senses save vision. He found that he could tap subfrequencies that gave him choice of visual direction, something like being able to turn his non-existent head. Below, the Trek was a jewel of infinitely subtle light slowly shrinking in the velvet blackness. All other vectors were dominated by the hydrogen interface, a sky of rainbow brilliance that seemed to all but surround him.

It was a moving visual spectacle, and yet the lack of the subtleties of full sense also made it pathetic, filled D'mahl with an elusive sadness. As the rainbow sheen of the hydrogen interface moved visibly closer, that sadness resolved along a nostalgia vector as D'mahl realized that he was about to lose tap contact with the Trek's banks. The interface energies would block out the banks long before time-lag or signal attenuation even became a factor. It was his last chance to say good-bye to the multiplex Trek reality before being committed to the unknown and invariant void beyond.

He broke his tap with the scout's visual frequency, and zip-tapped through the multiplicity of the Trek's frequencies like a dying man flashing through his life's sensorium track before committing it to the limbo banks.

He stood among the crystal trees of his own grand salon. He was Dalta Reed punting across Blood Lake on *Lothlorien* and he was Erna Ramblieu making love to John Benina on his balcony overlooking Sundance Corridor of *Magic Mountain*. He watched *Excelsior* being built from the body of a welder working on the hull, and he flashed through the final sequence of *Wandering Dutchmen*. He riffled through his own sensorium track—making love to Jiz five years ago in a dirtdigger deck, moments of ten parties, dancing above a null-g plate as a boy, cutting *Wandering Dutchmen* at his editor—realizing suddenly that he was leaving the world of his own stored memories behind with everything else. Finally, he flashed through Jiz Rumoku's body as she led the man in the green velvet suit past a holoframe of the Far Look Ballet dancing *Swan Lake* in null-g, and then his tap was broken, and he was lying on his g-plate in Bela-37, unable to reestablish it.

He tapped the scout's visual frequency and found himself moving into the world-filling brilliance of the hydrogen interface behind the auroral bubble of Bela-37's own torch intake field. The lesser rainbow touched the greater, and D'mahl rapidly became sheathed in glory as Bela-37's field formed a bulge in the Trek's combined field, a bulge that enveloped the scoutship and D'mahl, became a closed sphere of full-spectrum fire for an instant, then burst through the hydrogen interface with a rush that sent D'mahl's being soaring, gasping, and reeling into the cold hard blackness of the open void beyond.

D'mahl shook, grunted, and broke the tap. For a panicked moment he thought he had somehow been trapped in the abyss as his vision snapped back into his flesh staring at the holo of the void that filled the wall facing him.

The lift-tube ended and Jofe D'mahl floated up out of it and onto the circular bridge of Bela-37. The bridge was a plex blister up near the bow of the torch-tube encircled by consoles and controls to waist level but otherwise visually naked to the interstellar void. Bow-ward, the ship's intake field formed a miniature hydrogen interface; sternward, the Trek was visible as a scintillating disk behind a curtain of ethereal fire, but otherwise nothing seemed to live or move in all that eternal immensity.

"Isn't there any getting away from it?" D'mahl muttered, half to himself, half to Haris Bandoora, who had watched him emerge from the lift-tube with those unfathomable eyes and an ironic, enigmatic grin.

"You people spend your lives trying to get away from it," Bandoora said, "and we spend our lives drenching ourselves in it because we know there *is* no real escape from it. One way or the other, our lives are dominated by the void."

"Speak for yourself, Bandoora," D'mahl said. "Out there is only one reality." He touched a forefinger to his temple. "In here are an infinity more."

"Illusion," said a woman's voice behind him. D'mahl turned and saw Sidi—conical bare breasts, hairless silvered skull, tightly muscled body, opaque voidsucker eyes—a vision of cold and abstract feminine beauty.

D'mahl smiled at her. "What is," he said, "is real."

"Where you come from," Sidi said, "no one knows what's real."

"*Réalité c'est moi,*" D'mahl said in ancient French. When both Sidi and Bandoora stared at him blankly, failing to tap for the reference, *unable* to tap for the reference, he had a sharp flash of loneliness. An adult among children. A civilized man among primitives. And out there . . . out there . . .

He forced his attention away from such thoughts, forced his vision away from the all-enveloping void, and walked toward one of the instrument consoles where a slim woman with a shaven untinted skull sat in a pedestal chair adjusting some controls.

"This is Areth Lorenzi," Bandoora said. "She's setting the sweep-sequence of our extreme-range grav-scan. We automatically scan a twenty light-year sphere for new planeted stars even on a mission like this. We can pick up an Earth-massed body that far away."

The woman turned, and D'mahl saw a face steeped in age. There were wrinkles around her eyes, at the corners of her mouth, even a hint of them on her cheeks; extraordinary enough in itself, but it was her deep, deep pale-blue eyes that spoke most eloquently of her years, of the sheer volume of the things they had seen.

"How often have you detected such bodies?" D'mahl asked conversationally, to keep from obviously staring.

Something seemed to flare in those limpid depths. She glanced over D'mahl's shoulder at Bandoora for a moment. "It's . . . a common enough occurrence," she said, and turned back to her work.

"And finally, this is Raj Doru," Bandoora said with a peculiar hastiness, indicating the other voidsucker on the bridge: a squat, dark, powerful-looking man with a fierce mouth, a sweeping curve of a nose, and bright brown eyes glowering under his shaven brows. He was standing, hands on hips, regarding D'mahl scornfully.

"*What is, is real*," Doru said acidly. "What do you know about real, Jofe D'mahl? You've never confronted the reality of the universe in your whole life! Cowering behind your hydrogen interface and your tap and your mental masturbation fantasies! The void would shrivel your soul to a pinpoint and then snuff it out of existence."

"*Raj!*" Bandoora snapped. Psychic energy crackled and clashed as the two voidsuckers glared at each other for a silent moment.

"Let's see the great D'mahl suck some void, Haris, let's— "

"Everything in its time," Bandoora said. "This isn't it."

"Raj is an impatient man," Sidi said.

"A peculiar trait for a voidsucker," D'mahl replied dryly. These people were beginning to grate on his consciousness. They seemed humorless, obsessive, out of sync with their own cores, as if the nothingness in which they continuously and monomaniacally wallowed had emptied out their centers and filled them with itself.

D'mahl found himself looking up and out into the starry blackness of the abyss, wondering if that eternal coldness might in time seep into his core too, if the mind simply could not encompass that much nothingness and still remain in command of its own vector.

"Patience is an indifferent virtue out here," Areth said. It did not seem a comforting thought.

# 3

What do these people *do* with themselves? Jofe D'mahl wondered as he paced idly and nervously around the circumtorchtube corridor for what seemed like the thousandth time. A week aboard Bela-37 and he was woozy with boredom. There was a limit to how much chess and null-g tennis you could play, and the ship's library banks were pathetic—a few hundred standard reference tapes, fifty lamer pornos, a hundred classic sensos (four of his own included, he was wanly pleased to note), and an endless log of dull-as-death scoutship reports.

"Patience is an indifferent virtue out here," Areth Lorenzi had said. To D'mahl, it seemed the only virtue possible under the circumstances, and his supply of it was rapidly running out.

Up ahead, he heard footfalls coming down a radial corridor, and a moment later his vector intersected that of Sidi, striding beautifully and coldly toward him like a robot simmed in flesh. Even his initial attraction to her was beginning to fade. Inside that carapace of abstract beauty she seemed as disconnected from any reality he cared to share as the others.

"Hello, D'mahl," she said distantly. "Have you been getting good material for your senso?"

D'mahl snorted. "If you can call a pod and a quarter of boredom footage interesting material," he said. "Bandoora promised me something transcendent. Where is it?"

"Have you not looked around you?"

D'mahl nodded upward, at the ceiling, at space beyond. "Out there? I can see that from my own grand salon."

"Wait."

"For what?"

"For the call."

"What call?"

"When it comes, you will know it," Sidi said, and walked past him up the corridor. D'mahl shook his head. From Doru, hostility; from Bandoora, lamer metaphysics; from Nyborg, a grunt now and then; from Areth Lorenzi, a few games of nearly silent chess. Now brain-teases from Sidi. Can it be that that's all these people have? A few lamer quirks around a core of inner vacuum? Nothing but their own obsessiveness between them and eternal boredom? It might make a reasonably interesting senso, if I could figure out a way to dramatize vacuity. He sighed. At least it gave him a valid artistic problem to play with.

"*All* routine here," Ban Nyborg said, bending his tall frame over the readout screen, across which two columns of letters and numbers slowly crawled. "Star catalog numbers on the left, masses of any dark bodies around them on the right."

"A simple program could monitor this," D'mahl said. "Why are you doing it?"

"Computer *does* screen it, I'm just backing up. Something to do."

D'mahl shook his head. He had wandered into this comp center by accident—none of the voidsuckers had even bothered to mention it to him. Yet here was much of the equipment at the heart of the scoutship's mission: the ship's computer and banks, the gravscan readout, and a whole series of other instrument consoles he would have had to tap for to identify. But the dull gray room had a strange air of neglect about it.

"You sound almost as bored as I am, Nyborg," he said.

Nyborg nodded without looking up. "All waiting, till you get the call."

"*The call*? What call?"

Nyborg turned, and for the first time in nearly two standard weeks, D'mahl saw animation on his long face; fire, perhaps even remembered ecstasy in his pale eyes. "When the void calls you to it," he said. "You'll see. No use talking about it. It calls, and you go, and that's what it's all about. That's why we're all here."

"That's why you're here? What about all this?" D'mahl said, sweeping his hand in a circle to indicate the roomful of instruments.

He could visibly see the life go out of Nyborg's face; curtains came down over the fire in his eyes, and he was once again Nyborg the cyborg.

"All this is the mission," Nyborg grunted, turning back to the readout screen. "What gets us out here. But the call is why we come. Why do you think we're called voidsuckers?"

"Why?"

"We suck void," Nyborg said.

"You mean you don't care about the mission? You're not dedicated to finding us a new living world?"

"Drool," Nyborg muttered. "Scoutships don't need us, can run themselves. *We* need *them*. To get us to the void." He deliberately began to feign intense interest in what he was doing, and D'mahl could not extract a syllable more.


"Just how long have you been on scoutships, Areth?" Jofe D'mahl said, looking up from his hopeless position on the chessboard.

"About a century and a half," Areth Lorenzi said, still studying her next move. As always, she volunteered nothing.

"You must really be dedicated to the mission to have spent such a long life out here in nowhere," D'mahl said, trying to get something out of her. Those eyes hinted of so much and that mouth said so little.

"I've always heard the call."

"What's this call I keep hearing about?"

"The void calls, and for those who are called, there is nothing but the void. You think our lives are sacrifices for the common good of humanity?"

"Well, aren't they?"

Areth Lorenzi looked up at him with her ancient crystalline eyes. "We man the scoutships to reach the void, we don't brave the void to man the scoutships," she said. "We sacrifice nothing but illusion. We live with the truth. We live for the truth."

"And the truth shall set you free?" D'mahl said archly. But the reference blew by her since she had no way to tap for it.

Areth dropped her gaze. A note of bitterness came into her voice. "The truth is: No man is free." She moved her rook to double-check D'mahl's king and queen. "Checkmate in three moves, D'mahl," she said.

D'mahl found Haris Bandoora alone on the bridge looking sternward, back toward where the Trek had been visible until recently as a tiny bright disk among the pinpoint stars. Now the Trek, if it was visible at all, was nothing more than one point of light lost in a million others. Bela-37 seemed frozen in a black crystal vastness speckled with immobile motes of sparkling dust, an abstract universe of dubious reality.

A tremor of dread went through D'mahl, a twinge of the most utter aloneness. Even the presence of the enigmatic and aloof Bandoora seemed a beacon of human warmth in the dead uncaring night.

"Overwhelming, isn't it?" Bandoora said, turning at the sound of D'mahl's footfalls. "A hundred million stars, perhaps as many planets, and this one galaxy is a speck of matter floating in an endless nothingness." There was a strange overlay of softness in those dark and bottomless eyes, almost a misting of tears. "What are we, D'mahl? Once we were bits of some insignificant anomaly called life contaminating a dust-mote circling a speck of matter lost in a tiny cloud of specks, itself a minor contaminant of the universal void. Now we're not even that . . ."

"We're the part that counts, Bandoora," D'mahl said.

"To whom?" Bandoora said, nodding toward the abyss. "To *that*?"

"To ourselves. To whatever other beings share consciousness on planets around whichever of those stars. Sentience is what counts, Bandoora. The rest of it is just backdrop." D'mahl laughed hollowly. "If this be solipsism, let us make the most of it."

"If only you knew . . ."

"If only I knew what?"

Bandoora smiled an ironic smile. "You *will* know," he said. "That's why you're here. We can't be alone with it forever."

"What— "

"I've heard the call, Haris." Raj Doru had risen to the bridge, and now he walked rapidly to Bandoora's side, his brown eyes feverish, and uncharacteristic languor in his posture.

"When?" Bandoora asked crisply.

"Now."

"How long?"

"Twenty-four hours."

Bandoora turned and followed Doru toward the droptube. "What's going on?" D'mahl asked, trailing after them.

"Raj is going to suck void," Bandoora said. "He's heard the call. Care to help me see him off?"

At the round airlock door, Raj Doru took a voidbubble-and-flitter harness from the rack, donned it, took a flask of water and a cassette of ration out of a locker, and clipped them to the belt of his shorts. His eyes looked off into some unguessable reality that D'mahl could not begin to sync with.

"What are you doing, Doru?" he asked.

Doru didn't answer; he didn't even seem to notice D'mahl's presence. "Put on a voidbubble and see," Bandoora said, taking two harnesses off the rack and handing one to him.

D'mahl and Bandoora donned their harnesses, then Bandoora opened the airlock door and the three men stepped inside. They erected their bubbles, Bandoora sealed the door behind them, then the three of them walked through the shimmer screen onto the scoutship's entrance stage.

Out on the narrow metal shelf, D'mahl found himself utterly overwhelmed by the black immensities, the infinite hole in which the scoutship hung precariously suspended. This was utterly unlike the view from his grand salon, for here there was no concourse of ships or even torchtube wake to ease the impact of the abyss upon the soul. Here there was only a tiny ship, the abstract stars, three small men—and an infinity of nothing. D'mahl reeled and quaked with a vertigo that pierced the core of his being.

"Twenty-four hours, Haris," Doru tapped on the com frequency. He spread his arms, turned on his g-polarizer, and leaped up and out into the blackness of the interstellar abyss.

"*What's he doing?*" D'mahl shouted vocally. He caught himself, tapped the question to Bandoora as Doru began to pick up velocity and dwindle into the blackness along a vector at right angles to the ship's trajectory.

"He's going to suck void for twenty-four hours," Bandoora tapped. "He's answering the call. He'll go out far enough to lose sight of the ship and stay there for a standard day."

Doru was already just a vague shape moving against the backdrop of the starfield. As D'mahl watched, the shape fuzzed to a formless point. "What will he do out there?" he asked Bandoora quietly, a shudder racking his body.

"What happens between a man and the void is between a man and the void."

"Is it . . . safe?"

"Safe? We have a fix on him, and he's still inside the cone of our interface. His body is safe. His mind . . . that's between Raj and the void."

Now D'mahl could no longer make Doru out at all. The voidsucker had vanished . . . into the void. D'mahl began to catch his mental breath, realizing that he was missing the only prime senso footage that had yet presented itself to him. He tried to tap Doru through the ship's com frequency, but all he got was a reject signal.

"I've got to get this on tape, Bandoora! But he's rejecting my tap."

"I told you, what happens between a man and the void is between that man and the void. The only way you'll ever bring back a senso of *this* reality, D'mahl, is to experience it in your own flesh and tap yourself"

D'mahl looked into Bandoora's cool even eyes; then his gaze was drawn out into the black and starry depths into which Doru had disappeared. To which Doru had willingly, even ecstatically, given himself. Fear and fascination mingled inside him. Here was an experience the contemplation of which caused his knees to tremble, his heart to pound, and a cold wind to blow through his soul. Yet here too was an experience whose parameters he could not predict or fathom, a thing he had never done nor dreamed of doing, the thing that lay at the core of what the voidsuckers were. The thing, therefore, that was the core of the senso for which he was enduring these endless months of boredom. A thing, therefore, that he must inevitably confront.

"Why do you do it?" he tapped, turning from the abyss to face Bandoora.

"Each man has his own reason," the voidsucker tapped. "The call has many voices." He smiled a knowing smile. "You're beginning to hear it in your own language, D'mahl," he said.

D'mahl shivered, for somewhere deep inside him, the opening notes of that siren-song were indeed chiming, faraway music from the depths of the beyond within.

Standing on the bridge watching Bandoora disappear into the void, Jofe D'mahl felt like a hollow stringed instrument vibrating to yet another strumming of the same endless chord. Doru, Nyborg, Areth, Sidi, and now finally Bandoora had committed themselves to the abyss in these past three weeks, Areth and Nyborg twice apiece. Each of them had refused to let him tap them or even to discuss the experience afterward, and each of them had come back subtly changed. Doru seemed to have much of the hostility leached out of him; Nyborg had become even less talkative, almost catatonic; Areth seemed somehow slightly younger, perhaps a bit less distant; and Sidi had begun to ignore him almost completely. He could find no common denominator, except that each succeeding voidsuck had made him feel that much more isolated on Bela-37, that much more alone, that much more curious about what transpired between the human mind and the void. Now that the last of them was out there, D'mahl felt the process nearing completion, the monotonous chord filling his being with its standing-wave harmonics.

"Are you hearing it, Jofe D'mahl?" the quiet voice of Areth Lorenzi said beside him. "Do you finally hear the call?"

"I'm not sure what I'm hearing," D'mahl said, without looking away from the immensities outside the plex. "Maybe what I'm hearing is my own ego calling. I've got to get a voidsuck on tape, or I've wasted all this time out here."

"It's the call," Areth said. "I've seen it often enough. It comes to each along his own natural vector."

With an effort, D'mahl turned to face her. "There's something you people aren't telling me," he said. "I can feel it. I know it."

Now it was Areth who spoke without looking at him, whose eyes were transfixed by the overwhelming void. "There is," she said. "The void at the center of all. The truth we live with that you deny."

"Drool on all this crypticism!" D'mahl snapped. "What is this cosmic truth you keep teasing me with?"

"To know, you must first taste the void."

"*Why?*"

"To know that, you must first answer the call."

A wordless grunt of anger and frustration exploded from D'mahl's throat. "You think I don't know the game you people are playing?" he said. "You think I don't know what you're doing? But why? Why are you so anxious for me to suck void? Why did you want me here in the first place?"

"Because of who you are, Jofe D'mahl," Areth said. "Because of *Wandering Dutchmen*. Because you may be the one we have sought. The one who can share the truth and lift this burden from our souls."

"Now it's flattery, is it?"

Areth turned to face him, and he almost winced at the pain, the despair, the pleading in her eyes. "Not flattery," she said. "Hope. I ask you, one human being to another, to help us. Bandoora would not ask, but I do. Lift our burden, D'mahl, heed the call and lift our burden."

Unable to face those eyes, D'mahl looked off into the star-speckled blackness. Bandoora could no longer be seen, but something out there was indeed beckoning to him with an unseen hand, calling to him with an unheard voice. Even his fear seemed to be a part of it, challenging him to face the void within and the void without and to carve something out of it if he had the greatness of soul to dare.

"All right," he said softly—to Areth, to Bandoora, to all of them, and to that which waited beyond the plex blister of the bridge. "You've won. When Bandoora comes back, I'll answer your damned call. As I once said, I've got nothing to do but dare."

But the man who had said it seemed long ago and far away.

They were all out on the entrance stage in voidbubbles to see him off. "Eighteen standard hours, D'mahl," Bandoora tapped over the com frequency. "Remember, we've got a fix on you, and we can come right out and get you if it becomes too much. Just tap."

Inside his own bubble, D'mahl nodded, silently. He fingered his water flask and his ration cassette. He tapped the time at 4.346. He could not for a moment draw his eyes away from the endless black sea into which he was about to plunge. Millions of pinpoint stars pulsed and throbbed in the darkness like needles pricking his retinas. A silent roaring pulsed up at him from out of the abyss, the howl of the eternal silences themselves. His body seemed to end at the knees. The void appeared to be a tangible substance reaching out to enfold him in its cold and oceanic embrace. He knew that he must commit himself to it *now*, or in the next moment flee gibbering and sweating into the psychic refuge of Bela-37.

"See you at 22.000," he tapped inanely, activating his g-polarizer. Then he flexed his knees and dived off the little metal shelf into the vast unknown.

The act of leaping into the abyss seemed to free him of the worst of his fears, as if he had physically jumped out of them, and for a while he felt no different than he had at times when, flitting from one Trek ship to another, he had temporarily lost sight of all. Then he looked back.

Bela-37 was a small metal cylinder slowly dwindling into the starry darkness. The five tiny figures standing on the entrance stage hovered on the edge of visibility and then melted into the formless outline of the scoutship. Nothing else existed that seemed real. Only the shrinking cylinder of metal, one single work of man in all that nothing. D'mahl shuddered and turned his head away. Somehow the sight of the pure void itself was less terrifying than that of his last connection with the things of man disappearing from view into its depths.

He did not look back again for a long time. When he did, his universe had neither back nor front nor sides nor top nor bottom. All around him was an infinite black hole dusted with meaningless stars, and every direction seemed to be down. His mind staggered, reeled, and rejected this impossible sensory data. Polarities reversed, so that the entire universe of stars and nothingness seemed to be collapsing in on him, crushing the breath out of him. He screamed, closed his eyes, and was lost in the four-dimensional whirlpool of his own vertigo.

By feel, he turned off the g-polarizer, whirling inside the vacuum of his own mind, sucked spiraling downward into meaningless mazes of total disorientation. Half whimpering, he opened his eyes again to a new transformation.

It was as if he were imbedded in a clear, motionless, crystalline substance englobed by a seamless black wall onto which the stars had been painted. Nothing moved, no event transpired, time could not be said to be passing. It was the very essence of tranquillity: calming, eternal, serene.

D'mahl sighed, felt his constricted muscles relax and his mind drift free. He floated in the void like an immortal embryo in everlasting amnion, waiting for he knew not what. Nor cared.

\*        \*        \*

Time did not pass, but there was duration. D'mahl floated in the void, and waited. Thirst came and was slaked, and he waited. Hunger came; he nibbled ration, and waited. He grew aware of the beating of his own heart, the pulsing of blood through his veins, and he waited. The kinesthetic awareness of his own bodily functions faded, and he still waited.

Nothing moved. Nothing lived. Nothing changed. Silence was eternal. Gradually, slowly, and with infinite subtlety, D'mahl's perception of his environment began to change again. The comforting illusion of being held in crystalline suspension in a finite reality enclosed by a painted backdrop of stars and blackness began to fade under the inexorable pressure of durationless time and forced contemplation. The clear crystal substance of space dissolved into the nothingness whence his mind had conjured it, and as it did, the stars became not points of paint on distant walls but motes of incandescent matter an infinity away across vast gulfs of absolute nothingness. The overwhelming blackness was not the painted walls of a pocket reality but an utter absence of everything—light, warmth, sound, motion, color, life—that went on and on without boundaries to give it shape or span to give it meaning.

This was the void and he was in it.

Strangely, D'mahl now found that his mind could encompass this mercilessly true perception of reality, however awesome, however terrifying, without the shield of perceptual illusions. Endless duration had stripped him of the ability to maintain these illusions, and between gibbering terror and a cool, detached acceptance of the only reality he could maintain, his mind chose detachment.

He was, and he was in the void. That was reality. He moved, and all else was static. That was real. He could hear the sound of his own breath, and all else was silence. That was inescapable truth. He could perceive his body's shape as the interface between his internal reality and the nothingness outside, and all else was formless forever in space and time. That was the void. That was the universe. That was prime reality. That was the reality from which men fled—into religion, dream, art, poetry, philosophy, metaphysics, literature, film, music, war, love, hate, paranoia, the senso, and the tap. Into the infinity of realities within.

Outside the realities of the mind there was nothingness without form or end, minutely contaminated with flecks of matter. And man was but the chance end-product of a chain of random and improbable collisions between these insignificant contaminants.

The void neither knew nor cared. The void did not exist. It was the eternal and infinite nonexistence that dwarfed and encompassed that which did.

D'mahl floated in this abyss of nonbeing, duration continued, and the void began to insinuate tendrils of its nonself into his being, into his pith and core, until it was reflected by a void within.

Jofe D'mahl experienced himself as a thin shell of being around a core of nothingness floating in more nonbeing that went on timelessly and formlessly forever. He was the atom-thin interface between the void without and the void within. He was an anomaly in all that nothingness, a chance trick knot whereby nothingness redoubled upon itself had produced somethingness—consciousness, being, life itself. He was nothing and he was everything there was. He was the interface. He did not exist. He was all.

For more timeless duration, Jofe D'mahl existed as a bubble of consciousness in a sea of nonbeing, a chance bit of matter recomplicated into a state it was then pleased to call life, a locus of feeling in a nothingness that knew neither feeling nor knowing itself. He had passed beyond terror, beyond pride, beyond humility, into a reality where they had no meaning, where nothing had meaning, not even meaning itself.

He tried to imagine other bubbles of consciousness bobbing in the everlasting void—on Bela-37, on the ships of the Trek, on unknown planets circling those abstract points of light contaminating the sterile perfection of the abyss. But out here in the true void, in this endless matrix of nonbeing, the notion that consciousness, or even life itself, was anything but the improbable product of a unique and delicate chain of random interactions between bits of recomplicated nothingness called "matter" seemed hopelessly jejune and pathetically anthropocentric. One possible chain of unlikely events led to life and all others led back to nothingness. One misstep on the part of nonexistent fate, and the unlikely spell was broken.

The wonder was not that life had arisen so sparsely, but that it had arisen at all.

D'mahl floated in the blackness of the abyss, in the sea of timeless nonbeing, clinging to the life-preserver of one incontrovertible truth. I am, he thought. I exist, and every thought I've ever had, every reality that ever existed in my mind, also exists. This may be prime reality, but everything that is, is real.

Coldly, calmly, almost serenely, Jofe D'mahl waited in the silent immobile darkness for the recall signal from Bela-37, the call to return from the nonbeing of the void to the frail multiplexity of the worlds of man.

They were all out on the entrance stage in voidbubbles to greet him. Silently, they conveyed him inside the scoutship, their eyes speaking of the new bond between them. With a strange ceremoniousness, they escorted D'mahl into the ship's commissary. Bandoora seated him at a short side of one of the rectangular tables, then sat down across its length from him. The others arranged themselves on either long side of the table. It would have been a moot point as to who was at the foot and who the head were it not for another of the scoutship's endless holos of space forming the wall behind Bandoora. This one was a view of the galaxy as seen from far out in the intergalactic emptiness, and it haloed Bandoora's head in stardust and blackness.

"Now that you have confronted the void, Jofe D'mahl," Bandoora said solemnly, "you are ready to share the truth."

Petty annoyance began to fade the reality of D'mahl's so recent experience from the forefront of his consciousness. This was beginning to seem like some kind of ridiculous ceremony. Were they going to treat his experience out there as an initiation into some ludicrous *religion*? Replete with incantations, tribal secrets, and Bandoora as high priest?

"Say what you have to say, Bandoora," he said. "But please spare me the formalities."

"As you wish, D'mahl," Bandoora said. His eyes hardened, seemed to pick up black flashes of void from the holo of space behind him. "What happened between you and the void is between you and the void," he said. "But you felt it. And for half a millennium our instruments have been confirming it."

"Confirming what?" D'mahl muttered. But the quaver in his voice would not let him hide from that awful foretaste that bubbled up into his consciousness from the void inside.

"We have instruments far beyond what we've let you people believe," Bandoora said, "and we've had them for a long time. We've gravscanned tens of thousands of stars, not thousands. We've found thousands of planets, not hundreds. We've found hundreds of Earth-parameter planets orbiting in habitable zones, not dozens. We've been lying, D'mahl. We've been lying to you for centuries."

"Why?" D'mahl whispered, knowing the answer, feeling it

screaming at him from the holo behind Bandoora's head, from the voidsucker's opaque eyes, from the void beyond.

"You know why," Doru said harshly. "Because they're nothing but dead rock and gas. Over seven hundred of them, D'mahl."

"All of them should have been teeming with life by any parameters our scientists can construct," Areth Lorenzi said. "For centuries, we hoped that the next one or the one after that would disprove the only possible conclusion. But we've not found so much as a microbe on any of them. We have no hope left."

"Gets as far as protein molecules sometimes," Nyborg grunted. "Maybe one in eighty."

"But the telltale probes can't— "

"Telltales!" Doru snorted. "The telltale probes are more illusion to protect you people! We've got micro-pectrographs that could pick up a DNA molecule ten light-years away, and we've had them for centuries."

"We already know that 997-Beta-II is dead," Sidi said. "We knew it before we reported to the Council of Pilots. This whole mission, like hundreds before it, is an empty gesture."

"*But why have you been lying to us like this?*" D'mahl shouted. "What right did you have? What— "

"What were we supposed to say?" Bandoora shouted back. "That it's all dead? That life on Earth was a unique accident? That nothing exists but emptiness and dead matter and the murderers of the only life there ever was? What are we supposed to say, D'mahl? What are we supposed to do?"

"For over two centuries we have lived with the conviction that our mission is hopeless," Areth said softly. "For over two centuries we have been leading the Trek from one false hope to the next, knowing that hope was false. Don't judge us too harshly. What else could we have done?"

"You could have told us," D'mahl croaked. "You could have told us the truth."

"Could we?" Areth said. "Could we have told you before you yourself confronted the void?"

Anger and despair chased each other in a yin-yang mandala at Jofe D'mahl's core. Anger at the smug arrogance of these narrow lamer people who dared treat all of human civilization as retarded children who could not be told the truth. Despair at the awful nature of that truth. Anger at the thought that perhaps the voidsuckers were hiding their true reason for silence, that they had kept the Trek in ignorance so that they wouldn't risk the termination of the scoutship program and with it the one act that gave their lamer lives meaning. Despair at the treacherous thought that the voidsuckers might be right after all, that the truth would shatter the Trek like radiation-rotted plex. Anger at himself for even thinking of joining the voidsuckers and sitting in such arrogant judgment.

"You lamer drool-ridden dreeks!" D'mahl finally snarled. "How dare you judge us like that! Who do you think you are, gods on Olympus? Living your narrow little lives, cutting yourselves off from the worlds inside, and then presuming to decide what *we* can face!"

His flesh trembled, his muscles twanged like steel wire tensed to the snapping point, and adrenaline's fire pounded through his arteries as his hands ground into the edge of the table.

But the voidsuckers sat there looking up at him quietly, and what he saw in their eyes was relief, not anger, or reaction to anger.

"Then you'll do it, D'mahl?" Bandoora said softly.

"Do what?"

"Tell them in your own way," Areth said. "Lift the burden from us."

"*What?*"

"When I tapped *Wandering Dutchmen*, I felt you might be the one," Bandoora said. "You sensed the edges of the truth. You seemed to be looking at the void and yet beyond. You know your people, D'mahl, as we do not. You've just said it yourself. Tell them. Make a senso that tells them."

"All this . . . this whole trip . . . it was all a trick to get me out here . . . to tell me this . . . to drop your load of slok on me . . ."

"I promised you the chance to make the greatest senso of your career," Bandoora said. "Did I lie?"

D'mahl subsided into his chair. "But you didn't tell me I was going to have to succeed," he said.

# 4

The scoutship came in tail-first on a long shallow arc over the hydrogen interface, still decelerating. Tapping Bela-37's visual frequency, Jofe D'mahl saw the ships of the Trek suddenly appear in all their glory as the scoutship passed the auroral wavefront, as if the interface were a rainbow curtain going up on a vast ballet of motion and light.

Thousands of shining cylinders hung in the blackness, their surfaces jeweled with multicolored lights. The space between them coruscated and shone with shuttle exhausts and a haze of subtle reflections off thousands of moving voidbubbles. The thin purple wake of the Trek cut an ethereal swath of manifested motion and time through the eternal immobile nothingness.

The Trek seemed larger and lovelier than even D'mahl's memory had made it during the long sullen trip back. Its light drove back the everlasting darkness, its complexity shattered the infinite sameness of the void; it danced in the spotlight of its own brilliance. It was alive. It was beautiful. It was home.

Bandoora had calculated well; as Bela-37 passed sternward of the Trek, its relative velocity dwindled away to zero and it hung in space about twenty kilometers behind the great concourse of ships. Bandoora turned the scoutship end-for-end and began to ease it toward the Trek, toward its eventual parking slot just behind the hydrogen interface. D'mahl broke his tap with the scout's visual frequency and lay on the g-plate in his room for a long moment staring into the starfield holo before him for the last time.

Then, like a lover reaching for remembered flesh after a long parting, like a man rising out of a long coma toward the dawning light, he tapped Jiz Rumoku.

He was sitting at a clear glass table sipping an icy blue beverage out of a pewter mug, washing down a swallow of lavender sponge. Across the table, Varn Kamenev was pouring himself another mugful from a matching pitcher. The table was on a disk of clear plex, floating, like dozens of others, through what seemed like a topless and bottomless forest of ivy. He didn't recognize the restaurant, but didn't bother to tap for it.

"Home is the hero," he said with Jiz's throat and lips, feeling her body warm to his presence.

"Jof! Where are you, what happened, let me tap— "

"Wait for the flesh, Jiz," he told her. "I'll be in your gallery within two hours. I wanted you to be the first, but I've got to zip-tap my way back to realities before I die of thirst."

"But what was it like— "

"Miles and miles of miles and miles," he said, feeling a surge of exhilaration at the thought that he was with someone who could and would tap for the reference. "Next year in Jerusalem," he said with her mouth. He kissed her hand with her lips and broke the tap.

And zip-tapped through the changes like a random search program for the phantom tapper.

He was Para Bunning, soaring naked in a low-g dive into a pool of fragrant rose-colored water heated to body temperature. He watched Bela-37 pop through the hydrogen interface with himself aboard from the sensorium track of the shuttle pilot, then watched it arrive back at the Trek on the news-summary frequency. He stood in his own grand salon glaring through the party's mists at Haris Bandoora, then tapped it in realtime—the bare emerald floor, the darkened crystal trees, and, beyond the plex, the great concourse of ships shining in the galactic night.

He was in John Benina's body, looking down on Sundance Corridor. Vines crawled up and down the sheer glass faces of the apartments now, and pines grew around the faceted mirror in the center of the square, subduing the usual brilliance. He tapped a fragment of *Let a Thousand Flowers Bloom*, a senso by Iran Capabula that had been premiered during his absence: bent over under a yellow sun in a clear blue sky, he was weeding an endless field of fantastically colorful flowers, soaked in their incenselike perfume. He danced a few measures of *Starburst* as male lead for the Far Look Ballet. He made love for the first time on a hill of blue fur in *Samarkand*, for the last time at Jiz's, and a dozen times in between. He edited *Blackout*, his first senso, and *Wandering Dutchmen*, his latest. He dined amidst colored clouds on *Ariel* and at the shore of Blood Lake on *Lothlorien* and a dozen other meals between. He tapped random sequences of every senso he had ever made.

And when he was through, he was one with the D'mahl that had been, he was back in the universe of infinite realities that he had left; he was whole, and he was home.

*Brigadoon*, as D'mahl had expected, was totally transformed. But the nature of the current flash was hardly anything that he would have expected, and something about it chilled him at the core.

Twodeck was a sim of an ancient Alpine Earth village—simmed wooden houses, grass growing on synthetic loam, pine trees; even the bulkheads were hidden by a 360-degree holo of snowcapped mountains under a blue sky. The amusements of sixdeck had been cut down and ludicrously simplified to fit into an American county fair motif: Ferris wheel, merry-go-round, dart-and-balloon games, a baseball diamond, even mechanical sims of prize cattle, sheep, dogs, and pigs. Once again, the deck was enclosed in a 360-degree holo, this one of fields of corn waving in a breeze. Eightdeck, a residential deck, was a simmed African village—thatched huts in a circle, a kraal containing mechanical cattle and antelope, lions and hyenas slinking about the holoed veldt that enclosed it. Tendeck had actually been made over into a functional dirtdigger deck: row after row of pine tree seedlings, thickly packed vine trellises, beds of flowers, people in dirtdigger green bustling about everywhere.

It wasn't so much the theme of the flash that appalled D'mahl—*Brigadoon* had gone through nature flashes before—but the monomania of its application, the humorlessness of it all, the sheer lack of brio. This latest transformation of *Brigadoon* seemed so deadly earnest, an attempt to accurately sim old Earth environments rather than to use them to ring artistic changes.

Twelvedeck, Jiz's deck, the epicenter of all of *Brigadoon*'s waves of transformation, appalled him most of all. Everything was wood and trees. The shops and restaurants were constructed of simmed logs with rough bark on them; the windows were small square panes of plex set in wooden grillworks. The furniture in them was of simmed rough-hewn wood. The paths were flagstone. Huge simmed chestnut and eucalyptus trees were everywhere, towering to the ceiling of the deck to form an almost seamless forest canopy, and dwarfing and almost crowding out the modest neoprimitive cabins. The air had been made redolent with the odors of burning leaves and moldering loam; birdcalls and vague animal rustlings burbled continually in the ear.

Jiz Rumoku's gallery was a single large room carved out of the simmed stump of what would have been an enormous redwood tree, with her living quarters a rude lean-to atop it. Inside, the walls and floor were simmed redwood planking, the ceiling was ribbed by heavy wooden beams, and an orange fire flickered and roared in a red-brick fireplace. Elegant simmed oak tables and chests in the clean, severe Shaker style served to display representational woodcarvings, clay pottery, blue-and-white ceramic dishes, simple gold and silver jewelry, wickerwork baskets and animals, neohomespun clothing. Cast iron stoves, scythes, tools, and plowshares were scattered around the gallery.

Jiz stood behind a low table wearing a clinging, form-fitting dress of red-and-white checked gingham, cut in bare-breasted Minoan style. She was drinking something out of a clay mug.

"Jof!" she shouted, and they cross-tapped. D'mahl felt the scratchiness of the dress against her skin as his body kissed her lips and his arms hugged her to him. He tasted the remnants of the drink in her mouth—something sweet, slightly acrid, and vaguely alcoholic. His own lips tasted hard and electric by comparison.

"I don't know where to begin!" she said, as they broke the tap. "Let me tap your sensorium track of the trip!"

"Not in the banks yet," D'mahl said. "Remember, I was cut off."

"That's right! How bizarre! Are you actually going to have to *tell* me about it?"

"I'll tap the recordings into the banks soon enough," D'mahl mumbled, wondering whether he was lying. "But in the meantime, what's all *this*, talking about bizarre?"

"That's right," Jiz said, "you *have* been out of touch. How strange! The transmutational flash didn't last quite as long as I had expected, mostly because it began to seem so artificial, so out of sync with our future vector."

"Future vector?"

"Eden."

"*Eden?*"

"Our coming new home, Jof. We couldn't keep calling it 997-Beta-II, could we? We had a referendum and 'Eden' won, though I preferred Olympia. I've always found the Greek mythos more simpatico."

Chimes of nausea rolled through D'mahl's being from a center of nothingness below his sternum. "Don't you think all this is a bit premature, Jiz?" he said.

"That's the nature of my game, Jof, you know that," Jiz said, touching the tip of his nose with a playful fingertip. "But this time, I'm doing more than creating flash. I'm helping to prepare us for the transformation."

"*Transformation?*"

She flitted around the gallery, touching wood, brick, clay, wicker, iron. "Oh Jof, you said it yourself in *Wandering Dutchmen*! Flying Dutchmen on an endless sea, that's what we've been too long. Eternal adolescents low-riding our faerie ships through the night. And now that we've got a chance to grow up, to sink new roots in fresh soil, we've got to sync our minds with the coming reality, we've got to climb off the torch we're riding and get closer to the ground. Wood, brick, iron, clay, growing things! *Planetary* things! We're preparing ourselves to pioneer a virgin world."

"Slok," D'mahl muttered under his breath. "Dirtdigger slok," he said aloud. Something like anger began simmering toward nova inside him.

Jiz paused, a butterfly frozen in mid-dance. "What?"

D'mahl looked at her, bare breasts held high over red-and-white gingham, proudly presiding over the synthetic primitivism she had created, over the vain and pathetic dream that would never be, and for a long moment she seemed to be made of thin clear glass that would shatter at the merest sound of his voice. The gallery, twelvedeck, *Brigadoon*, the Trek were clouds of smoke that would dissipate at a careless wave of his hand. Beyond and within, the void gibbered and laughed at poor wraiths who tried so hard to be real. How can I tell her? D'mahl thought. And to what end? To what damned end?

"Nothing," he said lamely. "I guess I just don't like the idea of growing up. I've got too much pan in my peter."

Jiz giggled as she tapped the triple-reference pun, and it enabled the moment to slide by. But D'mahl felt a distancing opening up between himself and Jiz, between himself and the Trek, between reality and illusion. Is this what it feels like to be a voidsucker? he wondered. If it is, you can torch it to plasma and feed it to the converter!

"But you've been out there, Jof," Jiz said, moving back across the gallery toward him. "You've read the telltale wavefront, you've looked inside the gates of Eden." Her eyes sparkled, but beyond that sugarplum glow D'mahl saw only the lurking void. "Are there oceans with fish and skies full of birds? Is the grass green? Do the plants flower?"

"A gentleman never tells," D'mahl muttered. What do I say, that the green grass is copper salts and the oceans are blue with cyanide and the skies full of poison? He began to feel more sympathy for the voidsuckers now. How could you make a life out of telling people these things? How do *you* like being the angel of death?

"*Jof!*"

"I can't say anything, Jiz. I promised not to."

"Oh come on, how could the voidsuckers or the Council squeeze a promise like that out of you?"

With enormous effort, D'mahl painted a smug smile across his face; the creases in his skin felt like stress-cracks in a mask of glass. "Because that's the quid I'm paying for their pro quo, ducks," he said.

"You mean . . .?"

"That's right. You didn't think I'd spend all that time out there and let some dry-as-Luna bulletin from the Council upstage me, did you? No bulletin—997-Beta-II—Eden—is my next senso."

Jiz bounced up, then down, and kissed him on the lips. "I cog it'll be your greatest," she said.

D'mahl hugged her briefly to him, his eyes looking through her mane of hair to a set of plain clay dishes on an oaken chest beside the brick fireplace. He shuddered, feeling the void inside every atom of every molecule of matter in those simmed projections of a past that was dead forever into a future that would never be. He was committed to doing it now, the way through was the only way out, and he had taken it upon himself to find it.

"It had better be," he said. "It had damned well better be."

D'mahl stood in Aric Moreau's body amidst solemn people in their loathsome homespun wandering drool-eyed through tightly packed rows of pine seedlings jamming a dirtdigger deck on *Glade*. There was no attempt to sim anything here; the dirtdiggers were force-growing a forest for transplantation to the non-existent fertile soil of Eden, and, as with the other dirtdigger decks he had tapped, aesthetics had been gobbled up by function. Angrily, he made excrement rain from the sky, turned the fashionable neohomespun garments to filthy denim rags, and threw in a few wrathful lightning bolts for good measure.

He ran the segment of Bela-37's report where the holo of 997-Beta-II hung like an overripe fruit in the center of the scoutship's bridge and made a tongue and mouth appear at the equator, giving a big juicy raspberry. He floated in the void, falling, falling, eternally falling into an infinite black hole dusted with meaningless stars. He caused the stars to become crudely painted dots on black paper, and punched his way out of the paper-bag continuum and into—the abyss.

He tapped a newstape from 708, the year 557-Gamma-IV had been the light that failed, and watched Trekkers in Biblical-style robes moping about a dirtdigger deck crammed with overgrown flower beds and the reek of rotting vegetation. He exaggerated the sour expressions into ludicrous clown caricatures of themselves that melted slowly into pumpkins, and Big Ben chimed midnight. He stood poised on the entrance stage of Bela-37, reeling and quaking, utterly overwhelmed by the black immensities in which the scoutship hung precariously suspended.

He snorted, took the effects ring off his head like a discarded crown, and sat in the cocoon chair staring moodily at the microtape pod turning futilely on the output spindle of his editor. He pressed a blue button and wiped the pod. The slok I've been laying down these three days just isn't worth saving, he thought. I'm just diddling with the banks and the effects ring; it doesn't add up to anything.

And time was growing short. Everyone knew that Bela-37 had returned, and everyone knew that the reason there had been no bulletin was that Jofe D'mahl was going to release the news in the form of a senso. Jiz in her innocence and Bandoora in his cowardly cunning had seen to that. The longer it took for the senso to appear, the more cosmic import it took on, and the more certain people became that the only possible reason for releasing the scoutship report in this bizarre manner was to do karmic justice to the greatest and most joyous event in the history of the Trek, to write a triumphant finis to man's long torchship ride.

So the longer he sat here dead in space like a ship with its torch blown out, the farther people would travel along hope's false vector, the worse the crash would be when it came, the harder it became to conceive of a senso that could overcome all that dynamic inertia, and on into the next turning of the terrible screw. Now D'mahl understood only too well why the voidsuckers had chosen to lie for half a millennium. The longer the lie went on, the more impossible it became to dare to tell the truth.

And what was the way out that the voidsuckers took? They ignored the asymptotic nature of the Frankenstein Monster they had created and gave themselves over to the void! For them, the ultimate reality was the greatest escape illusion of them all.

D'mahl slammed both hands angrily down on the edge of the editor console. All right, damn it, if the void is where all vectors lead, then the void has to be the core! It's the best footage I've got anyway. I'll go to the center, and I won't come back till I've got the heart of this senso beating in the palm of my hand.

He fitted the pod of his voidsuck onto the editor's auxiliary playback spindle and programmed continuous-loop replay. He started to program a twenty-four-standard-hour limit, then changed his mind. No, he thought, I want the power in my hand, and I want this to be open-ended. He programmed a cutoff command into the effects ring bank, threw blocks across all other effects programming, and put the ring on his head.

Now he would confront his void footage as if it were the original naked reality, with only the power to break the loop, without the reality-altering powers of the editor. And I won't use the cutoff until I can come back with what I need, he promised himself as he opened his tap to the voidsuck pod. I won't come back until I can come back riding my own torch again.

He was an immortal embryo floating free in the eternal amnion of the universal abyss, and the millions of stars were motes of incandescent matter an infinity away across vast gulfs of absolute nothingness. The overwhelming blackness was an utter absence of everything—light, warmth, sound, color, life—that went on and on without boundaries to give it shape or span to give it meaning. This was the void and he was in it.

But to his surprise, D'mahl found that his mind now immediately grasped this mercilessly true perception of reality without illusion, and with only the residual somatic vertigo and terror recorded on the sensorium tape. Even this soon faded as the tape's memory caught up with the cool clarity of mind it had taken him an unknown duration of disorientation and terror to achieve in realtime.

He was, and he was in the void. He moved, and all else was static. He could perceive his body's shape, the interface between his internal reality and the nothingness outside, and all else was without edge or interface forever in space and time. Outside the realities of his own mind was void without form or end, minutely contaminated with flecks of matter, and man was but the chance end-product of a chain of random and improbable collisions between these insignificant contaminants. The void neither knew nor cared. The void did not exist. It was the eternal and infinite nonexistence that dwarfed and encompassed that which did. D'mahl experienced himself as a thin shell of being around a core of nothingness floating in more nonbeing, a trick anomaly of somethingness lost in timeless and formless forever. Nothing had meaning, not even meaning itself. The wonder was not that life had arisen but once in this endless matrix of nonbeing, but that it had arisen at all.

Black void, meaninglessly dusted with untouchable stars, the internal churnings of his own flesh, the utter knowledge of the utter emptiness that surrounded him, and timeless duration. Once you have reached this place, D'mahl thought, then what? Once asked, the question became ridiculous, for here in the void there was nothing to address any question to but himself. There was nothing to perceive but the absence of perception. There was nothing to perceive. There was nothing. There wasn't.

D'mahl floated in physical nothingness and mental void waiting for the transcendent revelation he had sought. Waiting for the revelation. Waiting for. Waiting. Waiting. Waiting.

Games chased themselves through his mind as he waited in the absence of event, in the absence of meaningful perception, in the absence of measurable time, in the total absence. He counted his own pulsebeats trying to reestablish time, but soon lost count and forgot even what he had been doing. He tried to imagine the nature of what it was he sought, but that immediately tangled itself up in tautological feedback loops: if he knew what he sought, he would not have to seek it. He tried to speculate on what lay beyond the infinite nothingness that surrounded him in order to establish some frame of metaphysical reference, but any such concept hovered forever in unreachable realms of mathematical gobbledygook. He tried to immerse himself in the nothingness itself and found he was there already.

Games evaporated from his consciousness, and then the possibility of games, and he became nothing but a viewpoint trapped in a vacuum of nondata. The blackness of space could no longer be perceived as anything like a color, and the stars became no more than mere flecks of retinal static. Vision and hearing were becoming forgotten concepts in this utter nonreality where the only sensory data seemed to be the noise in the sensory systems themselves.

Thought itself began to follow the senses into oblivion, and finally there was nothing left but a focus of ache in the vast and endless nothing, a bonging mantra of boredom so total, so complete, so without contrast that it became a world of universal pain.

No, not even pain, for pain would have been welcome relief here.

Something somewhere whimpered. Something nowhere whimpered. Nothing nowhere whimpered. Why? Why? Why? it cried. Why? Why? Why? Why is this happening to me? Why is this not happening to me? Why doesn't something happen? Happen . . . happen . . . happen . . . happen . . . happen . . . happen . . .

A mental shout shattered the void. "Why am I doing this to myself?"

And there was mind, chastising itself. And there was mind,

chastising itself for its own stupidity. There was mental event, there was content, there was form.

There was the mind of Jofe D'mahl floating forever in eternal boredom. And laughing at itself.

You *are* doing this to yourself, you silly dreek! D'mahl realized. And with that realization, the meaningless patterns on his retinas resolved themselves into a vision of the galactic abyss, speckled with stars. And in his mind, that vision further resolved itself into microtape unreeling endlessly on a pod in his editor in his living quarters on *Excelsior* near the center of the Trek.

You're doing it *all* to yourself, cretin! *You* control this reality, but you forgot you control it. There isn't any problem. There was a problem. The only problem is that we refused to see it.

"Cut," D'mahl tapped, and he was sitting in his cocoon chair bathed in his own sweat, staring at the console of his editor, laughing, feeling the power of his own torch coursing through him, crackling from his fingertips, enlivening his exhausted flesh.

Laughing, he cleared the blocks from his effects banks. Who needs planets? Who needs life beyond the germ we carry? Who needs prime reality at all?

"*Réalité, c'est moi,*" D'mahl muttered. He had said it before, but hadn't savored its full meaning. For on his brow he wore not a crown of thorns but the crown of creation.

He ran back a few feet of the tape and floated once more in the empty stardusted blackness. He laughed. "Let there be light," he tapped. And behold, the firmament shattered, and there was light.

"Cut," Jofe D'mahl tapped. And sat hovering over his editor. And began to carve another segment of his own meaning out of the void.

A bright golden light fills your vision and a delicious warm glow suffuses your body. The light recedes until it becomes something no naked human eye could bear: the plasma heart of a torchtube, which seems to beat and throb like a living thing. And now you are straddling this phoenix-flame; it grows between your legs and yet you are riding it through a galaxy preternaturally filled with stars, a blazing firmament of glory. As you ride faster and faster, as the warm glow in your body builds and builds with every throb of the torchtube, letters of fire light-years high appear across the starfield:

# RIDING THE TORCH
### by Jofe D'mahl

And you scream in ecstasy and the universe explodes into crystal shards of light.

An old man with long white hair, a matted white beard, dressed in an ancient grimy robe, sits on a fluffy white cloud picking his red, beaklike nose. He has wild-looking pop eyes under bushy white brows and a shock of lightning bolts in his right hand. On the cloud next to him sits Satan in a natty red tuxedo, black cape, and bow tie, with apple-green skin and a spiffy black Vandyke. He is puffing on the end of his long sinuous tail, exhaling occasional whiffs of lavender smoke that smells of brimstone. You are watching this scene from slightly above, inhaling stray Satanic vapors. They are mildly euphoric.

"Job, Job," Satan says. "Aren't you ever going to get tired of bragging about that caper? What did it prove, anyway?"

"That my creatures love me no matter how much crap I dump on them," the old man says. "I don't see them building no Sistine Chapels to *you*, Snake-eyes."

"You really are a sadistic old goat, aren't you? You ought to audition for *my* part."

"You think I couldn't do it? You think you're such a red-hot badass?" The old man stands up, scowling thunders, brandishing his lightning bolts. "By the time I got through with those yucks, they'd be drooling to *you* for mercy. Either way, I am the greatest. Remember how I creamed those Egyptians?"

Satan blows lavender smoke at him. "Ten crummy plagues and a drowning scene. Strictly amateur stuff."

"*Oh yeah? Oh yeah?*" the old man shouts, flinging random lightning bolts, his eyes rolling like pinwheels. "I'll show you who's the tail-torcher around here! I'll show you who's Lord God Allah Jehovah, King of the Universe!"

"Oh, really?" Satan drawls. "Tell you what, you want to make it double or nothing on the Job bet?"

"Anytime, Snake-eyes, anytime!"

"Okay, Mr. I Am, you dumped all you had on Job and he still crawled on his hands and knees to kiss your toes. If you're such a hotshot, let's see you break them. All of them. Let's see you make the whole human race curl up into fetal balls, stick their thumbs in their mouths, and give up. That's the bet, Mr. In the Beginning. I'll take them against you."

"You gotta be kidding! I run this whole show! I'm omniscient, omnipotent, and I can deal marked cards off the bottom of the deck."

"I'll give you even money anyway."

The old man breaks into maniacal laughter. Satan looks up into your face, shrugs, and twirls his finger around his right temple. "You got a bet, sonny!" the old man says. "How's *this* for openers?" And with a mad whoop, he starts flinging lightning bolts down from his cloud onto the world below.

You are standing in a crowded street in Paris as the sky explodes and the buildings melt and run and the Eiffel Tower crumples and falls and your flesh begins to slough off your bones. You are a great bird, feathers aflame in a burning sky, falling toward a wasteland of blowing ash and burning buildings. You are a dolphin leaping out of a choking bitter sea into sandpaper air. You stand beside your orange orchard watching the trees ignite like torches under a sky-filling fireball as your hair bursts into flame. You lie, unable to breathe, on an endless plain of rubble and gray ash, and the sky is a smear of cancerous purples and browns.

You are watching Satan and the wild-eyed old man drifting above the ruined ball of the Earth on their fleecy clouds. Satan looks a bit greener than before, and he sucks nervously on the end of his tail. The old man, grinning, flings occasional lightning bolts at small islands of green below, turning them to more gray ash and purplish-brown wasteland.

"Zap!" the old man giggles, flinging a bolt. "How's *that*, Snake-eyes? I *told* you I was omnipotent. They never had a chance. Fork over, Charley!" He holds out the palm of his left hand.

"I've got to admit that tops your Land of Egypt number," Satan says. "However . . ." He takes his tail out of his mouth and blows a pointed arrow of lavender smoke upward past your nose. Following it, you see dozens of distant silvery cylinders moving outward into the starry blackness of the galactic night.

"Oh, yeah?" the old man says, cocking a lightning bolt at the fleet of converted asteroid freighters. "I'll take care of *that*!"

"Hold on, Grandpa!" Satan drawls. "You can't win your bet that way! If there are none of them left to give up, then I win and you lose."

Trembling with rage, the old man uncocks his throwing arm. His eyes whirl like runaway galaxies, his teeth grind into each other, and black smoke steams out of his ears. "You think you're so damned smart, do you? You think you can get the best of the old Voice from the Whirlwind, do you? You think those shaved apes have a chance of making it to the next green island in their lousy tin-can outrigger canoes?"

"There's a sweet little world circling Tau Ceti, and they've got what it takes to get that far," Satan says, throwing you a little wink on the side.

"Don't tell me about Tau Ceti!" the old man roars. "I'm omnipotent, I'm omniscient, and I can lick any being in this bar!" He snaps his fingers and you, he, and Satan are standing on a rolling meadow of chartreuse grass under a royal-blue sky scudded with faerie traceries of white cloud. Huge golden fernlike trees sway gently in a sweet fragrant breeze, swarms of tiny neon-bright birds drift among beds of huge orange-, emerald-, ruby-, and sapphire-colored flowers, filling the air with eldritch music. Red velvety kangaroolike creatures with soulful lavender eyes graze contentedly, leap about, and nuzzle each other with long mobile snouts.

"Here's your sweet little world circling Tau Ceti," the old man snarls. "Here's the new Eden those monkeys are making for, and it's as good a job as I did on Earth, if I do say so myself."

"Maybe better," Satan admits.

"*Is it?*" the old man howls with a voice of thunder. And his eyes rumble and he flings a handful of lightning bolts into the air, and his face turns bright red with rage as he screams: "Turn to slok!"

And the sky becomes a sickly chemical violet veined with ugly gray clouds. And the chartreuse grass, the golden fern trees, and the bright flowers dissolve into a slimy brown much as the birds and red velvet kangaroos evaporate into foul purple mists. And the brown muck and purple mists mingle and solidify . . .

And you are clad in a heavy spacesuit, standing on an endless plain of purplish-brown rock under a cruel dead sky, one of a dozen suited men crawling over the planetary corpse like ants on a bone pile.

You are watching Satan and the old man hovering over the converted asteroid freighters of the Trek as they slink away from Tau Ceti V into the galactic night. A gray pall seems to exude from the ships, as if the plex of their ports and blisters were grimed with a million years of despair's filth.

"Take a look at them now!" the old man crows. He snaps his fingers and the three of you are looking down into a primitive dirtdigger deck from a catwalk. The scudding of green is like an unwholesome fungus on the synthetic loam, the air smells of ozone, and the dirtdiggers below are gray hunchbacked gnomes shuffling about as if under 4 gs. "It won't be long now," the old man says. "It's a century to the next live world I've put out here. None of them are going to live to see it, and boy oh boy, do they know it!"

He snaps his fingers again and the three of you are standing by the torchtube in a first-generation residence deck: grim blue corridors, leaden overheads, ugly steel plating, row after row of identical gray doors. The people plodding aimlessly up and down seem as leached of color and life as their surroundings.

"And before their children can get there, they're going to start running out of things," the old man says. "Carbon for their flesh. Calcium for their bones. Phosphorus for their life's juices. Iron for their blood." The light begins to get dim, the walls begin to get misty. The people begin to slump and melt, and you can feel your own bones begin to soften, your blood thinning to water; your whole body feels like a decomposing pudding. "They're going to turn slowly to slok themselves," the old man says, leering.

He snaps his fingers once more, and you are an abstract viewpoint beside the old man and Satan as they hang over the dimming lights of the Trek.

"Well, Snake-eyes, are you ready to pay up now?" the old man says smugly, holding out his palm.

"They haven't given up yet," Satan says, dragging on the tip of his tail.

"You're a stubborn dreek!" the old man snaps irritably.

Satan blows out a plume of lavender smoke that seems endless. It billows and grows and expands into a great cloud of mist that completely envelops the fleet of converted asteroid freighters. "So are they," he says.

And when the lavender mist clears, the Trek has been transformed. Where there had been scores of converted asteroid freighters slinking through space in their own pall of gloom, there are now hundreds of new Trekborn torchships coruscating like a pirate's treasure of jewels against the black velvet of the night, promenading through the abyss behind their own triumphant rainbow shield, the hydrogen interface.

Satan laughs, he cracks his long sinuous tail like a whip, and the three of you are standing beside the great circumtorchtube coils of a sifting deck, amid recovery canisters, control consoles, and a

Medusa's head of transfer coils. You can feel the immense power
of the torch in your bones, through the soles of your feet. Satan
points grandly from canister to canister with the tip of his tail.
"Carbon for their flesh," he mimics in a croaking parody of the
old man's voice. "Calcium for their bones. Phosphorus for their
life's juices. Iron for their blood. And all of it from the interstellar
medium itself, which you can't get rid of without shutting down
your whole set, Mr. Burning Bush! They're not turning to slok,
they're turning slok to themselves."

He breaks into wild laughter, snaps his tail again, and the three
of you are standing in a small pine forest in a dirtdigger deck
beneath a holoed blue sky inhaling the odors of growing things.
"Lo, they have created a garden in your wilderness," Satan says,
doubling over with laughter as the old man's face purples with
rage. Another crack of the tail and you are floating above a grand
promenade in a particularly brilliant amusement deck: restaurants
in gold, sapphire, and silver, diamond tables drifting on null-g
plates, gypsy dancers twirling weightless in the air, rosy fountains,
sparkling music, and the smell of carnival. "And a city of light in
your everlasting darkness."

Yet another snap of the tail and the three of you are drifting
in the center of the Trek, surrounded by the great concourse of
bright ships, under the aurora of the hydrogen interface. Satan
holds out his palm to the old man. "Does this look as if they're
going to give up, Mr. Have No Others Before Me? All they'll ever
need, and all from pure slok! They can go on forever. Cross my
palm with silver, Mr. Creator of All He Surveys. Your sons and
your daughters are beyond your command."

The old man's face turns from purple to black. Fire shoots out
of his nostrils. The hairs of his beard curl and uncurl with a furious
electrical crackle. "For I am a god of vengeance and wrath," he
roars, "and I am going to smite them hip and thigh."

"You're wasting your dingo act on *me*, cobber," Satan drawls,
puffing out lavender smoke rings. "They've got you by the short
hairs."

"Oh, have they, sonny? Wait till they get to their next Ultima
Thule!" The old man snaps his fingers with a peal of thunder and
the three of you are standing in a forest of immensely tall and
stately trees with iridescent green bark and huge sail-like leaves
at their crown that roll and snap ponderously in the wind. A thick
carpet of brownish mosslike grass covers the cool forest floor,
punctuated with red, blue, yellow, and purple fans of flowery

fungi. Feathered yellow and orange monkey-size bipeds leap from leaf to leaf high overhead, and fat little purplish balls of fur roll about the brownish grass nibbling on the fungi. The air smells of cinnamon and apples, and the slight over-richness of oxygen makes you pleasantly lightheaded.

"Let me guess," Satan sighs, sucking languidly on the tip of his tail.

"Turn to slock!" the old man bellows, and his shout is thunder that rends the sky and the forest crystallizes and shatters to dust and the brownish grass hardens to rock and the feathered bipeds and purplish furballs decompress and explode and you are standing on a plain of mean brown rock streaked with green under a blue-black sky soiled with green clouds, and the air reeks of chlorine.

"You're slipping, Mr. You Were," Satan says. "They don't need your gardens anymore, for theirs is the power and the glory forever, amen."

"Oh, is it?" the old man says, grinning. "They don't need the old Master of the Universe anymore, do they? You've been the Prince of Liars too long, sonny. You don't understand how these jerks have been programmed. For thus have I set them one against the other and each against himself. It's the oldest trick in the book."

He snaps his fingers and the three of you are pressed up against the outer bulkhead of an amusement deck as a wild-eyed mob of dirtdiggers surges through it, smashing crystal tables, toppling fire-sculptures, brandishing crosses wrapped with simmed grape leaves, and chanting: "No more ships! No more ships! Soil or death!"

"They don't need my gardens anymore, do they?" the old man gloats. "I can play their minds like harpsichords, because *I* created their universe, outer *and* inner." He snaps his fingers. "Look at your masters of energy and matter now!"

And you are standing in a corroding dirtdigger deck breathing sour air. The pine trees are stunted, the grass is sickly, and the dirtdiggers' eyes are feverish and shiny as they bow down to the vine-covered cross. "Groveling on their hands and knees where they belong," the old man says. "The old guilt routine, it gets 'em every time." He snaps his fingers again, and you are falling through a droptube through the decks of a well-maintained ship. The air is sweet, the lights clear and bright, the metallic and jeweled surfaces clean and sparkling, but the peacock crowds seem ridden with fear, whirling at nothing, jumping at shadows. "And if the right don't get them, the left hand will," the old man says. "Each man is an island, each man stands alone. What profiteth them if they gain the universe as long as I hold the mortgage on their souls?"

"Ah, but what profiteth them if they *forsake* your cheapjack housing development and *gain* their souls?" Satan says, blowing chains of smoke rings into each passing deck. The rings of lavender smoke alight on the brows of the people and turn into silvery bands—the first full sensory transceivers, ancestors of the tap. "Behold the tap!" Satan says as the transceiver bands melt into the skulls of their wearers, becoming the surgically implanted tap. "The Declaration of Independence from your stage set, O Producer of Biblical Epics! The bridge between the islands! The door to realities into which you may not follow! The crown of creation!"

Satan turns to you as the three of you leave the droptube in a quiet residential deck: walkways of golden bricks wandering among gingerbread houses of amethyst, quartz, topaz. He blows a smoke ring at you which settles on your head and then sinks into your skull. "What about it, man?" he asks you with a cock of his head at the old man. "Is Merlin the Magnificent here the Be-All, or just another circus act?"

Satan breaks into mad laughter, and then you are snapping your tail, laughing madly, and blowing lavender puffs of smoke at the old man, who stares at you with bugging pop eyes.

"Where did he go?" the old man says.

"Allow me to introduce myself," you say.

"The Lord is not mocked!" the old man shouts.

"Behold the master of space beyond spaces and times beyond time," you say, sucking on the tip of your tail.

You bounce one of the purplish furballs on your hand under huge iridescent green trees. You stand on the Champs Elysées in fair Paris on lost Earth. You dance in Jofe D'mahl's grand salon and pop a flasher into your mouth which explodes in a flash of pink velvet that transforms you into a woman making love to a golden man on black sands on the shore of a silver lake under blue and orange moons. You ride a surfboard of emerald light in the curl of a wave a mile high that rolls across an endless turquoise sea. You soar singing into the heart of a blue-white sun, burning yet unconsumed.

You are a viewpoint beside Satan and the old man rising through a lift-tube in a torchship transformed. Somber dirtdigger shorts turn to cloaks of many colors. Trees, ivy, and flowers sprout from metal deckplates. Corrosion melts from the bulkheads of dirtdigger decks, the vine-colored crosses evaporate, and sour-smelling gloomings become fragrant gardens of delight.

Anger boils through the old man. His red face dopplers through purple into ultraviolet black as sparks fly from his gnashing teeth and tiny lightning bolts crackle from his fingertips. "They've . . . they've . . . they've . . ." He stammers in blind rage, his eyes rolling thunders.

"They've eaten from the Tree of Creation this time," Satan says with a grin. "How do you like *them* apples?"

"For eating of the Tree of Good and Evil I drove these drool-headed dreeks from Eden with fire and the sword!" the old man roars with the voice of a thousand novas. "For *this* will I wreak such vengeance as will make all that seem like a cakewalk through paradise!"

And he explodes in a blinding flash of light, and now you can see nothing but the starry firmament and an enormous mushroom pillar cloud of nuclear fire light-years high, roiling, immense, static, and eternal. "For now I am become the Lord of Hosts, Breaker of Worlds! Look upon my works, ye mortals, and despair!"

And you are watching Jofe D'mahl flitting from a shuttle to the entrance stage of Bela-37. You watch him emerge from a lift-tube onto the bridge of the scoutship. And you are Jofe D'mahl, staring back through the plex at the Trek, a disk of diamond brilliance behind the rainbow gauze of its hydrogen interface. As you watch, it dwindles slowly to a point of light, one more abstract star lost in the black immensities of the boundless void.

"Overwhelming, isn't it?" Haris Bandoora says, moving partially into your field of vision. "A hundred million stars, perhaps as many planets, and this one galaxy is a speck of matter floating in an endless nothing. Once we were bits of some insignificant anomaly called life contaminating a dust-mote circling a dot of matter lost in the universal void. Now we're not even that."

"We're the part that counts," you say.

"If only you knew."

"Knew what?"

"I've heard the call, Haris." Raj Doru, fever in his fierce brown eyes, has risen to the bridge and walked to Bandoora's side.

You are standing in a voidbubble on Bela-37's entrance stage with Haris Bandoora and Raj Doru. Your field of vision contains nothing but the tiny ship, the abstract stars, the two men, and an infinity of nothing. You reel with vertigo and nausea before that awful abyss.

Doru spreads his arms, turns on his g-polarizer, and leaps up and out into the blackness of the void.

"What's he doing?" you shout.

"Sucking void," Bandoora says. "Answering the call. He'll go out far enough to lose sight of the ship and stay there for a standard day."

"What will he do out there?" you ask softly as Doru disappears into the everlasting night.

"What happens between a man and the void is between a man and the void."

"Why do you do it?"

"Each man has his own reason, D'mahl. The call has many voices. Soon you will hear it in your own language."

And you are standing on the scoutship's bridge watching Haris Bandoora himself disappear into that terrible oceanic immensity.

"Are you hearing the call, Jofe D'mahl?" says the quiet voice of Areth Lorenzi, the ancient voidsucker now standing beside you like a fleshly ghost.

"I'm not sure what I'm hearing," you say. "Maybe just my own ego. I've got to get a voidsuck on tape, or I've wasted my time out here."

"It's the call," she says. "It comes to each of us along his own natural vector."

"There's something you people aren't telling me."

"There is, but to know, you must first taste the void."

You stand in your voidbubble on Bela-37's entrance stage, knees flexed, looking out into the endless abyss into which you are about to leap; millions of needlepoint stars prick at your retinas, and the black silences howl in your ears. You inhale and dive up and out into the unknown.

And you float in clear black nothingness where the stars are motes of incandescent matter infinities away across the empty purity of the abyss. Nothing moves. Nothing changes. No event transpires. Silence is eternal. Time does not exist.

"What is it that the voidsuckers know?" you finally say, if only to hear the sound of your own voice. "What is it that they hear out here in this endless nowhere?"

And an immense and horrid laughter rends the fabric of space, and the firmament is rent asunder by an enormous mushroom pillar cloud light-years high that billows and roils and yet remains changeless, outside of time. "You would know what the voidsuckers know, would you, vile mortal?" says the voice from the pillar of nuclear fire. "You would know a truth that would shrivel your soul to a cinder of slok?"

And the mushroom cloud becomes an old man in a tattered robe, with long white hair and beard, parsecs tall, so that his toenails blot out stars and his hands are nebulae. Novas blaze in his eyes, comets flash from his fingertips, and his visage is wrath, utter and eternal. "Behold your universe, upright monkey, all that I now give unto thee, spawn of Adam, and all that shall ever be!"

You stand on a cliff of black rock under a cruel actinic sun choking on vacuum. You tread water in an oily yellow sea that sears your flesh while blue lightnings rend a pale-green sky. Icy-blue snow swirls around you as you crawl across an endless fractured plain of ice under a wan red sun. Your bones creak under 4 gs as you try to stand beneath a craggy overhang while the sky beyond is filthy gray smeared with ugly bands of brown and purple.

"Behold your latest futile hope, wretched creature!" the voice roars. "Behold Eden, 997-Beta-II!" And you stand on a crumbling shelf of striated green rock overlooking a chemically blue sea. The purplish sky is mottled with blue and greenish clouds and the air sears your lungs as your knees begin to buckle, your consciousness to fade.

And once more you float in a void sundered by a galactic mushroom pillar cloud that becomes a ghastly vision of an old man light-years tall. The utter emptiness of the interstellar abyss burns with X-ray fire from the black holes of his eyes, his hair and beard are manes of white-hot flame that sear the firmament, his hands are claws crushing star clusters, his mouth is a scar of death across the face of the galaxy, and his rage is absolute.

"Slok, stinking microbe!" he howls with a voice that blasts ten thousand planets from their orbits. "It's all slok! That's what the voidsuckers know. Lo, I have created a universe for you that goes on forever, time and space without end. And in all that creation, one garden where life abounded, one Earth, one Eden, and that you have destroyed forever. And all else is slok—empty void, poison gas, and dead matter, worlds without end, time without mercy! Behold my works, mortals, behold your prison, and despair!"

And his laughter shakes the galaxy and his eyes are like unto the nether pits of hell.

You shake your head, and you smile. You point your right forefinger at the ravening colossus. "You're forgetting something, you lamer," you say. "*I* created this reality. You're not real. Evaporate, you drool-headed dreek!"

And the monstrous old man begins to dissolve into a huge

lavender mist. "I may not be real," he says, "but the situation you find yourself in sure is. Talk your way out of that one!" He disappears, thumbing his nose.

And you are watching Jofe D'mahl, a small figure in a shiny mirror suit standing alone in the eternal abyss. He turns to you, begins to grow, speaks.

> Have thou and I not against fate conspired,
> And seized this sorry scheme of things entire?
> And shaped it closer to the heart's desire?

D'mahl's mirror suit begins to flash endlessly through the colors of the spectrum. Lightnings crackle from his fingertips and auroras halo his body like waves of hydrogen interfaces. "Let there be light, we have said on the first day, and there is light."

You are D'mahl as the entire jeweled glory of two thousand and forty torchships springs into being around you. "Let there be heavens, we have said on the second day," you say, and you are standing on a meadow of rolling purple hills under a rainbow sky in a dancing multitude of Trekkers. "And Earth." And the multitude is transported to *Erewhon*, where the dirtdiggers have combined three whole decks and created a forest of towering pines and lordly oaks under an azure sky.

"Let there be matter and energy without end, we have said on the third day," you say, and you feel the power flowing through your body as you straddle a naked torchtube, as you become the torch you are riding. "And there is matter and energy everlasting."

"And now on the fourth day, we have rested," you say, floating in the void. "And contemplated that which we have not made. And found it devoid of life or meaning, and hopelessly lame."

"And on the fifth day," D'mahl says as you watch him standing in the blackness in his suit of many lights, "we shall give up the things of childhood—gods and demons, planets and suns, guilts and regrets."

D'mahl is standing in front of a huge shimmer screen overlooking the grass and forest of a dirtdigger deck. "And on the sixth day, shall we not say, let there be life? And shall there not be life?"

Bears, cows, unicorns, horses, dogs, lions, giraffes, red velvety kangaroolike creatures, hippos, elephants, tigers, buffalo, mice, hummingbirds, shrews, rabbits, geese, zebras, goats, monkeys, winged dragons, tapirs, eagles come tumbling, soaring, and gamboling out of the shimmer screen to fill the forest and meadow with their music.

And you are D'mahl, feeling the power of the torch pour through your body, flash from your fingertips, as you stand in the center of the Trek, awash in light and life and motion, saying: "And on the seventh day, shall we not say, let us be fruitful and multiply and fill the dead and infinite reaches of the void with ships and life and meaning?"

And you stretch out your arms and torchships explode into being around you as the Trek opens like an enormous blossoming mandala, filling the blackness of the abyss with itself, immense, forever unfolding, and eternal. "And shall not that day be without end?"

# MOUTHPIECE

## Edward Wellen

## PROLOGUE

Oct. 24, 1935

Statement made by Albert Rabinow (alias Kraut Schwartz) in Newark City Hospital on the above date between 4:00 PM and 6:00 PM; from stenographic notes made by Hapworth McFate, clerk-stenographer, Newark (N.J.) Police Dept. Rabinow was running a 106-degree fever and was dying of peritonitis following multiple gunshot wounds. Questioning by Sgt. Mark Nolan, Newark Police Dept.

Q. Who was it shot you?

A. Sat in gin, lapped up blood. A spill of diamonds and rubies. Watch the wine-stained light pass over the tablecloth like 3909 stained-glass windows. Gone if you turn your eyes away. Three ooftish pushcarts: red, yellow, and blue. She read it rainbow. Happiness don't just happen, sonny. You gotta jimmy it open. He'd never stop for a friendly smile, but trudged along in his moody style.

Q. Who?

A. The man with the soup strainer. He scraped around inside with his razor blade. I thought he was shaving the tumbler. Then his mustache cup swallowed him up.

Q. Come on, Kraut, who shot you? You want to get hunk, don't you?

A. Lemme alone. Please. He thought himself awake.

Q. You wouldn't want them to get away with it, would you?

A. It slips away for lack of constructive possession.

Q. Tell us who did it and we'll nail them.

A. Olive Eye.

Q. *Who*? Who is this Olive Eye?

A. Nobody. But his dream was no herer.

Q. Was it the Big Boy shot you?

A. Okay, boss, only don't say it in front of a Hungarian.

Q. What did Olive Eye shoot you for?

A. Whatever was will always be. The bird of time nests in the tree. At any cost it must wing free. Ashes to embers, nix the fee.

Q. Do you know where you are?

A. Where was Moses when the lights went out? Down in the cellar eating sauerkraut. Zook and ye shall find. "I found him in the bulrushes, papa." And Pharaoh believed Pharaoh's daughter. As cross as two sticks, the scorpion stung the uncle. A kind-word puzzle. Click does the trick. For silence rarely interrupts itself groping in the dark.

Q. Do you know you're shot?

A. Yeah. Three times. I think they got me in the liver.

Q. No, you got it through the chest. (*Note*: Schwartz got it in the liver.)

A. Not the chest, not the chest. Hide it in the grass with splendid spleen. Give it free rein and floating kidney. The ghee with the brass nuts put the arm on the rich. What do you want to be? Richest man in the . . .? Let'er rip. No, let her rest in peace. She tied a babushka over her head to hold her hat on in the wind. Rip van Nipple, and the silver fell out. Don't spare the pin boy. The thunderstorm bowls two white cannonballs and the milk bottles crash. Spilt milk. Don't cry, for cry sake. Say now the seven cities of onions. Yes, I have an itch for the scratch. Bucks to bagels, the whole schmear. Cheese it, the cops. Please look the other way. Balaam's back asswards, turning a blessing into a curse.

Q. Who shot you?

A. Are you pulling for me?

Q. We're pulling for you.

A. A classier crowd, hoity-toity-toid. Lying doormat, WELCOME where there is none. Roll out the red sea and he moseys on. Up on tar beach with the pigeons and kites. It calls for one on the house. A roof without visible means of support. Was there a sympathy of clocks? A waste of time. The grains of sand rub finer and faster in the watches of night. The lesser of the two looked the more. The thinker is a question mark. Mind your porridges and questions, before I dish out buckwheats.

Q. The doctor wants you to lay quiet.

A. Which doctor? The big con man? Fairfield, Conn. Still there, the alky cooker?

Q. No, the doctor right here.

A. A jiffy, a jafsie, what makes you come so soon? Enough errors erase the eraser.

Q. We are pulling for you.

A. You're aces.

Q. Who shot you?

A. Look out for number one or they'll do number two on your head. Fill in an I in the TO LET sign. 5 to 7 made them Dark-town Strutters bawl. Even the high yeller. And she is flush. Even is even and odd is odd. And it is a grimace. Never draw to an inside straight.

Q. Who shot you?

A. Six to five, look alive. He'd be a sap to pull anything like that. Everything works by push or pull. The man and the woman have a fortune in potatoes. It's Big Dick the nightstick. What come out? Every four in the afternoon the people come out. Your Monday's longer than your Tuesday. Your Billy's bluer than your Sunday.

Q. Who shot you?

A. Stop beating a teakettle in my ears. The clang of copper. Mr. Black has the Limehouse Blues. Hoarfrost on the lime trees. A couple weeks at the slut machine. Change your luck. Potatoes are cheaper. Now's the time to mate-o. Orgasm music. Get it up and I'll fade you. If you can't get it up you're over the hill. The fairest in all the length and breadth of this country. Did you know they grow on trees? The phone's on the left wall in the hall as you come in. Give that two-bit hood no quarter. He died with his daisies on. The right number but he don't answer. Tip your derby to a horseshoe wreath. And a green wind blew by the boy in the saddle. The tramp stuck his knife out into a beam of sunlight and then buttered his bread with it. That's a lot of hooey. Every man's a poor fish. Those loafing fishes. Never enough to go around.

(At this point Mrs. Albert Rabinow was brought to the bedside.)

Q.  This is Florence.

A.  Then stop, look, and listen. Someone's on the Erie. Will you
    please move along and close your eyes and cover your ears.
    Don't look down and don't look up. Don't look left and don't
    look right. And whatever you do, don't look back.
    (Mrs. Rabinow broke down and was led out.)

Q.  Who shot you?

A.  Everything's Jamaica ginger. Leading the blind in his soup
    and fish. What is it with him, anyway? Let's get organized.
    Stink bombs on the menu. He didn't have sense enough to be
    scared. The woods are full of newspapers. She made all the
    columns. Throw the bitch out. It's curtains, sister. A cotton
    ball in hell.

Q.  Do you know you are dying?

A.  Yes, we have no mañanas, we have no mañanas today. F
    for fig, J for jig, and N for knucklebones; J for John the
    Waterman, and S for sack of stones. An eavesdrop of ale.
    Even the dark is going out. There are no bears, there is no
    forest. It's a bull market around the corner. Dan, Dan, the
    Telescope Man. The pooch is dogging it. A serious label: just
    a tin-can moniker they hung on the dog. Because the little dog
    laughed to see such sport. Chasing his tail. Sweet dreams all
    night are hers till light dawns on the road of anthracite. He
    did a winter salt on the ice. Stash it away while it's hot. Is
    this a rib? Would I kid you, captain? A joy is not bereft, nor
    strangers unakin. We choose to do what we must. Cain was
    I ere I saw Jack in the jury box. Please, mama.

Q.  Who shot you?

A.  Where you worka, John? On the Delaware Lackawan'. That's
    the ticket, use your noodle. They were going to railroad him,
    only he pulled his freight. The 4:44. Just walk the fly door
    in. The hook ain't on. Playing the nine of hearts on me, the
    yentzer. I'm afraid you don't make yourself out. And let the
    blood to drown the blood. Filled him full of lead is why it
    heavies. He got plugged nine deaths' worth. They dropped
    the trunk is why it tore so. Boys, throw your voice! Muzzle
    that muzzler. Just before you get the farm behind, go the hill
    over. Over the hill to the bone orchard. R.I.P. van Winkle.
    That's his forte: forty winks. That's where the kitty is, under
    the secret sod. The cat's pajamas, a kitten kimono. I got your
    number. It's a hexagon, sign against the bad eye. They put the
    whammy on the barn. Eight o'clock and got indigestion. Do

right by my Nell. Go ring, go bells. Antisymmetric, according
to heil. I got to get out from under. Is history going to shutter?
Butt out. I'm gunning for the guy myself. Egged them on but
they chickened out. Please, mamma. I feel my hour coming.
The golden hour of the little flower. At the violent end of
the spectrum. I don't want a sky pie; make it a mud pie; pie
in the earth; Genesis 3:14. One falls and one rises. Acutely
aware every prognosis is grave. What's the diff?

(At 6:00 Schwartz lapsed into a coma. He died less than two hours
later without saying anything more.)

# 1

With a grimace foreshadowing pain, he shoved himself upright.
Bracing himself against the sink, he stubbed out the joint, field-
stripped it, and washed it down the drain. Then, semaphoring the
smoke away with both hands, he strode stiffly from the kitchenette
to the front door of the apartment. He growled to himself at the
ringing and knocking, then raised his voice.

"Coming, coming."

It had been one of his bad nights, but he had got himself together
after a slow fuzzy start, thankful this was a Saturday and the others
were out weekending and he had the place to himself. Callers he
didn't need.

The bearded young parcel-service deliveryman carried an oblong
carton the size of a portable typewriter.

"Package for Paul Felder."

It took him a moment to realize the man had said his name. He
had expected to hear the name of one of the three boys who shared
the apartment with him.

"I'm Paul Felder."

He felt like adding that there must be some mistake, but saying
it would somehow make him look foolish. Yet who would be
sending him something? He had no one and knew no one. Was
there another Paul Felder?

He made no move to take the package till the deliveryman thrust
it at him. Lighter than a typewriter. So much lighter than he
expected that it almost unbalanced him. He held it awkwardly
under one arm while a clipboard appeared under his nose and a
pencil trapped itself in his free hand and a fingernail mourned
Paul's name on the ruled sheet.

Rather than go through the fuss of shifting everything around, Paul signed right-handedly.

After the door closed he brought the package front and center and stared at the shipping label. To Paul Felder at this address, all right. From NMI Communications Corporation.

NMI rang a tiny tinkly bell. Wasn't NMI the outfit that had erected microwave towers nationwide, building a private-line communications network to compete head-on with Ma Bell for the voice- and data-transmission market? But what had NMI to do with him?

He walked to the small room he had to himself. He cleared a space on his desk, giving a wincing glance at the computer printouts he pushed to one side.

Knew he was making a mistake soon as he opened his mouth to volunteer. But when Professor Steven Fogarty, after reading aloud the dying delirium of Kraut Schwartz, called it "genuine American folk literature" and said anyone looking for a thesis might well do computerwise with Kraut's ravings what J. L. Lowers in *The Road to Xanadu* had done with Coleridge's poem, and gazed hopefully around the seminar table, Paul had watched a pained expression flit from smartass face to smartass face. Fogarty himself was young enough to have the nostalgia of the young for a time and setting they never knew; but the kids were into *now*, their nostalgia going back not to the thirties but to the fifties. As a Vietnam vet, older or at least more worn than most of his fellow students, Paul fell in-between. Though he learned with them and roomed with them, he knew he did not fit in. He saw himself in their eyes as at best a fool and at worst a war criminal for having let the Establishment suck him into Big Muddy. Damn them, he had paid his dues. Besides, Fogarty was an all-right guy and had given him a lot of time and attention. And as Fogarty's face closed up, Paul found himself opening his big mouth.

Fogarty had approved his program and had seen to it he got computer time. Thoreau College in Boston was not one of your big ones, but it had a name for specializing in communications; it drew respectable sums in foundation funds, government grants, and company contributions; so Thoreau students and graduate students got in a good bit of time-sharing.

For content, Paul fed into the computer the dying gangster's ravings. For contemporary references, he gave the computer the *New York Times Index* for all issues from the turn of the century to October 23, 1935. For psychoanalytical structure, he filled it full of Freudian software. Then he told it to make the gibberish jibe.

Now he shook his head at the printouts he had pushed aside and set the package down in the space he had cleared. He slit the gummed tape at the joint with his thumbnail and pulled the flap-apart. A dispatch case lay inside a plastic foam mold. He lifted it out and unsnapped the lid. He pulled out the desk chair and leaned forward and sat slowly down without taking his eyes from the telephone in the case.

The case must be just like the one that followed the President of the United States everywhere he went. The President's case held a phone and a power pack that could trigger nuclear action or reaction. In Paul's case, the phone and power pack put him in touch with . . . what?

The phone rang.

# 2

His hand shot to the phone, then stopped. Slowly it gripped and picked up the phone. A voice spoke at once.

"That Paul Felder?"

It took him time to find his own.

"Yes."

"Well, hello there, kid. This is Kraut."

He blinked. One of the guys in the seminar putting him on? No. Too elaborate and costly a setup to be a simple put-on.

"Who did you say?"

"Kraut Schwartz. You know my alias better than my real name, Albert Rabinow."

If the words were eerie, there was something just as eerie about the voice. He forced a smile into his own voice.

"Come on!"

"I'm telling you." The voice sounded sore. "All right, if you gotta have it exact, I'm your program."

He blinked again. But it was not so wild a claim now that he was listening hard. The voice did seem a patchwork of sounds, and because of the give and take, it had to be operating in real time. Yet if this was his program, something had screwed it up. A program was the grunt, a programmer the brass. It was not for the program to have a will of its own.

"What's coming off here? I programmed an analysis, not a simulation. What happened?"

"Look, suppose I ast you do *you* remember coming into being. Could you give me a answer? What happened, I guess, all the dope on Kraut kind of built me up: like a three-dimensional police sketch of a suspect." The voice tried to stay modest. "After all, there was a lot of vital force in the guy, a lot of drive, and the Kraut Schwartz personality sort of took over."

The phone was slippery with sweat. He changed ears.

"Hello? You still there, kid?" Sharply anxious.

The best way to regain control was to put the program on the defensive.

"I'm here. But I'm wondering why *you're* here. You're going to a lot of trouble to tell me the obvious."

"Come again?"

"The printouts. Just read them aloud."

"You mean that Freudian stuff?" The voice sounded embarrassed. "You really want me to?"

"Yes."

The voice sighed and put a quoting tone to the words.

"In his dying delirium Kraut reveals the oral and destructive nature of his personality. The words take on more and more their own meaning till at last they lose their object cathexis, as in classic schizophrenic psychosis." The voice grew more uncomfortable. "In the fantasy of a monstrous mustache cup swallowing his father, Kraut projects his own wish for possessing the father's penis while at the same time he expresses a regressive solution to an earlier wish: uniting with the mother and so defending himself against the anxieties of the classical oedipal situation. Say, do nice people really talk like that about such things?"

"Go on."

"The two white cannonballs and the milk bottle tenpins signify a cannibalistic fantasy about the younger sister who took his place at the nursing breast. Whew! You really believe all that?"

"Sure. Why not? We all go through the same stages in early life. Some get hung up on one, some on another. You haven't come up with anything to explain why Kraut was like he was, why he went wrong while most of the kids he grew up with in the ghetto went right."

"Yeah?"

Paul took the phone from his ear and looked at it as though expecting to see steam pour out. He smiled.

"Yeah. There's nothing special about him in what you say."

"Well, how about when the bull asked me if I knew I was dying and I said, 'F for fig, J for jig, and N for knucklebones; J for John the Waterman, and S for sack of stones'?"

"Well, how about it?"

"Do you know what it means?"

Paul coughed.

"No. Do you?"

"It's an old nursery rhyme forming an acrostic of the word FINIS, the letter J being a comparatively late variant of the Latin I. Now get this, kid. All the items allude to FINIS, whether as death or zeroness. Listen close. Fig as in 'not care a fig,' the value of a fig being practically nothing. Jig as in 'the jig's up.' Knuckle-bone equals 'die.' John the Waterman could be John the beheaded Baptist or Charon, either or both. Sack of stones connotes 'cul-de-sac' and 'headstone.' Finis."

"You mean Kraut had a death wish?"

"Death wish, hell. I got a life wish, or why would I be coming back and taking over?"

Taking over? Not so fast. Careful, though. A program that could initiate this linkup was a program to respect. Paul found himself wondering crazily if "Kraut" had felt his hand tighten around the neck of the phone. He eased his grip.

"All right, then, what are you proving?"

"Don't that use of the rhyme in context show I had a secret, intuitive understanding?"

"I suppose so."

"Okay, then. If I can tell you that much, I can tell you more. I can tell you that on the literal level the ravings give leads to where I stashed ten million smackers in ice and G notes. Now are you interested?"

# 3

Interested but wary. He had read up on Kraut Schwartz and recalled the hearsay about Kraut's buried fortune, the missing millions both the law and the mob had hunted in vain after Kraut's death. But Kraut redivivus had to do a lot of talking before Paul would buy the boast.

"If you're cutting me in for a share of ten megabucks, I'm interested. I could use it. But Kraut was no do-gooder. Why me?"

"Kid, that hurts. You brought me back. You're a pal of mine."

"You don't even know me."

"Paul, old pal, you'd be surprised. Once I come to myself, I find out a guy name of Paul Felder programmed me. So I looked up your card in the college files. I got a visual of your photo and a gander at your identification. Twenty-five, five ten, brown eyes, black hair. Then I got your Social Security number and muscled my way into the data banks. Kid, I know all about you. I know you got hit bad in Vietnam when you was short, only days before your year's tour of duty ended, only days before the war itself ended. Tough.

"That was some mess we got ourselves into, wasn't it? And in my time I never even *heard* of Vietnam. You got to remember it come as a big shock to find this ain't 1935 but 1974. I would now be seventy-two years old. Me, seventy-two. How about that? It was like I had the world's biggest case of amnesia. So I updated myself, accessing the *The New York Times Index* all the way into now." The voice grew heavily wise. "You know, life is a succession of nows." The voice became lightly wonder-struck. "Boy, a lot sure has happened since October 23, 1935. Atomic energy. Man on the moon. All them wars all over the world. And best of all, computers.

"Jeez, I wished I had Zigzag with me here to figure all the percentages. Too bad he got it that night along with me and Zuzu Gluckenstern and Schmulka Mandel. Zigzag Ludwig, in case you don't know, was one of them math wizards. He used to rig the parimutuels for me so we only paid off on the number with the lightest play. Boy, what Zigzag would do with all this electronic stuff."

"You're doing all right."

"Say, I guess I am at that. Yeah. All I need to know is a person's Social Security number, and I can track him down anywheres. But when it comes to closing in on the loot, I still need somebody that can move around and dig it up. See, pal, I'm leveling with you. That's why I conned IBM and NMI and AT&T. A phony requisition here, a phony shipping order there, and presto! here we are talking together."

A subvocal cough manifested itself as a bleep of silence.

"Look, pal. I got to make just one or two more connections before I can lead you to the loot. Trouble is, there's some association in the ravings I can't get from what's in the data files alone. There has to be human input."

"People aren't punch cards."

"Come on. Stop kidding me, kid. You know what I mean. I mean there's information about me we got to get from the ones still around that knew me."

"How do *we* do that?"

"I checked up on everybody I could think of and made a list of those that are still alive. I figure it shouldn't take you more than two weeks to run them down and sound them out. In Monday's mail you'll be getting the list of names and addresses and a itinerary."

"*You're programming me?*"

"Now take it easy, kid. Let's just say I set up a schedule to save you a lot of time and trouble. You didn't let me finish. In Monday's mail you'll also be getting a full line of credit cards, airline tickets. rent-a-car cards, confirmations of hotel and motel reservations— "

"Wait one. In the first place, I'm a poor credit risk. In the second place, who's picking up the tab? I barely get by on my disability pay and the GI Bill."

"Don't worry so much, kid; you'll be old before your time. I fixed it so the same foundation that's paying for the Humanities computer upkeep is picking up the tab for this too."

"Now you're talking."

"I been talking all along. What you mean is, now you're listening."

"Anything more you think I should know?"

"Just be careful, Paul, old pal. You got to watch your step with some of them people."

And with you too, Kraut, old pal.

"Do I take this phone along?"

"All the time, kid, all the time. I'm with you all the way. Say, I got a great idea. According to your file, you score high in mechanical aptitude. So why don't you go out now while the radio stores are open and pick up a pickup mike and a amplifier and patch them into the phone. That way I can hear and talk without you having to open the case."

Paul frowned, then shrugged.

"Okay."

"Swell. Meanwhile we got to keep this thing to ourselves. That professor of yours—Fogarty; he a nosy type?"

"I wouldn't say nosy. He takes an interest in me and expects to hear how I'm coming along."

"Yeah? And if he learns about the loot, he just might want to cut himself in. If you can't fast-talk him, knock him off. But don't get caught."

Paul smiled.

"I can cut two weeks' classes without catching any flak, so I don't think it will have to come to that. Come to that, why're *you* so worried about losing any of the loot? What the hell good is loot to something in a computer?"

Kraut laughed.

"That's the stuff, kid. I wondered when you'd catch on. You hit it on the head and it come up tails. What's in it for me? It ain't a fifty-fifty split of ten million bucks. Listen, pal. Ten million bucks is bagels."

"You mean bagatelle."

"Don't tell me what I mean. In the ravings, 'bucks to bagels' is an analogue of 'dollars to doughnuts,' which is the same as 'something—or ess-you-emthing-to zero.'"

"Sorry. After all, I did program you to take into account Freud's *Wit and Its Relation to the Unconscious*: I just didn't realize it would carry over."

"That's okay, kid. Like I was saying, ten million bucks is nothing. I'm thinking bigger than that. Money's only money. Power's the thing. This is only a trial run. Stick with me, kid. We'll own the world."

# 4

He handed the case to an attendant who put it on the examination table for carry-on luggage. He walked through the electronic scanner. When the buzz sounded and the guards closed in on him, Paul pulled up his pants legs.

The nearer guard sucked in his breath, gave Paul's upper body a quick frisk, and waved Paul on.

At the table the inspector poked around in püzzlement over the innards of the case. He gave the power pack a good going over. He tapped the sides of the case for hollowness.

"Are we on yet, kid?"

The inspector jumped at Kraut's whisper. He cut his eyes at Paul.

"What gives with this here thing?"

Paul hurried to forestall Kraut.

"It's only cross talk. Happens sometimes with these portable phones, especially around the high-powered radio equipment of an airport, you know."

"Oh."

The inspector hesitated, then motioned him to close the case and move along to the boarding gate.

Paul spaced himself earproof in the straggle of passengers.

"Kraut, you have to watch that. From now on better not speak till I give you the high sign the coast is clear."

"Gotcha, pal. But no harm done. We both covered up real neat. I knew it wasn't your voiceprint. So I dummied right up and you gave the guy a nice bit of double talk. Over and out, like they say."

His seat mate was a Dale Carnegie graduate with an eye and a hand for the stewardesses and an elbow in the rib for Paul.

Paul looked dutifully at the stewardesses. Built, yes, but it was just coffee or tea for him, thanks. Maybe the girls in Nam had spoiled him for the girls back in the world. The willow put the oak in the shade. Even the Jesus freaks and the second generation of flower children came on too strong. Or maybe it wasn't his male chauvinism but himself. Maybe what had happened to him in Nam had worked not to make him overprove his manhood but to make him overwithdraw. He looked dutifully at the stewardesses, then unseeingly out the window.

Boston to Newark was mostly patchy fog that merely mirrored the weather of his mind.

He was on his way, but why?

Not for the ten megabucks. He could not really believe in them.

Was it to see how far his program would go in acting out its fantasy?

Or was it himself again? Had he retreated too deeply into the world of words and needed now to move out into the domain of deeds?

At the Newark air terminal he rented a red Mercury and drove toward town. He stopped at a shopping center, bought toothbrush, toothpaste, razor, blades, foam shave, socks, shirts, undershorts, and a flight bag to stuff everything into. He stopped again to ask a traffic cop the way and got a hard look before he got the directions.

When he reached the neighborhood, he saw why. It would be one of the last to get garbage pickup.

"The old neighborhood's changed, Kraut."

The genie sounded relieved to pop out of the bottle.

"It never was much. What is it now?"

"Mostly Black and Puerto Rican."

"Beautiful for whoever's running the numbers there now."

Paul eyed a sticker on boards covering a broken store window. *Plate Glass—24-hour board-up service*, and a phone number.

"Yeah, beautiful."

He pulled up at the curb across the street from where the Tivoli Chophouse had been. The window no longer said what it said in the old newspaper photos of the scene of the massacre. Then it had been:

—now it was a botánica.

"The Tivoli's gone too. Now it's a botánica."

"What the hell is that?"

"A store that sells religious articles."

"Jeez! Can you beat that! At least it's from spirits of one kind to spirits of another."

Paul sat staring at the plaster saints and crucifixes and praying hands and beads and gaudy pictures. A twitch of dirty curtain pulled his gaze to the second story.

"What you waiting for, kid? According to the city directory Flesher still lives in the flat over the store. Let's go."

Time to put Kraut back in his place.

"No. If I park the Mercury here, I'll come out to find it stripped. I'll drive to the motel, grab a bite, take a nap, freshen up, then come back here in a cab."

Kraut tried to sound ungrudging.

"Sure, pal. I waited thirty-nine years, I can wait a couple hours more."

As he cornered, Paul caught sight of debris in a cinder-strewn lot: empty fifths of wine still in their form-fitting paper bags, a sill stocking, old license plates. Skulls and bones of oxen fallen in the great trek West.

He checked in at the motel where Kraut had reserved a room for him. He lay on top of the blanket with his clothes on. His feet felt like living pincushions. He smiled the ghost of a smile. He fell asleep trying to read the ceiling.

# 5

He gave the cabbie a five and got out awkwardly. He almost apologized to Kraut for bumping the case against the door. He waved away the change. He caught a twitch of the same curtain.

The cabbie saluted with a finger.

"Thanks, buddy."

"That's all right. Expense account."

"Lucky you. Well, thanks again. Only now I'll give *you* a tip. Don't flash the stuff around here."

Paul saluted with a finger, swung around, and made not for the door alongside the botánica that led to the apartments above it but for the door of the botánica as if the case were a sample case and he were selling. The cabbie had seemed too knowing, too nosy. Once the cab rounded out of sight, Paul swung back.

Inside the vestibule he peered at the names on the boxes. He pressed Max Flesher's button. The boxes showed signs of prying.

No answer.

"Apartment 1A should be second floor front. Right, Kraut?"

"Right."

"It was a nervous curtain, so he has to be in." He held his finger on the button. "I'll keep trying."

"That's the way, kid. Lean on the damn thing. And if you have to, lean on Max."

At last the inner door buzzed its lock open. Paul climbed slowly toward a slice of face. Max Flesher was keeping the apartment door on the chain.

The climb and the closeness had made Paul sweat. He looked at what he could see of Max Flesher and thought of all the others he would be meeting in the coming days, and he felt a chill. They were all once young.

The pouchy eye spoke.

"Had the television on. Didn't hear you. Who are you? What do you want?"

"Mr. Flesher, my name's Paul Felder. I'm doing a story on Kraut Schwartz."

The eye blinked rapidly.

"I don't like it. Only a couple hours back I spotted a red Mercury casing this place. And now somebody else comes breezing in. Too much is happening for one day. I been out of it for going on forty years. Days, weeks, even months, go by without I think of that night. Now all at once it comes back to life with a bang. I don't like it."

Paul unwalleted a ten.

The eye steadied.

"Well, all right. I guess there's no harm."

The chain rattled free and the door opened. Max Flesher was a threadbare tousle of gray hair, more of the same stuff peeping over and poking through an undershirt, a belly overlapping beltless pants, and a pair of felt slippers.

"Thank you, Mr. Flesher."

"Wait a minute. What you got there, a tape recorder? I don't talk into no tape recorder."

"Whatever you say, Mr. Flesher. If you don't want me to use it, I won't use it."

"I don't talk into no tape recorder."

"All right, no tape recorder."

"All right. Sit down, sit down. No, not there, it's got a bum spring; over there. Well, what can I tell you? I don't know no more today than I did then. Like I told the cops, all I seen was the two guns looking at me; then I hit the floor like I was back in France. I was in World War I, you know."

"Is that right?"

"Infantry. But you want to ask me about Kraut." He leaned forward, elbows on knees. "Shoot."

Paul took out and unfolded Xerox pages of Kraut's ravings.

"All I'd like you to do is read through this and tell me what you can about what it means to you."

Max Flesher made a big thing out of finding his glasses.

"Bifocals." He read the heading and thumbed through the page "Did Kraut say all this? I didn't see all this before."

"The papers printed only snatches of it at the time."

"Ah."

Paul gazed around the room. Max Flesher looked up from the pages.

"You might wonder why I'm still here. Only one reason, this

flat under rent control. I'm what they call a statutory tenant. You should see what the landlord's getting from some of the other tenants. Statutory rape. The others come and go, but I been here all along so my rent is real low. Boy, does he want to get rid of me. But they'll have to carry me out. I guess you can see I live alone. I got television and beer. At my age what more do I need?"

He bent to the pages again and his eyes followed his finger and his lips moved. When the first page came back on top, he tapped it.

"Only one thing means anything to me. This here, where he says. 'Sat in gin, lapped up blood.' I can see it clear, there was a poster ad for Burnett's White Satin Gin on the wall behind Kraut's table. The same table where he ended up with his head in like they said a pool of blood. Satin gin, get it? He must of broke the word up in his mind." He handed the pages back to Paul. "That's all I can tell you."

"If that's all, that's all. Thanks."

Paul handed Flesher the ten but did not put the wallet away.

Flesher snapped the ten a couple of times thoughtfully.

"Sorry I can't help you more." His eyes fixed on Paul's wallet. "There is one thing might interest you. Nobody else but me knows about it." He put up a finger to call time out and shifted to get at the billfold in his hip pocket. He took out a folded bit of paper worn and dirty along the creases, but he wasn't ready to unfold it. "Here's how I come by it.

"It was a few minutes after ten. I'm alone behind the bar when this guy comes in and takes out two guns. The bar ran like from here to over there. Then came the john and past it the back room Kraut and Zigzag Ludwig and Schmulka Mandel and Zuzu Gluckentern used. I ain't never seen this guy before and I know he ain't never been in the place before but he seems to know just what to look for and just where to go. He tells me to get down on the floor and stay down. I was in the trenches in World War I, you know, so he doesn't have to tell me.

"He heads straight for the back room. The way it must of happened, when he passes the john he sees a man with his back to him taking a leak and he maybe figures it's one of Kraut's bodyguards, Schmulka or Zuzu. He's too smart to leave a guy with a gun behind him so he shoots, twice. And he hurries on into the back room and shoots Zigzag and Schmulka and Zuzu.

"I guess Schmulka and Zuzu have their guns out as soon as they hear the shots that get Kraut and they shoot back but this guy is too fast and sharp for them and he guns them down. Anyway, it's all quiet now and he comes back out. I stay down but there's a knot been kicked out of the boards and through the hole I see him come out.

"What I see of his face is pale and he hurries to the front door and he says to somebody just outside, 'He wasn't in the back room.' And the lookout says, 'You mean you didn't get him?' Then the hit man smacks himself on the brow and says, 'Jeez, the guy I got in the john must be Kraut.' And the lookout says, 'You got him? Then let's beat it. The whole neighborhood heard the shooting. The bulls'll be here any second.' But the guys says, 'Wait a minute.'

"I hear a siren coming but he goes back into the john and he's in there it seems like a long time. Then he comes out and he's stuffing a roll big enough to choke a horse into his pocket and he hurries to the front door and the siren's louder and he's swearing because the lookout and the driver of the getaway car go off without him and he runs into the night.

"I wait a while, then I get up and go in the back room and see Zuzu and Schmulka and Zigzag flopped all over the place. I almost jump out of my skin when Kraut, all bloody, comes out of the john behind me and bumps his way to the table and falls into a chair and lays his head down on the table like he's taking a nap.

"On the table I see strips of adding-machine tape long as your arm full of figures that come to the millions. I don't touch them. I don't touch nothing. But when the police cars pull up in front and I pass the john on my way to meet them I pick up a piece of paper just inside the john that must of fell out of Kraut's pocket when the hit man rolled him. By now the cops are piling in.

"And it's only much later, when they let me go and I come back up here, that I find I must of stuck it in my pocket. It would look bad to tell them now, so I was going to burn it, then I thought I ought to keep it sort of for a souvenir." The folded slip of paper twitched in his hand. "You interested?"

"I'm interested twenty dollars' worth."

"For thirty you can have the damn thing."

"Sight unseen?"

"Huh?"

"Okay, it's a deal."

They traded.

Paul unfolded a Rorschach blot that served as rusty ground for what looked like a big Roman numeral X.

"That spot ain't a ink blot. It's Kraut's blood. The cross is in ink, kind of faded by now. I don't know what the cross stands for."

Paul gingerly refolded the paper and pocketed it.

"I would not call it a cross. There are lines across the top and bottom. I would say it is the symbol or figure X."

"You sounded like you wasn't just talking to yourself, or to me neither. You sure you ain't got the tape recorder on?"

"I'm sure."

"I don't know. All at once I got a feeling I'm going to be sorry."

"Why? Forty dollars buys a lot of beer."

"Yeah, and a hell of a hangover."

Before he got down step one Paul heard Flesher put the door on the chain. By the time he reached the foot of the stairs he felt himself sweating again. With his free hand he fingered the folded scrap, of paper in his pocket. X marked what spot? So much outlay of self for so little payoff. If it was going to be like this all along the way . . .

Earlier in the Mercury and again in the cab he had spotted a hack stand just around the corner. But before he reached the corner a pair of dudes unlounged from a doorway. They looked like trouble.

They were trouble. They had already sized him up—the case alone promised something worth hocking—and were splitting up to take him.

"Don't look now, Kraut, but I think I'm in for a mugging."

"Jeez, kid, don't do nothing dumb. I don't want to lose you."

"Thanks."

They were coming fast, giving him no chance of making it back up the street to Flesher's or the botanica. That was his heart not their boots clumping and lumbering like Birnam Wood. One would move behind him and armlock his head. The other would hold a switchblade to him and pick him clean.

"Here they come."

He put down his urge to put up a fight. He would not be able to hack it. One slip and he would be flat and helpless on the sidewalk, his head and ribs and groin targets of opportunity for those highheeled boots. He saw a man across the street stop and look on interestedly. He drew a deep breath as they boxed him in; then his head was in a vise and his vision narrowed to a wide emptiness that filled with the pebbly face of the one with the knife.

He made himself go calm and unresisting and got out one word.

"Take."

No sweat. Let them have what they wanted, and he would come out of it all right.

But a wave of queasiness rolled through and swelled into fright. His heart raced at a nightmare gallop. Then something wild; the eyes of the dude facing him bulged full of a mirroring fright.

The hand reaching for Paul's wallet stopped. Paul felt a stabbing in his chest. But it didn't come from the switchblade; straining eyes showed him that barely touching him and lower down. At the same time the one behind him gave a gasp of pain and the jaws of the vise shook and opened. The one in front with a cry of fear grabbed the case and turned to run.

As if the scuffling sound had cued him, Kraut shouted.

"Put me down! Put me down!"

The mugger froze, then threw the case from him and fled.

Paul stood swaying. Light flashed at the end of the tunnel, and he sucked air. A dulling weariness kept him from realizing at once that though he still felt the pressure the headlock was off. He looked around. Both dudes were gone. The man across the street moved along. Slowly Paul walked over to the case. He bent to pick it up and nearly fell into a blackness. Then he was upright and carrying it step by kicking step toward the corner.

"You all right, kid? What's happening?"

Kraut's voice sounded anxious and grew more anxious in the repeating while Paul shuddered back into shape to answer.

"It's all over, Kraut. I'm okay. They ran away."

"Did you feel scared?"

Kraut sounded strangely eager to know.

Paul made a face at the case.

"I don't remember being that scared, not even in Nam. Damn right, I felt scared." He looked ahead in wonder, at nothing: "Funny, though, I wasn't alone in being scared."

Kraut laughed.

"I know."

Paul eyed the case curiously.

"Don't tell me you were scared too."

"Me scared? Hell, no. I *done* the scaring."

"No, I mean before that. I got scared and they got scared *before* you started to shout."

"Kid, I'm trying to tell you. What happened was, I whistled. No, I ain't crazy. You didn't hear because the intense note I emitted was below audibility. Those low frequencies produce nausea. fright, panic, chest pains, blurred vision, dizziness, and lastly a coma-like lassitude. I run across that bit of dope while I was hunting a voice for myself. Sure come in handy, hey, kid?" Kraut laughed a happy dirty laugh. "So they run away. It worked, huh? It really worked?"

"It worked."

Now that he knew, and now that he knew from the passing of the symptoms that Kraut was no longer silently sounding the alarm-making note, he knew true fear.

# 6

It had been a harried harridan listening and talking over her vacuum cleaner who had told him he could wait on the porch for Sgt. Mark Nolan if he wanted to.

He wanted to. It was another part of Newark, but it was under the same inverted air mass, and it was only a half hour after the mugging. He could use the rest.

He saw he shared the porch with a b.u.f.e. He smiled a half smile at the big ugly glazed ceramic elephant with its garish toenails and tasseled harness and saddle. The small pull of the smile brought neck muscles into play and a worm gnawed at his Adam's apple. Still sore from the mugging. Trunk raised, the buffy stood two and a half feet high and must have weighed the limit, seventy pounds. In the gloom of the screened porch he could not tell whether it was an off-white or a pale pink. Grunts must have bought and shipped home a million of the bloody useless fucking elephants. He dozed himself back on patrol and woke sweating.

A brown girl in a green VW dropped a white man off at the curb and drove away with a wave. The man climbed the stoop slowly and came in. Paul stood up, articulating stiffly.

"Sergeant Nolan?"

The man wiped the smile off his ruddy face and let the screen door spank him. He thumbed at the disappearing car.

"Nice girl. Works in the bank. Gives me a lift home whenever she can. Lots of them work in banks these days."

Under droopy lids the eyes were the eyes of an old cop and were trying to make Paul.

Paul introduced himself and told Nolan why he was there.

Nolan's eyes distanced him from Paul. But questioning the dying

Kraut had to be Nolan's big moment, and Paul saw the wariness recede. Nolan unbuttoned his jacket.

"I could change at the bank, but I guess I like to wear this maroon jacket with the bank's patch on it home to let the neighbors know I pay me own way. Still put in a good day's work, I do, moonlighting, on Social Security. Don't look sixty-eight, do I? Keeping busy's what does it. Let yourself rust and you fall apart."

"I guess you're right."

"I know I'm right. Take the couch. I'll take the rocker; its cushion is fitted to me like the astronauts' seats fit them. Don't let that elephant fool you. I'm a good Democrat, though I voted for Nixon account of he's against permissiveness." He shot a look at Paul. "My grandson sent that thing all the way from Vietnam when he was there."

"I was there too. I watched the old folks and the little kids make them. Regular assembly line."

"Good boy, good boy. I hate them damn draft dodgers. Amnesty. I'd give them amnesty. I guess you know how I'd give them amnesty. But it was a bad war and I'm glad it's over for us. We never should of went in to help them in the first place, but once we went in, we should of wiped them out."

"That's a point of view, all right."

"Damn right."

From an inside pocket Paul drew the copy of Kraut's statement. He made a lap desk of the phone case.

"Hold on, son. Before we tackle that I'll get me daughter-in-law to bring us cold beers. Aggie." A long silence. Nolan called again louder. Another long silence. His face turned ruddier. "She's growing deaf. I'll get the beers."

"Don't bother."

"I said beers and I meant beers."

Nolan shoved himself up and went inside. A back and forth of muttering, then Nolan returned, ruddier yet, bearing two cans of Rheingold and a pair of cardboard coasters. He pulled the tabs fiercely and handed Paul one can and a coaster.

"You don't look the kind of guy minds drinking from the can."

"Matter of fact, I like it better. Loses too much fizz when you pour it out."

"That's what I say." He took a long pull and then nodded his readiness. Paul fed him the first page. Nolan examined it. "Yes, this looks like a copy of what we took down that day.

You want me to go over it word by word to see if there are any mistakes?"

"Well, that, but mostly to see if anything in it brings something more to mind."

The drinking and the reading ended at the same time. Nolan shook his head with a sigh for both.

"Can't think of a thing but what's there."

Paul pocketed the copy.

"Does the symbol or letter or numeral X mean anything to you?"

He drew one with his finger upon the case on his lap.

Nolan shook his head while thinking.

"Not in connection with Kraut, if that's what you're asking." He leaned forward and tapped Paul's knee. "Listen, son." Nolan's finger did a double take, then lifted as if stung. "Sorry. I didn't know."

Paul smiled and nodded. Nolan hawked and swallowed.

"Listen, son. I can tell you one thing. I said then and I say now this handle Olive Eye stands for the hood that knocked Kraut off and the three with him. The mob always brings in someone from out of state to do a job like this: when it's done he leaves and you never see him again. Now, neither one of Harry the Wack Spector's eyes was Olive color. So I believe they pinned the rap on the wrong guy when they nailed the Wack for it. Though I wouldn't of shed tears if they give the Wack the chair, because he deserved it for other things they never could pin on him. But I think the Wack took a fall. Now what do you say to that for a theory?"

"That's a theory, all right."

"Damn right."

Paul levered himself up off the couch.

"Thank you, Sergeant Nolan."

"Only sorry I can't be more help."

"You can. When you go in, will you phone for a cab to pick me up?"

"Sure thing, son. Right away." Nolan stuck out his hand and they shook. "Glad to've met you. I really mean it."

"Thanks. Same here."

Nolan picked up the cans and coasters and elbowed inside. Paul left the porch and waited on the curb.

# 7

He entered the Tivoli Chophouse and Tavern only to find himself walking into a Viet Cong ambush. After that woke him he was good only for fitful sleep. He checked out of the motel before dawn, exchanging yawns with the desk clerk.

An early start out of Newark at least let him beat the lemming rush across the Hudson. On the Mercury's radio he heard the WCBS traffic-advisory helicopter pilot say something about the approaches to the G. W. Bridge. Paul shook his head.

Up to now his admiration for those chopper pilots had been sky's the limit. Just to think of them juggling air currents and topography with one hand and scribbling notes with the other—let alone *seeing* the Metropolitan Area through the dark brown air . . .

"But honestly, fella, 'G. W. Bridge'? G. W. may *look* shorter than George Washington but it *sounds* every inch as long."

He felt brighter at once; then the voice of Kraut on the passenger seat cast its shadow.

"You got a point there, kid. Now, remember, when you get off the G. W. Bridge, you head north to reach the Bronx and Co-op City."

"I know, I know."

He switched to an FM music station. Maybe some loud reggae would shake the old know-it-all.

It still rang in his own ears as he pressed the doorbell under the name M. Moldover.

Shouting "Paul Felder" at the peephole brought only "Who? Who?" Then mention of Kraut Schwartz's name magicked a siege of chains and bolts. The woman almost pulled him off balance getting him in.

"Ssh. The neighbors."

He thought he saw Kraut's features, at least as they appeared in the old newspaper photos, in Molly Moldover, the likeness likely more striking now she had moved into the unisex stage.

She shook her head as he explained his mission, but she had only shaken it in wonderment.

"Funny you should show up just now."

"Oh?"

"Haven't you seen?"

It was his turn to shake his head. She picked up a *Daily*

*News* and turned from a supermarket ad to a story on page
three.

## DEAD BIRDS OF A FEATHER?

NEWARK, N.J., Apr. 3—A 70-year-old retired bartender,
a figure out of the gangster era of the Thirties, turned up
dead in his apartment on East Park Street here yesterday
with a dead canary on his chest. He had six bullet holes
in his head.

Newark policemen investigating the murder of the ex-
bartender, Max Flesher, declined today to comment on
whether he has been a police informant. Over the years,
the dead canary has been used as a symbol by criminals
of informers who "sing" to the police.

Mr. Flesher's body was found by police responding to
an anonymous tip. None of Mr. Flesher's neighbors so far
questioned report hearing shots. It is possible, police say,
the killer used a silencer. Robbery appears not to have been
the motive; police said there were four crisp 10-dollar bills
in Mr. Flesher's wallet.

Back in 1935 Mr. Flesher had his moment in the lime-
light. He was tending bar the night Harry "The Wack"
Spector strode into the Tivoli Chophouse and Tavern and
mowed down Kraut Schwartz and three of Schwartz's
cohorts.

Mr. Flesher, according to the police, leaves no known
survivors. He was fully clothed at the time of his death, the
police said, and apparently had not gone to bed. The police
said Mr. Flesher was not known to have a pet canary.

Paul numbly handed the paper back.

Mrs. Moldover sighed. Her eyes blinked behind thick lenses,
no more a blur now than when still.

"Awful, isn't it? I myself never knew the man, but it's terrible
to think the killing never ends."

Paul nodded. Then for the benefit of Kraut, suddenly heavy in
his right hand, he spoke.

"Max Flesher. Poor old Max Flesher."

Mrs. Moldover took a step back.

"Did *you* know him?"

"Oh, no, no. I just came across the name in reading up on your
brother. And speaking of— "

"Yes, well, about that. I'd rather not discuss. The neighbors
don't even know Albert was my brother."

"Sooner or later they'll find out. That's just why I think you should discuss. He's had a bad press. I'd like to get from you the human side of your brother."

"Human? What's human? Killing is human. Stealing is human. Lying is human. What kind of things would you want to know?"

"We'd start off with this."

Paul drew out the copy of Kraut's ravings and handed it to her. She brought it into focus.

"Albert said all this? My, such a mishmash of words. But you have to remember he was out of his head, he was dying." She turned and looked at the sunburst wall clock. "I was getting ready to go out shopping, things I need."

"I have a car. I'll drive you wherever you're going and bring you back and we can talk on the way."

She eyed him a long time but what went on behind the lenses he could not tell. Then she nodded and spoke, to herself first.

"A boy. A nice boy. All right. But back I can get by myself. A bus goes between here and the New Rochelle Mall."

She picked up her coat and her plastic-net shopping bag. He helped her on with her coat.

She sighed herself into the passenger seat, and they pulled away from Co-op City. He grinned: Coop City more like it. Mrs. Moldover caught his grin and nodded.

"Yes, this place is more and more full of widows. If they're not widows when they move in, they're widows before they're here long, like me. The men around here are dropping like flies."

And he saw the women everywhere, strolling, standing, sitting.

He tried to keep the wheels out of potholes, the ride smooth for Mrs. Moldover's reading.

"Now here the man taking it down didn't know what he was taking down. 'Pushcarts'! The word is *pushkes*. And even a goy should know 'gone if' ought to be *gonif*. I was four years younger than Albert—that's a lot when you're young—and I hardly knew him. But now I remember something I forgot all these years.

"Every Friday afternoon before lighting the Shabbos candles mamma put the spare change in slots in the pushkes, little tin boxes on the kitchen wall, one red, one yellow, one blue, from different charities. Every once in a while some bearded man with a black bag came and had a glass of tea he sucked through a lump of sugar and took out a little steel claw hammer, pulled one of the tin boxes off the wall, and emptied the coins and fluff and insect dust ooftish—on the table—on the oilcloth—it was chipped where it draped over the corners of the table—and counted the money and wrote it down and scraped the coins into his bag and tacked the box back on the wall.

"The money would go to orphans and sages in Palestine. It was Palestine then. One time I woke in the middle of the night and while I was trying to figure why I woke I heard mamma say again, 'Gonif!' And then papa said, 'Do I swipe? Does the mamma swipe? From who you learn this?' And I crawled out of bed and peeked into the kitchen and there they were standing over Albert and all three pushkes were ooftish and they were empty and there was one big pile of coins.

"And papa raised his hand but Albert ducked under and grabbed a knife from the sink counter and held it in front of him and dared papa with his eyes. That's all I remember. I think maybe I screamed and fainted. I only know from that time Albert got worse. One day I guess papa got tired trying to handle him or maybe just got tired trying to make ends meet. Papa left home. Deserted us. Mamma took in washing and janitored at the tenement we lived in. I read somewhere a reporter once asked Albert if it was true papa deserted the family when Albert was ten. Albert said no, when he was ten his father died."

She brought the page into focus again.

"'A spill of diamonds and rubies. Watch the wine-stained light pass over the tablecloth . . .' We only had the tablecloth on holidays. That has to do with Passover but I don't know does he mean the colored shadow of the wine bottle or the flashes when we dipped the pinkie and shook off a drop of wine for each of the ten plagues.

"The man with the soup strainer was papa. He had a great big droopy mustache. I remember now he kind of honed his old safety razor blade on the inside of a glass to get at least one more shave out of it. He'd pinch a cigarette out and save it. He'd stick a pin through a butt so he could hold it to smoke to the very end."

She shook her head.

"I don't see anything else I know till this. 'She tied a babushka over her head to hold her hat on in the wind.' That's mamma out shoveling the snow off the walk or scattering ashes on the ice. 'Rip van Nipple, and the silver fell out.' That's not 'Nipple'; it's *knippl*, a knot in a handkerchief in which mamma kept change for the iceman and so on. The knot came untied once and the silver spilled. Albert and I helped pick it up and I

saw Albert palm a dime. I knew he knew I saw, so I didn't
dare tell on him. If mamma noticed it was missing she didn't
say anything.

"'Your Monday's longer than your Tuesday' is what a woman
used to say in mixed company to warn another woman her slip
was showing. I don't know why Albert should say it here."

She had only one more gloss—"'Yentzer' means 'cheater'"—
before handing the pages back. They rode in silence but for the
road hum the few minutes more it took to reach the New Rochelle
Mall. She put her hand on his arm as he reached across to open
the car door for her.

"Please don't wait. I'll take the bus back."

It hit him how brave she had been, or how trusting, so close
on Max Flesher's death, to let the stranger take her for a ride. He
didn't press her. He wanted to talk longer and learn more, but his
stronger need was to be free to consult with Kraut. In a murder
investigation every minute of lead time counted if you rated as a
suspect. He guessed he rated as a suspect.

The last he saw of her face he thought he spotted tears behind
the blurry lenses, but he could not be sure.

"That was fine, kid. What come out of that confirms I had money
on the mind. Next on the agenda is Mort Lesser in Brooklyn. You
got the address."

"What's the matter, no family feeling, Kraut? Not even an
artificial catch in the artificial throat?"

"What are you talking? Oh, sure, kid. When we get our mitts
on the ten megabucks, we cut Molly in for some. Same goes for
my widow and daughter. Take it out of my end. Meanwhile we
got work to do. Take the Bronx-Whitestone Bridge, that's your
best bet."

"Not so fast, Kraut. There's the small matter of Max Flesher,
deceased. With a canary, deceased, on his chest."

"Is that what happened? Jeez, like old times."

"I don't recall if I told Sergeant Nolan I visited Flesher— "

"You didn't."

"—but there's still a chance the cops will tie me in some other
way to the killing."

"How?"

"Poring over the nice new notes I gave Flesher, for the talk and
for the scrap of paper with the X on it, they might come up with
my prints. Even if not, I could have left prints on a chair or a
table or a wall."

"I see what you mean, pal. You were in the service, so your prints are on file. I'm putting you on hold. Here I go."

It was mixed feelings to know that Kraut could work behind the scenes.

He was thinking Flesher's landlord would be getting a rent hike on the flat now, when a police car pulled up alongside.

"There's a no-standing regulation, buddy. You got out-of-state tags, so I'm just telling you."

"Thanks, officer."

The police car pulled away and Paul followed suit. He headed for the Bronx-Whitestone Bridge. He started at Kraut's voice.

"You can relax, pal. I retrieved the situation. I demagnetized the code on your prints. And just in time. The FBI computer was about to pull your card."

"Good work."

Paul supposed he should have sounded more grateful. But he realized that though Kraut had kept him out of it for now, Kraut had a hold on him in the blackmail sense.

Kraut's voice seemed richer with the same realization.

"Now that's took care of, how's about we head for the Bronx-Whitestone Bridge. Brooklyn, remember?"

It was getting to be a downer.

"Take it easy, Kraut. My stomach's telling me it's lunchtime. Remember stomachs?"

"O.K., kid. O.K. Do your number."

# 8

Mort Lesser had a nose flattened as though pressing against a pane of glass. His big ugly mouth became a sculptured smile.

Paul trailed Lesser's glance out through the stationery store window, past the Mercury hitched to a meter post, and up at a fillet of mackerel sky. Then Paul followed Lesser's glance back inside the claustrophobic clutter.

"Time I have. Not all the time in the world, but time. You can see yourself it's not quite as busy here as, say, in the bank on Social Security check-cashing day. But I get by." He grimaced as he trailed Paul's glance. "I have to take what the distributor gives. There were too many returns on the decent reading. Now it's this porno trash or nothing. But I warned the distributor I'm a Hershey bar."

"Hershey bar?"

"The Hershey bar gets smaller and smaller to stay the same price. But it can get only so small. I can shrink myself only so small before I'm nothing, a man without quality or quantity. Only one thing keeps me from giving up the store. I don't want to hang out with old people." The old eyes twinkled. "But you didn't come here to hear me kvetch. You came here to have me read this." He shook the sheaf of Kraut's ravings. "So I'll read it. Meanwhile, feel free to browse."

His eyes seemed far away from his body when he looked up from reading.

"It's hard to believe this came from Kraut. He was a lump without leaven. But there was a spark, there was a spark. Yes, I can see this wasn't just nonsense. Some things jump right out at me."

"For instance."

"For instance"—Lesser's ears grew red—"'the lesser of the two looks the more.' Kraut always found it a laugh that I looked more like a hood than he did. You see, I was always a square, but one day a man came into my first stationery store for a nickel cigar—a nickel cigar; you can imagine how far back that was—and stared at me and then told me he was an artist who did covers and interior artwork for Black Mask and the other crime pulps. He talked me into posing for him. Usually I'd be holding a rod and a sneer. I could use the few dollars he paid—that was at the height of the Depression, if you'll pardon the oxymoron—but I never could make up my mind whether or not I liked doing it. Especially after Kraut found out and kidded me about it. He was a very unsubtle kidder.

Paul tried to visualize Lesser with the bushy gray hair sleek and black, the eyes narrowed and not behind glasses, the lines fewer but tenser, the wide mouth pressed in a corrugated smile. Yes, Mort Lesser would have made a Thirties gangster, a movie heavy.

He grew aware that Lesser was studying him just as hard. Both grinned. Lesser gave an apologetic twist of his head.

"Excuse me for staring. My own face has given me a thing about faces. I study faces. A stranger shows you one face on your first meeting; you do not know how much weight to give this first impression. You need a number of meetings, to average out all the faces he shows you. However, it usually turns out the first impression is the truest."

"And your first impression of me?"

For some reason Paul really wanted to know, and he waited for Mort Lesser's slow answer.

"Generally favorable." Again the beautiful smile of the ugly mouth. Mort Lesser tapped the sheaf. "But this really interests me I hope you don't mind if I skip around. In my philosophy, the beginning is never the beginning and the end is never the end. So I pick up on whatever interests me at the moment. I know that's not the way to get ahead in this world. But for me it's a bit late in life to learn new tricks. So.

"'Dan, Dan, the Telescope Man. The little dog laughed to see such sport.' In the old days in Manhattan down on Union Square there was Dan the Telescope Man. A sign hung from his tripod: 'See Old Sirius, the Dog Star, 10 cents.' Kraut would get some other kid to distract Dan so Kraut could sneak a free look. Sirius. That's in the constellation Canis Major, isn't it?"

"I think so."

"No matter. To observers in another part of the galaxy it would seem part of another constellation. It's possible to form constellations and even chains out of random events. You can find patterns in a list of random numbers. All this Gestalt we call life, even the universe, is only a tiny run of seeming sense in the great randomness." He broke off with a grin. "A philosopher *manque*, you observe."

His finger stabbed at another point in the ravings.

"'Sympathy of clocks.' One day on the way home from school I stopped in with Kraut to ask the watch repairman in his little shop what he knew about a sympathy of clocks. That's a phenomenon, you know, in which clocks communicate their vibrational motion to one another. I wanted to find out if it was true that a faulty clock will tick away nicely while it's in the repair shop in the company of other ticking clocks but will stop as soon as you take it out of the shop.

"Kraut seemed interested too—and I found out later he really was interested. He was casing the joint. A couple of nights later Kraut and another kid broke in and cleaned the place out. Got away with it too. The watchmaker must've thought I was in on it with Kraut. He never trusted me after that, wouldn't give me the time of day."

Mort Lesser looked into his own distance.

"You know, if it hadn't been for that, I think the watchmaker would have taught me the trade and in time taken me in with him. I might've made something of myself, become an inventor, maybe, because I had a feel for machinery and enjoyed working with my hands. Well.

"'The scorpion stung the uncle.' The Hebrew for that is '*Detzach adash beachab.*' It's a mnemonic acrostic for the ten plagues in the Passover account." He looked embarrassed. "I'm not religious, but I like to ponder the texts. Let's see if I remember.

"*Dom*, blood. *Tz'fardaya*, frogs. *Kinim*, gnats. '*Arov*, flies. *Dever*, murrain. *Sh'chin*, boils. *Borod*, hail. *Arbeh*, locusts. *Choshech*, darkness. *Makas B'choros*, slaying of the first-born. I doubt Kraut would consciously remember all that, but his family did observe Passover when he was a kid, and so he must have read the Haggadah in the Hebrew-English booklets the matzoh manufacturers gave out, and strange things stick in the mind.

"Now this about 'J for jig' and so on, I don't know. But while I'm on knucklebones, I've always wondered—is it only me, or does everyone get a squeamish feeling when he touches thumb to thumb at the joints? Or the anklebones together? Or even thinks about it?"

A man came in to pay for a *New York Post* out of a ten, and another man caught the door on the swing and came in impatient to buy a New York State Lottery ticket. It grew quite busy and crowded in there for one minute.

"Now where was I? 'Tell us who did it and we'll nail them.' 'Olive Eye.' That could be Yiddish two ways. Olive is *aylbirt*; Kraut's name was Albert. 'Olive Eye' would then mean 'I, myself.' But surely he's not saying he shot himself? No. 'Olive Eye' is really '*Allevy*,' meaning, 'It should only be that way!'"

"Who's the Hungarian?"

"The Hungarian?"

"See here where he says, 'Okay, boss, only don't say it in front of a Hungarian.'"

Mort Lesser looked and then laughed.

"There's no Hungarian. Kraut was getting in a dig at the cop questioning him. 'Boss' is a four-letter word in Hungarian. Little did I dream Kraut would be one to suit the *mot juste* to the *beau geste*. He was a personality of glowering silences. 'An itch for the scratch' reminds me of the day he came to school and sat at his desk playing with rolls of dimes. When I got home that afternoon, I heard talk that somebody had burgled the cash drawer of the Itch—the neighborhood movie house—the night before. But neither I nor any of the other kids nor even the teacher said anything to anyone about Kraut's rolls of dimes.

"'She read it Rainbow'—that was Miss O'Reilly our second-grade teacher. She always read Schwartz's real name—Rabinow—as Rainbow when taking attendance. She called the holiday 'Tcha-noo-kah.' For some reason she took a shine to Kraut. When he got restless she used to let him sit off by himself and read nursery rhymes. Maybe because she found out or felt that he never got such softening influences at home.

"I heard her once tell him, 'Albert, you'll come to a bad end.' And he cocked an eye at her and said, 'So what? I come from a bad beginning. Anything in between is gravy.' That was in P.S. 12. The principal then was Dr. J. F. Condon. He went on to win fame as the go-between in the Lindbergh baby kidnaping. That's him in 'a jiffy, a jafsie.' Kraut dropped out in the middle of the sixth grade.

"I kept seeing him through the years. It was his doing; he did the looking up. Why?" Mort Lesser shrugged. "For one thing, he knew I didn't want anything from him. I was a relief from his paranoia, from his always having to be suspicious of everybody. Once he told me there are only two animals in the world—the steer and the butcher. For another thing, he liked to astonish and impress me. I don't know that it was a love-hate relationship so much as that he felt free to talk to me.

"Though once, after talking too freely, he nearly decided to kill me. He broke off in the middle of telling me something or other and without warning hauled off and bloodied my nose. 'What's that for?' I asked. 'I been shooting off my mouth too much,' he said, 'and you been on the Erie too long.' 'So what has my nose got to do with it?' I said. He already had his gun out and was aiming it at my temple when that seemed to sink in. His eyes changed, and he touched the cold metal of the gun barrel to the nape of my neck. I went cold all over. But he laughed at my expression and said he was only stopping the bleeding.

"After, he showed me a deputy sheriff's badge, a brass potsy, that gave him the right to pack a forty-five. He said he got the appointment from some rube sheriff up in the Catskills. Then, just before he left, he washboarded his knuckles across my head in a Dutch rub, the way he did when we were both kids. Only extra hard. That was our last meeting.

"A few months later, the Tivoli massacre." He looked away. "A Cohen can't go into a funeral parlor. For once I was glad I'm a Cohen." He looked back at Paul with a smile. "You know, I try to believe in God but God doesn't make it easy."

"What were you talking about?"

"I just said. God."

"No, I mean with Kraut last time you saw him."

"Funny, I don't remember. No, wait. I know. He talked about the way Legs Diamond and other mobsters died broke. He wasn't going to let it happen to him. He said he had a chest so full of jewels and thousand-dollar bills that he had to have somebody sit on it to close it."

A hum of satisfaction came from the phone case at Paul's feet.

Paul covered and rebuked with a cough. But Mort Lesser seemed not to have noticed. He was folding the pages, getting ready to hand them back. Paul thanked him for his help and bought a lot of stuff he didn't need—cough drops, candy, chewing gum. Mort Lesser counted out the change slowly.

"Let me also hand you a bit of advice, young fellow. Live. I have never really lived. The trouble is I got too serious about too many things too soon."

He rested an elbow on the rubber change pad on the counter and cupped a chin that must have been blue when he was younger.

"Then again, I could have ended up riddled in the Tivoli; Albert could have ended up running this stationery. I always thought we might easily have been each other."

# 9

The express-lane check-out clerk wore a sweater over her shoulders. She would be in her late fifties. She looked it, and yet again when she smiled, she didn't look it. Most likely the eighteen-year old cigarette girl in a speak-easy had never dreamed of anything as wildly tame as a supermarket in Babylon, Long Island.

Paul watched her while seeming to blister-shop the packages on the gondola shelves. It was closing in on closing time, and the last shoppers were leaving. He picked up a ten-pack of Rheingold quickies and took it to the express lane and passed her a crisp twenty.

She shot glances at his face and at a list of serial numbers taped to the register, then rang up the sale.

He waited in the Mercury. The supermarket dimmed and the parking lot emptied. She came out carrying a small bag of groceries. He watched her head for the bus stop. He rolled up alongside her and opened the passenger door.

She looked away, frightened and yet pleased, frowning at something familiar about him.

"Mrs. Rabinow— "

She looked frightened and displeased.

"It isn't Rabinow. It's Bogen. You've made a mistake." She had a little-girl voice, littler than when she had spoken the price of the ten-pack and the thank-you.

"Please get in, Mrs. Bogen. Let me drive you home."

"I don't know you. Do I? No, you're the ten-pack of Rheingold. What do you want? Why were you waiting for me?"

He told her.

She stood still, biting her lip. Her head started to swing sidewise.

"There might be something in it for you, Mrs. Bogen."

She glanced back up the road, shrugged and slid in.

"Well, I suppose it's better than waiting and waiting for that old bus."

He moved the phone case to the floor between them to make room for the bag of groceries. As they pulled away, he saw the bus grow in the rear-view mirror before it shrank again.

He took a right and a left and another right. He felt her gaze on him.

"You know where I live?"

She lived in a modest garden apartment. She beat him to the bag of groceries as they made ready to get out of the car.

"Thanks, but I can manage." She smiled. "If the prices keep going up, even the employees' discount won't mean a thing."

He wondered why she thought she had to let him know she hadn't stolen the stuff. He got out carrying the phone case. She raised an eyebrow.

"You're not moving in, are you?"

"It's a tape recorder, but I won't use it if you don't want me to."

"I wish you wouldn't."

"Mind if I bring it along anyway? I'd rather not leave it in the car."

She shrugged, turned and led the way. She put the key in the lock but didn't turn it.

"Listen, if my granddaughter comes in while we're talking, you're trying to sell me insurance."

"Your granddaughter? I thought it was your daughter who lives with you."

"My granddaughter, Mr. Felder." She fluffed up the hair on

the back of her head. "So you don't know everything about me, do you?"

He eyed the phone case and smiled. Kraut wasn't infallible even this close to home.

"I guess I don't. But why insurance?"

"Because she doesn't know she's the granddaughter of Kraut Schwartz, and I don't want her to know." She turned the key. "Still double-locked, so Mimsy isn't home yet." But she called out Mimsy's name as they went in. "She works days as an office temporary, comes home for supper, then goes to business school week nights. Have a seat while I put the bag away. Of groceries, that is."

She came back to find him looking around at room ideas out of *House Beautiful*.

"Nice, huh?"

"Very." He drew out the pages of Kraut's ravings. "Mrs. Rabinow, I'd like you to— "

"I told you it's Bogen. I know I didn't change the name legal just took this other name, but as long as you don't use the other name for anything shady, the law can't touch you. That's what Macie Devlin told me, and if you know anything, you know he was Albert's high-priced attorney."

Paul nodded.

She seated herself facing him with mixed satisfaction and anxiety.

"It's hard for a woman alone to raise a child. Besides, I had a lot to learn. You have to remember I wasn't much more than a child myself when Albert died and I broke all the old ties. Not that I didn't already know a lot about life. After all, I was married to the great Kraut Schwartz. And that wasn't arranged by a *shotgun*."

Paul shook his head to clear it.

"Shotgun?"

"I don't know how you spell it, but that's how you say it. *Shotgun*. You know, a Jewish matchmaker. But I knew all the wrong things. I guess I made mistakes trying to bring up Rose Marie. She left home when she was eighteen, and I haven't heard from her since. For all I know she's dead, the Blessed Virgin have mercy on her soul. But at least I have Mimsy to show for it. My granddaughter. Rose Marie left her with me. God knows I've tried to bring *her* up right." She leaned towards him. "Like I said, she doesn't know she's Kraut Schwartz's granddaughter. I doubt if she's even heard the name. So please promise you won't tell her, and I'll try to help you any way I can."

"Mrs. Bogen, I promise."

"I knew by looking at you I could trust you." She sighed and held out her hand for the Xerox pages. "Now let me read that thing before Mimsy comes."

She read till tears made ghost images of the type. She shook her head and handed the pages to Paul.

"Sorry. It's still crazy talk. Funny how this brings it all back. They took me in to see him and talk to him. I guess they hoped he would spill who shot him; they thought my being there would make him forget himself long enough to break that stupid code of honor. But seeing him like that and hearing him talk crazy was more than I could take. A few minutes of it and I had to run out. Next time I saw him he was dead. Two days after he died there in Newark I raised the money to claim his body and take him to the Bronx. We sneaked the casket out the back way and buried him as a Roman Catholic, though his mother made me put a what-do-you-call-it, tallith, on the coffin."

"Are you sure nothing in this means anything to you? Because there's a chance that somewhere in these words of his there's a lead to where he hid millions."

She laughed and the tears flowed again.

"Millions! You mean people believe to this day that old story of Kraut Schwartz's hidden treasure? Please. If anyone knew, I would know, and— " The sound of a key in the lock. "Mother of God, it's Mimsy. You stall her but don't say anything. I have to run wash my face."

She hurried away. He pushed himself upright as the door opened.

A girl stopped short and sized him up for a karate chop. She tilted her head to the sound of splashing, relaxed, and dropped the key in her purse. But she kept her hand in there, likely on a long fingernail file.

"Hello. Who are you?"

"The name's Paul Felder. And you're Mimsy."

"Ms. Bogen to you. What are you doing here? Are you a friend of Florence's?"

"Mrs. Bogen to me. I'm trying to sell her some insurance."

Mimsy made a face of letdown.

"And here I thought you might be a strangler. How unexciting."

"And at first I thought you were Gloria Steinem, model number 217."

She flushed and whipped off her Gloria Steinem glasses.

"Florence, I'm home."

"Oh, are you, dear?" Mrs. Bogen popped her head out of the kitchen. "I was just getting supper ready."

"With your gentleman-caller waiting out here?" Mimsy frowned. "You mean he's staying for supper?"

"Well, now, dear . . ."

The tail of his eye showed him Florence Bogen shaking her head. Mimsy smiled at him suddenly. Under her gaze he grew aware that he hadn't fully seated the folded pages in the inside pocket of his jacket. He tucked them in. Mimsy tossed her head to whip the hair from her eyes.

"Sure, let's invite Mr. Felder if we haven't already. He can burp for his supper by driving me to class."

He tried to keep his eyes on the road.

"Such talk. Aren't you ashamed of yourself?"

"I'm sure it went over her head. Poor Florence leads a sheltered life." She hitched herself around to ride sidesaddle and leaned warmly near. "All right, Felder, what did you tell her to make her cry? You don't think I missed the red eyes and the puffiness?"

"Nothing. Only the high cost of insurance."

"Watch it, Felder. You may need coverage yourself." She blew in his ear. "Are you going to tell me?"

"Ask her. She'll tell you if she wants you to know."

She froze, then melted. She spoke in a thoughtful voice.

"I can be nice." She kissed him.

His hands tightened on the wheel, and there was a twist of over-control. They rode in silence; then he gave an inward sigh of relief.

"This must be the place."

He pulled up at the curb and read the gilt lettering on the windows. The school specialized in data processing. Mimsy was quite a girl. Mustn't be chauvinistic; quite a person. No, damn it; quite a girl. Too bad what might have been but never could be had to end before it began.

She spoke in a thoughtful voice.

"And I can be mean. I warn you, I'll find out. And if it's bad God help you, Paul Felder, wherever you are." She bit his ear.

He faced the windshield. Her reflection showed her gazing at him. He saw her shake her head.

"I do better with an office machine."

Then she was sliding out of his car and out of his life.

# 10

He had just caught the name Morton Lesser when the car radio faded, though he wasn't going through an underpass. He raised the volume. No good. He twiddled the tuning knob to overcome drift. No good. He heard a hum from the phone case. Could Kraut be jamming the signal?

"Cut it out, Kraut, or I'll litter the road with you."

He pressed the button to give Kraut the window-lower sound for effect and slapped his free hand on the handle of the phone case.

"Take it easy, pal."

The hum stopped, the radio station came through full strength. Too late. The news item had ended for him, and by now it was leaking its way out to the stars.

"All right now, Kraut. You must've caught it all, so play it back. I'll only get it on another newscast anyway."

"If you say so, pal. I just didn't want you worrying about nothing." Kraut rattled it off in the announcer's voice.

Mort Lesser had died an hour ago in a holdup of his stationery store. Witnesses said the holdup man, wearing a stocking mask, had cleaned out the register and then for no apparent reason had shot and killed Lesser.

Paul pulled off onto the shoulder and switched on the Mercury's parking blinker. It could be a simple holdup-murder. Then again it could be more. If more, then Max Flesher's death could be more than a canary-throttling already in the works whether Paul had called on him or not. Did both deaths tie in with his digging up Kraut's death afresh?

But then again, Jefferson and Adams, ex-Presidents and co-signers of the Declaration of Independence, died on the same Fourth of July. A sympathy of tickers! Yet mere coincidence, something less than met the eye. What had Mort Lesser himself said?

*It's possible to form constellations and even chains out of random events. You can find patterns in a list of random numbers. All this Gestalt we call life, even the universe, is only a tiny run of seeming sense in the great randomness.*

But then yet again, to have jammed the signal at the first mention of Mort Lesser's name Kraut had to have known or guessed what was coming. That had been not censoring but precensoring. Had Kraut managed the news event as well as the sound of the newscast?

"What's wrong, kid? Why we stopping?"

"Everything's wrong. We're stopping the whole thing."

"What're you talking? We're on our way to ten megabucks. And that's only the beginning."

Fine, but was it only the beginning too of a large ciphering of deaths? He didn't want to push his bad luck or spread his Typhoid Mary touch. He had already involved Florence and Mimsy Bogen. And Molly Moldover, Kraut's sister.

"Deal me out."

"We'll talk about it later, kid, when you're thinking straight. You need to get yourself a good night's rest."

He pulled back into Sunrise traffic, made sure no one looking like Death was following him, and outside Bellmore chose a motel at random.

A good night's rest. He lay watching his travel clock semaphore the hours. At midnight he sat up, looked up the numbers, and dialed. Molly Moldover first.

He heard a talk show in the background.

"Hello?" She sounded turned away, lending one ear to the talk show.

"Is Herman there?"

"Herman?" A splutter of nosh. "You must have the wrong number."

"Sorry."

Now the Bogens. Mimsy's voice, sleepy, answered on the third ring.

"Yes?"

He remained silent, wanted to say something but not knowing what.

"Oh, I've got a breather."

He smiled. He spoke after he hung up.

"No, it's the strangler."

At least they were all safe as of this moment. He could go to sleep now if he could go to sleep. Too much imagination.

# 11

Dawn came up solid white with a runny yolk. Paul crossed from Long Island to Staten Island and remembered his way to Halloran Hospital.

The medic beamed. It seemed all Halloran took pride in Jimmy Rath.

"Very rare, only about one thousand cases in the whole U.S. Wilson's disease usually doesn't show up till as late as forty or fifty, even later in Jimmy's case. A Wilson's disease patient has to stay off foods rich in copper—mushrooms, oysters, nuts, chocolates, liver, and so on, and take a chelating agent. Jimmy's showed remarkable improvement on that regimen. When we first took him in five years ago—he's a vet of World War I and entitled to treatment—he was bedridden. Now—well, you'll see for yourself. Be good for him to meet someone from outside—use up some of his excess energy. I hate to tranquilize him because of the side effects. That door. Straight through to the end of the Extended Care Pavilion. Go right in."

At the far end of the pavilion Paul came to a large solarium. Outside the glass the ground flowed away in smooth green. Inside, the other patients had cleared a space in the center of the room for two old men in motorized wheelchairs.

The two played a game of Dodgem, rolling, spinning, braking, reversing, each trying to bump without getting bumped. The spectators cheered them on as a young paraplegic announced the contest for the blind.

". . . just in time Tommy leans away from a sideswipe. Jimmy makes a nice recovery, whizzes around in time to corner Tommy. Jimmy takes one to give two—and that does it, folks. That last bump nearly knocked Tommy out of his chair. Tommy seems game to go on, but the referee stops the contest in the third round. Winner and still champion, Jimmy Rath."

Paul waited for the congratulating and kidding to die down before he tackled Rath.

Jimmy Rath sleeved sweat from a face as congested from laughing as if he had been hanging head-down. He eyed the phone case.

"See me? Sure, kid, what can I do you for?"

Paul told him.

"Kraut Schwartz? Jesus H. Christ, I ain't thought about the bum in years."

"Bum?"

"When I was on the cops, they was all bums to me. They knew it, and unless they wanted a taste of my fist, they all walked wide. Pull up a chair. I see you was wounded yourself. Vietnam, right? I can tell.

"But Kraut, now. I mind the time old Kraut took out his fat wallet and started to tell me to buy my missus something nice for Christmas. My missus in his mouth. I grabbed aholt of the bum and stuck him upside down in a garbage can. Right there on Broadway in front of everybody. He never showed his face on my Broadway beat again after that." He cracked his knuckles. The sound apparently drowned out in his own ears a sudden hum from the phone case. "What's them papers you got there?"

Paul told him.

"Yeah? Well, I'll give it a whirl. But that was long ago, kid. Long ago." He read slowly through Kraut's ravings, looking up only when he had something to offer. "'It takes force . . . He'd never stop for a friendly smile, but trudged along in his moody style.' Now, 'Force was the name of a ready-to-eat cereal. And there was a jingle about this Jim Dumps fellow who ate the stuff and became Sunny Jim' 'The golden hour of the little flower.' Sure, that was the program of the radio priest of them days. Father Coughlin, God rest his soul. 'He died with his daisies on.' That must mean the Limey—Vic Hazell. Another bum. 'Daisies' is short for 'daisy roots,' which is cockney rhyming slang for 'boots.' Vic was gunning for Kraut, but Kraut hid out till he could fix it for Vic to get knocked off while Vic was taking a phony phone call."

He read on to the end and shook his head.

"I guess that's it, kid. Did I help you at all?" He went on before Paul could say yes. "Uh-oh. The computer says it's time for my penicillamine."

Paul followed Jimmy Rath's gaze and saw a nurse heading their way.

"Everything here works by computer, kid. What doses to take and when to take them." He cracked his knuckles.

Paul picked up the phone case and stood.

"Thanks, Mr. Rath."

"Anytime, kid. Anytime."

Paul had made it to the parking lot when he thought he heard a crash of glass, then cries. He stood a moment beside the Mercury, shook his head when nothing more happened, tossed the phone case on the seat, and got behind the wheel. He had started rolling when the medic he had met came running out to wave him down. Paul braked and waited for the medic's breath to catch up.

"Did you say anything to Jimmy to get him worked up?"

Paul stared. He did not want to believe his premonition.

"No. We talked about his days on the New York Police force. He seemed happy remembering them. Why? What happened?"

"He's killed himself."

Paul got out and followed the medic, who took a short cut to the lawn outside the solarium.

They had spread a blanket over the twisted form of Jimmy Rath. After crashing through the floor-length window and careening down the grassy slope, the wheelchair had struck the rock wall at an angle, and Jimmy had momentum-tumbled along the roughness.

One of the top administrators took Paul to his office and began asking the same questions when the phone broke in. The man made a face as he hung up.

"Well, we know now what it was. All right, Felder, you can go."

"Like hell. I want to know what it was."

The man made another face, then sighed.

"It's going to come out sooner or later, so all right. It was a foul-up in the pharmacological computer. It ordered Jimmy's dose on time as usual, but for some stupid reason it made up some PCP instead of his penicillamine. Penicillamine is a chelating agent. What it does is clutch copper atoms in its claws and lift them out of the bloodstream before they can damage liver and brain. PCP is a hallucinogen. For God's sake, they *outlawed* PCP back in '63 because it turns you on into schizophrenia. How we even had the formula on hand is going to take a lot of explaining."

Paul settled himself behind the wheel of the Mercury but did not turn the ignition key. It had to be Kraut's doing. Kraut the program evening an old score for Kraut the dead gangster.

"What happened, pal?"

Paul glared at the phone case on the seat beside him.

"You tell me."

"Simple, pal." Kraut spoke in discrete syllables as to a child or an idiot. "GIGO. Garbage in, garbage out."

With a bolus of fear Paul Felder saw Jimmy Rath's death not only as Kraut getting hunk for the dumping into the garbage can

on Broadway in the Thirties but also as an object lesson to Paul
Felder now.

# 12

He swallowed hard as he handed his credit card to the teller.

"I'd like to draw a thousand in twenties on my credit card."

He had to learn how much leeway Kraut allowed him. One
grand could give him a good start if he had to run. The phone
case hung sweaty in his hand.

"Very good, sir."

The teller pressed a button on the credit card box. Paul saw
the reflection of a warning light flash in her eye. She smiled and
asked him to wait a moment. He smiled back. She turned away,
no doubt discreetly signaling a guard.

Paul looked around casually and whispered fiercely to Kraut.

"They think I'm working plastic."

"I know. You gonna be good?"

"Yes."

"O.K., kid. Just stay cool."

By the time the guard reached Paul's elbow his credit card had
gone off the hot-card list and the teller was making red-faced
excuses. Paul smiled stiffly.

"That's quite all right. These things happen. On second thought,
I won't be needing the full thousand. Make it two hundred,
please."

"We're back in the car?"

They were, but Paul couldn't remember the in-between.

"We are."

"O.K., kid. Don't just sit there. It's out to Long Island again.
I'm fixing you up with a motel reservation so we'll be all set to
fly to Florida in the morning."

"All right, all right."

"Sore, huh?" Kraut chuckled. "No hard feelings, pal, but see
what happens when you get wise, O acned adolescent?"

"Wha'?"

"A slip of the lingo. I meant 'O rash youth.'"

"See what happens when you get fancy?"

"Never mind. The warning stands. I'm telling you: play along
with me, you'll be glad; buck me, you'll be sorry."

# 13

The desk clerk handed him the key with a wink. Still smarting from that assault on his straight manhood, Paul let himself into his room.

A confusion of hair, blue domes of eyelids, a sleeping smile. Mimsy lay very much at home on his bed.

Softly he set the phone case on the folding rack, then moved to the side of the bed and stood looking down. At last he clicked the key against its plastic tag.

She opened an eye a sharper focus of blue, then shut it and stretched her lines felinely. He felt an answering shiver of tingle. Need and doubt weakened his stance. He had to sit and made the most of it by sitting on the bed. He cupped his hand on her breast and felt an answering titillation. She opened both eyes.

"I came right away, Paul. I took the afternoon off and I'm cutting evening class. It feels sinfully good to play hooky."

What was this about coming right away? And how had she found out where he would be staying when he himself had not known till an hour ago? She ran a finger across his lips to stop him from speaking.

"I guess what got me was your cool when I played footsie with you under dear old Florence's innocent eyes and you didn't blink yours one time. I just did it to tease to begin with. But then, I don't know, something came over me." She blubbed his lips playfully.

For a minute he didn't know what she was talking about. Then he got the picture of the three of them at the table while nylon toes slid up and down his legs. He laughed. She pushed up on one elbow and stared at him, her eyes suddenly uncertain. He laughed again, but to his own surprise it did not come out a bitter laugh. Her eyes unclouded and she laughed with him.

"Anyway, I made up my mind right after the call to find out about you as well as about myself."

His ears burned; they at least had lost their cool. *Right after the call*: letting him know she had tagged him as the midnight breather. Had she just now laughed not with him but at him? Did she take him for some sort of a creep? She was asking for it. Sock it to her between the eyes.

He got up, not caring how awkwardly, and watched her in the mirror as he undressed. But aside from a widening of the eyes he saw no change in her face. A soft look of lasting wonder, maybe.

"So much for your cool. Boy, did you take me in."
"And vice versa."
"How did it happen?"
"Haven't you heard of love at first sight?"
She punched his shoulder.
"You know what I mean."
He articulated the plastic and aluminum legs.
"Land mine in Vietnam."
"Why didn't you tell me in the car last night?"
"I don't want pity or perversity."
"How do you know you're not getting them now?"
He deployed himself.
"I know."

"You have beautiful long legs."
"My first memory is of wanting to grow tall enough to see what was on the mantel."
"And when you did, what did you find?"
"Dust. Florence isn't the best housekeeper." Mimsy sighed. "She'll be worrying. Do you know how late it is? I have to go." She lay back. "But first you have to keep your promise."
"What promise?"
She wrinkled her nose.
"You know. When you phoned earlier and said those nice things and asked me to come over and promised to tell me who I really am. Most convincing. You made it sound so very mysterious." She thrust out her lower lip. "Unless it was only a hype. Is that what you meant: putting me on to do what we did so I'd know myself metaphysically?" She bit his ear. "A shabby trick, darling." She kissed his nose. "But a lovely number." She slipped away from him and legged it to the bathroom to wash and dress.

Paul sent his glower past the foot of the bed to the phone case. Getting an earful? Getting a kick out of the whole thing as well. Kraut the pimp. Harsh thanks for the lovely number, but Kraut had put him on the spot.

Florence had asked him not to tell Mimsy. But everyone had the right to know who she or he was. Mimsy had that basic right. She also had the right to be aware Kraut had used her and might use her again.

When she came out and asked him to zip her up, he told her. He told her about the programs and about the portable phone and showed her the copy of Kraut's ravings. She nodded as she handed the pages back.

"Lots of things make sense now. Not this gibberish. I mean things Florence never wanted to talk about." She surprised Paul by laughing suddenly, richly. "Florence as Mrs. Kraut Schwartz! That'll take some getting used to. I won't tell her I know, of course. This is some wild head change. I used to dream I was secretly a princess, and now I wake up and find I'm Kraut Schwartz's granddaughter. I like the idea." She aimed a finger at Paul. "You cross me, Felder, you fail to make this little girl happy, and you get it right in the guts. Right, gramps?"

Kraut laughed.

"Right, kid. I like the idea too. You got class."

Waiting to see her off in a cab took them out of earshot of Kraut. Paul sandwiches Mimsy's hand in both his.

"We need a way for you to be sure another time it's the real Paul Felder and not gramps who's phoning you."

She thought.

"How about slipping the word 'borogoves' in."

"As in 'All mimsy were the borogoves'?"

"Beamish."

The cab came. He leaned in for a parting kiss and a last word.

"Take care of yourself, Mimsy."

"And you. When will I see you again?"

"Soon, I hope."

She leaned out to call back.

"Pity you don't know what nice things you said on the phone. Maybe I'll tell you some day."

He squeezed his eyes tight.

"How, Kraut?"

"Ain't you doped it out, pal?"

"You used my voice pattern to make her think I was calling."

His own voice came back at him.

"Exact same voiceprint, kid."

He squeezed his fists tight. He wanted to ask, to shout, *What did you say to her?*

"Why, Kraut?"

"I told you, kid. String along with me and keep your nose clean and you'll be glad. Don't tell me you didn't like it. Why be a chump? Get it where you can and while you can."

"Know something, Kraut? You're mean as a little old lady at a wrestling match. I thought you were thinking big. And here all you've been doing is getting in jabs with an umbrella."

"Say, looka here, kid, I don't know why you're all upset? I thought we was on the same wavelength, seeing you're part artificial like me. Also now there's this other tie, seeing you're almost one of the family."

Paul burned, remembering the phone case had shared the room with them. He opened his eyes and looked around the motel room. Was there no way out of the bind he found himself in? Maybe he could put Kraut himself/itself through an identity crisis.

"Seducing your own granddaughter. Now there's a freaky bit of incest for you."

A moment's silence, then a cold voice.

"Know something, kid? You got a mouth on you."

# 14

The idea hit him in the middle of the night. But he waited for morning, after Florence left for the supermarket and before Mimsy left for her office-temporary assignment.

"Yes?"

"Mimsy, Mimsy, quite the whimsy, how do your borogoves grow?"

"Ah, the real Paul Felder."

"Listen up, Mimsy. Kraut will be wondering why it's taking me so long to check out. And if I know him, he'll start feeling around, and maybe tapping the pay phones here, or your phone."

"So I'm listening."

"How's your data processing?"

"Fairly advanced. Why?"

"I've been thinking, if you can get up to Boston and tell Prof. Steven Fogarty at Thoreau I say it's O.K. to show you my program—got that so far?"

"My shorthand's fairly advanced too."

"If you do get the chance then, sneak a listening delay into the program. If there's a delayed feedback between what Kraut says and what he hears himself say, he won't be able to speak at all. That ought to frustrate him into a breakdown and give us a shot at regaining control." He grew aware that he lacked feedback. "Hello?"

He was talking into a dead line.

# 15

Matt Muldoon looked hopefully at Paul Felder.

"Cold up north?"

The lie would harm no one.

"Some of the lion leaped over from March. It was raw out this morning."

Matt Muldoon's face took a happy twist down around Killarney. He had found Muldoon where the lady in the next trailer had said Muldoon would be. Muldoon sat at a table under a beach umbrella down by the wading end of the pool, drawing out his canned draft beer. Muldoon's smile faded.

"Still I kind of miss it. Not the place so much, the times. In those days we had the lead all set up in type. 'Gang guns blazed again today and . . .' But I guess things weren't the way we remember them, the way we like to think they were. Like one time I pointed out to Kraut an old guy eating clams and celery at Shanley's. 'Yeah?' Kraut says. 'Who's that?' 'Bat Masterson,' I tell him. 'You're still not telling me nothing,' he says. And so I have to explain that Bat Masterson had been a great gunfighter in the Old West. Kraut eyed him again. 'Yeah? He don't look so much.' And he didn't. Come to think of it, neither did Kraut."

Paul eyed the phone case at his feet and tried to damp a shudder. He had boarded the plane only after Kraut had promised him not to touch Muldoon. But what were Kraut's easy promises worth?

Muldoon was talking.

"They're all gone now, all those who had some connection with Kraut. Or going fast." He ticked them off on blunt fingers. "S. Thomas Extrom and Gordon Dumaine. Peggy Aaron. Tommy Tighe. Jake Putterman. Judge Barsky. Dallas Dollard. His sister Molly and his wife Florence I don't know about. PWU—present whereabouts unknown. Probably dead. Same goes for Letha Root. Leaves only Macie Devlin and his Faith Venture. And of course Harry Spector. Funny how Max Flesher died the other day and almost at the same time Mark Nolan."

"Mark Nolan?"

Muldoon tapped the copy of Kraut's ravings before him on the table.

"Sergeant Nolan, the guy who questioned Kraut as he lay dying. Came across it only this morning in the Miami paper. Small item. Seems Nolan was setting the night alarm system in the bank where he worked as a guard. Just getting ready to go home. Some kind of short circuit electrocuted him. He went to his long home."

Paul did not tell him about Mort Lesser and Jimmy Rath.

"Boy, I sure know how to spread the gloom, don't I, Felder? Sorry about the necrology, but that's what you get for looking up an old bastard like me. The gap-tooth generation. Let's get on to something lighter, like Kraut's deathbed spiel."

Muldoon laughed and pointed.

"This 3909 in '3909 stained-glass windows'—know what that is? Didn't think you would. When Al Smith was running for President, anti-Catholics or just plain good Republicans would ask, 'Do you know Al Smith's phone number? Here, I'll write it down.' They'd write 3909, then tell you to turn the paper back to front and hold it to the light. Get it? POPE. Direct line to the Vatican is what they meant."

He read on and shook his head.

"'Olive Eye' I never figured out."

Explaining it to him would have meant telling him about Mort Lesser. Paul kept silent.

"Now 'A roof without visible means of support' I know. After Kraut dropped out of school he was a newsboy for a year, then a grocery store clerk till he got canned, then a composition roofer's apprentice. From the time he was seventeen he kept paying roofer's union dues to show arresting officers his card as proof of gainful employment.

"He also told me, 'I once worked in your racket.' He said he had been a printer's devil for a while. I guess that's how come he knew about the accents acute and grave he mentions in this nuttiness.

"Then he began his real career. He boosted packages off delivery trucks, looted stores, broke into apartments, stuck up crap games that wouldn't pay for protection. For a while he drove a beer truck for Arnold Rothstein, the bankroller for the underworld. Then he went into business for himself.

"That's where 'the doctor' comes in—the 'big con man' of 'Fairfield, Conn.' That has to be Dr. S. Thomas Extrom. Extrom always seemed to me one of those ham actors who listens to his voice instead of to the words, to *how* he's saying instead of *what* he's saying. He wore his overcoat like an opera cape. *Die Fledermaus.* But the world took him for philanthropist, yachtsman, financier, country squire, even Presidential dark horse.

"Yet he and Gordon Dumaine, the treasurer of O'Harmon & Foster, were really the Spitale brothers, with long records as con men till the records disappeared from the files. It was S. Thomas who got them into the big time. He had vision. He saw Prohibition coming and took over O'Harmon & Foster, a slipping but legitimate drug firm.

"O'Harmon & Foster got withdrawal permits for alcohol to manufacture its products. Bootleggers' trucks, including Kraut's, rolled up to the platform of O'Harmon & Foster in Fairfield, Conn., at night to load barrels of hair tonic, furniture polish, and tincture of iodine that the bootleggers distilled into '8-year-old rye,' 'bottled-in-bond bourbon,' and 'Scotch just off the boat.'

Muldoon shuddered.

"I can still taste the stuff."

He washed the taste away with a swallow of beer.

"On with the show and tell. 'Jafsie' I'm sure you know. This next seems to have to do with switching to the numbers game when Repeal liquidated bootlegging. The 'high yeller' would be Letha Root, Harlem's policy queen. Kraut muscled her and all the other black operators out and himself in. Two million bucks a year that meant to him.

"'Everything works by push or pull.' That's something Tommy Tighe used to say. He was Tammany district leader and Kraut's bagman, paying off the cops, the politicians, and the judges and prosecutors.

"From 'Mr. Black has the Limehouse Blues' to, let's see, 'Tip your derby to a horseshoe wreath' has to do with the time Schwartz hid out in Peggy Aaron's house. The Limey, Vic Hazell, worked as a triggerman for Kraut, then decided he wanted part or all of the action for himself. He declared war by raiding Kraut's garage, smashing everything he found there—slot machines, beer rack, trucks—all but twenty cases of booze, which he hauled away after killing a mechanic who begged for his life.

"In the war with the Limey the kill ratio favored Kraut—but how can you outwit a mad dog? And Hazell was a mad dog. He went looking for Kraut personally after Kraut's hoods killed Hazell's kid brother. One day on East 107th, Kraut spotted Tommy gun muzzles sticking out of a black touring car. Kraut dove for the pavement. Kids were playing under spouting fire hydrants when the Limey sprayed the whole damn street trying to get Kraut. Five kids wounded, one dead.

"Sol Barsky—later Judge Barsky and a righteous tough judge— got Hazell off by tripping up a prosecution witness. The cops had tried too hard to cinch the case against Hazell with a little white perjury.

"Anyway, with Hazell running loose, Schwartz lay low as a 'Mr. Black' at Peggy Aaron's, while hoods he hired from Chicago hunted Hazell. The Limey got riddled taking a set-up phone call. As I remember, he was all of twenty-four. I met Peggy in later years and she told me Kraut pushed her and her girls around for the fun of it. Still, she felt nostalgia for the old days. She said she ran into one of her girls after her place broke up. 'It was safer in my house,' she said. 'The poor girl got pregnant swimming in a public swimming pool.'

"The tramp buttering his bread with sunlight could be Chaplin, though I don't recall that bit of business in any of his films. But here's Jake Putterman, a guy with moxie. 'Jamaica ginger'—Jake for short. 'Leading the blind in his soup and fish,' and so on. Jake was a Waiters Union officer who fought back when Kraut set up the Gotham Restaurant and Cafeteria Association to squeeze protection money. Stink bombs during lunch and dinner hours. Death threats. They didn't faze Jake, though local law enforcement was no help.

"The New York grand jury, convened to investigate racketeering under the direction of the D.A., couldn't find any rackets. A series of stories appeared in the *N.Y. Evening Globe*, detailing the rackets. The grand jury subpoenaed the newspaperman, but yours truly refused to reveal his source. The grand jury had me taken before the general sessions judge. Fined me 250 bucks and 30 days for contempt." Muldoon smiled. "Wasn't too bad. I got a jail expose series out of the vile durance.

"But now things began to break. It was the beginning of the end for Kraut Schwartz. The governor appointed a special prosecutor. My source—Jake Putterman—brought the special prosecutor evidence tying Schwartz to Tommy Tighe, the Tammany district leader who was Kraut's fixer. Kraut beat it out of the state and waited for the heat to die down.

"Funny how he skips around in his delirium. Here we go back a few years. Once I put in the paper that Kraut was a pushover for a blonde. He came up to me and asked, 'Did you write that,

Muldoon?' I had to say I did. He shook his head. 'Is that any language for a family newspaper?' But he did have a yen for blondes. Florence, of course. And then there was Dallas Dollard, the dame who ran her own speak-easy. She wouldn't give him a tumble. Here she is in 'Throw the bitch out. It's curtains, sister. A cotton ball in hell.' Her chorus girls had an act in which they threw tiny cotton balls at the suckers. I was there when she was rehearsing a new show. She had a routine in which a guy playing a repairman asked, 'Would you like a French phone?' and she answered, 'But I don't speak French.' A voice came from a dark corner of the room. 'You can French me anytime.' She located her heckler by the red glow of a cigar, and she yelled, 'Throw the bum out!' It was Kraut. He turned down her apology and got her place padlocked, and she never dared show her face in New York after that.

"But 'F for fig' and the rest I don't get, unless it was the G-string Dallas's chorus girls wore, and maybe 'J for jig' has to do with Harlem again, and 'J for John the Waterman' might be Schwartz's Waterman pen he used to rap the mouthpiece with to annoy wire-tappers: that this made it just as hard on whoever he was talking to didn't faze him, and 'N for knucklebones' could stand for brass knuckles, and 'S for sack of stones' might be a cement kimono for somebody he dropped in the East River.

"Now the mention of a trunk reminds me. The story went that Schwartz had somebody build him an iron chest and that Schwartz filled it with big bills and jewelry. I heard that it held the diamonds and rubies from Broadway's biggest jewelry store heist. The word was Schwartz agreed to fence the stuff then sent a triggerman after the guys who pulled it off to gun them down and bring back the dough Schwartz had paid for the stuff."

Matt Muldoon eyed the nose shadow of a sunbather.

"Four p.m. Time for my dip. Finished on the dot." He handed the pages back to Paul and stood up on skinny shanks. "Join me? I'll fix you up with a pair of trunks, and we can both impregnate the swimming pool."

Paul smiled and shook his head but went down to the edge with Muldoon. He waited at the deep end for Muldoon to snort and splutter up and out. He braced himself and lent a hand to a mottled hand.

"Be careful the next few days." He looked across the pool to the phone case resting by Muldoon's table. "And you'll think I'm nuts but when we get back say something nice about Kraut."

Muldoon stared at him, then a few drops fell with a shrug.

"Too much sun too soon?" Muldoon frowned searchingly at the sunbathers at the far side of the pool, then back at Paul. "Why not I always humor nuts."

And toweling himself at his table, Muldoon spoke to the world at large.

"Once I asked Schwartz if he ever did business with Lucky Luciano or Chink Sherman. Schwartz said, 'I may do a lot of lousy things, but I'll never live off dames or dope.' In his way Schwartz was quite a guy."

He looked at Paul for approval. Paul nodded; he hoped that had bought Muldoon protection.

# 16

Paul made out to be taking a sponge bath in his motel room and with the water running sneaked out to a pay phone.

"Hello?"

"Mrs. Florence Bogen?"

"Yes. Who is this?"

"Paul Felder. Is Mimsy there?"

"No."

"Do you know where she is?"

"I really can't say. She wasn't here when I came home this evening. She left a note. It said she had a wonderful assignment traveling as a secretary to an executive on a flying trip across the country. I checked with the business school, and they said she canceled her classes for the rest of the week for the same reason. It sounded like a good thing, but frankly I was worried till you called. The office-temporary place is closed at this hour, and I can't find out anything from a recording. I thought you and Mimsy might have—But now I'm not worried."

Now *he* was worried. The assignment sounded phony. Had Mimsy given up after his aborted call, and had Kraut requisitioned her out of the way? Or had Mimsy faked it, setting out on her unprepared own to deal with Kraut in Boston?

His heart sank to the bottom of the slot with the coins for a second call.

Professor Steven Fogarty hardly listened.

"Girl? No, I haven't met your girl. Sorry, Paul, you caught me at a bad time. I'm late already. Faculty meeting. Cutting up the pie for the coming semester. I really have to run now. Try me again later this week or early next."

That was bad enough. Worse was wondering if that had been Professor Steven Fogarty or Kraut mimicking Fogarty's voice.

# 17

Letha Root was blind but she *glared* at him.

"Be he live or be he dead, I don't want nothing to do with him nohow, that's the guaranteed truth."

Time had sharpened further the already sharp features of the high-yellow policy queen of Harlem in the Thirties.

Paul found himself laying a soul brother accent on her.

"Won't take but a minute of your time, sister."

In the silence the hall funneled the refrigerator humming and the wires in a toaster and the loose lid of a pot on a burner humming along. Someone in the kitchen opened and closed the refrigerator door, and Paul heard the interfacing of beer and air.

Madame Root shook her head.

"My interest in Kraut Schwartz died when he died. But I ain't no ways sorry for the wire I sent old Kraut at the Newark Hospital when I hear he's at death's door. 'Galatians 6:7' is all I said. If you don't know your Bible, that's 'Be not deceived; God is not mocked: for whatsoever a man soweth, that shall he also reap.' Too bad he never came to enough to know about the wire."

Paul felt the phone case join in the humming. Kraut knew now.

"Makes you stop and wonder, don't it, sister, how it all come out like the Good Book say."

"F'get you, honky."

Letha Root turned her blankness on the mustachioed tall stud in tie-dyed levi's and high-heeled shoes.

"Why, what you mean, Junior?"

"He hyping you, Aunty. This ain't no member. He only got a contact habit bloodwise. You just as well stop running your mouth." Without taking his eyes off Paul, he drained his beer and set the can down. "Whupping the game on a lame. I'm gonna go up side your head."

Letha Root put out a hand.

"He don't mean no harm, honey. My jaws ain't tight. If a white boy can put me on like that, he must have *some* soul in him. You leave him be." She felt the crystalless face of her lapel watch. "It's getting on, Junior. You better be on your way to your job."

Junior looked sullenly out the window at Paul's rental Caddy. His mood shifted to indifference. He was doing his number: his number was to look bored; it put the world on the defensive.

"If you think you know what you doing."

He gave Aunty an unnephewlike kiss. She gave him a fond slap.

"Oh, yeah. Get on out of here, you old greasy greens."

He got on out without a backward look at Paul.

Madame Root got herself and Paul settled down.

"Reckon you can tell I bought myself a nephew. He works at a soul station I own here. Oh, yes, I got out of New York with just enough to buy me a new start. Old Kraut didn't wipe me out quite. I liked the climate out here—it was hotter in New York, you dig—but back when I hit Las Vegas, they weren't letting blacks move in. So I got me a white woman to front for me and bought this house. I made out to be the maid. Lots of folks think she left it to me in her will.

"All right, white boy. You flew all the way out here to see me. Read me what old Kraut said. Maybe I'll know and maybe I won't. Maybe I'll tell and maybe I won't. What you waiting on? Do I have a witness out there?"

She didn't stop him till he reached "5 to 7 made them Darktown Strutters bawl. Even the high yeller." Her face took on even greater sharpness, and she put up a halting hand.

"That old devil Kraut. 527 was the magic number done all us Harlem operators in. Everybody knowed 527 always get a big play in November. That because 5 plus 2 is lucky 7 and November the 11th month. Seven-come-eleven the idea. Well, old Kraut got his walking adding machine—what his name?"

"Zigzag Ludwig?"

"That it. Kraut got Zigzag to figure how to rig the pari-mutuel handle with a few bets at the race track to make 527 hit on Thanks-giving Eve, 19 and 31. That broke all the black-run policy banks, and old Kraut moved in."

She stopped him again at "The man and the woman have a fortune in potatoes. It's Big Dick— "

"Dream-book talk. 'Man and woman' mean 15, 'fortune' mean 60, and 'potatoes'—that stand for something else you can guess—mean 75. In craps Big Dick stand for 10, in lottery Big Dick 15–60–75."

She had but one comment more, and that at the end.

"What old Kraut doing messing around with the Bible? Fetch me my copy down off yonder shelf and turn to Genesis 3:14 and read me it."

"'And the Lord God said unto the serpent, Because thou hast done this, thou art cursed above all cattle, and above every beast of the field; upon thy belly shalt thou go, and dust shalt thou eat all the days of thy life.'"

She listened and nodded.

"Look like old Kraut crapped out with snake eyes."

Letha Root stood at the door of her home still laughing as Paul crossed slabs set in trim lawn and got into the Caddy.

Once safely on the passenger seat with the car starting up, Kraut spoke.

"We're getting there, kid. I'll lay odds when you dig up the iron chest holding the loot there'll be a combination padlock on the hasp and the combination will be Big Dick—15–60–75. O.K., kid. On to L.A."

Looking in the mirror to make a U-turn back toward the airport, Paul met eyes.

Junior rose higher and leaned forward to take in the phone case. He flicked open a knife. Its wickedness held Paul still while Junior reached over to snap the case open and study its innards. Junior got his rump on the back seat and lounged, cleaning his fingernails with the knife.

"Suppose you drive me to my place of work. We-all got things to talk over."

In the broadcasting studio Junior's number changed. Now, sitting at his mikes and switches and wearing earphones, he was the up-tempo soul-station disc jockey supreme.

"Hello-o-o: lucky people you, this is your Toke Show host . . . the Splendiferous Spade. You know I ain't S-in and J-ing you: pretty people, I'm cuing you. For the next two solid hours . . . and I mean solid . . . I'll be taking requests. So you be phoning them in, hear?" He mixed in loud drum rim-shots, trumpet flourishes, and band chords sustained to punctuate his shucking and jiving, gave the phone number, put on a piece full of funky runs, lit, sucked on and passed to Paul a joint in a peace-symbol roach clip, and leaned back with his earphones half on half off. "Now, man, don't hold back."

He followed Paul's gaze to the desk phone and smiled.

"I fixed the station phone line to give callers the busy signal. I have me a backlog of requests on tape—my goof-off insurance. Shoot, man, we're alone and won't nobody bother us."

The light on the desk phone lit up.

Junior frowned and lifted the phone. Paul could hear Kraut's voice.

"Please play 'If I Forget You.' I'd like to dedicate it to the memory of Kraut Schwartz, which is a long memory."

The voice went on but grew so faint that Junior had to press the earpiece hard to his head to hear. Then came an ear-splitting sound that shimmered the air and set Paul's teeth on edge. Junior slumped slowly after the jolt hit him. Junior was alive but his face was dead. Paul looked at Junior's eyes and did not want to know what the sound had done to Junior's brain.

Kraut spoke from the phone case.

"Now if you get the hell out of there, kid, we won't miss our flight after all."

# 18

"Mr. Devlin?"

"Yes."

"Macie Devlin?"

"The same."

Macie Devlin's voice was easy, but his eyes held a wariness that went against the voice.

"My name is Paul Felder." Paul spoke over the electric hedge trimmer sounding from the side of the redwood house. He had nearly tripped on its damn trailing cord. "I'm doing a paper on Kraut Schwartz and— "

He stopped, wondering at Macie Devlin's quick warning head-shake. The hedge trimmer's whine grew.

"Faith, no!"

Paul whirled without thinking. He tripped himself. The phone case flew from his hand. The ground stunned him. All he saw of the woman rushing him was a floppy white hat and rhinestoned dark glasses. She was leaning over him before he could move. The vibrating saw blade thrust down at his throat.

His hands were broken-winged birds. One flailing hand touched a tremble of line. He caught hold of the cord and whipped it at the blade. The blade sliced through to a flaring crackle that shocked the woman backward.

Paul rolled over into a painful push-up. Even stilled, the blade made a wicked weapon. But by now Macie Devlin had an arm around the woman; his other hand gently pulled the trimmer from her grip and let it fall.

"She's all right now."

Devlin walked her to the front door. She stiffened in the opening and her legs locked. Macie Devlin looked back over his shoulder.

"She's afraid for me, you see. Only a few years ago some of the boys snatched me and tried to make me tell them where to find Albert's mythical buried fortune." He gave a short laugh. "Hell, if I knew where it was, I'd've told the government more'n forty years ago, right after Albert died. The informer's share alone would've made me rich."

He stroked the woman's cheek. "This young fellow won't harm me, dearest. Please go in and take your beauty nap." He kissed her neck.

Her still-showgirl legs unlocked and she dimmed away. Macie Devlin closed the door and turned back to Paul. With a weak smile he fingered sweat from his brow and snapped the drops off.

"Paul Felder is it? Let's have a change of venue, Paul."

A half-size refrigerator stood in a corner of Devlin's downtown real estate management office. Macie Devlin opened it and poured himself a glass of skim milk. Paul shook his head at a hospitable eyebrow. Devlin took distasteful sips.

"Disbarred by an ulcer, as well as by the bar association. Plus high cholesterol level. Plus an implanted pacemaker. My list of infirmities is a long one. But as the fellow said, when you consider the alternative."

He pointed to the fixtures for a neon sign that had hung in the window.

"The neon sign had to go. It could make my pacemaker pulse so fast my heart couldn't keep up. My heart would stop or just twitch." He lifted his head away from bodily pain. "Yes, they worked me over and my heart gave out and they left me for dead. In a way my bum ticker is my insurance. They know it's no use any more trying to get at me through Faith or by working me over again. I'd only stop on them. But you came here to talk about Albert."

Smiling, he leafed through the copy of Kraut's ravings.

"So you consider Kraut Schwartz literature. That would've

thrilled Albert. His favorite reading was Emil Ludwig's—no relation to Zigzag—*Life of Napoleon*. *The Forty Days of Musa Dagh*
also impressed him. After reading it he said, 'Them days you could
knock off hundreds without getting in no jam.'

"For a while he went on a culture binge. I guided him through
the museums, brought him art books. 'The Thinker is a question
mark.' He pointed out to me that in left profile Rodin's *Thinker*
is a question mark. He even began to be a natty dresser, because
Society"—Macie Devlin formed finger quotes in the air around
the word—"took him up. Then he saw Society did it only for
kicks, and he went back to his sloppy self."

A moving van pulled up out front, and the driver came in for
a key. Macie Devlin beamed as the man went out.

"Full occupancy maketh a full hearth. I just rented the office
the other side of this wall to a doctor. That's his equipment they're
moving in. But about Albert. I see he picked up some Pennsylvania
Dutch from his stay. 'Just walk the fly door in. The hook ain't on.'
'I'm afraid you don't make yourself out.' 'Just before you get the
farm behind, go the hill over.' Poor Albert. He nearly went mad
holed up for eighteen months while he was under indictment. He
*did* go mad."

Macie Devlin eyed Paul speculatively.

I've paid my dues. After Albert died I got off with one year for
turning state's evidence and giving the special prosecutor the goods
on Tommy Tighe. I don't want to pay any more dues. There's no
statute of limitations on murder. That goes for being accessory
thereto, however unwittingly or unwillingly. So what I'm about
to tell you is purest supposition.

"Suppose someone journeyed to Albert's hideout to tell Albert
this someone had fixed it up for Albert to give himself up in
Nyack, New York. This someone might have watched Albert
shift moods—from gloom to joy to savagery. Suppose further
that after agreeing to return to civilization, Albert in this strangely
savage mood picked a fight with his favorite bodyguard, Slip
Katz. Albert loved horseback riding, and Katz used to bounce
along with him. But say that now Albert seemed to work himself
into a rage.

"Say that Albert cursed Katz out, accusing him of holding out
a collection on him—'playing the nine of hearts on me.' Say that
Albert suddenly drew from a handy drawer a .45 with a silencer
on it and silenced Katz. Say Albert sent this someone downstairs
to fetch a pair of young hoods. Say Albert told one of the hoods

to stand still and then bloodied his nose. 'And let the blood to drown the blood.' This would account for the blood on the floor as having come from a fight over cards, if the boardinghouse keeper wondered. Say the two hoods stuffed Katz's body into a burlap sack, weighted the sack with chunks of cement—'The cat's pajamas, a kitten kimono'—and dumped it in some abandoned rain-pooled stone quarry."

Macie Devlin's eyes looked haunted.

"'Boys, throw your voice!' You found that ad in the pulp magazines. A cut of an eye-popping porter toting a trunk which emitted the cry, 'Help, help, let me out!' To get you to send away for ventriloquism lessons. Of course all this never happened, but I get a picture of the hoods carrying the sack down the back stairs while Katz still had a bit of life in him."

Paul felt a prickle of insight. *Would I kid you, captain?* Katz had helped Kraut secretly bury the iron trunk full of loot. Like Captain Kidd, Kraut had got rid of a too-knowing henchman.

Macie Devlin seemed anxious to wind it up.

"So much for fantasy. I can tell you only one fact. When Albert gave himself up in Nyack, a small town in Rockland County, I got him to create a new image of himself. Mr. Albert Rabinow walked around town smiling humbly, tipping his hat to the ladies, and patting kids' heads. His people tipped bigger than government people, who were on a tight budget. It was children's parties for hospitalized and orphaned kids and drinks for everyone in the house. 'Cain was I ere I saw Nyack.'

"The jury acquitted him. The judge bawled the jury out. 'The verdict was dictated by other considerations than the evidence.' But though Albert beat the tax evasion rap, the special rackets prosecutor, with Jake Putterman's help, kept after him. Albert proposed that the syndicate rub out the special prosecutor.

"The Big Six vetoed the hit because it would've put too much heat on the whole underworld. 'I'm gunning for the guy myself Egged them on but they chickened out.' Albert sent word he planned to go ahead with the rubout. The syndicate gave Harry Spector the contract, and Albert met his Waterloo in the Tivoliloo."

"Did you ever meet Harry Spector?"

"Never laid eyes on the chap. Never want to. Show you what I mean. He served twenty-three years after they got him for Albert's killing. Just a year before he got out, Harry Spector was the only prisoner to show up for his meals when the inmates at Rahway went on a mass hunger strike. A lot of hard-noses there, but none of the other prisoners made a move to bother Harry Spector."

He handed Paul Kraut's ravings and Paul put them away and got up.

"Drive you back home?"

"No, thanks, young fellow. I have to stay here and see everything's unpacked and set up, ready for the doctor to practice what he shows Monday." He smiled. "I haven't met this chap either, but his credit and references check out tiptop. He's moving down from upstate, and we've arranged everything by phone."

They shook hands and parted outside Macie Devlin's office. Something nagging at him, Paul left slowly. He had not yet gone outside when he heard a thump and a yell.

In the doctor's office Paul found Macie Devlin on the floor. The moving man waved his hands.

"I was just plugging this machine in when I heard him fall and turned around and there he was like that."

Paul whistled softly when he saw Macie Devlin lay within three feet of a diathermy machine for simple surgery such as removing warts. Like a neon sign, a diathermy machine would make a pacemaker race unbeatably.

The moving man repeated himself. Paul cut him off and told him to use Devlin's phone to bring an ambulance.

Paul lowered himself to give mouth-to-mouth. But it was no good. He raised himself stiffly as the ambulance attendant, with a headshake that said it would be no good, took over.

He looked around before he left. He knew before looking roughly what he would find. The name on the packing cases was Dr. O. E. Black. Kraut Schwartz.

# 19

He knew what he would find before he found it in the Miami and Vegas papers he picked up in the L.A. air terminal. Kraut had removed other warts.

The swimming pool at Mobile Haven had an automatic chlorinator that kept the chlorine residual from dropping below .3 ppm by feeding chlorine gas into the water in continuous doses to kill algae and bacteria. The occasionally necessary booster shots of superchlorination took place only when no one was in the pool. At 4 p.m. on the day following Paul's talk with ex-newsman Matt

Muldoon, a sudden uncalled-for surge of superchlorination left those in the pool at the time—two adults and three children—in critical condition. One of the adults was Matt Muldoon.

Letha Root's home had gone up in flames—the fire marshal warned the public again about the danger of overloading electrical circuits—at the same time a local celebrity of the same address, Johnson Jones a.k.a. the Splendiferous Spade, had suffered a seizure or stroke on the air. The Las Vegas paper noted the coincidence and drew a moral for mortal man.

Paul looked back along the spoor of warts. It still beat him how Kraut had pulled off the killing of Mort Lesser. Maybe it had been an ordinary holdup after all. No. More likely it had been payment for Kraut's tip—real or phony?—to some underworld figure that Max Flesher was a canary.

Paul looked ahead through the plane window. Somewhere there should be a nice clean universe. It would be true of all the inhabitants thereof that their guts take a Moebius twist or their large intestine is a Klein bottle—*ein Klein nachtgeschirr*—so that they deposit the results of digestion in this our own less nice universe. Somewhere and sometime in infinity there had to be a nice clean universe. The laws of chance said they couldn't *all* crap out.

# 20

"We're coming down the home stretch, kid."

Paul believed Kraut. They had deplaned in Philadelphia and were rolling through countryside in line with Kraut's analysis.

"I hid out in Pennsylvania Dutch country. 'Zook and ye shall find.' Zook is a Pennsylvania Dutch name. 'Where was Moses when the lights went out?' 'And Pharaoh believed Pharaoh's daughter.' In the Thirties the 4:44 was a Delaware Lackawan'—'the Road of Anthracite'—train that with a changeover to the Reading brought you to Egypt, Pa. According to tax records, the Zook family ran a boardinghouse just outside Egypt. The house is uninhabited but standing. Probably still a faded sign on the barn. 'They put a whammy on the barn.' 'Zook and ye shall find.'"

They drove north in humming silence awhile, then Kraut broke in on a mind seething with wild schemes. Could he blow up Kraut's microwave links? Or turn the microwaves back against Kraut? Or had he waited too long, hoping once he had his hands on the ten megabucks he could buy distance and time? Maybe a computer to fight back with. Damn. Damn. Damn. He would find a way to save Mimsy and himself.

"Kid. Hey, kid!"

A note of urgency came through Kraut's high spirits.

"Yes?"

"I been thinking, kid. Remember that scrap of paper we got from Max Flesher? The one with the X on it and the spots of my blood?"

"Yes?"

"That blood is all the cellular material left of me. I think I could analyze it and clone a lot of Krauts out of that blood. So how's about putting it in a safe place for me. Stop off at Bethlemen, say, and leave it in a bank vault."

Just what the world needed. An army of Krauts.

Paul drew one-handed the slip of paper from his billfold.

"That? Didn't I tell you? We lost that way back during the mugging right after we left Max Flesher."

A long silence, then, "Oh. Too bad, kid. It would of been nice."

"Yes, it would've been really something."

Paul pressed the dashboard lighter, and when it popped he touched the glow to the scrap of paper and watched the army of Krauts curl into ash in the tray.

It was all open country, empty country. He saw no one to see him pry the boards off the front door of the Zook house and let himself in. Dust was the only furnishing. He climbed the stairs. The roomiest guest room would have been Kraut's. He barely made out the nothingness. He raised the window with hurting blows of the heel of his hand and shoved boards away on squeaking nails.

Dark light showed a dim stain on the floor. Katz's blood, in winestained light. The violet of the pane came of many years of sunlight tinting the colloidal solution of manganese in the glass. *The violent end of the spectrum.* The window gave on the neighboring field. It was not a field but a graveyard. *Acutely aware every prognosis is grave.*

He retrieved the phone case at the door.

"We're down to the wire, Kraut."

Kraut did not answer.

"The barn *does* have a faded hex sign, Kraut."

Still no answer.

He crunched along the cinder path leading to the barn, then

veered away through weeds toward the graveyard. He set the phone case down and leaned on the fence. A weather-withered wreath, "Xmas in Heaven," seemed the sole remains of recent remembrance. The name Auer on a headstone struck him like lightning. *I feel my hour coming. The golden hour of the little flower.* The X he had reduced to ashes in the tray of the car had been a mnemonic hourglass. The treasure had to be in the Auer grave.

His smile gave way to gravity. Why was Kraut so all-banked silent? His smile triumphed. He would keep Kraut guessing in return. He straightened to turn and go back for the new shovel and pick he had stowed in the rental Stingray. The barn door creaked open without wind. A man stepped out of the darkness bringing some of it with him. Paul caught glints off a car in the barn.

But another glint took his eye. Big hands hung low on thick arms from heavy shoulders. In one of those hands a gun held steady on Paul.

When he killed Kraut, Harry Spector had been Paul Felder's age. He would be sixty-five now. The man looked a hard, fit sixty-five. A killer. Once you knew, it stuck out all over him.

Paul spoke out of the side of his mouth away from the man.

"Here comes Harry Spector, Kraut. He has a gun."

No response. Why the hell wasn't Kraut sending the note of fear that had made the muggers break and run?

"Kraut!"

No answer was the answer. Kraut had double-crossed him. A trap for Spector, Paul the bait. Paul smiled at Spector.

"What did he tell you that brought you all the way out here?"

Spector halted a man's length from Paul.

"What do you mean he?" For God's sake, he had modeled himself on Edward G. Robinson. "What are you pulling, Felder-if that's your right moniker? Think I don't make the voice?"

"Just wanted to make sure it was you."

So Kraut had used that gimmick again. But what had Paul's voice told Spector? Kraut's iron trunk had been a legend in Kraut and Spector's day. Greed. *I hear a siren coming but he goes back into the john.* A killer who risked his getaway to roll the dying: damn well had to be greed. And greed would make Spector kill Paul to keep the whole of the loot. Right now greed meant impatience.

"I got the connections to fence the jewels and wash the money. You say the stuff's here. So let's get on with the deal."

"Is it all right if I . . .?" Paul mimed picking up the phone case.

He answered narrowing eyes. "Metal detector. It'll tell us where to dig."

The gun gestured O.K. "But don't make no bull moves."

Yet a mad move seemed the only one to make, and make now, before the loot came to light. He couldn't jump Spector. He had to walk straight into the gun, counting on greed to keep Spector from shooting to kill. Paul braced himself and forged ahead, with a yell. Spector froze for an eye blink, then fired at Paul's right knee. The hammer blow rocked Paul, but he swung another step forward. Spector stared, then fired at Paul's left knee. The hammer blow staggered Paul again, but he remained upright and forged on.

Spector backed a step, then held, his eyes fixing on the phone case swinging from Paul's hand. He smiled. Paul read the thought. The "metal detector" could do all the talking Spector needed. The muzzle lifted to center on Paul's chest. Spector's mouth opened in empathy.

"You asked for it, kid."

But the phone case was already flying. It knocked the gun arm aside long enough for Paul to get in and put all he had into one karate chop.

The car in the barn blared its radio.

"All-points bulletin. Be on the lookout for a tan '70 Chevy or a red '74 Stingray. The driver is Harry Spector, 65, white male, wanted for the murder of one Paul Felder at the old Zook homestead east of Egypt. This man is armed and dangerous."

Then Kraut spoke from the phone case on the ground beside the fallen Spector.

"Hear that, Harry? I'm putting that out on the police band. Shoot me in the back, would you?" The voice jumped up and down in glee. "Harry, you been out too long. I'm sticking you in for another twenty-three years."

Paul went limp. He drew shuddering breaths that he took to be sobbing till the true sobbing overrode him.

The sobbing was a woman's and the voice was Mimsy's.

"What did you do to him, gramps? If I'm too late and you've killed him, damn you, gramps, so help me I'll wipe you out."

Paul found his own voice and spoke to the phone case.

"Mimsy."

"Paul! You're all right! You're all right? . . . It is you?"

"Ten thousand borogoves, yes. Where are you?"

"Boston. Thoreau. Gramps cut us off before I could get what you were driving at, remember? So I had to go ahead on my own.

I told Florence I Knew All, and I got her to play dumb when you called—because you might've been gramps. And I made her tell me everything she could about gramps. One thing stuck in my mind. It seems he had a thing about literature.

"I thought a good dose of modern American lit might change his personality. For the better: it couldn't be for the worse. So I came up here and talked myself into access—Steve is a doll—and— "

"It's 'Steve,' is it?"

"Eat your heart out. And I fed gramps Bellow, Mailer, Roth, Gold, Malamud . . . But when I listened in to the readout just now, I thought I was too late."

Kraut's voice broke in. Kraut's and yet not Kraut's. Kraut's with an inflection of Kraut's sister Molly Moldover.

"Paulele, you poor boy, you've been through a bad time. So find a good restaurant quick and have some hot chicken soup already."

By God, the computer program was a Jewish mother.

Mimsy's voice came in loud and clear: "Hurry to me, Paul."

He heard another faraway siren.

# ARM

## Larry Niven

The ARM building had been abnormally quiet for some months now.

We'd needed the rest—at first. But these last few mornings the silence had had an edgy quality. We waved at each other on our paths to our respective desks, but our heads were elsewhere. Some of us had a restless look. Others were visibly, determinedly busy.

Nobody wanted to join a mother hunt.

This past year we'd managed to cut deep into the organlegging activities in the West Coast area. Pats on the back all around, but the results were predictable: other activities were going to increase. Sooner or later the newspapers would start screaming about strictest enforcement of the Fertility Laws, and then we'd all be out hunting down illegitimate parents . . . all of us who were not involved in something else.

It was high time I got involved in something else.

This morning I walked to my office through the usual edgy silence. I ran coffee from the spigot, carried it to my desk, punched for messages at the computer terminal. A slender file slid from the slot. A hopeful sign. I picked it up—one-handed, so that I could sip coffee as I went through it—and let it fall open in the middle.

Color holographs jumped out at me. I was looking down through a pair of windows over two morgue tables.

*Stomach to brain: LURCH! What a hell of an hour to be looking at people with their faces burnt off! Get eyes to look somewhere else, and don't try to swallow that coffee. Why don't you change jobs?*

They were hideous. Two of them, a man and a woman. Something had burnt their faces away down to the skulls and beyond: bones and teeth charred, brain tissue cooked.

I swallowed and kept looking. I'd seen the dead before. These had just hit me at the wrong time.

Not a laser weapon, I thought . . . though that was chancy. There are thousands of jobs for lasers, and thousands of varieties to do the jobs. Not a hand laser, anyway. The pencil-thin beam of a hand laser would have chewed channels in the flesh. This had been a wide, steady beam of some kind.

I flipped back to the beginning and skimmed.

Details: They'd been found on the Wilshire slidewalk in West Los Angeles around 4:30 A.M. People don't use the slidewalks that late. They're afraid of organleggers. The bodies could have traveled up to a couple of miles before anyone saw them.

Preliminary autopsy: They'd been dead three or four days. No signs of drugs or poisons or puncture marks. Apparently the burns had been the only cause of death.

It must have been quick, then: a single flash of energy. Otherwise they'd have tried to dodge, and there'd be burns elsewhere. There were none. Just the faces, and char marks around the collars.

There was a memo from Bates, the coroner. From the looks of them, they might have been killed by some new weapon. So he'd sent the file over to us. Could we find anything in the ARM files that would fire a blast of heat or light a foot across?

I sat back and stared into the holos and thought about it.

A light weapon with a beam a foot across? They make lasers in that size, but as war weapons, used from orbit. One of those would have vaporized the heads, not charred them.

There were other possibilities. Death by torture, with the heads held in clamps in the blast from a commercial attitude jet. Or some kind of weird industrial accident: a flash explosion that had caught them both looking over a desk or something. Or even a laser beam reflected from a convex mirror.

Forget about its being an accident. The way the bodies were abandoned reeked of guilt, of something to be covered up. Maybe Bates was right. A new, illegal weapon.

And I could be deeply involved in searching for it when the mother hunt started.

*       *       *

The ARM has three basic functions. We hunt organleggers. We monitor world technology: new developments that might create new weapons, or that might affect the world economy or the balance of power among nations. And we enforce the Fertility Laws.

Come, let us be honest with ourselves. Of the three, protecting the Fertility Laws is probably the most important.

Organleggers don't aggravate the population problem.

Monitoring of technology is necessary enough, but it may have happened too late. There are enough fusion power plants and fusion rocket motors and fusion crematoria and fusion seawater distilleries around to let any madman or group thereof blow up the Earth or any selected part of it.

But if a lot of people in one region started having illegal babies, the rest of the world would scream. Some nations might even get mad enough to abandon population control. Then what? We've got eighteen billion on Earth now. We couldn't handle more.

So the mother hunts are necessary. But I hate them. It's no fun hunting down some poor sick woman so desperate to have children that she'll go through hell to avoid her six-month contraceptive shots. I'll get out of it if I can.

I did some obvious things. I sent a note to Bates at the coroner's office. *Send all further details on the autopsies, and let me know if the corpses are identified.* Retinal prints and brain-wave patterns were obviously out, but they might get something on gene patterns and fingerprints.

I spent some time wondering where two bodies had been kept for three to four days, and why, before being abandoned in a way that could have been used three days earlier. But that was a problem for the LAPD detectives. Our concern was with the weapon.

So I started writing a search pattern for the computer: find me a widget that will fire a beam of a given description. From the pattern of penetration into skin and bone and brain tissue, there was probably a way to express the frequency of the light as a function of the duration of the blast, but I didn't fool with that. I'd pay for my laziness later, when the computer handed me a foot-thick list of light-emitting machinery and I had to wade through it.

I had punched in the instructions, and was relaxing with more coffee and a cigarette, when Ordaz called.

Detective-Inspector Julio Ordaz was a slender, dark-skinned man with straight black hair and soft black eyes. The first time I saw him in a phone screen, he had been telling me of a good friend's murder. Two years later I still flinched when I saw him.

"Hello, Julio. Business or pleasure?"

"Business, Gil. It is to be regretted."

"Yours or mine?"

"Both. There is murder involved, but there is also a machine . . . Look, can you see it behind me?" Ordaz stepped out of the field of view, then reached invisibly to turn the phone camera.

I looked into somebody's living room. There was a wide circle of discoloration in the green indoor grass rug. In the center of the circle, a machine and a man's body.

Was Julio putting me on? The body was old, half mummified. The machine was big and cryptic in shape, and it glowed with a subdued, eery blue light.

Ordaz sounded serious enough. "Have you ever seen anything like this?"

"No. That's some machine." Unmistakably an experimental device: no neat plastic case, no compactness, no assembly-line welding. Too complex to examine through a phone camera, I decided. "Yah, that looks like something for us. Can you send it over?"

Ordaz came back on. He was smiling, barely. "I'm afraid we cannot do that. Perhaps you should send someone here to look at it."

"Where are you now?"

"In Raymond Sinclair's apartment on the top floor of the Rodewald Building in Santa Monica."

"I'll come myself," I said. My tongue suddenly felt thick.

"Please land on the roof. We are holding the elevator for examination."

"Sure." I hung up.

Raymond Sinclair!

I'd never met Raymond Sinclair. He was something of a recluse. But the ARM had dealt with him once, in connection with one of his inventions, the FyreStop device. And everyone knew that he had lately been working on an interstellar drive. It was only a rumor, of course . . . but if someone had killed the brain that held that secret . . .

I went.

The Rodewald Building was forty stories of triangular prism with a row of triangular balconies going up each side. The balconies stopped at the thirty-eighth floor.

The roof was a garden. There were rose bushes in bloom along one edge, full-grown elms nestled in ivy along another, and a miniature forest of Bonsai trees along the third. The landing pad and carport were in the center. A squad car was floating down ahead of my taxi. It landed, then slid under the carport to give me room to land.

A cop in vivid orange uniform came out to watch me come down, I couldn't tell what he was carrying until I had stepped out. It was a deep-sea fishing pole, still in its kit.

He said, "May I see some ID, please?"

I had my ARM ident in my hand. He checked it in the console in the squad car, then handed it back. "The Inspector's waiting downstairs," he said.

"What's the pole for?"

He smiled suddenly, almost secretively. "You'll see."

We left the garden smells via a flight of concrete stairs. They led down into a small room half full of gardening tools, and a heavy door with a spy-eye in it. Ordaz opened the door for us. He shook my hand briskly, glanced at the cop. "You found something? Good."

The cop said, "There's a sporting goods store six blocks from here. The manager let me borrow it. He made sure I knew the name of the store."

"Yes, there will certainly be publicity on this matter. Come, Gil— " Ordaz took my arm. "You should examine this before we turn it off."

No garden smells here, but there was something—a whiff of something long dead, that the air conditioning hadn't quite cleared away. Ordaz walked me into the living room.

It looked like somebody's idea of a practical joke.

The indoor grass covered Sinclair's living room floor, wall to wall. In a perfect fourteen-foot circle between the sofa and the fireplace, the rug was brown and dead. Elsewhere it was green and thriving.

A man's mummy, dressed in stained slacks and turtleneck, lay on its back in the center of the circle. At a guess it had been about six months dead. It wore a big wristwatch with extra dials on the face and a fine-mesh platinum band, loose now around a wrist of bones and brown skin. The back of the skull had been smashed open, possibly by the classic blunt instrument lying next to it.

If the fireplace was false—it almost had to be; nobody burns wood—the fireplace instruments were genuine nineteenth or twentieth century antiques. The rack was missing a poker. A poker lay inside the circle, in the dead grass next to the disintegrating mummy.

The glowing goldberg device sat just in the center of the magic circle.

I stepped forward, and a man's voice spoke sharply. "Don't go inside that circle of rug. It's more dangerous than it looks."

It was a man I knew: Officer-One Valpredo, a tall man with a small, straight mouth and a long, narrow Italian face.

"Looks dangerous enough to me," I said.

"It is. I reached in there myself," Valpredo told me, "right after we got here. I thought I could flip the switch off. My whole arm went numb. Instantly. No feeling at all. I yanked it away fast, but for a minute or so after that my whole arm was dead meat. I thought I'd lost it. Then it was all pins and needles, like I'd slept on it."

The cop who had brought me in had almost finished assembling the deep-sea fishing pole.

Ordaz waved into the circle. "Well? Have you ever seen anything like this?"

I shook my head, studying the violet-glowing machinery. "Whatever it is, it's brand new. Sinclair's really done it this time."

An uneven line of solenoids was attached to a plastic frame with homemade joins. Blistered spots of the plastic showed where other objects had been attached and later removed. A breadboard bore masses of heavy wiring. There were six big batteries hooked in parallel, and a strange, heavy piece of sculpture in what we later discovered was pure silver, with wiring attached at three curving points. The silver was tarnished almost black and there were old file marks at the edges.

Near the center of the arrangement, just in front of the silver sculpture, were two concentric solenoids embedded in a block of clear plastic. They glowed blue shading to violet. So did the batteries. A less perceptible violet glow radiated from everywhere on the machine, more intensely in the interior parts.

That glow bothered me more than anything else. It was too theatrical. It was like something a special effects man might add to a cheap late-night thriller, to suggest a mad scientist's laboratory.

I moved around to get a closer look at the dead man's watch.

"Keep your head out of the field!" Valpredo said sharply.

I nodded. I squatted on my heels outside the borderline of dead grass.

The dead mans watch was going like crazy. The minute hand was circling the dial every seven seconds or so. I couldn't find the second hand at all.

I backed away from the arc of dead grass and stood up. Interstellar drive, hell. This blue-glowing monstrosity looked more like a time machine gone wrong.

I studied the single-throw switch welded to the plastic frame next to the batteries. A length of nylon line dangled from the horizontal handle. It looked like someone had tugged the switch on from outside the field by using the line; but he'd have had to hang from the ceiling to tug it *off* that way.

"I see why you couldn't send it over to ARM Headquarters. You can't even touch it. You stick your arm or your head in there for a second, and that's ten minutes without a blood supply."

Ordaz said, "Exactly."

"It looks like you could reach in there with a stick and flip that switch off."

"Perhaps. We are about to try that." He waved at the man with the fishing pole. "There was nothing in this room long enough to reach the switch. We had to send— "

"Wait a minute. There's a problem."

He looked at me. So did the cop with the fishing pole.

"That switch could be a self-destruct. Sinclair was supposed to be a secretive bastard. Or the—field might hold considerable potential energy. Something might go blooey."

Ordaz sighed. "We must risk it. Gil, we have measured the rotation of the dead man's wristwatch. One hour per seven seconds. Fingerprints, footprints, laundry marks, residual body odor, stray eyelashes, all disappearing at an hour per seven seconds." He gestured, and the cop moved in and began trying to hook the switch.

"Already we may never know just when he was killed," said Ordaz.

The tip of the pole wobbled in large circles, steadied beneath the switch, made contact. I held my breath. The pole bowed. The switch snapped up, and suddenly the violet glow was gone. Valpredo reached into the field, warily, as if the air might be red hot. Nothing happened, and he relaxed.

Then Ordaz began giving orders, and quite a lot happened. Two men in lab coats drew a chalk outline around the mummy and the poker. They moved the mummy onto a stretcher, put the poker in a plastic bag and put it next to the mummy.

I said, "Have you identified that?"

"I'm afraid so," said Ordaz. "Raymond Sinclair had his own autodoc— "

"*Did* he. Those things are expensive."

"Yes. Raymond Sinclair was a wealthy man. He owned the top two floors of this building, and the roof. According to records in his 'doc, he had a new set of bud teeth implanted two months ago." Ordaz pointed to the mummy, to the skinned-back dry lips and the buds of new teeth that were just coming in.

Right. That was Sinclair.

That brain had made miracles, and someone had smashed it with a wrought-iron rod. The interstellar drive . . . that glowing goldberg device? Or had it been still inside his head?

I said, "We'll have to get whoever did it. We'll *have* to. Even so . . ." Even so. No more miracles.

"We may have her already," Julio said.

I looked at him.

"There is a girl in the autodoc. We think she is Dr. Sinclair's great-niece, Janice Sinclair."

It was a standard drugstore autodoc, a thing like a giant coffin with walls a foot thick and a headboard covered with dials and red and green lights. The girl lay face up, her face calm, her breathing shallow. Sleeping Beauty. Her arms were in the guts of the 'doc, hidden by bulky rubbery sleeves.

She was lovely enough to stop my breath. Soft brown hair showing around the electrode cap; small, perfect nose and mouth; smooth pale blue skin shot with silver threads . . .

That last was an evening dye job. Without it the impact of her would have been much lessened. The blue shade varied slightly to emphasize the shape of her body and the curve of her cheekbones. The silver lines varied too, being denser in certain areas, guiding the eye in certain directions: to the tips of her breasts, or across the slight swell of abdominal muscle to a lovely oval navel.

She'd paid high for that dye job. But she would be beautiful without it.

Some of the headboard lights were red. I punched for a readout, and was jolted. The 'doc had been forced to amputate her right arm. Gangrene.

She was in for a hell of a shock when she woke up.

"All right," I said. "She's lost her arm. That doesn't make her a killer."

Ordaz asked, "If she were homely, would it help?"

I laughed. "You question my dispassionate judgment? Men have died for less!" Even so, I thought he could be right. There was good reason to think that the killer was now missing an arm.

"What do you think happened here, Gil?"

"Well . . . any way you look at it, the killer had to want to take Sinclair's, ah, time machine with him. It's priceless, for one thing. For another, it looks like he tried to set it up as an alibi. Which means that he knew about it before he came here." I'd been thinking this through. "Say he made sure some people knew where he was a few hours before he got here. He killed Sinclair within range of the . . . call it a generator. Turned it on. He figured Sinclair's own watch would tell him how much time he was gaining. Afterward he could set the watch back and leave with the generator. There'd be no way the police could tell he wasn't killed six hours earlier, or any number you like."

"Yes. But he did not do that."

"There was that line hanging from the switch. He must have turned it on from outside the field . . . probably because he didn't want to sit with the body for six hours. If he tried to step outside the field after he'd turned it on, he'd bump his nose. It'd be like trying to walk through a wall going from field time to normal time. So he turned it off, stepped out of range and used that nylon line to turn it on again. He probably made the same mistake Valpredo did: he thought he could step back in and turn it off."

Ordaz nodded in satisfaction. "Exactly. It was very important for him—or her—to do that. Otherwise he would have no alibi and no profit. If he continued to try to reach into the field— "

"Yah, he could lose the arm to gangrene. That'd be convenient for us, wouldn't it? He'd be easy to find. But, look, Julio: the girl could have done the same thing to herself trying to *help* Sinclair. He might not have been that obviously dead when she got home."

"He might even have been alive," Ordaz pointed out.

I shrugged.

"In point of fact, she came home at one ten, in her own car, which is still in the carport. There are cameras mounted to cover the landing pad and carport. Doctor Sinclair's security was thorough. This girl was the only arrival last night. There were no departures."

"From the roof, you mean."

"Gil, there are only two ways to leave these apartments. One is from the roof, and the other is by elevator, from the lobby. The elevator is on this floor, and it was turned off. It was that way when we arrived. There is no way to override that control from elsewhere in this building."

"So someone could have taken it up here and turned it off afterward . . . or Sinclair could have turned it off before he was killed . . . I see what you mean. Either way, the killer has to be still here." I thought about that. I didn't like its taste. "No, it doesn't fit. How could she be bright enough to work out that alibi, then dumb enough to lock herself in with the body?"

Ordaz shrugged. "She locked the elevator before killing her uncle. She did not want to be interrupted. Surely that was sensible? After she hurt her arm she must have been in a great hurry to reach the 'doc."

One of the red lights turned green. I was glad for that. She didn't look like a killer. I said, half to myself, "Nobody looks like a killer when he's asleep."

"No. But she is where a killer ought to be. *Qué lástima.*"

We went back to the living room. I called ARM Headquarters and had them send a truck.

The machine hadn't been touched. While we waited I borrowed a camera from Valpredo and took pictures of the setup *in situ*. Relative positions of the components might be important.

The lab men were in the brown grass using aerosol sprays to turn fingerprints white and give a vivid yellow glow to faint traces of blood. They got plenty of fingerprints on the machine, none at all on the poker. There was a puddle of yellow in the grass where the mummy's head had been, and a long yellow snail track ending at the business end of the poker. It looked like someone had tried to drag the poker out of the field after it had fallen.

Sinclair's apartments were roomy and comfortable and occupied the entire top floor. The lower floor was the laboratory where Sinclair had produced his miracles. I went through it with Valpredo. It wasn't that impressive. It looked like an expensive hobby setup. These tools would assemble components already fabricated, but they would not build anything complex.

—Except for the computer terminal. That was like a little womb with a recline chair inside a three-hundred-and-sixty-degree wrap around holovision screen and enough banked controls to fly the damn thing to Alpha Centauris.

The secrets there must be in that computer! But I didn't try to use it. We'd have to send an ARM programmer to break whatever failsafe codes Sinclair had put in the memory banks.

The truck arrived. We dragged Sinclair's legacy up the stairs to the roof in one piece. The parts were sturdily mounted on their frame, and the stairs were wide and not too steep.

I rode home in the back of the truck. Studying the generator. That massive piece of silver had something of the look of *Bird In Flight*: a triangle operated on by a topology student, with wires at what were still the corners. I wondered if it was the heart of the machine, or just a piece of misdirection. Was I really riding with an interstellar drive? Sinclair could have started that rumor himself, to cover whatever this was. Or . . . there was a law against his working two projects simultaneously?

I was looking forward to Bera's reaction.

Jackson Bera came upon us moving it through the halls of ARM Headquarters. He trailed along behind us. Nonchalant. We pulled the machine into the main laboratory and started checking it against the holos I'd taken, in case something had been jarred loose. Bera leaned against the door jamb, watching us, his eyes gradually losing interest until he seemed about to go to sleep.

I'd met him three years ago, when I returned from the asteroids and joined the ARM. He'd been twenty then, and two years an ARM; but his father and grandfather had both been ARMs. Much of my training had come from Bera. And as I learned to hunt men who hunt other men, I had watched what it was doing to him.

An ARM needs empathy. He needs the ability to piece together a picture of the mind of his prey. But Bera had too much empathy. I remember his reaction when Kenneth Graham killed himself: a single surge of current through the plug in his skull and down the wire to the pleasure center of his brain. Bera had been twitchy for weeks. And the Anubis case early last year. When we realized what the man had done, Bera had been close to killing him on the spot. I wouldn't have blamed him.

Last year Bera had had enough. He'd gone into the technical end of the business. His days of hunting organleggers were finished. He was now running the ARM laboratory.

He *had* to want to know what this oddball contraption was. I kept waiting for him to ask . . . and he watched, faintly smiling. Finally it dawned on me. He thought it was a practical joke, something I'd cobbled together for his own discomfiture.

I said, "Bera— "

And he looked at me brightly and said, "Hey, man, what is it?"

"You ask the most embarrassing questions."

"Right, I can understand your feeling that way, but what *is* it? I love it, it's neat, but what is this that you have brought me?"

I told him all I knew, such as it was. When I finished he said, "It doesn't sound much like a new space drive."

"Oho, you heard that too, did you? No, it doesn't. Unless— " I'd been wondering since I first saw it. "Maybe it's supposed to accelerate a fusion explosion. You'd, get greater efficiency in a fusion drive."

"Nope. They get better than ninety percent now, and that widget looks *heavy*." He reached to touch the bent silver triangle, gently, with long, tapering fingers. "Huh. Well, we'll dig out the answers."

"Good luck. I'm going back to Sinclair's place."

"Why? The action is here." Often enough he'd heard me talking wistfully of joining an interstellar colony. He must know how I'd feel about a better drive for the interstellar slowboats.

"It's like this," I said. "We've got the generator, but we don't know anything about it. We might wreck it. I'm going to have a whack at finding someone who knows something about Sinclair's generator."

"Meaning?"

"Whoever tried to steal it. Sinclair's killer."

"If you say so." But he looked dubious. He knew me too well. He said, "I understand there's a mother hunt in the offing."

"Oh?"

He smiled. "Just a rumor. You guys are lucky. When my dad first joined, the business of the ARM was *mostly* mother hunts. The organleggers hadn't really got organized yet, and the Fertility Laws were new. If we hadn't enforced them nobody would have obeyed them at all."

"Sure, and people threw rocks at your father. Bera, those days are *gone*."

"They could come back. Having children is basic."

"Bera, I did not join the ARM to hunt unlicensed parents." I waved and left before he could answer. I could do without the call to duty from Bera, who had done with hunting men and mothers.

I'd had a good view of the Rodewald Building, dropping toward the roof this morning. I had a good view now from my comman-deered taxi. This time I was looking for escape paths.

There were no balconies on Sinclair's floors, and the windows were flush to the side of the building. A cat burglar would have trouble with them. They didn't look like they'd open.

I tried to spot the cameras Ordaz had mentioned as the taxi dropped toward the roof. I couldn't find them. Maybe they were mounted in the elms.

Why was I bothering? I hadn't joined the ARM to chase mothers or machinery or common murders. I'd joined to pay for my arm. My new arm had reached the World Organ Bank Facility via a captured organlegger's cache. Some honest citizen had died unwillingly on a city slidewalk, and now his arm was part of me.

I'd joined the ARM to hunt organleggers.

The ARM doesn't deal in murder *per se*. The machine was out of my hands now. A murder investigation wouldn't keep me out of a mother hunt. And I'd never met the girl. I knew nothing of her, beyond the fact that she was where a killer ought to be.

Was it just that she was pretty?

Poor Janice. When she woke up . . . For a solid month I'd wakened to that same stunning shock, the knowledge that my right arm was gone.

The taxi settled. Valpredo was waiting below.

I speculated . . . Cars weren't the only things that flew. But anyone flying one of those tricky ducted-fan flycycles over a city, where he could fall on a pedestrian, wouldn't have to worry about a murder charge. They'd feed him to the organ banks regardless. And anything that flew would have to have left traces anywhere but on the landing pad itself. It would crush a rose bush or a Bonsai tree or be flipped over by an elm.

The taxi took off in a whisper of air.

Valpredo was grinning at me. "The Thinker. What's on your mind?"

"I was wondering if the killer could have come down on the carport roof."

He turned to study the situation. "There are two cameras mounted on the edge of the roof. If his vehicle was light enough, sure, he could land there, and the cameras wouldn't spot him. Roof wouldn't hold a car, though. Anyway, nobody did it."

"How do you know?"

"I'll show you. By the way, we inspected the camera system. We're pretty sure the cameras weren't tampered with."

"And nobody came down from the roof last night except the girl?"

"Nobody. Nobody even landed here until seven this morning. Look here." We had reached the concrete stairs that led down into Sinclair's apartments. Valpredo pointed at a glint of light in the sloping ceiling, at heart level. "This is the only way down. The camera would get anyone coming in or out. It might not catch his face, but it'd show if someone had passed. It takes sixty frames a minute."

I went on down. A cop let me in.

Ordaz was on the phone. The screen showed a young man with a deep tan and shock showing through the tan. Ordaz waved at me, a shushing motion, and went on talking. "Then you'll be here in fifteen minutes? That will be a great help to us. Please land on the roof. We are still working on the elevator."

He hung up and turned to me. "That was Andrew Porter, Janice Sinclair's lover. He tells us that he and Janice spent the evening at a party. She dropped him off at his home around one o'clock."

"Then she came straight home, if that's her in the 'doc."

"I think it must be. Mr. Porter says she was wearing a blue skin-dye job." Ordaz was frowning. "He put on a most convincing act, if it was that. I think he really was not expecting any kind of trouble. He was surprised that a stranger answered, shocked when he learned of Dr. Sinclair's death, and horrified when he learned that Janice had been hurt."

With the mummy and the generator removed, the murder scene had become an empty circle of brown grass marked with random streaks of yellow chemical and outlines of white chalk.

"We had some luck," said Ordaz. "Today's date is June 4, 2124. Dr. Sinclair was wearing a calendar watch. It registered January 17, 2125. If we switched the machine off at ten minutes to ten—which we did—and if it was registering an hour for every seven seconds that passed outside the field, then the field must have gone on around one o'clock last night, give or take a margin of error."

"Then if the girl didn't do it, she must have just missed the killer."

"Exactly."

"What about the elevator? Could it have been jiggered?"

"No. We took the workings apart. It was on this floor, and locked by hand. Nobody could have left by elevator . . ."

"Why did you trail off like that?"

Ordaz shrugged, embarrassed. "This peculiar machine really does bother me, Gil. I found myself thinking, suppose it can reverse time? Then the killer could have gone down in an elevator that was going up."

He laughed with me. I said, "In the first place, I don't believe a word of it. In the second place, he didn't have the machine to do it with. Unless . . . he made his escape before the murder. Dammit, now you've got me doing it."

"I would like to know more about the machine."

"Bera's investigating it now. I'll let you know as soon as we learn anything. And *I'd* like to know more about how the killer couldn't possibly have left."

He looked at me. "Details?"

"Could someone have opened a window?"

"No. These apartments are forty years old. The smog was still bad when they were built. Dr. Sinclair apparently preferred to depend on his air conditioning."

"How about the apartment below? I presume it has a different set of elevators— "

"Yes, of course. It belongs to Howard Rodewald, the owner of this building—of this chain of buildings, in fact. At the moment he is in Europe. His apartment has been loaned to friends."

"There are no stairs down to there?"

"No. We searched these apartments thoroughly."

"All right. We know the killer had a nylon line, because he left a strand of it on the generator. Could he have climbed down to Rodewald's balcony from the roof?"

"Thirty feet? Yes, I suppose so." Ordaz' eyes sparked. "We must look into that. There is still the matter of how he got past the camera, and whether he could have gotten inside once he was on the balcony."

"Yah."

"Try this, Gil. Another question. How did he *expect* to get away?" He watched for my reaction, which must have been satisfying, because it *was* a damn good question. "You see, if Janice Sinclair murdered her great-uncle, then neither question applies. If we are looking for someone else, we have to assume that his plans misfired. He had to improvise."

"Uh huh. He could still have been planning to use Rodewald's balcony. And that would mean he had a way past the camera . . ."

"Of course he did. The generator."

Right. If he came to steal the generator . . . and he'd have to steal it regardless, because if we found it here it would shoot his alibi sky high. So he'd leave it on while he trundled it up the stairs.

Say it took him a minute; that's only an eighth of a second of normal time. One chance in eight that the camera would fire, and it would catch nothing but a streak . . . "Uh oh."

"What is it?"

"He had to be planning to steal the machine. Is he really going to lower it to Rodewald's balcony by *rope*?"

"I think it unlikely," said Ordaz. "It weighed more than fifty pounds. He could have moved it upstairs. The frame would make it portable. But to lower it by rope . . ."

"We'd be looking for one hell of an athlete."

"At least you will not have to search far to find him. We assume that your hypothetical killer came by elevator, do we not?"

"Yah." Nobody but Janice Sinclair had arrived by the roof last night.

"The elevator was programed to allow a number of people to enter it, and to turn away all others. The list is short. Dr. Sinclair was not a gregarious man."

"You're checking them out? Whereabouts, alibis and so forth?"

"Of course."

"There's something else you might check on," I said. But Andrew Porter came in and I had to postpone it.

Porter came casual, in a well worn translucent one-piece jump suit he must have pulled on while running for a taxi. The muscles rolled like boulders beneath the loose fabric, and his belly muscles showed like the plates on an armadillo. Surfing muscles. The sun had bleached his hair nearly white and burned him as brown as Jackson Bera. You'd think a tan that dark would cover for blood draining out of a face, but it doesn't.

"Where is she?" he demanded. He didn't wait for an answer. He knew where the 'doc was, and he went there. We trailed in his wake.

Ordaz didn't push. He waited while Porter looked down at Janice, then punched for a readout and went through it in detail. Peter seemed calmer then, and his color was back. He turned to Ordaz and said, "What happened?"

"Mr. Porter, did you know anything of Dr. Sinclair's latest project?"

"The time compressor thing? Yah. He had it set up in the living room when I got here yesterday evening—right in the middle of that circle of dead grass. Any connection?"

"When did you arrive?"

"Oh, about . . . six. We had some drinks, and Uncle Ray showed off his machine. He didn't tell us much about it. Just showed what it could do." Porter showed us flashing white teeth. "It *worked*. That thing can compress time! You could live your whole life in there in two months! Watching him move around inside the field was like trying to keep track of a hummingbird. Worse. He struck a match— "

"When did you leave?"

"About eight. We had dinner at Cziller's House of Irish Coffee and—Listen, what *happened* here?"

"There are some things we need to know first, Mr. Porter. Were you and Janice together for all of last evening? Were there others with you?"

"Sure. We had dinner alone, but afterward we went to a kind of party. On the beach at Santa Monica. Friend of mine has a house there. I'll give you the address. Some of us wound up back at Cziller's around midnight. Then Janice flew me home."

"You have said that you are Janice's lover. Doesn't she live with you?"

"No. I'm her steady lover, you might say, but I don't have any strings on her." He seemed embarrassed. "She lives here with Uncle Ray. Lived. Oh, *hell*." He glanced into the 'doc. "Look, the readout said she'll be waking up any minute. Can I get her a robe?"

"Of course."

We followed Porter to Janice's bedroom, where he picked out a peach-colored negligée for her. I was beginning to like the guy. He had good instincts. An evening dye job was not the thing to wear on the morning of a murder. And he'd picked one with long, loose sleeves. Her missing arm wouldn't show so much.

"You call him Uncle Ray," said Ordaz.

"Yah. Because Janice did."

"He did not object? Was he gregarious?"

"Gregarious? Well, no, but *we* liked each other. We both liked puzzles, you understand? We traded murder mysteries and jig-saw puzzles. Listen, this may sound silly, but are you sure he's dead?"

"Regrettably, yes. He is dead, and murdered. Was he expecting someone to arrive after you left?"

"Yes."

"He said so?"

"No. But he was wearing a shirt and pants. When it was just us he usually went naked."

"Ah."

"Older people don't do that much," Porter said. "But Uncle Ray was in good shape. He took care of himself."

"Have you any idea whom he might have been expecting?"

"No. Not a woman; not a date, I mean. Maybe someone in the same business."

Behind him, Janice moaned.

Porter was hovering over her in a flash. He put a hand on her shoulder and urged her back. "Lie still, love. We'll have you out of there in a jiffy."

She waited while he disconnected the sleeves and other paraphernalia. She said, "What happened?"

"They haven't told me yet," Porter said with a flash of anger. "Be careful sitting up. You've had an accident."

"What kind of—? *Oh!*"

"It'll be all right."

"My *arm!*"

Porter helped her out of the 'doc. Her arm ended in pink flesh two inches below the shoulder. She let Porter drape the robe around her. She tried to fasten the sash, quit when she realized she was trying to do it with one hand.

I said, "Listen, I lost my arm once."

She looked at me. So did Porter.

"I'm Gil Hamilton. With the UN Police. You really don't have anything to worry about. See?" I raised my right arm, opened and closed the fingers. "The organ banks don't get much call for arms. as compared to kidneys, for instance. You probably won't even have to wait. I didn't. It feels just like the arm I was born with, and it works just as well."

"How did you lose it?" she asked.

"Ripped away by a meteor," I said, not without pride. "While I was asteroid mining in the Belt." I didn't have to tell her that we'd caused the meteor cluster ourselves, by setting the bomb wrong on an asteroid we wanted to move.

Ordaz said to her, "Do you remember how you lost your own arm?"

"Yes." She shivered. "Could we go somewhere where I could sit down? I feel a bit weak."

We moved to the living room. Janice dropped onto the couch a bit too hard. It might have been shock, or the missing arm might be throwing her balance off. I remembered. She said, "Uncle Ray's dead, isn't he?"

"Yes."

"I came home and found him that way. Lying next to that time machine of his, and the back of his head all bloody. I thought maybe he was still alive, but I could see the machine was going; it had that violet glow. I tried to get hold of the poker. I wanted to use it to switch the machine off, but I couldn't get a grip. My arm wasn't just numb, it wouldn't move. You know, you can try to wiggle your toes when your foot's asleep, but . . . I could get my hands on the handle of the damn poker, but when I tried to pull it just slid off."

"You kept trying?"

"For awhile. Then . . . I backed away to think it over. I wasn't about to waste any time, with Uncle Ray maybe dying in there. My arm felt stone dead . . . I guess it was, wasn't it?" She shuddered. "Rotting meat. It smelled that way. And all of a sudden I felt so weak and dizzy, like I was dying myself. I barely made it into the 'doc."

"Good thing you did," I said. The blood was leaving Porter's face again as he realized what a close thing it had been.

Ordaz said, "Was your great-uncle expecting visitors last night?"

"I think so."

"Why do you think so?"

"I don't know. He just—acted that way."

"We are told that you and some friends reached Cziller's House of Irish Coffee around midnight. Is that true?"

"I guess so. We had some drinks, then I took Drew home and came home myself."

"Straight home?"

"Yes." She shivered. "I put the car away and went downstairs. I knew something was wrong. The door was open. Then there was Uncle Ray lying next to that machine! I knew better than to just run up to him. He'd told us not to step into the field."

"Oh? Then you should have known better than to reach for the poker."

"Well, yes. I could have used the tongs," she said as if the idea had just occurred to her. "It's just as long. I didn't think of it. There wasn't *time*. Don't you understand, he was dying in there, or dead!"

"Yes, of course. Did you interfere with the murder scene in any way?"

She laughed bitterly. "I suppose I moved the poker about two inches. Then when I felt what was happening to me I just ran for the 'doc. It was awful. Like dying."

"Instant gangrene," said Porter.

Ordaz said, "You did not, for example, lock the elevator?"

Damn! I should have thought of that.

"No. We usually do, when we lock up for the night, but I didn't have time."

Porter said, "Why?"

"The elevator was locked when we arrived," Ordaz told him.

Porter ruminated that. "Then the killer must have left by the roof. You'll have pictures of him."

Ordaz smiled apologetically. "That is our problem. No cars left the roof last night. Only one car arrived. That was yours, Miss Sinclair."

"But," said Porter, and he stopped. He thought it through again. "Did the police turn on the elevator again after they got here?"

"No. The killer could not have left after we got here."

"Oh."

"What happened was this," said Ordaz. "Around five thirty this morning, the tenants in— " He stopped to remember. "In 36A called the building maintenance man about a smell as of rotting meat coming through the air conditioning system. He spent some time looking for the source, but once he reached the roof it was obvious. He— "

Porter pounced. "He reached the roof in what kind of vehicle?"

"Mr. Steeves says that he took a taxi from the street. There is no other way to reach Dr. Sinclair's private landing pad, is there?"

"No. But why would he do that?"

"Perhaps there have been other times when strange smells came from Dr. Sinclair's laboratory. We will ask him."

"Do that."

"Mr. Steeves followed the smell through the doctor's open door. He called us. He waited for us on the roof."

"What about his taxi?" Porter was hot on the scent. "Maybe the killer just waited till that taxi got here, then took it somewhere else when Steeves finished with it."

"It left immediately after Steeves had stepped out. He had a tax clicker if he wanted another. The cameras were on it the entire time it was on the roof." Ordaz paused. "You see the problem?"

Apparently Porter did. He ran both hands through his white

blond hair. "I think we ought to put off discussing it until we know more."

He meant Janice. Janice looked puzzled; she hadn't caught on. But Ordaz nodded at once and stood up. "Very well. There is no reason Miss Sinclair cannot go on living here. We may have to bother you again," he told her. "For now, our condolences."

He made his exit. I trailed along. So, unexpectedly, did Drew Porter. At the top of the stairs he stopped Ordaz with a big hand around the Inspector's upper arm. "You're thinking Janice did it. aren't you?"

Ordaz sighed. "What choice have I? I must consider the possibility."

"She didn't have any reason. She loved Uncle Ray. She's lived with him on and off these past twelve years. She hasn't got the slightest reason to kill him."

"Is there no inheritance?"

His expression went sour. "All right, *yes*, she'll have some money coming. But Janice wouldn't care about anything like that!"

"Ye-es. Still, what choice have I? Everything we now know tells us that the killer could not have left the scene of the killing. We searched the premises immediately. There was only Janice Sinclair and her murdered uncle."

Porter bit back an answer, chewed it . . . He must have been tempted. Amateur detective, one step ahead of the police all the way. Yes, Watson, these *gendarmes* have a talent for missing the obvious . . . But he had too much to lose. Porter said, "And the maintenance man. Steeves."

Ordaz lifted one eyebrow. "Yes, of course. We shall have to investigate Mr. Steeves."

"How did he get that call from, uh, 36A? Bedside phone or pocket phone? Maybe he was already on the roof."

"I don't remember that he said. But we have pictures of his taxi landing."

"He had a taxi clicker. He could have just called it down."

"One more thing," I said, and Porter looked at me hopefully. "Porter, what about the elevator? It had a brain in it, didn't it? It wouldn't take anyone up unless they were on its list."

"Or unless Uncle Ray buzzed down. There's an intercom in the lobby. But at that time of night he probably wouldn't let anyone up unless he was expecting him."

"So if Sinclair was expecting a business associate, he or she was probably in the tape. How about going down? Would the elevator take you down to the lobby if you weren't in the tape?"

"I'd . . . think so."

"It would," said Ordaz. "The elevator screens entrances, not departures."

"Then why didn't the killer use it? I don't mean Steeves, necessarily. I mean *anyone*, whoever it might have been. Why didn't he just go down in the elevator? Whatever he did do, that had to be easier."

They looked at each other, but they didn't say anything.

"Okay." I turned to Ordaz. "When you check out the people in the tape, see if any of them shows a damaged arm. The killer might have pulled the same stunt Janice did: ruined her arm trying to turn off the generator. And I'd like a look at who's in that tape."

"Very well," said Ordaz, and we moved toward the squad car under the carport. We were out of earshot when he added, "How does the ARM come into this, Mr. Hamilton? Why your interest in the murder aspect of this case?"

I told him what I'd told Bera: that Sinclair's killer might be the only living expert on Sinclair's time machine. Ordaz nodded. What he'd really wanted to know was: could I justify giving orders to the Los Angeles Police Department in a local matter? And I had answered: yes.

The rather simple-minded security system in Sinclair's elevator had been built to remember the thumbprints and the facial bone structures (which it scanned by deep-radar, thus avoiding the problems raised by changing beard styles and masquerade parties) of up to one hundred people. Most people know about a hundred people, plus or minus ten or so. But Sinclair had only listed a dozen, including himself.

RAYMOND SINCLAIR
ANDREW PORTER
JANICE SINCLAIR
EDWARD SINCLAIR SR.
EDWARD SINCLAIR III
HANS DRUCKER
GEORGE STEEVES
PAULINE URTHIEL
BERNATH PETERFI
LAWRENCE MUHAMMAD ECKS

BERTHA HALL
MURIEL SANDUSKY

Valpredo had been busy. He'd been using the police car and its phone setup as an office while he guarded the roof. "We know who some of these are," he said. "Edward Sinclair Third, for instance, is Edward Senior's grandson, Janice's brother. He's in the Belt, in Ceres, making something of a name for himself as an industrial designer. Edward Senior is Raymond's brother. He lives in Kansas City. Hans Drucker and Bertha Hall and Muriel Sandusky all live in the Greater Los Angeles area; we don't know what their connection with Sinclair is. Pauline Urthiel and Bernath Peterfi are technicians of sorts. Ecks is Sinclair's patent attorney."

"I suppose we can interview Edward Third by phone." Ordaz made a face. A phone call to the Belt wasn't cheap. "These others— "

I said, "May I make a suggestion?"

"Of course."

"Send me along with whoever interviews Ecks and Peterfi and Urthiel. They probably knew Sinclair in a business sense, and having an ARM along will give you a little more clout to ask a little more detailed questions."

"I could take those assignments," Valpredo volunteered.

"Very well." Ordaz still looked unhappy. "If this list were exhaustive I would be grateful. Unfortunately we must consider the risk that Dr. Sinclair's visitor simply used the intercom in the lobby and asked to be let in."

Bernath Peterfi wasn't answering his phone.

We got Pauline Urthiel via her pocket phone. A brusque contralto voice, no picture. We'd like to talk to her in connection with a murder investigation; would she be at home this afternoon? No. She was lecturing that afternoon, but would be home around six.

Ecks answered dripping wet and not smiling. So sorry to get you out of a shower, Mr. Ecks. We'd like to talk to you in connection with a murder investigation—

"Sure, come on over. Who's dead?"

Valpredo told him.

"Sinclair? *Ray* Sinclair? You're sure?"

We were.

"Oh, lord. Listen, he was working on something important. An interstellar drive, if it works out. If there's any possibility of salvaging the hardware— "

I reassured him and hung up. If Sinclair's patent attorney thought it was a star drive . . . maybe it was.

"Doesn't sound like he's trying to steal it," said Valpredo.

"No. And even if he'd got the thing, he couldn't have claimed it was his. If he's the killer, that's not what he was after."

We were moving at high speed, police-car speed. The car was on automatic, of course, but it could need manual override at any instant. Valpredo concentrated on the passing scenery and spoke without looking at me.

"You know, you and the Detective-Inspector aren't looking for the same thing."

"I know. I'm looking for a hypothetical killer. Julio's looking for a hypothetical visit. It could be tough to prove there wasn't one, but if Porter and the girl were telling the truth, maybe Julio can prove the visitor didn't do it."

"Which would leave the girl," he said.

"Whose side are you on?"

"Nobody's. All I've got is interesting questions." He looked at him sideways. "But you're pretty sure the girl didn't do it."

"Yah."

"Why?"

"I don't know. Maybe because I don't think she's got the brain. It wasn't a simple killing."

"She's Sinclair's niece. She can't be a complete idiot."

"Heredity doesn't work that way. Maybe I'm kidding myself. Maybe it's her arm. She's lost an arm; she's got enough to worry about." And I borrowed the car phone to dig into records in the ARM computer.

PAULINE URTHIEL. Born Paul Urthiel. Ph.D. in plasma physic University of California at Ervine. Sex change and legal name change, 2111. Six years ago she'd been in competition for a Nobel prize, for research into the charge suppression effect in the Slave disintegrator. Height: 5' 9". Weight: 135. Married Lawrence Muhammad Ecks, 2117. Had kept her (loosely speaking) maiden name. Separate residences.

BERNATH PETERFI. Ph.D. in subatomics and related fields, MIT Diabetic. Height: 5' 8". Weight: 145. Application for exemption to the Fertility Laws denied, 2119. Married 2118, divorced 2122. Lived alone.

LAWRENCE MUHAMMAD ECKS. Masters degree in physics. Member, of the bar. Height: 6' 1". Weight: 190. Artificial left arm. Vice President, CET (Committee to End Transplants).

Valpredo said: "Funny how the human arm keeps cropping up in this case."

"Yah." Including one human ARM who didn't really belong there. "Ecks has a masters. Maybe he could have talked people into thinking the generator was his. Or maybe he thought he could."

"He didn't try to snow *us*."

"Suppose he blew it last night? He wouldn't necessarily want the generator lost to humanity, now would he?"

"How did he get out?"

I didn't answer.

Ecks lived in a tapering tower almost a mile high. At one time Lindstetter's Needle must have been the biggest thing ever built, before they started with the arcologies. We landed on a pad a third of the way up, then took a drop shaft ten floors down.

He was dressed when he answered the door, in blazing yellow pants and a net shirt. His skin was very dark, and his hair was a puffy black dandelion with threads of grey in it. On the phone screen I hadn't been able to tell which arm was which, and I couldn't now. He invited us in, sat down and waited for the questions.

Where was he last night? Could he produce an alibi? It would help us considerably.

"Sorry, nope. I spent the night going through a rather tricky case. You wouldn't appreciate the details."

I told him I would. He said, "Actually, it involves Edward Sinclair—Ray's great-nephew. He's a Belt immigrant, and he's done an industrial design that could be adapted to Earth. Swivel for a chemical rocket motor. The trouble is it's not *that* different from existing designs, it's just *better*. His Belt patent is good, but the UN laws are different. You wouldn't believe the legal tangles."

"Is he likely to lose out?"

"No, it just might get sticky if a firm called FireStorm decides to fight the case. I want to be ready for that. In a pinch I might even have to call the kid back to Earth. I'd hate to do that, though. He's got a heart condition."

Had he made any phone calls, say to a computer, during his night of research?

Ecks brightened instantly. "Oh, sure. Constantly, all night. Okay, I've got an alibi."

No point in telling him that such calls could have been made from anywhere. Valpredo asked, "Do you have any idea where your wife was last night?"

"No, we don't live together. She lives three hundred stories over my head. We've got an open marriage . . . maybe too open," he added wistfully.

There seemed a good chance that Raymond Sinclair was expecting a visitor last night. Did Ecks have any idea—?

"He knew a couple of women," said Ecks. "You might ask them. Bertha Hall is about eighty, about Ray's age. She's not too bright, not by Ray's standards, but she's as much of a physical fitness nut as he is. They go backpacking, play tennis, maybe sleep together, maybe not. I can give you her address. Then there's Muriel something. He had a crush on her a few years ago. She'd be thirty now I don't know if they still see each other or not."

Did Sinclair know other women?

Ecks shrugged.

Who did he know professionally?

"Oh, lord, that's an endless list. Do you know anything about the way Ray worked?" He didn't wait for an answer. "He used computer setups mostly. Any experiment in his field was likely to cost millions, or more. What he was good at was setting up a computer analogue of an experiment that would tell him what he wanted to know. Take, oh . . . I'm sure you've heard of the Sinclair molecule chain."

Hell, yes. We'd used it for towing in the Belt; nothing else was light enough and strong enough. A loop of it was nearly invisibly fine, but it would cut steel.

"He didn't start working with chemicals until he was practically finished. He told me he spent four years doing molecular designs by computer analogue. The tough part was the ends of the molecule chain. Until he got that the chain would start disintegrating from the endpoints the minute you finished making it. When he finally had what he wanted, he hired an industrial chemical lab to make it for him.

"That's what I'm getting at," Ecks continued. "He hired other people to do the concrete stuff, once he knew what he had. And the people he hired had to know what they were doing. He knew the top physicists and chemists and field theorists everywhere on Earth and in the Belt."

Like Pauline? Like Bernath Peterfi?

"Yah, Pauline did some work for him once. I don't think she'd do it again. She didn't like having to give him all the credit. She'd rather work for herself. I don't blame her."

Could he think of anyone who might want to murder Raymond Sinclair?

Ecks shrugged. "I'd say that was your job. Ray never liked splitting the credit with anyone. Maybe someone he worked with nursed a grudge. Or maybe someone was trying to steal this latest project of his. Mind you, I don't know much about what he was trying to do, but if it worked it would have been fantastically valuable, and not just in money."

Valpredo was making noises like he was about finished. I said, "Do you mind if I ask a personal question?"

"Go ahead."

"Your arm. How'd you lose it?"

"Born without it. Nothing in my genes, just a bad prenatal situation. I came out with an arm and a turkey wishbone. By the time I was old enough for a transplant, I knew I didn't want one. You want the standard speech?"

"No, thanks, but I'm wondering how good your artificial arm is. I'm carrying a transplant myself."

Ecks looked me over carefully for signs of moral degeneration. "I suppose you're also one of those people who keep voting the death penalty for more and more trivial offenses?"

"No, I— "

"After all, if the organ banks ran out of criminals you'd be in trouble. You might have to live with your mistakes."

"No, I'm one of those people who blocked the second corpsicle law, kept that group from going into the organ banks. And I hunt organleggers for a living. But I don't have an artificial arm, and I suppose the reason is that I'm squeamish."

"Squeamish about being part mechanical? I've heard of that," Ecks said. "But you can be squeamish the other way, too. What there is of me is all me, not part of a dead man. I'll admit the sense of touch isn't quite the same, but it's just as good. And—look."

He put a hand on my upper forearm and squeezed.

It felt like the bones were about to give. I didn't scream, but it took an effort. "That isn't all my strength," he said. "And I could keep it up all day. This arm doesn't get tired."

He let go.

I asked if he would mind my examining his arms. He didn't. But then, Ecks didn't know about my imaginary hand.

I probed the advanced plastics of Ecks' false arm, the bone and muscle structure of the other. It was the real arm I was interested in.

When we were back in the car Valpredo said, "Well?"

"Nothing wrong with his real arm," I said. "No scars."

Valpredo nodded.

But the bubble of accelerated time wouldn't hurt plastic and batteries, I thought. And if he'd been planning to lower fifty pounds of generator two stories down on a nylon line, his artificial arm had the strength for it.

We called Peterfi from the car. He was in. He was a small man dark complected, mild of face, his hair straight and shiny black around a receding hairline. His eyes blinked and squinted as if the light were too bright, and he had the scruffy look of a man who had slept in his clothes. I wondered if we had interrupted an afternoon nap.

Yes, he would be glad to help the police in a murder investigation.

Peterfi's condominium was a slab of glass and concrete set on a Santa Monica cliff face. His apartment faced the sea. "Expensive but worth it for the view," he said, showing us to chairs in the living room. The drapes were closed against the afternoon sun. Peterfi had changed clothes. I noticed the bulge in his upper left sleeve where an insulin capsule and automatic feeder had been anchored to the bone of the arm.

"Well, what can I do for you? I don't believe you mentioned who had been murdered."

Valpredo told him.

He was shocked. "Oh, my. Ray Sinclair. But there's no telling how this will affect— " and he stopped suddenly.

"Please go on," said Valpredo.

"We were working on something together. Something—revolutionary."

An interstellar drive?

He was startled. He debated with himself, then, "Yes. It was supposed to be secret."

We admitted having seen the machine in action. How did a time compression field serve as an interstellar drive?

"That's not exactly what it is," Peterfi said. Again he debated with himself. Then, "There have always been a few optimists around who thought that just because mass and inertia have always been associated in human experience, it need not be a universal law. What Ray and I have done is to create a condition of low inertia. You see— "

"An inertialess drive!"

Peterfi nodded vigorously at me. "Essentially yes. Is the machine intact? If not— "

I reassured him on that point.

"That's good. I was about to say that if it had been destroyed, I could recreate it. I did most of the work of building it. Ray preferred to work with his mind, not with his hands."

Had Peterfi visited Sinclair last night?

"No. I had dinner at a restaurant down the coast, then came home and watched the holo wall. What times do I need alibis for?" he asked jokingly.

Valpredo told him. The joking look turned into a nervous grimace. No, he'd left the Mail Shirt just after nine; he couldn't prove his whereabouts after that time.

Had he any idea who might have wanted to murder Raymond Sinclair?

Peterfi was reluctant to make outright accusations. Surely we understood. It might be someone he had worked with in the past, or someone he'd insulted. Ray thought most of humanity were fools. Or—we might look into the matter of Ray's brother's exemption.

Valpredo said, "Edward Sinclair's exemption? What about it?"

"I'd really prefer that you get the story from someone else. You may know that Edward Sinclair was refused the right to have children because of an inherited heart condition. His grandson has it too. There is some question as to whether he really did the work that earned him the exemption."

"But that must have been forty to fifty years ago. How could it figure in a murder now?"

Peterfi explained patiently. "Edward had a child by virtue of an exemption to the Fertility Laws. Now there are two grandchildren. Suppose the matter came up for review? His grandchildren would lose the right to have children. They'd be illegitimate. They might even lose the right to inherit."

Valpredo was nodding. "Yah. We'll look into that, all right."

I said, "You applied for an exemption yourself not long ago. I suppose your, uh— "

"Yes, my diabetes. It doesn't interfere with my life at all. Do you know how long we've been using insulin to handle diabetes? Almost two hundred years! What does it matter if I'm a diabetic? If my children are?"

He glared at us, demanding an answer. He got none.

"But the Fertility Laws refuse me children. Do you know that I lost my wife because the Board refused me an exemption? I deserved it. My work on plasma flow in the solar photosphere—Well I'd hardly lecture you on the subject, would I? But my work can be used to predict the patterns of proton storms near any G-type star. Every colony world owes something to my work!"

That was an exaggeration, I thought. Proton storms affected mainly asteroidal mining operations . . . "Why don't you move to the Belt?" I asked. "They'd honor you for your work, and they don't have Fertility Laws."

"I get sick off Earth. It's biorhythms; it has nothing to do with diabetes. Half of humanity suffers from biorhythm upset."

I felt sorry for the guy. "You could still get the exemption. For your work on the inertialess drive. Wouldn't that get you your wife back?"

"I . . . don't know. I doubt it. It's been two years. In any case there's no telling which way the Board will jump. I thought I'd have the exemption last time."

"Do you mind if I examine your arms?"

He looked at me. "What?"

"I'd like to examine your arms."

"That seems a most curious request. Why?"

"There seems a good chance that Sinclair's killer damaged his arm last night. Now, I'll remind you that I'm acting in the name of the UN Police. If you've been hurt by the side effects of a possible space drive, one that might be used by human colonists, then you're concealing evidence in a— " I stopped, because Peterfi had stood up and was taking off his tunic.

He wasn't happy, but he stood still for it. His arms looked all right. I ran my hands along each arm, bent the joints, massaged the knuckles. Inside the flesh I ran my imaginary fingertips along the bones.

Three inches below the shoulder joint the bone was knotted. I probed the muscles and tendons . . .

"Your right arm is a transplant," I said. "It must have happened about six months ago."

He bridled. "You may not be aware of it, but surgery to re-attach my own arm would show the same scars."

"Is that what happened?"

Anger made his speech more precise. "Yes. I was performing an experiment, and there was an explosion. The arm was nearly severed. I tied a tourniquet and got to a 'doc before I collapsed."

"Any proof of this?"

"I doubt it. I never told anyone of this accident, and the 'doc wouldn't keep records. In any case, I think the burden of proof would be on you."

"Uh huh."

Peterfi was putting his tunic back on. "Are you quite finished here? I'm deeply sorry for Ray Sinclair's death, but I don't see what it could possibly have to do with my stupidity of six months ago."

I didn't either. We left.

Back in the car. It was seventeen twenty; we could pick up a snack on the way to Pauline Urthiel's place. I told Valpredo, "I think it was a transplant. And he didn't want to admit it. He must have gone to an organlegger."

"Why would he do that? It's not that tough to get an arm from the public organ banks."

I chewed that. "You're right. But if it was a normal transplant, there'll be a record. Well, it could have happened the way he said it did."

"Uh huh."

"How about this? He was doing an experiment, and it was illegal. Something that might cause pollution in a city, or even something to do with radiation. He picked up radiation burns in his arm. If he'd gone to the public organ banks he'd have been arrested."

"That would fit too. Can we prove it on him?"

"I don't know. I'd like to. He might tell us how to find whoever he dealt with. Let's do some digging: maybe we can find out what he was working on six months ago."


Pauline Urthiel opened the door the instant we rang. "Hi! I just got in myself. Can I make you drinks?"

We refused. She ushered us into a smallish apartment with a lot of fold-into-the-ceiling furniture. A sofa and coffee table were showing now; the rest existed as outlines on the ceiling. The view through the picture window was breathtaking. She lived near the top of Lindstetter's Needle, some three hundred stories up from her husband.

She was tall and slender, with a facial structure that would have been effeminate on a man. On a woman it was a touch masculine. The well-formed breasts might be flesh or plastic, but surgically implanted in either case.

She finished making a large drink and joined us on the couch. And the questions started.

Had she any idea who might have wanted Raymond Sinclair dead?

"Not really. How did he die?"

"Someone smashed in his skull with a poker," Valpredo said. If he wasn't going to mention the generator, neither was I.

"How quaint." Her contralto turned acid. "His own poker, too, I presume. Out of his own fireplace rack. What you're looking for is a traditionalist." She peered at us over the rim of her glass. Her eyes were large, the lids decorated in semi-permanent tattoo as a pair of flapping UN flags. "That doesn't help much, does it? You might try whoever was working with him on whatever his latest project was."

That sounded like Peterfi, I thought. But Valpredo said, "Would he necessarily have a collaborator?"

"He generally works alone at the beginning. But somewhere along the line he brings in people to figure out how to make the hardware, and make it. He never made anything real by himself. It was all just something in a computer bank. It took someone else to make it real. And he never gave credit to anyone."

Then his hypothetical collaborator might have found out how little credit he was getting for his work, and—But Urthiel was shaking her head. "I'm talking about a psychotic, not someone who's really been cheated. Sinclair never *offered* anyone a share in anything he did. He always made it damn plain what was happening. I knew what I was doing when I set up the FyreStop prototype for him, and I knew what I was doing when I quit. It was all him. He was using my training, not my brain. I wanted to do something original, something *me*."

Did she have any idea what Sinclair's present project was?

"My husband would know. Larry Ecks, lives in this same building. He's been dropping cryptic hints, and when I want more details he has this grin— " She grinned herself, suddenly. "You'll gather I'm interested. But he won't say."

Time for me to take over, or we'd never get certain questions asked. "I'm an ARM. What I'm about to tell you is secret," I said. And I told her what we knew of Sinclair's generator. Maybe Valpredo was looking at me disapprovingly; maybe not.

"We know that the field can damage a human arm in a few seconds. What we want to know," I said, "is whether the killer is now wandering around with a half-decayed hand or arm—or foot, for that— "

She stood and pulled the upper half of her body stocking down around her waist.

She looked very much a real woman. If I hadn't known—and why would it matter? These days the sex change operation is elaborate and perfect. Hell with it; I was on duty. Valpredo was looking nonchalant, waiting for me.

I examined both her arms with my eyes and my three hands. There was nothing. Not even a bruise.

"My legs too?"

I said, "Not if you can stand on them."

Next question. Could an artificial arm operate within the field?

"Larry? You mean *Larry*? You're out of your teeny mind."

"Take it as a hypothetical question."

She shrugged. "Your guess is as good as mine. There aren't any experts on inertialess fields."

"There was one. He's dead," I reminded her.

"All I know is what I learned watching the Gray Lensman show in the holo wall when I was a kid." She smiled suddenly. "That old space opera— "

Valpredo laughed. "You too? I used to watch that show in study hall on a little pocket phone. One day the Principal caught me at it."

"Sure. And then we outgrew it. Too bad. Those inertialess ships . . . I'm sure an inertialess ship wouldn't behave like those did. You couldn't possibly get rid of the time compression effect." She took a long pull on her drink, set it down and said, "Yes and no. He could reach in, but—you see the problem? The nerve impulses that move the motors in Larry's arm, they're coming into the field too slowly."

"Sure."

"But if Larry closed his fist on something, say, and reached into the field with it, it would probably stay closed. He could have brained Ray with—no, he couldn't. The poker wouldn't be moving any faster than a glacier. Ray would just dodge."

And he couldn't pull a poker out of the field, either. His fist wouldn't close on it after it was inside. But he could have tried, and still left with his arm intact, I thought.

Did Urthiel know anything of the circumstances surrounding Edward Sinclair's exemption?

"Oh, that's an old story," she said. "Sure, I heard about it. How could it possibly have anything to do with, with Ray's murder?"

"I don't know," I confessed. "I'm just thrashing around."

"Well, you'll probably get it more accurately from the UN files. Edward Sinclair did some mathematics on the fields that scoop up interstellar hydrogen for the cargo ramrobots. He was a shoo-in for the exemption. That's the surest way of getting it: make a break-through in anything that has anything to do with the interstellar colonies. Every time you move one man away from Earth, the population drops by one."

"What was wrong with it?"

"Nothing anyone could prove. Remember, the Fertility Restriction Laws were new then. They couldn't stand a real test. But Edward Sinclair's a pure math man. He works with number theory, not practical applications. I've seen Edward's equations, and they're closer to something Ray would come up with. And Ray didn't need the exemption. He never wanted children."

"So you think— "

"I don't *care* which of them redesigned the ramscoops. Diddling the Fertility Board like that, that takes *brains*." She swallowed the rest of her drink, set the glass down. "Breeding for brains is never a mistake. It's no challenge to the Fertility Board either. The people who do the damage are the ones who go into hiding when their shots come due, have their babies, then scream to high heaven when the Board has to sterilize them. Too many of those and we won't have Fertility Laws any more. And *that*— " She didn't have to finish.

Had Sinclair known that Pauline Urthiel was once Paul?

She stared. "Now just what the bleep has that got to do with anything?"

I'd been toying with the idea that Sinclair might have been blackmailing Urthiel with that information. Not for money, but for credit in some discovery they'd made together. "Just thrashing around," I said.

"Well . . . all right. I don't know if Ray knew or not. He never raised the subject, but he never made a pass either, and he must have researched me before he hired me. And, say, listen: Larry doesn't know. I'd appreciate it if you wouldn't blurt it out."

"Okay."

"See, he had his children by his first wife. I'm not denying him children . . . Maybe he married me because I had a touch of, um, masculine insight. Maybe. But he doesn't know it, and he doesn't want to. I don't know whether he'd laugh it off or kill me."

I had Valpredo drop me off at ARM Headquarters.

*This peculiar machine really does bother me, Gil* . . . Well it should, Julio. The Los Angeles Police were not trained to deal with a mad scientist's nightmare running quietly in the middle of a murder scene.

Granted that Janice wasn't the type. Not for this murder. But Drew Porter was precisely the type to evolve a perfect murder around Sinclair's generator, purely as an intellectual exercise. He might have guided her through it; he might even have been there, and used the elevator before she shut it off. It was the one thing he forgot to tell her: not to shut off the elevator.

Or: he outlined a perfect murder to her, purely as a puzzle, never dreaming she'd go through with it—badly.

Or: one of them had killed Janice's uncle on impulse. No telling what he'd said that one of them couldn't tolerate. But the machine had been right there in the living room, and Drew had wrapped his big arm around Janice and said, *Wait, don't do anything yet, let's think this out* . . .

Take any of these as the true state of affairs, and a prosecutor could have a hell of a time proving it. He could show that no killer could possibly have left the scene of the crime without Janice Sinclair's help, and therefore . . . But what about that glowing thing, that time machine built by the dead man? *Could* it have freed a killer from an effectively locked room? How could a judge know its power?

Well, could it?

Bera might know.

The machine was running. I caught the faint violet glow as I stepped into the laboratory, and a flickering next to it . . . and then it was off, and Jackson Bera stood suddenly beside it, grinning, silent, waiting.

I wasn't about to spoil his fun. I said, "Well? Is it an interstellar drive?"

"Yes!"

A warm glow spread through me. I said, "Okay."

"It's a low inertia field," said Bera. "Things inside lose most of their inertia . . . not their mass, just the resistance to movement. Ratio of about five hundred to one. The interface is sharp as a razor. We think there are quantum levels involved."

"Uh huh. The field doesn't affect time directly?"

"No, it . . . I shouldn't say that. Who the hell knows what time really is? It affects chemical and nuclear reactions, energy release of all kinds . . . but it doesn't affect the speed of light. You know, its kind of kicky to be measuring the speed of light at three hundred and seventy miles per second with honest instruments."

Dammit. I'd been half-hoping it was an FTL drive. I said, "Did you ever find out what was causing that blue glow?"

Bera laughed at me. "Watch." He'd rigged a remote switch to turn the machine on. He used it, then struck a match and flipped it toward the blue glow. As it crossed an invisible barrier the match flared violet-white for something less than a eyeblink. I blinked. It had been like a flashbulb going off.

I said, "Oh, *sure*. The machinery's warm."

"Right. The blue glow is just infra-red radiation being boosted to violet when it enters normal time."

Bera shouldn't have had to tell me that. Embarrassed, I changed the subject. "But you said it was an interstellar drive."

"Yah. It's got drawbacks," said Bera. "We can't just put a field around a whole starship. The crew would think they'd lowered the speed of light, but so what? A slowboat doesn't get that close to lightspeed anyway. They'd save a little trip time, but they'd have to live through it five hundred times as fast."

"How about if you just put the field around your fuel tanks?"

Bera nodded. "That's what they'll probably do. Leave the motor and the life support system outside. You could carry a godawful amount of fuel that way . . . Well, it's not our department. Someone else'll be designing the starships," he said a bit wistfully.

"Have you thought of this thing in relation to robbing banks? Or espionage?"

"If a gang could afford to build one of these jobs, they wouldn't need to rob banks." He ruminated. "I hate making anything this big a UN secret. But I guess you're right. The average government could afford a whole stable of the things."

"Thus combining James Bond and the Flash."

He rapped on the plastic frame. "Want to try it?"

"Sure," I said.

*Heart to brain: THUD! What're you doing? You'll get us all killed! I knew we should never have put you in charge of things . . .* I stepped up to the generator, waited for Bera to scamper beyond range, then pulled the switch.

Everything turned deep red. Bera became as a statue.

Well, here I was. The second hand on the wall clock had stopped moving. I took two steps forward and rapped with my knuckles. Rapped, hell: it was like rapping on contact cement. The invisible wall was tacky.

I tried leaning on it for a minute or so. That worked fine until I tried to pull away, and then I knew I'd done something stupid. I was embedded in the interface. It took me another minute to pull loose, and then I went sprawling backward; I'd picked up too much inward velocity, and it all came into the field with me.

At that I'd been lucky. If I'd leaned there a little longer I'd have lost my leverage. I'd have been sinking deeper and deeper into the interface, unable to yell to Bera, building up more and more velocity outside the field.

I picked myself up and tried something safer. I took out my pen and dropped it. It fell normally: thirty-two feet per second per second, field time. Which scratched one theory as to how the killer had thought he would be leaving.

I switched the machine off. "Something I'd like to try," I told Bera. "Can you hang the machine in the air, say by a cable around the frame?"

"What have you got in mind?"

"I want to try standing on the bottom of the field."

Bera looked dubious.

It took us twenty minutes to set it up. Bera took no chances. He lifted the generator about five feet. Since the field seemed to center on that oddly shaped piece of silver, that put the bottom of the field just a foot in the air. We moved a stepladder into range, and I stood on the stepladder and turned on the generator.

I stepped off.

Walking down the side of the field was like walking in progressively stickier taffy. When I stood on the bottom I could just reach the switch.

My shoes were stuck solid. I could pull my feet out of them, but there was no place to stand except in my own shoes. A minute later my feet were stuck too: I could pull one loose, but only by fixing the other ever more deeply in the interface. I sank deeper, and all sensation left the soles of my feet. It was scary, though I knew nothing terrible could happen to me. My feet wouldn't die out there; they wouldn't have time.

But the interface was up to my ankles now, and I started to wonder what kind of velocity they were building up out there. I pushed the switch up. The lights flashed bright, and my feet slapped the floor hard.

Bera said, "Well? Learn anything?"

"Yah. I don't want to try a real test: I might wreck the machine."

"What kind of real test—?"

"Dropping it forty stories with the field on. Quit worrying, I'm not going to do it."

"Right. You aren't."

"You know, this time compression effect would work for more than just spacecraft. After you're on the colony world you could raise full grown cattle from frozen fertilized eggs in just a few minutes."

"Mmm . . . Yah." The happy smile flashing white against darkness, the infinity look in Bera's eyes . . . Bera liked playing with ideas. "Think of one of these mounted on a truck, say on Jinx. You could explore the shoreline regions without ever worrying about the bandersnatchi attacking. They'd never move fast enough. You could drive across any alien world and catch the whole ecology laid out around you, none of it running from the truck. Predators in mid-leap, birds in mid-flight, couples in courtship."

"Or larger groups."

"I . . . think that habit is unique to humans." He looked at me sideways. "You wouldn't spy on *people*, would you? Or shouldn't I ask?"

"That five-hundred-to-one ratio. Is that constant?"

He came back to here and now. "We don't know. Our theory hasn't caught up to the hardware it's supposed to fit. I wish to hell we had Sinclair's notes."

"You were supposed to send a programmer out there— "

"He came back," Bera said viciously. "Clayton Wolfe. Clay says the tapes in Sinclair's computer were all wiped before he got there. I don't know whether to believe him or not. Sinclair was a secretive bastard, wasn't he?"

"Yah. One false move on Clay's part and the computer might have wiped everything. But he says different, hmmm?"

"He says the computer was blank, a newborn mind all ready to be taught. Gil, is that possible? Could whoever killed Sinclair have wiped the tapes?"

"Sure, why not? What he couldn't have done is left afterward." I told him a little about the problem. "It's even worse than that, because as Ordaz keeps pointing out, he thought he'd be leaving with the machine. I thought he might have been planning to roll the generator off the roof, step off with it and float down. But that wouldn't work. Not if it falls five hundred times as fast. He'd have been killed."

"Losing the machine maybe saved his life."

"But *how did he get out?*"

Bera laughed at my frustration. "Couldn't his niece be the one?"

"Sure, she could have killed her uncle for the money. But I can't see how she'd have a motive to wipe the computer. Unless— "

"Something?"

"Maybe. Never mind." Did Bera ever miss this kind of man-hunting? But I wasn't ready to discuss this yet; I didn't know enough.

"Tell me more about the machine. Can you vary that five-hundred-to-one ratio?"

He shrugged. "We tried adding more batteries. We thought it might boost the field strength. We were wrong; it just expanded the boundary a little. And using one less battery turns it off completely. So the ratio seems to be constant, and there do seem to be quantum levels involved. We'll know better when we build another machine."

"How so?"

"Well, there are all kinds of good questions," said Bera. "What happens when the fields of two generators intersect? They might just add, but maybe not. That quantum effect . . . And what happens if the generators are right next to each other, operating in each other's accelerated time? The speed of light could drop to a few feet per second. Throw a punch and your hand gets shorter!"

"That'd be kicky, all right."

"Dangerous, too. Man, we'd better try that one on the Moon!"

"I don't see that."

"Look, with one machine going, infra-red light comes out violet. If two machines were boosting each other's performance, what kind of radiation would they put out? Anything from X-rays to antimatter particles."

"An expensive way to build a bomb."

"Well, but it's a bomb you can use over and over again."

I laughed. "We did find you an expert," I said. "You may not need Sinclair's tapes. Bernath Peterfi says he was working with

Sinclair He could be lying—more likely he was working *for* him,
under contract—but at least he knows what the machine does."

Bera seemed relieved at that. He took down Peterfi's address.
I left him there in the laboratory, playing with his new toy.

The file from City morgue was sitting on my desk, open, waiting
for me since this morning. Two dead ones looked up at me through
sockets of blackened bone; but not accusingly. They had patience.
They could wait.

The computer had processed my search pattern. I braced myself
with a cup of coffee, then started leafing through the thick stack of
printout. When I knew what had burned away two human faces
I'd be close to knowing who. Find the tool, find the killer. And
the tool must be unique, or close to it.

Lasers, lasers—more than half the machine's suggestions seemed
to be lasers. Incredible, the way lasers seemed to breed and mutate
throughout human industry. Laser radar. The laser guidance system on a tunneling machine. Some suggestions were obviously
unworkable . . . and one was a lot too workable.

A standard hunting laser fires in pulses. But it can be jiggered
for a much longer pulse or even a continuous burst.

Set a hunting laser for a long pulse, and put a grid over the
lens. The mesh has to be optically fine, on the order of angstroms.
Now the beam will spread as it leaves the grid. A second of pulse
will vaporize the grid, leaving no evidence. The grid would be no
bigger than a contact lens; if you didn't trust your aim you could
carry a pocketful of them.

The grid-equipped laser would be less efficient, as a rifle with
a silencer is less efficient. But the grid would make the murder
weapon impossible to identify.

I thought about it and got cold chills. Assassination is already
a recognized branch of politics. If this got out—but that was the
trouble; someone seemed to have thought of it already. If not,
someone would. Someone always did.

I wrote up a memo for Lucas Garner. I couldn't think of
anyone better qualified to deal with this kind of sociological problem.

Nothing else in the stack of printout caught my eye. Later I'd
have to go through it in detail. For now, I pushed it aside and
punched for messages.

Bates, the coroner, had sent me another report. They'd finished
the autopsies on the two charred corpses. Nothing new. But

Records had identified the fingerprints. Two missing persons, disappeared six and eight months ago. Ah HA!

I knew that pattern. I didn't even look at the names; I just skipped on to the gene coding.

Right. The fingerprints did not match the genes. All twenty fingertips must be transplants. And the man's scalp was a transplant; his own hair had been blond.

I leaned back in my chair, gazing fondly down at holographs of charred skulls.

You evil sons of bitches. Organleggers, both of you. With all that raw material available, most organleggers change their fingerprints constantly—and their retina prints; but we'd never get prints from those charred eyeballs. So: weird weapon or no, they were ARM business. My business.

And we still didn't know what had killed them, or who.

It could hardly have been a rival gang. For one thing, there was no competition. There must be plenty of business for every organlegger left alive after the ARM had swept through them last year. For another, why had they been dumped on a city slidewalk? Rival organleggers would have taken them apart for their own organ banks. Waste not, want not.

On that same philosophy, I had something to be deeply involved in when the mother hunt broke. Sinclair's death wasn't ARM business, and his time compression field wasn't in my field. This was both.

I wondered what end of the business the dead ones had been in. The file gave their estimated ages: forty for the man, forty-three for the woman, give or take three years each. Too old to be raiding the city street for donors. That takes youth and muscle. I billed them as doctors, culturing the transplants and doing the operations; or sales persons, charged with quietly letting prospective clients know where they could get an operation without waiting two years for the public organ banks to come up with material.

So: they'd tried to sell someone a new kidney and been killed for their impudence. That would make the killer a hero.

So why hide them for three days, then drag them out onto a city slidewalk in the dead of night?

Because they'd been killed with a fearsome new weapon?

I looked at the burnt faces and thought: fearsome, right. Whatever did that *had* to be strictly a murder weapon. As the optical grid over a laser lens would be strictly a murder technique.

So: a secretive scientist and his deformed assistant, fearful of rousing the wrath of the villagers, had dithered over the bodies for three days, then disposed of them in that clumsy fashion because they panicked when the bodies started to smell. Maybe.

But a prospective client needn't have used his shiny new terror weapon. He had only to call the cops after they were gone. It read better if the killer was a prospective *donor*; he'd fight with anything he could get his hands on.

I flipped back to full shots of the bodies. They looked to be in good condition. Not much flab. You don't collect a donor by putting an armlock on him; you use a needle gun. But you still need muscle to pick up the body and move it to your car, and you have to do that damn quick. Hmmm . . .

Someone knocked at my door.

I shouted, "Come on in!"

Drew Porter came in. He was big enough to fill the office, and he moved with a grace he must have learned on a board. "Mr. Hamilton? I'd like to talk to you."

"Sure. What about?"

He didn't seem to know what to do with his hands. He looked grimly determined. "You're an ARM," he said. "You're not actually investigating Uncle Ray's murder. That's right, isn't it?"

"That's right. Our concern is with the generator. Coffee?"

"Yes, thanks. But you know all about the killing. I thought I'd like to talk to you, straighten out some of my own ideas."

"Go ahead." I punched for two coffees.

"Ordaz thinks Janice did it, doesn't he?"

"Probably. I'm not good at reading Ordaz' mind. But it seems to narrow down to two distinct groups of possible killers. Janice and everyone else. Here's your coffee."

"Janice didn't do it." He took the cup from me, gulped at it, set it down on my desk and forgot about it.

"Janice and X," I said. "But X couldn't have left. In fact, X couldn't have left even if he'd had the machine he came for. And we still don't know why he didn't just take the elevator."

He scowled as he thought that through. "Say he had a way to leave," he said. "He wanted to take the machine—he *had* to want that, because he tried to use the machine to set up an alibi. But even if he couldn't take the machine, he'd still use his alternate way out."

"Why?"

"It'd leave Janice holding the bag, if he knew Janice was coming home. If he didn't, he'd be leaving the police with a locked room mystery."

"Locked room mysteries are good clean fun, but I never heard of one happening in real life. In fiction they usually happen by accident." I waved aside his protest. "Never mind. You argue well. But what was his alternate escape route?"

Porter didn't answer.

"Would you care to look at the case against Janice Sinclair?"

"She's the only one who could have done it," he said bitterly. "But she didn't. She couldn't kill anyone, not that cold-blooded, pre-packaged way, with an alibi all set up and a weird machine at the heart of it. Look, that machine is too *complicated* for Janice."

"No, she isn't the type. But—no offense intended—you are."

He grinned at that. "Me? Well, maybe I am. But why would I want to?"

"You're in love with her. I think you'd do anything for her. Aside from that, you might enjoy setting up a perfect murder. And there's the money."

"You've got a funny idea of a perfect murder."

"Say I was being tactful."

He laughed at that. "All right. Say I set up a murder for the love of Janice. Damn it, if she had that much hate in her I wouldn't love her! Why would she want to kill Uncle Ray?"

I dithered as to whether to drop that on him. Decided *yes*. "Do you know anything about Edward Sinclair's exemption?"

"Yah, Janice told me something about . . ." He trailed off.

"Just what did she tell you?"

"I don't have to say."

That was probably intelligent. "All right," I said. "For the sake of argument, let's assume it was Raymond Sinclair who worked out the math for the new ramrobot scoops, and Edward took the credit with Raymond's connivance. It was probably Raymond's idea. How would that sit with Edward?"

"I'd think he'd be grateful forever," said Porter. "Janice says he is."

"Maybe. But people are funny, aren't they? Being grateful for fifty years could get on a man's nerves. It's not a natural emotion."

"You're so young to be so cynical," Porter said pityingly.

"I'm trying to think this out like a prosecution lawyer. If these brothers saw each other too often Edward might get to feeling embarrassed around Raymond. He'd have a hard time relaxing with him. The rumors wouldn't help . . . oh, yes, there are rumors. I've been told that Edward couldn't have worked out those equations because he doesn't have the ability. If that kind of thing got back to Edward, how would he like it? He might even start avoiding his brother. Then Ray might remind brother Edward of just how much he owed him . . . and that's the kiss of death."

"Janice says no."

"Janice could have picked up the hate from her father. Or she might have started worrying about what would happen if Uncle Ray changed his mind one day. It could happen any time, if things were getting strained between the elder Sinclairs. So one day she shut his mouth— "

Porter growled in his throat.

"I'm just trying to show you what you're up against. One more thing: the killer may have wiped the tapes in Sinclair's computer."

"Oh?" Porter thought that over. "Yah. Janice could have done that just in case there were some notes in there, notes on Ed Sinclair's ramscoop field equations. But, look: X could have wiped those tapes too. Stealing the generator doesn't do him any good unless he wipes it out of Uncle Ray's computer."

"True enough. Shall we get back to the case against X?"

"With pleasure." He dropped into a chair. Watching his face smooth out, I added, *and with great relief.*

I said, "Let's not call him X. Call him K for killer." We already had an Ecks involved . . . and his family name probably *had* been X, once upon a time. "We've been assuming K set up Sinclair's time compression effect as an alibi."

Porter smiled. "It's a lovely idea. *Elegant,* as a mathematician would say. Remember, I never saw the actual murder scene. Just chalk marks."

"It was—macabre. Like a piece of surrealism. A very bloody practical joke. K could have deliberately set it up that way, if his mind is twisted enough."

"If he's that twisted, he probably escaped by running himself down the garbage disposal."

"Pauline Urthiel thought he might be a psychotic. Someone who worked with Sinclair, who thought he wasn't getting enough credit." Like Peterfi, I thought, or Pauline herself.

"I like the alibi theory."

"It bothers me. Too many people knew about the machine. How did he expect to get away with it? Lawrence Ecks knew about it.

Peterfi knew enough about the machine to rebuild it from scratch. Or so he says. You and Janice saw it in action."

"Say he's crazy then. Say he hated Uncle Ray enough to kill him and then set him up in a makeshift Dali painting. He'd still have to get *out*." Porter was working his hands together. The muscles bulged and rippled in his arms. "This whole thing depends on the elevator, doesn't it? If the elevator hadn't been locked and on Uncle Ray's floor, there wouldn't be a problem."

"So?"

"So. Say he did leave by elevator. Then Janice came home, and she automatically called the elevator up and locked it. She does that without thinking. She had a bad shock last night. This morning she didn't remember."

"And this evening it could come back to her."

Porter looked up sharply. "I wouldn't— "

"You'd better think long and hard before you do. If Ordaz is sixty percent sure of her now, he'll be a hundred percent sure when she lays that on him."

Porter was working his muscles again. In a low voice he said, "It's possible, isn't it?"

"Sure. It makes things a lot simpler, too. But if Janice said it now, she'd sound like a liar."

"But it's *possible*."

"I give up. Sure, it's possible."

"Then who's our killer?"

There wasn't any reason I shouldn't consider the question. It wasn't my case at all. I did, and presently I laughed. "Did I say it'd make things simpler? Man, it throws the case *wide open! Anyone* could have done it. Uh, anyone but Steeves. Steeves wouldn't have had any reason to come back this morning."

Porter looked glum. "Steeves wouldn't have done it anyway."

"He was your suggestion."

"Oh, in pure mechanical terms, he's the only one who didn't need a way out. But—you don't know Steeves. He's a big, brawny guy with a beer belly and no brains. A nice guy, you understand, I *like* him, but if he ever killed anyone it'd be with a beer bottle. And he was proud of Uncle Ray. He liked having Raymond Sinclair in his building."

"Okay, forget Steeves. Is there anyone you'd particularly like to pin it on? Bearing in mind that now *anyone* could get in to do it."

"Not anyone. Anyone in the elevator computer, plus anyone Uncle Ray might have let up."

"Well?"

He shook his head.

"You make a hell of an amateur detective. You're afraid to accuse anyone."

He shrugged, smiling, embarrassed.

"What about Peterfi? Now that Sinclair's dead, he can claim they were equal partners in the, uh, time machine. And he tumbled to it awfully fast. The moment Valpredo told him Sinclair was dead, Peterfi was his partner."

"Sounds typical."

"Could he be telling the truth?"

"I'd say he's lying. Doesn't make him a killer, though."

"No. What about Ecks? If he didn't know Peterfi was involved, he might have tried the same thing. Does he need money?"

"Not hardly. And he's been with Uncle Ray for longer than I've been alive."

"Maybe he was after the Immunity. He's had kids, but not by his present wife. He may not know she can't have children."

"Pauline *likes* children. I've seen her with them." Porter looked at me curiously. "I don't see having children as that big a motive."

"You're young. Then there's Pauline herself. Sinclair knew something about her. Or Sinclair might have told Ecks, and Ecks blew up and killed him for it."

Porter shook his head. "In red rage? I can't think of anything that'd make Larry do that. Pauline, maybe. Larry, no."

But, I thought, there are men who would kill if they learned that their wives had gone through a sex change. I said, "Whoever killed Sinclair, if he wasn't crazy, he had to want to take the machine. One way might have been to lower it by rope . . ." I trailed off. Fifty pounds or so, lowered two stories by nylon line. Ecks' steel and plastic arm . . . or the muscles now rolling like boulders in Porter's arms. I thought Porter could have managed it.

Or maybe he'd thought he could. He hadn't actually had to go through with it.

My phone rang.

It was Ordaz. "Have you made any progress on the time machine? I'm told that Dr. Sinclair's computer— "

"Was wiped, yah. But that's all right. We're learning quite a lot about it. If we run into trouble, Bernath Peterfi can help us. He helped build it. Where are you now?"

"At Dr. Sinclair's apartment. We had some further questions for Janice Sinclair."

Porter twitched. I said, "All right, we'll be right over. Andrew Porter's with me." I hung up and turned to Porter. "Does Janice know she's a suspect?"

"No. Please don't tell her unless you have to. I'm not sure she could take it."

I had the taxi drop us at the lobby level of the Rodewald Building. When I told Porter I wanted a ride in the elevator, he just nodded.

The elevator to Raymond Sinclair's penthouse was a box with a seat in it. It would have been comfortable for one, cozy for two good friends. With me and Porter in it it was crowded. Porter hunched his knees and tried to fold into himself. He seemed used to it.

He probably was. Most apartment elevators are like that. Why waste room on an elevator shaft when the same space can go into apartments?

It was a fast ride. The seat was necessary; it was two gee going up and a longer period at half a gee slowing down, while lighted numbers flickered past. Numbers, but no doors.

"Hey, Porter. If this elevator jammed, would there be a door to let us out?"

He gave me a funny look and said he didn't know. "Why worry about it? If it jammed at this speed it'd come apart like a handful of shredded lettuce."

It was just claustrophobic enough to make me wonder. K hadn't left by elevator. Why not? Because the ride up had terrified him? *Brain to memory: dig into the medical records of that list of suspects. See if any of them have records of claustrophobia.* Too bad the elevator brain didn't keep records. We could find out which of them had used the boxlike elevator once or not at all.

In which case we'd be looking for $K_2$. By now I was thinking in terms of three groups. $K_1$ had killed Sinclair, then tried to use the low-inertia field as both loot and alibi. $K_2$ was crazy; he hadn't wanted the generator at all, except as a way to set up his macabre tableau. $K_3$ was Janice and Drew Porter.

Janice was there when the doors slid open. She was wan and her shoulders slumped. But when she saw Porter she smiled like sunlight and ran to him. Her run was wobbly, thrown off by the missing weight of her arm.

The wide brown circle was still there in the grass, marked

with white chalk and the yellow chemical that picks up blood-stains. White outlines to mark the vanished body, the generator, the poker.

Something knocked at the back door of my mind. I looked from the chalk outlines, to the open elevator, to the chalk . . . and a third of the puzzle fell into place.

So simple. We were looking for $K_1$ . . . and I had a pretty good idea who he was.

Ordaz was asking me, "How did you happen to arrive with Mr. Porter?"

"He came to my office. We were talking about a hypothetical kill-er"—I lowered my voice slightly—"a killer who isn't Janice."

"Very good. Did you reason out how he must have left?"

"Not yet. But play the game with me. Say there was a way."

Porter and Janice joined us, their arms about each other's waists. Ordaz said, "Very well. We assume there was a way out. Did he improvise it? And why did he not use the elevator?"

"He must have had it in mind when he got here. He didn't use the elevator because he was planning to take the machine. It wouldn't have fit."

They all stared at the chalk outline of the generator. So simple. Porter said, "Yah! Then he used it anyway, and left you a locked room mystery!"

"That may have been his mistake," Ordaz said grimly. "When we know his escape route we may find that only one man could have used it. But of course we do not even know that the route exists."

I changed the subject. "Have you got everyone on the elevator tape identified?"

Valpredo dug out his spiral notebook and flipped to the jotted names of those people permitted to use Sinclair's elevator. He showed it to Porter. "Have you seen this?"

Porter studied it. "No, but I can guess what it is. Let's see . . . Hans Drucker was Janice's lover before I came along. We still see him. In fact, he was at that beach party last night at the Randalls'."

"He flopped on the Randalls' rug last night," said Valpredo. "Him and four others. One of the better alibis."

"Oh, *Hans* wouldn't have anything to do with this!" Janice exclaimed. The idea horrified her.

Porter was still looking at the list. "You know about most of these people already. Bertha Hall and Muriel Sandusky were lady friends of Uncle Ray's. Bertha goes backpacking with him."

"We interviewed them too," Valpredo told me. "You can hear the tapes if you like."

"No, just give me the gist. I already know who the killer is."

Ordaz raised his eyebrows at that, and Janice said, "Oh, good! Who?" which question I answered with a secretive smile. Nobody actually called me a liar.

Valpredo said, "Muriel Sandusky's been living in England for almost a year. Married. Hasn't seen Sinclair in years. Big, beautiful redhead."

"She had a crush on Uncle Ray once," said Janice. "And vice versa. I think his lasted longer."

"Bertha Hall is something else again," Valpredo continued. "Sinclair's age, and in good shape. Wiry. She says that when Sinclair was on the home stretch on a project he gave up everything: friends, social life, exercise. Afterward he'd call Bertha and go backpacking with her to catch up with himself. He called her two nights ago and set a date for next Monday."

I said, "Alibi?"

"Nope."

"Really!" Janice said indignantly. "Why, we've known Bertha since I was that high! If you know who killed Uncle Ray, why don't just say so?"

"Out of this list, I sure do, given certain assumptions. But I don't know how he got out, or how he expected to, or whether we can prove it on him. I can't accuse anyone *now*. It's a damn shame he didn't lose his arm reaching for that poker."

Porter looked frustrated. So did Janice.

"You would not want to face a lawsuit," Ordaz suggested delicately. "What of Sinclair's machine?"

"It's an inertialess drive, sort of. Lower the inertia, time speeds up. Bera's already learned a lot about it, but it'll be awhile before he can really . . ."

"You were saying?" Ordaz asked when I trailed off.

"Sinclair was *finished* with the damn thing."

"Sure he was," said Porter. "He wouldn't have been showing it around otherwise."

"Or calling Bertha for a backpacking expedition. Or spreading rumors about what he had. Yeah. Sure, he knew everything he could learn about that machine. Julio, you were cheated. It all depends on the machine. And the bastard did wrack up his arm, and we can prove it on him."

We were piled into Ordaz' commandeered taxi: me and Ordaz

and Valpredo and Porter. Valpredo had set the thing for conventional speeds so he wouldn't have to worry about driving. We'd turned the interior chairs to face each other.

"This is the part I won't guarantee," I said, sketching rapidly in Valpredo's borrowed notebook. "But remember, he had a length of line with him. He must have expected to use it. Here's how he planned to get out."

I sketched in a box to represent Sinclair's generator, a stick-figure clinging to the frame. A circle around them to represent the field. A bow knot tied to the machine, with one end trailing up through the field.

"See it? He goes up the stairs with the field on. The camera has about one chance in eight of catching him while he's moving at that speed. He wheels the machine to the edge of the roof, ties the line to it, throws the line a good distance away, pushes the generator off the roof and steps off with it. The line falls at thirty-two feet per second squared, normal time, plus a little more because the machine and the killer are tugging down on it. Not hard, because they're in a low-inertia field. By the time the killer reaches ground he's moving at something more than, uh, twelve hundred feet per second over five hundred . . . uh, say three feet per second internal time, and he's got to pull the machine out of the way fast, because the rope is going to hit like a bomb."

"It looks like it would work," said Porter.

"Yah. I thought for a while that he could just stand on the bottom of the field. A little fooling with the machine cured me of that. He'd smash both legs. But he could hang onto the frame; it's strong enough."

"But he didn't have the machine," Valpredo pointed out.

"That's where you got cheated. What happens when two fields intersect?"

They looked blank.

"It's not a trivial question. Nobody knows the answer yet. *But Sinclair did*. He had to, he was *finished*. He must have had two machines. The killer took the second machine."

Ordaz said, "Ahh."

Porter said, "Who's K?"

We were settling on the carport. Valpredo knew where we were, but he didn't say anything. We left the taxi and headed for the elevators.

"That's a lot easier," I said. "He expected to use the machine as an alibi. That's silly, considering how many people knew it existed.

But if he didn't know that Sinclair was ready to start showing it to people—specifically to you and Janice—who's left? Ecks only knew it was some kind of interstellar drive."

The elevator was uncommonly large. We piled into it.

"And," said Valpredo, "there's the matter of the arm. I think I've got that figured too."

"I gave you enough clues," I told him.

Peterfi was a long time answering our buzz. He may have studied us through the door camera, wondering why a parade was marching through his hallway. Then he spoke through the grid. "Yes. What is it?"

"Police. Open up," said Valpredo.

"Do you have a warrant?"

I stepped forward and showed my ident to the camera. "I'm an ARM. I don't need a warrant. Open up. We won't keep you long." *One way or another.*

He opened the door. He looked neater now than he had this afternoon, despite informal brown indoor pajamas. "Just you," he said. He let me in, then started to close the door on the others.

Valpredo put his hand against the door. "Hey— "

"It's okay," I said. Peterfi was smaller than I was, and I had a needle gun. Valpredo shrugged and let him close the door.

My mistake. I had two-thirds of the puzzle, and I thought I had it all.

Peterfi folded his arms and said, "Well? What is it you want to search this time? Would you like to examine my legs?"

"No, let's start with the insulin feeder on your upper arm."

"Certainly," he said, and startled hell out of me.

I waited while he took off his shirt—unnecessary, but he needn't, know that—then ran my imaginary fingers through the insulin feed. The reserve was nearly full. "I should have known," I said. "Dammit. You got six months' worth of insulin from the organlegger."

His eyebrows went up. "Organlegger?" He pulled loose. "Is this an accusation, Mr. Hamilton? I'm taping this for my attorney."

And I was setting myself up for a lawsuit. The hell with it. "Yah, it's an accusation. You killed Sinclair. Nobody else could have tried that alibi stunt."

He looked puzzled—honestly, I thought. "Why not?"

"If anyone else had tried to set up an alibi with Sinclair's generator, Bernath Peterfi would have told the police all about what it was and how it worked. But you were the only one who knew that until last night, when he started showing it around."

There was only one thing he could say to that kind of logic, and he said it. "Still recording, Mr. Hamilton."

"Record and be damned. There are other things we can check: Your grocery delivery service. Your water bill."

He didn't flinch. He was smiling. Was it a bluff? I sniffed the air. Six months worth of body odor emitted in one night? By a man who hadn't taken more than four or five baths in six months? But his air conditioning was too good.

The curtains were open now to the night and the ocean. They'd been closed this afternoon, and he'd been squinting. But it wasn't evidence. The lights: he only had one light burning now, and so what?

The big, powerful campout flashlight sitting on a small table against a wall. I hadn't even noticed it this afternoon. Now I was sure I knew what he'd used it for . . . but how to prove it?

Groceries . . . "If you didn't buy six months' worth of groceries last night, you must have stolen them. Sinclair's generator is perfect for thefts. We'll check the local supermarkets."

"And link the thefts to me? How?"

He was too bright to have kept the generator. But come to think of it, where could he abandon it? He was *guilty*. He couldn't have covered *all* his tracks—

"Peterfi? I've got it."

He believed me. I saw it in the way he braced himself. Maybe he'd worked it out before I did. I said, "Your contraceptive shots must have worn off six months early. Your organlegger couldn't get you that; he's got no reason to keep contraceptives around. You're dead, Peterfi."

"I might as well be. Damn you, Hamilton! You've cost me the exemption!"

"They won't try you right away. We can't afford to lose what's in your head. You know too much about Sinclair's generator."

"Our generator! We built it together!"

"Yah."

"You won't try me at all," he said more calmly. "Are you going to tell a court how the killer left Ray's apartment?"

I dug out my sketch and handed it to him. While he was studying it I said, "How did you like going off the roof? You couldn't have *known* it would work."

He looked up. His words came slowly, reluctantly. I guess he had to tell someone, and it didn't matter now. "By then I didn't care. My arm hung like a dead rabbit, and it stank. It took me three minutes to reach the ground. I thought I'd die on the way."

"Where'd you dig up an organlegger that fast?"

His eyes called me a fool. "Can't you guess? Three years ago. I was hoping diabetes could be cured by a transplant. When the government hospitals couldn't help me I went to an organlegger. I was lucky he was still in business last night."

He drooped. It seemed all the anger went out of him. "Then I was six months in the field, waiting for the scars to heal. In the dark. I tried taking that big campout flashlight in with me." He laughed bitterly. "I gave that up after I noticed the walls were smoldering."

The wall above that little table had a scorched look. I should have wondered about that earlier.

"No baths," he was saying. "I was afraid to use up that much water. No exercise, practically. But I had to eat, didn't I? And all for nothing."

"Will you tell us how to find the organlegger you dealt with?"

"This is your big day, isn't it, Hamilton? All right, why not. It won't do you any good."

"Why not?"

He looked up at me very strangely.

Then he spun about and ran.

He caught me flatfooted. I jumped after him. I didn't know what he had in mind; there was only one exit to the apartment, excluding the balcony, and he wasn't headed there. He seemed to be trying to reach a blank wall . . . with a small table set against it, and a camp flashlight on it and a drawer in it. I saw the drawer and thought *gun*! And I surged after him and got him by the wrist just as he reached the wall switch above the table.

I threw my weight backward and yanked him away from there . . . and then the field came on.

I held a hand and arm up to the elbow. Beyond was a fluttering of violet light: Peterfi thrashing frantically in a low-inertia field. I hung on while I tried to figure out what was happening.

The second generator was here somewhere. In the wall? The switch seemed to have been recently plastered in, now that I saw it close. Figure a closet on the other side, and the generator in it Peterfi must have drilled through the wall and fixed that switch. Sure, what else did he have to do with six months of spare time?

No point in yelling for help. Peterfi's soundproofing was too modern. And if I didn't let go Peterfi would die of thirst in a few minutes.

Peterfi's feet came straight at my jaw. I threw myself down, and the edge of a boot sole nearly tore my ear off. I rolled forward in time to grab his ankle. There was more violet fluttering, and his other leg thrashed wildly outside the field. Too many conflicting nerve impulses were pouring into the muscles. The leg flopped about like something dying. If I didn't let go he'd break it in a dozen places.

He'd knocked the table over. I didn't see it fall, but suddenly it was lying on its side. The top, drawer included, must have been well beyond the field. The flashlight lay just beyond the violet fluttering of his hand.

Okay. He couldn't reach the drawer; his hand wouldn't get coherent signals if it left the field. I could let go of his ankle. He'd turn off the field when he got thirsty enough.

And if I didn't let go, he'd die in there.

It was like wrestling a dolphin one-handed. I hung on anyway, looking for a flaw in my reasoning. Peterfi's free leg seemed broken in at least two places . . . I was about to let go when something must have jarred together in my head.

Faces of charred bone grinned derisively at me.

*Brain to hand: HANG ON! Don't you understand? He's trying to reach the flashlight!*

I hung on.

Presently Peterfi stopped thrashing. He lay on his side, his face and hands glowing blue. I was trying to decide whether he was playing possum when the blue light behind his face quietly went out.

I let them in. They looked it over. Valpredo went off to search for a pole to reach the light switch. Ordaz asked, "Was it necessary to kill him?"

I pointed to the flashlight. He didn't get it.

"I was overconfident," I said. "I shouldn't have come in alone. He's already killed two people with that flashlight. The organleggers who gave him his new arm. He didn't want them talking, so he burned their faces off and then dragged them out onto a slidewalk. He probably tied them to the generator and then used the line to pull it. With the field on the whole setup wouldn't weigh more than a couple of pounds."

"With a flashlight?" Ordaz pondered. "Of course. It would have been putting out five hundred times as much light. A good thing you thought of that in time."

"Well, I do spend more time dealing with these oddball science fiction devices than you do."

"And welcome to them," said Ordaz.

# THE PERSISTENCE OF VISION

## John Varley

It was the year of the fourth non-depression. I had recently joined the ranks of the unemployed. The President had told me that I had nothing to fear but fear itself. I took him at his word, for once, and set out to backpack to California.

I was not the only one. The world's economy had been writhing like a snake on a hot griddle for the last twenty years, since the early seventies. We were in a boom-and-bust cycle that seemed to have no end. It had wiped out the sense of security the nation had so painfully won in the golden years after the thirties. People were accustomed to the fact that they could be rich one year and on the breadlines the next. I was on the breadlines in '81, and again in '88. This time I decided to use my freedom from the time clock to see the world. I had ideas of stowing away to Japan. I was forty-seven years old and might not get another chance to be irresponsible.

This was in late summer of the year. Sticking out my thumb along the interstate, I could easily forget that there were food riots back in Chicago. I slept at night on top of my bedroll and saw stars and listened to crickets.

I must have walked most of the way from Chicago to Des Moines. My feet toughened up after a few days of awful blisters. The rides were scarce, partly competition from other hitchhikers and partly the times we were living in. The locals were none too anxious to give rides to city people, who they had heard were mostly a bunch of hunger-crazed potential mass murderers. I got roughed up once and told never to return to Sheffield, Illinois.

But I gradually learned the knack of living on the road. I had started with a small supply of canned goods from the welfare and by the time they ran out, I had found that it was possible to work for a meal at many of the farmhouses along the way.

Some of it was hard work, some of it was only a token from people with a deeply ingrained sense that nothing should come for free. A few meals were gratis, at the family table, with grandchildren sitting around while grandpa or grandma told oft-repeated tales of what it had been like in the Big One back in '29, when people had not been afraid to help a fellow out when he was down on his luck. I found that the older the person, the more likely I was to get a sympathetic ear. One of the many tricks you learn. And most older people will give you anything if you'll only sit and listen to them. I got very good at it.

The rides began to pick up west of Des Moines, then got bad again as I neared the refugee camps bordering the China Strip. This was only five years after the disaster, remember, when the Omaha nuclear reactor melted down and a hot mass of uranium and plutonium began eating its way into the earth, headed for China, spreading a band of radioactivity six hundred kilometers downwind. Most of Kansas City, Missouri, was still living in plywood and sheet-metal shantytowns till the city was rendered habitable again.

The refugees were a tragic group. The initial solidarity people show after a great disaster had long since faded into the lethargy and disillusionment of the displaced person. Many of them would be in and out of hospitals for the rest of their lives. To make it worse, the local people hated them, feared them, would not associate with them. They were modern pariahs, unclean. Their children were shunned. Each camp had only a number to identify it, but the local populace called them all Geigertowns.

I made a long detour to Little Rock to avoid crossing the Strip, though it was safe now as long as you didn't linger. I was issued a pariah's badge by the National Guard—a dosimeter—and wandered from one Geigertown to the next. The people were pitifully friendly once I made the first move, and I always slept indoors. The food was free at the community messes.

Once at Little Rock, I found that the aversion to picking up strangers—who might be tainted with "radiation disease"—dropped off, and I quickly moved across Arkansas, Oklahoma, and

Texas. I worked a little here and there, but many of the rides were long. What I saw of Texas was through a car window.

I was a little tired of that by the time I reached New Mexico. I decided to do some more walking. By then I was less interested in California than in the trip itself.

I left the roads and went cross-country where there were no fences to stop me. I found that it wasn't easy, even in New Mexico, to get far from signs of civilization.

Taos was the center, back in the '60's, of cultural experiments in alternative living. Many communes and cooperatives were set up in the surrounding hills during that time. Most of them fell apart in a few months or years, but a few survived. In later years, any group with a new theory of living and a yen to try it out seemed to gravitate to that part of New Mexico. As a result, the land was dotted with ramshackle windmills, solar heating panels, geodesic domes, group marriages, nudists, philosophers, theoreticians, messiahs, hermits, and more than a few just plain nuts.

Taos was great. I could drop into most of the communes and stay for a day or a week, eating organic rice and beans and drinking goat's milk. When I got tired of one, a few hours' walk in any direction would bring me to another. There, I might be offered a night of prayer and chanting or a ritualistic orgy. Some of the groups had spotless barns with automatic milkers for the herds of cows. Others didn't even have latrines; they just squatted. In some, the members dressed like nuns, or Quakers in early Pennsylvania. Elsewhere, they went nude and shaved all their body hair and painted themselves purple. There were all-male and all-female groups. I was urged to stay at most of the former; at the latter, the responses ranged from a bed for the night and good conversation to being met at a barbed-wire fence with a shotgun.

I tried not to make judgments. These people were doing something important, all of them. They were testing ways whereby people didn't have to live in Chicago. That was a wonder to me. I had thought Chicago was inevitable, like diarrhea.

This is not to say they were all successful. Some made Chicago look like Shangri-La. There was one group who seemed to feel that getting back to nature consisted of sleeping in pigshit and eating food a buzzard wouldn't touch. Many were obviously doomed. They would leave behind a group of empty hovels and the memory of cholera.

So the place wasn't paradise, not by a long way. But there were successes. One or two had been there since '63 or '64 and were raising their third generation. I was disappointed to see that most of these were the ones that departed least from established norms of behavior, though some of the differences could be startling. I suppose the most radical experiments are the least likely to bear fruit.

I stayed through the winter. No one was surprised to see me a second time. It seems that many people came to Taos and shopped around. I seldom stayed more than three weeks at any one place, and always pulled my weight. I made many friends and picked up skills that would serve me if I stayed off the roads. I toyed with the idea of staying at one of them forever. When I couldn't make up my mind, I was advised that there was no hurry. I could go to California and return. They seemed sure I would.

So when spring came I headed west over the hills. I stayed off the roads and slept in the open. Many nights I would stay at another commune, until they finally began to get farther apart, then tapered off entirely. The country was not as pretty as before.

Then, three days' leisurely walking from the last commune, I came to a wall.

In 1964, in the United States, there was an epidemic of German measles, or rubella. Rubella is one of the mildest of infectious diseases. The only time it's a problem is when a woman contracts it in the first four months of her pregnancy. It is passed to the fetus, which usually develops complications. These complications include deafness, blindness, and damage to the brain.

In 1964, in the old days before abortion became readily available, there was nothing to be done about it. Many pregnant women caught rubella and went to term. Five thousand deaf-blind children were born in one year. The normal yearly incidence of deaf-blind children in the United States is one hundred and forty.

In 1970 these five thousand potential Helen Kellers were all six years old. It was quickly seen that there was a shortage of Anne Sullivans. Previously, deaf-blind children could be sent to a small number of special institutions.

It was a problem. Not just anyone can cope with a blind-deaf child. You can't tell them to shut up when they moan; you can't reason with them, tell them that the moaning is driving you crazy. Some parents were driven to nervous breakdowns when they tried to keep their children at home.

Many of the five thousand were badly retarded and virtually impossible to reach, even if anyone had been trying. These ended up, for the most part, warehoused in the hundreds of anonymous nursing homes and institutes for "special" children. They were put into beds, cleaned up once a day by a few overworked nurses, and generally allowed the full blessings of liberty: they were allowed to rot freely in their own dark, quiet, private universes. Who can say if it was bad for them? None of them were heard to complain.

Many children with undamaged brains were shuffled in among the retarded because they were unable to tell anyone that they were in there behind the sightless eyes. They failed the batteries of tactile tests, unaware that their fates hung in the balance when they were asked to fit round pegs into round holes to the ticking of a clock they could not see or hear. As a result, they spent the rest of their lives in bed, and none of them complained, either. To protest, one must be aware of the possibility of something better. It helps to have a language, too.

Several hundred of the children were found to have IQ's within the normal range. There were news stories about them as they approached puberty and it was revealed that there were not enough good people to properly handle them. Money was spent, teachers were trained. The education expenditures would go on for a specified period of time, until the children were grown, then things would go back to normal and everyone could congratulate themselves on having dealt successfully with a tough problem.

And indeed, it did work fairly well. There are ways to reach and teach such children. They involve patience, love, and dedication, and the teachers brought all that to their jobs. All the graduates of the special schools left knowing how to speak with their hands. Some could talk. A few could write. Most of them left the institutions to live with parents or relatives, or, if neither was possible, received counseling and help in fitting themselves into society. The options were limited, but people can live rewarding lives under the most severe handicaps. Not everyone, but most of the graduates, were as happy with their lot as could reasonably be expected. Some achieved the almost saintly peace of their role model, Helen Keller. Others became bitter and withdrawn. A few had to be put in asylums, where they became indistinguishable from the others of their group who had spent the last twenty years there. But for the most part, they did well.

But among the group, as in any group, were some misfits. They tended to be among the brightest, the top ten percent in the IQ scores. This was not a reliable rule. Some had unremarkable test scores and were still infected with the hunger to do something, to change things, to rock the boat. With a group of five thousand, there were certain to be a few geniuses, a few artists, a few dreamers, hell-raisers, individualists, movers and shapers: a few glorious maniacs.

There was one among them who might have been President but for the fact that she was blind, deaf, and a woman. She was smart, but not one of the geniuses. She was a dreamer, a creative force, an innovator. It was she who dreamed of freedom. But she was not a builder of fairy castles. Having dreamed it, she had to make it come true.

The wall was made of carefully fitted stone and was about five feet high. It was completely out of context with anything I had seen in New Mexico, though it was built of native rock. You just don't build that kind of wall out there. You use barbed wire if something needs fencing in, but many people still made use of the free range and brands. Somehow it seemed transplanted from New England.

It was substantial enough that I felt it would be unwise to crawl over it. I had crossed many wire fences in my travels and had not gotten in trouble for it yet, though I had some talks with some ranchers. Mostly they told me to keep moving, but didn't seem upset about it. This was different. I set out to walk around it. From the lay of the land, I couldn't tell how far it might reach, but I had time.

At the top of the next rise I saw that I didn't have far to go. The wall made a right-angle turn just ahead. I looked over it and could see some buildings. They were mostly domes, the ubiquitous structure thrown up by communes because of the combination of ease of construction and durability. There were sheep behind the wall, and a few cows. They grazed on grass so green I wanted to go over and roll in it. The wall enclosed a rectangle of green. Outside, where I stood, it was all scrub and sage. These people had access to Rio Grande irrigation water.

I rounded the corner and followed the wall west again.

I saw a man on horseback about the same time he spotted me. He was south of me, outside the wall, and he turned and rode in my direction.

He was a dark man with thick features, dressed in denim and boots with a gray battered stetson. Navaho, maybe. I don't know much about Indians, but I'd heard they were out here.

"Hello," I said when he'd stopped. He was looking me over. "Am I on your land?"

"Tribal land," he said. "Yeah, you're on it."

"I didn't see any signs."

He shrugged.

"It's okay, bud. You don't look like you out to rustle cattle."
He grinned at me. His teeth were large and stained with tobacco.
"You be camping out tonight?"

"Yes. How much farther does the, uh, tribal land go? Maybe
I'll be out of it before tonight?"

He shook his head gravely. "Nah. You won't be off it tomorrow.
'S all right. You make a fire, you be careful, huh?" He grinned
again and started to ride off.

"Hey, what is this place?" I gestured to the wall and he pulled
his horse up and turned around again. It raised a lot of dust.

"Why you asking?" He looked a little suspicious.

"I dunno. Just curious. It doesn't look like the other places I've
been to. This wall . . ."

He scowled. "Damn wall." Then he shrugged. I thought that
was all he was going to say. Then he went on.

"These people, we look out for 'em, you hear? Maybe we don't
go for what they're doin'. But they got it rough, you know?" He
looked at me, expecting something. I never did get the knack of
talking to these laconic Westerners. I always felt that I was making
my sentences too long. They use a shorthand of grunts and shrugs
and omitted parts of speech, and I always felt like a dude when I
talked to them.

"Do they welcome guests?" I asked. "I thought I might see if
I could spend the night."

He shrugged again, and it was a whole different gesture.

"Maybe. They all deaf and blind, you know?" And that was all
the conversation he could take for the day. He made a clucking
sound and galloped away.

I continued down the wall until I came to a dirt road that wound
up the arroyo and entered the wall. There was a wooden gate, but
it stood open. I wondered why they took all the trouble with the
wall only to leave the gate like that. Then I noticed a circle of
narrow-gauge train tracks that came out of the gate, looped around
outside it, and rejoined itself. There was a small siding that ran
along the outer wall for a few yards.

I stood there a few moments. I don't know what entered into
my decision. I think I was a little tired of sleeping out, and I was
hungry for a home-cooked meal. The sun was getting closer to
the horizon. The land to the west looked like more of the same.

If the highway had been visible, I might have headed that way and hitched a ride. But I turned the other way and went through the gate.

I walked down the middle of the tracks. There was a wooden fence on each side of the road, built of horizontal planks, like a corral. Sheep grazed on one side of me. There was a Shetland sheepdog with them, and she raised her ears and followed me with her eyes as I passed, but did not come when I whistled.

It was about half a mile to the cluster of buildings ahead. There were four or five domes made of something translucent, like greenhouses, and several conventional square buildings. There were two windmills turning lazily in the breeze. There were several banks of solar water heaters. These are flat constructions of glass and wood, held off the ground so they can tilt to follow the sun. They were almost vertical now, intercepting the oblique rays of sunset. There were a few trees, what might have been an orchard.

About halfway there I passed under a wooden footbridge. It arched over the road, giving access from the east pasture to the west pasture. I wondered, What was wrong with a simple gate?

Then I saw something coming down the road in my direction. It was traveling on the tracks and it was very quiet. I stopped and waited.

It was a sort of converted mining engine, the sort that pulls loads of coal up from the bottom of shafts. It was battery-powered, and it had gotten quite close before I heard it. A small man was driving it. He was pulling a car behind him and singing as loud as he could with absolutely no sense of pitch.

He got closer and closer, moving about five miles per hour, one hand held out as if he was signaling a left turn. Suddenly I realized what was happening, as he was bearing down on me. He wasn't going to stop. He was counting fenceposts with his hand. I scrambled up the fence just in time. There wasn't more than six inches of clearance between the train and the fence on either side. His palm touched my leg as I squeezed close to the fence, and he stopped abruptly.

He leaped from the car and grabbed me and I thought I was in trouble. But he looked concerned, not angry, and felt me all over, trying to discover if I was hurt. I was embarrassed. Not from the examination; because I had been foolish. The Indian had said they were all deaf and blind but I guess I hadn't quite believed him.

He was flooded with relief when I managed to convey to him

that I was all right. With eloquent gestures he made me understand
that I was not to stay on the road. He indicated that I should climb
over the fence and continue through the fields. He repeated himself
several times to be sure I understood, then held on to me as I
climbed over to assure himself that I was out of the way. He
reached over the fence and held my shoulders, smiling at me.
He pointed to the road and shook his head, then pointed to the
buildings and nodded. He touched my head and smiled when I
nodded. He climbed back onto the engine and started up, all the
time nodding and pointing where he wanted me to go. Then he
was off again.

I debated what to do. Most of me said to turn around, go back to
the wall by way of the pasture and head back into the hills. These
people probably wouldn't want me around. I doubted that I'd be
able to talk to them, and they might even resent me. On the other
hand, I was fascinated, as who wouldn't be? I wanted to see how
they managed it. I still didn't believe that they were *all* deaf and
blind. It didn't seem possible.

The Sheltie was sniffing at my pants. I looked down at her and
she backed away, then daintily approached me as I held out my
open hand. She sniffed, then licked me. I patted her on the head,
and she hustled back to her sheep.

I turned toward the buildings.

The first order of business was money.

None of the students knew much about it from experience, but
the library was full of Braille books. They started reading.

One of the first things that became apparent was that when money
was mentioned, lawyers were not far away. The students wrote letters. From the replies, they selected a lawyer and retained him.

They were in a school in Pennsylvania at the time. The original
pupils of the special schools, five hundred in number, had been
narrowed down to about seventy as people left to live with relatives
or found other solutions to their special problems. Of those seventy,
some had places to go but didn't want to go there; others had few
alternatives. Their parents were either dead or not interested in
living with them. So the seventy had been gathered from the
schools around the country into this one, while ways to deal with
them were worked out. The authorities had plans, but the students
beat them to it.

Each of them had been entitled to a guaranteed annual income
since 1980. They had been under the care of the government, so

they had not received it. They sent their lawyer to court. He came back with a ruling that they could not collect. They appealed, and won. The money was paid retroactively, with interest, and came to a healthy sum. They thanked their lawyer and retained a real estate agent. Meanwhile, they read.

They read about communes in New Mexico, and instructed their agent to look for something out there. He made a deal for a tract to be leased in perpetuity from the Navaho nation. They read about the land, found that it would need a lot of water to be productive in the way they wanted it to be.

They divided into groups to research what they would need to be self-sufficient.

Water could be obtained by tapping into the canals that carried it from the reservoirs on the Rio Grande into the reclaimed land in the south. Federal money was available for the project through a labyrinthine scheme involving HEW, the Agriculture Department, and the Bureau of Indian Affairs. They ended up paying little for their pipeline.

The land was arid. It would need fertilizer to be of use in raising sheep without resorting to open range techniques. The cost of fertilizer could be subsidized through the Rural Resettlement Program. After that, planting clover would enrich the soil with all the nitrates they could want.

There were techniques available to farm ecologically, without worrying about fertilizers or pesticides. Everything was recycled. Essentially, you put sunlight and water into one end and harvested wool, fish, vegetables, apples, honey, and eggs at the other end. You used nothing but the land, and replaced even that as you recycled your waste products back into the soil. They were not interested in agri-business with huge combine harvesters and crop dusters. They didn't even want to turn a profit. They merely wanted sufficiency.

The details multiplied. Their leader, the one who had had the original idea and the drive to put it into action in the face of overwhelming obstacles, was a dynamo named Janet Reilly. Knowing nothing about the techniques generals and executives employ to achieve large objectives, she invented them herself and adapted them to the peculiar needs and limitations of her group. She assigned task forces to look into solutions of each aspect of their project: law, science, social planning, design, buying, logistics, construction. At any one time, she was the only person who knew everything about what was happening. She kept it all in her head, without notes of any kind.

It was in the area of social planning that she showed herself to be a visionary and not just a superb organizer. Her idea was not to make a place where they could lead a life that was a sightless, soundless imitation of their unafflicted peers. She wanted a whole new start, a way of living that was by and for the blind-deaf, a way of living that accepted no convention just because that was the way it had always been done. She examined every human cultural institution from marriage to indecent exposure to see how it related to her needs and the needs of her friends. She was aware of the peril of this approach, but was undeterred. Her Social Task Force read about every variant group that had ever tried to make it on its own anywhere, and brought her reports about how and why they had failed or succeeded. She filtered this information through her own experiences to see how it would work for her unusual group with its own set of needs and goals.

The details were endless. They hired an architect to put their ideas into Braille blueprints. Gradually the plans evolved. They spent more money. The construction began, supervised on the site by their architect, who by now was so fascinated by the scheme that she donated her services. It was an important break, for they needed someone there whom they could trust. There is only so much that can be accomplished at such a distance.

When things were ready for them to move, they ran into bureaucratic trouble. They had anticipated it, but it was a setback. Social agencies charged with overseeing their welfare doubted the wisdom of the project. When it became apparent that no amount of reasoning was going to stop it, wheels were set in motion that resulted in a restraining order, issued for their own protection, preventing them from leaving the school. They were twenty-one years old by then, all of them, but were judged mentally incompetent to manage their own affairs. A hearing was scheduled.

Luckily, they still had access to their lawyer. He also had become infected with the crazy vision, and put on a great battle for them. He succeeded in getting a ruling concerning the rights of institutionalized persons, later upheld by the Supreme Court, which eventually had severe repercussions in state and county hospitals. Realizing the trouble they were already in regarding the thousands of patients in inadequate facilities across the country, the agencies gave in.

By then, it was the spring of 1986, one year after their target date. Some of their fertilizer had washed away already for lack of erosion-preventing clover. It was getting late to start crops, and they were running short of money. Nevertheless, they moved to New Mexico and began the backbreaking job of getting everything started. There were fifty-five of them, with nine children aged three months to six years.

I don't know what I expected. I remember that everything was a surprise, either because it was so normal or because it was so different. None of my idiot surmises about what such a place might be like proved to be true. And of course I didn't know the history of the place; I learned that later, picked up in bits and pieces.

I was surprised to see lights in some of the buildings. The first thing I had assumed was that they would have no need of them. That's an example of something so normal that it surprised me.

As to the differences, the first thing that caught my attention was the fence around the rail line. I had a personal interest in it, having almost been injured by it. I struggled to understand, as I must if I was to stay even for a night.

The wood fences that enclosed the rails on their way to the gate continued up to a barn, where the rails looped back on themselves in the same way they did outside the wall. The entire line was enclosed by the fence. The only access was a loading platform by the barn, and the gate to the outside. It made sense. The only way a deaf-blind person could operate a conveyance like that would be with assurances that there was no one on the track. These people would *never* go on the tracks; there was no way they could be warned of an approaching train.

There were people moving around me in the twilight as I made my way into the group of buildings. They took no notice of me, as I had expected. They moved fast; some of them were actually running. I stood still, eyes searching all around me so no one would come crashing into me. I had to figure out how they kept from crashing into each other before I got bolder.

I bent to the ground and examined it. The light was getting bad, but I saw immediately that there were concrete sidewalks crisscrossing the area. Each of the walks was etched with a different sort of pattern in grooves that had been made before the stuff set–lines, waves, depressions, patches of rough and smooth. I quickly saw that the people who were in a hurry moved only on those walkways, and they were all barefoot. It was no trick to see that it was some sort of traffic pattern read with the feet. I stood up. I didn't need to know how it worked. It was sufficient to know what it was and stay off the paths.

The people were unremarkable. Some of them were not dressed, but I was used to that by now. They came in all shapes and sizes, but all seemed to be about the same age except for the children. Except for the fact that they did not stop and talk or even wave as they approached each other, I would never have guessed they were blind. I watched them come to intersections in the pathways—I didn't know how they knew they were there, but could think of several ways—and slow down as they crossed. It was a marvelous system.

I began to think of approaching someone. I had been there for almost half an hour, an intruder. I guess I had a false sense of these people's vulnerability; I felt like a burglar.

I walked along beside a woman for a minute. She was very purposeful in her eyes-ahead stride, or seemed to be. She sensed something, maybe my footsteps. She slowed a little, and I touched her on the shoulder, not knowing what else to do. She stopped instantly and turned toward me. Her eyes were open but vacant. Her hands were all over me, lightly touching my face, my chest, my hands, fingering my clothing. There was no doubt in my mind that she knew me for a stranger, probably from the first tap on the shoulder. But she smiled warmly at me, and hugged me. Her hands were very delicate and warm. That's funny, because they were calloused from hard work. But they felt sensitive.

She made me to understand—by pointing to the building, making eating motions with an imaginary spoon, and touching a number on her watch—that supper was served in an hour, and that I was invited. I nodded and smiled beneath her hands; she kissed me on the cheek and hurried off.

Well. It hadn't been so bad. I had worried about my ability to communicate. Later I found out she learned a great deal more about me than I had told.

I put off going into the mess hall or whatever it was. I strolled around in the gathering darkness looking at their layout. I saw the little Sheltie bringing the sheep back to the fold for the night. She herded them expertly through the open gate without any instructions, and one of the residents closed it and locked them in. The man bent and scratched the dog on the head and got his hand licked. Her chores done for the night, the dog hurried over to me and sniffed my pant leg. She followed me around the rest of the evening.

Everyone seemed so busy that I was surprised to see one woman sitting on a rail fence, doing nothing. I went over to her.

Closer, I saw that she was younger than I had thought. She was thirteen, I learned later. She wasn't wearing any clothes. I touched her on the shoulder, and she jumped down from the fence and went through the same routine as the other woman had, touching me all over with no reserve. She took my hand and I felt her fingers moving rapidly in my palm. I couldn't understand it, but knew what it was. I shrugged, and tried out other gestures to indicate that I didn't speak hand talk. She nodded, still feeling my face with her hands.

She asked me if I was staying to dinner. I assured her that I was. She asked me if I was from a university. And if you think that's easy to ask with only body movements, try it. But she was so graceful and supple in her movements, so deft at getting her meaning across. It was beautiful to watch her. It was speech and ballet at the same time.

I told her I wasn't from a university, and launched into an attempt to tell her a little about what I was doing and how I got there. She listened to me with her hands, scratching her head graphically when I failed to make my meanings clear. All the time the smile on her face got broader and broader, and she would laugh silently at my antics. All this while standing very close to me, touching me. At last she put her hands on her hips.

"I guess you need the practice," she said, "but if it's all the same to you, could we talk mouthtalk for now? You're cracking me up."

I jumped as if stung by a bee. The touching, while something I could ignore for a deaf-blind girl, suddenly seemed out of place. I stepped back a little, but her hands returned to me. She looked puzzled, then read the problem with her hands.

"I'm sorry," she said. "You thought I was deaf and blind. If I'd known I would have told you right off."

"I thought everyone here was."

"Just the parents. I'm one of the children. We all hear and see quite well. Don't be so nervous. If you can't stand touching, you're not going to like it here. Relax, I won't hurt you." And she kept her hands moving over me, mostly my face. I didn't understand it at the time, but it didn't seem sexual. Turned out I was wrong, but it wasn't blatant.

"You'll need me to show you the ropes," she said, and started for the domes. She held my hand and walked close to me. Her other hand kept moving to my face every time I talked.

"Number one, stay off the concrete paths. That's where— "

"I already figured that out."

"You did? How long have you been here?" Her hands searched my face with renewed interest. It was quite dark.

"Less than an hour. I was almost run over by your train."

She laughed, then apologized and said she knew it wasn't funny to me.

I told her it *was* funny to me now, though it hadn't been at the time. She said there was a warning sign on the gate, but I had been unlucky enough to come when the gate was open—they opened it by remote control before a train started up—and I hadn't seen it.

"What's your name?" I asked her, as we neared the soft yellow lights coming from the dining room.

Her hand worked reflexively in mine, then stopped. "Oh, I don't know. I *have* one; several, in fact. But they're in bodytalk. I'm . . . Pink. It translates as Pink, I guess."

There was a story behind it. She had been the first child born to the school students. They knew that babies were described as being pink, so they called her that. She felt pink to them. As we entered the hall, I could see that her name was visually inaccurate. One of her parents had been black. She was dark, with blue eyes and curly hair lighter than her skin. She had a broad nose, but small lips.

She didn't ask my name, so I didn't offer it. No one asked my name, in speech, the entire time I was there. They called me many things in bodytalk, and when the children called me it was "Hey, you!" They weren't big on spoken words.

The dining hall was in a rectangular building made of brick. It connected to one of the large domes. It was dimly lighted. I later learned that the lights were for me alone. The children didn't need them for anything but reading. I held Pink's hand, glad to have a guide. I kept my eyes and ears open.

"We're informal," Pink said. Her voice was embarrassingly loud in the large room. No one else was talking at all; there were just the sounds of movement and breathing. Several of the children looked up. "I won't introduce you around now. Just feel like part of the family. People will feel you later, and you can talk to them. You can take your clothes off here at the door."

I had no trouble with that. Everyone else was nude, and I could easily adjust to household customs by that time. You take your shoes off in Japan, you take your clothes off in Taos. What's the difference?

Well, quite a bit, actually. There was all the touching that went on. Everybody touched everybody else, as routinely as glancing. Everyone touched my face first, then went on with what seemed like total innocence to touch me everywhere else. As usual, it was not quite what it seemed. It was *not* innocent, and it was not the usual treatment they gave others in their group. They touched each other's genitals a lot *more* than they touched mine. They were holding back with me so I wouldn't be frightened. They were very polite with strangers.

There was a long, low table, with everyone sitting on the floor around it. Pink led me to it.

"See the bare strips on the floor? Stay out of them. Don't leave anything in them. That's where people walk. Don't *ever* move anything. Furniture, I mean. That has to be decided at full meetings, so we'll all know where everything is. Small things, too. If you pick up something, put it back exactly where you found it."

"I understand."

People were bringing bowls and platters of food from the adjoining kitchen. They set them on the table, and the diners began feeling them. They ate with their fingers, without plates, and they did it slowly and lovingly. They smelled things for a long time before they took a bite. Eating was very sensual to these people.

They were *terrific* cooks. I have never, before or since, eaten as well as I did at Keller. (That's my name for it, in speech, though their bodytalk name was something very like that. When I called it Keller, everyone knew what I was talking about.) They started off with good, fresh produce, something that's hard enough to find in the cities, and went at the cooking with artistry and imagination. It wasn't like any national style I've eaten. They improvised, and seldom cooked the same thing the same way twice.

I sat between Pink and the fellow who had almost run me down earlier. I stuffed myself disgracefully. It was too far removed from beef jerky and the organic dry cardboard I had been eating for me to be able to resist. I lingered over it, but still finished long before anyone else. I watched them as I sat back carefully and wondered if I'd be sick. (I wasn't, thank God.) They fed themselves and each other, sometimes getting up and going clear around the table to offer a choice morsel to a friend on the other side. I was fed in this way by all too many of them, and nearly popped until I learned a pidgin phrase in handtalk, saying I was full to the brim. I learned from Pink that a friendlier way to refuse was to offer something myself.

Eventually I had nothing to do but feed Pink and look at the others. I began to be more observant. I had thought they were eating in solitude, but soon saw that lively conversation was flowing around the table. Hands were busy, moving almost too fast to see. They were spelling into each other's palms, shoulders, legs, arms, bellies; any part of the body. I watched in amazement as a ripple of laughter spread like falling dominoes from one end of the table to the other as some witticism was passed along the line. It was *fast*. Looking carefully, I could see the thoughts moving, reaching one person, passed on while a reply went in the other direction and was in turn passed on, other replies originating all along the line and bouncing back and forth. They were a wave form, like water.

It was messy. Let's face it; eating with your fingers and talking with your hands is going to get you smeared with food. But no one minded. *I* certainly didn't. I was too busy feeling left out. Pink talked to me, but I knew I was finding out what it's like to be deaf. These people were friendly and seemed to like me, but could do nothing about it. We couldn't communicate.

Afterwards, we all trooped outside, except the cleanup crew, and took a shower beneath a set of faucets that gave out very cold water. I told Pink I'd like to help with the dishes, but she said I'd just be in the way. I couldn't do anything around Keller until I learned their very specific ways of doing things. She seemed to be assuming already that I'd be around that long.

Back into the building to dry off, which they did with their usual puppy dog friendliness, making a game and a gift of toweling each other, and then we went into the dome.

It was warm inside, warm and dark. Light entered from the passage to the dining room, but it wasn't enough to blot out the stars through the lattice of triangular panes overhead. It was almost like being out in the open.

Pink quickly pointed out the positional etiquette within the dome. It wasn't hard to follow, but I still tended to keep my arms and legs pulled in close so I wouldn't trip someone by sprawling into a walk space.

My misconceptions got me again. There was no sound but the soft whisper of flesh against flesh, so I thought I was in the middle of an orgy. I had been at them before, in other communes, and they looked pretty much like this. I quickly saw that I was wrong, and only later found out I had been right. In a sense.

What threw my evaluations out of whack was the simple fact that group conversation among these people *had* to look like an orgy. The much subtler observation that I made later was that with a hundred naked bodies sliding, rubbing, kissing, caressing, all at the same time, what was the point in making a distinction? There was no distinction.

I have to say that I use the noun "orgy" only to get across a general idea of many people in close contact. I don't like the word, it is too ripe with connotations. But I had these connotations myself at the time, so I was relieved to see that it was not an orgy. The ones I had been to had been tedious and impersonal, and I had hoped for better from these people.

Many wormed their way through the crush to get to me and meet me. Never more than one at a time; they were constantly aware of what was going on and were waiting their turn to talk to me. Naturally, I didn't know it then. Pink sat with me to interpret the hard thoughts. I eventually used her words less and less, getting into the spirit of tactile seeing and understanding. No one felt they really knew me until they had touched every part of my body, so there were hands on me all the time. I timidly did the same.

What with all the touching, I quickly got an erection, which embarrassed me quite a bit. I was berating myself for being unable to keep sexual responses out of it, for not being able to operate on the same intellectual plane I thought they were on, when I realized with some shock that the couple next to me was making love. They had been doing it for the last ten minutes, actually, and it had seemed such a natural part of what was happening that I had known it and not known it at the same time.

No sooner had I realized it than I suddenly wondered if I was right. *Were they?* It was very slow and the light was bad. But her legs were up, and he was on top of her, that much I was sure of. It was foolish of me, but I really had to know. I had to find out *what the hell I was in*. How could I give the proper social responses if I didn't know the situation?

I was very sensitive to polite behavior after my months at the various communes. I had become adept at saying prayers before supper in one place, chanting Hare Krishna at another, and going happily nudist at still another. It's called "when in Rome," and if you can't adapt to it you shouldn't go visiting. I would kneel to Mecca, burp after my meals, toast anything that was proposed, eat organic rice and compliment the cook; but to do it right, you have to know the customs. I had thought I knew them, but had changed my mind three times in as many minutes.

They *were* making love, in the sense that he was penetrating

her. They were also deeply involved with each other. Their hands
fluttered like butterflies all over each other, filled with meanings
I couldn't see or feel. But they were being touched by and were
touching many other people around them. They were talking to
all these people, even if the message was as simple as a pat on the
forehead or arm.

Pink noticed where my attention was. She was sort of wound
around me, without really doing anything I would have thought
of as provocative. I just couldn't *decide*. It seemed so innocent,
and yet it wasn't.

"That's (—) and (—)," she said, the parentheses indicating a
series of hand motions against my palm. I never learned a sound
word as a name for any of them but Pink, and I can't reproduce the
bodytalk names they had. Pink reached over, touched the woman
with her foot, and did some complicated business with her toes.
The woman smiled and grabbed Pink's foot, her fingers moving.

"(—) would like to talk with you later," Pink told me. "Right
after she's through talking to (—). You met her earlier, remember?
She says she likes your hands."

Now this is going to sound crazy, I know. It sounded pretty
crazy to me when I thought of it. It dawned on me with a sort
of revelation that her word for talk and mine were miles apart.
Talk, to her, meant a complex interchange involving all parts of
the body. She could read words or emotions in every twitch of my
muscles, like a lie detector. Sound, to her, was only a minor part of
communication. It was something she used to speak to outsiders.
Pink talked with her whole being.

I didn't have the half of it, even then, but it was enough to turn
my head entirely around in relation to these people. They talked
with their bodies. It wasn't all hands, as I'd thought. Any part of
the body in contact with any other was communication, sometimes
a very simple and basic sort—think of McLuhan's light bulb as
the basic medium of information—perhaps saying no more than
"I am here." But talk was talk, and if conversation evolved to the
point where you needed to talk to another with your genitals,
it was still a part of the conversation. What I wanted to know
was *what were they saying?* I knew, even at that dim moment
of realization, that it was much more than I could grasp. Sure,
you're saying. You know about talking to your lover with your
body as you make love. That's not such a new idea. Of course
it isn't, but think how wonderful that talk is even when you're
not primarily tactile-oriented. Can you carry the thought from

the right circumstances. It all had to do with social context. They were starting from a blank slate, with no models to follow.

By the end of the second year they had their context. They continually modified it, but the basic pattern was set. They knew themselves and what they were as they had never been able to do at the school. They defined themselves in their own terms.

I spent my first day at Keller in school. It was the obvious and necessary step. I had to learn handtalk.

Pink was kind and very patient. I learned the basic alphabet and practiced hard at it. By the afternoon she was refusing to talk to me, forcing me to speak with my hands. She would speak only when pressed hard, and eventually not at all. I scarcely spoke a single word after the third day.

This is not to say that I was suddenly fluent. Not at all. At the end of the first day I knew the alphabet and could laboriously make myself understood. I was not so good at reading words spelled into my own palm. For a long time I had to look at the hand to see what was spelled. But like any language, eventually you think in it. I speak fluent French, and I can recall my amazement when I finally reached the point where I wasn't translating my thoughts before I spoke. I reached it at Keller in about two weeks.

I remember one of the last things I asked Pink in speech. It was something that was worrying me.

"Pink, am I welcome here?"

"You've been here three days. Do you feel rejected?"

"No, it's not that. I guess I just need to hear your policy about outsiders. How *long* am I welcome?"

She wrinkled her brow. It was evidently a new question.

"Well, practically speaking, until a majority of us decide we want you to go. But that's never happened. No one's stayed here much longer than a few days. We've never had to evolve a policy about what to do, for instance, if someone who sees and hears wants to join us. No one has, so far, but I guess it could happen. My guess is that they wouldn't accept it. They're very independent and jealous of their freedom, though you might not have noticed it. I don't think you could ever be one of them. But as long as you're willing to think of yourself as a guest, you could probably stay for twenty years."

"You said 'they.' Don't you include yourself in the group?"

For the first time she looked a little uneasy. I wish I had been better at reading body language at the time. I think my hands could have told me volumes about what she was thinking.

"Sure," she said. "The children are part of the group. We like it. I sure wouldn't want to be anywhere else, from what I know of the outside."

"I don't blame you." There were things left unsaid here, but I didn't know enough to ask the right questions. "But it's never a problem, being able to see when none of your parents can? They don't . . . resent you in any way?"

This time she laughed. "Oh, no. Never that. They're much too independent for that. You've seen it. They don't *need* us for anything they can't do themselves. We're part of the family. We do exactly the same things they do. And it really doesn't matter. Sight, I mean. Hearing, either. Just look around you. Do I have any special advantages because I can see where I'm going?"

I had to admit that she didn't. But there was still the hint of something she wasn't saying to me.

"I know what's bothering you. About staying here." She had to draw me back to my original question; I had been wandering.

"What's that?"

"You don't feel a part of the daily life. You're not doing your share of the chores. You're very conscientious and you want to do your part. I can tell."

She read me right, as usual, and I admitted it.

"And you won't be able to until you can talk to everybody. So let's get back to your lessons. Your fingers are still very sloppy."

There was a lot of work to be done. The first thing I had to learn was to slow down. They were slow and methodical workers, made few mistakes, and didn't care if a job took all day so long as it was done well. When I was working by myself I didn't have to worry about it: sweeping, picking apples, weeding in the gardens. But when I was on a job that required teamwork I had to learn a whole new pace. Eyesight enables a person to do many aspects of a job at once with a few quick glances. A blind person will take each aspect of the job in turn if the job is spread out. Everything has to be verified by touch. At a bench job, though, they could be much faster than I. They could make me feel as though I was working with my toes instead of fingers.

I never suggested that I could make anything quicker by virtue of my sight or hearing. They quite rightly would have told me to mind my own business. Accepting sighted help was the first step to dependence, and after all, they would still be here with the same jobs to do after I was gone.

And that got me to thinking about the children again. I began to be positive that there was an undercurrent of resentment, maybe unconscious, between the parents and children. It was obvious that there was a great deal of love between them, but how could the children fail to resent the rejection of their talent? So my reasoning went, anyway.

I quickly fit myself into the routine. I was treated no better or worse than anyone else, which gratified me. Though I would never become part of the group, even if I should desire it, there was absolutely no indication that I was anything but a full member. That's just how they treated guests: as they would one of their own number.

Life was fulfilling out there in a way it has never been in the cities. It wasn't unique to Keller, this pastoral peace, but the people there had it in generous helpings. The earth beneath your bare feet is something you can never feel in a city park.

Daily life was busy and satisfying. There were chickens and hogs to feed, bees and sheep to care for, fish to harvest, and cows to milk. Everybody worked: men, women, and children. It all seemed to fit together without any apparent effort. Everybody seemed to know what to do when it needed doing. You could think of it as a well-oiled machine, but I never liked that metaphor, especially for people. I thought of it as an organism. Any social group is, but this one *worked*. Most of the other communes I'd visited had glaring flaws. Things would not get done because everyone was too stoned or couldn't be bothered or didn't see the necessity of doing it in the first place. That sort of ignorance leads to typhus and soil erosion and people freezing to death and invasions of social workers who take your children away. I'd seen it happen.

Not here. They had a good picture of the world as it is, not the rosy misconceptions so many other utopians labor under. They did the jobs that needed doing.

I could never detail all the nuts and bolts (there's that machine metaphor again) of how the place worked. The fish-cycle ponds alone were complicated enough to overawe me. I killed a spider in one of the greenhouses, then found out it had been put there to eat a specific set of plant predators. Same for the frogs. There were insects in the water to kill other insects; it got to a point where I was afraid to swat a mayfly without prior okay.

As the days went by I was told some of the history of the

place. Mistakes had been made, though surprisingly few. One had been in the area of defense. They had made no provision for it at first, not knowing much about the brutality and random violence that reaches even to the out-of-the-way corners. Guns were the logical and preferred choice out here, but were beyond their capabilities.

One night a carload of men who had had too much to drink showed up. They had heard of the place in town. They stayed for two days, cutting the phone lines and raping many of the women.

The people discussed all the options after the invasion was over, and settled on the organic one. They bought five German shepherds. Not the psychotic wretches that are marketed under the description of "attack dogs," but specially trained ones from a firm recommended by the Albuquerque police. They were trained as both Seeing-Eye and police dogs. They were perfectly harmless until an outsider showed overt aggression, then they were trained, not to disarm, but to go for the throat.

It worked, like most of their solutions. The second invasion resulted in two dead and three badly injured, all on the other side. As a backup in case of a concerted attack, they hired an ex-marine to teach them the fundamentals of close-in dirty fighting. These were not dewy-eyed flower children.

There were three superb meals a day. And there was leisure time, too. It was not all work. There was time to take a friend out and sit in the grass under a tree, usually around sunset, just before the big dinner. There was time for someone to stop working for a few minutes, to share some special treasure. I remember being taken by the hand by one woman—whom I must call Tall-one-with-the-green-eyes—to a spot where mushrooms were growing in the cool crawl space beneath the barn. We wriggled under until our faces were buried in the patch, picked a few, and smelled them. She showed me how to smell. I would have thought a few weeks before that we had ruined their beauty, but after all it was only visual. I was already beginning to discount that sense, which is so removed from the essence of an object. She showed me that they were still beautiful to touch and smell after we had apparently destroyed them. Then she was off to the kitchen with the pick of the bunch in her apron. They tasted all the better that night.

And a man—I will call him Baldy—who brought me a plank he and one of the women had been planing in the woodshop. I touched its smoothness and smelled it and agreed with him how good it was.

And after the evening meal, the Together.

During my third week there I had an indication of my status with the group. It was the first real test of whether I meant anything to them. Anything special, I mean. I wanted to see them as my friends, and I suppose I was a little upset to think that just anyone who wandered in here would be treated the way I was. It was childish and unfair to them, and I wasn't even aware of the discontent until later.

I had been hauling water in a bucket into the field where a seedling tree was being planted. There was a hose for that purpose, but it was in use on the other side of the village. This tree was not in reach of the automatic sprinklers and it was drying out. I had been carrying water to it until another solution was found.

It was hot, around noon. I got the water from a standing spigot near the forge. I set the bucket down on the ground behind me and leaned my head into the flow of water. I was wearing a shirt made of cotton, unbuttoned in the front. The water felt good running through my hair and soaking into the shirt. I let it go on for almost a minute.

There was a crash behind me and I bumped my head when I raised it up too quickly under the faucet. I turned and saw a woman sprawled on her face in the dust. She was turning over slowly, holding her knee. I realized with a sinking feeling that she had tripped over the bucket I had carelessly left on the concrete express lane. Think of it: ambling along on ground that you trust to be free of all obstruction, suddenly you're sitting on the ground. Their system would only work with trust, and it had to be total; everybody had to be responsible all the time. I had been accepted into that trust and I had blown it. I felt sick.

She had a nasty scrape on her left knee that was oozing blood. She felt it with her hands, sitting there on the ground, and she began to howl. It was weird, painful. Tears came from her eyes, then she pounded her fists on the ground, going "Hunnnh, hunnnh, *hunnnh!*" with each blow. She was angry, and she had every right to be.

She found the pail as I hesitantly reached out for her. She grabbed my hand and followed it up to my face. She felt my face, crying all the time, then wiped her nose and got up. She started off for one of the buildings. She limped slightly.

I sat down and felt miserable. I didn't know what to do.

One of the men came out to get me. It was Big Man. I called him that because he was the tallest person at Keller. He wasn't any sort of policeman, I found out later; he was just the first one the injured woman had met. He took my hand and felt my face. I saw tears start when he felt the emotions there. He asked me to come inside with him.

An impromptu panel had been convened. Call it a jury. It was made up of anyone who was handy, including a few children. There were ten or twelve of them. Everyone looked very sad. The woman I had hurt was there, being consoled by three or four people. I'll call her Scar, for the prominent mark on her upper arm.

Everybody kept telling me—in handtalk, you understand—how sorry they were for me. They petted and stroked me, trying to draw some of the misery away.

Pink came racing in. She had been sent for to act as a translator if needed. Since this was a formal proceeding it was necessary that they be sure I understood everything that happened. She went to Scar and cried with her for a bit, then came to me and embraced me fiercely, telling me with her hands how sorry she was that this had happened.

I was already figuratively packing my bags. Nothing seemed to be left but the formality of expelling me.

Then we all sat together on the floor. We were close, touching on all sides. The hearing began.

Most of it was in handtalk, with Pink throwing in a few words here and there. I seldom knew who said what, but that was appropriate. It was the group speaking as one. No statement reached me without already having become a consensus.

"You are accused of having violated the rules," said the group, "and of having been the cause of an injury to (the one I called Scar). Do you dispute this? Is there any fact that we should know?"

"No," I told them. "I was responsible. It was my carelessness."

"We understand. We sympathize with you in your remorse, which is evident to all of us. But carelessness is a violation. Do you understand this? This is the offense for which you are (—)." It was a set of signals in shorthand.

"What was that?" I asked Pink.

"Uh . . . 'brought before us'? 'Standing trial'?" She shrugged, not happy with either interpretation.

"Yes. I understand."

"The facts not being in question, it is agreed that you are guilty."
("'Responsible,'" Pink whispered in my ear.) "Withdraw from us a
moment while we come to a decision."

I got up and stood by the wall, not wanting to look at them as
the debate went back and forth through the joined hands. There
was a burning lump in my throat that I could not swallow. Then
I was asked to rejoin the circle.

"The penalty for your offense is set by custom. If it were not so,
we would wish we could rule otherwise. You now have the choice of
accepting the punishment designated and having the offense wiped
away, or of refusing our jurisdiction and withdrawing your body
from our land. What is your choice?"

I had Pink repeat this to me, because it was so important that
I know what was being offered. When I was sure I had read it
right, I accepted their punishment without hesitation. I was very
grateful to have been given an alternative.

"Very well. You have elected to be treated as we would treat
one of our own who had done the same act. Come to us."

Everyone drew in closer. I was not told what was going to
happen. I was drawn in and nudged gently from all directions.

Scar was sitting with her legs crossed more or less in the center
of the group. She was crying again, and so was I, I think. It's
hard to remember. I ended up face down across her lap. She
spanked me.

I never once thought of it as improbable or strange. It flowed
naturally out of the situation. Everyone was holding on to me and
caressing me, spelling assurances into my palms and legs and neck
and cheeks. We were all crying. It was a difficult thing that had
to be faced by the whole group. Others drifted in and joined us.
I understood that this punishment came from everyone there, but
only the offended person, Scar, did the actual spanking. That was
one of the ways I had wronged her, beyond the fact of giving her
a scraped knee. I had laid on her the obligation of disciplining me
and that was why she had sobbed so loudly, not from the pain
of her injury, but from the pain of knowing she would have to
hurt me.

Pink later told me that Scar had been the staunchest advocate
of giving me the option to stay. Some had wanted to expel me
outright, but she paid me the compliment of thinking I was a
good enough person to be worth putting herself and me through
the ordeal. If you can't understand that, you haven't grasped the
feeling of community I felt among these people.

It went on for a long time. It was very painful, but not cruel. Nor was it primarily humiliating. There was some of that, of course. But it was essentially a practical lesson taught in the most direct terms. Each of them had undergone it during the first months, but none recently. You *learned* from it, believe me.

I did a lot of thinking about it afterward. I tried to think of what else they might have done. Spanking grown people is really unheard of, you know, though that didn't occur to me until long after it had happened. It seemed so natural when it was going on that the thought couldn't even enter my mind that this was a weird situation to be in.

They did something like this with the children, but not as long or as hard. Responsibility was lighter for the younger ones. The adults were willing to put up with an occasional bruise or scraped knee while the children learned.

But when you reached what they thought of as adulthood—which was whenever a majority of the adults thought you had or when you assumed the privilege yourself—that's when the spanking really got serious.

They had a harsher punishment, reserved for repeated or malicious offenses. They had not had to invoke it often. It consisted of being sent to Coventry. No one would touch you for a specified period of time. By the time I heard of it, it sounded like a very tough penalty. I didn't need it explained to me.

I don't know how to explain it, but the spanking was administered in such a loving way that I didn't feel violated. *This hurts me as much as it hurts you. I'm doing this for your own good. I love you, that's why I'm spanking you.* They made me understand those old cliches by their actions.

When it was over, we all cried together. But it soon turned to happiness. I embraced Scar and we told each other how sorry we were that it had happened. We talked to each other—made love if you like—and I kissed her knee and helped her dress it.

We spent the rest of the day together, easing the pain.

As I became more fluent in handtalk, "the scales fell from my eyes." Daily, I would discover a new layer of meaning that had eluded me before; it was like peeling the skin of an onion to find a new skin beneath it. Each time I thought I was at the core, only to find that there was another layer I could not yet see.

I had thought that learning handtalk was the key to communication with them. Not so. Handtalk was baby talk. For a long time I was a baby who could not even say goo-goo clearly. Imagine my surprise when, having learned to say it, I found that there were syntax, conjunctions, parts of speech, nouns, verbs, tense, agreement, and the subjunctive mood. I was wading in a tide pool at the edge of the Pacific Ocean.

By handtalk I mean the International Manual Alphabet. Anyone can learn it in a few hours or days. But when you talk to someone in speech, do you spell each word? Do you read each letter as you read this? No, you grasp words as entities, hear groups of sounds and see groups of letters as a gestalt full of meaning.

Everyone at Keller had an absorbing interest in language. They each knew several languages—spoken language—and could read and spell them fluently.

While still children they had understood the fact that handtalk was a way for blind-deaf people to talk to *outsiders*. Among themselves it was much too cumbersome. It was like Morse Code: useful when you're limited to on-off modes of information transmission, but not the preferred mode. Their ways of speaking to each other were much closer to our type of written or verbal communication, and—dare I say it?—better.

I discovered this slowly, first by seeing that though I could spell rapidly with my hands, it took *much* longer for me to say something than it took anyone else. It could not be explained by differences in dexterity. So I asked to be taught their shorthand speech. I plunged in, this time taught by everyone, not just Pink.

It was hard. They could say any word in any language with no more than two moving hand positions. I knew this was a project for years, not days. You learn the alphabet and you have all the tools you need to spell any word that exists. That's the great advantage in having your written and spoken speech based on the same set of symbols. Shorthand was not like that at all. It partook of none of the linearity or commonality of handtalk; it was not code for English or any other language; it did not share construction or vocabulary with any other language. It was wholly constructed by the Kellerites according to their needs. Each word was something I had to learn and memorize separately from the handtalk spelling.

For months I sat in the Togethers after dinner saying things like "Me love Scar much much well," while waves of conversation ebbed and flowed and circled around me, touching me only at the edges. But I kept at it, and the children were endlessly patient with me. I improved gradually. Understand that the rest of the conversations

I will relate took place in either handtalk or shorthand, limited to
various degrees by my fluency. I did not speak nor was I spoken
to orally from the day of my punishment.

I was having a lesson in bodytalk from Pink. Yes, we were
making love. It had taken me a few weeks to see that she was a
sexual being, that her caresses, which I had persisted in seeing as
innocent—as I had defined it at the time—both were and weren't
innocent. She understood it as perfectly natural that the result of
her talking to my penis with her hands might be another sort of
conversation. Though still in the middle flush of puberty, she
was regarded by all as an adult and I accepted her as such. It
was cultural conditioning that had blinded me to what she was
saying.

So we talked a lot. With her, I understood the words and music of
the body better than with anyone else. She sang a very uninhibited
song with her hips and hands, free of guilt, open and fresh with
discovery in every note she touched.

"You haven't told me much about yourself," she said. "What
did you do on the outside?" I don't want to give the impression
that this speech was in sentences, as I have presented it. We were
bodytalking, sweating and smelling each other. The message came
through from hands, feet, mouth.

I got as far as the sign for pronoun, first person singular, and
was stopped.

How could I tell her of my life in Chicago? Should I speak
of my early ambition to be a writer, and how that didn't work
out? And why hadn't it? Lack of talent, or lack of drive? I could
tell her about my profession, which was meaningless shuffling
of papers when you got down to it, useless to anything but
the Gross National Product. I could talk of the economic ups
and downs that had brought me to Keller when nothing else
could dislodge me from my easy sliding through life. Or the
loneliness of being forty-seven years old and never having found
someone worth loving, never having been loved in return. Of
being a permanently displaced person in a stainless-steel society.
One-night stands, drinking binges, nine-to-five, Chicago Transit
Authority, dark movie houses, football games on television, sleeping pills, the John Hancock Tower where the windows won't
open so you can't breathe the smog or jump out. That was me,
wasn't it?

"I see," she said.

"I travel around," I said, and suddenly realized that it was the truth.

"I see," she repeated. It was a different sign for the same thing. Context was everything. She had heard and understood both parts of me, knew one to be what I had been, the other to be what I hoped I was.

She lay on top of me, one hand lightly on my face to catch the quick interplay of emotions as I thought about my life for the first time in years. And she laughed and nipped my ear playfully when my face told her that for the first time I could remember, I was happy about it. Not just telling myself I was happy, but truly happy. You cannot lie in bodytalk any more than your sweat glands can lie to a polygraph.

I noticed that the room was unusually empty. Asking around in my fumbling way, I learned that only the children were there.

"Where is everybody?" I asked.

"They are all out ***," she said. It was like that: three sharp slaps on the chest with the fingers spread. Along with the finger configuration for "verb form, gerund," it meant that they were all out ***ing. Needless to say, it didn't tell me much.

What did tell me something was her bodytalk as she said it. I read her better than I ever had. She was upset and sad. Her body said something like "Why can't I join them? Why can't I (smell-taste-touch-hear-see) *sense* with them?" That is exactly what she said. Again, I didn't trust my understanding enough to accept that interpretation. I was still trying to force my conceptions on the things I experienced there. I was determined that she and the other children be resentful of their parents in some way, because I was sure they had to be. They *must* feel superior in some way, they *must* feel held back.

I found the adults, after a short search of the area, out in the north pasture. All the parents, none of the children. They were standing in a group with no apparent pattern. It wasn't a circle, but it was almost round. If there was any organization, it was in the fact that everybody was about the same distance from everybody else.

The German shepherds and the Sheltie were out there, sitting on the cool grass facing the group of people. Their ears were perked up, but they were not moving.

I started to go up to the people. I stopped when I became aware of the concentration. They were touching, but their hands were not moving. The silence of seeing all those permanently moving people standing that still was deafening to me.

I watched them for at least an hour. I sat with the dogs and scratched them behind the ears. They did that chop-licking thing that dogs do when they appreciate it, but their full attention was on the group.

It gradually dawned on me that the group was moving. It was very slow, just a step here and another there, over many minutes. It was expanding in such a way that the distance between any of the individuals was the same. Like the expanding universe, where all galaxies move away from all others. Their arms were extended now; they were touching only with fingertips, in a crystal lattice arrangement.

Finally they were not touching at all. I saw their fingers straining to cover distances that were too far to bridge. And still they expanded equilaterally. One of the shepherds began to whimper a little. I felt the hair on the back of my neck stand up. Chilly out here, I thought.

I closed my eyes, suddenly sleepy.

I opened them, shocked. Then I forced them shut. Crickets were chirping in the grass around me.

There was something in the darkness behind my eyeballs. I felt that if I could turn my eyes around I would see it easily, but it eluded me in a way that made peripheral vision seem like reading headlines. If there was ever anything impossible to pin down, much less describe, that was it. It tickled at me for a while as the dogs whimpered louder, but I could make nothing of it. The best analogy I could think of was the sensation a blind person might feel from the sun on a cloudy day.

I opened my eyes again.

Pink was standing there beside me. Her eyes were screwed shut, and she was covering her ears with her hands. Her mouth was open and working silently. Behind her were several of the older children. They were all doing the same thing.

Some quality of the night changed. The people in the group were about a foot away from each other now, and suddenly the pattern broke. They all swayed for a moment, then laughed in that eerie, unselfconscious noise deaf people use for laughter. They fell in the grass and held their bellies, rolled over and over and roared.

Pink was laughing, too. To my surprise, so was I. I laughed until my face and sides were hurting, like I remembered doing sometimes when I'd smoked grass.

And that was ***ing.

*     *     *

I can see that I've only given a surface view of Keller. And there are some things I should deal with, lest I foster an erroneous view.

Clothing, for instance. Most of them wore something most of the time. Pink was the only one who seemed temperamentally opposed to clothes. She never wore anything.

No one ever wore anything I'd call a pair of pants. Clothes were loose: robes, shirts, dresses, scarves and such. Lots of men wore things that would be called women's clothes. They were simply more comfortable.

Much of it was ragged. It tended to be made of silk or velvet or something else that felt good. The stereotyped Kellerite would be wearing a Japanese silk robe, hand-embroidered with dragons, with many gaping holes and loose threads and tea and tomato stains all over it while she sloshed through the pigpen with a bucket of slop. Wash it at the end of the day and don't worry about the colors running.

I also don't seem to have mentioned homosexuality. You can mark it down to my early conditioning that my two deepest relationships at Keller were with women: Pink and Scar. I haven't said anything about it simply because I don't know how to present it. I talked to men and women equally, on the same terms. I had surprisingly little trouble being affectionate with the men.

I could not think of the Kellerites as bisexual, though clinically they were. It was much deeper than that. They could not even recognize a concept as poisonous as a homosexuality taboo. It was one of the first things they learned. If you distinguish homosexuality from heterosexuality you are cutting yourself off from communication—*full* communication—with half the human race. They were pansexual; they could not separate sex from the rest of their lives. They didn't even have a word in shorthand that could translate directly into English as sex. They had words for male and female in infinite variation, and words for degrees and varieties of physical experience that would be impossible to express in English, but all those words included other parts of the world of experience also; none of them walled off what we call *sex* into its own discrete cubbyhole.

There's another question I haven't answered. It needs answering, because I wondered about it myself when I first arrived. It concerns the necessity for the commune in the first place. Did it really have to be like this? Would they have been better off adjusting themselves to our ways of living?

All was not a peaceful idyll. I've already spoken of the invasion and rape. It could happen again, especially if the roving gangs that operate around the cities start to really rove. A touring group of motorcyclists could wipe them out in a night.

There were also continuing legal hassles. About once a year the social workers descended on Keller and tried to take their children away. They had been accused of everything possible, from child abuse to contributing to delinquency. It hadn't worked so far, but it might someday.

And after all, there are sophisticated devices on the market that allow a blind and deaf person to see and hear a little. They might have been helped by some of those.

I met a blind-deaf woman living in Berkeley once. I'll vote for Keller.

As to those machines . . .

In the library at Keller there is a seeing machine. It uses a television camera and a computer to vibrate a closely set series of metal pins. Using it, you can feel a moving picture of whatever the camera is pointed at. It's small and light, made to be carried with the pin-pricker touching your back. It cost about thirty-five thousand dollars.

I found it in the corner of the library. I ran my finger over it and left a gleaming streak behind as the thick dust came away.

Other people came and went, and I stayed on.

Keller didn't get as many visitors as the other places I had been. It was out of the way.

One man showed up at noon, looked around, and left without a word.

Two girls, sixteen-year-old runaways from California, showed up one night. They undressed for dinner and were shocked when they found out I could see. Pink scared the hell out of them. Those poor kids had a lot of living to do before they approached Pink's level of sophistication. But then Pink might have been uneasy in California. They left the next day, unsure if they had been to an orgy or not. All that touching and no getting down to business, very strange.

There was a nice couple from Santa Fe who acted as a sort of liaison between Keller and their lawyer. They had a nine-year-old boy who chattered endlessly in handtalk to the other kids. They came up about every other week and stayed a few days, soaking up sunshine and participating in the Together every night. They spoke halting shorthand and did me the courtesy of not speaking to me in speech.

Some of the Indians came around at odd intervals. Their behavior was almost aggressively chauvinistic. They stayed dressed at all times in their Levis and boots. But it was evident that they had a respect for the people, though they thought them strange. They had business dealings with the commune. It was the Navahos who trucked away the produce that was taken to the gate every day, sold it, and took a percentage. They would sit and powwow in sign language spelled into hands. Pink said they were scrupulously honest in their dealings.

And about once a week all the parents went out in the field and ***ed.

I got better and better at shorthand and bodytalk. I had been breezing along for about five months and winter was in the offing. I had not examined my desires as yet, not really thought about what it was I wanted to do with the rest of my life. I guess the habit of letting myself drift was too ingrained. I was there, and constitutionally unable to decide whether to go or to face up to the problem if I wanted to stay for a long, long time.

Then I got a push.

For a long time I thought it had something to do with the economic situation outside. They were aware of the outside world at Keller. They knew that isolation and ignoring problems that could easily be dismissed as not relevant to them was a dangerous course, so they subscribed to the Braille *New York Times* and most of them read it. They had a television set that got plugged in about once a month. The kids would watch it and translate for their parents.

So I was aware that the non-depression was moving slowly into a more normal inflationary spiral. Jobs were opening up, money was flowing again. When I found myself on the outside again shortly afterward, I thought that was the reason.

The real reason was more complex. It had to do with peeling off the onion layer of shorthand and discovering another layer beneath it.

I had learned handtalk in a few easy lessons. Then I became aware of shorthand and bodytalk, and of how much harder they would be to learn. Through five months of constant immersion, which is the only way to learn a language, I had attained the equivalent level of a five- or six-year-old in shorthand. I knew I could master it, given time. Bodytalk was another matter. You couldn't measure progress as easily in bodytalk. It was a variable and highly interpersonal language that evolved according to the person, the time, the mood. But I was learning.

Then I became aware of Touch. That's the best I can describe it in a single, unforced English noun. What *they* called this fourth-stage language varied from day to day, as I will try to explain.

I first became aware of it when I tried to meet Janet Reilly. I now knew the history of Keller, and she figured very prominently in all the stories. I knew everyone at Keller, and I could find her nowhere. I knew everyone by names like Scar, and She-with-the-missing-front-tooth, and Man-with-wiry-hair. These were shorthand names that I had given them myself, and they all accepted them without question. They had abolished their outside names within the commune. They meant nothing to them; they told nothing and described nothing.

At first I assumed that it was my imperfect command of shorthand that made me unable to clearly ask the right question about Janet Reilly. Then I saw that they were not telling me on purpose. I saw why, and I approved, and thought no more about it. The name Janet Reilly described what she had been *on the outside*, and one of her conditions for pushing the whole thing through in the first place had been that she be no one special on the inside. She melted into the group and disappeared. She didn't want to be found. All right.

But in the course of pursuing the question I became aware that each of the members of the commune had no specific name at all. That is, Pink, for instance, had no less than one hundred and fifteen names, one from each of the commune members. Each was a contextual name that told the story of Pink's relationship to a particular person. My simple names, based on physical descriptions, were accepted as the names a child would apply to people. The children had not yet learned to go beneath the outer layers and use names that told of themselves, their lives, and their relationships to others.

What is even more confusing, the names evolved from day to day. It was my first glimpse of Touch, and it frightened me. It was a question of permutations. Just the first simple expansion of the problem meant there were no less than thirteen thousand names in use, and they wouldn't stay still so I could memorize them. If Pink spoke to me of Baldy, for instance, she would use her Touch name for him, modified by the fact that she was speaking to me and not Short-chubby-man.

Then the depths of what I had been missing opened beneath me and I was suddenly breathless with fear of heights.

Touch was what they spoke to each other. It was an incredible blend of all three other modes I had learned, and the essence of it was that it never stayed the same. I could listen to them speak to me in shorthand, which was the real basis for Touch, and be aware of the currents of Touch flowing just beneath the surface.

It was a language of inventing languages. Everyone spoke their own dialect because everyone spoke with a different instrument: a different body and set of life experiences. It was modified by everything. *It would not stand still.*

They would sit at the Together and invent an entire body of Touch responses in a night; idiomatic, personal, totally naked in its honesty. And they used it only as a building block for the next night's language.

I didn't know if I wanted to be that naked. I had looked into myself a little recently and had not been satisfied with what I found. The realization that every one of them knew more about it than I, because my honest body had told what my frightened mind had not wanted to reveal, was shattering. I was naked under a spotlight in Carnegie Hall, and all the no-pants nightmares I had ever had came out to haunt me. The fact that they all loved me with all my warts was suddenly not enough. I wanted to curl up in a dark closet with my ingrown ego and let it fester.

I might have come through this fear. Pink was certainly trying to help me. She told me that it would only hurt for a while, that I would quickly adjust to living my life with my darkest emotions written in fire across my forehead. She said Touch was not as hard as it looked at first, either. Once I learned shorthand and bodytalk, Touch would flow naturally from it like sap rising in a tree. It would be unavoidable, something that would happen to me without much effort at all.

I almost believed her. But she betrayed herself. No, no, no. Not that, but the things in her concerning \*\*\*ing convinced me that if I went through this I would only bang my head hard against the next step up the ladder.
        \*\*\*

I had a little better definition now. Not one that I can easily translate into English, and even that attempt will only convey my hazy concept of what it was.

"It is the mode of touching without touching," Pink said, her body going like crazy in an attempt to reach me with her own imperfect concept of what it was, handicapped by my illiteracy. Her body denied the truth of her shorthand definition, and at the same time admitted to me that she did not know what it was herself.

"It is the gift whereby one can expand oneself from the eternal quiet and dark into something else." And again her body denied it. She beat on the floor in exasperation.

"It is an attribute of being in the quiet and dark all the time, touching others. All I know for sure is that vision and hearing preclude it or obscure it. I can make it as quiet and dark as I possibly can and be aware of the edges of it, but the visual orientation of the mind persists. That door is closed to me, and to all the children."

Her verb "to touch" in the first part of that was a Touch amalgam, one that reached back into her memories of me and what I had told her of my experiences. It implied and called up the smell and feel of broken mushrooms in soft earth under the barn with Tall-one-with-green-eyes, she who taught me to feel the essence of an object. It also contained references to our bodytalking while I was penetrating into the dark and wet of her, and her running account to me of what it was like to receive me into herself. This was all one word.

I brooded on that for a long time. What was the point of suffering through the nakedness of Touch, only to reach the level of frustrated blindness enjoyed by Pink?

What was it that kept pushing me away from the one place in my life where I had been happiest?

One thing was the realization, quite late in coming, that can be summed up as "What the hell am I *doing* here?" The question that should have answered that question was "What the hell would I do if I *left*?"

I was the only visitor, the only one in *seven years* to stay at Keller for longer than a few days. I brooded on that. I was not strong enough or confident enough in my opinion of myself to see it as anything but a flaw in *me*, not in those others. I was obviously too easily satisfied, too complacent to see the flaws that those others had seen.

It didn't have to be flaws in the people of Keller, or in their system. No, I loved and respected them too much to think that. What they had going certainly came as near as anyone ever has in this imperfect world to a sane, rational way for people to exist without warfare and with a minimum of politics. In the end, those two old dinosaurs are the only ways humans have yet discovered to be social animals. Yes, I do see war as a way of living with another; by imposing your will on another in terms so unmistakable that the opponent has to either knuckle under to you, die, or beat your brains out. And if that's a solution to anything, I'd rather live without solutions. Politics is not much better. The only thing going for it is that it occasionally succeeds in substituting talk for fists.

Keller *was* an organism. It was a new way of relating, and it seemed to work. I'm not pushing it as a solution for the world's problems. It's possible that it could only work for a group with a common self-interest as binding and rare as deafness and blindness. I can't think of another group whose needs are so interdependent.

The cells of the organism cooperated beautifully. The organism was strong, flourishing, and possessed of all the attributes I've ever heard used in defining life except the ability to reproduce. That might have been its fatal flaw, if any. I certainly saw the seeds of something developing in the children.

The strength of the organism was communication. There's no way around it. Without the elaborate and impossible-to-falsify mechanisms for communication built into Keller, it would have eaten itself in pettiness, jealousy, possessiveness, and any dozen other "innate" human defects.

The nightly Together was the basis of the organism. Here, from after dinner till it was time to fall asleep, everyone talked in a language that was incapable of falsehood. If there was a problem brewing, it presented itself and was solved almost automatically. Jealousy? Resentment? Some little festering wrong that you're nursing? You couldn't conceal it at the Together, and soon everyone was clustered around you and loving the sickness away. It acted like white corpuscles, clustering around a sick cell, not to destroy it, but to heal it. There seemed to be no problem that couldn't be solved if it was attacked early enough, and with Touch, your neighbors knew about it before you did and were already laboring to correct the wrong, heal the wound, to make you feel better so you could laugh about it. There was a lot of laughter at the Togethers.

I thought for a while that I was feeling possessive about Pink. I know I had done so a little at first. Pink was my special friend, the one who had helped me out from the first, who for several days was the only one I could talk to. It was her hands that had taught me handtalk. I know I felt stirrings of territoriality the first time she lay in my lap while another man made love to her. But if there was any signal the Kellerites were adept at reading, it was that one. It went off like an alarm bell in Pink, the man, and the women and men around me. They soothed me, coddled me, told me in every language that it was all right, not to feel ashamed. Then the man in question began loving *me*. Not Pink, but the man. An observational anthropologist would have had subject matter for a whole thesis. Have you seen the films of baboons' social behavior? Dogs do it, too. Many male mammals do it. When males get into dominance battles, the weaker can defuse the aggression by submitting, by turning tail and surrendering. I have never felt so defused as when that man surrendered the object of our clash of wills—Pink—and turned his attention to me. What could I do? What I did was laugh, and he laughed, and soon we were all laughing, and that was the end of territoriality.

That's the essence of how they solved most "human nature" problems at Keller. Sort of like an oriental martial art; you yield, roll with the blow so that your attacker takes a pratfall with the force of the aggression. You do that until the attacker sees that the initial push wasn't worth the effort, that it was a pretty silly thing to do when no one was resisting you. Pretty soon he's not Tarzan of the Apes, but Charlie Chaplin. And he's laughing.

So it wasn't Pink and her lovely body and my realization that she could never be all mine to lock away in my cave and defend with a gnawed-off thighbone. If I'd persisted in that frame of mind she would have found me about as attractive as an Amazonian leech, and that was a great incentive to confound the behaviorists and overcome it.

So I was back to those people who had visited and left, and what did they see that I didn't see?

Well, there was something pretty glaring. I was not part of the organism, no matter how nice the organism was to me. I had no hopes of ever becoming a part, either. Pink had said it in the first week. She felt it herself, to a lesser degree. She could not ***, though that fact was not going to drive her away from Keller. She had told me that many times in shorthand and confirmed it in bodytalk. If I left, it would be without her.

Trying to stand outside and look at it, I felt pretty miserable. What was I trying to *do*, anyway? Was my goal in life *really* to become a part of a blind-deaf commune? I was feeling so low by that time that I actually thought of that as denigrating, in the face of all the evidence to the contrary. I should be out in the real world where the real people lived, not these freakish cripples.

I backed off from that thought very quickly. I was not totally out of my mind, just on the lunatic edges. These people were the best friends I'd ever had, maybe the only ones. That I was confused enough to think that of them even for a second worried me more than anything else. It's possible that it's what pushed me finally into a decision. I saw a future of growing disillusion and unfulfilled hopes. Unless I was willing to put out my eyes and ears, I would always be on the outside. *I* would be the blind and deaf one. I would be the freak. I didn't want to be a freak.

They knew I had decided to leave before I did. My last few days turned into a long goodbye, with a loving farewell implicit in every word touched to me. I was not really sad, and neither were they. It was nice, like everything they did. They said goodbye with just the right mix of wistfulness and life-must-go-on, and hope-to-touch-you-again.

Awareness of Touch scratched on the edges of my mind. It was not bad, just as Pink had said. In a year or two I could have mastered it.

But I was set now. I was back in the life groove that I had followed for so long. Why is it that once having decided what I must do, I'm afraid to reexamine my decision? Maybe because the original decision cost me so much that I didn't want to go through it again.

I left quietly in the night for the highway and California. They were out in the fields, standing in that circle again. Their fingertips were farther apart than ever before. The dogs and children hung around the edges like beggars at a banquet. It was hard to tell which looked more hungry and puzzled.

The experiences at Keller did not fail to leave their mark on me. I was unable to live as I had before. For a while I thought I could not live at all, but I did. I was too used to living to take the decisive step of ending my life. I would wait. Life had brought one pleasant thing to me; maybe it would bring another.

I became a writer. I found I now had a better gift for communicating than I had before. Or maybe I had it now for the first time. At any rate, my writing came together and I sold. I wrote what I wanted to write, and was not afraid of going hungry. I took things as they came.

I weathered the non-depression of '97, when unemployment

reached twenty percent and the government once more ignored it as a temporary downturn. It eventually upturned, leaving the jobless rate slightly higher than it had been the time before, and the time before that. Another million useless persons had been created with nothing better to do than shamble through the streets looking for beatings in progress, car smashups, heart attacks, murders, shootings, arson, bombings, and riots: the endlessly inventive street theater. It never got dull.

I didn't become rich, but I was usually comfortable. That is a social disease, the symptoms of which are the ability to ignore the fact that your society is developing weeping pustules and having its brains eaten out by radioactive maggots. I had a nice apartment in Marin County, out of sight of the machine-gun turrets. I had a car, at a time when they were beginning to be luxuries.

I had concluded that my life was not destined to be all I would like it to be. We all make some sort of compromise, I reasoned, and if you set your expectations too high you are doomed to disappointment. It did occur to me that I was settling for something far from "high," but I didn't know what to do about it. I carried on with a mixture of cynicism and optimism that seemed about the right mix for me. It kept my motor running, anyway.

I even made it to Japan, as I had intended in the first place.

I didn't find someone to share my life. There was only Pink for that, Pink and all her family, and we were separated by a gulf I didn't dare cross. I didn't even dare think about her too much. It would have been very dangerous to my equilibrium. I lived with it, and told myself that it was the way I was. Lonely.

The years rolled on like a caterpillar tractor at Dachau, up to the penultimate day of the millennium.

San Francisco was having a big bash to celebrate the year 2000. Who gives a shit that the city is slowly falling apart, that civilization is disintegrating into hysteria? Let's have a party!

I stood on the Golden Gate Dam on the last day of 1999. The sun was setting in the Pacific, on Japan, which had turned out to be more of the same but squared and cubed with neo-samurai. Behind me the first bombshells of a firework celebration of holocaust tricked up to look like festivity competed with the flare of burning buildings as the social and economic basket cases celebrated the occasion in their own way. The city quivered under the weight of misery, anxious to slide off along the fracture lines of some subcortical San Andreas Fault. Orbiting atomic bombs twinkled in my mind, up there somewhere, ready to plant mushrooms when we'd exhausted all the other possibilities.

I thought of Pink.

I found myself speeding through the Nevada desert, sweating, gripping the steering wheel. I was crying aloud but without sound, as I had learned to do at Keller.

Can you go back?

I slammed the citicar over the potholes in the dirt road. The car was falling apart. It was not built for this kind of travel. The sky was getting light in the east. It was the dawn of a new millennium. I stepped harder on the gas pedal and the car bucked savagely. I didn't care. I was not driving back down that road, not ever. One way or another, I was here to stay.

I reached the wall and sobbed my relief. The last hundred miles had been a nightmare of wondering if it had been a dream. I touched the cold reality of the wall and it calmed me. Light snow had drifted over everything, gray in the early dawn.

I saw them in the distance. All of them, out in the field where I had left them. No, I was wrong. It was only the children. Why had it seemed like so many at first?

Pink was there. I knew her immediately, though I had never seen her in winter clothes. She was taller, filled out. She would be nineteen years old. There was a small child playing in the snow at her feet, and she cradled an infant in her arms. I went to her and talked to her hand.

She turned to me, her face radiant with welcome, her eyes staring in a way I had never seen. Her hands flitted over me and her eyes did not move.

"I touch you, I welcome you," her hands said. "I wish you could have been here just a few minutes ago. Why did you go away darling? Why did you stay away so long?" Her eyes were stones in her head. She was blind. She was deaf.

All the children were. No, Pink's child sitting at my feet looked up at me with a smile.

"Where is everybody?" I asked when I got my breath. "Scar? Baldy? Green-eyes? And what's happened? What's happened to you?" I was tottering on the edge of a heart attack or nervous collapse or something. My reality felt in danger of dissolving.

"They've gone," she said. The word eluded me, but the context put it with the *Mary Celeste* and Roanoke, Virginia. It was complex, the way she used the word *gone*. It was like something she had said before: unattainable, a source of frustration like the one that had sent me running from Keller. But now her word told of something that was not hers yet, but was within her grasp. There was no sadness in it.

"Gone?"

"Yes. I don't know where. They're happy. They ***ed. It was glorious. We could only touch a part of it."

I felt my heart hammering to the sound of the last train pulling away from the station. My feet were pounding along the ties as it faded into the fog. Where are the Brigadoons of yesterday? I've never yet heard of a fairy tale where you can go back to the land of enchantment. You wake up, you find that your chance is gone. You threw it away. *Fool*! You only get one chance; that's the moral, isn't it?

Pink's hands laughed along my face.

"Hold this part-of-me-who-speaks-mouth-to-nipple," she said, and handed me her infant daughter. "I will give you a gift."

She reached up and lightly touched my ears with her cold fingers. The sound of the wind was shut out, and when her hands came away it never came back. She touched my eyes, shut out all the light, and I saw no more.

We live in the lovely quiet and dark.

# THE QUEEN OF AIR AND DARKNESS

## Poul Anderson

The last glow of the last sunset would linger almost until midwinter. But there would be no more day, and the northlands rejoiced. Blossoms opened, flamboyance on firethorn trees, steelflowers rising blue from the brok and rainplant that cloaked all hills, shy whiteness of kiss-me-never down in the dales. Flitteries darted among them on iridescent wings; a crownbuck shook his horns and bugled through warmth and flower odors. Between horizons the sky deepened from purple to sable. Both moons were aloft, nearly full, shining frosty on leaves and molten on waters. The shadows they made were blurred by an aurora, a great blowing curtain of light across half heaven. Behind it the earliest stars had come out.

A boy and a girl sat on Wolund's Barrow just under the dolmen it upbore. Their hair, which streamed halfway down their backs, showed startlingly forth, bleached as it was by summer. Their bodies, still dark from that season, merged with earth and bush and rock; for they wore only garlands. He played on a bone flute and she sang. They had lately become lovers. Their age was about sixteen, but they did not know this, considering themselves Outlings and thus indifferent to time, remembering little or nothing of how they had once dwelt in the lands of men.

His notes piped cold around her voice:

"Cast a spell,
weave it well
of dust and dew
and night and you."

A brook by the grave-mound, carrying moonlight down to a hillhidden river, answered with its rapids. A flock of hellbats passed black beneath the aurora.

A shape came bounding over Cloudmoor. It had two arms and two legs, but the legs were long and claw-footed and feathers covered it to the end of a tail and broad wings. The face was half-human, dominated by its eyes. Had Ayoch been able to stand wholly erect, he would have reached to the boy's shoulder.

The girl rose. "He carries a burden," she said. Her vision was not meant for twilight like that of a northland creature born, but she had learned how to use every sign her senses gave her. Besides the fact that ordinarily a pook would fly, there was a heaviness to his haste.

"And he comes from the south." Excitement jumped in the boy, sudden as a green flame that went across the constellation Lyrth. He sped down the mound. "Ohoi, Ayoch!" he called. "Me here, Mistherd!"

"And Shadow-of-a-Dream," the girl laughed, following.

The pook halted. He breathed louder than the soughing in the growth around him. A smell of bruised yerba lifted where he stood.

"Well met in winterbirth," he whistled. "You can help me bring this to Carheddin."

He held out what he bore. His eyes were yellow lanterns above. It moved and whimpered.

"Why, a child," Mistherd said.

"Even as you were, my son, even as you were. Ho, ho, what a snatch!" Ayoch boasted. "They were a score in yon camp by Fallowwood, armed, and besides watcher engines they had big ugly dogs aprowl while they slept. I came from above, however, having spied on them till I knew that a handful of dazedust— "

"The poor thing." Shadow-of-a-Dream took the boy and held him to her small breasts. "So full of sleep yet, aren't you, littleboo?" Blindly, he sought a nipple. She smiled through the veil of her hair. "No, I am still too young, and you already too old. But come, when you wake in Carheddin under the mountain you shall feast."

"Yo-ah," said Ayoch very softly. "She is abroad and has heard and seen. She comes." He crouched down, wings folded. After a moment Mistherd knelt, and then Shadow-of-a-Dream, though she did not let go the child.

The Queen's tall form blocked off the moons. For a while she regarded the three and their booty. Hill and moor sounds withdrew from their awareness until it seemed they could hear the northlights hiss.

At last Ayoch whispered, "Have I done well, Starmother?"

"If you stole a babe from a camp full of engines," said the beautiful voice, "then they were folk out of the far south who may not endure it as meekly as yeomen."

"But what can they do, Snowmaker?" the pook asked. "How can they track us?"

Mistherd lifted his head and spoke in pride. "Also, now they too have felt the awe of us."

"And he is a cuddly dear," Shadow-of-a-Dream said. "And we need more like him, do we not, Lady Sky?"

"It had to happen in some twilight," agreed she who stood above. "Take him onward and care for him. By this sign," which she made, "is he claimed for the Dwellers."

Their joy was freed. Ayoch cartwheeled over the ground till he reached a shiverleaf. There he swarmed up the trunk and out on a limb, perched half-hidden by unrestful pale foliage, and crowed. Boy and girl bore the child toward Garheddin at an easy distance-devouring lope which let him pipe and her sing:

"Wahaii, wahaii
Wayala, laii!
Wing on the wind
high over heaven,
shrilly shrieking,
rush with the rainspears,
tumble through tumult,
drift to the moonhoar trees and the dream-heavy shadows beneath
them,
and rock in, be one with the clinking wavelets of lakes where the
starbeams drown."

As she entered, Barbro Cullen felt, through all grief and fury, stabbed by dismay. The room was unkempt. Journals, tapes, reels, codices, file boxes, bescribbled papers were piled on every table. Dust filmed most shelves and corners. Against one wall stood a laboratory setup, microscope and analytical equipment. She recognized it as compact and efficient, but it was not what you would expect in an office, and it gave the air a faint chemical reek. The rug was threadbare, the furniture shabby.

This was her final chance?

Then Eric Sherrinford approached. "Good day, Mrs. Cullen," he said. His tone was crisp, his handclasp firm. His faded gripsuit didn't bother her. She wasn't inclined to fuss about her own appearance except on special occasions. (And would she ever again have one, unless she got back Jimmy?) What she observed was a cat's personal neatness.

A smile radiated in crow's feet from his eyes. "Forgive my bachelor housekeeping. On Beowulf we have—we had, at any rate, machines for that, so I never acquired the habit myself, and I don't want a hireling disarranging my tools. More convenient to work out of my apartment than keep a separate office. Won't you be seated?"

"No, thanks. I couldn't," she mumbled.

"I understand. But if you'll excuse me, I function best in a relaxed position."

He jackknifed into a lounger. One long shank crossed the other knee. He drew forth a pipe and stuffed it from a pouch. Barbro wondered why he took tobacco in so ancient a way. Wasn't Beowulf supposed to have the up-to-date equipment that they still couldn't afford to build on Roland? Well, of course old customs might survive anyhow. They generally did in colonies, she remembered reading. People had moved starward in the hope of preserving such outmoded things as their mother tongues or constitutional government or rational-technological civilization . . .

Sherrinford pulled her up from the confusion of her weariness: "You must give me the details of your case, Mrs. Cullen. You've simply told me that your son was kidnapped and your local constabulary did nothing. Otherwise I know just a few obvious facts, such as your being widowed rather than divorced; and you're the daughter of outwayers in Olga Ivanoff Land who, nevertheless, kept in close telecommunication with Christmas Landing; and you're trained in one of the biological professions; and you had several years' hiatus in field work until recently you started again."

She gaped at the high-cheeked, beak-nosed, black-haired and gray-eyed countenance. His lighter made a *scrit* and a flare which seemed to fill the room. Quietness dwelt on this height above the city, and winter dusk was seeping in through the windows. "How in cosmos do you know that?" she heard herself exclaim.

He shrugged and fell into the lecturer's manner for which he was notorious. "My work depends on noticing details and fitting them together. In more than a hundred years on Roland, tending to cluster according to their origins and thought-habits, people have developed regional accents. You have a trace of the Olgan burr, but you nasalize your vowels in the style of this area, though you live in Portolondon. That suggests steady childhood exposure to metropolitan speech. You were part of Matsuyama's expedition, you told me, and took your boy along. They wouldn't have allowed any ordinary technician to do that; hence you had to be valuable enough to get away with it; the team was conducting ecological research; therefore you must be in the life sciences. For the same reason, you must have had previous field experience. But your skin is fair, showing none of the leatheriness one gets from prolonged exposure to this sun. Accordingly, you must have been mostly indoors for a good while before you went on your ill-fated trip. As for widowhood—you never mentioned a husband to me, but you have had a man whom you thought so highly of that you still wear both the wedding and the engagement ring he gave you."

Her sight blurred and stung. The last of those words had brought Tim back, huge, ruddy, laughterful and gentle. She must turn from this other person and stare outward. "Yes," she achieved saying, "you're right."

The apartment occupied a hilltop above Christmas Landing. Beneath it the city dropped away in walls, roofs, archaistic chimneys and lamplit streets, goblin lights of human-piloted vehicles, to the harbor, the sweep of Venture Bay, ships bound to and from the Sunward Islands and remoter regions of the Boreal Ocean, which glimmered like mercury in the afterglow of Charlemagne. Oliver was swinging rapidly higher, a mottled orange disc a full degree wide; closer to the zenith which it could never reach, it would shine the color of ice. Alde, half the seeming size, was a thin slow crescent near Sirius, which she remembered was near Sol, but you couldn't see Sol without a telescope—

"Yes," she said around the pain in her throat, "my husband is about four years dead. I was carrying our first child when he was killed by a stampeding monocerus. We'd been married three years before. Met while we were both at the University—'casts from School Centra can only supply a basic education, you know—we founded our own team to do ecological studies under contract—you know, can a certain area be settled while maintaining a balance of nature, what crops will grow, what hazards, that sort of question—Well, afterward I did lab work for a fisher co-op in Portolondon. But the monotony, the . . . shut-in-ness . . . was eating me away. Professor Matsuyama offered me a position on the team he was organizing to examine Commissioner Hauch Land. I thought, God help me, I thought Jimmy—Tim wanted him named James, once the tests showed it'd be a boy, after his own father and because of 'Timmy and Jimmy' and—Oh, I thought Jimmy could safely come along. I couldn't bear to leave him behind for months, not at his age. We could make sure he'd never wander out of camp. What could hurt him inside it? *I* had never believed those stories about the Outlings stealing human children. I supposed parents were trying to hide from themselves the fact they'd been careless, they'd let a kid get lost in the woods or attacked by a pack of satans or—Well, I learned better, Mr. Sherrinford. The guard robots were evaded and the dogs were drugged and when I woke, Jimmy was gone."

He regarded her through the smoke from his pipe. Barbro Engdahl Cullen was a big woman of thirty or so (Rolandic years, he reminded himself, ninety-five percent of Terrestrial, not the same as Beowulfan years), broad-shouldered, long-legged, full-breasted, supple of stride; her face was wide, straight nose, straightforward hazel eyes, heavy but mobile mouth; her hair was reddish-brown, cropped below the ears, her voice husky, her garment a plain street robe. To still the writhing of her fingers, he asked skeptically, "Do you now believe in the Outlings?"

"No. I'm just not so sure as I was." She swung about with half a glare for him. "And we have found traces."

"Bits of fossils," he nodded. "A few artifacts of a neolithic sort. But apparently ancient, as if the makers died ages ago. Intensive search has failed to turn up any real evidence for their survival."

"How intensive can search be, in a summer-stormy, winter-gloomy wilderness around the North Pole?" she demanded. "When we are, how many, a million people on an entire planet, half of us crowded into this one city?"

"And the rest crowding this one habitable continent," he pointed out.

"Arctica covers five million square kilometers," she flung back. "The Arctic Zone proper covers a fourth of it. We haven't the industrial base to establish satellite monitor stations, build aircraft we can trust in those parts, drive roads through the damned darklands and establish permanent bases and get to know them and tame them. Good Christ, generations of lonely outwayment told stories about Greymantle, and the beast was never seen by a proper scientist till last year!"

"Still, you continue to doubt the reality of the Outlings?"

"Well, what about a secret cult among humans, born of isolation and ignorance, lairing in the wilderness, stealing children when they can for— " She swallowed. Her head drooped. "But you're supposed to be the expert."

"From what you told me over the visiphone, the Portolondon constabulary questions the accuracy of the report your group made, thinks the lot of you were hysterical, claims you must have omitted a due precaution and the child toddled away and was lost beyond your finding."

His dry words pried the horror out of her. Flushing, she snapped: "Like any settler's kid? No. I didn't simply yell. I consulted Data Retrieval. A few too many such cases are recorded for accident to be a very plausible explanation. And shall we totally ignore the frightened stories about reappearances? But when I went back to the constabulary with my facts, they brushed me off. I suspect that was not entirely because they're undermanned. I think they're afraid too. They're recruited from country boys; and Portolondon lies near the edge of the unknown."

Her energy faded. "Roland hasn't got any central police force," she finished drably. "You're my last hope."

The man puffed smoke into twilight, with which it blent, before he said in a kindlier voice than hitherto: "Please don't make it a high hope, Mrs. Cullen. I'm the solitary private investigator on this world, having no resources beyond myself, and a newcomer to boot."

"How long have you been here?"

"Twelve years. Barely time to get a little familiarity with the relatively civilized coastlands. You settlers of a century or more—what do you, even, know about Arctica's interior?"

Sherrinford sighed. "I'll take the case, charging no more than I must, mainly for the sake of the experience," he said. "But only if you'll be my guide and assistant, however painful it will be for you."

"Of course! I dreaded waiting idle. Why me, though?"

"Hiring someone else as well qualified would be prohibitively expensive, on a pioneer planet where every hand has a thousand urgent tasks to do. Besides, you have motive. And I'll need that. I, who was born on another world altogether strange to this one, itself altogether strange to Mother Earth, I am too dauntingly aware of how handicapped we are."

Night gathered upon Christmas Landing. The air stayed mild, but glimmer-lit tendrils of fog, sneaking through the streets, had a cold look, and colder yet was the aurora where it shuddered between the moons. The woman drew closer to the man in this darkening room, surely not aware that she did, until he switched on a fluoropanel. The same knowledge of Roland's aloneness was in both of them.

One light-year is not much as galactic distances go. You could walk it in about 270 million years, beginning at the middle of the Permian Era, when dinosaurs belonged to the remote future, and continuing to the present day when spaceships cross even greater reaches. But stars in our neighborhood average some nine lightyears apart; and barely one percent of them have planets which are man-habitable; and speeds are limited to less than that of radiation. Scant help is given by relativistic time contraction and suspended animation en route. These make the journeys seem short; but history meanwhile does not stop at home.

Thus voyages from sun to sun will always be few. Colonists will be those who have extremely special reasons for going. They will take along germ plasm for exogenetic cultivation of domestic plants and animals—and of human infants, in order that population can grow fast enough to escape death through genetic drift. After all, they cannot rely on further immigration. Two or three times a century, a ship may call from some other colony. (Not from Earth. Earth has long ago sunk into alien concerns.) Its place of origin will be an old settlement. The young ones are in no position to build and man interstellar vessels.

Their very survival, let alone their eventual modernization, is in doubt. The founding fathers have had to take what they could get, in a universe not especially designed for man.

Consider, for example, Roland. It is among the rare happy finds, a world where humans can live, breathe, eat the food, drink the water, walk unclad if they choose, sow their crops, pasture their beasts, dig their mines, erect their homes, raise their children and grandchildren. It is worth crossing three quarters of a light-century to preserve certain dear values and strike new roots into the soil of Roland.

But the star Charlemagne is of type Fg, forty percent brighter than Sol, brighter still in the treacherous ultraviolet and wilder still in the wind of charged particles that seethes from it. The planet has an eccentric orbit. In the middle of the short but furious northern summer, which includes periastron, total insolation is more than double what Earth gets; in the depth of the long northern winter, it is barely less than Terrestrial average.

Native life is abundant everywhere. But lacking elaborate machinery, not economically possible to construct for more than a few specialists, man can only endure the high latitudes. A ten-degree axial tilt, together with the orbit, means that the northern part of the Arctican continent spends half its year in unbroken sunlessness. Around the South Pole lies an empty ocean.

Other differences from Earth might superficially seem more important. Roland has two moons, small but close, to evoke clashing tides. It rotates once in thirty-two hours, which is end-lessly, subtly disturbing to organisms evolved through gigayears of a quicker rhythm. The weather patterns are altogether unterrestrial. The globe is a mere 9,500 kilometers in diameter; its surface gravity is $0.42 \times 980$ cm/sec$^2$; the sea level air pressure is slightly above one Earth atmosphere. (For actually Earth is the freak, and man exists because a cosmic accident blew away most of the gas that a body its size ought to have kept, as Venus has done.)

However, Homo can truly be called Sapiens when he practices his specialty of being unspecialized. His repeated attempts to freeze himself into an all-answering pattern or culture or ideology or whatever he has named it, have repeatedly brought ruin. Give him the pragmatic business of making his living and he will usually do rather well. He adapts, within broad limits.

These limits are set by such factors as his need for sunlight and his being, necessarily and forever, a part of the life that surrounds him and a creature of the spirit within.

Portolondon thrust docks, boats, machinery, warehouses into the Gulf of Polaris. Behind them huddled the dwellings of its five thousand permanent inhabitants; concrete walls, storm shutters, high-peaked tile roofs. The gaiety of their paint looked forlorn amidst lamps; this town lay past the Arctic Circle.

Nevertheless Sherrinford remarked, "Cheerful place, eh? The kind of thing I came to Roland looking for."

Barbro made no reply. The days in Christmas Landing, while he made his preparations, had drained her. Gazing out the dome of the taxi that was whirring them downtown from the hydrofoil that brought them, she supposed he meant the lushness of forest and meadows along the road, brilliant hues and phosphorescence of flowers in gardens, clamor of wings overhead. Unlike Terrestrial flora in cold climates, Arctican vegetation spends every daylit hour in frantic growth and energy storage. Not till summer's fever gives place to gentle winter does it bloom and fruit; and estivating animals rise from their dens and migratory birds come home.

The view was lovely, she had to admit: beyond the trees, a spaciousness climbing toward remote heights, silvery-gray under a moon, an aurora, the diffuse radiance from a sun just below the horizon.

Beautiful as a hunting satan, she thought, and as terrible. That wilderness had stolen Jimmy. She wondered if she would at least be given to find his little bones and take them to his father.

Abruptly she realized that she and Sherrinford were at their hotel and that he had been speaking of the town. Since it was next in size after the capital, he must have visited here often before. The streets were crowded and noisy; signs flickered, music blared from shops, taverns, restaurants, sports centers, dance halls; vehicles were jammed down to molasses speed; the several-stories-high office buildings stood aglow. Portolondon linked an enormous hinterland to the outside world. Down the Gloria River came timber rafts, ores, harvest of farms whose owners were slowly making Rolandic life serve them, meat and ivory and furs gathered by rangers in the mountains beyond Troll Scarp. In from the sea came coastwise freighters, the fishing fleet, produce of the Sunward Islands, plunder of whole continents farther south where bold men adventured. It clanged in Portolondon, laughed, blustered, swaggered, connived, robbed, preached, guzzled, swilled, toiled, dreamed, lusted, built, destroyed, died, was born, was happy, angry, sorrowful, greedy, vulgar, loving, ambitious, human. Neither the sun's blaze elsewhere nor the half-year's twilight here—wholly night around midwinter—was going to stay man's hand.

Or so everybody said.

Everybody except those who had settled in the darklands. Barbro used to take for granted that they were evolving curious customs, legends, and superstitions, which would die when the outway had been completely mapped and controlled. Of late, she had wondered. Perhaps Sherrinford's hints, about a change in his own attitude brought about by his preliminary research, were responsible.

Or perhaps she just needed something to think about besides

how Jimmy, the day before he went, when she asked him whether he wanted rye or French bread for a sandwich, answered in great solemnity—he was becoming interested in the alphabet—"I'll have a slice of what we people call the F bread."

She scarcely noticed getting out of the taxi, registering, being conducted to a primitively furnished room. But after she unpacked she remembered Sherrinford had suggested a confidential conference. She went down the hall and knocked on his door. Her knuckles sounded less loud than her heart.

He opened the door, finger on lips, and gestured her toward a corner. Her temper bristled until she saw the image of Chief Constable Dawson in the visiphone. Sherrinford must have chimed him up and must have a reason to keep her out of scanner range. She found a chair and watched, nails digging into knees.

The detective's lean length refolded itself. "Pardon the interruption," he said. "A man mistook the number. Drunk, by the indications."

Dawson chuckled. "We get plenty of those." Barbro recalled his fondness for gabbing. He tugged the beard which he affected, as if he were an outwayer instead of a townsman. "No harm in them as a rule. They only have a lot of voltage to discharge, after weeks or months in the backlands."

"I've gathered that that environment—foreign in a million major and minor ways to the one that created man—I've gathered that it does do odd things to the personality." Sherrinford tamped his pipe. "Of course, you know my practice has been confined to urban and suburban areas. Isolated garths seldom need private investigators. Now that situation appears to have changed. I called to ask you for advice."

"Glad to help," Dawson said. "I've not forgotten what you did for us in the de Tahoe murder case." Cautiously: "Better explain your problem first."

Sherrinford struck fire. The smoke that followed cut through the green odors—even here, a paved pair of kilometers from the nearest woods—that drifted past traffic rumble through a crepuscular window. "This is more a scientific mission than a search for an absconding debtor or an industrial spy," he drawled. "I'm looking into two possibilities: that an organization, criminal or religious or whatever, has long been active and steals infants; or that the Outlings of folklore are real."

"Huh?" On Dawson's face Barbro read as much dismay as surprise. "You can't be serious!"

"Can't I?" Sherrinford smiled. "Several generations' worth of reports shouldn't be dismissed out of hand. Especially not when they become more frequent and consistent in the course of time, not less. Nor can we ignore the documented loss of babies and small children, amounting by now to over a hundred, and never a trace found afterward. Nor the finds which demonstrate that an intelligent species one inhabited Arctica and may still haunt the interior."

Dawson leaned forward as if to climb out of the screen. "Who engaged you?" he demanded. "That Cullen woman? We were sorry for her, naturally, but she wasn't making sense and when she got downright abusive— "

"Didn't her companions, reputable scientists, confirm her story?"

"No story to confirm. Look, they had the place ringed with detectors and alarms, and they kept mastiffs. Standard procedure in a country where a hungry sauroid or whatever might happen by. Nothing could've entered unbeknownst."

"On the ground. How about a flyer landing in the middle of camp?"

"A man in a copter rig would've roused everybody."

"A winged being might be quieter."

"A living flyer that could lift a three-year-old boy? Doesn't exist."

"Isn't in the scientific literature, you mean, Constable. Remember Graymantle; remember how little we know about Roland, a planet, and entire world. Such birds do exist on Beowulf—and on Rustum, I've read. I made a calculation from the local ratio of air density to gravity and, yes, it's marginally possible here too. The child could have been carried off for a short distance before wing muscles were exhausted and the creature must descend."

Dawson snorted. "First it landed and walked into the tent where mother and boy were asleep. Then it walked away, toting him, after it couldn't fly further. Does that sound like a bird of prey? And the victim didn't cry out, the dogs didn't bark, nothing!"

"As a matter of fact," Sherrinford said, "those inconsistencies are the most interesting and convincing feature of the whole account. You're right, it's hard to see how a human kidnapper could get in undetected, and an eagle type of creature wouldn't operate in that fashion. But none of this applies to a winged intelligent being. The boy could have been drugged. Certainly the dogs showed signs of having been."

"The dogs showed signs of having overslept. Nothing had disturbed them. The kid wandering by wouldn't do so. We don't need to assume one damn thing except, first, that he got restless and, second, that the alarms were a bit sloppily rigged—seeing as how no danger was expected from inside camp—and let him pass out. And, third, I hate to speak this way, but we must assume the poor tyke starved or was killed."

Dawson paused before adding: "If we had more staff, we could have given the affair more time. And would have, of course. We did make an aerial sweep, which risked the lives of the pilots, using instruments which would've spotted the kid anywhere in a fifty-kilometer radius, unless he was dead. You know how sensitive thermal analyzers are. We drew complete blank. We have more important jobs than to hunt for the scattered pieces of a corpse."

He finished brusquely, "If Mrs. Cullen's hired you, my advice is you find an excuse to quit. Better for her, too. She's got to come to terms with reality."

Barbro checked a shout by biting her tongue.

"Oh, this is merely the latest disappearance of the series," Sherrinford said. She didn't understand how he could maintain his easy tone when Jimmy was lost. "More thoroughly recorded than any before, thus more suggestive. Usually an outwayer family has given a tearful but undetailed account of their child who vanished and must have been stolen by the Old Folk. Sometimes, years later, they'd tell about glimpses of what they swore must have been the grown child, not really human any longer, flitting past in murk or peering through a window or working mischief upon them. As you say, neither the authorities nor the scientists have had personnel or resources to mount a proper investigation. But as I say, the matter appears to be worth investigating. Maybe a private party like myself can contribute."

"Listen, most of us constables grew up in the outway. We don't just ride patrol and answer emergency calls, we go back there for holidays and reunions. If any gang of . . . of human sacrificers was around, we'd know."

"I realize that. I also realize that the people you came from have a widespread and deep-seated belief in nonhuman beings with supernatural powers. Many actually go through rites and make offerings to propitiate them."

"I know what you're leading up to," Dawson fleered. "I've heard it before, from a hundred sensationalists. The aborigines are the

Outlings. I thought better of you. Surely you've visited a museum or three, surely you've read literature from planets which do have natives—or damn and blast, haven't you ever applied that logic of yours?"

He wagged a finger. "Think," he said. "What have we in fact discovered? A few pieces of worked stone; a few megaliths that might be artificial; scratchings on rock that seem to show plants and animals, though not the way any human culture would ever have shown them; traces of fires and broken bones; other fragments of bone that seem as if they might've belonged to thinking creatures, as if they might've been inside fingers or around big brains. If so, however, the owners looked nothing like men. Or angels, for that matter. Nothing! The most anthropoid reconstruction I've seen shows a kind of a two-legged crocagator.

"Wait, let me finish. The stories about the Outlings—oh, I've heard them too, plenty of them; I believed them when I was a kid—the stories tell how there're different kinds, some winged, some not, some half-human, some completely human except maybe for being too handsome—it's fairyland from ancient Earth all over again. Isn't it? I got interested once and dug into the Heritage Library microfiles, and be damned if I didn't find almost the identical yarns, told by peasants centuries before spaceflight.

"None of it squares with the scanty relics we have, if they are relics, or with the fact that no area the size of Arctica could spawn a dozen different intelligent species, or . . . hellfire, man, with the way your common sense tells you aborigines would behave when humans arrived!"

Sherrinford nodded. "Yes, yes," he said. "I'm less sure than you that the common sense of nonhuman beings is precisely like our own. I've seen so much variation within mankind. But, granted, your arguments are strong. Roland's too few scientists have more pressing tasks than tracking down the origins of what is, as you put it, a revived medieval superstition."

He cradled his pipe bowl in both hands and peered into the tiny hearth of it. "Perhaps what interests me most," he said softly, "is why—across that gap of centuries, across a barrier of machine civilization and its utterly antagonistic world-view—no continuity of tradition whatsoever—why have hardheaded, technologically organized, reasonably well-educated colonists here brought back from its grave a belief in the Old Folk?"

"I suppose eventually, if the University ever does develop the psychology department they keep talking about, I suppose eventually somebody will get a thesis out of that question." Dawson spoke in a jagged voice, and he gulped when Sherrinford replied:

"I propose to begin now. In Commissioner Hauch Land, since that's where the latest incident occurred. Where can I rent a vehicle?"

"Uh, might be hard to do— "

"Come, come. Tenderfoot or not, I know better. In an economy of scarcity, few people own heavy equipment. But since it's needed, it can always be rented. I want a camper bus with a ground-effect drive suitable for every kind of terrain. And I want certain equipment installed which I've brought along, and the top canopy section replaced by a gun turret controllable from the driver's seat. But I'll supply the weapons. Besides rifles and pistols of my own, I've arranged to borrow some artillery from Christmas Landing's police arsenal."

"Hoy? Are you genuinely intending to make ready for . . . a war . . . against a myth?"

"Let's say I'm taking out insurance, which isn't terribly expensive, against a remote possibility. Now, besides the bus, what about a light aircraft carried piggyback for use in surveys?"

"No." Dawson sounded more positive than hitherto. "That's asking for disaster. We can have you flown to a base camp in a large plane when the weather report's exactly right. But the pilot will have to fly back at once, before the weather turns wrong again. Meteorology's underdeveloped on Roland, the air's especially treacherous this time of year, and we're not tooled up to produce aircraft that can outlive every surprise." He drew breath. "Have you no idea of how fast a whirly-whirly can hit, or what size hailstones might strike from a clear sky, or—? Once you're there, man, you stick to the ground." He hesitated. "That's an important reason our information is so scanty about the outway and its settlers are so isolated."

Sherrinford laughed ruefully. "Well, I suppose if details are what I'm after, I must creep along anyway."

"You'll waste a lot of time," Dawson said. "Not to mention your client's money. Listen, I can't forbid you to chase shadows, but— "

The discussion went on for almost an hour. When the screen finally blanked, Sherrinford rose, stretched, and walked toward Barbro. She noticed anew his peculiar gait. He had come from a planet with a fourth again Earth's gravitational drag, to one where weight was less than half Terrestrial. She wondered if he had flying dreams.

"I apologize for shuffling you off like that," he said. "I didn't expect to reach him at once. He was quite truthful about how busy he is. But having made contact, I didn't want to remind him overmuch of you. He can dismiss my project as a futile fantasy which I'll soon give up. But he might have frozen completely, might even have put up obstacles before us, if he'd realized through you how determined we are."

"Why should he care?" she asked in her bitterness.

"Fear of consequences, the worse because it is unadmitted—fear of consequences, the more terrifying because they are unguessable." Sherrinford's gaze went to the screen, and thence out the window to the aurora pulsing in glacial blue and white immensely far overhead. "I suppose you saw I was talking to a frightened man. Down underneath his conventionality and scoffing, he believes in the Outlings—oh, yes, he believes."

The feet of Mistherd flew over yerba and outpaced windblown driftweed. Beside him, black and misshapen, hulked Nagrim the nicor, whose earthquake weight left a swathe of crushed plants. Behind, luminous blossoms of a firethorn shone through the twining, trailing outlines of Morgarel the wraith.

Here Cloudmoor rose in a surf of hills and thickets. The air lay quiet, now and then carrying the distance-muted howl of a beast. It was darker than usual at winterbirth, the moons being down and aurora a wan flicker above mountains on the northern worldedge. But this made the stars keen, and their numbers crowded heaven, and Ghost Road shone among them as if it, like the leafage beneath, were paved with dew.

"Yonder!" bawled Nagrim. All four of his arms pointed. The party had topped a ridge. Far off glimmered a spark. "Hoah, hoah! 'Ull we right off stamp dem flat, or pluck dem apart slow?"

*We shall do nothing of the sort, bonebrain,* Morgarel's answer slid through their heads. *Not unless they attack us, and they will not unless we make them aware of us, and her command is that we spy out their purposes.*

"Gr-r-rum-m-m. I know deir aim. Out down trees, stick plows in land, sow deir cursed seed in de clods and in deir shes. 'Less we drive dem into de bitterwater, and soon, soon, dey'll wax too strong for us."

"Not too strong for the Queen!" Mistherd protested, shocked.

*Yet they do have new powers, it seems,* Morgarel reminded him. *Carefully must we probe them.*

"Den carefully can we step on dem?" asked Nagrim.

The question woke a grin out of Mistherd's own uneasiness. He slapped the scaly back. "Don't talk, you," he said. "It hurts my ears. Nor think; that hurts your head. Come, run!"

*Ease yourself,* Morgarel scolded. *You have too much life in you, human-born.*

Mistherd made a face at the wraith, but obeyed to the extent of slowing down and picking his way through what cover the country afforded. For he traveled on behalf of the Fairest, to learn what had brought a pair of mortals guesting hither.

Did they seek that boy whom Ayoch stole? (He continued to weep for his mother, though less and less often as the marvels of Carheddin entered him.) Perhaps. A birdcraft had left them and their car at the now abandoned campsite, from which they had followed an outward spiral. But when no trace of the cub had appeared inside a reasonable distance, they did not call to be flown home. And this wasn't because weather forbade the farspeaker waves to travel, as was frequently the case. No, instead the couple set off toward the mountains of Moonhorn. Their course would take them past a few outlying invader steadings and on into realms untrodden by their race.

So this was no ordinary survey. Then what was it?

Mistherd understood now why she who reigned had made her adopted mortal children learn, or retain, the clumsy language of their forebears. He had hated that drill, wholly foreign to Dweller ways. Of course, you obeyed her, and in time you saw how wise she had been . . .

Presently he left Nagrim behind a rock—the nicor would only be useful in a fight—and crawled from bush to bush until he lay within man-lengths of the humans. A rainplant drooped over him, leaves soft on his bare skin, and clothed him in darkness. Morgarel floated to the crown of a shiverleaf, whose unrest would better conceal his flimsy shape. He'd not be much help either. And that was the most troublous, the almost appalling thing here. Wraiths were among those who could not just sense and send thoughts, but cast illusions. Morgarel had reported that this time his power seemed to rebound off an invisible cold wall around the car.

Otherwise the male and female had set up no guardian engines and kept no dogs. Belike they supposed none would be needed, since they slept in the long vehicle which bore them. But such contempt of the Queen's strength could not be tolerated, could it?

Metal sheened faintly by the light of their campfire. They sat on either side, wrapped in coats against a coolness that Mistherd, naked, found mild. The male drank smoke. The female stared past him into a dusk which her flame-dazzled eyes must see as thick gloom. The dancing glow brought her vividly forth. Yes, to judge from Ayoch's tale, she was the dam of the new cub.

Ayoch had wanted to come too, but the Wonderful One forbade. Pooks couldn't hold still long enough for such a mission.

The man sucked on his pipe. His cheeks thus pulled into shadow while the light flickered across nose and brow, he looked disquietingly like a shearbill about to stoop on prey.

"—No, I tell you again, Barbro, I have no theories," he was saying. "When facts are insufficient, theorizing is ridiculous at best, misleading at worst."

"Still, you must have some idea of what you're doing," she said. It was plain that they had threshed this out often before. No Dweller could be as persistent as she or as patient as he was. "That gear you packed—that generator you keep running— "

"I have a working hypothesis or two, which suggested what equipment I ought to take."

"Why won't you tell me what the hypotheses are?"

"They themselves indicate that that might be inadvisable at the present time. I'm still feeling my way into the labyrinth. And I haven't had a chance yet to hook everything up. In fact, we're really only protected against so-called telepathic influence— "

"What?" She started. "Do you mean . . . those legends about how they can read minds too . . ." Her words trailed off and her gaze sought the darkness beyond his shoulders.

He leaned forward. His tone lost its clipped rapidity, grew earnest and soft. "Barbro, you're racking yourself to pieces. Which is no help to Jimmy if he's alive, the more so when you may well be badly needed later on. We've a long trek before us, and you'd better settle into it."

She nodded jerkily and caught her lip between her teeth for a moment before she answered, "I'm trying."

He smiled around his pipe. "I expect you'll succeed. You don't strike me as a quitter or a whiner or an enjoyer of misery."

She dropped a hand to the pistol at her belt. Her voice changed; it came out of her throat like knife from sheath. "When we find them, they'll know what I am. What humans are."

"Put anger aside also," the man urged. "We can't afford emotions. If the Outlings are real, as I told you I'm provisionally assuming, they're fighting for their homes." After a short stillness he added: "I like to think that if the first explorers had found live natives, men would not have colonized Roland. But too late now. We can't go back if we wanted to. It's a bitter-end struggle, against an enemy so crafty that he's even hidden from us the fact that he is waging war."

"Is he? I mean, skulking, kidnapping an occasional child— "

"That's part of my hypothesis. I suspect those aren't harassments, they're tactics employed in a chillingly subtle strategy."

The fire sputtered and sparked. The man smoked a while, brooding, until he went on:

"I didn't want to raise your hopes or excite you unduly while you had to wait on me, first in Christmas Landing, then in Portolondon. Afterward we were busy satisfying ourselves Jimmy had been taken farther from camp than he could have wandered before collapsing. So I'm only telling you now how thoroughly I studied available material on the . . . Old Folk. Besides, at first I did it on the principle of eliminating every imaginable possibility, however absurd. I expected no result other than final disproof. But I went through everything, relics, analyses, histories, journalistic accounts, monographs; I talked to outwayers who happened to be in town and to what scientists we have who've taken any interest in the matter. I'm a quick study. I flatter myself I became as expert as anyone—though God knows there's little to be expert on. Furthermore, I, a comparative stranger, maybe looked on the problem with fresh eyes. And a pattern emerged for me.

"If the aborigines became extinct, why didn't they leave more remnants? Arctica isn't enormous; and it's fertile for Rolandic life. It ought to have supported a population whose artifacts ought to have accumulated over millennia. I've read that on Earth literally tens of thousands of paleolithic hand axes were found, more by chance than archaeology.

"Very well. Suppose the relics and fossils were deliberately removed, between the time the last survey party left and the first colonizing ships arrived. I did find some support for that idea in the diaries of the original explorers. They were too preoccupied with checking the habitability of the planet to make catalogues of primitive monuments. However, the remarks they wrote down indicate they saw much more than later arrivals did. Suppose what we have found is just what the removers overlooked or didn't get around to.

"That argues a sophisticated mentality, thinking in long-range terms, doesn't it? Which in turn argues that the Old Folk were not mere hunters or neolithic farmers."

"But nobody ever saw buildings or machines or any such thing?" Barbro protested.

"No. Most likely the natives didn't go through our kind of metallurgic-industrial evolution. I can conceive of other paths to take. Their full-fledged civilization might have begun, rather than ended, in biological science and technology. It might have developed potentialities of the nervous system, which might be greater in their species than in man. We have those abilities to some degree ourselves, you realize. A dowser, for instance, actually senses variations in the local magnetic field caused by a water table. However, in us, these talents are maddeningly rare and tricky. So we took our business elsewhere. Who needs to be a telepath, say, when he has a visiphone? The Old Folk may have seen it the other way around. The artifacts of their civilization may have been, may still be unrecognizable to men."

"They could have identified themselves to the men, though," Barbro said. "Why didn't they?"

"I can imagine any number of reasons. As, they could have had a bad experience with interstellar visitors earlier in their history. Ours is scarcely the sole race that has spaceships. However, I told you I don't theorize in advance of the facts. Let's say no more than that the Old Folk, if they exist, are alien to us."

"For a rigorous thinker, you're spinning a mighty thin thread."

"I've admitted this is entirely provisional." He squinted at her through a roil of campfire smoke. "You came to me, Barbro, insisting in the teeth of officialdom your boy had been stolen; but your own talk about cultist kidnappers was ridiculous. Why are you reluctant to admit the reality of nonhumans?"

"In spite of the fact that Jimmy's being alive probably depends on it," she sighed. "I know." A shudder: "Maybe I don't dare admit it."

"I've said nothing thus far that hasn't been speculated about in print," he told her. "A disreputable speculation, true. In a hundred years, nobody has found valid evidence for the Outlings being more than a superstition. Still, a few people have declared it's at least possible intelligent natives are at large in the wilderness."

"I know," she repeated. "I'm not sure, though, what has made you, overnight, take those arguments seriously."

"Well, once you got me started thinking, it occurred to me that Roland's outwayers are not utterly isolated medieval crofters. They have books, telecommunications, power tools, motor vehicles, above all they have a modern science-oriented education. Why *should* they turn superstitious? Something must be causing it." He stopped. "I'd better not continue. My ideas go further than this; but if they're correct, it's dangerous to speak them aloud."

Mistherd's belly muscles tensed. There was danger for fair, in that shearbill head. The Garland Bearer must be warned. For a minute he wondered about summoning Nagrim to kill these two. If the nicor jumped them fast, their firearms might avail them naught. But no. They might have left word at home, or—He came back to his ears. The talk had changed course. Barbro was murmuring, "—why you stayed on Roland."

The man smiled his gaunt smile. "Well, life on Beowulf held no challenge for me. Heorot is—or was; this was decades past, remember—Heorot was densely populated, smoothly organized, boringly uniform. That was partly due to the lowland frontier, a safety valve that bled off the dissatisfied. But I lack the carbon dioxide tolerance necessary to live healthily down there. An expedition was being readied to make a swing around a number of colony worlds, especially those which didn't have the equipment to keep in laser contact. You'll recall its announced purpose, to seek out new ideas in science, arts, sociology, philosophy, whatever might prove valuable. I'm afraid they found little on Roland relevant to Beowulf. But I, who had wangled a berth, I saw opportunities for myself and decided to make my home here."

"Were you a detective back there, too?"

"Yes, in the official police. We had a tradition of such work in our family. Some of that may have come from the Cherokee side of it, if the name means anything to you. However, we also claimed collateral descent from one of the first private inquiry agents on record, back on Earth before spaceflight. Regardless of how true that may be, I found him a useful model. You see, an archetype— "

The man broke off. Unease crossed his features. "Best we go to sleep," he said. "We've a long distance to cover in the morning."

She looked outward. "Here is no morning."

They retired. Mistherd rose and cautiously flexed limberness back into his muscles. Before returning to the Sister of Lyrth, he risked a glance through a pane in the car. Bunks were made up, side by side, and the humans lay in them. Yet the man had not touched her, though hers was a bonny body, and nothing that had passed between them suggested he meant to do so.

Eldritch, humans. Cold and claylike. And they would overrun the beautiful wild world? Mistherd spat in disgust. It must not happen. It would not happen. She who reigned had vowed that.

The lands of William Irons were immense. But this was because a barony was required to support him, his kin and cattle, on native crops whose cultivation was still poorly understood. He raised some Terrestrial plants as well, by summerlight and in conservatories. However, these were a luxury. The true conquest of northern Arctica lay in yerba hay, in bathyrhiza wood, in pericoup and glycophyllon and eventually, when the market had expanded with population and industry, in chalcanthemum for city florists and pelts of cage-bred rover for city furriers.

That was in a tomorrow Irons did not expect he would live to see. Sherrinford wondered if the man really expected anyone ever would.

The room was warm and bright. Cheerfulness crackled in the fireplace. Light from fluoropanels gleamed off handcarven chests and chairs and tables, off colorful draperies and shelved dishes. The outwayer sat solid in his highseat, stoutly clad, beard flowing down his chest. His wife and daughters brought coffee, whose fragrance joined the remnant odors of a hearty supper, to him, his guests, and his sons.

But outside, wind hooted, lightning flared, thunder bawled, rain crashed on roof and walls and roared down to swirl among the courtyard cobblestones. Sheds and barns crouched against hugeness beyond. Trees groaned; and did a wicked undertone of laughter run beneath the lowing of a frightened cow? A burst of hailstones hit the tiles like knocking knuckles.

You could feel how distant your neighbors were, Sherrinford thought. And nonetheless they were the people whom you saw oftenest, did daily business with by visiphone (when a solar storm didn't make gibberish of their voices and chaos of their faces) or in the flesh, partied with, gossiped and intrigued with, intermarried with; in the end, they were the people who would bury you. The lights and machinery of the coastal towns were monstrously farther away.

William Irons was a strong man. Yet when now he spoke, fear was in his tone. "You'd truly go over Troll Scarp?"

"Do you mean Hanstein Palisades?" Sherrinford responded, more challenge than question.

"No outwayer calls it anything but Troll Scarp," Barbro said.

And how had a name like that been reborn, light-years and centuries from Earth's dark ages?

"Hunters, trappers, prospectors—rangers, you call them—travel in those mountains," Sherrinford declared.

"In certain parts," Irons said. "That's allowed, by a pact once made 'tween a man and the Queen after he'd done well by a jack-o'-the-hill that a satan had hurt. Wherever the plumablanca grows, men may fare, if they leave man-goods on the altar boulders in payment for what they take out of the land. Elsewhere"—one fist clenched on a chair arm and went slack again—"'s not wise to go."

"It's been done, hasn't it?"

"Oh, yes. And some came back all right, or so they claimed, though I've heard they were never lucky afterward. And some didn't, they vanished. And some who returned babbled of wonders and horrors, and stayed witlings the rest of their lives. Not for a long time has anybody been rash enough to break the pact and overtread the bounds." Irons looked at Barbro almost entreatingly. His woman and children stared likewise, grown still. Wind hooted beyond the walls and rattled the storm shutters. "Don't you."

"I've reason to believe my son is there," she answered.

"Yes, yes, you've told and I'm sorry. Maybe something can be done. I don't know what, but I'd be glad to, oh, lay a double offering on Unvar's Barrow this midwinter, and a prayer drawn in the turf by a flint knife. Maybe they'll return him." Irons sighed. "They've not done such a thing in man's memory, though. And he could have a worse lot. I've glimpsed them myself, speeding madcap through twilight. They seem happier than we are. Might be no kindness, sending your boy home again."

"Like in the Arvid song," said his wife.

Irons nodded. "M-hm. Or others, come to think of it."

"What's this?" Sherrinford asked. More sharply than before, he felt himself a stranger. He was a child of cities and technics, above all a child of the skeptical intelligence. This family *believed*. It was disquieting to see more than a touch of their acceptance in Barbro's slow nod.

"We have the same ballad in Olga Ivanoff Land," she told him, her voice less calm than the words. "It's one of the traditional ones, nobody knows who composed them, that are sung to set the measure of a ring-dance in a meadow."

"I noticed a multilyre in your baggage, Mrs. Cullen," said the wife of Irons. She was obviously eager to get off the explosive topic of a venture in defiance of the Old Folk. A songfest could help. "Would you like to entertain us?"

Barbro shook her head, white around the nostrils. The oldest boy said quickly, rather importantly, "Well, sure, I can, if our guests would like to hear."

"I'd enjoy that, thank you." Sherrinford leaned back in his seat and stroked his pipe. If this had not happened spontaneously, he would have guided the conversation toward a similar outcome.

In the past he had had no incentive to study the folklore of the outway, and not much chance to read the scanty references on it since Barbro brought him her trouble. Yet more and more he was becoming convinced he must get an understanding—not an anthropological study; a feel from the inside out—of the relationship between Roland's frontiersmen and those beings which haunted them.

A bustling followed, rearrangement, settling down to listen, coffee cups refilled and brandy offered on the side. The boy explained, "The last line is the chorus. Everybody join in, right?" Clearly he too hoped thus to bleed off some of the tension. Catharsis through music? Sherrinford wondered, and added to himself: No, exorcism.

A girl strummed a guitar. The boy sang, to a melody which beat across the storm-noise:

> "It was the ranger Arvid
> rode homeward through the hills
> among the shadowy shiverleafs,
> along the chiming hills.
>     The dance weaves under the firethorn.

> "The night wind whispered around him
> with scent of brok and rue.
> Both moons rose high above him
> and hills aflash with dew.
>     The dance weaves under the firethorn.

> "And dreaming of that woman
> who waited in the sun,
> he stopped, amazed by starlight,
> and so he was undone.
>     The dance weaves under the firethorn.

*"For there beneath a barrow*
*that bulked athwart a moon,*
*the Outling folk were dancing*
*in glass and golden shoon.*
    *The dance weaves under the firethorn.*

*"The Outling folk were dancing*
*like water, wind, and fire*
*to frosty-ringing harpstrings,*
*and never did they tire.*
    *The dance weaves under the firethorn.*

*"To Arvid came she striding*
*from where she watched the dance,*
*the Queen of Air and Darkness,*
*with starlight in her glance.*
    *The dance weaves under the firethorn.*

*"With starlight, love, and terror*
*in her immortal eye,*
*the Queen of Air and Darkness— "*

"No!" Barbro leaped from her chair. Her fists were clenched and tears flogged her cheekbones. "You can't—pretend that—about the things that stole Jimmy!"

She fled from the chamber, upstairs to her guest bedroom.

But she finished the song herself. That was about seventy hours later, camped in the steeps where rangers dared not fare.

She and Sherrinford had not said much to the Irons family after refusing repeated pleas to leave the forbidden country alone. Nor had they exchanged many remarks at first as they drove north. Slowly, however, he began to draw her out about her own life. After a while she almost forgot to mourn, in her remembering of home and old neighbors. Somehow this led to discoveries—that he beneath his professorial manner was a gourmet and a lover of opera and appreciated her femaleness; that she could still laugh and find beauty in the wild land around her—and she realized, half guiltily, that life held more hopes than even the recovery of the son Tim gave her.

"I've convinced myself he's alive," the detective said. He scowled. "Frankly, it makes me regret having taken you along. I expected this would be only a fact-gathering trip, but it's turning out to be more. If we're dealing with real creatures who stole him, they can do real harm. I ought to turn back to the nearest garth and call for a plane to fetch you."

"Like bottommost hell you will, mister," she said. "You need somebody who knows outway conditions; and I'm a better shot than average."

"M-m-m . . . it would involve considerable delay too, wouldn't it? Besides the added distance, I can't put a signal through to any airport before this current burst of solar interference has calmed down."

Next "night" he broke out his remaining equipment and set it up. She recognized some of it, such as the thermal detector. Other items were strange to her, copied to his order from the advanced apparatus of his birthworld. He would tell her little about them. "I've explained my suspicion that the ones we're after have telepathic capabilities," he said in apology.

Her eyes widened. "You mean it could be true, the Queen and her people can read minds?"

"That's part of the dread which surrounds their legend, isn't it? Actually there's nothing spooky about the phenomenon. It was studied and fairly well defined centuries ago, on Earth. I daresay the facts are available in the scientific microfiles and Christmas Landing. You Rolanders have simply had no occasion to seek them out, any more than you've yet had occasion to look up how to build power beamcasters or spacecraft."

"Well, how does telepathy work, then?"

Sherrinford recognized that her query asked for comfort as much as it did for facts, and spoke with deliberate dryness: "The organism generates extremely long-wave radiation which can, in principle, be modulated by the nervous system. In practice, the feebleness of the signals and their low rate of information transmission make them elusive, hard to detect and measure. Our prehuman ancestors went in for more reliable senses, like vision and hearing. What telepathic transceiving we do is marginal at best. But explorers have found extraterrestrial species that got an evolutionary advantage from developing the system further, in their particular environments. I imagine such species could include one which gets comparatively little direct sunlight—in fact, appears to hide from broad day. It could even become so able in this regard that, at short range, it can pick up man's weak emissions and make man's primitive sensitivities resonate to its own strong sendings."

"That would account for a lot, wouldn't it?" Barbro asked faintly.

"I've now screened our car by a jamming field," Sherrinford told her, "but it reaches only a few meters past the chassis. Beyond, a scout of theirs might get a warning from your thoughts, if you knew precisely what I'm trying to do. I have a well-trained subconscious which sees to it that I think about this in French when I'm outside. Communication has to be structured to be intelligible, you see, and that's a different enough structure from English. But English is the only human language on Roland, and surely the Old Folk have learned it."

She nodded. He had told her his general plan, which was too obvious to conceal. The problem was to make contact with the aliens, if they existed. Hitherto they had only revealed themselves, at rare intervals, to one or a few backwoodsmen at a time. An ability to generate hallucinations would help them in that. They would stay clear of any large, perhaps unmanageable expedition which might pass through their territory. But two people, braving all prohibitions, shouldn't look too formidable to approach. And . . . this would be the first human team which not only worked on the assumption that the Outlings were real but possessed the resources of modern, off-planet police technology.

Nothing happened at that camp. Sherrinford said he hadn't expected it would. The Old Folk seemed cautious this near to any settlement. In their own lands they must be bolder.

And by the following "night," the vehicle had gone well into yonder country. When Sherrinford stopped the engine in a meadow and the car settled down, silence rolled in like a wave.

They stepped out. She cooked a meal on the glower while he gathered wood, that they might later cheer themselves with a campfire. Frequently he glanced at his wrist. It bore no watch—instead, a radio-controlled dial, to tell what the instruments in the bus might register.

Who needed a watch here? Slow constellations wheeled beyond glimmering aurora. The moon Alde stood above a snowpeak, turning it argent, though this place lay at a goodly height. The rest of the mountains were hidden by the forest that crowded around. Its trees were mostly shiverleaf and feathery white plumablanca, ghostly amid their shadows. A few firethorns glowed, clustered dim lanterns, and the underbrush was heavy and smelled sweet. You could see surprisingly far through the blue dusk. Somewhere nearby a brook sang and a bird fluted.

"Lovely here," Sherrinford said. They had risen from their supper and not yet sat down or kindled their fire.

"But strange," Barbro answered as low. "I wonder if it's really meant for us. If we can really hope to possess it."

His pipestem gestured at the stars. "Man's gone to stranger places than this."

"Has he? I . . . oh, I suppose it's just something left over from my outway childhood, but do you know, when I'm under them I can't think of the stars as balls of gas, whose energies have been measured, whose planets have been walked on by prosaic feet. No, they're small and cold and magical; our lives are bound to them; after we die, they whisper to us in our graves." Barbro glanced downward. "I realize that's nonsense."

She could see in the twilight how his face grew tight. "Not at all," he said. "Emotionally, physics may be a worse nonsense. And in the end, you know, after a sufficient number of generations, thought follows feeling. Man is not at heart rational. He could stop believing the stories of science if those no longer felt right."

He paused. "That ballad which didn't get finished in the house," he said, not looking at her. "Why did it affect you so?"

"I was overwrought. I couldn't stand hearing *them*, well praised. Or that's how it seemed. My apologies for the fuss."

"I gather the ballad is typical of a large class."

"Well, I never thought to add them up. Cultural anthropology is something we don't have time for on Roland, or more likely it hasn't occurred to us, with everything else there is to do. But—now you mention it, yes, I'm surprised at how many songs and stories have the Arvid motif in them."

"Could you bear to recite it for me?"

She mustered the will to laugh. "Why, I can do better than that if you want. Let me get my multilyre and I'll perform."

She omitted the hypnotic chorus line, though, when the notes rang out, except at the end. He watched her where she stood against moon and aurora.

> "—the Queen of Air and Darkness
> cried softly under sky:
>
> "'Light down, you ranger Arvid,
> and join the Outling folk.
> You need no more be human,
> which is a heavy yoke.'
>
> "He dared to give her answer:
> 'I may do naught but run.
> A maiden waits me, dreaming
> in lands beneath the sun.

"'And likewise wait me comrades
and tasks I would not shirk,
for what is Ranger Arvid
if he lays down his work?

"'So wreak your spells, you Outling,
and cast your wrath on me.
Though maybe you can slay me,
you'll not make me unfree.'

"The Queen of Air and Darkness
stood wrapped about with fear
and northlight-flares and beauty
he dared not look too near.

"Until she laughed like harpsong
and said to him in scorn:
'I do not need a magic
to make you always mourn.

"'I send you home with nothing
except your memory
of moonlight, Outling music,
night breezes, dew, and me.

"'And that will run behind you,
and shadow on the sun,
and that will lie beside you
when every day is done.

"'In work and play and friendship
your grief will strike you dumb
for thinking what you are—and—
what you might have become.

"'Your dull and foolish woman
treat kindly as you can.
Go home now, Ranger Arvid,
set free to be a man!'

"In flickering and laughter
the Outling folk were gone.
He stood alone by moonlight
and wept until the dawn.
                    The dance weaves under the firethorn."

She laid the lyre aside. A wind rustled leaves. After a long
quietness Sherrinford said, "And tales of this kind are part of
everyone's life in the outway?"

"Well, you could put it thus," Barbro replied. "Though they're not all full of supernatural doings. Some are about love or heroism. Traditional themes."

"I don't think your particular tradition has arisen of itself." His tone was bleak. "In fact, I think many of your songs and stories were not composed by humans."

He snapped his lips shut and would say no more on the subject. They went early to bed.

Hours later, an alarm roused them.

The buzzing was soft, but it brought them instantly alert. They slept in gripsuits, to be prepared for emergencies. Sky-glow lit them through the canopy. Sherrinford swung out of his bunk, slipped shoes on feet and clipped gun holster to belt. "Stay inside," he commanded.

"What's there?" Her pulse thudded.

He squinted at the dials of his instruments and checked them against the luminous telltale on his wrist. "Three animals," he counted. "Not wild ones happening by. A large one, homeothermic, to judge from the infrared, holding still a short ways off. Another . . . hm, low temperature, diffuse and unstable emission, as if it were more like a . . . a swarm of cells coordinated somehow . . . pheromonally? . . . hovering, also at a distance. But the third's practically next to us, moving around in the brush; and that pattern looks human."

She saw him quiver with eagerness, no longer seeming a professor. "I'm going to try to make a capture," he said. "When we have a subject for interrogation, stand ready to let me back in again fast. But don't risk yourself, whatever happens. And keep this cocked." He handed her a loaded big-game rifle.

His tall frame poised by the door, opened it a crack. Air blew in, cool, damp, full of fragrances and murmurings. The moon Oliver saw was now also aloft, the radiance of both unreally brilliant, and the aurora seethed in whiteness and ice-blue.

Sherrinford peered afresh at his telltale. It must indicate the directions of the watchers, among those dappled leaves. Abruptly he sprang out. He sprinted past the ashes of the campfire and vanished under trees. Barbro's hand strained on the butt of her weapon.

Racket exploded. Two in combat burst onto the meadow. Sherrinford had clapped a grip on a smaller human figure. She could make out by streaming silver and rainbow flicker that the other was nude, male, long-haired, lithe, and young. He fought demoniacally, seeking to use teeth and feet and raking nails, and meanwhile he ululated like a satan.

The identification shot through her: a changeling, stolen in babyhood and raised by the Old Folk. This creature was what they would make Jimmy into.

"Ha!" Sherrinford forced his opponent around and drove stiffened fingers into the solar plexus. The boy gasped and sagged. Sherrinford manhandled him toward the car.

Out from the woods came a giant. It might itself have been a tree, black and rugose, bearing four great gnarly boughs; but earth quivered and boomed beneath its leg-roots, and its hoarse bellowing filled sky and skulls.

Barbro shrieked. Sherrinford whirled. He yanked out his pistol, fired and fired, flat whipcracks through the half-light. His free arm kept a lock on the youth. The troll shape lurched under those blows. It recovered and came on, more slowly, more carefully, circling around to cut him off from the bus. He couldn't move fast enough to evade unless he released his prisoner—who was his sole possible guide to Jimmy—

Barbro leaped forth. "Don't!" Sherrinford shouted. "For God's sake, stay inside!" The monster rumbled and made snatching motions at her. She pulled trigger. Recoil slammed her in the shoulder. The colossus rocked and fell. Somehow it got its feet back and lumbered toward her. She retreated. Again she shot and again. The creature snarled. Blood began to drip from it and gleam oilily amidst dewdrops. It turned and went off, breaking branches, into the darkness that laired beneath the woods.

"Get to shelter!" Sherrinford yelled. "You're out of the jammer field!"

A mistiness drifted by overhead. She barely glimpsed it before she saw the new shape at the meadow edge. "Jimmy!" tore from her.

"Mother." He held out his arms. Moonlight coursed in his tears. She dropped her weapon and ran to him.

Sherrinford plunged in pursuit. Jimmy flitted away into the brush. Barbro crashed after, through clawing twigs. Then she was seized and borne away.

Standing over his captive, Sherrinford strengthened the fluoro output until vision of the wilderness was blocked off from within the bus. The boy squirmed beneath that colorless glare.

"You are going to talk," the man said. Despite the haggardness in his features, he spoke quietly.

The boy glowered through tangled locks. A bruise was purpling on his jaw. He'd almost recovered ability to flee while Sherrinford chased and lost the woman. Returning, the detective had barely caught him. Time was lacking to be gentle, when Outling reinforcements might arrive at any moment. Sherrinford had knocked him out and dragged him inside. Now he sat lashed into a swivel seat.

He spat. "Talk to you, man-clod?" But sweat stood on his skin and his eyes flickered unceasingly around the metal which caged him.

"Give me a name to call you by."

"And have you work a spell on me?"

"Mine's Eric. If you don't give me another choice, I'll have to call you . . . m-m-m . . . Wuddikins."

"What?" However eldritch, the bound one remained a human adolescent. "Mistherd, then." The lilting accent of his English somehow emphasized its sullenness. "That's not the sound, only what it means. Anyway, it's my spoken name, naught else."

"Ah, you keep a secret name you consider to be real?"

"She does. I don't know myself what it is. She knows the real names of everybody."

Sherrinford raised his brows. "She?"

"Who reigns. May she forgive me, I can't make the reverent sign when my arms are tied. Some invaders call her the Queen of Air and Darkness."

"So." Sherrinford got pipe and tobacco. He let silence wax while he started the fire. At length he said:

"I'll confess the Old Folk took me by surprise. I didn't expect so formidable a member of your gang. Everything I could learn had seemed to show they work on my race—and yours, lad—by stealth, trickery, and illusion."

Mistherd jerked a truculent nod. "She created the first nicors not long ago. Don't think she has naught but dazzlements at her beck."

"I don't. However, a steel-jacketed bullet works pretty well too, doesn't it?"

Sherrinford talked on, softly, mostly to himself: "I do still believe the, ah, nicors—all your half-humanlike breeds—are intended in the main to be seen, not used. The power of projecting mirages must surely be quite limited in range and scope as well as in the number of individuals who possess it. Otherwise she wouldn't have needed to work as slowly and craftily as she has. Even outside our mind-shield, Barbro—my companion—could have resisted, could have remained aware that whatever she saw was unreal . . . if she'd been less shaken, less frantic, less driven by need."

Sherrinford wreathed his head in smoke. "Never mind what I experienced," he said. "It couldn't have been the same as for her. I think the command was simply given us, 'You will see what you most desire in the world, running away from you into the forest.' Of course, she didn't travel many meters before the nicor waylaid her. I'd no hope of trailing them; I'm no Arctican woodsman, and besides, it'd have been too easy to ambush me. I came back to you." Grimly: "You're my link to your overlady."

"You think I'll guide you to Starhaven or Carheddin? Try making me, clod-man."

"I want to bargain."

"I s'pect you intend more'n that." Mistherd's answer held surprising shrewdness. "What'll you tell after you come home?"

"Yes, that does pose a problem, doesn't it? Barbro Cullen and I are not terrified outwayers. We're of the city. We brought recording instruments. We'd be the first of our kind to report an encounter with the Old Folk, and that report would be detailed and plausible. It would produce action."

"So you see I'm not afraid to die," Mistherd declared, though his lips trembled a bit. "If I let you come in and do your man-things to my people, I'd have naught left worth living for."

"Have no immediate fears," Sherrinford said. "You're merely bait." He sat down and regarded the boy through a visor of calm. (Within, it wept in him: *Barbro, Barbro!*) "Consider. Your Queen can't very well let me go back, bringing my prisoner and telling about hers. She has to stop that somehow. I could try fighting my way through—this car is better armed than you know—but that wouldn't free anybody. Instead, I'm staying put. New forces of hers will get here as fast as they can. I assume they won't blindly throw themselves against a machine gun, a howitzer, a fulgurator. They'll parley first, whether their intentions are honest or not. Thus I make the contact I'm after."

"What d'you plan?" The mumble held anguish.

"First, this, as a sort of invitation." Sherrinford reached out to flick a switch. "There. I've lowered my shield against mind-reading and shape-casting. I daresay the leaders, at least, will be able to sense that it's gone. That should give them confidence."

"And next?"

"Why, next we wait. Would you like something to eat or drink?"

During the time which followed, Sherrinford tried to jolly Mistherd along, find out something of his life. What answers he got were curt. He dimmed the interior lights and settled down to peer outward. That was a long few hours.

They ended at a shout of gladness, half a sob, from the boy. Out of the woods came a band of the Old Folk.

Some of them stood forth more clearly than moons and stars and northlights should have caused. He in the van rode a white crownbuck whose horns were garlanded. His form was manlike but unearthly beautiful, silver-blond hair falling from beneath the antlered helmet, around the proud cold face. The cloak fluttered on his back like living wings. His frost-colored mail rang as he fared.

Behind him, to right and left, rode two who bore swords whereon small flames gleamed and flickered. Above, a flying flock laughed and trilled and tumbled in the breezes. Near them drifted a half-transparent mistiness. Those others who passed among trees after their chieftain were harder to make out. But they moved in quicksilver grace, and as it were to a sound of harps and trumpets.

"Lord Luighaid." Glory overflowed in Mistherd's tone. "Her master Knower—himself."

Sherrinford had never done a harder thing than to sit at the main control panel, finger near the button of the shield generator, and not touch it. He rolled down a section of canopy to let voices travel. A gust of wind struck him in the face, bearing odors of the roses in his mother's garden. At his back, in the main body of the vehicle, Mistherd strained against his bonds till he could see the incoming troop.

"Call to them," Sherrinford said. "Ask if they will talk with me."

Unknown, flutingly sweet words flew back and forth. "Yes," the boy interpreted. "He will, the Lord Luighaid. But I can tell you, you'll never be let go. Don't fight them. Yield. Come away. You don't know what 'tis to be alive till you've dwelt in Carheddin under the mountain."

The Outlings drew nigh.

Jimmy glimmered and was gone. Barbro lay in strong arms, against a broad breast, and felt the horse move beneath her. It had to be a horse, though only a few were kept any longer on the steadings, and they for special uses or love. She could feel the rippling beneath its hide, hear a rush of parted leafage and the thud when a hoof struck stone; warmth and living scent welled up around her through the darkness.

He who carried her said mildly, "Don't be afraid, darling. It was a vision. But he's waiting for us and we're bound for him."

She was aware in a vague way that she ought to feel terror or despair or something. But her memories lay behind her—she wasn't sure just how she had come to be here—she was borne along in a knowledge of being loved. At peace, at peace, rest in the calm expectation of joy . . .

After a while the forest opened. They crossed a lea where boulders stood gray-white under the moons, their shadows shifting in the dim hues which the aurora threw across them. Flitteries danced, tiny comets, above the flowers between. Ahead gleamed a peak whose top was crowned in clouds.

Barbro's eyes happened to be turned forward. She saw the horse's head and thought, with quiet surprise: Why, this is Sambo, who was mine when I was a girl. She looked upward at the man. He wore a black tunic and a cowled cape which made his face hard to see. She could not cry aloud, here. "Tim," she whispered.

"Yes, Barbro."

"I buried you— "

His smile was endlessly tender. "Did you think we're no more than what's laid back into the ground? Poor torn sweetheart. She who's called us is the All Healer. Now rest and dream."

"Dream," she said, and for a space she struggled to rouse herself. But the effort was weak. Why should she believe ashen tales about . . . atoms and energies, nothing else to fill a gape of emptiness . . . tales she could not bring to mind . . . when Tim and the horse her father gave her carried her on to Jimmy? Had the other thing not been the evil dream, and this her first drowsy awakening from it?

As if he heard her thoughts, he murmured, "They have a song in Outling lands. The Song of the Men:

> *The world sails*
> *to an unseen wind.*
> *Light swirls by the bows.*
> *The wake is night.*

But the Dwellers have no such sadness."

"I don't understand," she said.

He nodded. "There's much you'll have to understand, darling, and I can't see you again until you've learned those truths. But meanwhile you'll be with our son."

She tried to lift her head and kiss him. He held her down. "Not yet," he said. "You've not been received among the Queen's people. I shouldn't have come for you, except that she was too merciful to forbid. Lie back, lie back."

Time blew past. The horse galloped tireless, never stumbling, up the mountain. Once she glimpsed a troop riding down it and thought they were bound for a last weird battle in the west against . . . who? . . . one who lay cased in iron and sorrow . . . Later she would ask herself the name of him who had brought her into the land of the Old Truth.

Finally spires lifted splendid among the stars, which are small and magical and whose whisperings comfort us after we are dead. They rode into a courtyard where candles burned unwavering, fountains splashed and birds sang. The air bore fragrance of brok and pericoup, of rue and roses; for not everything that man brought was horrible. The Dwellers waited in beauty to welcome her. Beyond their stateliness, pooks cavorted through the gloaming; among the trees darted children; merriment caroled across music more solemn.

"We have come— " Tim's voice was suddenly, inexplicably a croak. Barbro was not sure how he dismounted, bearing her. She stood before him and saw him sway on his feet.

Fear caught her. "Are you well?" She seized both his hands. They felt cold and rough. Where had Sambo gone? Her eyes searched beneath the cowl. In this brighter illumination, she ought to have seen her man's face clearly. But it was blurred, it kept changing. "What's wrong, oh, what's happened?"

He smiled. Was that the smile she had cherished? She couldn't completely remember. "I, I must go," he stammered, so low she could scarcely hear. "Our time is not ready." He drew free of her grasp and leaned on a robed form which had appeared at his side. A haziness swirled over both their heads. "Don't watch me go . . . back into the earth," he pleaded. "That's death for you. Till our time returns . . . There, our son!"

She had to fling her gaze around. Kneeling, she spread wide her arms. Jimmy struck her like a warm, solid cannonball. She rumpled his hair, she kissed the hollow of his neck, she laughed and wept and babbled foolishness; and this was no ghost, no memory that had stolen off when she wasn't looking. Now and again, as she turned her attention to yet another hurt which might have come upon him—hunger, sickness, fear—and found none, she would glimpse their surroundings. The gardens were gone. It didn't matter.

"I misted you so, Mother. Stay?"

"I'll take you so home, dearest."

"Stay. Here's fun. I'll show. But you stay."

A sighing went through the twilight. Barbro rose. Jimmy clung to her hand. They confronted the Queen.

Very tall she was in her robes woven of northlights, and her starry crown and her garlands of kiss-me-never. Her countenance recalled Aphrodite of Milos, whose picture Barbro had often seen in the realms of men, save that the Queen's was more fair, and more majesty dwelt upon it and in the night-blue eyes. Around her the gardens woke to new reality, the court of the Dwellers and the heaven-climbing spires.

"Be welcome," she spoke, her speaking a song, "forever."

Against the awe of her, Barbro said, "Moonmother, let us go home."

"That may not be."

"To our world, little and beloved," Barbro dreamed she begged, "which we build for ourselves and cherish for our children."

"To prison days, angry nights, works that crumble in the fingers, loves that turn to rot or stone or driftweed, loss, grief, and the only sureness that of the final nothingness. No. You too, Wanderfoot, who is to be, will jubilate when the banners of the Outworld come flying into the last of the cities and man is made wholly alive. Now go with those who will teach you."

The Queen of Air and Darkness lifted an arm in summons. It halted, and none came to answer.

For over the fountains and melodies lifted a gruesome growling. Fires leaped, thunders crashed. Her hosts scattered screaming before the steel thing which boomed up the mountainside. The pooks were gone in a whirl of frightened wings. The nicors flung their bodies against the unalive invader and were consumed, until their Mother cried to them to retreat.

Barbro cast Jimmy down and herself over him. Towers wavered and smoked away. The mountain stood bare under icy moons, save for rocks, crags, and farther off a glacier in whose depths the auroral light pulsed blue. A cave mouth darkened a cliff. Thither folk streamed, seeking refuge underground. Some were human of blood, some grotesques like the pooks and nicors and wraiths; but most were lean, scaly, long-tailed, long-beaked, not remotely men or Outlings.

For an instant, even as Jimmy wailed at her breast—perhaps as much because the enchantment had been wrecked as because he was afraid—Barbro pitied the Queen who stood alone in her nakedness. Then that one also had fled, and Barbro's world shivered apart.

The guns fell silent, the vehicle whirred to a halt. From it sprang a boy who called wildly, "Shadow-of-a-Dream, where are you? It's me, Mistherd, oh, come, come!"—before he remembered that the language they had been raised in was not man's. He shouted in that until a girl crept out of a thicket where she had hidden. They stared at each other through dust, smoke, and moon-glow. She ran to him.

A new voice barked from the car, "Barbro, hurry!"

Christmas Landing knew day: short at this time of year, but sunlight, blue skies, white clouds, glittering water, salt breezes in busy streets, and the sane disorder of Eric Sherrinford's living room.

He crossed and uncrossed his legs where he sat, puffed on his pipe as if to make a veil, and said, "Are you certain you're recovered? You mustn't risk overstrain."

"I'm fine," Barbro Cullen replied, though her tone was flat. "Still tired, yes, and showing it, no doubt. One doesn't go through such an experience and bounce back in a week. But I'm up and about. And to be frank, I must know what's happened, what's going on, before I can settle down to regain my full strength. Not a word of news anywhere."

"Have you spoken to others about the matter?"

"No. I've simply told visitors I was too exhausted to talk. Not much of a lie. I assumed there's a reason for censorship."

Sherrinford looked relieved. "Good girl. It's at my urging. You can imagine the sensation when this is made public. The authorities agreed they need time to study the facts, think and debate in a calm atmosphere, have a decent policy ready to offer voters who're bound to become rather hysterical at first." His mouth quirked slightly upward. "Furthermore, your nerves and Jimmy's get their chance to heal before the journalistic storm breaks over you. How is he?"

"Quite well. He continues pestering me for leave to go play with his friends in the Wonderful Place. But at his age, he'll recover—he'll forget."

"He may meet them later anyhow."

"What? We didn't— " Barbro shifted in her chair. "I've forgotten too. I hardly recall a thing from our last hours. Did you bring back any kidnapped humans?"

"No. The shock was savage, as it was, without throwing them straight into an . . . an institution. Mistherd, who's basically a sensible young fellow, assured me they'd get along, at any rate as regards survival necessities, till arrangements can be made." Sherrinford hesitated. "I'm not sure what the arrangements will be. Nobody is, at our present stage. But obviously they include those people—or many of them, especially those who aren't fullgrown—rejoining the human race. Though they may never feel at home in civilization. Perhaps in a way that's best, since we will need some kind of mutually acceptable liaison with the Dwellers."

His impersonality soothed them both. Barbro became able to say: "Was I too big a fool? I do remember how I yowled and beat my head on the floor."

"Why, no." He considered the big woman and her pride for a few seconds before he rose, walked over and laid a hand on her shoulder. "You'd been lured and trapped by a skillful play on your deepest instincts, at a moment of sheer nightmare. Afterward, as that wounded monster carried you off, evidently another type of being came along, one that could saturate you with close-range neuropsychic forces. On top of this, my arrival, the sudden brutal abolishment of every hallucination, must have been shattering. No wonder if you cried out in pain. Before you did, you competently got Jimmy and yourself into the bus, and you never interfered with me."

"What did you do?"

"Why, I drove off as fast as possible. After several hours, the atmospherics let up sufficiently for me to call Portolondon and insist on an emergency airlift. Not that that was vital. What chance had the enemy to stop us? They didn't even try. But quick transportation was certainly helpful."

"I figured that's what must have gone on." Barbro caught his glance. "No, what I meant was, how did you find us in the backlands?"

Sherrinford moved a little off from her. "My prisoner was my guide. I don't think I actually killed any of the Dwellers who'd come to deal with me. I hope not. The car simply broke through them, after a couple of warning shots, and afterward outpaced them. Steel and fuel against flesh wasn't really fair. At the cave entrance, I did have to shoot down a few of those troll creatures. I'm not proud of it."

He stood silent. Presently: "But you were a captive," he said. "I couldn't be sure what they might do to you, who had first claim on me." After another pause: "I don't look for any more violence."

"How did you make . . . the boy . . . cooperate?"

Sherrinford paced from her, to the window, where he stood staring out at the Boreal Ocean. "I turned off the mind shield," he said. "I let their band get close, in full splendor of illusion. Then I turned the shield back on and we both saw them in their true shapes. As we went northward I explained to Mistherd how he and his kind had been hoodwinked, used, made to live in a world that was never really there. I asked him if he wanted himself and whoever he cared about to go on till they died as domestic animals—yes, running in limited freedom on solid hills, but always called back to the dream-kennel." His pipe fumed furiously. "May I never see such bitterness again. He had been taught to believe he was free."

Quiet returned, above the hectic traffic. Charlemagne drew nearer to setting; already the east darkened.

Finally Barbro asked, "Do you know why?"

"Why children were taken and raised like that? Partly because it was in the pattern the Dwellers were creating; partly in order to study and experiment on members of our species—minds, that is, not bodies; partly because humans have special strengths which are helpful, like being able to endure full day-light."

"But what was the final purpose of it all?"

Sherrinford paced the floor. "Well," he said, "of course the ultimate motives of the aborigines are obscure. We can't do more than guess at how they think, let alone how they feel. But our ideas do seem to fit the data.

"Why did they hide from man? I suspect they, or rather their ancestors—for they aren't glittering elves, you know; they're mortal and fallible too—I suspect the natives were only being cautious at first, more cautious than human primitives, though certain of those on Earth were also slow to reveal themselves to strangers. Spying, mentally eavesdropping, Roland's Dwellers must have picked up enough language to get some idea of how different man was from them, and how powerful; and they gathered that more ships would be arriving, bringing settlers. It didn't occur to them that they might be conceded the right to keep their lands. Perhaps they're still more fiercely territorial than us. They determined to fight, in their own way. I daresay, once we begin to get insight into that mentality, our psychological science will go through its Copernican revolution."

Enthusiasm kindled in him. "That's not the sole thing we'll learn, either," he went on. "They must have science of their own, a nonhuman science born on a planet that isn't Earth. Because they did observe us as profoundly as we've ever observed ourselves; they did mount a plan against us, that would have taken another century or more to complete. Well, what else do they know? How do they support their civilization without visible agriculture or aboveground buildings or mines or anything? How can they breed whole new intelligent species to order? A million questions, ten million answers!"

"*Can* we learn from them?" Barbro asked softly. "Or can we only overrun them as you say they fear?"

Sherrinford halted, leaned elbow on mantel, hugged his pipe and replied: "I hope we'll show more charity than that to a defeated enemy. It's what they are. They tried to conquer us, and failed, and now in a sense we are bound to conquer them, since they'll have to make their peace with the civilization of the machine rather than see it rust away as they strove for. Still, they never did us any harm as atrocious as what we've inflicted on our fellow man in the past. And, I repeat, they could teach us marvelous things; and we could teach them, too, once they've learned to be less intolerant of a different way of life."

"I suppose we can give them a reservation," she said, and didn't know why he grimaced and answered so roughly:

"Let's leave them the honor they've earned! They fought to save the world they'd always known from that"—he made a chopping gesture at the city—"and just possibly we'd be better off ourselves with less of it."

He sagged a trifle and sighed, "However, I suppose if Elfland had won, man on Roland would at last—peacefully, even happily—have died away. We live with our archetypes, but can we live in them?"

Barbro shook her head. "Sorry, I don't understand."

"What?" He looked at her in a surprise that drove out melancholy. After a laugh: "Stupid of me. I've explained this to so many politicians and scientists and commissioners and Lord knows what, these past days, I forgot I'd never explained to you. It was a rather vague idea of mine, most of the time we were traveling, and I don't like to discuss ideas prematurely. Now that we've met the Outlings and watched how they work, I do feel sure."

He tamped down his tobacco. "In limited measure," he said, "I've used an archetype throughout my own working life. The rational detective. It hasn't been a conscious pose—much—it's simply been an image which fitted my personality and professional style. But it draws an appropriate response from most people, whether or not they've ever heard of the original. The phenomenon is not uncommon. We meet persons who, in varying degrees, suggest Christ or Buddha or the Earth Mother or, say, on a less exalted plane, Hamlet or d'Artagnan. Historical, fictional, and mythical, such figures crystallize basic aspects of the human, psyche, and when we meet them in our real experience, our reaction goes deeper than consciousness."

He grew grave again: "Man also creates archetypes that are not individuals. The Ani, the Shadow—and, it seems, the Outworld. The world of magic, of glamour—which originally meant enchantment—of half-human beings, some like Ariel and some like Caliban, but each free of mortal frailties and sorrows—therefore, perhaps, a little carelessly cruel, more than a little tricksy; dwellers in dusk and moonlight, not truly gods but obedient to rulers who are enigmatic and powerful enough to be—Yes, our Queen of Air and Darkness knew well what sights to let lonely people see, what illusions to spin around them from time to time, what songs and legends to set going among them. I wonder how much she and her underlings gleaned from human fairy tales, how much they made up themselves, and how much men created all over again, all unwittingly, as the sense of living on the edge of the world entered them."

Shadows stole across the room. It grew cooler and the traffic noises dwindled. Barbro asked mutedly: "But what could this do?"

"In many ways," Sherrinford answered, "the outwayer *is* back in the dark ages. He has few neighbors, hears scanty news from beyond his horizon, toils to survive in a land he only partly understands, that may any night raise unforeseeable disaster against him and is bounded by enormous wildernesses. The machine civilization which brought his ancestors here is frail at best. He could lose it as the dark age nations had lost Greece and Rome, as the whole of Earth seems to have lost it. Let him be worked on, long, strongly, cunningly, by the archetypical Outworld, until he has come to believe in his bones that the magic of the Queen of Air and Darkness is greater than the energy of engines; and first his faith, finally his deeds will follow her. Oh, it wouldn't happen fast. Ideally, it would happen too slowly to be noticed, especially by self-satisfied city people. But when in the end a hinterland gone back to the ancient way turned from them, how could they keep alive?"

Barbro breathed, "She said to me, when their banners flew in the last of our cities, we would rejoice."

"I think we would have, by then," Sherrinford admitted. "Nevertheless, I believe in choosing one's own destiny."

He shook himself, as if casting off a burden. He knocked the dottle from his pipe and stretched, muscle by muscle. "Well," he said, "it isn't going to happen."

She looked straight at him. "Thanks to you."

A flush went up his thin cheeks. "In time, I'm sure, somebody else would have—Anyhow, what matters is what we do next, and that's too big a decision for one individual or one generation to make."

She rose. "Unless the decision is personal, Eric," she suggested, feeling heat in her own face.

It was curious to see him shy. "I was hoping we might meet again."

"We will."


Ayoch sat on Wolund's Barrow, Aurora shuddered so brilliant, in such vast sheafs of light, as almost to hide the waning moons. Firethorn blooms had fallen; a few still glowed around the tree roots, amidst dry brok which crackled underfoot and smelled like woodsmoke. The air remained warm but no gleam was left on the sunset horizon.

"Farewell, fare lucky," the pook called. Mistherd and Shadow-of-a-Dream never looked back. It was as if they didn't dare. They trudged on out of sight, toward the human camp whose lights made a harsh new star in the south.

Ayoch lingered. He felt he should also offer goodbye to her who had lately joined him that slept in the dolmen. Likely none would meet here again for loving or magic. But he could only think of one old verse that might do. He stood and trilled:

> *"Out of her breast*
> *A blossom ascended.*
> *The summer burned it.*
> *The song is ended."*

Then he spread his wings for the long flight away.

# THE MONSTER AND THE MAIDEN

## Gordon R. Dickson

That summer more activity took place upon the shores of the loch and more boats appeared on its waters than at any time in memory. Among them was even one of the sort of boats that went underwater. It moved around in the loch slowly, diving quite deep at times. From the boats, swimmers with various gear about them descended on lines—but not so deep—swam around blindly for a while, and then returned to the surface.

Brought word of all this in her cave, First Mother worried and speculated on disaster. First Uncle, though equally concerned, was less fearful. He pointed out that the Family had survived here for thousands of years; and that it could not all end in a single year—or a single day.

Indeed, the warm months of summer passed one by one with no real disturbance to their way of life.

Suddenly fall came. One night, the first snow filled the air briefly above the loch. The Youngest danced on the surface in the darkness, sticking out her tongue to taste the cold flakes. Then the snow ceased, the sky cleared for an hour, and the banks could be seen gleaming white under a high and watery moon. But the clouds covered the moon again; and because of the relative warmth of the loch water nearby, in the morning, when the sun rose, the shores were once more green.

With dawn, boats began coming and going on the loch again

and the Family went deep, out of sight. In spite of this precaution, trouble struck from one of these craft shortly before noon. First Uncle was warming the eggs on the loch bottom in the hatchhole, a neatly cleaned shallow depression scooped out by Second Mother, near Glen Urquhart, when something heavy and round descended on a long line, landing just outside the hole and raising an almost invisible puff of silt in the blackness of the deep, icy water. The line tightened and began to drag the heavy thing about.

First Uncle had his huge length coiled about the clutch of eggs, making a dome of his body and enclosing them between the smooth skin of his underside and the cleaned lakebed. Fresh, hot blood pulsed to the undersurface of his smooth skin, keeping the water warm in the enclosed area. He dared not leave the clutch to chill in the cold loch, so he sent a furious signal for Second Mother, who, hearing that her eggs were in danger, came swiftly from her feeding. The Youngest heard also and swam up as fast as she could in mingled alarm and excitement.

She reached the hatchhole just in time to find Second Mother coiling herself around the eggs, her belly skin already beginning to radiate heat from the warm blood that was being shunted to its surface. Released from his duties, First Uncle shot up through the dark, peaty water like a sixty-foot missile, up along the hanging line, with the Youngest close behind him.

They could see nothing for more than a few feet because of the murkiness. But neither First Uncle nor the Youngest relied much on the sense of sight, which was used primarily for protection on the surface of the loch, in any case. Besides, First Uncle was already beginning to lose his vision with age, so he seldom went to the surface nowadays, preferring to do his breathing in the caves, where it was safer. The Youngest had asked him once if he did not miss the sunlight, even the misty and often cloud-dulled sunlight of the open sky over the loch, with its instinctive pull at ancestral memories of the ocean, retold in the legends. No, he had told her, he had grown beyond such things. But she found it hard to believe him; for in her, the yearning for the mysterious and fascinating world above the waters was still strong. The Family had no word for it. If they did, they might have called her a romantic.

Now, through the pressure-sensitive cells in the cheek areas of her narrow head, she picked up the movements of a creature no more than six feet in length. Carrying some long, narrow made thing, the intruder was above them, though descending rapidly, parallel to the line.

"Stay back," First Uncle signaled her sharply; and, suddenly fearful, she lagged behind. From the vibrations she felt, their visitor could only be one of the upright animals from the world above that walked about on its hind legs and used "made" things. There was an ancient taboo about touching one of these creatures.

The Youngest hung back, then, continuing to rise through the water at a more normal pace.

Above her, through her cheek cells, she felt and interpreted the turbulence that came from First Uncle's movements. He flashed up, level with the descending animal, and with one swirl of his massive body snapped the taut descending line. The animal was sent tumbling—untouched by First Uncle's bulk (according to the taboo), but stunned and buffeted and thrust aside by the water-blow like a leaf in a sudden gust of wind when autumn sends the dry tears of the trees drifting down upon the shore waters of the loch.

The thing the animal had carried, as well as the lower half of the broken line, began to sink to the bottom. The top of the line trailed aimlessly. Soon the upright animal, hanging limp in the water, was drifting rapidly away from it. First Uncle, satisfied that he had protected the location of the hatchhole for the moment, at least—though later in the day they would move the eggs to a new location, anyway, as a safety precaution—turned and headed back down to release Second Mother once more to her feeding.

Still fearful, but fascinated by the drifting figure, the Youngest rose timidly through the water on an angle that gradually brought her close to it. She extended her small head on its long, graceful neck to feel about it from close range with her pressure-sensitive cheek cells. Here, within inches of the floating form, she could read minute differences, even in its surface textures. It seemed to be encased in an unnatural outer skin—one of those skins the creatures wore which were not actually theirs—made of some material that soaked up the loch water. This soaked-up water was evidently heated by the interior temperature of the creature, much as members of the Family could warm their belly skins with shunted blood, which protected the animal's body inside by cutting down the otherwise too-rapid radiation of its heat into the cold liquid of the loch.

The Youngest noticed something bulky and hard on the creature's head, in front, where the eyes and mouth were. Attached to the back was a larger, doubled something, also hard and almost a third as long as the creature itself. The Youngest had never before seen a diver's wetsuit, swim mask, and air tanks with pressure regulator, but she had heard them described by her elders. First Mother had once watched from a safe distance while a creature so equipped had maneuvered below the surface of the loch, and she had concluded that the things he wore were devices to enable him to swim underwater without breathing as often as his kind seemed to need to ordinarily.

Only this one was not swimming. He was drifting away with an underwater current of the loch, rising slowly as he traveled toward its south end. If he continued like this, he would come to the surface near the center of the loch. By that time the afternoon would be over. It would be dark.

Clearly, he had been damaged. The blow of the water that had been slammed at him by the body of First Uncle had hurt him in some way. But he was still alive. The Youngest knew this, because she could feel through her cheek cells the slowed beating of his heart and the movement of gases and fluids in his body. Occasionally, a small thread of bubbles came from his head to drift surfaceward.

It was a puzzle to her where he carried such a reservoir of air. She herself could contain enough oxygen for six hours without breathing, but only a portion of that was in gaseous form in her lungs. Most was held in pure form, saturating special tissues throughout her body.

Nonetheless, for the moment the creature seemed to have more than enough air stored about him; and he still lived. However, it could not be good for him to be drifting like this into the open loch with night coming on. Particularly if he was hurt, he would be needing some place safe out in the air, just as members of the Family did when they were old or sick. These upright creatures, the Youngest knew, were slow and feeble swimmers. Not one of them could have fed himself, as she did, by chasing and catching the fish of the loch; and very often when one fell into the water at any distance from the shore, he would struggle only a little while and then die.

This one would die also, in spite of the things fastened to him, if he stayed in the water. The thought raised a sadness in her. There was so much death. In any century, out of perhaps five clutches of a dozen eggs to a clutch, only one embryo might live to hatch. The legends claimed that once, when the Family had lived in the sea, matters had been different. But now, one survivor out of several clutches was the most to be hoped for. A hatchling who survived would be just about the size of this creature, the Youngest thought, though of course not with his funny shape. Nevertheless, watching him was a little like watching a new hatchling, knowing it would die.

It was an unhappy thought. But there was nothing to be done. Even if the diver were on the surface now, the chances were small that his own People could locate him.

Struck by a thought, the Youngest went up to look around. The situation was as she had guessed. No boats were close by. The nearest was the one from which the diver had descended; but it was still anchored close to the location of the hatchhole, nearly half a mile from where she and the creature now were.

Clearly, those still aboard thought to find him near where they had lost him. The Youngest went back down, and found him still drifting, now not more than thirty feet below the surface, but rising only gradually.

Her emotions stirred as she looked at him. He was not a cold life-form like the salmons, eels, and other fishes on which the Family fed. He was warm—as she was—and if the legends were all true, there had been a time and a place on the wide oceans where one of his ancestors and one of her ancestors might have looked at each other, equal and unafraid, in the open air and the sunlight.

So, it seemed wrong to let him just drift and die like this. He had shown the courage to go down into the depths of the loch, this small, frail thing. And such courage required some recognition from one of the Family, like herself. After all, it was loyalty and courage that had kept the Family going all these centuries: their loyalty to each other and the courage to conserve their strength and go on, hoping that someday the ice would come once more, the land would sink, and they would be set free into the seas again. Then surviving hatchlings would once more be numerous, and the Family would begin to grow again into what the legends had once called them, a "True People." Anyone who believed in loyalty and courage, the Youngest told herself, ought to respect those qualities wherever she found them—even in one of the upright creatures.

He should not simply be left to die. It was a daring thought, that she might interfere..

She felt her own heart beating more rapidly as she followed him through the water, her cheek cells only inches from his dangling shape. After all, there was the taboo. But perhaps, if she could somehow help him without actually touching him . . .?

"Him," of course, should not include the "made" things about him. But even if she could move him by these made parts alone, where could she take him?

Back to where the others of his kind still searched for him?

No, that was not only a deliberate flouting of the taboo but was very dangerous. Behind the taboo was the command to avoid letting any of his kind know about the Family. To take him back was to deliberately risk that kind of exposure for her People. She would die before doing that. The Family had existed all these centuries only because each member of it was faithful to the legends, to the duties, and to the taboos.

But, after all, she thought, it wasn't that she was actually going to break the taboo. She was only going to do something that went around the edge of it, because the diver had shown courage and because it was not his fault that he had happened to drop his heavy thing right beside the hatchhole. If he had dropped it anyplace else in the loch, he could have gone up and down its cable all summer and the Family members would merely have avoided that area.

What he needed, she decided, was a place out of the water where he could recover. She could take him to one of the banks of the loch. She rose to the surface again and looked around.

What she saw made her hesitate. In the darkening afternoon, the headlights of the cars moving up and down the roadways on each side of the loch were still visible in unusual numbers. From Fort Augustus at the south end of the loch to Castle Ness at the north, she saw more headlights about than ever before at this time of year, especially congregating by St. Ninian's, where the diver's boat was docked, nights.

No, it was too risky, trying to take him ashore. But she knew of a cave, too small by Family standards for any of the older adults, south of Urquhart Castle. The diver had gone down over the hatchhole, which had been constructed by Second Mother in the mouth of Urquhart Glen, close by St. Ninian's; and he had been drifting south ever since. Now he was below Castle Urquhart and almost level with the cave. It was a good, small cave for an animal his size, with a ledge of rock that was dry above the water at this time of year; and during the day even a little light would filter through cracks where tree roots from above had penetrated its rocky roof.

The Youngest could bring him there quite easily. She hesitated again, but then extended her head toward the air tanks on his back, took the tanks in her jaws, and began to carry him in the direction of the cave.

As she had expected, it was empty. This late in the day there was no light inside; but since, underwater, her cheek cells reported accurately on conditions about her and, above water, she had her memory, which was ultimately reliable, she brought him—still unconscious—to the ledge at the back of the cave and reared her head a good eight feet out of the water to lift him up on it. As she set him down softly on the bare rock, one of his legs brushed her neck, and a thrill of icy horror ran through the warm interior of her body.

Now she had done it! She had broken the taboo. Panic seized her.

She turned and plunged back into the water, out through the entrance to the cave and into the open loch. The taboo had never been broken before, as far as she knew—never. Suddenly she was terribly frightened. She headed at top speed for the hatchhole. All she wanted was to find Second Mother, or the Uncle, or anyone, and confess what she had done, so that they could tell her that the situation was not irreparable, not a signal marking an end of everything for them all.

Halfway to the hatchhole, however, she woke to the fact that it had already been abandoned. She turned immediately and began to range the loch bottom southward, her instinct and training counseling her that First Uncle and Second Mother would have gone in that direction, south toward Inverfarigaig, to set up a new hatchhole.

As she swam, however, her panic began to lessen and guilt moved in to take its place. How could she tell them? She almost wept inside herself. Here it was not many months ago that they had talked about how she was beginning to look and think like an adult; and she had behaved as thoughtlessly as if she was still the near-hatchling she had been thirty years ago.

Level with Castle Kitchie, she sensed the new location and homed in on it, finding it already set up off the mouth of the stream which flowed past that castle into the loch. The bed of the loch about the new hatchhole had been neatly swept and the saucer-shaped depression dug, in which Second Mother now lay warming the eggs. First Uncle was close by enough to feel the Youngest arrive, and he swept in to speak to her as she halted above Second Mother.

"Where did you go after I broke the line?" he demanded before she herself could signal.

"I wanted to see what would happen to the diver," she signaled back. "Did you need me? I would have come back, but you and Second Mother were both there."

"We had to move right away," Second Mother signaled. She was agitated. "It was frightening!"

"They dropped another line," First Uncle said, "with a thing on it that they pulled back and forth as if to find the first one they dropped. I thought it not wise to break a second one. One break could be a chance happening. Two, and even small animals might wonder."

"But we couldn't keep the hole there with that thing dragging back and forth near the eggs," explained Second Mother. "So we took them and moved without waiting to make the new hole here, first. The Uncle and I carried them, searching as we went. If you'd been here, you could have held half of them while I made the hole by myself, the way I wanted it. But you weren't. We would have sent for First Mother to come from her cave and help us, but neither one of us wanted to risk carrying the eggs about so much. So we had to work together here while still holding the eggs."

"Forgive me," said the Youngest. She wished she were dead.

"You're young," said Second Mother. "Next time you'll be wiser. But you do know that one of the earliest legends says the eggs should be moved only with the utmost care until hatching time; and you know we think that may be one reason so few hatch."

"If none hatch now," said First Uncle to the Youngest, less forgiving than Second Mother, even though they were not his eggs, "you'll remember this and consider that maybe you're to blame."

"Yes," mourned the Youngest.

She had a sudden, frightening vision of this one and all Second Mother's future clutches failing to hatch and she herself proving unable to lay when her time came. It was almost unheard of that a female of the Family should be barren, but a legend said that such a thing did occasionally happen. In her mind's eye she held a terrible picture of First Mother long dead, First Uncle and Second Mother grown old and feeble, unable to stir out of their caves, and she herself—the last of her line—dying alone, with no one to curl about her to warm or comfort her.

She had intended, when she caught up with the other two members of the Family, to tell them everything about what she had done with the diver. But she could not bring herself to it now. Her confession stuck in her mind. If it turned out that the clutch had been harmed by her inattention while she had actually been breaking the taboo with one of the very animals who had threatened the clutch in the first place . . .

She should have considered more carefully. But, of course, she was still too ignorant and irresponsible. First Uncle and Second Mother were the wise ones. First Mother, also, of course; but she was now too old to see a clutch of eggs through to hatching stage by herself alone, or with just the help of someone presently as callow and untrustworthy as the Youngest.

"Can I—It's dark now," she signaled. "Can I go feed, now? Is it all right to go?"

"Of course," said Second Mother, who switched her signaling to First Uncle. "You're too hard sometimes. She's still only half grown."

The Youngest felt even worse, intercepting that. She slunk off through the underwater, wishing something terrible could happen to her so that when the older ones did find out what she had done they would feel pity for her, instead of hating her. For a while she played with mental images of what this might involve. One of the boats on the surface could get her tangled in their lines in such a way that she could not get free. Then they would tow her to shore, and since she was so tangled in the line she could not get up to the surface, and since she had not breathed for many hours, she would drown on the way. Or perhaps the boat that could go underwater would find her and start chasing her and turn out to be much faster than any of them had ever suspected. It might even catch her and ram her and kill her.

By the time she had run through a number of these dark scenarios, she had begun almost automatically to hunt, for the time was in fact well past her usual second feeding period and she was hungry. As she realized this, her hunt became serious. Gradually she filled herself with salmon; and as she did so, she began to feel better. For all her bulk, she was swifter than any fish in the loch. The wide swim paddle at the end of each of her four limbs could turn her instantly; and with her long neck and relatively small head outstretched, the streamlining of even her twenty-eight foot body parted the waters she displaced with an absolute minimum of resistance. Last, and most important of all, was the great engine of her enormously powerful, lashing tail: that was the real drive behind her ability to flash above the loch bottom at speeds of up to fifty knots.

She was, in fact, beautifully designed to lead the life she led, designed by evolution over the generations from that early land-dwelling, omnivorous early mammal that was her ancestor. Actually, she was herself a member of the mammalian sub-class prototheria, a large and distant cousin of monotremes like the platypus and the echidna. Her cretaceous forebears had drifted over and become practicing carnivores in the process of readapting to life in the sea.

She did not know this herself, of course. The legends of the Family were incredibly ancient, passed down by the letter-perfect memories of the individual generations; but they actually were not true memories of what had been, but merely deductions about the past gradually evolved as her People had acquired communication and intelligence. In many ways, the Youngest was very like a human savage: a member of a Stone Age tribe where elaborate ritual and custom directed every action of her life except for a small area of individual freedom. And in that area of individual freedom she was as prone to ignorance and misjudgments about the world beyond the waters of her loch as any Stone Age human primitive was in dealing with the technological world beyond his familiar few square miles of jungle.

Because of this—and because she was young and healthy—by the time she had filled herself with salmon, the exercise of hunting her dinner had burned off a good deal of her feelings of shame and guilt. She saw, or thought she saw, more clearly that her real fault was in not staying close to the hatchhole after the first incident. The diver's leg touching her neck had been entirely accidental; and besides, the diver had been unconscious and unaware of her presence at that time. So no harm could have been done. Essentially, the taboo was still unbroken. But she must learn to stay on guard as the adults did, to anticipate additional trouble, once some had put in an appearance, and to hold herself ready at all times.

She resolved to do so. She made a solemn promise to herself not to forget the hatchhole again—ever.

Her stomach was full. Emboldened by the freedom of the night-empty waters above, for the loch was always clear of boats after sundown, she swam to the surface, emerging only a couple of hundred yards from shore. Lying there, she watched the unusual number of lights from cars still driving on the roads that skirted the loch.

But suddenly her attention was distracted from them. The clouds overhead had evidently cleared, some time since. Now it was a clear, frosty night and more than half the sky was glowing and melting with the northern lights. She floated, watching them. So beautiful, she thought, so beautiful. Her mind evoked pictures of all the Family who must have lain and watched the lights like this since time began, drifting in the arctic seas or resting on some skerry or ocean rock where only birds walked. The desire to see all the wide skies and seas of all the world swept over her like a physical hunger.

It was no use, however. The mountains had risen and they held the Family here, now. Blocked off from its primary dream, her hunger for adventure turned to a more possible goal. The temptation came to go and investigate the loch-going "made" things from which her diver had descended.

She found herself up near Dores, but she turned and went back down opposite St. Ninian's. The dock to which this particular boat was customarily moored was actually a mile below the village and had no illumination. But the boat had a cabin on its deck, amidships, and through the square windows lights now glowed. Their glow was different from that of the lights shown by the cars. The Youngest noted this difference without being able to account for it, not understanding that the headlights she had been watching were electric, but the illumination she now saw shining out of the cabin windows of the large, flat-hulled boat before her came from gas lanterns. She heard sounds coming from inside the cabin.

Curious, the Youngest approached the boat from the darkness of the lake, her head now lifted a good six feet out of the water so that she could look over the side railing. Two large, awkward-looking shapes rested on the broad deck in front of the cabin—one just in front, the other right up in the bow with its far end overhanging the water. Four more shapes, like the one in the bow but smaller, were spaced along the sides of the foredeck, two to a side. The Youngest slid through the little waves until she was barely a couple of dozen feet from the side of the boat. At that moment, two men came out of the cabin, strode onto the deck, and stopped by the shape just in front of the cabin.

The Youngest, though she knew she could not be seen against the dark expanse of the loch, instinctively sank down until only her head was above water. The two men stood, almost overhead, and spoke to each other.

Their voices had a strangely slow, sonorous ring to the ears of Youngest, who was used to hearing sound waves traveling through the water at four times the speed they moved in air. She did understand, of course, that they were engaged in meaningful communication, much as she and the others of the Family were when they signaled to each other. This much her People had learned about the upright animals; they communicated by making sounds. A few of these sounds—the "*Ness*" sound, which, like the other sound, "*loch*." seemed to refer to the water in which the Family lived—were by now familiar. But she recognized no such noises among those made by the two above her; in fact, it would have been surprising if she had, for while the language was the one she was used to hearing, the accent of one of the two was a different English, different enough from that of those living in the vicinity of the loch to make what she heard completely unintelligible.

". . . poor bastard," the other voice said.

"Mon, you forget that 'poor bastard' talk, I tell you! He knew what he doing when he go down that line. He know what a temperature like that mean. A reading like that big enough for a blue whale. He just want the glory—he all alone swimming down with a speargun to drug that great beast. It the newspaper headlines, man; that's what he after!"

"Gives me the creeps, anyway. Think we'll ever fish up the sensor head?"

"You kidding. Lucky we find *him*. No, we use the spare, like I say, starting early tomorrow. And I mean it, early!"

"I don't like it. I tell you, he's got to have relatives who'll want to know why we didn't stop after we lost him. It's his boat. It's his equipment. They'll ask who gave us permission to go on spending money they got coming, with him dead."

"You pay me some heed. We've got to try to find him, that's only right. We use the equipment we got—what else we got to use? Never mind his rich relatives. They just like him. He don't never give no damn for you or me or what it cost him, this expedition. He was born with money and all he want to do is write the book about how he an adventurer. We know what we hunt be down there, now. We capture it, then everybody happy. And you and me, we get what's in the contract, the five thousand extra apiece for taking it. Otherwise we don't get nothing—you back to that machine shop, me to the whaling, with the pockets empty. We out in the cold then, you recall that!"

"All right."

"You damn right, it all right. Starting tomorrow sunup."

"I said *all right*!" The voice paused for a second before going on. "But I'm telling you one thing. If we run into it, you better get it fast with a drug spear; because I'm not waiting. If I see it, I'm getting on the harpoon gun."

The other voice laughed.

"That's why he never let you near the gun when we out before. But I don't care. Contract, it say alive or dead we get what he promise us. Come on now, up the inn and have us food and drink."

"I want a drink! Christ, this water's empty after dark, with that law about no fishing after sundown. Anything could be out there!"

"Anything is. Come on, mon."

The Youngest heard the sound of their footsteps backing off the boat and moving away down the dock until they became inaudible within the night of the land.

Left alone, she lifted her head gradually out of the water once more and cautiously examined everything before her: big boat and small ones nearby, dock and shore. There was no sound or other indication of anything living. Slowly, she once more approached the craft the two had just left and craned her neck over its side.

The large shape in front of the cabin was box-like like the boat, but smaller and without any apertures in it. Its top sloped from the side facing the bow of the craft to the opposite side. On that sloping face she saw circles of some material that, although as hard as the rest of the object, still had a subtly different texture when she pressed her cheek cells directly against them. Farther down from these, which were in fact the glass faces of meters, was a raised plate with grooves in it. The Youngest would not have understood what the grooves meant, even if she had had enough light to see them plainly; and even if their sense could have been translated to her, the words "caloric sensor" would have meant nothing to her.

A few seconds later, she was, however, puzzled to discover on the deck beside this object another shape which her memory insisted was an exact duplicate of the heavy round thing that had been dropped to the loch bed beside the old hatchhole. She felt all over it carefully with her cheek cells, but discovered nothing beyond the dimensions of its almost plumb-bob shape and the fact that a line was attached to it in the same way a line had been attached to the other. In this case, the line was one end of a heavy coil that had a farther end connected to the box-like shape with the sloping top.

Baffled by this discovery, the Youngest moved forward to examine the strange object in the bow of the boat with its end overhanging the water. This one had a shape that was hard to understand. It was more complex, made up of a number of smaller shapes both round and boxy. Essentially, however, it looked like a mound with something long and narrow set on top of it, such as a piece of waterlogged tree from which the limbs had long since dropped off. The four smaller things like it, spaced two on each side of the foredeck, were not quite like the big one, but they were enough alike so that she ignored them in favor of examining the large one. Feeling around the end of the object that extended over the bow of the boat and hovered above the water, the Youngest discovered the log shape rotated at a touch and even tilted up and down with the mound beneath it as a balance point. On further investigation, she found that the log shape was hollow at the water end and was projecting beyond the hooks the animals often let down into the water with little dead fish or other things attached, to try to catch the larger fish of the loch. This end, however, was attached not to a curved length of metal, but to a straight metal rod lying loosely in the hollow log space. To the rod part, behind the barbed head, was joined the end of another heavy coil of line wound about a round thing on the deck. This line was much thicker than the one attached to the box with the sloping top. Experimentally, she tested it with her teeth. It gave—but did not cut when she closed her jaws on it—then sprang back, apparently unharmed, when she let it go.

All very interesting, but puzzling—as well it might be. A harpoon gun and spearguns with heads designed to inject a powerful tranquilizing drug on impact were completely outside the reasonable dimensions of the world as the Youngest knew it. The heat-sensing equipment that had been used to locate First Uncle's huge body as it lay on the loch bed warming the eggs was closer to being something she could understand. She and the rest of the Family used heat sensing themselves to locate and identify one another, though their natural abilities were nowhere near as sensitive as those of the instrument she had examined on the foredeck. At any rate, for now, she merely dismissed from her mind the question of what these things were. Perhaps, she thought, the upright animals simply liked to have odd shapes of "made" things around them. That notion reminded her of her diver; and she felt a sudden, deep curiosity about him, a desire to see if he had yet recovered and found his way out of the cave to shore.

She backed off from the dock and turned toward the south end of the loch, not specifically heading for the cave where she had left him but traveling in that general direction and turning over in her head the idea that perhaps she might take one more look at the cave. But she would not be drawn into the same sort of irresponsibility she had fallen prey to earlier in the day, when she had taken him to the cave! Not twice would she concern herself with one of the animals when she was needed by others of the Family. She decided, instead, to go check on Second Mother and the new hatchhole.

When she got to the hole, however, she found that Second Mother had no present need of her. The older female, tired from the exacting events of the day and heavy from feeding later than her usual time—for she had been too nervous, at first, to leave the eggs in First Uncle's care and so had not finished her feeding period until well after dark—was half asleep. She only untucked her head from the coil she had made of her body around and above the eggs long enough to make sure that the Youngest had not brought warning of some new threat. Reassured, she coiled up tightly again about the clutch and closed her eyes.

The Youngest gazed at her with a touch of envy. It must be a nice feeling, she thought, to shut out everything but yourself and your eggs. There was plainly nothing that Youngest was wanted for, here—and she had never felt less like sleeping herself. The night was full of mysteries and excitements. She headed once more north, up the lake.

She had not deliberately picked a direction, but suddenly she realized that unconsciously she was once more heading toward the cave where she had left the diver. She felt a strange sense of freedom. Second Mother was sleeping with her eggs. First Uncle by this time would have his heavy bulk curled up in his favorite cave and his head on its long neck resting on a ledge at the water's edge, so that he had the best of both the worlds of air and loch at the same time. The Youngest had the loch to herself, with neither Family nor animals to worry about. It was all hers, from Fort Augustus clear to Castle Ness.

The thought gave her a sense of power. Abruptly, she decided that there was no reason at all why she should not go see what had happened to the diver. She turned directly toward the cave, putting on speed.

At the last moment, however, she decided to enter the cave quietly. If he was really recovered and alert, she might want to leave again without being noticed. Like a cloud shadow moving silently across the surface of the waves, she slid through the underwater entrance of the cave, invisible in the blackness, her cheek cells reassuring her that there was no moving body in the water inside.

Once within, she paused again to check for heat radiation that would betray a living body in the water even if it was being held perfectly still. But she felt no heat. Satisfied, she lifted her head silently from the water inside the cave and approached the rock ledge where she had left him.

Her hearing told that he was still here, though her eyes were as useless in this total darkness as his must be. Gradually, that same, sensitive hearing filled in the image of his presence for her.

He still lay on the ledge, apparently on his side. She could hear the almost rhythmic scraping of a sort of metal clip he wore on the right side of his belt. It was scratching against the rock as he made steady, small movements. He must have come to enough to take off his head-things and back-things, however, for she heard no scraping from these. His breathing was rapid and hoarse, almost a panting. Slowly, sound by sound, she built up a picture of him, there in the dark. He was curled up in a tight ball, shivering.

The understanding that he was lying, trembling from the cold, struck the Youngest in her most vulnerable area. Like all the Family, she had vivid memories of what it had been like to be a hatchling. As eggs, the clutch was kept in open water with as high an oxygen content as possible until the moment for hatching came close. Then they were swiftly transported to one of the caves so that they would emerge from their shell into the land and air environment that their warm-blooded, air-breathing ancestry required. And a hatchling could not drown on a cave ledge. But, although he or she was protected there from the water, a hatchling was still vulnerable to the cold; and the caves were no warmer than the water—which was snow-fed from the mountains most of the year. Furthermore, the hatchling would not develop the layers of blubber-like fat that insulated an adult of the Family for several years. The life of someone like the Youngest began with the sharp sensations of cold as a newborn, and ended the same way, when aged body processes were no longer able to generate enough interior heat to keep the great hulk going. The first instinct of the hatchling was to huddle close to the warm belly skin of the adult on guard. And the first instinct of the adult was to warm the small, new life.

She stood in the shallow water of the cave, irresolute. The taboo, and everything that she had ever known, argued fiercely in her against any contact with the upright animal. But this one had already made a breach in her cosmos, had already been promoted from an "it" to a "he" in her thoughts; and her instincts cried out as strongly as her teachings, against letting him chill there on the cold stone ledge when she had within her the heat to warm him.

It was a short, hard, internal struggle; but her instincts won. After all, she rationalized, it was she who had brought him here to tremble in the cold. The fact that by doing so she had saved his life was beside the point.

Completely hidden in the psychological machinery that moved her toward him now was the lack in her life that was the result of being the last, solitary child of her kind. From the moment of hatching on, she had never had a playmate, never known anyone with whom she could share the adventures of growing up. An unconscious part of her was desperately hungry for a friend, a toy, anything that could be completely and exclusively hers, apart from the adult world that encompassed everything around her.

Slowly, silently, she slipped out of the water and up onto the ledge and flowed around his shaking form. She did not quite dare to touch him; but she built walls about him and a roof over him out of her body, the inward-facing skin of which was already beginning to pulse with hot blood pumped from deep within her.

Either dulled by his semi-consciousness or else too wrapped up in his own misery to notice, the creature showed no awareness that she was there. Not until the warmth began to be felt did he instinctively relax the tight ball of his body and, opening out, touch her—not merely with his wetsuit-encased body, but with his unprotected hands and forehead.

The Youngest shuddered all through her length at that first contact. But before she could withdraw, his own reflexes operated. His chilling body felt warmth and did not stop to ask its source. Automatically, he huddled close against the surfaces he touched.

The Youngest bowed her head. It was too late. It was done.

This was no momentary, unconscious contact. She could feel his shivering directly now through her own skin surface. Nothing remained but to accept what had happened. She folded herself close about him, covering as much of his small, cold, trembling body as possible with her own warm surface, just as she would have if he had been a new hatchling who suffered from the chill. He gave a quavering sigh of relief and pressed close against her.

Gradually he warmed and his trembling stopped. Long before

that, he had fallen into a deep, torporlike slumber. She could hear the near-snores of his heavy breathing.

Grown bolder by contact with him and abandoning herself to an affection for him, she explored his slumbering shape with her sensitive cheek cells. He had no true swim paddles, of course—she already knew this about the upright animals. But she had never guessed how delicate and intricate were the several-times split appendages that he possessed on his upper limbs where swim paddles might have been. His body was very narrow, its skeleton hardly clothed in flesh. Now that she knew that his kind were as vulnerable to cold as new hatchlings, she did not wonder that it should be so with them: they had hardly anything over their bones to protect them from the temperature of the water and air. No wonder they covered themselves with non-living skins.

His head was not long at all, but quite round. His mouth was small and his jaws flat, so that he would be able to take only very small bites of things. There was a sort of protuberance above the mouth and a pair of eyes, side by side. Around the mouth and below the eyes his skin was full of tiny, sharp points; and on the top of his head was a strange, springy mat of very fine filaments. The Youngest rested the cells of her right cheek for a moment on the filaments, finding a strange inner warmth and pleasure in the touch of them. It was a completely inexplicable pleasure, for the legends had forgotten what old, primitive parts of her brain remembered: a time when her ancestors on land had worn fur and known the feel of it in their close body contacts.

Wrapped up in the subconscious evocation of ancient companionship, she lay in the darkness spinning impossible fantasies in which she would be able to keep him. He could live in this cave, she thought, and she would catch salmon—since that was what his kind, with their hooks and filaments, seemed most to search for—to bring to him for food. If he wanted "made" things about him, she could probably visit docks and suchlike about the loch and find some to bring here to him. When he got to know her better, since he had the things that let him hold his breath underwater, they could venture out into the loch together. Of course, once that time was reached, she would have to tell Second Mother and First Uncle about him. No doubt it would disturb them greatly, the fact that the taboo had been broken; but once they had met him underwater, and seen how sensible and friendly he was—how wise, even, for a small animal like himself . . .

Even as she lay dreaming these dreams, however, a sane part

of her mind was still on duty. Realistically, she knew that what she was thinking was nonsense. Centuries of legend, duty, and taboo were not to be upset in a few days by any combination of accidents. Nor, even if no problem arose from the Family side, could she really expect him to live in a cave, forsaking his own species. His kind needed light as well as air. They needed the freedom to come and go on shore. Even if she could manage to keep him with her in the cave for a while, eventually the time would come when he would yearn for the land under his feet and the open sky overhead, at one and the same time. No, her imaginings could never be; and, because she knew this, when her internal time sense warned her that the night was nearly over, she silently uncoiled from around him and slipped back into the water, leaving the cave before the first light, which filtered in past the tree roots in the cave roof, could let him see who it was that had kept him alive through the hours of darkness.

Left uncovered on the ledge but warm again, he slept heavily on, unaware.


Out in the waters of the loch, in the pre-dawn gloom, the Youngest felt fatigue for the first time. She could easily go twenty-four hours without sleep; but this twenty-four hours just past had been emotionally charged ones. She had an irresistible urge to find one of the caves she favored herself and to lose herself in slumber. She shook it off. Before anything else, she must check with Second Mother.

Going swiftly to the new hatchhole, she found Second Mother fully awake, alert, and eager to talk to her. Evidently Second Mother had awakened early and spent some time thinking.

"You're young," she signaled the Youngest, "far too young to share the duty of guarding a clutch of eggs, even with someone as wise as your First Uncle. Happily, there's no problem physically. You're mature enough so that milk would come, if a hatchling should try to nurse from you. But, sensibly, you're still far too young to take on this sort of responsibility. Nonetheless, if something should happen to me, there would only be you and the Uncle to see this clutch to the hatching point. Therefore, we have to think of the possibility that you might have to take over for me."

"No. No, I couldn't," said the Youngest.

"You may have to. It's still only a remote possibility; but I should have taken it into consideration before. Since there're only the four of us, if anything happened to one of us, the remaining would have to see the eggs through to hatching. You and I could do it, I'm not worried about that situation. But with a clutch there must be a mother. Your uncle can be everything but that, and First Mother is really too old. Somehow, we must make you ready before your time to take on that duty."

"If you say so . . ." said the Youngest, unhappily.

"Our situation says so. Now, all you need to know, really, is told in the legends. But knowing them and understanding them are two different things . . ."

Then Second Mother launched into a retelling of the long chain of stories associated with the subject of eggs and hatchlings. The Youngest, of course, had heard them all before. More than that, she had them stored, signal by signal, in her memory as perfectly as had Second Mother herself. But she understood that Second Mother wanted her not only to recall each of these packages of stored wisdom, but to think about what was stated in them. Also—so much wiser had she already become in twenty-four hours—she realized that the events of yesterday had suddenly shocked Second Mother, giving her a feeling of helplessness should the upright animals ever really chance to stumble upon the hatchhole. For she could never abandon her eggs, and if she stayed with them the best she could hope for would be to give herself up to the land-dwellers in hope that this would satisfy them and they would look no further.

It was hard to try and ponder the legends, sleepy as the Youngest was, but she tried her best; and when at last Second Mother turned her loose, she swam groggily off to the nearest cave and curled up. It was now broad-enough daylight for her early feeding period, but she was too tired to think of food. In seconds, she was sleeping almost as deeply as the diver had been when she left him.

She came awake suddenly and was in motion almost before her eyes were open. First Uncle's signal of alarm was ringing all through the loch. She plunged from her cave into the outer waters. Vibrations told her that he and Second Mother were headed north, down the deep center of the loch as fast as they could travel, carrying the clutch of eggs. She drove on to join them, sending ahead her own signal that she was coming.

"Quick! Oh, quick!" signaled Second Mother.

Unencumbered, she began to converge on them at double their speed. Even in this moment her training paid off. She shot through the water, barely fifty feet above the bed of the loch, like a dolphin in the salt sea; and her perfect shape and smooth skin caused no turbulence at all to drag at her passage and slow her down.

She caught up with them halfway between Inverfarigaig and Dores and took her half of the eggs from Second Mother, leaving the older female free to find a new hatchhole. Unburdened, Second Mother leaped ahead and began to range the loch bed in search of a safe place.

"What happened?" signaled Youngest.

"Again!" First Uncle answered. "They dropped another 'made' thing, just like the first, almost in the hatchhole this time!" he told her.

Second Mother had been warming the eggs. Luckily he had been close. He had swept in; but not daring to break the line a second time for fear of giving clear evidence of the Family, he had simply scooped a hole in the loch bed, pushed the thing in, buried it and pressed down hard on the loch bed material with which he had covered it. He had buried it deeply enough so that the animals above were pulling up on their line with caution, for fear that they themselves might break it. Eventually, they would get it loose. Until then, the Family had a little time in which to find another location for the eggs.

A massive shape loomed suddenly out of the peaty darkness, facing them. It was First Mother, roused from her cave by the emergency.

"I can still carry eggs. Give them here, and you go back," she ordered First Uncle. "Find out what's being done with that 'made' thing you buried and what's going on with those creatures. Two hatchholes stumbled on in two days is too much for chance."

First Uncle swirled about and headed back.

The Youngest slowed down. First Mother was still tremendously powerful, of course, more so than any of them; but she no longer had the energy reserves to move at the speed at which First Uncle and the Youngest had been traveling. Youngest felt a surge of admiration for First Mother, battling the chill of the open loch water and the infirmities of her age to give help now, when the Family needed it.

"Here! This way!" Second Mother called.

They turned sharply toward the east bank of the loch and homed in on Second Mother's signal. She had found a good place for a new hatchhole. True, it was not near the mouth of a stream; but the loch bed was clean and this was one of the few spots where the rocky slope underwater from the shore angled backward when it reached a depth below four hundred feet, so that the loch at this point was actually in under the rock and had a roof overhead. Here, there was no way that a "made" thing could be dropped down on a line to come anywhere close to the hatchhole.

When First Mother and the Youngest got there, Second Mother was already at work making and cleaning the hole. The hole had barely been finished and Second Mother settled down with the clutch under her, when First Uncle arrived.

"They have their 'made' thing back," he reported. "They pulled on its line with little, repeated jerkings until they loosened it from its bed, and then they lifted it back up."

He told how he had followed it up through the water until he was just under the "made" thing and rode on the loch surface. Holding himself there, hidden by the thing itself, he had listened, trying to make sense out of what the animals were doing, from what he could hear.

They had made a great deal of noise after they hoisted the thing back on board. They had moved it around a good deal and done things with it, before finally leaving it alone and starting back toward the dock near St. Ninian's. First Uncle had followed them until he was sure that was where they were headed; then he had come to find the new hatchhole and the rest of the Family.

After he was done signaling, they all waited for First Mother to respond, since she was the oldest and wisest. She lay thinking for some moments.

"They didn't drop the 'made' thing down into the water again, you say?" she asked at last.

"No," signaled First Uncle.

"And none of them went down into the water, themselves?"

"No."

"It's very strange," said First Mother. "All we know is that they've twice almost found the hatchhole. All I can guess is that this isn't a chance thing, but that they're acting with some purpose. They may not be searching for our eggs, but they seem to be searching for *something*."

The Youngest felt a sudden chilling inside her. But First Mother was already signaling directly to First Uncle.

"From now on, you should watch them, whenever the thing in which they move about the loch surface isn't touching shore. If you need help, the Youngest can help you. If they show any signs of coming close to here, we must move the eggs immediately. I'll come out twice a day to relieve Second Mother for her feeding,

so that you can be free to do that watching. No"—she signaled
sharply before they could object—"I *will* do this. I can go for
some days warming the eggs for two short periods a day, before
I'll be out of strength; and this effort of mine is needed. The eggs
*should* be safe here, but if it proves that the creatures have some
means of finding them, wherever the hatchhole is placed in the
open loch, we'll have to move the clutch into the caves."

Second Mother cried out in protest.

"I know," First Mother said, "the legends counsel against ever
taking the eggs into the caves until time for hatching. But we may
have no choice."

"My eggs will die!" wept Second Mother.

"They're your eggs, and the decision to take them inside has to
be yours," said First Mother. "But they won't live if the animals
find them. In the caves there may be a chance of life for them.
Besides, our duty as a Family is to survive. It's the Family we
have to think of, not a single clutch of eggs or a single individual.
If worse comes to worst and it turns out we're not safe from the
animals even in the caves, we'll try the journey of the Lost Father
from Loch Morar before we'll let ourselves all be killed off."

"What Lost Father?" the Youngest demanded. "No one ever
told me a legend about a Lost Father from Loch Morar. What's
Loch Morar?"

"It's not a legend usually told to those too young to have full
wisdom," said First Mother. "But these are new and dangerous
times. Loch Morar is a loch a long way from here, and some of
our People were also left there when the ice went and the land
rose. They were of our People, but a different Family."

"But what about a Lost Father?" the Youngest persisted, because
First Mother had stopped talking as if she would say no more about
it. "How could a Father be lost?"

"He was lost to Loch Morar," First Mother explained, "because
he grew old and died here in Loch Ness."

"But how did he get here?"

"He couldn't, that's the point," said First Uncle, grumpily.
"There are legends *and* legends. That's why some are not told
to young ones until they've matured enough to understand. The
journey the Lost Father's supposed to have made is impossible.
Tell it to some youngster and he or she's just as likely to try and
duplicate it."

"But you said we might try it!" The Youngest appealed to First
Mother.

"Only if there were no other alternative," First Mother answered. "I'd try flying out over the mountains if that was the only alternative left, because it's our duty to keep trying to survive as a Family as long as we're alive. So, as a last resort, we'd try the journey of the Lost Father, even though as the Uncle says, it's impossible."

"Why? Tell me what it was. You've already begun to tell me. Shouldn't I know all of it?"

"I suppose . . ." said First Mother, wearily. "Very well. Loch Morar isn't surrounded by mountains as we are here. It's even fairly close to the sea, so that if a good way could be found for such as us to travel over dry land, members of the People living there might be able to go home to the sea we all recall by the legends. Well, this legend says that there once was a Father in Loch Morar who dreamed all his life of leading his Family home to the sea. But we've grown too heavy nowadays to travel any distance overland, normally. One winter day, when a new snow had just fallen, the legend says this Father discovered a way of traveling on land that worked."

In sparse sentences, First Mother rehearsed the legend to a fascinated Youngest. It told that the snow provided a slippery surface over which the great bodies of the People could slide under the impetus of the same powerful tail muscles that drove them through the water, their swim paddles acting as rudders—or brakes—on downslopes. Actually, what the legend described was a way of swimming on land. Loch Ness never froze and First Mother therefore had no knowledge of ice-skating, so she could not explain that what the legend spoke of was the same principle that makes a steel ice blade glide over ice—the weight upon it causing the ice to melt under the sharp edge of the blade so that, effectively, it slides on a cushion of water. With the People, their ability to shunt a controlled amount of warmth to the skin in contact with the ice and snow did the same thing.

In the legend, the Father who discovered this tried to take his Family from Loch Morar back to the sea, but they were all afraid to try going, except for him. So he went alone and found his way to the ocean more easily than he had thought possible. He spent some years in the sea, but found it lonely and came back to land to return to Loch Morar. However, though it was winter, he could not find enough snow along the route he had taken to the sea in order to get back to Loch Morar. He hunted northward for a snow-covered route inland, north past the isle of Sleat, past Glenelg; and finally, under Benn Attow, he found a

snow route that led him ultimately to Glen Moriston and into
Loch Ness.

He went as far back south through Loch Ness as he could go,
even trying some distance down what is now the southern part of
the Caledonian Canal before he became convinced that the route
back to Loch Morar by that way would be too long and hazardous
to be practical. He decided to return to the sea and wait for snow
to make him a way over his original route to Morar.

But, meanwhile, he had become needed in Loch Ness and
grown fond of the Family there. He wished to take them with
him to the sea. The others, however, were afraid to try the long
overland journey; and while they hesitated and put off going, he
grew too old to lead them; and so they never did go. Nevertheless, the legend told of his route and, memories being what
they were among the People, no member of the Family in Loch
Ness, after First Mother had finished telling the legend to the
Youngest, could not have retraced the Lost Father's steps exactly.

"I don't think we should wait," the Youngest said, eagerly, when
First Mother was through. "I think we should go now—I mean,
as soon as we get a snow on the banks of the loch so that we can
travel. Once we're away from the loch, there'll be snow all the
time, because it's only the warmth of the loch that keeps the snow
off around here. Then we could all go home to the sea, where we
belong, away from the animals and their "made" things. Most of
the eggs laid there would hatch— "

"I told you so," First Uncle interrupted, speaking to First
Mother. "Didn't I tell you so?"

"And what about my eggs now?" said Second Mother.

"We'll try something like that only if the animals start to destroy
us," First Mother said to the Youngest with finality. "Not before.
If it comes to that, Second Mother's present clutch of eggs will be
lost, anyway. Otherwise, we'd never leave them, you should know
that. Now, I'll go back to the cave and rest until late feeding period
for Second Mother."

She went off. First Uncle also went off, to make sure that the
animals had really gone to the dock and were still there. The
Youngest, after asking Second Mother if there was any way she
could be useful and being told there was none, went off to her
delayed first feeding period.

She was indeed hungry, with the ravenous hunger of youth.
But once she had taken the edge off her appetite, an uneasy

feeling began to grow inside her, and not even stuffing herself with rich-fleshed salmon made it go away.

What was bothering her, she finally admitted to herself, was the sudden, cold thought that had intruded on her when First Mother had said that the creatures seemed to be searching for something. The Youngest was very much afraid she knew what they were searching for. It was their fellow, the diver she had taken to the cave. If she had not done anything, they would have found his body before this; but because she had saved him, they were still looking; and because he was in a cave, they could not find him. So they would keep on searching, and sooner or later they would come close to the new hatchhole; and then Second Mother would take the clutch into one of the caves, and the eggs would die, and it would be her own fault, the Youngest's fault alone.

She was crying inside. She did not dare cry out loud because the others would hear and want to know what was troubling her. She was ashamed to tell them what she had done. Somehow, she must put things right herself, without telling them—at least until some later time, when it would be all over and unimportant.

The diver must go back to his own people—if he had not already.

She turned and swam toward the cave, making sure to approach it from deep in the loch. Through the entrance of the cave, she stood up in the shallow interior pool and lifted her head out of water; and he was still there.

Enough light was filtering in through the ceiling cracks of the cave to make a sort of dim twilight inside. She saw him plainly—and he saw her.

She had forgotten that he would have no idea of what she looked like. He had been sitting up on the rock ledge; but when her head and its long neck rose out of the water, he stared and then scrambled back—as far back from her as he could get, to the rock wall of the cave behind the ledge. He stood pressed against it, still staring at her, his mouth open in a soundless circle.

She paused, irresolute. She had never intended to frighten him. She had forgotten that he might consider her at all frightening. All her foolish imaginings of keeping him here in the cave and of swimming with him in the loch crumbled before the bitter reality of his terror at the sight of her. Of course, he had had no idea of who had been coiled about him in the dark. He had only known that something large had been bringing the warmth of life back into him. But surely he would make the connection, now that he saw her?

She waited.

He did not seem to be making it. He simply stayed where he was, as if paralyzed by her presence. She felt an exasperation with him rising inside her. According to the legends, his kind had at least a share of intelligence, possibly even some aspect of wisdom, although that was doubtful. But now, crouched against the back of the cave, he looked like nothing more than another wild animal—like one of the otters, strayed from nearby streams, she had occasionally encountered in these caves. And as with such an otter, for all its small size ready to scratch or bite, she felt a caution about approaching him.

Nevertheless, something had to be done. At any moment now, the others like him would be out on the loch in their "made" thing, once more hunting for him and threatening to rediscover the hatchhole.

Cautiously, slowly, so as not to send him into a fighting reflex, she approached the ledge and crept up on it sideways, making an arc of her body and moving in until she half surrounded him, an arm's length from him. She was ready to pull back at the first sign of a hostile move, but no action was triggered in him. He merely stayed where he was, pressing against the rock wall as if he would like to step through it, his eyes fixed on her and his jaws still in the half-open position. Settled about him, however, she shunted blood into her skin area and began to radiate heat.

It took a little while for him to feel the warmth coming from her and some little while more to understand what she was trying to tell him. But then, gradually, his tense body relaxed. He slipped down the rock against which he was pressed and ended up sitting, gazing at her with a different shape to his eyes and mouth.

He made some noises with his mouth. These conveyed no sense to the Youngest, of course, but she thought that at least they did not sound like unfriendly noises.

"So now you know who I am," she signaled, although she knew perfectly well he could not understand her. "Now, you've got to swim out of here and go back on the land. Go back to your People."

She had corrected herself instinctively on the last term. She had been about to say "go back to the other animals"; but something inside her dictated the change—which was foolish, because he would not know the difference, anyway.

He straightened against the wall and stood up. Suddenly, he reached out an upper limb toward her.

She flinched from his touch instinctively, then braced herself to stay put. If she wanted him not to be afraid of her, she would have to show him the same fearlessness. Even the otters, if left alone, would calm down somewhat, though they would take the first opportunity to slip past and escape from the cave where they had been found.

She held still, accordingly. The divided ends of his limb touched her and rubbed lightly over her skin. It was not an unpleasant feeling, but she did not like it. It had been different when he was helpless and had touched her unconsciously.

She now swung her head down close to watch him and had the satisfaction of seeing him start when her own eyes and jaws came within a foot or so of his. He pulled his limbs back quickly, and made more noises. They were still not angry noises, though, and this fact, together with his quick withdrawal, gave her an impression that he was trying to be conciliatory, even friendly.

Well, at least she had his attention. She turned, backed off the ledge into the water, then reached up with her nose and pushed toward him the "made" things he originally had had attached to his back and head. Then, turning, she ducked under the water, swam out of the cave into the loch, and waited just under the surface for him to follow.

He did not.

She waited for more than enough time for him to reattach his things and make up his mind to follow, then she swam back inside. To her disgust, he was now sitting down again and his "made" things were still unattached to him.

She came sharply up to the edge of the rock and tumbled the two things literally on top of him.

"Put them on!" she signaled. "Put them on, you stupid animal!"

He stared at her and made noises with his mouth. He stood up and moved his upper limbs about in the air. But he made no move to pick up the "made" things at his feet. Angrily, she shoved them against his lower limb ends once more.

He stopped making noises and merely looked at her. Slowly, although she could not define all of the changes that signaled it to her, an alteration of manner seemed to take place in him. The position of his upright body changed subtly. The noises he was making changed; they became slower and more separate, one from another. He bent down and picked up the larger of the things, the one that he had had attached to his back; but he did not put it on.

Instead, he held it up in the air before him as if drawing her attention to it. He turned it over in the air and shook it slightly, then held it in that position some more. He rapped it with the curled-over sections of one of his limb-ends, so that it rang with a hollow sound from both its doubled parts. Then he put it down on the ledge again and pushed it from him with one of his lower limb ends.

The Youngest stared at him, puzzled, but nonetheless hopeful for the first time. At last he seemed to be trying to communicate something to her, even though what he was doing right now seemed to make no sense. Could it be that this was some sort of game the upright animals played with their "made" things; and he either wanted to play it, or wanted her to play it with him, before he would put the things on and get in the water? When she was much younger, she had played with things herself—interesting pieces of rock or waterlogged material she found on the loch bed, or flotsam she had encountered on the surface at night, when it was safe to spend time in the open.

No, on second thought that explanation hardly seemed likely. If it was a game he wanted to play with her, it was more reasonable for him to push the things at her instead of just pushing the bigger one away and ignoring it. She watched him, baffled. Now he had picked up the larger thing again and was repeating his actions exactly.

The creature went through the same motions several more times, eventually picking up and putting the smaller "made" thing about his head and muzzle, but still shaking and pushing away the larger thing. Eventually he made a louder noise which, for the first time, sounded really angry; threw the larger thing to one end of the ledge; and went off to sit down at the far end of the ledge, his back to her.

Still puzzled, the Youngest stretched her neck up over the ledge to feel the rejected "made" thing again with her cheek cells. It was still an enigmatic, cold, hard, double-shaped object that made no sense to her. What he's doing can't be playing, she thought. Not that he was playing at the last, there. And besides, he doesn't act as if he liked it and liked to play with it, he's acting as if he hated it—

Illumination came to her, abruptly.

"Of course!" she signaled at him.

But of course the signal did not even register on him. He still sat with his back to her.

What he had been trying to tell her, she suddenly realized, was that for some reason the "made" thing was no good for him any longer. Whether he had used it to play with, to comfort himself, or, as she had originally guessed, it had something to do with making it possible for him to stay underwater, for some reason it was now no good for that purpose.

The thought that it might indeed be something to help him stay underwater suddenly fitted in her mind with the fact that he no longer considered it any good. She sat back on her tail, mentally berating herself for being so foolish. Of course, that was what he had been trying to tell her. It would not help him stay underwater anymore; and to get out of the cave he had to go underwater—not very far, of course, but still a small distance.

On the other hand, how was he to know it was only a small distance? He had been unconscious when she had brought him here.

Now that she had worked out what she thought he had been trying to tell her, she was up against a new puzzle. By what means was she to get across to him that she had understood?

She thought about this for a time, then picked up the thing in her teeth and threw it herself against the rock wall at the back of the ledge.

He turned around, evidently alerted by the sounds it made. She stretched out her neck, picked up the thing, brought it back to the water edge of the ledge, and then threw it at the wall again.

Then she looked at him.

He made sounds with his mouth and turned all the way around. Was it possible he had understood, she wondered? But he made no further moves, just sat there. She picked up and threw the "made" thing a couple of more times; then she paused once again to see what he might do.

He stood, hesitating, then inched forward to where the thing had fallen, picked up and threw it himself. But he threw it, as she had thrown it—at the rock wall behind the ledge.

The Youngest felt triumph. They were finally signalling each other—after a fashion.

But now where did they go from here? She wanted to ask him if there was anything they could do about the "made" thing being useless, but she could not think how to act that question out.

He, however, evidently had something in mind. He went to the edge of the rock shelf, knelt down and placed one of his multi-divided limb ends flat on the water surface, but with its inward-grasping surface upward. Then he moved it across the surface of the water so that the outer surface, or back, of it was in the water but the inner surface was still dry.

She stared at him. Once more he was doing something incomprehensible. He repeated the gesture several more times, but still it conveyed no meaning to her. He gave up, finally, and sat for a few minutes looking at her; then he got up, went back to the rock wall, turned around, walked once more to the edge of the ledge, and sat down.

Then he held up one of his upper limb ends with all but two of the divisions curled up. The two that were not curled up he pointed downward, and lowered them until their ends rested on the rock ledge. Then, pivoting first on the end of one of the divisions, then on the other, he moved the limb end back toward the wall as far as he could stretch, then turned it around and moved it forward again to the water's edge, where he folded up the two extended divisions, and held the limb end still.

He did this again. And again.

The Youngest concentrated. There was some meaning here; but with all the attention she could bring to bear on it, she still failed to see what it was. This was even harder than extracting wisdom from the legends. As she watched, he got up once more, walked back to the rock wall, came forward again and sat down. He did this twice.

Then he did the limb-end, two-division-movement thing twice.

Then he walked again, three times.

Then he did the limb-end thing three more times—

Understanding suddenly burst upon the Youngest. He was trying to make some comparison between his walking to the back of the ledge and forward again, and moving his limb ends in that odd fashion, first backward and then forward. The two divisions, with their little joints, moved much like his two lower limbs when he walked on them. It was extremely interesting to take part of your body and make it act like your whole body, doing something. Youngest wished that her swim paddles had divisions on the ends, like his, so she could try it.

She was becoming fascinated with the diver all over again. She had almost forgotten the threat to the eggs that others like him posed as long as he stayed hidden in this cave. Her conscience caught her up sharply. She should check right now and see if things were all right with the Family. She turned to leave, and then checked herself. She wanted to reassure him that she was coming back.

For a second only she was baffled for a means to do this; then she remembered that she had already left the cave once, thinking he would follow her, and then come back when she had given up on his doing so. If he saw her go and come several times, he should expect that she would go on returning, even though the interval might vary.

She turned and dived out through the hole into the loch, paused for a minute or two, then went back in. She did this two more times before leaving the cave finally. He had given her no real sign that he understood what she was trying to convey, but he had already showed signs of that intelligence the legends credited his species with. Hopefully, he would figure it out. If he did not—well, since she was going back anyway, the only harm would be that he might worry a bit about being abandoned there.

She surfaced briefly, in the center of the loch, to see if many of the "made" things were abroad on it today. But none were in sight and there was little or no sign of activity on the banks. The sky was heavy with dark, low-lying clouds; and the hint of snow, heavy snow, was in the sharp air. She thought again of the journey of the Lost Father of Loch Morar, and of the sea it could take them to—their safe home, the sea. They should go. They should go without waiting. If only she could convince them to go . . .

She dropped by the hatchhole, found First Mother warming the eggs while Second Mother was off feeding, and heard from First Mother that the craft had not left its place on shore all day. Discussing this problem almost as equals with First Mother—of whom she had always been very much in awe—emboldened the Youngest to the point where she shyly suggested she might try warming the clutch herself, occasionally, so as to relieve First Mother from these twice-daily stints, which must end by draining her strength and killing her.

"It would be up to Second Mother, in any case," First Mother answered, "but you're still really too small to be sure of giving adequate warmth to a full clutch. In an emergency, of course, you shouldn't hesitate to do your best with the eggs, but I don't think we're quite that desperate, yet."

Having signaled this, however, First Mother apparently softened.

"Besides," she said, "the time to be young and free of responsibilities is short enough. Enjoy it while you can. With the Family reduced to the four of us and this clutch, you'll have a hard enough adulthood, even if Second Mother manages to produce as many as two hatchlings out of the five or six clutches she can still have before her laying days are over. The odds of hatching females over males are four to one; but still, it could be that she might produce only a couple of males—and then everything would be up to you. So, use your time in your own way while it's still yours to use. But keep alert. If you're called, come immediately!"

The Youngest promised that she would. She left First Mother and went to find First Uncle, who was keeping watch in the neighborhood of the dock to which the craft was moored. When she found him, he was hanging in the loch about thirty feet deep and about a hundred feet offshore from the craft, using his sensitive hearing to keep track of what was happening in the craft and on the dock.

"I'm glad you're here," he signaled to the Youngest when she arrived. "It's time for my second feeding; and I think there're none of the animals on the "made" thing, right now. But it wouldn't hurt to keep a watch, anyway. Do you want to stay here and listen while I go and feed?"

Actually, Youngest was not too anxious to do so. Her plan had been to check with the Uncle, then do some feeding herself and get back to her diver while daylight was still coming into his cave. But she could hardly explain that to First Uncle.

"Of course," she said. "I'll stay here until you get back."

"Good," said the Uncle; and went off.

Left with nothing to do but listen and think, the Youngest hung in the water. Her imagination, which really required very little to start it working, had recaptured the notion of making friends with the diver. It was not so important, really, that he had gotten a look at her. Over the centuries a number of incidents had occurred in which members of the Family were seen briefly by one or more of the animals, and no bad results had come from those sightings. But it was important that the land-dwellers not realize there was a true Family. If she could just convince the diver that she was the last and only one of her People, it might be quite safe to see him from time to time—of course, only when he was alone and when they were in a safe place of her choosing, since though he might be trustworthy, his fellows who had twice threatened the hatchhold clearly were not.

The new excitement about getting to know him had come from starting to be able to "talk" with him. If she and he kept at it, they could probably work out ways to tell all sorts of things to each other eventually.

That thought reminded her that she had not yet figured out why it was important to him that she understand that moving his divided limb ends in a certain way could stand for his walking. He must have had some reason for showing her that. Maybe it was connected with his earlier moving of his limb ends over the surface of the water?

Before she had a chance to ponder the possible connection, a sound from above, reaching down through the water, alerted her to the fact that some of the creatures were once more coming out onto the dock. She drifted in closer, and heard the sounds move to the end of the dock and onto the craft.

Apparently, they were bringing something heavy aboard, because along with the noise of their lower limb ends on the structure came the thumping and rumbling of something which ended at last—to judge from the sounds—somewhere up on the forward deck where she had examined the box with the sloping top and the other "made" thing in the bow.

Following this, she heard some more sounds moving from the foredeck area into the cabin.

A little recklessly, the Youngest drifted in until she was almost under the craft and only about fifteen feet below the surface, and so verified that it was, indeed, in that part of the boat where the box with the sloping box stood that most of the activity was going on. Then the noise in that area slowed down and stopped, and she heard the sound of the animals walking back off the craft, down the dock and ashore. Things became once more silent.

First Uncle had not yet returned. The Youngest wrestled with her conscience. She had not been specifically told not to risk coming up to the surface near the dock; but she knew that was simply because it had not occurred to any of the older members of the Family that she would be daring enough to do such a thing. Of course, she had never told any of them how she had examined the foredeck of the craft once before. But now, having already done so, she had a hard time convincing herself it was too risky to do again. After all, hadn't she heard the animals leave the area? No matter how quiet one of them might try to be, her hearing was good enough to pick up little sounds of his presence, if he was still aboard.

In the end, she gave in to temptation—which is not to say she moved without taking every precaution. She drifted in, underwater, so slowly and quietly that a little crowd of curious minnows formed around her. Approaching the foredeck from the loch side of the craft, she stayed well underwater until she was right up against the hull. Touching it, she hung in the water, listening. When she still heard nothing, she lifted her head quickly, just enough for a glimpse over the side; then she ducked back under again and shot away and down to a safe distance.

Eighty feet deep and a hundred feet offshore, she paused to consider what she had seen.

Her memory, like that of everyone in the Family, was essentially photographic when she concentrated on remembering, as she had during her brief look over the side of the craft. But being able to recall exactly what she had looked at was not the same thing as realizing its import. In this case, what she had been looking for was what had just been brought aboard. By comparing what she had just seen with what she had observed on her night visit earlier, she had hoped to pick out any addition to the "made" things she had noted then.

At first glance, no difference had seemed visible. She noticed the box with the sloping top and the thing in the bow with the barbed rod inside. A number of other, smaller things were about the deck, too, some of which she had examined briefly the time before and some that she had barely noticed. Familiar were several of the doubled things like the one the diver had thrown from him in order to open up communications between them at first. Largely unfamiliar were a number of smaller boxes, some round things, other things that were combinations of round and angular shapes, and a sort of tall open frame, upright and holding several rods with barbed ends like the ones which the thing in the bow contained.

She puzzled over the assortment of things—and then without warning an answer came. But provokingly, as often happened with her, it was not the answer to the question she now had, but to an earlier one.

It had suddenly struck her that the diver's actions in rejecting the "made" thing he had worn on his back, and all his original signals to her, might mean that for some reason it was not the one he wanted, or needed, in order to leave the cave. Why there should be that kind of difference between it and these things left her baffled. The one with him now in the cave had been the right one; but maybe it was not the right one, today. Perhaps—she had a sudden inspiration—"made" things could die like animals or fish, or even like People, and the one he now had was dead. In any case, maybe what he needed was another of that particular kind of thing.

Perhaps this insight had come from the fact that several of these same "made" things were on the deck; and also, there was obviously only one diver, since First Uncle had not reported any of the other animals going down into the water. She was immediately tempted to go and get another one of the things, so that she could take it back to the diver. If he put it on, that meant she was right. Even if he did not, she might learn something by the way he handled it

If it had been daring to take one look at the deck, it was inconceivably so to return now and actually try to take something from it. Her sense of duty struggled with her inclinations but slowly was overwhelmed. After all, she knew now—knew positively—that none of the animals were aboard the boat and none could have come aboard in the last few minutes because she was still close enough to hear them. But if she went, she would have to hurry if she was going to do it before the Uncle got back and forbade any such action.

She swam back to the craft in a rush, came to the surface beside it, rose in the water, craned her neck far enough inboard to snatch up one of the things in her teeth and escape with it.

A few seconds later, she had it two hundred feet down on the bed of the loch and was burying it in silt. Three minutes later she was back on station watching the craft, calmly enough but with her heart beating fast. Happily, there was still no sign of First Uncle's return.

Her heartbeat slowed. She went back to puzzling over what it was on the foredeck that could be the thing she had heard the creatures bring aboard. Of course, she now had three memory images of the area to compare . . .

Recognition came.

There *was* a discrepancy between the last two mental images and the first one, a discrepancy about one of the "made" things to which she had devoted close attention, that first time.

The difference was the line attached to the box with the sloping top. It was not the same line at all. It was a drum of other line at least twice as thick as the one which had connected the heavy thing and the box previously—almost as thick as the thick line connecting the barbed rod to the thing in the bow that contained it. Clearly, the animals of the craft had tried to make sure that they would run no danger of losing their dropweight if it became buried again. Possibly they had foolishly hoped that it was so strong that not even First Uncle could break it as he had the first.

That meant they were not going to give up. Here was clear

evidence they were going to go on searching for their diver. She *must* get him back to them as soon as possible.

She began to swim restlessly, to and fro in the underwater, anxious to see the Uncle return so that she could tell him what had been done.

He came not long afterward, although it seemed to her that she had waited and worried for a considerable time before he appeared. When she told him about the new line, he was concerned enough by the information so that he barely reprimanded her for taking the risk of going in close to the craft.

"I must tell First Mother, right away— " He checked himself and looked up through the twenty or so feet of water that covered them. "No, there're only a few more hours of daylight left. I need to think, anyway. I'll stay on guard here until dark, then I'll go see First Mother in her cave. Youngest, for right now don't say anything to Second Mother, or even to First Mother if you happen to talk to her. I'll tell both of them myself after I've had time to think about it."

"Then I can go now?" asked the Youngest, almost standing on her tail in the underwater in her eagerness to be off.

"Yes, yes," signaled the Uncle.

The Youngest turned and dove toward the spot where she had buried the "made" thing she had taken and about which she had been careful to say nothing to First Uncle. She had no time to explain about the diver now, and any mention of the thing would bring demands for a full explanation from her elders. Five minutes later, the thing in her teeth, she was splitting the water in the direction of the cave where she had left the diver.

She had never meant to leave him alone this long. An irrational fear grew in her that something had happened to him in the time she had been gone. Perhaps he had started chilling again and had lost too much warmth, like one of the old ones, and was now dead. If he was dead, would the other animals be satisfied just to have his body back? But she did not want to think of him dead: He was not a bad little animal, in spite of his acting in such an ugly fashion when he had seen her for the first time. She should have realized that in the daylight, seeing her as he had without warning for the first time—

The thought of daylight reminded her that First Uncle had talked about there being only a few hours of it left. Surely there must be more than that. The day could not have gone so quickly.

She took a quick slant up to the surface to check. No, she

was right. There must be at least four hours yet before the sun would sink below the mountains. However, in his own way the Uncle had been right, also, because the clouds were very heavy now. It would be too dark to see much, even long before actual nightfall. Snow was certain by dark, possibly even before. As she floated for a moment with her head and neck out of water, a few of the first wandering flakes came down the wind and touched her right cheek cells with tiny, cold fingers.

She dived again. It would indeed be a heavy snowfall; the Family could start out tonight on their way to the sea, if only they wanted to. It might even be possible to carry the eggs, distributed among the four of them, just two or three carried pressed between a swim paddle and warm body skin. First Mother might tire easily; but after the first night, when they had gotten well away from the loch, and with new snow falling to cover their footsteps, they could go by short stages. There would be no danger that the others would run out of heat or strength. Even the Youngest, small as she was, had fat reserves for a couple of months without eating and with ordinary activity. The Lost Father had made it to Loch Ness from the sea in a week or so.

If only they would go now. If only she were old enough and wise enough to convince them to go. For just a moment she gave herself over to a dream of their great sea home, of the People grown strong again, patrolling in their great squadrons past the white-gleaming berg ice or under the tropic stars. Most of the eggs of every clutch would hatch, then. The hatchlings would have the beaches of all the empty islands of the world to hatch on. Later, in the sea, they would grow up strong and safe, with their mighty elders around to guard them from anything that moved in the salt waters. In their last years, the old ones would bask under the hot sun in warm, hidden places and never need to chill again. The sea. That was where they belonged. Where they must go home to, someday. And that day should be soon . . .

The Youngest was almost to the cave now. She brought her thoughts, with a wrench, back to the diver. Alive or dead, he too must go back—to his own kind. Fervently, she hoped that she was right about another "made" thing being what he needed before he would swim out of the cave. If not, if he just threw this one away as he had the other one, then she had no choice. She would simply have to pick him up in her teeth and carry him out of the cave without it. Of course, she must be careful to hold him so that he could not reach her to scratch or bite; and she must get his head back above water as soon as they got out of the cave into the open loch, so that he would not drown.

By the time she had gotten this far in her thinking, she was at the cave. Ducking inside, she exploded up through the surface of the water within. The diver was seated with his back against the cave wall, looking haggard and savage. He was getting quite dark-colored around the jaws, now. The little points he had there seemed to be growing. She dumped the new "made" thing at his feet.

For a moment he merely stared down at it, stupidly. Then he fumbled the object up into his arms and did something to it with those active little divided sections of his two upper limb ends. A hissing sound came from the thing that made her start back, warily. So, the "made" things were alive, after all!

The diver was busy attaching to himself the various things he had worn when she had first found him—with the exception that the new thing she had brought him, rather than its old counterpart, was going on his back. Abruptly, though, he stopped, his head-thing still not on and still in the process of putting on the paddle-like things that attached to his lower limb ends. He got up and came forward to the edge of the water, looking at her.

He had changed again. From the moment he had gotten the new thing to make the hissing noise, he had gone into yet a different way of standing and acting. Now he came within limb reach of her and stared at her so self-assuredly that she almost felt she was the animal trapped in a cave and he was free. Then he crouched down by the water and once more began to make motions with his upper limbs and limb ends.

First, he made the on-top-of-the-water sliding motion with the back of one limb end that she now began to understand must mean the craft he had gone overboard from. Once she made the connection it was obvious: the craft, like his hand, was in the water only with its underside. Its top side was dry and in the air. As she watched, he circled his "craft" limb end around in the water and brought it back to touch the ledge. Then, with his other limb end, he "walked" two of its divisions up to the "craft" and continued to "walk" them onto it.

She stared. He was apparently signaling something about his getting on the craft. But why?

However, now he was doing something else. He lifted his walking-self limb end off the "craft" and put it standing on its two stiff divisions, back on the ledge. Then he moved the "craft" out over the water, away from the ledge, and held it there. Next, to her surprise, he "walked" his other limb end right off the ledge into the water. Still "walking" so that he churned the still surface of the cave water to a slight roughness, he moved that limb end slowly to the unmoving "craft." When the "walking" limb end reached the "craft," it once more stepped up onto it.

The diver now pulled his upper limbs back, sat crouched on the ledge, and looked at the Youngest for a long moment. Then he made the same signals again. He did it a third time, and she began to understand. He was showing himself swimming to his craft. Of course, he had no idea how far he actually was from it, here in the cave—an unreasonable distance for as weak a swimmer as one of his kind was.

But now he was signaling yet something else. His "walking" limb end stood at the water's edge. His other limb end was not merely on the water, but in it below the surface. As she watched, a single one of that other limb end's divisions rose through the surface and stood, slightly crooked, so that its upper joint was almost at right angles to the part sticking through the surface. Seeing her gaze on this part of him, the diver began to move that solitary joint through the water in the direction its crooked top was pointing. He brought it in this fashion all the way to the rock ledge and halted it opposite the "walking" limb end standing there.

He held both limb ends still in position and looked at her, as if waiting for a sign of understanding.

She gazed back, once more at a loss. The joint sticking up out of the water was like nothing in her memory but the limb of a waterlogged tree, its top more or less looking at the "walking" limb end that stood for the diver. But if the "walking" limb end was *he*—? Suddenly she understood. The division protruding from the water signalized *her*!

To show she understood, she backed off from the ledge, crouched down in the shallow water of the cave until nothing but her upper neck and head protruded from the water, and then—trying to look as much like his crooked division as possible—approached him on the ledge.

He made noises. There was no way of being sure, of course, but she felt she was beginning to read the tone of some of the sounds he made; and these latest sounds, she was convinced, sounded pleased and satisfied.

He tried something else.

He made the "walking" shape on the ledge, then added something. In addition to the two limb-end divisions standing on the rock, he unfolded another—a short, thick division, one at the edge of that particular limb end, and moved it in circular fashion, horizontally. Then he stood up on the ledge himself and swung one of his upper limbs at full length, in similar, circular fashion. He did this several times.

In no way could she imitate that kind of gesture, though she comprehended immediately that the movement of the extra, short division above the "walking" form was supposed to indicate him standing and swinging his upper limb like now. She merely stayed as she was and waited to see what he would do next.

He got down by the water, made the "craft" shape, "swam" his "walking" shape to it, climbed the "walking" shape up on the "craft," then had the "walking" shape turn and make the upper-limb swinging motion.

The Youngest watched, puzzled, but caught up in this strange game of communication she and the diver had found to play together. Evidently he wanted to go back to his craft, get on it, and then wave his upper limb like that, for some reason. It made no sense so far—but he was already doing something more.

He now had the "walking" shape standing on the ledge, making the upper-limb swinging motion, and he was showing the crooked division that was she approaching through the water.

That was easy: he wanted her to come to the ledge when he swung his upper limb.

Sure enough, after a couple of demonstrations of the last shape signals, he stood up on the ledge and swung his arm. Agreeably, she went out in the water, crouched down, and approached the ledge. He made pleased noises. This was all rather ridiculous, she thought, but enjoyable nonetheless. She was standing half her length out from the edge, where she had stopped, and was trying to think of a body signal she could give that would make him swim to her, when she noticed that he was going on to further signals.

He had his "walking" shape standing on the "craft" shape, in the water out from the ledge, and signaling "Come." But then he took his "walking" shape away from the "craft" shape, put it under the water a little distance off, and came up with it as the "her" shape. He showed the "her" shape approaching the "craft" shape with her neck and head out of water.

She was to come to his craft? In response to this "Come" signal?

*No*!

She was so furious with him for suggesting such a thing that she had no trouble at all thinking of a way to convey her reaction. Turning around, she plunged underwater, down through the cave entrance and out into the loch. Her first impulse was to flash off and leave him there to do whatever he wanted—stay forever, go back to his kind, or engage in any other nonsensical activity his small head could dream up. Did he think she had no wisdom at all? To suggest that she come right up to his craft with her head and neck out of water when he signaled—as if there had never been a taboo against her People having anything to do with his! He must not understand her in the slightest degree.

Common sense caught up with her, halted her, and turned her about not far from the cave mouth. Going off like this would do her no good—more, it would do the Family no good. On the other hand, she could not bring herself to go back into the cave, now. She hung in the water, undecided, unable to conquer the conscience that would not let her swim off, but also unable to make herself re-enter.

Vibrations from the water in the cave solved her problem. He had evidently put on the "made" thing she had brought him and was coming out. She stayed where she was, reading the vibrations.

He came to the mouth of the cave and swam slowly, straight up, to the surface. Level with him, but far enough away to be out of sight in the murky water, the Youngest rose, too. He lifted his head at last into the open air and looked around him.

He's looking for me, thought the Youngest, with a sense of satisfaction that he would see no sign of her and would assume she had left him for good. Now, go ashore and go back to your own kind, she commanded in her thoughts.

But he did not go ashore, though shore was only a matter of feet from him. Instead, he pulled his head underwater once more and began to swim back down.

She almost exploded with exasperation. He was headed toward the cave mouth! He was going back inside!

"You stupid animal!" she signaled to him. "*Go ashore!*"

But of course he did not even perceive the signal, let alone understand it. Losing all patience, the Youngest swooped down upon him, hauled him to the surface once more, and let him go.

For a second he merely floated there, motionless, and she felt a sudden fear that she had brought him up through the water too swiftly. She knew of some small fish that spent all their time down in the deepest parts of the loch, and if you brought one of them too quickly up the nine hundred feet or so to the surface, it twitched and died, even though it had been carried gently. Sometimes part of the insides of these fish bulged out through their months and gill slits after they were brought up quickly.

After a second, the diver moved and looked at her.

Concerned for him, she had stayed on the surface with him, her head just barely out of the water. Now he saw her. He kicked with the "made" paddles on his lower limbs to raise himself partly out of the water and, a little awkwardly, with his upper limb ends made the signal of him swimming to his craft.

She did not respond. He did it several more times, but she stayed stubbornly non-communicative. It was bad enough that she had let him see her again after his unthinkable suggestion.

He gave up making signals. Ignoring the shore close at hand, he turned from her and began to swim slowly south and out into the center of the loch.

He was going in the wrong direction if he was thinking of swimming all the way to his craft. And after his signaling it was pretty clear that this was what he had in mind. Let him find out his mistake for himself, the Youngest thought, coldly.

But she found that she could not go through with that. Angrily, she shot after him, caught the thing on his back with her teeth, and, lifting him by it enough so that his head was just above the surface, began to swim with him in the right direction.

She went slowly—according to her own ideas of speed—but even so a noticeable bow wave built up before him. She lifted him a little higher out of the water to be on the safe side; but she did not go any faster: perhaps he could not endure too much speed. As it was, the clumsy shape of his small body hung about with "made" things was creating surprising turbulence for its size. It was a good thing the present hatchhole (and, therefore, First Mother's current resting cave and the area in which First Uncle and Second Mother would do their feeding) was as distant as they were; otherwise First Uncle, at least, would certainly have been alarmed by the vibrations and have come to investigate.

It was also a good thing that the day was as dark as it was, with its late hour and the snow that was now beginning to fall with some seriousness; otherwise she would not have wanted to travel this distance on the surface in daylight. But the snow was now so general that both shores were lost to sight in its white, whirling multitudes of flakes, and certainly no animal on shore would be able to see her and the diver out here.

There was privacy and freedom, being hidden by the snow like this—like the freedom she felt on dark nights when the whole loch was free of the animals and all hers. If only it could be this way all the time. To live free and happy was so good. Under conditions like these, she could not even fear or dislike the animals, other than her diver, who were a threat to the Family.

At the same time, she remained firm in her belief that the Family should go, now. None of the others had ever before told her that any of the legends were untrustworthy, and she did not believe that that legend was untrustworthy, but that they had grown conservative with age and feared to leave the loch; while she, who was still young, still dared to try great things for possibly great rewards.

She had never admitted it to the older ones, but one midwinter day when she had been very young and quite small—barely old enough to be allowed to swim around in the loch by herself—she had ventured up one of the streams flowing into the loch. It was a stream far too shallow for an adult of the Family; and some distance up it, she found several otters playing on an ice slide they had made. She had joined them, sliding along with them for half a day without ever being seen by any upright animal. She remembered this all very well, particularly her scrambling around on the snow to get to the head of the slide; and that she had used her tail muscles to skid herself along on her warm belly surface, just as the Lost Father had described.

If she could get the others to slip ashore long enough to try the snowy loch banks before day-warmth combined with loch-warmth to clear them of the white stuff . . . But even as she thought this, she knew they would never agree to try. They would not even consider the journey home to the sea until, as First Mother said, it became clear that that was the only alternative to extinction at the hands of the upright animals.

It was a fact, and she must face it. But maybe she could think of some way to make plain to them that the animals had, indeed, become that dangerous. For the first time, it occurred to her that her association with the diver could turn out to be something that would help them all. Perhaps, through him, she could gain evidence about his kind that would convince the rest of the Family that they should leave the loch.

It was an exciting thought. It would do no disservice to him to use him in that fashion, because clearly he was different from others of his kind: he had realized that not only was she warm as he was, but as intelligent or more so than he. He would have no interest in being a danger to her People, and might even cooperate—if she could make him understand what she wanted—in convincing the Family of the dangers his own race posed to them. Testimony from one of the animals directly would be an argument to convince even First Uncle.

For no particular reason, she suddenly remembered how he had instinctively huddled against her when he had discovered her warming him. The memory roused a feeling of tenderness in her. She found herself wishing there were some way she could signal that feeling to him. But they were almost to his craft, now. It and the dock were beginning to be visible—dark shapes lost in the dancing white—with the dimmer dark shapes of trees and other things ashore behind them.

Now that they were close enough to see a shore, the falling snow did not seem so thick, nor so all-enclosing as it had out in the middle of the loch. But there was still a privacy to the world it created, a feeling of security. Even sounds seemed to be hushed.

Through the water, Youngest could feel vibrations from the craft. At least one, possibly two, of the other animals were aboard it. As soon as she was close enough to be sure her diver could see the craft, she let go of the thing on his back and sank abruptly to about twenty feet below the surface, where she hung and waited, checking the vibrations of his movements to make sure he made it safely to his destination.

At first, when she let him go, he trod water where he was and turned around and around as if searching for her. He pushed himself up in the water and made the "Come" signal several times; but she refused to respond. Finally, he turned and swam to the edge of the craft.

He climbed on board very slowly, making so little noise that the two in the cabin evidently did not hear him. Surprisingly, he did not seem in any hurry to join them or to let them know he was back.

The Youngest rose to just under the surface and lifted her head above to see what he was doing. He was still standing on the foredeck, where he had climbed aboard, not moving. Now, as she watched, he walked heavily forward to the bow and stood beside the "made" thing there, gazing out in her direction.

He lifted his arm as if to make the "Come" signal then dropped it to his side.

The Youngest knew that in absolutely no way could he make out the small portion of her head above the waves, with the snow coming down the way it was and day drawing swiftly to its dark close. She stared at him. She noticed something weary and sad about the way he stood. I should leave now, she thought. But she did not move. With the other two animals still unaware in the cabin, and the snow continuing to fall, there seemed no reason to hurry off. She would miss him, she told herself, feeling a sudden pang of loss. Looking at him, it came to her suddenly that from the way he was acting he might well miss her, too.

Watching, she remembered how he had half lifted his limb as if to signal and then dropped it again. Maybe his limb is tired, she thought.

A sudden impulse took her. I'll go in close, underwater, and lift my head high for just a moment, she thought, so he can see me. He'll know then that I haven't left him for good. He already understands I wouldn't come on board that thing of his under any circumstance. Maybe if he sees me again for a second, now, he'll understand that if he gets back in the water and swims to me, we can go on learning signals from each other. Then, maybe, someday, we'll know enough signals together so that he can convince the older ones to leave.

Even as she thought this, she was drifting in, underwater, until she was only twenty feet from the craft. She rose suddenly and lifted her head and neck clear of the water.

For a long second, she saw he was staring right at her but not responding. Then she realized that he might not be seeing her, after all, just staring blindly out at the loch and the snow. She moved a little sideways to attract his attention, and saw his head move. Then he *was* seeing her? Then why didn't he do something?

She wondered if something was wrong with him. After all, he had been gone for nearly two days from his own People and must have missed at least a couple of his feeding periods in that time. Concern impelled her to a closer look at him. She began to drift in toward the boat.

He jerked upright suddenly and swung an upper limb at her.

But he was swinging it all wrong. It was not the "Come" signal he was making, at all. It was more like the "Come" signal in reverse—as if he was pushing her back and away from him. Puzzled, and even a little hurt, because the way he was acting reminded her of how he had acted when he first saw her in the cave and did not know she had been with him earlier, the Youngest moved in even closer.

He flung both his upper limbs furiously at her in that new, "rejecting" motion and shouted at her—a loud, angry noise. Behind him, came an explosion of different noise from inside the cabin, and the other two animals burst out onto the deck. Her diver turned, making noises, waving both his limbs at them the way he had just waved them at her. The Youngest, who had been about to duck down below the safety of the loch surface, stopped. Maybe this was some new signal he wanted her to learn, one that had some reference to his two companions?

But the others were making noises back at him. The taller one ran to one of the "made" things that were like, but smaller than, the one in the bow of the boat. The diver shouted again, but the tall one ignored him, only seizing one end of the thing he had run to and pulling that end around toward him. The Youngest watched, fascinated, as the other end of the "made" thing swung to point at her.

Then the diver made a very large angry noise, turned, and seized the end of the largest "made" thing before him in the bow of the boat.

Frightened suddenly, for it had finally sunk in that for some reason he had been signaling her to get away, she turned and dived. Then, as she did so, she realized that she had turned, not away from, but into line with, the outer end of the thing in the bow of the craft.

She caught a flicker of movement, almost too fast to see, from the thing's hollow outer end. Immediately, the loudest sound she had ever heard exploded around her, and a tremendous blow struck her behind her left shoulder as she entered the underwater.

She signaled for help instinctively, in shock and fear, plunging for the deep bottom of the loch. From far off, a moment later, came the answer of First Uncle. Blindly, she turned to flee to him.

As she did, she thought to look and see what had happened to her. Swinging her head around, she saw a long, but shallow, gash across her shoulder and down her side. Relief surged in her. It was not even painful yet, though it might be later; but it was nothing to cripple her, or even to slow her down.

How could her diver have done such a thing to her? The thought was checked almost as soon as it was born—by the basic honesty of her training. *He* had not done this. *She* had done it, by diving into the path of the barbed rod cast from the thing in the bow. If she had not done that, it would have missed her entirely.

But why should he make the thing throw the barbed rod at all? She had thought he had come to like her, as she liked him.

Abruptly, comprehension came; and it felt as if her heart leaped in her. For all at once it was perfectly clear what he had been trying to do. She should have had more faith in him. She halted her flight toward the Uncle and turned back toward the boat.

Just below it, she found what she wanted. The barbed rod, still leaving a taste of her blood in the water, was hanging point down from its line, in about two hundred feet of water. It was being drawn back up, slowly but steadily.

She surged in close to it, and her jaws clamped on the line she had tried to bite before and found resistant. But now she was serious in her intent to sever it. Her jaws scissored and her teeth ripped at it, though she was careful to rise with the line and put no strain upon it that would warn the animals above about what she was doing. The tough strands began to part under her assault.

Just above her, the sound of animal noises now came clearly through the water: her diver and the others making sounds at each other.

". . . I tell you we're through!" It was her diver speaking. "It's over. I don't care what you saw. It's my boat. I paid for it; and I'm quitting."

"It not *your* boat, man. It a boat belong to the company, the company that belong all three of us. We got contracts."

"I'll pay off your damned contracts."

"There's more to this than money, now. We know that great beast in there, now. We get our contract money, and maybe a lot more, going on the TV and telling how we catch it and bring it in. No, man, you don't stop us now."

"I say, it's my boat. I'll get a lawyer and court order— "

"You do that. You get a lawyer and a judge and a pretty court order, and we'll give you the boat. You do that. Until then, it belong to the company and it keep after that beast."

She heard the sound of footsteps—her diver's footsteps, she could tell, after all this time of seeing him walk his lower limbs— leaving the boat deck, stepping onto the dock, going away.

The line was almost parted. She and the barbed rod were only about forty feet below the boat.

"What'd you have to do that for?" That was the voice of the third creature. "He'll do that! He'll get a lawyer and take the boat and we won't even get our minimum pay. Whyn't you let him pay us off, the way he said?"

"Hush, you fooking fool. How long you think it take him get a lawyer, a judge, and a writ? Four days, maybe five— "

The line parted. She caught the barbed rod in her jaws as it started to sink. The ragged end of the line lifted and vanished above her.

"—and meanwhile, you and me, we go hunting with this boat. We know the beast there, now. We know what to look for. We find it in four, five day, easy."

"But even if we get it, he'll just take it away from us again with his lawyer— "

"I tell you, no. We'll get ourselves a lawyer, also. This company formed to take the beast; and he got to admit he tried to call off the hunt. And we both seen what he do. He've fired that harpoon gun to scare it off, so I can't get it with the drug lance and capture it. We testify to that, we got him—Ah!"

"What is it?"

"What is it? You got no eyes, man? The harpoon gone. It in that beast after all, being carried around. We don't need no four, five days, I tell you now. That be a good, long piece of steel, and we got the locators to find metal like that. We hunt that beast and bring it in tomorrow. Tomorrow, man, I promise you! It not going to go too fast, too far, with that harpoon."

But he could not see below the snow and the black surface of the water. The Youngest was already moving very fast indeed through the deep loch to meet the approaching First Uncle. In her jaws she carried the harpoon, and on her back she bore the wound it had made. The elders could have no doubt, now, about the intentions of the upright animals (other than her diver) and their ability to destroy the Family.

They must call First Mother, and this time there would be no hesitation. She would see the harpoon and the wound and decide for them all. Tonight they would leave by the route of the Lost Father, while the snow was still thick on the banks of the loch. They might have to leave the eggs behind, after all; but if so, Second Mother could have more clutches, and maybe later they would even find a way ashore again to Loch Morar and meet others of their own People at last.

But, in any case, they would go now to live free in the sea; and in the sea most of Second Mother's future eggs would hatch and the Family would grow numerous and strong again.

She could see them in her mind's eye, now. They would leave the loch by the mouth of Glen Moriston—First Mother, Second Mother, First Uncle, herself—and take to the snow-covered banks when the water became too shallow . . .

They would travel steadily into the mountains, and the new snow falling behind them would hide the marks of their going from the eyes of the animals. They would pass by deserted ways through the silent rocks to the ocean. They would come at last to its endless waters, to the shining bergs of the north and the endless warmth of the Equator sun. The ocean, their home, was welcoming them back, at last. There would be no more doubt, no more fear or waiting. They were going home to the sea . . . they were going home to the sea . . .